John Tremaine, John Rice, Thomas Vickers

Pleas of the Crown in Matters Criminal & Civil

containing a large collection of modern precedents - Vol. 1

John Tremaine, John Rice, Thomas Vickers

Pleas of the Crown in Matters Criminal & Civil
containing a large collection of modern precedents - Vol. 1

ISBN/EAN: 9783337267995

Printed in Europe, USA, Canada, Australia, Japan

Cover: Foto ©Andreas Hilbeck / pixelio.de

More available books at **www.hansebooks.com**

PLEAS OF THE CROWN

IN MATTERS

CRIMINAL AND CIVIL:

CONTAINING

A LARGE COLLECTION

OF

MODERN PRECEDENTS;

TO WIT.

APPEALS,	REPLICATIONS,
CERTIORARI'S,	REJOYNDERS, &c.
CONVICTIONS,	TRAVERSES,
DEMURRERS,	WRITS of HABEAS CORPUS
INDICTMENTS,	———MANDAMUS,
INFORMATIONS,	———QUO WARRANTO,
PLEAS in ABATEMENT,	———RESTITUTION, &c.
———— BAR,	and PLEADINGS thereupon.

With a great Variety of PRECEDENTS under many other Heads,
relating to the CROWN LAW.

The Whole collected
By the Late Sir JOHN TREMAINE, Kt. Serjeant at Law

Digested and Revised,
By the Late Mr. JOHN RICE, of Furnivals Inn.

And Translated into English,
By THOMAS VICKERS, Esq. Barrister at Law.

With a new INDEX.

DUBLIN:
PRINTED BY H. WATTS, LAW BOOKSELLER, NO. 3. CHRIST-
CHURCH-LANE, 1793.

THE HONOURABLE

WILLIAM DOWNES,

ONE OF THE JUSTICES

OF HIS MAJESTY'S COURT

OF

KING'S BENCH

IN

IRELAND;

THIS WORK

IS,

WITH HIS PERMISSION,

RESPECTFULLY DEDICATED,

by his obedient,

obliged and

humble servant,

THOMAS VICKERS.

THE Editor prefents to the Profeffors of the
Law, the tranflation of a book of Entries of
eftablifhed reputation, which he trufts will be found
to be faithful and accurate. In it he has preferved
the paging of the original, as well to facilitate
collation, as for the fake of uniformity in citation.
He has divided the work into two parts, and annexed a new index to each; he has introduced a
few notes at the end of fome of the Precedents,
in addition to thofe which they have in the original; and, wherever he difcovered, what appeared
to him to be any error or defect, he has been careful to point it out by a marginal note, ftating alfo
where neceffary, what he conceived to be the
proper amendment or addition. He hopes that
the great labour beftowed by him upon this work,
is fome fmall claim to the favour and protection
of his readers. Juft cenfure he ought not, and
does not wifh to avert: but he trufts that the li-
beral and ingenuous will fhield him from unde-
ferved condemnation.

DUBLIN, *April* 20th. 1793.

ERRATA.

8, l. 31, dele *and* after *called*
9, l. 9, for *O,* read *P.*
for *O,* read *P.*
13, for *O,* read *P.*
19, for *O.* read *P.*
11, l. 14, read *ſaid* before *lady.*
15, dele the word *ſaid*
13, l. 4, for *Banqury,* read *Banbury*
27, after *the* inſert *ſaid*
17, l. 10, after *the* inſert *ſaid*
before *collar-* inſert *ſaid*
18, before *kill* inſert *did*
41, after *juſtice* add *s*
43, after *him* add *ſelf*
18 l. 45, for *and* read *ſhe*
19 l. 24, for *comes* read *come*
20 l. 4, for *made* read *aſſigned*
20, for *made* read *aſſigned*
52, after *right* inſert *and*
22, l. 22, for *he* read *the*
24, l. 6, for *county* read *country*
48, (beginning the line) after *that* inſert *the*
26 l. 50, for *comes* read *come*
51, after *aforeſaid* inſert *as*
31, l. 11, for *nex* read *next*
3d marginal note, for *juratorum*
read *juratores*
32, l. 40, (at the end) dele *to*
39, l. 27, after *his* inſert *ſaid*
56, l. 18, for *boing* read *being*
31, after *ſubornation* add *&c.*
57, l. 41 for *li* read *it*
44, for *J* read *S*
67, laſt line but 4, after *prayer* add *s*
94, In the margin, before *women,*
read *the*
96, l. 8, dele *and*
105, margin (the king againſt Chamberlaine) for *Information*
read *Indictment*
124, l 48, for *county* read *city*
128, l. 16, aft. *Jeffreys* inſert *for* 100*l.*

130, l. 31, for *was* read *hath been*
37, for *was* read *hath been*
134, l. 31, for *publiſh* read *publick*
137. laſt l. but 8, dele *at*
139, L 11, for *Thomas* read *John*
140, l. 25, for *ſecurity* read *ſeizure*
149, l. 19, after *Mary* inſert *I*
175, l. 26, dele *s* in *conventicles*
184, l. 27, for *I* read *S*
38, after *faciatis* inſert *of*
185, l. 23, for *Edward* read *Edmu*
38, for *Edward* read *Edmu*
193, l. 5, after *king* inſert *his cro*
and *dignity*
198, l. 27, for *in* read *great*
200, l. 1 for *where* read *when*
201, l. 15, for *where* read *when*
20, for *and others* read *&c.*
204, l. 24, for *on* read *in*
219, l. 40, after *juſtice* inſert *to*
220, l. 5, for *Aldick* read *Abdick*
224, l. 37, for *them* read *him*
for *their* read *his*
244, l. 13, (margin) for *dicharg*
read *charged*
248, l. 11, after *attorney* inſert *gene*
254, l. 25, for *upou* read *upon*
273, l. 18, (margin) for *counſell*
read *counſellor*
274, l. 2, for *hadns* read *hands*
276, l. 31, for firſt *or* read *nor*
281, l. 28, for *fellow* read *fellows*
287, l. 21, dele firſt *ſaid* in the li
300, laſt l. but 6 dele *ment* in t
beginning of the line
310, l. 51, after *who* read *is*
314, l. 38, for *verif* read *verify*
320, l. 9, dele *y* at the end of the li
338. l. 7, for *your* read *our*
8, for *our* read *your*
346, l. 16, after *then* inſert *were*
348, l. 2, for *of* read *and*
349, l. 25, for *at* read *of*

SUBSCRIBERS NAMES,

A.
Antifell, Chrift. Efq;

B.
Baker, William, Efq;
Barrington, Jonah, Efq;
Batty, John Efpine, Efq;
Bell, James Wm. Efq;
Beresford, Marcus, Efq;
   one of his Majefty's
   council at Law.
Betty, William, Efq;
Blackburne, Anth. Efq;
Bloffet, John, Efq;
Boyd, Abraham, Efq;
Boyd, John, Efq;
Boyd, the Hon. Rob. one
   of his Majefty's juftices
   of the court of K. B.
Browne, Arth. Efq; S. F.
   T. C. D.
Browne, Geo. Jof. Efq;
Burne, John, Efq.
Burroughs, Fran. Efq;
Burrowes, Peter, Efq;
Burfton, Beresford, Efq;
   one of his Majefty's
   council at Law.
Butler, the Hon. Simon,
   one of his Majefty's
   council at Law.

C.
Chamberlaine, W. T. Efq;
Clonmell, the Rt. Hon.
   Ld. Vif. Ld. C. J. of
   his Majefty's ct. of K. B.
Colles, Rich. Efq;
Conroy, Phil. J. J. Efq;
Crofton, Morgan, Efq;

Curran, Jn. Philpot, Efq;
   one of his Majefty's
   council at Law.

D.
Dobbs, Francis, Efq;
Downs, the Hon. Wm.
   one of his Majefty's
   juft. of the ct. of K. B.
Doyne, Phil. Efq;
Drifcoll, Tim. Efq;
Duquery, Henry, Efq;
   one of his Majefty's
   council at Law.
Dwyer, Anth. Efq;

E.
Egan, Jn. Efq; one of
   his Majefty's council at
   Law.
Evans, Mr. Jn. Att.

F.
Fitzgerald, the Rt. Hon.
   Ja. his Majefty's prime
   Serjeant at Law.
Filgate, Townly P. Efq.
Fitton Rich. Efq;
Fletcher, Wm. Efq;
Foote, Lundy, Efq;
Fox, Luke, Efq;
Frankland, Rich. Efq;
Frizzell, Cha. Fraz. Efq;
Furlong, Mr. Wm. Att.

G.
Gabbet, Jof. Efq;
Garnett, C. K. Efq;
Grace, George, Efq;
Grady, Hen. Deane Efq;

SUBSCRIBERS NAMES.

Greene, Fra. Wm. Efq;
Guinnefs, Rich. Efq;
George, Denis, Efq; Recorder of the city of
Dublin.

H.

Hamilton, John, Efq;
Hewit, the Hon. Jof. one
of his Majefty's juftices
of the court of K. B.
Hone, I. T. Efq;
Hodgkinfon, Fran. 'Efq;
F. T. C. D.

J.

Jamefon, Jofeph, Efq;
Jebb, Rich. Efq;
Jenkins, Mr. Rob. Att.
Johnfon, Rob. Efq;
Jones, Mr. Wm. B. S. 12
copies.
Joy, Henry, Efq;

K.

Kemmis, Tho. Efq; his
Majefty's crown Solicitor.
King, Steuart, Efq;
Kirwan, John, Efq;

L.

Laffan, James, Efq;
Leland, John, Efq;
Lill, J. G. Efq.

M.

Marfden, Alex. Efq;
Mac-Cartney, A. C. Efq;
Mac-Nally, Leon. Efq;
Monck, Wm. S. Efq;
Moore, Arth. Efq;
Moore, Mr. Ja. B. S. 6
copies.

P.

Parfons, John, Efq;

Pearfon, Matthew, Efq;
Phillips, Mr. Sam. Att.
Pigeon, Peter, Efq;
Ponfonby, Geo. Efq.; one
of his Majefty's council
at Law.
Powell, Eyre Bur. Efq;

Q.

Quin, Tho. Efq;

R.

Radcliffe, John, Efq;
Rice, Mr. John, B. S. 50
copies.
Ridgeway, Wm. Efq;
Redford, Arch. Efq;

S.

Sanders, Rob. S. Efq;
Sankey, Wm. Efq;
Sheares, Henry, Efq;
Skerrett, Ja. Efq;
Smith, Mich. Efq;
Smith, William, Efq;

T.

Thompfon, Fred. Efq;
Toler, Jn. Efq; his Majefty's Solicitor Gen.
Townfend, Jn. S. Efq;

U.

Upton, S. W. Efq;
Vicars, George, Efq;

W.

Walker, Wm. Efq;
White, Jn. Efq;
Williams, Chrift. S. Efq;
Williams, Geo. Efq;
Wolfe, the Rt. Hon. Arthur, his Majefty's Attorney General.
Wynne, Wm. Efq;

Y.

Yelverton, the Rt. Hon.
Barry, Ld. chief Baron
of his Majefty's court
of Exchequer.

PLEAS of the CROWN,

IN

Matters Criminal and Civil.

Indictments for High Treason.

To wit. THE jurors for our lord the king, upon their oath present, that *T. H.* late of, &c. in the county aforesaid, &c. not having the fear of God in his heart nor weighing the duty of his allegiance, but being moved and seduced by the inftigation of the devil, and intirely withdrawing the love and true obedience, which a true and faithful fubject of our lord Charles, by the grace of God of England, Scotland, France, and Ireland, king, defender of the faith, &c. fhould, and of right ought to bear towards the faid lord the king, and devifing, and as much as in him lay intending, to difturb the peace and public tranquility of this kingdom of England; on the 10th day of Auguft, in the 20th year of the reign of the faid lord now king of England, &c. at Silferton, in the county aforefaid, traiteroufly did compafs, imagine, and intend to raife and levy war, rebellion, and infurrection againft the faid lord the king, within this kingdom of England; and to fulfil and bring to effect, his faid treafons, imaginations, and intentions aforefaid, he, the faid *T. H.* afterwards, to wit, on the faid 10th day of Auguft, in the twentieth year aforefaid, with force and arms, &c. at S. aforefaid, in the county aforefaid, with a great multitude of perfons, to the jurors aforefaid unknown, to wit, to the number of ten perfons armed and arrayed in a warlike manner, to wit, with drums, trumpets,

Indictment for levying war againft the King.

25 Ed. 3. Stat. 5. C. 2.

A   piftols,

piftols, ftaves, blunderbuffes, fwords, and other arms, as well offenfive as defenfive, being then and there unlawfully and traiteroufly affembled and gathered, againft the faid lord the king, at S. aforefaid, in the county aforefaid, on the 10th day of Auguft, in the 20th year aforefaid, traiteroufly did prepare, levy, and ordain public war againft the faid lord the king, his fupreme and undoubted lord, againft the peace of the faid lord the king, his crown and dignity, and alfo againft the form of the ftatute in fuch cafe made and provided.

---

*P. 2.

*REX v. AYLIFFE.

Michaelmas, 36th Charles II.

Indictment for confpiring to depofe the King and murder him

London, **{** **T**HAT John Ayliffe of, &c. as a falfe traitor
To wit. **}** againft the moft illuftrious and moft excellent Prince, our lord Charles, by the grace of God, king of, &c. and his natural lord ; not having the fear of God in his heart, nor weighing the duty of his allegiance, but being moved and feduced by the inftigation of the devil, and intirely withdrawing the love and true and due obedience, which a true and faithful fubject of the faid lord the king towards the faid lord the king fhould, and of right ought to bear, and as much as in him lay, intending to difturb the peace and common tranquility of this kingdom of England, and to move and excite war and rebellion againft the faid lord the king, and to fubvert the government of the faid lord the king in this kingdom of England, and to depofe and deprive the faid lord the king of his royal title, honour and name, and of the imperial crown of his kingdom of England, and to bring and put the faid lord the king to death and final deftruction, on the 2d day of March, in the 35th year of the reign of the faid lord Charles the 2d, now king of England, and at divers other days and times, as well before as after, at the parifh, &c. malicioufly and traiteroufly, with divers other traitors, to the jurors aforefaid unknown, did confpire compafs, imagine, and intend, not only to deprive and depofe the faid lord the king his fupreme lord of his royal eftate, title, power, and government, but alfo the faid lord the king to kill, and to bring and put to death, and to alter, change, and entirely fubvert the antient government of this kingdom of England, and to caufe and procure a miferable

flaughter

slaughter among the subjects of the said lord the king, through-out his whole kingdom of England, and to move and levy war, insurrection, and rebellion against the said lord the king, within this kingdom of England, and to fulfil, perfect, and bring to effect, his said most wicked and traiterous contrivings, imaginations and purposes, he the said John Ayliffe as a false traitor, then and there, and at divers other days and times, as well before as after, maliciously, traiterously and advisedly did assemble himself with, meet and consult, with the other traitors as aforesaid, to the jurors aforesaid unknown, and with the same did treat of and concerning the executing and fulfilling their said treasons and traiterous compassings, imaginations and purposes as aforesaid; and that the said *J. A.* as a false traitor, maliciously, traiterously and advisedly then and there as aforesaid, and at divers other days and times, as well before as after, did assume upon himself, and to the aforesaid other traitors did promise that he would be aiding and assisting in the execution of their aforesaid treasons, and traiterous compassings, imaginations and purposes, and in procuring of arms and armed men to fulfil and bring to effect their said treasons and traiterous compassings, imaginations and purposes; and to fulfil and bring to effect his said most wicked treasons, compassings, imaginations and purposes as aforesaid, * he the said *J. A.* as a false traitor, maliciously, traiterously and advisedly then and there did procure and prepare certain arms, to wit; blunderbusses, carabines and pistols, against the duty of his allegiance, against the peace of our said Lord the now King his crown, &c. and also against the form of the statute, &c.

Overt acts, treating with other traitors, &c.

Promising his assistance, and to procure men and arms.

P. 3.

And actually procuring arms.

The King *v.* Mary Speke.

Hillary, 4th. James II.

Somerset,
To wit.
THAT whereas James Scott, who was lately called or named by the name of James Duke of Monmouth, and divers other false traitors, to the jurors aforesaid unknown, not having the fear of God in their hearts, nor weighing the duty of their allegiance, but being moved and seduced by the instigation of the devil, and entirely withdrawing the love and true and due obedience, which true and faithful subjects of our lord James the 2d now king of England, towards the said lord the king, should and of right ought to bear, and devising and as much as in them lay intending to disturb the peace and public tranquility of this kingdom of England, on the

For aiding and assisting the Duke of Monmouth, and others in open rebellion against the King.

day

day of   in the year, &c. at &c. in the county, &c. traiteroufly had compaffed, imagined and intended not only intirely to depofe and difinherit the faid lord the king their fupreme
and natural lord of his royal eftate, title, power and government, but alfo to bring the faid lord the king to death and
final deftruction, and to levy and raife againft the faid lord
the king, war, rebellion and infurrection, within this realm
of England, and in order to fulfil, perfect, and bring to effect
their faid treafons, confpiracies and imaginations, he the faid
James Scott who was lately called or named by the name of
James Duke of Monmouth, and the faid divers other traitors to
the jurors aforefaid unknown, afterwards to wit, on the
day of   in the year, &c. and in the county aforefaid, with a
great multitude of perfons, to the jurors aforefaid unknown,
to the number of 4000 perfons at leaft, armed and arrayed in
a warlike manner; to wit, with colours, drums, bills, fcythes
and guns; and with other arms as well offenfive as defenfive;
then and there unlawfully and traiteroufly had collected and
affembled themfelves againft the faid lord the king their fupreme, true, natural and undoubted lord, and at *Ilminfter*, in
the county aforefaid, on the day aforefaid, in the year aforefaid, had traiteroufly prepared, levyed and ordained public
war againft the faid lord the now king, againft the duty of
their allegiance, and againft the peace of the faid lord the
now king, his crown and dignity, &c. And that Mary
Speke, the wife of George Speke, late of *Whitelackington*,
in the county aforefaid, Efq. well knowing the faid James
Scott, then to be a falfe traitor againft the faid lord the now
* P. 4.   king, and * with many other falfe traitors to the jurors aforefaid
unknown, to the number of 4000 perfons at leaft, then and
there unlawfully had affembled and collected, and then and
there unlawfully, unjuftly, and traiteroufly had prepared,
levied and raifed war, infurrection and rebellion againft
the faid lord the king, within this realm of England. Neverthelefs the faid Mary Speke, the wife of George Speke, for
the comforting, affifting, aiding and fupporting of the faid
James Scott, lately called or named by the name of James
Duke of Monmouth, and of the other falfe traitors as aforefaid, in the war, rebellion and infurrection aforefaid, by them
then and there as aforefaid, levied and raifed on the   day
of   &c. in the year, &c. and on divers other days and
times, at, &c. in the county, &c. falfely, unlawfully and traiteroufly did convey and carry, and did caufe to be conveyed and
carried to the faid James Scott, lately called or named by the
name of James Duke of Monmouth, and to the other falfe
traitors as aforefaid, cart loads of bread and of cheefe, and
other great quantities of provifions, and alfo on the faid day
                                                    and

and year, &c. at, &c. for the intentions aforesaid ; falsely, unlawfully and traiterously did deliver and send, and did cause
to be delivered and sent, a certain mare being a mare of the
said George Speke to the aforesaid James Scott, and to the
other false traitors as aforesaid, * or to some one of them,
against the peace of the said lord the now king his crown and
dignity, &c. and also against the form of the statute, &c.

> * Quere, if this part of this indictment could be supported, being in the disjunctive, vide 2nd Hawkins 321 322 and 5th mod. 137 Rex vertus Stocker

---

The King *against* Horsley.

Michaelmas, 1 James II.

Surry, THAT *William Horsley,* late of, &c. being a
To wit, false traitor against the most illustrious and
most excellent Prince, our lord James the 2d. by the grace of
God of England, Scotland, France and Ireland, king, and
his natural lord, not having the fear of God in his heart, nor
weighing the duty of his allegiance, but being moved and seduced by the instigation of the devil, and entirely withdrawing
the cordial love, and true, due and natural obedience which a
true and faithful subject of the said lord the king towards the
said lord the king, should and of right ought to bear, and contriving, practising, and as much as in him lay, intending to molest and disturb the peace and public tranquility of this kingdom of England, and to raise, move and procure war and rebellion against the said lord the now king, and to subvert the government of the said lord the king of this kingdom of England,
and to depose and deprive the said lord the king of his royal
title, honour and name, and of the imperial crown of this
realm of England, and to bring and put the said lord the king
to death and final destruction, on the 10th day of July, in the
year, &c. and at divers other days and times as well after as
before, at the parish, &c. falsely, maliciously and traiterously
with one James Scott, late Duke of Monmouth, and with
divers other rebels and traitors, to the jurors aforesaid unknown, did conspire, compass, imagine and intend, not only
to deprive and depose the said lord the king, his supreme natural lord of his royal estate, power, title and government of his
his kingdom of England, but also to slay and to bring, and put
to death the said lord the king, and to alter, change and entirely
subvert the antient government of * this kingdom of England,
and to cause and procure a miserable slaughter among the subjects of the said lord the king, throughout his entire realm
of England ; and to move, promote and assist the insurrection
and

> Indictment. For traitorously conspiring the deposition, death and destruction of the king:

> * P. 5.

and rebellion, against the said lord the king, by the aforesaid
J. S. and other rebels and traitors within this kingdom of
England, begun, moved and stirred up, and to fulfil perfect
and bring to effect the said most wicked and diabolical treasons, and his traiterous, compassings, imaginations and purposes aforesaid ; and to move and persuade other subjects
of the said lord the king, to be aiding and assisting to the said
James Scott, and to the other traitors as aforesaid ; he the said
William Horsely, then and there, and at divers other days and
times as well before as after, at   in the county aforesaid, &c. falsely, unlawfully, wickedly, traiterously and seditiously did imprint, and did cause to be imprinted and published a certain false, seditious and traiterous libel, to move the
subjects of the said lord the king, of his realm of England,
to levy war against the said lord the now king ; in which false
seditions and traiterous libel, among other things there were
contained, these false, seditious and traiterous English sentences, to wit, " Now therefore we *(meaning the said James*
" *Scott, and the other rebels and traitors aforesaid)* do solemnly de-
" clare and proclaim war against James Duke of York, *(mean-*
" *ing the most serene lord James the second, the now king of Eng-*
" *land)* as a murderer and assassinate of innocent men, a po-
" pish usurper of the crown, *(meaning the imperial crown of this*
" *kingdom of England)* traytor to the nation, and tyrant over
" the people ; and we would have none that appear under
" his banner, to flatter themselves with expectation of for-
" giveness, it being our firm resolution to prosecute him ;
" *(meaning the said most serene lord the now king)* and his ad-
" herents, without giving way to treaties or accommodati-
" ons, until we have brought him *(meaning the said lord the*
" *now king)* and them to undergo what the rules of the con-
" stitution, and the statutes of the realm, as well as the laws
" of nature, scripture and nations adjudge to be the punish-
" ment due to the enemies of God, mankind, their country,
" and all things that are honourable, virtuous and good ;"——
against the duty of his allegiance, against the peace of the
said lord the now king, his crown and dignity, &c. and also
against the form of the statute in such case made and provided.

The

The King *against* Hayes.

Michaelmas, 36th. Charles II.

London,
To wit.
THAT *Joseph Hayes*, late of London, merchant, as a false traitor against the most illustrious and most excellent prince, the lord Charles the second, by the grace of God, king, &c. and his natural lord, not having the fear of God in his heart, nor weighing the duty of his allegiance, but being moved and seduced by the instigation of the devil, and entirely withdrawing the love, and true, due and natural obedience which a true and faithful subject of the said lord the king, towards the said lord the king should and of right ought to bear, and as much as in him lay, intending to molest and disturb the peace and public * tranquility of this realm of England, and to move and raise war and rebellion against the said lord the king, and to subvert the government of the said lord the king, in this kingdom of England, and to expel, depose and deprive the said lord the king of his royal title, honour and name, and of the imperial crown of his kingdom of England, and to bring and put the said lord the king to death and final destruction, on the 31st day of August, in the 35th year of the reign of the lord Charles 2d. the now king of England, &c. at the parish of St. Michael Bassishaw, in the ward of Bassishaw, London, well-knowing that one Thomas Armstrong, late of London, kt. as a false traitor had traiterously conspired and imagined the death and final destruction of the said lord the king, and for the same treason had traiterously fled, he the aforesaid *Joseph Hayes* afterwards, to wit, on the said 31st day of Aug. in the 35th year of the reign of the said lord the now king as aforesaid, and at divers other days and times as well after as before, at the parish of St. Michael Bassishaw, in the ward of Bassishaw, London, aforesaid, knowingly, maliciously, seditiously and traiterously did comfort, maintain, and support the said *Thomas Armstrong* and the said *Joseph Hayes*, then and there for the comforting, maintaining and supporting the aforesaid *Tho-*

mas

Indictment.
For conspiring the deposition, death and destruction of the King.

\# P. 6.

Overt act. Comforting and supporting Sir Th. Armstrong, whom he knew to have committed treason, and to have fled for the same.

An affift-
ing him
with mo-
ney.

mas *Armftrong*, malicioufly, feditioufly and traiteroufly did
pay, and did caufe to be paid to the faid *Thomas Armftrong*,
a fum amounting to the fum of one hundred and fifty pounds,
of the lawful money of England, againft the duty of his allegiance, againft the peace of the faid lord the king, his crown
and dignity, &c. and alfo againft the form of the ftatute, &c.

Indictments for Murder.

The King *againft* Green, and others.

Michaelmas, 30th Charles II.

Indictment.

For the
murder of
SirEdmund.
buiy God-
frey, by
ftrangling
him with a
handker-
chief.

* P. 7.

To wit. THE Jurors for the lord the king, upon their
oath prefent, That *Ro ert Green* of the parifh
of *St. Mary* in the Strand, in the county of *Middlefex*, labourer, *Laurence Hill* late of the faid parifh aforefaid, in the county aforefaid labourer, *Dominick Kelly* late of the parifh aforefaid, in the county aforefaid, clerk, and *Philbert Vernat* late of
the parifh aforefaid, in the county aforefaid labourer, not having the fear of God before their eyes, but being moved and feduced by the inftigation of the devil, on the 12th day of October, in the 30th year of the reign of the lord Charles 2d. by
the grace of God, king, &c. with force and arms, at the parifh of St. Mary in the Strand aforefaid, in the county aforefaid, in and upon one Edmundbury Godfrey, knt. in the peace
of God, and of the faid lord the king, then and there being,
felonioufly, wilfully, and of their malice aforethought, did
make an affault, and that the aforefaid Robert Green, a certain linen handkerchief, of the value of 6d. about the neck of
the faid Edmundbury Godfrey, then and there felonioufly,
wilfully, and of his malice aforethought, * did fold and faften,
and that the aforefaid Robert Green, with the aforefaid handkerchief fo by him, the faid Robert Green folded and faftened
about the neck of him, the faid Edmundbury Godfrey, then
and there, him, the aforefaid Edmundbury Godfrey, felonioufly,

ly, wilfully, and of his malice aforesaid, did choak and strangle, by which choaking and strangling of him, the said Edmundbury Godfrey aforesaid, by him the said Robert Green, in the form aforesaid committed and perpetrated, he the aforesaid Edmundbury Godfrey, then and there instantly died. And that the aforesaid Laurence Hill, Dominick Kelly, and Philbert Vernat, feloniously, wilfully, and of their malice aforethought, were present, aiding and abetting, comforting, assisting, and maintaining the aforesaid Robert Green, him the said Edmundbury Godfrey, in the form aforesaid, feloniously, wilfully, and of his malice aforethought, to slay and murder, and so the jurors aforesaid, upon their oath aforesaid say, that the said Robert Green, Laurence Hill, Dominick Kelly, and Philbert Vernat, in the manner and form aforesaid, him, the said Edmundbury Godfrey feloniously, wilfully, and of their malice aforethought, did slay and murder, against the peace of the said lord the now king, his crown and dignity, &c.

The trial and conviction of the defendants, on this indictment, is in State Trials, 2 vol. 214.

The King *against* Thurston.

Indictment.

To wit. BE it remembered, that at the goal delivery of our lord the king, of and for his county of Suffolk, holden at Bury St. Edmund's, in the county aforesaid, on Monday the 11th day of March, in the 14th year of the reign of our lord Charles the 2d, by the grace of God, king, &c. before Matthew Hale, kt. chief baron of the Exchequer of the said lord the king, and Edward Atkyns, kt. one of the barons of the Exchequer, of the said lord the king, justices of the said lord the king, assigned to deliver his goal of his said county of Suffolk of the prisoners being therein, and justices of the said lord the king, assigned to preserve the peace in the said county, and also to hear and determine divers felonies, trespasses, and other misdeeds in the said county perpetrated, by the oath of Francis Coppinger, K. M. S. B. (and 16 others) good and lawful men of the county aforesaid, impanelled and sworn to enquire for the said lord the king, and for the body of the county aforesaid, it is presented, That Anthony Thurston, late of West-haven, in the county aforesaid, labourer, not having the fear of God before his eyes, but being moved and seduced by the instigation of the devil, on the 30th day of May, in the 12th year of the reign of our lord Charles the 2d. by the grace of God, king of England, &c. with force and arms, at W. aforesaid, in the county aforesaid, in and upon one Edw.

For murder, by stabbing the deceased with a knife.

B   Rowe,

Rowe, in the peace of God and our said lord the king, then and there being feloniously, wilfully, and of his malice aforethought did make an assault; and the aforesaid Anthony Thurston, with a certain knife of the value of 1d. which he, the said Anthony Thurston, then and there in his right hand had and held, him the aforesaid Edward Rowe, in and upon the left side of the body of him the said Edward Rowe, under the ribs of the said left side of the body of him the said Edward Rowe, then and there feloniously, wilfully, and of his malice, aforethought, did strike, thrust, stab, and penetrate, giving to the said Edward Rowe, then and there with the knife aforesaid, in and upon the left side of the body of him the said

***P. 8.**

Edward Rowe, one mortal wound of the * breadth of one inch, and of the depth of six inches, of which said mortal wound, the aforesaid Edward Rowe, at W——— aforesaid, in the county aforesaid, instantly died, and so the aforesaid A. T. the aforesaid E. R. in the manner and form aforesaid, feloniously, wilfully and of his malice aforethought, did kill and murder, against the peace of the said lord the now king his

Capias awarded.

crown and dignity, &c. Whereupon the sheriff of the county aforesaid, is commanded that he do not omit, &c. but that he take him, &c. to answer, &c. &c. Afterwards, to wit, on Tuesday the 15th day of July, in the 14th year of the reign of our lord Charles the 2d, by the grace of God, king, &c. at the general goal delivery of our lord the king, for his said county of Suffolk, then held at Bury St. Edmund's, in the said county, before Thomas Twysden, kt. one of the justices of the lord the king assigned to hold pleas before the king himself, and Richard Levinz, Esq, justices of our said lord the king assigned to deliver his goal of his county of Suffolk aforesaid, of the prisoners being therein; cometh the aforesaid Anthony Thurston, under the custody of R. W. Esq. sheriff of the county aforesaid, (into whose custody heretofore for the cause aforesaid, and for other certain causes he had been committed) brought here to the bar in his proper person, and being forthwith demanded of the premises above charged against him, how he will acquit himself

Plea not guilty.

thereof; he saith he is not guilty thereof, and for good and evil puts himself upon the country. Therefore, immediately let a jury come here before the justices aforesaid, &c. and the jurors of the jury aforesaid, by the sheriff of the county aforesaid, for this purpose impanelled; to wit, W. C. T. B. J. B. (and 9 others) being called and come, who being elected, tried and sworn to speak the truth of, and concerning the premisses; say upon their oath, that before the perpetration of the felony and murder aforesaid, in the indictment

Special verdict, That ca. sa. issued out of the Upper

aforesaid, mentioned, to wit, in the term of St. Hilary, in the year of our Lord 1659, a certain writ of *capias ad satisfaciendum*, issued out of the court, lately called the court of Upper

Bench,

Bench, upon a judgment entered in the said court, directed to
the sheriff of Suffolk, to take the aforesaid A. T. in execution, at the suit of one William Hacon; the tenor of which
writ, follows in these words—" *The keepers of the liberty of
England by the authority of parliament, to the sheriff of Suffolk,
greeting, We command you to take Anthony Thurston, if he shall be
found in your bailiwick, and him safely keep, so that you have his
body before us in the Upper Bench, at Westminster, on Saturday
next, after the morrow of the Ascension of our Lord, to satisfy
William Hacon of seven pounds, five shillings, which were adjudged
to the said William, for his damages which he hath sustained as well
by not performing of certain promises and assumptions to the said
William, by the said Anthony made, as for his costs and charges by
him, about his suit in that behalf expended; whereof he is convicted
as appeareth unto us of record, and that you have there this writ,
witness R. Newdigate, at Westminster, the 13th February, in the
year of Lord 1659. Wrightwick and Henly.*" As by the writ
aforesaid to the jurors aforesaid, in evidence exhibited more
fully appears; and further, ⌐the jurors aforesaid upon their
oath aforesaid. say that J. W. esq; at that time sheriff of the
county aforesaid, by virtue of the said writ afterwards, and before the return of the said writ, and before the perpetration of
the felony and murder aforesaid, in the indictment aforesaid
specified; made his certain warrant under the seal of his office, to one W. P. his bailiff, to take and arrest the aforesaid
A. T. according to the command of the said writ, and that the
said W. P. by virtue of the * warrant aforesaid afterwards, and
before the return of the said writ, to wit, on the 30th. day of
May, in the 12th year of the reign of the said lord, the now
king aforesaid, at W. aforesaid, in the county aforesaid, took
and arrested the said A. T. and him in execution by virtue of
the warrant aforesaid, then and there had; and further the jurors aforesaid, say upon their oath aforesaid, that the said E. R.
then and there, by the command and at the request of the said
W. O. came to the aid and assistance of the said W. O. to lead
the said A. T. (so being in execution as aforesaid)to the goal of
the lord the king of the county aforesaid; and the jurors
aforesaid, further say upon their oath aforesaid, that the aforesaid A. T. then and there being under arrest, and in custody of
the said W. O. and in execution in the manner and form aforesaid, the said A. T. then and there, with the knife aforesaid,
struck the said E. R. and then and there gave to the said E. R.
the mortal wound aforesaid, in the indictment aforesaid mentioned, of which mortal wound the said E. R. then and there instantly died, (the said E. R. being then and there aiding and assisting the said W. O. to conduct the said A. T. so being then in
execution to the goal of the said lord the king in the county afore-
ors. But whether upon the whole matter aforesaid, by the jurors aforesaid, in the form aforesaid found, the said A. T. is

Bench, in
Hillary
term, 1659,
against the
prisoner,
that the
sheriff of
Suffolk
made a
warrant
therein, to
one of his
bailiffs who
arrested the
prisoner,
and the de-
ceased at
the bailiffs
request, af-
sisted in
carrying
the prisoner
to goal, and
in so doing,
the prisoner
stabbed the
deceased,
and killed
him, but
whether
murder or
not, &c.

* P. 9.

B 2

guilty

guilty of the felony and murder aforesaid, in the indictment aforesaid specified or not, the jurors aforesaid are intirely ignorant, and therefore they pray the advice of the justices aforesaid, and of the court, &c. and if upon the whole matter aforesaid, by the jury aforesaid, in form aforesaid found, it shall appear, to the justices aforesaid, and to the court, &c. that the aforesaid A. T. is guilty of the felony and murder aforesaid, then the jurors aforesaid say upon their oath aforesaid, that the said A. T. is guilty of the felony and murder aforesaid in the indictment aforesaid, specified in the manner and form as by the indictment aforesaid, is above supposed against him, and that the said A. T. at the time of the perpetration of the felony and murder aforesaid, or at any time after, had no goods or chattels, lands or tenements, to the knowledge of the said jurors; and if upon the whole matter aforesaid, by the jurors aforesaid, in the form aforesaid found, it shall appear to the justices aforesaid, and to the court, &c. that the said A. T. is not guilty of the murder aforesaid, then the jurors aforesaid, say upon their oath, that the said A. T. is not guilty of the murder aforesaid, as the said A. T. by pleading above hath alledged, but that the said A. T. is guilty of the felony and homicide only, and that the said A. T. at the time of the perpetration of the felony and homicide aforesaid, or at any time afterwards, had no goods or chattels, lands or tenements, to the knowledge of the jurors aforesaid, and because, &c.

This case is reported in 1 Keble 454, 455, *and* 1 Levinz 91. *The court gave no judgment upon the point, whether killing the bailiff who arrested him by a warrant under the usurped government, was murder or not, the proceedings being afterwards confirmed by an act of parliament, but the defendant got a pardon.*

The King and Queen *against* Bigglefton.

The Palace of the lord the king, and the lady the queen, and the verge of the same, to wit.

Indictment for murder, by knocking down an old woman standing in the crowd to receive the king and queen's maundy money, whereby she was trod to death by the crowd.

THE jurors for the lord the king, and the lady the queen present upon their oath, that Michael Bigglefton, late of the parish of St. Martin, in the fields, in the county of Middlesex, labourer, not having the fear of God before his eyes, but being moved and seduced by the instigation of the devil, on the 13th day of April, in the 5th year of the reign of the lord William and the lady Mary, the now king and queen of England, &c. at the parish aforesaid, in the county aforesaid, and within the verge of the palace, of the said lord the king and

and the lady the queen, (the said palace then and there being at Whitehall, in the parish aforesaid, and county aforesaid, and the said lady the queen in her royal person, then and there at Whitehall aforesaid, in the parish aforesaid, and county aforesaid, living and abiding) in and upon one Joyce Barker, in the peace of God, and of the said lord the king, and the lady the queen, then and there being, feloniously, wilfully, and of his malice aforethought, did make an assault, and that the said M. B. with a certain wooden staff of the value of one penny, which he the said M. B. then and there in his hands had and held, her the aforesaid J. B. [she the said J. B. then and there, at the parish aforesaid, in the county aforesaid, and within the verge aforesaid, among a great concourse of people, to the number of 500 persons at the least, to the jurors aforesaid unknown, then and there standing, and being to receive a certain charity, of the said lord the king, and the lady the queen, commonly called the maundy money] in and upon the forehead of the said J. B. near the left eye of the said J. B. then and there feloniously, wilfully, and of his malice aforethought, did strike and knock, whereby, she the said J. B. then and there at the parish aforesaid, in the county aforesaid, and within the verge aforesaid, among the concourse of persons aforesaid, then and there assembled and collected as aforesaid, fell to the ground ; and the jurors aforesaid, upon their oath aforesaid, further say, that thereupon many of the persons aforesaid, [so as aforesaid then and there collected and assembled] to the jurors aforesaid unknown, her the said J. B. so fallen to the ground, by the stroke and knock given to the said J. B. by the said M B. as aforesaid, and then and there lying and being prostrate upon the ground, in and upon the neck, shoulders, breast, belly, sides and back of the said J. B. with the feet of the said persons unknown, as aforesaid, then and there at the parish aforesaid, in the county aforesaid, and within the verge aforesaid, on and upon the ground there most grievously did tread and bruise, of which striking and knocking of her the said J. B. by the said M. B. with the wooden staff aforesaid, in and upon the forehead of her the said J. B. as aforesaid, and of the aforesaid treading and bruising of the said J. B. as aforesaid, by the persons aforesaid, with their feet in and upon the neck, shoulders, breast, body, sides and back of the said J. B. she the said J. B. then and there instantly died, and so * **P.** 11.
the jurors aforesaid, * upon their oath aforesaid, say that he the said M. B. her the aforesaid J. B. in manner and form aforesaid, at the parish aforesaid, in the county aforesaid, and within the verge aforesaid, feloniously, wilfully, and of his malice aforethought, did kill and murder, against the peace of the said lord the now king, and the lady the now queen their crown and dignity, &c.

This indict-
ment under
22 Hen. 8.
c. 12.

The

The King *against* Knowles, otherwise Earl of Banbury.

Hilary, 4 & 5 William and Mary.

Indictment for murder against the Earl of Banbury, by the name of Charles Knowles, esq; found at Hick's-Hall in Middlesex, and removed by Certiorari into the King's-Bench, where the defendant being arraigned thereon pleads misnomer in abatement of the indictment, *viz.* that he is Earl of Banbury, and sets out the King's Letters patent to his ancestors and the descents to himself, the Attorney-general replies, that the defendant petitioned the House of Lords to be tried there, for the said crime, and

Middlesex, HERETOFORE to wit, on Wednesday, to wit, to wit. the 7th day of September, in the fourth year of the reign of our lord William, and our lady Mary, by the grace of God, of England, &c. king and queen, at the general sessions of the peace of the said lord the king, and the lady the said queen, holden by adjournment for the county of Middlesex, at Hick's-Hall, in St. John-street, in the county aforesaid, before Char. Lee, kt. Lancelot Johnson, and others, their fellows, justices of the said lord the king, and the said lady the queen, assigned to preserve the peace in the county aforesaid, and also to hear and determine divers felonies, trespasses, and other misdeeds, in the said county perpetrated, upon the oath of twelve good and lawful men of the county aforesaid, then and there charged and sworn to inquire for the said lord the king, and the said lady the queen, and for the body of the county aforesaid, it is presented, that Charles Knowles, late of the parish of St. Giles, in the fields, in the county of Middlesex, Esquire, not having the fear of God before his eyes, but being moved and seduced by the instigation of the devil, on the 6th day of December, in the 4th year of the reign of our lord and lady, William and Mary, king and queen, &c. with force and arms, at the parish aforesaid, in the county aforesaid, in and upon one Philip Lawson, gent. in the peace of God, and of the said lord the king, and the said lady the queen, then and there being, feloriously, wilfully, and of his malice aforethought, did make an assault; and that the said Charles Knowles, with a certain sword, made of iron and steel, of the value of five shillings, which he the said Charles Knowles, then and there in his right hand, had and held drawn, him the said Philip Lawson, in and upon the left part of the body of the said Philip Lawson, then and there feloniously, wilfully, and of his malice aforethought, did thrust and stab, giving to the said P. L. then and there, with the drawn sword as aforesaid, in and upon the left side of the body of the said P. L. as aforesaid, nigh the ribs called the short ribs, of him the said P. L. one mortal wound of the breadth of one inch, and of the depth of six inches, of which said mortal wound, the said P. L. then and there instantly died, and so the jurors aforesaid, say upon their oath aforesaid,

that

that the aforesaid C. K. him the said P. L. in the manner and form aforesaid, then and there feloniously, wilfully, and of his malice aforethought, did kill and murder against the peace of the said lord the now king, and the said lady the now queen, their crown and dignity, &c. Which indictment the said lord the now king, and the said lady the now queen, afterwards for * certain causes, have caused to come before them, to be determined, &c. Wherefore, the sheriff of the county aforesaid, is commanded, that he do not omit, &c. but that he do take, &c. to answer, &c. And now, to wit, on the Tuesday next after the octave of St. Hilary, in this same term, before the lord the king, and the lady the queen at Westminster; cometh Charles, Earl of Banbury, under the custody of William Richardson, gent. keeper of the goal of the lord the king, and the lady the queen of Newgate, by virtue of a writ of the lord the king, and the lady the queen, of *habeas corpus ad subjiciendum*, &c. to him directed, into whose custody for the cause aforesaid, he had been before committed, by the name of Charles, Earl of Banbury, otherwise called Charles Knowles, Esquire, brought to the bar here in his proper person, and being immediately demanded of the premisses above charged against him, how he will acquit himself thereof, he saith, that he is the person in the indictment aforesaid mentioned, and intended by the name of Charles Knowles, of the parish of St. Giles, in the fields, in the county of Middlesex, Esquire, and against whom the indictment aforesaid is found, and preferred, for the murder and felony aforesaid, and saith that he ought not to be compelled to answer to that indictment, because he saith that the lord Charles the 1st, late king of England, &c. by his letters patent, under the great seal of England, bearing date the 18th day of Aug. in the 2d year of his reign, which letters patent, sealed under the great seal of the said late king of England, the said C. Earl of B. brings here into court; of his special favour, certain knowledge, and mere motion, advanced, made and created William at that time Viscount Wallingford, to the state, degree, dignity and honour of Earl of Banbury; and to the said William, by the said letters patent, gave, granted and appointed, the state, style, title, dignity and honour of Earl of Banbury, and invested, and really ennobled him, the said William, with the same name, title, stile, state, honour and dignity of an Earl, by girding on of a sword, and by putting on of a cap of honour, and of a golden coronet, to have and to hold, the same name, state, degree, dignity, stile, title and honour of Earl of Banbury, with all and singular, the pre-eminences and other honours to the same name, state, degree, dignity, stile, title and honour of an Earl, belonging or appertaining to the aforesaid William, and to the heirs male of his body issuing for ever;

willing

that thereon it was adjudged that he had no right to the said Earldom, to * P. 12. this replication the defendant demurs, and the Attorney general joins in demurrer.

The plea in abatement, misnomer for that defendant is a peer.

willing and by the said letters patent, granting for himself his heirs and successors, that the said William, and his heirs male aforesaid, and each and every of them, should successively have and bear, the name, state, degree, honour and title aforesaid, and that each and every of them successively should be called by the name of Earl of Banbury, as by the said letters patent more fully appears, by virtue of which letters patent aforesaid, the said William was Earl of Banbury, and was seized of the estate, degree, title and honour of Earl of Banbury, in his demesne as of fee tail, to wit, to him and to the heirs male of his body, and being so seized, the said William, Earl of Banbury died so seized, to wit, at the parish of St. Giles, in the fields aforesaid, in the county of Middlesex aforesaid, after whose death the state, degree, title and honour of Earl of Banbury aforesaid, descended to Edward Knowles, the son and heir male of the body of the said William, Earl of Banbury, whereby the said Edward was Earl of Banbury, and seized of the state, degree, title and honour of Earl of Banbury aforesaid, in his demesne as of fee tail, to * P. 13. wit, to him and the heirs * male of the body of the said William, to wit, at the parish of St. Gile's, in the fields aforesaid, and being so seized thereof, the said Edward Earl of Banqury, died seized, without heir male of his body, to wit, at the parish aforesaid, after whose death the state, degree, title and honour of Earl of Banbury aforesaid, descended to Nicholas Knowles, as heir male of the body of the said William, Earl of Banbury, to wit, as brother and heir to the said Edward, the son and heir to the said William, whereby the said Nicholas was Earl of Banbury, and seized of the state, degree and honour of Earl of Banbury aforesaid, in his demesne as of fee tail, to wit, to him and the heirs male of the body of the aforesaid William, late Earl of Banbury, to wit, at the parish of St. Giles, in the fields aforesaid, and being so seized, the said Nicholas, Earl of Banbury, afterwards died so seized thereof, to wit, at the parish aforesaid, after whose death the state, degree and honour of Earl of Banbury aforesaid, descended to the said Charles, as heir male issuing of the body of the said William, late Earl of Banbury, to wit, the son and heir of Nicholas, late Earl of Banbury, the brother and heir of the said Edward, the son and heir of the said William, whereby the said Charles at the time of the caption of the indictment aforesaid, was and as yet, is seized of, and in the state, degree and honour of Earl of Banbury aforesaid, in his demesne as of fee tail, to wit, to him and the heirs male of the body of the said William, and Earl of Banbury as yet is, to wit, at the parish of St. Giles, in the fields, and this he is ready to verify; wherefore, because, that he is not named in the indictment aforesaid, by the aforesaid name of Earl of Banbury, he prays judgment of

the

Indictments for Murder.

the indictment aforesaid, and if he to the indictment aforesaid,
ought to be compelled any further to answer, &c.

Creswell Levinz.
Bartholmew Shower.

And J. Somers, kt. attorney-general of the lord the now king, Replication
and the lady the now queen, who for the lord the now king, and That de-
the lady the now queen, in this behalf prosecutes, by protesting fendant pe-
not acknowledging any thing in the plea of the aforesaid Cha. tition at the
to be true, saith, that the said Charles Knowles in the indict- House of
ment aforesaid named to that indictment ought to answer, be- Lords, to
cause he saith that he the said Charles Knowles, by the name be tried
of Charles, Earl of Banbury, heretofore, to wit, on the 13th there, and
day of December, in the 4th year of the reign of the said that it was
lord and lady the now king and queen, did exhibit his certain resolved,
petition in writing, to the lords spiritual and temporal in par- defendant
liament, then and as yet, held and assembled at Westminster, had no right
in the county of Middlesex, alledging and pretending by the to the title,
said petition, that he the said Charles, by hereditary right, and that the
then was Earl of Banbury, and one of the peers of this realm petition
of England, and that at that time, he was indicted for should be
the death of the said P. L. wherefore the said Charles, most dismissed.
humbly besought the said lords spiritual and temporal, then
and there in the said parliament assembled, that he the said
Charles, of and for the death of the said P. L. might be tried
by the peers of the said realm, and thereupon it was in such
wise proceeded, that afterwards on Tuesday the 17th day of
January, in the 4th year of the reign of the said lord and
lady the now king and queen, by the said lords, spiritual and
temporal, in the said parliament, then and * there assembled * P. 14.
according to the law and custom of parliament, it was
resolved, ordered and considered, that the said Charles,
had not any right to the said title and honour of Earl of
Banbury, and that the said petition from thenceforth should
be dismissed, as by the record thereof, among the records of
parliament here at Westminster aforesaid, remaining more
fully appears, and this he is ready to verify, wherefore, he
prays judgment, and that the indictment aforesaid, may be
adjudged good, and that the aforesaid C. K. may further
answer to that indictment.

J. Somers.
T. Trevor.
J. Tremaine.

And the aforesaid Charles in his proper person cometh and Demurrer.
saith, that the said plea, of the said Attorney-general, of
the lord and lady, the now king and queen, in form aforesaid above, by replying pleaded, and the matter therein contained are not sufficient in law to compel the said Charles to

C

that

the said indictment any farther to answer. Wherefore, for want of a sufficient replication to the plea aforesaid, of the said Charles in this behalf pleaded, the said Charles as before prays judgment of the said indictment, and that he of the indictment aforesaid, by the court here may be dismissed and discharged, &c.

Joinder.   And Edward Ward, esquire, attorney-general of the said lord and lady, the now king and queen, who for the said lord and lady the king and queen in this behalf prosecutes, saith, that the plea aforesaid of the attorney-general of the said lord and lady, the now king and queen, in form aforesaid above, by replying pleaded, and the matter therein contained, are good and sufficient in law to compel the said Charles to the said indictment further to answer; which plea above, by replying pleaded, and the matter therein contained, the said attorney-general, of the said lord and lady, the now king and queen, on the behalf of the said lord and lady, the now king and queen, is ready to verify as the court, &c.

Edward Ward.
Thomas Trevor.
John Tremaine.

The court of King's-Bench, after several arguments, gave judgment, that the replication was insufficient, and the defendant remains untried to this day.

---

* Appeals of Murder.

Goreing v. *Deering.*

Michaelmas, 1st James II.   *Roll* 23.

Appeal of murder, by the widow of the deceased.   *Middlesex,* **C**HARLES DEERING, late of the parish of St. Martin's in the fields, in the county of Middlesex, esquire, was attached by his body to answer Mary Goreing, widow, who was the wife of Henry Goreing; esq; of the death of the said Henry Goreing heretofore her husband, whereof she appealeth him, and there are pledges to prosecute John Stone, of New Inn, in the county of Middlesex, gentleman, and Thomas Jones of the parish of St. Clement Danes, in the county of Middlesex, gentleman, and thereupon the said Mary, by Thomas Bathurst her attorney, according to the form of the statute in that case made and provided, instantly appealeth, the aforesaid C. D. for this, that when the said H. G. was in the peace of God, and of the

lord

lord the now king, at the parish of St. Martin in the Fields, in the county of Middlesex, on the 10th day of June, in the 1st year of the reign of the lord James the 2d. king, &c. about the eighth hour after mid-day of the said day, there, to wit. at the parish of St. Martin in the Fields, in the county of Middlesex came, the said C. D. feloniously, and as a felon of the said lord the now king, and of his malice afore-thought, and with premeditated lying in wait, against the peace of the said lord the now king, his crown and dignity, on the said 10th day of June, in the 1st year of the reign of the said lord the now king aforesaid, about the eighth hour after mid-day of the said day, and in and upon the said H. G. then with force and arms, &c. at the parish of St. Martin in the Fields, in the county of Middlesex aforesaid, did make an assault, and the said C. D. then and there with a certain sword, called a Rapier, to the value of five shillings, which he the said C. D. in his right hand then and there, to it, on the 10th day of June, in the 1st year, &c. at the parish of St. Martin in the Fields aforesaid, and in the county of Middlesex aforesaid, had and held, him the said H. G. in and upon the left side of the neck of him the said H. G. near the collar-bone of him the said H. G. then and there feloniously, wilfully, and of his malice aforethought, did thrust and stab, and then and there gave to him the said H. G. one mortal wound, of the depth of four inches, and of the breadth of one inch, of which mortal wound he the said H.G. then and there instantly died. And so the aforesaid C. D. him the aforesaid H. G. on the 10th day of June, in the 1st year, &c. at the parish, &c. in the said county of Middlesex, in the manner and form aforesaid, feloniously, wilfully, and of his malice aforethought, did kill and murder against the peace of the said lord now king, his crown and dignity. And as soon as the said Charles Deering, the said felony had committed he fled, and the said Mary him freshly pursued from vill to vill, unto the four nearest vills, and fur-ther, until, &c. And if the said Charles Deering * the felony   *** P. 16.** and murder aforesaid, to him in form aforesaid charged will deny, the said Mary is ready this to prove against him, as the court, &c. And the aforesaid Charles Deering in his pro-per person, comes and defends the force and injury, when, &c. and all the felony, and murder, and whatsoever, &c ——— And he prays Oyer of the writ of appeal; and it is read to him in these words. To wit. James the 2d. by the grace of God, king, &c. to the sheriff of Middlesex, greeting. For as much as Mary Goreing, widow, who was the wife of Henry Goreing, esquire, hath given us security to prosecute her suit, by John Stone of New Inn, in your county, gentleman, and Thomas Jones, of the parish of St. Clement Danes, in your county, gentleman, therefore, We command you, that you attach C. D. late of the parish, &c. in your county, esquire,

by

Defendant prays oyer of the writ of appeal and the re-turn there-of.

by his body, according to the law and cuſtom of England, ſo that you may have him before us, from the day of St. Michael in three weeks, whereſoever we ſhall then be in England, to anſwer to the ſaid Mary, of the death of the ſaid H. G. heretofore her huſband, whereof ſhe appealeth him, and have there then this writ. Witneſs Ourſelf, at Weſtminſter, the 8th day of July, in the 1ſt year of our reign, Layton. Alſo, he prays Oyer of the return of the ſaid writ, and to him in like manner it is read in theſe words, to wit: By virtue of this writ to me directed, I have attached the within named C. D. eſq; by his body, which body I have ready before the within written king, &c. at the day within contained, whereſoever, &c. as within it is to me commanded. The anſwer of William Goſlin, kt. and Peter Vandeput, knt. ſheriff. That writ as above indorſed, was delivered by the aforeſaid late ſheriff, to me the now ſheriff undernamed. on his departure from office. The anſwer of Benjamin Thorowgood, knt. and Thomas Kinſey, knt. ſheriff; which being read and heard, the ſaid Charles Deering ſaith, that the ſaid Mary Goreing ought not to have or maintain againſt him her appeal aforeſaid, for the death of the ſaid Henry Goreing, heretofore her huſband; becauſe he ſaith, that heretofore, to wit, at the general quarter ſeſſions of the peace, of the lord the king, held for the county of Middleſex, at Hick's-hall, in St. John-ſtreet, in the county aforeſaid, on Monday the 13th of July, in the 1ſt year of the reign of our lord James the 2d. king, &c. before William Earl Craven, &c. and others their fellow juſtices of the ſaid lord the king, aſſigned to preſerve the peace in the ſaid county; and alſo to hear and determine divers felonies, treſpaſſes and other miſdeeds in the ſaid county perpetrated, by the oath of Edward Porter, John Weſton, (and 15 others) good and lawful men, of the county aforeſaid, then and there ſworn and charged to enquire for the ſaid lord the king. and the body of the county aforeſaid; the ſaid C. D. by the name of C. D. late of, &c. eſq; was indicted for the death of the ſaid H. G. which indictment follows in theſe words, to wit, Middleſex, to wit, The jurors for the lord the king upon their oath preſent, that C. D. late of, &c. in the county of Middleſex, eſq; not having the fear of God before his eyes, but being moved and ſeduced by the inſtigation of the devil, on the 10th day of June, in the 1ſt year of the reign of our lord James the 2d. king, &c. with force and arms, &c. at the pariſh aforeſaid, in the county aforeſaid, in and upon one H G eſq; in the peace of God, and of our ſaid lord the king, then and there being, * feloniouſly, wilfully, and of his malice aforethought, did make an aſſault; and that the ſaid C. D. with a certain ſword made of iron and ſteel, of the value of 5s. which he the ſaid C. D. then and there in his right hand had and held drawn, him the ſaid H. G. in and upon the left part of the neck of him the ſaid H. G. near to the

* P. 17.

collar-

collar-bone of him the said H. G, feloniously, wilfully, and of his malice aforethought, did strike and stab, giving to the said H. G. then and there with the sword aforesaid, in and upon the left part of the neck of him the said H. G. near the collar-bone of him the said H. G. one mortal wound of the breadth of one inch, and of the depth of six inches, of which mortal wound he the said H. G. then and there instantly died, and so the jurors aforesaid say upon their oath aforesaid, that the aforesaid C. D. him the aforesaid H. G. in manner and form aforesaid, feloniously, wilfully, and of his malice aforethought, kill and murder, against the peace of the said lord the now king, his crown and dignity. Whereupon the sheriff of the county aforesaid, was commanded that he should not omit, &c. but that he should take him, to answer, &c. and that afterwards, to wit, at the delivery of the goal of the said lord the king, of Newgate, held for the county aforesaid, at Justice-hall in the Old-bailey, in the suburbs of the city of London, on Thursday, to wit, the 16th day of July, in the 1st. year aforesaid, before James Smith, knight, mayor of the city of London, Thomas Jones, knight, chief justice of the said lord the king of the Bench, W. M. J. M. and others their fellow-justices, of the said lord the king, assigned to deliver his goal of Newgate of the prisoners being therein, the aforesaid justices of the said lord the king, assigned to preserve the peace in the said county, and also to hear and determine divers felonies, trespasses and misdemeanors within the said county perpetrated, by their proper hands did deliver the indictment aforesaid, into the said court of goal delivery aforesaid, of record to be determined. Whereupon at the said delivery of the goal of the said lord the king of Newgate, held for the county aforesaid, at Justice-hall aforesaid, on the said Thursday the 16th day of July, in the 1st year of the reign of the said lord the now king aforesaid, before the said justice of the said lord the king assigned to deliver his goal of Newgate of the prisoners being therein, came the said C. D. in his proper person, and surrendered him prisoner in the goal of the said lord the king of Newgate, for the county of Middlesex aforesaid, under the custody of William Gostlin, kt. and Peter Vandeput, kt. sheriff of the co. of Middlesex aforesaid, who for the cause aforesaid, was brought there to the bar by the said sheriff, and was committed to the said sheriff, and forthwith being demanded of the felony and murder aforesaid, in the indictment aforesaid above specified, how he would acquit himself thereof, the said C. D. then and there said, that he was not guilty thereof, and thereof for good and evil he put himself upon the country, and thereupon by the said court then and there, the sheriff of the county of Middlesex aforesaid was commanded, that he should cause a jury immediately to come thereupon, before the said justices of the said lord the

William,
Earl Craven
&c. ut su-
pra.

king

king laſt-mentioned, to the ſaid court of goal delivery there, and the jurors of the jury by the ſaid ſheriff, for that purpoſe returned and impanelled, to wit, Thomas Whifield (and eleven others) being called came, who being elected, tried, and ſworn to ſpeak the truth of and concerning the premiſſes, then ſaid upon * their oath, that the aforeſaid C. D. was guilty of man-ſlaughter and of the felonious killing of the ſaid H. G. in the in-dictment aforeſaid named; and that the ſaid C. D. had no goods or chattels, lands or tenements, to the knowledge of the jurors aforeſaid, but the ſaid jurors then ſaid, that the ſaid C. D. was not guilty of the murder aforeſaid, to him charged in the indictment ſpecified as the ſaid C. D. for himſelf by pleading alledged, and that he never for the cauſe aforeſaid fled, as by the record thereof in its full force and effect now being and a-mong the records of the ſaid court of goal-delivery, before the juſtices of the goal-delivery of Newgate, for the county afore-ſaid, at Juſtice-hall aforeſaid, in the pariſh of St. Sepulchre, in the ward of Farrington without London, remaining, among other things in the ſaid record mentioned more fully appears. And the ſaid C. D. further ſaith, that no judgment of and up-on the premiſſes is as yet given; and that he there then was, and as yet is a clerk; and then and there at the ſaid goal-deli-very, before the juſtices laſt mentioned, was ready to read as a clerk, if that court would admit him to his book in that be-half; and as yet is ready to read as a clerk in bar of any judg-ment of death upon the conviction of manſlaughter aforeſaid, and this he is ready to verify; wherefore he prays judgment, if the ſaid M. G. her appeal ought to have or maintain againſt him, for the death of the ſaid H. G. &c. with this, that the ſaid C. D. will verify, that he the ſaid C. D. now appealed, and the ſaid C. D. in the indictment above ſpecified named, and in form aforeſaid convicted, are one and the ſame perſon, and not another nor a different perſon, and that the ſaid H. G. for and concerning whoſe death, he the ſaid C. D. now is appealed, and the aforeſaid H. G. in the indictment aforeſaid named, and for whoſe death the ſaid C. D. in form aforeſaid is convicted, are one and the ſame perſon, and not another nor a different perſon, and that the aforeſaid wound, in the appeal aforeſaid, by which it is ſuppoſed that the ſaid H. G. was killed, and the atoreſaid wound by which it is ſuppoſed in the indictment aforeſaid, that the ſaid H. G. was killed, are one and the ſame wound, and not another nor a different wound, and prays allowance of the premiſſes, &c. And as to the felony and murder aforeſaid, the ſaid C. D. faith, that he is not guil-ty thereof, and thereof for good and evil, he puts himſelf up-on the country, and the ſaid Mary doth the like, &c.

And the ſaid Mary Goreing, as to the plea aforeſaid, of the ſaid Charles Decring of the conviction aforeſaid, in manner and form aforeſaid above, by pleading pleaded; ſaith, that

And

* P. 18.

Net guilty as to the murder.

Demurrer.

the the faid Mary, by any thing, by the faid Charles Deering thereupon above, by pleading pleaded, ought not to be precluded from having her appeal aforefaid againſt him the faid Charles Deering, becaufe ſhe faith, that the plea aforefaid, by him the faid Charles Deering, in manner and form aforefaid, in bar of the appeal aforefaid above by pleading pleaded, and the matter in the fame contained, are not fufficient in law, to which plea ſhe the faid Mary hath no neceſſity, neither is ſhe bound by the law of the land in any manner to anſwer, wherefore for want of a fufficient anſwer in this behalf the faid Mary prays judgment, and execution to be had againſt the faid C. D. of and upon the premiſſes, &c.

H. Pollexfen.

* And the faid Charles Deering, as to the plea of him the faid C. D. of the conviction aforefaid, above-pleaded, faith, that the faid plea in manner and form aforefaid above pleaded, and the matter in the fame contained are good and fuſſicient in law, to preclude the faid M. G. from having her appeal aforefaid againſt him, the faid C. D. and entirely to defeat the faid appeal, which plea and the matter therein contained, the faid C. D. is ready to verify and to prove as the court, &c. And becaufe the faid M. G. to that plea doth not anſwer, nor it hitherto in any manner doth deny, the faid C. D. as before prays judgment, &c. and that the faid M. G. may be precluded from her appeal againſt him, the faid C. D. And becaufe the court of the faid lord the king here, is not yet adviſed to give their judgment of and upon the premiſſes, day thereupon is given to the parties aforefaid, before the faid lord the king, to the octave of St. Hilary whereſoever, &c. to hear their judgment of and upon the premiſſes, &c. becaufe the court of the faid lord the king, here thereupon not as yet, &c. And as to the trial of the iſſue aforefaid, between the parties aforefaid, above joined to be tried by the country, let the procefs thereupon ceafe, until that the matter aforefaid, in form aforefaid, above pleaded, by the judgement of the court, in fome lawful manner be determined. And thereupon before the faid lord the king at Weſtminſter, comes E. S. of, &c. E. T. of, &c. and W. W. of, &c. in their proper perfons, and mainprized to have the body of the faid C. D. before the faid lord the king, on the octave of St. Hilary aforefaid, whereſoever, &c. and fo from day to day until, &c. to wit, each of the mainpernors aforefaid, body for body, &c.

Judgment was given for the plaintiff by all the judges (except Street juſtice) for that the court was not bound to aſk the priſoner what he had to ſay, why judgment of death ſhould not be given againſt him, to let him in to obtain the benefit of his clergy. This cafe is reported 3 Mod. 156; and mentioned, 2 Shower, 507; but vide the next cafe of Armſtrong againſt Liſle, and the report thereof, where this cafe is mentioned, and the law now ſettled to be quite otherwiſe.

* P. 19.

Joinder

Continuan-
ces

― Armſtrong

* P. 20.   * Armſtrong v. Liſle.

Michaelmas, 8 William III.   Roll 561.

<table>
<tr><td>

Appeal of
Murder, by
the brother
and heir at
law, by bil,
at the aſſi-
zes.

Certiorari
to remove
the appeal
into the
King's-
Bench.
</td><td>

Cumberland,
To wit.
</td></tr>
</table>

THE lord the king hath ſent to his juſtices made by his letters patent, to inquire by the oath of good and lawful men of the county of Cumberland, and by other ways, methods and means by which they might or could better know, of certain treaſons, miſpriſions of treaſons, inſurrections, rebellions, counterteitings, clippings, waſhings, falſe coinings, and other falſities of the monies of this kingdom of England, and of other kingdoms and dominions whatſoever, and aſſigned to hear and determine certain murders, burglaries, manſlaughters, killings, felonies, rapes of women, unlawful meetings and conventicles, unlawful uttering of words, combinations, miſpriſions, confederacies, falſe allegations, and all other miſdeeds, offences and injuries, whatſoever, and alſo to his juſtices aſſigned to deliver his goal of the county of Cumberland aforeſaid, of the priſoners being therein, and to each and every of them, his writ in theſe words, to wit, William the 3d, by the grace of God of England, &c to our juſtices made, by our letters patent, to inquire by the oath of good and lawful men of the county of Cumberland, and by other ways, methods and means by which they could or might better know of certain treaſons, miſpriſions of treaſon, inſurrections, rebellions, counterfeitings, clippings, waſhings, falſe coinings, and other falſities of the money of this kingdom of England, and of other kingdoms, and dominions whatſoever, and aſſigned to hear and determine certain murders, felonies, manſlaughters, killings, burglaries, rapes of women, unlawful meetings and conventicles, unlawful uttering of words, combinations, miſpriſions, confederacies, falſe allegations, and all other miſdeeds, offences and injuries whatſoever, and alſo to our juſtices aſſigned to deliver our goal of the county of Cumberland aforeſaid, of the priſoners being therein, and to each and every of them greeting, We willing for certain cauſes, that all and ſingular indictments, inquiſitions, records, convictions and appeals of certain felonies, murders and manſlaughters, whereof Thomas Liſle is indicted, charged, appealed or convicted before you, and alſo that all indictments and records of acquittal, againſt the form of the ſtatute made for the taking away of the benefit of clergy, from manſlaughter in certain caſes, whereof the ſaid

Thomas

Thomas Lifle is indicted and acquitted before you, as it is said, be determined before us and not elsewhere, command you and each and every of you, that you or one of you send all and singular indictments, inquisitions, records, convictions and appeals, and records of acquittal aforesaid, with all things touching them by whatsoever name the said T. L. is named in the same, under your seals, or under the seal of one of you, before us at Westminster, on Thursday in 15 days of St. Martin, together with this writ, that we may cause to be done further thereupon, that which of right, according to the law and custom of our realm of England, we shall see to be done. Witness John Holt, kt. at Westminster, the * 6th day of No- *** P. 21.** vember, in the 8th year of our reign. Winter, Aflry. The an- **The return.** fwer of Edward Ward, kt. chief baron of the Exchequer, and one of the justices within specified ; the execution of this writ appears in a certain schedule to this writ annexed, Edward Ward.

Cumberland, to wit.—Be it remembered, that at the general **The bill of** delivery of the goal of the lord the king, of his county of **appeal.** Cumberland, held for the county of Cumberland aforesaid, at the city of Carlisle, in the county aforesaid, on Saturday the 15th day of August, in the 8th year of the reign of our lord William the 3d, king, &c. before Edward Ward, kt. chief baron of the Exchequer, and John Turton, kt. one of the justices of the said lord the king assigned to hold pleas before the king himself, justices of the said lord the king, assigned to deliver his goal there of the prisoners being therein, John Armstrong, brother and heir of Richard Armstrong, deceased, in his proper person by his bill without writ, instantly appealeth Thomas Lisle, in the custody of John Ponsonby, Esquire, sheriff of the county aforesaid, brought here to the bar in his proper person, of the death of the aforesaid Richard Armstrong his brother, and there are pledges to prosecute the said bill, to wit, John Doe and Richard Doe, which bill follows in these words, to wit, Cumberland to wit, John Armstrong, brother and heir of Richard Armstrong, late of Pedderhill, in the county of Cumberland, gent. deceased, in his proper person instantly appealeth Thomas Lisle, late of, &c. gent. for this, that when the said R. A. was in the peace of God, and the said lord the king at the city of Carlisle, in the county aforesaid, on the 4th day of November, in the 7th year of the reign of the lord William the 3d, the now king, &c. about the eleventh hour after mid day of the said day, there then came the said T. L. feloniously, as a felon of the said lord the now king, lying in wait, and with premeditated assault, against the peace of the said lord the now king his crown and dignity, on the same day, year, hour and place, and then and there, with force and arms, &c. feloriously, wilfully, and of his malice aforethought, upon him the said R. A.

D

did

did make an assault, and the said T. L. with a certain sword, called a rapier, made of iron and steel, of the value of five shillings, which he the said T. L. then and there, had and held drawn, him the said R. A. in and upon the left part of the body of him the said R. A. above and nigh the left pap of him the said R. A. then and there violently, feloniously, wilfully, and of his malice aforethought, did strike, stab and thrust, (which R. A. at that time had not any weapon drawn, nor then had first struck the said T. L.) and he the said T. L. then and there with the sword aforesaid, feloniously, wilfully, and of his malice aforethought, did give to the said R. A. in and upon the said left part of the body of the said R. A. above and nigh the said left pap of the said R. A. one mortal wound of the breadth of half of one inch, and of the depth of seven inches, of which mortal wound the said R. A. then and there, instantly died, and so the said T. L. on the said 4th day of November, in the 7th year of the reign of the said lord the now king, about the eleventh hour after mid-day, of the said day, at the city of Carlisle aforesaid, in the county aforesaid,

* P. 22. in manner and form aforesaid, feloniously, wilfully, and * of his malice aforethought, him the aforesaid R. A. who had not any weapon drawn, nor had first struck the said T. L. as aforesaid, did kill, slay and murder against the peace of the said lord the now king, his crown and dignity, &c. and as soon as the said felon, the felony and murder aforesaid had committed, he fled, and the aforesaid J. A. him freshly pursued from vill to vill, unto the four nearest vills, and further until, &c. and if the said felon the felony and murder aforesaid, to him in form aforesaid, charged will deny the said J. A. is ready to

Defendant prove this against him, as the court, &c. on which Thursday,
brought in 15 days of St. Martin, before the lord the king, at West-
into the minster, the said T. L. under the custody of the sheriff of
King's- Cumberland, was brought here to the bar, by virtue of the
Bench, by writ of the said lord the king, to the said sheriff in that be-
the sheriff half directed, to have the body of the said T. L. then before
of Cumber- the said lord the king, wheresoever, &c. to answer, &c. and to do
land, on a and to receive, &c. and thereupon the said T. L. for the cause
habeas cor- aforesaid, upon the appeal aforesaid, returned as aforesaid, by
pus, and the said court of the said lord the king, before the king him-
committed self, was immediately committed to the marshal of the mar-
to the mar- shalsea of the said lord the king, before the king himself,
shal. there to remain of and upon the premisses, until, &c. And after-
wards to wit, on the octave of the purification of the blessed Virgin Mary, in the term of St. Hilary next following, comes the said T. L. in the custody of the marshal, &c. and prays

Scire facias the writ of the lord the king, to be directed to the sheriff of
against the Cumberland, to forewarn the said J. A. to be before the said
appellant to lord the king to prosecute his appeal, &c. and it is granted to
prosecute. him; whereupon, the sheriff of the county of Cumberland
aforesaid,

aforesaid, is commanded, that by good, &c. he give notice to the said J. A. that he be before the said lord the king, from the day of Easter, in fifteen days, wheresoever, &c. to prosecute his appeal aforesaid At which day, before the king at Westminster, comes the said T. L. under the custody of the marshal, &c. and the sheriff of the county of Cumberland aforesaid, returns that by virtue of the writ aforesaid, to him directed, by good, &c. that he hath given notice to the said J. A. to be before the lord the king, at the day aforesaid, wheresoever, &c. to prosecute his appeal aforesaid; and the said J. A. when solemnly called, comes in his proper person, and saith that he is ready to prosecute his appeal against the said T. L. and prays that the said T. L. may to it thereupon answer, &c. and the said T. L. defends the force and injury, when, &c. and all the felony and murder, and whatsoever, &c. and saith that the said J. A. ought not to maintain his appeal against him the said T. L. for the death of the said R. A. because he saith, that heretofore, to wit, at the general delivery of the goal of the lord the king, for his county of Cumberland, holden for the county of Cumberland aforesaid, at the city of Carlisle, in the said county on Saturday the 15th day of August, in the 8th year of the reign of the lord William, &c. before E. W. kt. chief baron of the Exchequer, of the said lord the king, and J. T. kt. one of the justices of the said lord the king, assigned to hold pleas before the king himself, justices of the said lord the king, assigned to deliver his goal there of the prisoners being therein, &c. by the oath of Sir John Ballanton, kt. (and 21 others) good and lawful men of the county aforesaid, sworn and charged to inquire and present for the said lord the king, and for the body of the county aforesaid, it was presented, that T. L. late of, &c. gent. not having the fear of God before his eyes, but being moved and seduced by the * instigation of the devil, on the 4th day of November, in the 7th year of the reign of our lord William, &c. with force and arms, &c. at the city of Carlisle, in the county aforesaid, in and upon one Richard Armstrong, in the peace of God, and of the said lord the king, then and there being, feloniously, wilfully, and of his malice aforethought, did make an assault, and that the said T. L. then and there, with a certain sword, of the value of 5s. which he the said T. L. then and there, in his right hand, had and held drawn, him the said R. A. in and upon the left part of the body of him the said R. A. above and nigh to the left pap of him the said R. A. then and there, violently, feloniously, wilfully, and of his malice aforethought, did strike, stab and thrust in, giving to the said R. A. then and there, with the drawn sword aforesaid, in and upon the said left part of the body of him the said R. A. and above and nigh to the said left pap of him the said R. A. one mortal wound, of the breadth of half

of

of one inch, and of the depth of seven inches, of which mortal wound, the said R. A. then and there instantly died, and so the jurors aforesaid, upon their oath aforesaid, did say that the said T. L. him the said R. A. in manner and form aforesaid, feloniously, wilfully, and of his malice aforethought, did kill and murder against the peace of the said lord the now king, his crown and dignity, &c. And the said T. L. then and there under the custody of John Ponsonby, Esquire, at that time sheriff of Cumberland aforesaid, into whose custody for the cause aforesaid, he had been formerly committed, came before the said justices, brought to the bar in his proper person, and forthwith being demanded of the premisses above, by the indictment aforesaid, charged against him, how he would acquit himself thereof, the said T. L. then said that he was not guilty thereof, and thereof for good and evil put himself upon the country; and the jurors of the jury thereupon, by the sheriff of the county aforesaid, in that behalf, then and there returned and impanelled, to wit, John Bullman, gent. (and 11 others) being called, came, who being elected, tried and sworn to speak the truth of and concerning the premisses, then upon their oath said, that the said T. L. was not guilty of the murder aforesaid, in the indictment aforesaid, above specified, in the manner and form, as he the said T. L. above by pleading alledged, nor that he ever fled for that cause, but the said jurors upon their oath aforesaid, then and there said that the said T. L. was guilty of felony and manslaughter only, to wit, of the felonious killing of the said R. A. and that he the said T. L. had no goods or chattles, lands or tenements, at the time of the perpetration of the felony and manslaughter aforesaid, or at any time afterwards, to the knowledge of the said jurors, as by the record thereof, in its full force and effect now being among other things more fully appears, [which record the lord the now king, for certain causes, hath caused to come into his court here, before the king himself, by virtue of his writ of certiorari, and which in the said court of the said lord the king, before the king himself, among the indictments of the term of St. Hilary, in the 8th year of the reign of the said lord the king, now remains filed of record] And the said T. L. further saith, that no judgment of and upon the premisses aforesaid, in the indictment aforesaid to him above charged at the said general delivery of the goal, was given, but the said T. L. further saith, that
P. 24. he the said T. L. then was and yet is a clk. and then and there, at the said general delivery of the goal of the county of Cumberland aforesaid, before the said justices assigned to deliver the said goal, prayed the benefit of clergy might be allowed to him for the manslaughter aforesaid, whereof, by the jury of the county as aforesaid, then he was convicted, and he presented himself ready to read as a clerk, if the said court would admit him to his

book

book in that behalf; and the said T. L. further faith, that some
time ago, to wit, on the Monday next after the morrow of the
purification of the blessed virgin Mary, in the term of St.
Hilary, in the 8th year of the reign of the said lord the now
king, he the said T. L. in his proper person, came here into
the court of the said lord the king, before the king himself, in
the custody of the marshal of the marshalsea of the said lord
the king, which said T. L. was committed to the custody of
the said marshal (into whose custody the said T. L. before
that time, to wit, on Thursday in 15 days of St. Martin last
past, brought here to the bar by virtue of a writ of the said
lord the king, to have the body of the said T. L. in the court
of the said lord the king, &c. to the sheriff of the county of
Cumberland aforesaid directed, was by the court aforesaid
committed) and immediately by the said court here being demanded, if he had or knew any thing to say for himself, wherefore the said court of the lord the king, before the king himself, should not proceed to judgment and execution against him
the said T. L. of and upon the premisses in the said record of
conviction of manslaughter against him the said T. L. for the
death of the said R. A. (which record the said lord the king for
certain causes heretofore, into the said court of the said lord
the king, before the king himself, hath caused to come by his
writ of certiorari as aforesaid, and which record in the said
court of the said lord the king, before the king himself, at that
time remained, and now still remains) he the said T. L. then
and there said that he was a clerk, and there prayed the benefit
of clergy to be allowed him in that behalf, and thereupon by
the court aforesaid, the book being delivered to the said T. L.
then and there, the said T. L. then and there read as a clerk,
and then and there it was considered by the court aforesaid,
that the said T. L. should be burned in his left hand, and the
said T. L. then and there was burned in his left hand, as by
the record thereof, in the said court of the said lord the king,
before the king himself, more fully appears, and this the said
T. L. is ready to verify, wherefore he prays judgment if the
said J. A. ought to have or maintain his appeal aforesaid,
against the said T. L. of the death aforesaid, &c. with this,
that said T. L. will verify, that he the said T. L. now appealed, and the said T. L. in the indictment above-named,
and in the form aforesaid, convicted and burned, are one and
the same person, and not another, nor different, and that the
aforesaid R. A. for whose death the said T. L. is now appealed, and the said R. A. in the indictment aforesaid above-
named, and for whose death the said T. L. in form aforesaid,
was convicted, are one and the same person, and not another nor
different, and that the wound of which in the appeal aforesaid,
it is supposed that the said R. A. died, and the wound aforesaid,
of which in the indictment aforesaid, it is supposed that the
said

R. A. died, are one and the same mortal wonnd, and not another or different, and prays the allowance of the premisses aforesaid. And as to the felony and murder aforesaid, the said T. L. saith, * that he is not guilty thereof, and thereof for good and evil puts himself upon the country, and the aforesaid J. A. doth the like, &c.

*P. 25.

Not guilty as to the murder.

R. Webb.
St. John Broderick.

Replication that the defendant refused to plead at the assizes.

And the aforesaid J. A. as to the plea of the said T. L. of conviction aforesaid, in manner and form aforesaid, above pleaded, saith, that he by any thing by the said T. L. above by pleading alledged, ought not to be precluded from having his appeal aforesaid, of the death of R. A. his brother aforesaid, against the said T. L. because, by protesting, not acknowledging any such record as the said T. L. above, by pleading hath alledged in bar of appeal aforesaid, for plea the said J. A. saith, that after the bill aforesaid, of the appeal aforesaid, before the justices aforesaid, at the said court of general goal delivery was preferred, he the said J. A. without delay, prosecuted the said bill of appeal, in the said court of general goal delivery, before the justices aforesaid, and then and there instantly prayed that the said T. L. to the bill of appeal, so preferred and prosecuted as aforesaid, at the said then present general goal delivery should answer, and the said T. L. having had oyer of the bill of appeal aforesaid then appeared gratis, but to the bill of appeal aforesaid, entirely refused to plead or to answer during the general goal delivery aforesaid, as by the record thereof, among other things more fully appears, [which record the lord the king for certain causes, here into his court before the king himself, by his writ of certiorari hath caused to come, and which in the said court of the lord the king, before the king himself now remains] and this the said J. A. is ready to verify, wherefore, he prays judgment and execution upon the premisses, to be awarded against the said T. L. &c.

Bartholomew Shower.
John Cheshire.

Demurrer.

And the said T. L. by protesting, not acknowledging, any such record as the said J. A. above, by replying hath alledged, for plea the said T. L. saith, that the plea aforesaid, of the said J. A. in manner and form aforesaid, above by replying pleaded, and the matter therein contained are not sufficient in law for him the said J A. to have or maintain his appeal aforesaid, against the said T. L. and that he the said T. L. to the plea aforesaid, in manner and form aforesaid above, by replying pleaded, hath no necessity, neither is he bound by the law of the land, in any manner to answer, and this he is ready

to

to verify, wherefore, for want of a sufficient replication of the said J. A. in this behalf, he the aforesaid T. L. (as before) prays judgment, &c. and that the said J. A. may be precluded from having his appeal aforesaid. against the said T. L, and that the said T. L. by the court, may be dismissed of the premisses, &c.

R. Webb.
St. John Broderick.

And the said J. A saith, that the plea aforesaid, by him the said J. A. in manner and form aforesaid above by replying pleaded, and the matter therein contained are * good and sufficient in law, for him the said J. A. to have and maintain his appeal aforesaid, against the said T. L. which plea, and the matter therein contained, the said J. A. is ready to verify, and prove as the court, &c. wherefore, because the said T. L. to that plea doth not answer, nor it hitherto in any manner doth deny, the said J. A. as before prays judgment and execution upon the premisses to be awarded, against the said T. L. &c. And because the court of the said lord the now king, here, are not yet advised to give their judgment, of and upon the premisses, whereupon the parties aforesaid above, have put themselves upon the judgment of the court, day thereupon is given to the parties aforesaid, before the said lord the king, until the morrow of the Holy Trinity, wheresoever, &c. to hear their judgment of and upon the premisses, because the court of the said lord the now king. here thereof, not as yet, &c. to wit, to the said T. L. in the custody of the marshal, &c. and as to the trial of the issue aforesaid, between the parties aforesaid above-joined, to be tried by the country, let the process thereupon cease, until the matter aforesaid, in the form aforesaid pleaded by the judgment of the court be determined in some lawful manner, &c. and thereupon before the said lord the king, come W. L. of, &c. B. H. of &c. W. B. of, &c. and J. W. of, &c. in their proper persons, and mainprised, and each of them mainprised to have the body of the said T. L. before the said lord the king, at the same term, and so from day to day until, &c. to wit, each of the mainpernors aforesaid, body for body, &c. and thereupon the said J. A. according to the form of the statute in such case made and provided, puts in his place Michael Johnson, his attorney, to prosecute his appeal aforesaid, against the said Thomas Lisle, &c. at which day, before the lord the king at Westminster, come as well the said J. A. by his attorney aforesaid, as the aforesaid Thomas Lisle, in his proper person, but because that the court of the said lord the now king here, are not yet advised to give their judgment of and upon the premisses, whereupon the parties aforesaid, have put themselves upon the judgment of the court, therefore day is given

25

Curia advi-sari usque Michaelmas as well to the aforefaid J. A. as to the faid T. L. to wit, to the faid T. L. by the bail as before, &c. before the faid lord the king, from the day of St. Michael, in three weeks, wherefoever, &c. to hear their judgment of and upon the premiffes, becaufe that the court of the faid lord the now king here, thereupon, not as yet, &c. and as to the trial of

Ceffat pro-ceffus. the iffue aforefaid, between the parties aforefaid above-joined, to be tried by the country, let the procefs thereupon ceafe, until the matter aforefaid, in the form aforefaid pleaded by the judgment of the court, be determined in fome lawful manner.

Judgment for the de-fendant. At which day before the lord the king at Weftminfter, comes as well the faid J. A. by his attorney aforefaid the faid T. L. in his proper perfon, whereupon all and fingular the premiffes being feen, and by the court of the faid lord the now king here, more fully underftood, and mature deliberation being thereupon had, becaufe that it feems to the court of the faid lord the now king here, that the plea aforefaid by the faid J. A. in the manner and form above, by replying pleaded, and the matter therein contained, are not fufficient in law, for him the faid J. A. to have or maintain his appeal aforefaid, againft the faid T. L. it is confidered that the faid J. A. take nothing by his bill of appeal aforefaid, but for his falfe plaint be thereupon taken, and that the faid T. L. may go thence without day, &c.

This cafe is elaborately and learnedly reported by the Lord Chief Juftice Holt, in Keyling's Reports, 93.

---

* P. 27.   * Orbell, (widow) *againft* Ward.

Hilary, 3 & 4 of James II.

Appeal by writ, by the widow of the deceafed *Middlefex,* GEORGE Ward, late of the parifh of St. James, To wit, Weftminfter, in the county of Middlefex, gt. was attached by his body, to anfwer Elizabeth Orbell, widow, who was the wife of Ifaac Orbell, gentleman, of the death of the faid Ifaac Orbell, heretofore her hufband, whereof fhe appealeth him, and there are pledges to profecute, to wit, J B. &c. and thereupon the faid Elizabeth, by F. H. her attorney, according to the form of the ftatute, in fuch cafe made and provided, inftantly appealeth the faid G. W. for this, that when the faid Ifaac Orbell was in the peace of God, and of

our

our lord the king, in the parish of St. James, within the liberties of Westminster, in the county aforesaid, on the 13th day of July, in the 3d year of the reign of our lord James the 2d, &c. on the ninth hour after mid-day, of the said day, there to wit, at the parish of St. James, within the liberties of Westminster, in the county aforesaid, came the said George Ward, feloniously, and as a felon of the said lord the now king, wilfully, and of his malice aforethought, and with premeditated lying in wait, against the peace of the said lord the now king, his crown and dignity; on the 13th day of June, in the 3d year of the reign of our said lord the now king, at the ninth hour, after mid-day of the said day, and in and upon the said I. O. then with force and arms, &c. at the parish, &c. in the county aforesaid, did make an assault, and the said G. W. then and there, with a certain sword, of the value of 5s. which he the said G. W. then and there, to wit, on the 13th day of June, in the 3d year of the reign of our lord James the 2d, at the parish aforesaid, and in the county aforesaid, in his right hand, had and held, him the said I. O. in and upon the left part of the belly, of him the said I. O. nigh to the navel of him the said I. O. then and there feloniously, wilfully, and of his malice aforethought, did strike, and thrust, and gave to the said I. O. then and there, in and upon the said left part of the belly of him the said I. O. then and there, nigh to the said navel of him the said I. O. with the sword aforesaid, one mortal wound, of the breadth of half of one inch, and of the depth of six inches, of which mortal wound, the said I. O. from the 13th day of June, in the 3d year aforesaid, until the 16th day of the said month of June, in the 3d year aforesaid, at the parish aforesaid, in the county aforesaid, did languish, and languishing did live, and then to wit, on the said 16th day of June, in the 3d year aforesaid, at the parish aforesaid, &c. and in the county aforesaid, &c. he the said I. O. of the mortal wound aforesaid, died, and so the said G. W. him the said I. O. on the said 16th day of June, in the 3d year aforesaid, at the parish aforesaid, and in the county aforesaid, in the manner and form aforesaid, feloniously, wilfully, and of his malice aforethought, did kill and murder, against the peace of the said lord the now king, his crown and dignity, and as soon as the said G. W. the felony and murder aforesaid, had committed, he the said G. W. fled, and she the said Elizabeth him freshly pursued, from vill to vill, unto the four nearest vills, and further until &c. and if the said G. W. the felony and murder aforesaid, to him in form aforesaid, charged will deny, the said Elizabeth is ready to prove it against him, as the court, &c.

* And the said George Ward comes in his proper person, and prays oyer of the writ of appeal aforesaid, and the re-

* P. 28.
Prayer of
turn oyer of the

Writ of appeal, and of the return thereof.

Writ against the defendant, by the name of George Ward, late of the parish of St. James Westminster.

turn of the said writ, and they are read to him in these words, " *To the sheriff of Middlesex, greeting, for as much as Elizabeth Orbell, who was the wife of Isaac Orbell, hath given us security to prosecute her complaint, by J. B. late of the parish of St. James, Westminster, in your county, gentleman, and R. O. of, &c. thereafore, we command you, that you attach George Ward, late of the parish of St. James, Westminster, in your county, gentleman, by his body, according to the law and custom of England, so that you may have him before us, on the octave of St. Hilary, wheresoever, &c. to answer to the said Elizabeth, of the death of the said I. O. heretofore her husband, and whereof she appealeth him, and have there then this writ, witness, &c.*" The execution of this writ appears in a certain schedule to this writ annexed, the answer of Basill Firebrass, kt. and J. P. kt. sheriff, *Middlesex, to wit, I, B. F. and J. P. sheriff of the county of Middlesex, to the the said lord the king at Westminster, humbly certify, that by virtue of the said writ to me directed, which is annexed to this schedule, I attached the said George Ward, in the said writ named, by his body, according to the law and custom of England, whose body in the prison of the said lord the king, under my safe custody, I had and detained until afterwards, to wit, on the 21st day of December, in the 3d year of the reign of our lord James the 2d, &c. I received a certain writ, of the said lord the king, of habeas corpus cum causâ, to me directed, to have the body of the said G. W. before Robert Wright, kt. chief justice of the said lord the king, assigned to hold pleas in the court of the said lord the king, before the king himself, at his chamber, situate in Serjeant's-inn, in Chancery-lane, London, immediately after the receipt of the said writ; by virtue of which writ, on the receipt thereof, and immediately after, to wit, on the 20th day of December aforesaid, I had in my safe custody before the chief justice aforesaid, at the time aforesaid, the body of the said George Ward, together with the day and cause of the caption and detention of the said George Ward, in the form aforesaid, which chief justice then received from me, the body of the said G. W. charged with the cause aforesaid, and me exonerated from any further custody of the said G. W. therefore I cannot have the body of the said G. W. before the said lord the king, at the day and place in the writ aforesaid contained, according to the command of that writ, by the said sheriff*; which being read and heard the said George Ward, by C. G. his attorney, defends the force and injury, when, &c. and all the felony, and whatsoever, &c. and prays judgment of the original writ aforesaid, because he saith that he the said G. W. by the said writ is appealed by the name of G. W. late of the parish of St. James, Westminster, in the county of Middlesex, gentleman, whereas in truth and in fact, within the county of Middlesex, there is a certain parish known and called by the name of the parish of St. James, *within the liberties of Westminster*, but in the

Defendant pleads in abatement that there is

said

said county of Middlesex, there is not had, nor on the day of *no such* the suing out the original writ of appeal aforesaid, or ever *parish.* afterwards was there had any parish, vill or place, called or named by the name of the parish of St. James, Westminster only, as the said Elizabeth by her writ aforesaid supposes, and this the said G. is ready to verify, wherefore he prays judgment of the said writ, and that the writ aforesaid may be quashed.

H. *Pollexfen.*
Samp. Ward.

* And the said Elizabeth Orbell saith, that the plea afore- * P. 29. said, of the said G. W. above pleaded, and the matter there- *Demurrer.* in contained, are not sufficient in law to quash the writ afore- said, and that she to the plea aforesaid, of the said G. W. in manner and form aforesaid pleaded hath no necessity, neither is she bound by the law of the land to answer the said plea, and this she is ready to verify, wherefore, for want of a sufficient answer in this behalf, the said Elizabeth prays judgment against the said G. W. of and upon the premisses, and that the said writ may be adjudged good, &c.

Creswell Levinz.

And the said G. W. saith, that the plea aforesaid, by him Joinder. the said G. W. in abatement of the original writ aforesaid above pleaded, and the matter therein contained, are good and sufficient in law to quash the original writ aforesaid, of the said E. O. which plea, and the matter therein contained, the said G. is ready to verify and prove as the court, &c. and be- cause the said Elizabeth doth not answer the said plea, nor it in any manner hitherto doth deny the said G. as before prays judgment, and that the said writ may be quashed, &c. *Curia ad-* And because the court of the said lord the king here, are not *visare.* yet advised to give their judgment of and upon the premisses, therefore day is given to the parties aforesaid, before the said lord the king, from the day of Easter in 15 days, wheresoever, &c. to hear their judgment of and upon the premisses, because the court of the said lord the now king here, thereupon not as yet, &c.

Judgment for the defendant. Reported Shower's Reports 47. 1 Salk. 59.

E 2

Killegrew

Killegrew *againſt* Vincent.

Pleas before the lord the king, at Weſtminſter, *of the term of the Holy Trinity, in the 4th year of the reign of the lord* James *the 2d. the now king of* England, &c.

<table>
<tr>
<td valign="top">

Appeal by the widow of the deceaſed.

Not guilty pleaded, and at the trial at the aſſiſes the defendant was found not guilty.

* P. 30.

</td>
<td valign="top">

Cornwall. BE it remembered, that on Friday next after the To wit. Morrow of the Holy Trinity, in this ſame term, before the lord the king, at Weſtminſter, came Ann Killegrew, widow, who was the wife of George Killegrew, late of &c. eſquire, in her proper perſon, and brought here into the court of the ſaid lord the king then there, her certain bill againſt Walter Vincent, late of, &c. eſquire, in the cuſtody of the marſhal, &c. of the death of the ſaid G. K. heretofore her huſband; and there are pledges to proſecute, to wit. W. T. of, &c. baronet, and F. T. of, &c. eſquire; which bill follows in theſe words, to wit,—Cornwall, to wit. A. K. widow, who was the wife of G. K. late of, &c. eſquire, inſtantly appealeth, W. V. late of, &c. eſquire, being in the cuſtody of the marſhal of the marſhalſea, of the lord the king, before the king himſelf, for this, that when the ſaid G. K. was in the peace of God and of the ſaid lord the king, at the vill of. &c. in the county of Cornwall aforeſaid, on the 20th day of March, in the 4th year of the reign of our lord James the 2d, the now * king, &c. at the 7th hour after mid-day, of the ſaid day there to wit, at the vill &c. in the co. of Cornwall aforeſaid, came the ſaid W. V. feloniouſly, and as a felon of our ſaid lord the now king, wilfully, and of his malice aforethought, and with premeditated lying in wait, againſt the peace of the ſaid lord the now king, his crown and dignity, on the 20th day of March, in the 4th year of the reign, &c. at the 7th hour after mid day of the ſaid day, and in and upon the ſaid G. K. then with force and arms, &c. at, &c. in the county of Cornwall aforeſaid, did make an aſſault, and the ſaid W. V. then and there with a certain ſword, of the value of 5 ſhillings, which he the ſaid W. V. then and there, to wit, on the 20th day of March aforeſaid, in the 4th year of the reign, &c. at, &c. in his right-hand had and held, him the ſaid G. K. in and upon the right ſide of the body of him the ſaid G. K. under the right arm of him, the ſaid G. K. then and there feloniouſly, wilfully, and of his malice aforethought, did ſtrike

and

</td>
</tr>
</table>

and thruft, and gave to the faid G. K. then and there with the fword aforefaid, one mortal wound of the breadth of one inch, and of the depth of eight inches, of which mortal wound the faid G. K. then and there inftantly died, and fo the aforefaid W. V. him the faid G. K. on the faid 20th day of March, in the 4th year, &c. at, &c. in the manner and form aforefaid, felonioufly, wilfully and of his malice aforethought, did kill and murder, againft the peace of the faid lord the now king, his crown and dignity : and as foon as the faid W. V. had committed the felony and murder aforefaid he fied, and the faid Ann him freihly purfued from vill to vill, unto the four neareft vills, and further until, &c. And if the faid W. V. the felony and murder aforefaid, to him in manner and form aforefaid charged will deny, the faid Ann is ready to prove this againft him, as the court, &c.

And the faid Walter Vincent comes in his proper perfon, and defends the force and injury, when, &c. and all the felony and murder, and whatfoever, &c. and faith that he is not guilty thereof, and thereof, for good and evil, puts himfelf upon the country, and the faid Ann doth the like ; therefore let a jury come before the lord the king at Weftminfter, on the Wednefday next after three weeks of the Holy Trinity, who neither, &c. to recognize, &c. becaufe as well, &c. The fame day is given to the parties aforefaid there, &c. and thereupon before the lord the king at Weftminfter, comes A. B. of, &c. C. D. of, &c. G. H. of, &c. in their proper perfons, and mainprized to have the body of the faid W. V. before the faid lord the king, at Weftminfter, on the faid day, and fo from day to day until that, &c. each of the mainpernors aforefaid, body for body. *Plea not guilty.*

* Pleas before the lord the king at Weftminfter, of the term of the Holy Trinity, in the 4th year of the reign of the lord James the 2d the now king of England, &c. *** P. 31.**

Cornwall, to wit.—The jury between A. K. widow, who was the wife of G. K. late of, &c. efq; appellant, by her attorney, and W. V. late of, &c. efq; to recognize upon their oath, whether the faid W. V. be guilty of the death of the faid G. K. heretofore the hufband of the faid Ann, whereof fhe the faid Ann hath appealed him in the court of the faid lord the king before the king himfelf, or not, is refpited, before the faid lord the king at Weftminfter, until the Tuefday next after three weeks of St. Michael, unlefs the juftices of the faid lord the king, affigned to take affizes in the county aforefaid, fhall firft come, to wit, on Monday the 20th day of Auguft, at Launceftor, in the county aforefaid, by the form of the ftatute, &c. for the default of jurors, &c. therefore let the fheriff *The Juiata.*

have

have their bodies, &c. The same day is given to the parties aforesaid, to wit, to the said W. V. by his bail as before, &c.

Postea.

Afterwards at the day and place within contained, before Edward Atkyns, knt. chief baron of the Exchequer of the lord the king, and R. B. knt. one of the justices of the said lord the king, assigned to hold pleas before the king himself, according to the form of the statute, &c. come as well the within written A. K. widow, as the within mentioned W. V. esq; in their proper persons, and the jurors of the jury, whereof mention is within made, being called likewise come, who being elected, tried and sworn to speak the truth of and concerning the premisses within contained, say upon their oath, that the said W.

Not guilty.

V. is not guilty of the felony and murder within written, as the said W. V. within thereupon, by pleading hath alledged, therefore, &c.

The Distringas Juratorum in an appeal.

James, &c. to the sheriff of Cornwall, greeting. We command you, that you distrain William Vivian, esquire, and the other jurors summoned in our court before us, between A. K. widow, who was the wife of G. K. late of, &c. appellant, and W. V. late of, &c. to recognize upon their oath whether the said W. be guilty of the death of the said G heretofore the husband of the said A. whereof the said A. hath appealed him in our court before us, or not, by all their goods and chattels within their bailiwick, so that neither they, nor any by them, lay hands on them until that you shall have other command from us thereupon, and that you answer to us of the issues of the same, so that you have their bodies before us on the Tuesday next after three weeks of St. Michael, or before our justices assigned to take assises in your county, if they shall first come on Monday the 20th day of August, at Launceston, in your county, according to the form of the statute in that case made and provided, to make the said jury, and to hear their judgment of many defaults: and have you there the names of the jurors and this writ. Witness, R Wright, kt. at Westminster, the 4th day of July, in the fourth year of our reign.

Henly.

† Appeal

Appeal *of* Robbery.   *** P. 32.**

H. B.   againſt   J. O.

31 Charles the 2d.

Derby, AND the ſaid H. ſaith, that the ſaid J. ought Counter-
To wit, not to be admitted to wage battle in this appeal plea to a
with the ſaid H. becauſe he ſaith that heretofore, to wit, at the wager of
general ſeſſions of the peace, for the town of D. aforeſaid, in battle, on
the county aforeſaid, holden on the 7th day of June, in the not guilty,
31ſt year, &c. at the town of D. aforeſaid, at the Guildhall an appeal of
there, before R. W. eſq; mayor of the lord the king of the town Robbery.
aforeſaid, S. D. knt. recorder of the town, and others their fellows, juſtices of the ſaid lord the king, to preſerve the peace
there, and alſo aſſigned to hear and determine divers felonics,
treſpaſſes and other miſdeeds, within the town aforeſaid perpetrated, by the oath, I. D. gent. L. S. gent. &c. good and
lawful men of the ſaid town, then and there ſworn and charged
to enquire for the ſaid lord the king, and the body of the town
aforeſaid, it was preſented, that the ſaid J. O. by the name,
&c. on the 10th day of March, in the 31ſt year, &c. with force
and arms at the town of D. aforeſaid, in the county aforeſaid,
the ſhop of H. D. in the town aforeſaid, in the county aforeſaid, adjoining to the manſion-houſe of the ſaid H. B. in the
town of D. aforeſaid, and parcel of the ſaid manſion-houſe,
(Hellen the wife of the ſaid H. then being in the ſaid manſion-
houſe) feloniouſly entered, and twenty ſnaffles, of the value
of 8s. 4d. ſeven pair of ſpurs, of the value of 6s. 11d. two
whips, of the value of 6s. two ſurcingles, &c. of the proper
goods and chattels of the ſaid H. B. then and there found,
felonic uſly did ſteal, take, and carry away, againſt the peace
of the ſaid lord the now king his crown and dignity; the
record of which indictment, now for certain cauſes is tranſmit-
ted into the court of the ſaid lord the king, before the king
himſelf, by virtue of the writ of the ſaid lord the king, of
                                                certiorari,

eertiorari, and now here in the said court of the said lord the king himself, remains of record, as by the record here in the said court of the said lord the king, now remaining fully appears, and this he is ready to verify by the said record, wherefore he prays judgment, and that the said J. O. may not be admitted to wage battle, with this that the said H. will to verify that the said J. O. in the indictment aforesaid, and the said J. O. now appealed, is one and the same person, and not another nor different person, and that the goods and merchandize in the indictment aforesaid, above specified, and the goods and merchandize in the appeal of the said H. B. above mentioned, are the same goods and merchandize, and not other nor different.

Simon Degge.

See Pulton de pace Regis et Regni, 185 b. to 187 b, Staunford's Pleas of the Crown, 178 b, for what causes the appellant shall counterplead battle, and that an indictment found is a good counterplea.

---

* Indictments for Felony.

The King against Ringrofe.

<table>
<tr>
<td style="vertical-align:top; width:18%">Indictment for Felony, on the stat. 22 & 23 C. 2, c. 1. commonly called the Coventry Act against the person who did the fact, and the aiders and abetters.</td>
<td>

To wit. THE jurors, &c. that D. R. of, &c. W. D. of, &c. and M. D. of &c. on the 21st of February, in the 29th year, &c. not having the fear of God before their eyes, but contriving and maliciously intending one J. R. then and as yet being a subject of our said lord the king, to maim and disfigure, with force and arms, &c. at, &c. in and upon the said J. R. then and as yet being a subject of our said lord the now king, on purpose, and of their malice aforethought, and by lying in wait, unlawfully and feloniously did make an assault, and that the said D. R. with a certain knife, of the value of 1d. which he the said D. R. then and there, in his right hand had and held, then and there with force and arms, &c. on purpose, and of his malice aforethought, and by lying in wait, unlawfully and feloniously did cut and

disable.

</td>
</tr>
</table>

disable the right eye of her the said J. R. with intention in so doing, to maim and disfigure her the said J. R. and the jurors aforesaid, further say upon their oath aforesaid, that the said W. D. and M. D. with force and arms, &c. on purpose, and of their malice aforethought, and by lying in wait, unlawfullyand feloniously then and there, were present, abetting, aflifting and comforting the said D. R. to commit and perpetrate the felony aforesaid, in manner and form aforesaid committed, and so the jurors aforesaid, upon their oath aforesaid, further say, that the said D. R. W. D. and M. D. on the 20th day of February, in the 29th year, &c. at, &c. with force and arms, &c. on purpose, and of their malice aforethought, and by lying in wait, unlawfully and feloniously did do, commit and perpetrate, and each of them did do, commit and perpetrate the felony aforesaid, in form aforesaid committed upon the said J. R. against the form of the statute, &c. and against the peace, &c.

The King and Queen *against* Campbell and * P. 34. others.

The Second of William and Mary.

Middlesex, THE jurors, &c. that James Campbell, late of,   Indictment
To wit.   &c. Archibald Montgomery, late of, &c. John for stealing, Johnston, late of, &c. otherwise called Captain Johnston, late and marrying an of, &c. otherwise called Sir John Johnston, late of, &c. on Heirefs. the 14th day of November, in the 2d year, &c. with force and (*Stubbs.* arms, &c, at the parish of St. Giles, in the fields, &c. in and 587.) upon Mary Wharton. spinster, then and as yet being within the age of 14 years, and a maiden, and the only daughter and heir of one P. W. efquire, then deceased, and then and there having fubftance in moveable goods, to the value of one thousand pounds, and in lands and tenements, to the value of one thousand five hundred pounds by the year, and in the peace of God, and of the said lord the king and the said lady the queen, then and there being, violently did make an affault, and her the said M. W. then and there did put in great fear of her life, and her the said M. W. then and there, with force and arms, &c. from the said parish of St. Giles, in the fields, unlawfully, felonioufly, and against the will of the said M. W. violently did take, force, and carry away, with intention

F

that

that he the said J. C. for the lucre of the subftance aforefaid, her the faid M. W. felonioufly might marry and take to wife, and that the faid J. C. afterwards to wit, on the faid 14th day of November, in the fecond year aforefaid, at the parifh of St. Margaret's, Weftminfter, &c. by the affent, confent, procurement and abetment of the faid A. M. J. J. and of W. C. late of, &c. doctor in divinity, S. C. wife of, &c, and G. W. late of, &c. fpinfter, felonioufly, and for the lucre of the faid fubftance, her the faid M. W. felonioufly did marry and take to wife, to the great difpleafure of almighty God, againft the laws of the faid lord the king and the lady the queen; to the great difparagement of the faid Mary, and to the utter forrow and affliction of her friends, and to the evil example of all perfons in the like cafe offending, and againft the form of the ftatute, in fuch cafe made and provided, and alfo againft the peace of the faid lord and lady the now king and queen, their crown and dignity; and the jurors aforefaid, upon their oath aforefaid, further fay, that the faid A. M. J. J. otherwife called, &c. W. C. S. C. and G. W. on the faid 14th day of November, in the 2d year aforefaid, at the parifh of St. Margaret, &c. aforefaid, knowingly and felonioufly were affenting to, aiding, procuring, affifting, abetting and maintaining the faid J. C. felonioufly to commit and perpetrate the felony aforefaid, in the form aforefaid, againft the form of the ftatute, in fuch cafe made and provided, and againft the peace of the faid lord the now king and the lady the now queen, their crown and dignity, &c.

P. 35. *All the defendants (except Campbell, who fled) were tried at the Old-Bailey, upon this indictment, before Sir Henry Pollexfen, Chief Juftice of the Common Pleas, and the other Judges then * prefent. Sir John Johnfton, a Scotch knight, was found guilty and executed on a gibbet, before the lady's door in great Queen-ftreet, the reft were acquitted. Note, The ftatute upon which this is founded, is the 3d of H 7. c. 2. which makes this offence felony, and the ftatute 39 Eliz. c. 2. takes away clergy from the principal, procurers, and acceffaries before, fee the cafe of the lady Fulwood and others, (cited and made ufe of by the counfel for the king in this cafe) Cro. Ch. 483, 484, 488, 492, wherein are good obfervations and refolutions u on this ftatute; Sir John Johnfton was a ftranger to the Englifh laws, and when he was called to judgment was much furprifed, and afked if it was a hanging matter, but neverthelefs fentence was given againft him, and he was executed.*

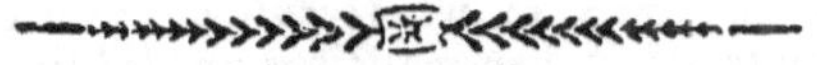

Indictments and Informations for Sedition.

1. By Acts.   2. Libels.   3. Words.

The King *against* Bradden and another.

Michaelmas, 35th Charles.   *Roll.* 54.

1. By Acts.

To wit. THAT whereas, Arthur, Earl of Essex, was on the 12th day of January, in the 35th year, &c. committed to the tower of London, the prison of the lord the king, for certain high treasons, by him supposed to have been committed, and the said A. E. of E. being a prisoner in the tower of London aforesaid, for high treason aforesaid, on the 13th day of January, in the 35th year of the reign of the said lord the king aforesaid, not having the fear of God before his eyes, but being moved and seduced by the instigation of the devil, at the tower of London aforesaid, in the county aforesaid, himself feloniously, and as a felon of himself, did kill and murder, as by the inquisition taken at the tower of London aforesaid, in the county of Middlesex aforesaid, on the 14th day of July, in the year aforesaid, before Edward Farnham, esquire, then coroner of the said lord the king, of the liberties of the tower of London, on view of the body of the said A. E. of E. before the said lord the king, remaining of record, more fully appears, nevertheless one Laurence Bradden, of the Middle-Temple, London, gentleman, and Hugh Speke, of Lincoln's-Inn, in the county of Middlesex, gentleman, not ignorant of the premisses, but devising and maliciously, and seditiously * intending the government of the said lord the king of this kingdom of England, to bring into hatred, detestation and contempt, on the 15th day of August, in the 35th year of the reign of the said lord the now king aforesaid, and at divers other days and times, as well before as after, at the parish, &c. with force and arms, &c. falsely, unlawfully, seditiously and maliciously did conspire, and endeavour to cause

Information for conspiring and endeavouring to persuade others that on an inquisition taken before the coroner, whereby it was found that the Earl of Essex, a prisoner in the tower, for High Treason, was felo de se was unduly taken, and that he was murdered by others to the * P. 36 disparagement of th king's government

the

the subjects of the said lord the king, of this kingdom of England, to believe that the inquisition aforesaid, was unduly taken, and that the said A E. of E. was killed and murdered by certain persons unknown, in whose custody he was, and to perfect and bring to effect their malicious and seditious devices, designs and intentions aforesaid, they the said L. B. and H.S. at the parish, &c. on the said 15th day of August, in the 35th year aforesaid, falsely, unlawfully, seditiously and maliciously did conspire to procure certain false witnesses to prove that the said A. E. of E. was not a felon of himself, but that the said A. E. E. was killed and murdered by certain persons unknown, and to persuade other subjects of the said lord the king, to believe this to be true, they the said L. B and H.S. falsely, maliciously and seditiously then and there in writing declared, and caused to be declared, that the said L. B. was the person who was prosecuting the murder of the said A. E. E. to the great scandal and contempt of the government of the said lord the king, of this kingdom of England, to the evil example of all others in the like case offending, and against the peace of the said lord the now king, his crown and dignity, &c. wherefore the said attorney-general of the said lord the now king, &c.

The trial of the defendant upon this information, is at large in the State Trials, vol. 3d, 267 to 312.

---

* P. 37.

* The King *against* John Hampden.

Indictment for conspiring with others, to raise an insurrection within this kingdom, and consulting and agreeing to send a messenger into Scotland to invite some ill-disposed persons there, to come hither to consult about, and assistance from France.

Middlesex,
to wit.

THAT John Hampden, late of the parish of gent. being a pernicious and seditious man, and a person of a depraved mind, and also of an impious, unquiet and turbulent disposition, and devising, practising, and falsely, unlawfully, unjustly, maliciously, turbulently and seditiously intending to disturb, molest and disquiet the peace of the said lord the now king, and the public tranquility of this kingdom of England, and as much as in him lay, to move, stir up, and procure sedition within this kingdom of England, and to endanger the government of the said lord the king, in this kingdom of England, and that the said John Hampden to fulfil, perfect, and bring to effect, his most wicked, detestable and seditious intentions aforesaid, on the last day of June, in the 35th year of the reign, &c. and at divers other days and times, as well before as after, with force and arms, &c. at the parish, &c. unlawfully, unjustly, maliciously and seditiously did assemble, meet, consult, conspire, and confederate himself, with divers evil-disposed subjects of

the

the said lord the king, to the jurors aforesaid unknown, and with the same did treat of and concerning the executing, perfecting, and bringing to effect, his wicked and seditious compassings, imaginations, and purposes aforesaid; and further the said John Hampden to fulfil and bring to effect his most wicked, detestable and seditious devices, practices and intentions aforesaid, then and there, to wit, on the last day of June aforesaid, in the 35th year of the reign, &c. aforesaid, and at divers other days and times as well before as after, at the parish aforesaid, in the county aforesaid, with force and arms, &c. falsely, unlawfully, maliciously and seditiously did consult, counsel, conspire, and confederate to make an insurrection within this kingdom of England, and to provide and procure arms, and armed men, to be prepared at different places within this kingdom of England, to fulfil and perfect his said most wicked, detestable, and seditious intentions, compassings, imaginations and purposes aforesaid, and that the said J. H. to fulfil, perfect and bring to effect his most wicked, detestable, and seditious intentions aforesaid, afterwards to wit, on the said last day of June, in the 35th year, &c. aforesaid, at the parish aforesaid, in the county aforesaid, with force and arms, &c falsely, unlawfully, unjustly, wickedly, maliciously and seditiously, did consult, agree and consent, that a certain person to the jurors aforesaid unknown, should be sent into Scotland to invite and incite divers evil-disposed subjects of the said lord the king, of his kingdom of Scotland, to come into this kingdom of England, to advise and consult with the said John Hampden, and with the said other evil-disposed subjects of the said lord the king in this kingdom of England, of bringing and supplying aid and assistance from the said kingdom of Scotland, to promote, do, and perfect his said most wicked, detestable and seditious compassings and imaginations aforesaid, in manifest contempt of the laws of this kingdom of England, to the evil and pernicious example of all others in like case offending, and against the peace of the said lord the now king, his crown and dignity.

---

* The King *against* Gerrard.　　　　* P. 38.

Michaelmas, 1st James 2d. *Roll.* 83.

Middlesex, **T**HAT Gilbert Gerrard, late of, &c. baronet, to wit. being a pernicious and seditious man, and a person of a depraved mind, and also of an impious unquiet disposition,

Information for conspiring to disturb the public peace

of the king-disposition, and devising, practising, and falsely, unlawfully,
dom, and unjustly, maliciously, turbulently and seditiously intending, to
holding con-disquiet, molest and disturb the peace and public tranquility
sultations to of this kingdom of England, and as much as in him lay, to
raise an in-excite, move and procure sedition and rebellion within this
surrection, kingdom of England, and to endanger the government of this
and procure kingdom of England, and that the said G. G. to fulfil perfect,
arms and
men to that and bring to effect his most wicked, detestable, seditious and
purpose. diabolical intentions aforesaid, on the 30th day of May, in
the 35th year of the reign of Charles the 2d, late king, &c.
and at divers other days and times as well before as after,
with force and arms, &c. at the parish, &c. unlawfully, unjustly, maliciously and seditiously did assemble, meet, consult,
conspire and confederate himself with divers evil-disposed subjects of the said late lord the king, as yet unknown, and with
the said persons then and there did treat of and concerning the
executing, fulfilling, perfecting and bringing to effect his said
most wicked, detestable, seditious and diabolical contrivances,
devices and intentions aforesaid, and that the said G. G. to
fulfil, perfect, and bring to effect, his most wicked, detestable,
seditious and diabolical contrivances, devices and intentions
aforesaid, then and there, to wit, on the 30th May, in the
35th year of the reign of the lord, &c. late king, &c. and at
divers other days and times, as well after as before, at the
parish aforesaid, &c. with force and arms, &c. unlawfully,
unjustly, wickedly, maliciously, seditiously and diabolically,
did consult, consent, conspire and confederate to make an insurrection within this kingdom of England, and to procure
and provide arms, and armed men, to be prepared at different
places within this kingdom of England, to fulfil, perfect,
and bring to effect his said most wicked, detestable, seditious
and diabolical intentions, purposes, imaginations and purposes,
in contempt of the laws of this kingdom of England, to the
evil and pernicious example of all persons in the like case offending, and against the peace as well of the said late lord the
king, as of the lord the now king, their crowns and dignities,
&c. whereupon the said attorney-general of the said lord the
now king, &c.

---

* P. 39.   * The King *against the* Earl of Macclesfield.

Hilary, 4th James II.

Information
for conspir-To wit. THAT Charles, Earl of Macclesfield, late of,
ing with   &c. being a seditious person of a depraved
Lord Grey,   mind,

mind, and also of an impious, unquiet, turbulent, factious and seditious disposition, and devising, practising and falsely, maliciously, unlawfully, wickedly, unjustly and seditiously intending to disquiet, molest and disturb the peace of the lord the king Charles the 2d, late king, &c. and the public tranquility of this kingdom of England, and to excite, move and procure, insurrection and rebellion within this kingdom of England, and to endanger the government of the said late lord the king, in this kingdom of England, and that the said Charles, Earl of Macclesfield, to fulfil, perfect, and bring to effect his most wicked, detestable and seditious intentions aforesaid, on the 30th day of May, in the 35th year of the reign of Charles the 2d, late king, &c. and at divers other days and times as well before as after, with force and arms, &c. at the parish, &c. falsely, unlawfully, unjustly, wickedly, maliciously, factiously and seditiously did assemble, meet, consult and confederate himself with Ford, late Lord Grey, and with divers other evil-disposed persons, to the attorney-general of the said lord the now king, as yet unknown, and with the said persons, then and there did treat of and concerning the perfecting, fulfilling and bringing to effect his said most wicked and seditious compassings, imaginations and purposes, and that the said C. E. of M. further to fulfil, perfect and bring to effect his most wicked, detestable and seditious contrivances, devices, and intentions, then and there to wit, on the said 30th day of May, in the 35th year, &c. and at different other days and times, as well before as after, at the parish, &c. with force and arms, &c. falsely, unlawfully, unjustly, wickedly, maliciously, factiously and seditiously did consult, consent, conspire, and confederate with the said Ford, Lord Grey, and with diver other evil-disposed persons, to make an insurrection and rebellion within this kingdom of England, and to procure and provide arms, and armed men, to be prepared in different places within this kingdom of England, to fulfil, perfect and bring to effect, his said most wicked and seditious compassings, intentions and purposes aforesaid, and that the said C. E. of M. further to fulfil, perfect and bring to effect, his most wicked, detestable, seditious and diabolical contrivances, devices and intentions aforesaid, afterwards, to wit, on the said 30th day of May, in the 35th year, &c. at, &c. falsely, unlawfully, wickedly, unjustly, factiously and seditiously assumed upon himself, and to the aforesaid evil-disposed persons promised, that he would be personally aiding and assisting to fulfil and promote the said his most wicked, detestable and seditious intentions and compassings aforesaid, in contempt of the laws, &c. to the evil example, &c. and against the peace, &c.

The

* P. 40.　　　　　* *The* King *against* Trenchard.

Hilary the 2d. *of* James *the 2d.*

<table>
<tr><td>Information for the like.</td><td>

London, THAT John Trenchard, late of, &c. esquire, To wit. being a pernicious and sediticus person, of a depraved mind, and also of an impious, unquiet, turbulent, factious and seditious disposition, and devising, practising and falsely, maliciously, unlawfully, wickedly and seditiously intending to disquiet and disturb the peace of the lord Charles the 2d late king of England, &c. and the public tranquillity of this kingdom of England, and to stir up, move and procure insurrection and rebellion within this kingdom of England, and to endanger the government of the said late lord the king in this kingdom of England, and that the said J. T. to fulfil, perfect, and bring to effect his most wicked, detestable and seditious intentions aforesaid, on the 30th day of May, in the 35th year of the reign of the lord Charles the 2d, late king, &c. and at divers other days and times, as well before as after, with force and arms, &c. at, &c. unlawfully, unjustly, wickedly, maliciously, factiously and seditiously, did assemble, meet, consult and confederate himself with Ford, late lord Grey, and with divers other evil-disposed persons to the Attorney-general aforesaid, of the said lord the now king as yet unknown, and with the said Ford, late lord Grey, and with the aforesaid other evil-disposed persons, then and there did treat of and concerning the fulfilling, perfecting, and bringing to effect, his said most wicked and seditious compassings, imagirations, and purposes aforesaid, and then and there, to wit, on the day and year, &c. aforesaid, and at divers other days and times, as well before as after, at the parish, &c. with force and arms, &c. with the aforesaid late lord Grey, and with the other evil disposed persons aforesaid, to the said attorney-general of the said lord the now king as yet unknown, falsely, unlawfully, unjustly, wickedly, maliciously, factiously and seditiously did consult, consent, conspire and confederate to stir up, move and levy insurrection, rebellion and war against the said late lord the king, and to provide and procure arms and armed men, to be prepared in divers places in this said kingdom of England : And that the said J. T. further to fulfil, perfect, and bring to effect his said most wicked, detestable, seditious and diabolical devices,

practices

</td></tr>
</table>

practises and intentions aforesaid, afterwards, to wit. on the
day and year, &c. aforesaid, at the parish &c. with force
and arms, &c. falsely, unlawfully, unjustly, wickedly, factiously, and seditiously assumed upon himself, and to the said
Ford, lord G. and to the other evil-disposed persons as aforesaid unknown, promised and undertook, that he would be
personally aiding and assisting, to fulfil, perfect, and promote
his said most wicked, detestable, and seditious compassings and
intentions aforesaid, in manifest contempt of the laws of this
kingdom of England, to the evil example of all others in like
case offending, and against the peace, &c.

The King *against* Blake.

* P. 41.

Michaelmas, 1st James *the* 2d.

Middlesex, **T**HAT Samuel Blake, late of, &c. draper, being
To wit. a pernicious and seditious man, and a person
of a depraved mind, and of an impious, unquiet and turbulent
disposition, and devising, practising, and falsely, maliciously,
wickedly, and diabolically intending not only to disquiet, molest and disturb the peace and public tranquility of this kingdom of England, but also to stir up, move and procure war and
rebellion against the most serene lord James the 2d. &c. his
natural lord within this kingdom of England, and to subvert,
change, and alter the government of the said lord the now king
of this his kingdom of England, and to depose and deprive
the said lord the king of his style, title, honour, and Royal
name, and of the imperial crown of this kingdom of England,
and to put and bring the said lord the king to death and final
destruction, and to fulfil, perfect, and bring to effect, his most
wicked, detestable, and diabolical contrivances, devices and
intentions, he the said S. B, on the 1st day of June, in the 1st
year, &c. with force and arms, &c. falsely, unlawfully, unjustly, wickedly, and diabolically, at the parish, &c. did give
and deliver, and did cause to be given and delivered to one
John Evans, a great sum of money, to wit, the sum of eleven
pounds, and fifteen shillings of the lawful money of England,
under the condition, and for the intention and purpose, that he
the said J. E. instantly should purchase a horse and pistols,

Information
for advanc-
ing money
to a man to
buy a horse
and arms to
go and assist
the duke of
Monmouth
in rebellion

G

and

and without delay should travel into the western parts of this kingdom of England, and should join himself, the said J. E. to one James Scott, otherwise called James Duke of Monmouth, and to other traitors and rebels, at that time traiterously assembling, to wit, at Lyme Regis, in the county of Dorset, in the western parts of this kingdom of England, in the treasons of the said traitors, against his most serene lord the now king, to aid and assist the said James Scott, otherwise called James duke of Monmouth, and the other traitors and rebels aforesaid, to do, perfect, and bring to effect their treasons aforesaid, against the duty of his allegiance, and against the peace of the said lord the now king his crown and dignity, &c.

* P. 43.   * *The* King *against* Wildman.

Information for conspiring to raise rebellion in the kingdom.

Middlesex, To wit. THAT John Wildman. late of, &c, being a seditious and pernicious person, of a depraved, mind, and also of an impious, unquiet, turbulent, factious and seditious disposition, and devising, practising, and falsely, unlawfully, wickedly, and seditiously intending to disquiet, molest and disturb the peace of the said lord the now king, and the common tranquillity of this kingdom of England, and to stir up, move and procure sedition and rebellion within this kingdom of England, and to endanger the government of the said lord the king of this kingdom of England, and that the said J W. to fulfil, perfect, and bring to effect his most wicked, detestable, and seditious devices and intentions aforesaid, on the 20th day of May in the 1st year of the reign of the lord James, &c. and at divers other days and times, as well before as after, with force and arms, &c. at the parish, &c. falsely, unlawfully, wickedly, maliciously, unjustly, factiously, and seditiously did assemble, meet, consult, and confederate himself with one Wm· Disney, and with divers other evil-disposed persons to the attorney-general aforesaid, of the said lord the now king, as yet unknown, and with the said persons then and there did treat of and concerning the fulfilling, perfecting and bringing to effect, his most wicked and seditious compassings, imaginations, intentions and purposes aforesaid,

and

and then and there, to wit, on the said 20th day of May, in the 1ft year, &c. and at divers other days and times as well before as after, at the parish, &c. with force and arms, &c. falsely, unlawfully, unjustly, wickedly, factiously, maliciously, and seditiously did consult, consent, conspire and confederate, with the said W. D. and the divers other evil-disposed persons aforesaid unknown, to make an insurrection and rebellion within this kingdom of England, and to procure and provide arms and armed men to be prepared in divers places in this kingdom of England, to fulfil, perfect and bring to effect, his most wicked, detestable, seditious and diabolical contrivances, devices and intentions aforesaid; And that the said J. W. further to fulfil, perfect and bring to effect his most wicked, detestable, seditious and diabolical contrivances, devices and intentions aforesaid, afterwards, to wit, on the 20th day of May, in the 1ft year, &c. aforesaid, at, &c. with force and arms, &c. falsely, unlawfully, unjustly, wickedly, factiously and seditiously assumed upon himself, and to the aforesaid evil-disposed persons promised, that he the said J. W. would be personally aiding and assisting in the fulfilling, perfecting and promoting his said most wicked, detestable and seditious intentions, purposes and compassings aforesaid, and then and there did send a certain person unknown, into parts beyond the seas, to wit, into Holland in parts beyond the seas, to one * James late duke of Monmouth, to incite and procure the said James late duke of Monmouth to invade this kingdom of England, with a great number of armed men, and to move, procure, and levy war and rebellion against the said lord the now king within this kingdom of England, to the evil and pernicious example of all others in like case offending, and against the peace, &c.

* P. 43.

The King *against* Nevill.

Hilary, the 30th & 31ft Charles II.

2. By Libels.

To wit. THAT in the term of St. Michael, in the 30th year, &c. in the court of the said lord the king, before the king himself, at Westminster, in the county of Middlesex, one Edward Coleman, late of, &c. gentleman, in

Information for writing, composing and publishing a seditious libel.

*entitled the
Glorified
Martyr, to
bring into
contempt
the treason
committed
by Edward
Coleman,
and the ver-
dict and
judgment
whereon he
was execu-
ted for the
same.*

the due manner, by the oath of twelve jurors, good and law-ful men of the county of Middlesex aforesaid, was indicted for divers high treasons, in falsely, maliciously, subtely and traiterously purposing, compassing, imagining and intending to justify sedition and rebellion within this kingdom of England and entirely to deprive, depose and disinherit the said lord the now king, from his royal state, title, power and government of this kingdom, and to bring and put the said lord the king to death and final destruction, and to change and alter at his will and pleasure, the government of the said kingdom, and the true worship of God in the said kingdom, certainly by the laws of the said kingdom established, and totally to subvert and destroy the state of this kingdom of England, well ordered and instituted in all its parts, and to levy and procure war against the said lord the king, within this realm of England; and that the said E. C. afterwards to wit, in the term of St. Michael, in the 30th year, &c. aforesaid, in the said court of the said lord the king, before the king himself, at Westminster, in the county of Middlesex aforesaid, in the due manner, by the oath of 12 jurors of the country, was convicted of the said high treasons, and afterwards was drawn, hanged and quartered. And that one Henry Nevill, of, &c. otherwise called Henry Payne, of, &c. well-knowing the premisses aforesaid, but being a pernicious and seditious man, and contriving and maliciously intending to diminish the said crime and offence of treason, and also to bring and draw the verdict and judgment aforesaid, in the lawful manner aforesaid, against the said E. C. for the high treasons aforesaid, had, obtained and given, into hatred and scandal, with all the liege subjects of the said lord the king, and to cause and procure the said E. C. who for the treason aforesaid, by him, as aforesaid committed, in the form aforesaid, was rightly and justly punished, to be reputed and worshiped within this kingdom of England, as a most glorious martyr of God, by wicked and superstitious men of the Roman religion, on the 10th day of January, in the 30th year, &c. at the parish, &c. * falsely, unlawfully, unjustly, wickedly, maliciously, scandalously and seditiously did make, compose and write, and did cause to be made, composed and written a certain false, malicious, scandalous, libellous and seditious libel, entitled the Glorified Martyr, E. C. [by which two letters E. C. the said H. N. did intend, and did design the said E. C. to be understood, who for high treason as aforesaid, was lawfully convicted and attainted, and afterwards drawn, hanged and quartered, to be understood] the tenor of which false, malicious, scandalous, libellous and seditious libel follows, to wit, " *To the glorified martyr, E. C. Hail glorious soul to whom the crown is given, all hail thou mighty favorite of heaven, triumphant martyr, from the endless throne, where thou must reign with Christ disturbed by none;*

P. 44.

look

*look down a while and view upon his knee, an understanding friend
to truth and thee; pardon the boasted title since that love, which gives
it here must needs confirm it above; for that's a flaming charity
which sure, since boundless here must endless there endure; but ah!
alas great saint I own with shame, that ill I then, worse now deserve
that name; whilst here on earth my troubles kept me still, from friend-
ship's laws, and now my causes will; but what you pardoned then
on fortune's score, be pleased on passions now to pity move. And for
those goods which here you did design, without reward or least desert
of mine, obtain me more from our great Lord and thine; not that I
hope to equal thee in place, tho' I could wish it with the like disgrace;
I barely hope to view that holy ring, where crowned saints do hallelu-
jahs sing; prepare me some low place in that bright quire, where tho'
I might not sing I might admire.''*

And the said attorney-general of the said lord the king, for
our said lord the king further gives the court here to understand and to be informed, that the said H. N. &c. otherwise
called H. P. &c afterwards to wit, on the said 10th day of
January, in the 30th year, &c. at the parish, &c. knowingly
the said false, feigned, malicious, scandalous, libellous and seditious libel, falsely, unlawfully, unjustly, wickedly, maliciously, scandalously and seditiously to divers liege subjects of the
said lord the king, then and there did publish, and did cause to
be published, in manifest contempt of the laws of this kingdom of England, to the pernicious example of all others in
like case offending, and against the peace, &c. Whereupon
the said attorney-general of the said lord the king, for the
said lord the king, prays the consideration of the court here
in the premisses, and the due process of law to be awarded
against the said H. N. otherwise called H. P. in this behalf, to
make him answer to the said lord the king, &c.

---

* The King *against* Baxter.

* P. 45.

London, } **T**HAT Richard Baxter, late of, &c. clerk, being
To wit.   a factious and seditious person, of a wicked Information
mind, and also of an impious, unquiet and turbulent disposition, for a Libel,
and conversation, and devising, practising, and intending, as in Notes on
much as in him lay, not only to disquiet, molest and disturb the the New
Testament.
      peace

peace and public tranquility of the said lord the king, within this kingdom of England, and to move, procure, and stir up sedition, discord and malevolence among the liege and faithful subjects of the said lord the king, but also to bring into hatred and scandal, and to render useless the sincere, pious, blessed and peaceable protestant religion, used within this kingdom of England, and the prelates, bishops, and other clergymen of the English church, established by the laws of this kingdom, and the new testament of our lord and saviour Jesus Christ, and that the said R. B. to fulfil, perfect, and bring to effect his most wicked, detestable and diabolical intentions aforesaid, on the 14th day of February, in the 1st year of the reign of our lord James the 2d with force and arms, &c. at, &c. falsely, unlawfully, unjustly, wickedly, factiously, seditiously and irreligiously did make, compose, write, imprint and publish, and did cause to be made, composed, written, imprinted and published a certain false, seditious, libellous, factious and irreligious book, intitled, *" a Paraphrase on the " New Testament, with notes doctrinal and practical,"* in which false, seditious, libellous, factious and irreligious book, among other things were contained these false, factious, malicious, scandalous and seditious sentences, of and concerning the said prelates, bishops, and other clergymen of the church of this kingdom of England, in these English words following, to wit, *" Note, are not these preachers and prelates,* (meaning the bishops and other clergymen of the said church of this kingdom of England) *then the least and basest that preach and tread'd wn christian love of all that dissent from any of their presumptions, and so preach down not the least but the great command ?"* And the said attorney-general of the said lord the king, for the lord the king further gives the court here to understand and to be informed, that in another place in the said false, scandalous, seditious and irreligious book, among other things there were contained these false, libellous, scandalous, seditious and irreligious sentences following, of and concerning the said clergymen of the said church of this kingdom of England, to wit, *" Note, it is folly to doubt whether there be devils, while devils incarnate live here among us,* (meaning the clergymen of the said church of this kingdom of England) *what else but devils sure could make ceremonious hypocrites,* (meaning the clergymen aforesaid) *consult with politick royalists,* (meaning the liege and faithful subjects of the said lord the king of his kingdom of England) *to destroy the Son of God for saving men's health and lives by miracle ? Quere, whether if this withered hand had been their own, they would have plotted to kill him, that would have cured them by a miracle, as a sabbath-breaker ? and whether their successors,* (meaning the prelates, bishops, and other clergymen of the church of this * kingdom of England, who have in order succeeded) *would silence and imprison godly ministers,* (meaning the said R. B. and

other

(margin: 1st Count.)

(margin: 2d Count.)

*(margin: * P. 46.)*

other factious and seditious perfons within this kingdom of England, arguing againſt the laws of this kingdom, and the liturgy of the church eſtabliſhed within this kingdom) *if they could cure them of their fickneſſes, and help them to preferment, and give them money to feed their luſts ?"* And the ſaid attorney-general of the ſaid lord the king, for the ſaid lord the king, further gives the court here to underſtand, and to be informed, that in another place in the ſaid falfe, ſcandalous, libellous and ſeditious book, there were among other things contained theſe other falfe, libellous, ſcandalous, ſeditious and irreligious Engliſh ſentences following, of and concerning the biſhops aforeſaid, and the miniſters of juſtice of this kingdom of England, to wit, " *Note, men that preach in Chriſt's name* (meaning him the ſaid R. B. and other factious and ſeditious perfons within this kingdom of England, arguing againſt the laws of this kingdom, and the liturgy of the church of this kingdom as by law eſtabliſhed) *therefore are not to be filenced tho' faulty, if they* (meaning again the ſaid evil-difpoſed, factious and ſeditious perfons) *do more good than harm ; dreadful then is the caſe of them* (meaning the biſhops and miniſters of juſtice within this kingdom of England) *that filence Chriſt's faithful miniſters,"* (meaning him the ſaid R. B. and the other factious and ſeditious perfons aforeſaid). And the ſaid attorney-general of the ſaid lord the king, for the ſaid lord the king, further gives the court here to underſtand, and to be informed, that to excite the people of this kingdom of England to affemble in unlawful conventicles, and to defame the juſtice of this kingdom in puniſhing unlawful conventicles, in another place in the ſaid falfe, ſcandalous, ſeditious and irreligious book, among other things there were contained theſe other falfe, libellous, ſcandalous, ſeditious and irreligious Engliſh ſentences following, to wit, (1.) Note, " *It was well they confidered what might be ſaid againſt them, which now moſt chriſtians do not in their diſputes. (2.) Theſe perfecutors and the Romans had ſome charity and confideration, in that they were reſtrained by the fear of the people, and did not accuſe and fine them as for routs, riots and ſeditions. (3.) They that deny neceſſary premiſſes are not to be diſputed with."* And the ſaid attorney-general of the ſaid lord the now king, for the ſaid lord the king, gives the court here to underſtand, and to be informed that in another place in the ſaid falfe, ſcandalous, ſeditious and irreligious book, among other things there were contained theſe other falfe, libellous, ſcandalous, ſeditious and irreligious Engliſh ſentences following, of and concerning the biſhops, and other clergymen of this kingdom of England, to wit, " *Let not theſe proud hypocrites,* (meaning the biſhops and other clergymen of the church of this kingdom of England) *deceive you,* (meaning the ſubjects of the ſaid lord the king of this kingdom of England) *who by their long liturgies and ceremonies* (meaning the liturgies and ceremonies of the church of this kingdom of England) *and claim*

of

of superiority, do but cloak their worldliness, pride and oppression, and are religious to their greater damnation." And the said attorney-general of the said lord the now king, for the said lord the now king, further gives the court here to understand and to be informed that in another place in the said false, scandalous, seditious and irreligious book, among other things there were contained these other false, scandalous, libellous, seditious and irreligious English sentences following, of and concerning the clergy of this kingdom of England, (2.) *" Priests now are many* (meaning the clergy of the * church of this kingdom of England) *but labourers few; what men are they that have, and silence the faithfullest labourers ?* (meaning him the said R. B. and the other factious and seditious persons aforesaid) *suspecting that they are not for their interest ?"* (meaning the interest of the clergy of the church of this kingdom of England.) And the said attorney-general of the said lord the now king, for the said lord the now king, further gives the court here to understand and to be informed that in another place in the said false, scandalous, seditious and irreligious book, among other things there were contained these other false, libellous, scandalous, seditious and irreligious sentences following, of and concerning the clergy of this kingdom of England, to wit, (3.) Note, *" Christ's ministers use God's ordinances to save men, and the devil's clergy* (meaning the clergy of the church of this kingdom of England) *use them for snares, mischiefs and murder.* (2.) *They* (meaning the clergy of the church of this kingdom of England) *will not let the people,* (meaning the subjects of this kingdom of England) *be neuters between God and the devil, but force them* (meaning the subjects of this kingdom of England) *to be informing persecutors."* And the said attorney-general of the said lord the now king, for the said king further gives the court here to understand to be informed that in another place in the said false, scandalous, seditious and irreligious book, among other things were contained these other false, libellous, scandalous, seditious and irreligious English sentences following, of and concerning the laws of this kingdom of England, against unlawful conventicles, and to stir up the people to assemble in unlawful conventicles, to wit, (2.) Note, *" To be dissenters and disputants against errors and tyrannical impositions upon conscience* (meaning the laws and statutes of this kingdom of England, provided and enacted against factious persons, and dissenters to the liturgy of the church of this kingdom of England) *is no fault but a great duty."* To the great displeasure of Almighty God, in manifest contempt of the laws of this kingdom of England, to the evil and pernicious example of all others in the like case offending, and against the peace of the said lord the king his crown and dignity, whereupon the said attorney-general of the said lord the now king prays the consideration of the court here, in the premisses, and the due process of law to be

awarded

awarded againſt him the ſaid R. B. in this behalf, to make him to anſwer to the ſaid lord the king, touching and concerning the premiſſes, &c.

The defendant was found guilty upon this information, and after exceptions taken in arreſt of judgment and over-ruled, the court gave judgment, and fined him 500 l. and ordered him to give ſecurity for his good behaviour for 7 years. The caſe is reported in 3 Mod. 68.

☞ *See in Rapin's Hiſtory of England, vol. 12, p. 15. the extraordinary language of Lord Chief Juſtice Jefferies at the trial.*

---

* The King *againſt* Williams. * P. 48.

Trinity, 36th Charles II.

Middleſex, THAT William Williams, late of Weſtminſter, in the county of Middleſex, eſquire, being a pernicious and ſeditious man, and deviſing, and falſely, maliciouſly and ſeditiouſly intending to diſquiet, moleſt and difturb the peace and public tranquility of this kingdom of England, and to make, move, ſtir up and procure ſedition, diſcord and malevolence between the ſaid lord the now king, and his ſubjects of this kingdom of England, and alſo to bring and draw the moſt excellent and ſerene prince, James, Duke of York and Albany, the only brother of the ſaid lord the king into the greateſt hatred, contempt and ſcandal with the ſaid lord the king, and with the liege and faithful ſubjects of the ſaid lord the king, and to fulfil, perfect and bring to effect his moſt wicked, deteſtable and diabolical intentions, practiſes and devices, he the ſaid W. W. on the 9th day of November, in the 34th year of the reign of the lord Charles the 2d, the now king, &c. at the pariſh of St. Martin in the fields, in the county of Middleſex, with force and arms, &c. falſely, unlawfully, unjuſtly, wickedly, maliciouſly, ſcandalouſly, ſeditiouſly and diabolically, for his own proper gain, did cauſe and appoint, to be printed and publiſhed a certain falſe, ſcandalous, ſeditious and defamatory libel, intituled " *The information of Thomas Dangerfield, gentleman,*" in which libel, among other things there was contained as follows, " *The information of Thomas Dangerfield, gent. About the months September or October 1679, when Mrs. Cellier and myſelf (meaning the ſaid Thomas Dangerfield, in the information aforeſaid*

To wit. Information for printing and publiſhing a ſeditious Libel, reflecting on the Duke of York the King's brother.

H   mentioned)

mentioned) *waited on my lord Peterborough* (meaning Henry Earl of Peterborough) *to be introduced to his highness the Duke of York, his lordship enquired of me,* (again meaning the said T. D.) *if the lady Powis had given me* (again meaning the said T. D.) *any directions how to discourse the Duke,* (meaning the said James, Duke of York) *I,* (meaning himself the said T. D.) *replied, she* (meaning the said lady Powis) *had*; *then he* (meaning the said Earl of Peterborough) *desired to know what they were, upon which I* (meaning the said T. D.) *shewed his lordship a little book, in which was contained a scheme, and the pretended discovery which I* (meaning the said T. D.) *had made in the Presbyterian plot, which book his lordship carefully perused, and finding some omission therein, he* (meaning the said Earl of Peterborough) *ordered me* (meaning the said T. D.) *to write while his lordship did dictate to me* (meaning him the said T. D.) *these words, to wit, that the presbyterian party intended to make an insurrection in the North, and so to join with an army of Scots : immediately after this his lordship took us* (meaning the said T. D. and M. Cellier, in the information aforesaid, in like manner mentioned) *into the Duke's closet,* (mean-
* P. 49. ing the * Duke of York aforesaid) *at Whitehall, where we* (meaning the said T. D. and Mrs. Cellier) *both kissed his hand* (meaning the hand of the said James, Duke of York) *and me,* (meaning the said T. D.) *he,* (meaning the said Duke of York) *took from the ground, for I* (meaning the said T. D.) *was kneeling, then I gave his highness* (meaning the said Duke) *the aforementioned little book, which he* (meaning the said Duke) *after some perusal thereof thanked me* (meaning the said T. D.) *for ; and also for my diligence for the catholick cause, and did advise me* (meaning the said T. D.) *to go on; and wished good success to all my undertakings, adding in these very words, viz.—" That the Presbyterian plot was a thing of most mighty consequence, and if well managed, would be very conducible to the safety of the catholick cause, and I* (meaning the said Duke) *do not question but the effects of it will answer your expectation, especially in the northern parts, where I* (meaning the said Duke) *am well assured the major part of the gentry are my* (meaning the said Duke) *friends, and have given sufficient demonstration of their affections to me,* (meaning the said Duke) *as also of their intentions to prosecute this Presbyterian plot to the utmost, for they are no strangers to the design ; immediately after this his highness* (meaning the said Duke of York) *ordered Mrs. Cellier and myself, in the hearing of my lord Peterborough, who was privy to the whole discourse, to be very careful of what we* (meaning the said T. D. and Mrs. C.) *communicated to the persons who were to be witnesses in that new plot, lest we* (meaning the said T. D. and Mrs. C.) *should be caught in the subornation, and so bring a terrible odium on the catholicks, and make ourselves* (meaning the said T. D. and Mrs. C.) *uncapable of any further service. After this the Duke* (meaning the said Duke) *informed us,* (meaning the said T. D. and Mrs. C.) *that in a month or two's time, the*
commissions

*commissions would be ready, but ordered us, (meaning the said
T. D. and Mrs. C.) in the mean time to bring our part to bear with
the commissioners, and particularly ordered me, (meaning the said
T. D.) to find out some persons (as there were enough sure among the
catholicks, as well as elsewhere) which were fit to be trusted, and
that should accept of such commissions, which should be delivered to
them by a person appointed for that purpose, but not to be known to
them to be any other but a presbyterian, so that when occasion should
require, they might together with those which we (meaning the said
T. D. and Mrs. C.) then had, be ready to swear in the plot, and
that the presbyterians were raising forces against the king and government, and had given out commissions for that purpose; and in order
to this, I (meaning the said T. D.) did in some short time after
procure one Bedford, Curtis, Grey, Hill, Hopkins, and others, to
accept of such commissions when they should be ready; whose business in the mean time was to spread reports in the coffee-houses, that
the Popish plot was a contrivance of the presbyterians, &c. now for
our (meaning the said T. D. and Mrs. C.) * encouragement, in* P. 50
the prosecution of that sham plot, the Duke (meaning the said Duke
of York) promised that he would take care that money should not be
wanting, but ordered us (meaning the said T. D. and Mrs. C.)
to use all the expedition the thing would allow to make a discovery
thereof to the king's attorney; after which the Duke, (meaning the
said Duke of York) said the catholick party would be eased of
the charge, in regard he (meaning the said Duke) was sure it
would be defrayed some other way; then the Duke (meaning the
said Duke) made divers vows, and bitter execrations to stand by us
(meaning the said T. D. and Mrs. C.) in the thing, and engaged
on his honour to be our rewarder, adding, that such considerable services were not to be slighted, and further promised, that to whose lot
soever it should happen to be imprisoned, according to their fidelity and
stedfastness in the cause, so much the more should their reward be
augmented, and that all care possible should be used to support and
preserve them, but particularly desiring me (meaning the said T. D)
to keep up to the courageous and active character which his highness
(meaning the said Duke) had heard of me; all which I (meaning the said T. D) promised to do, whereupon we (meaning the
said T. D. and Mrs. C.) withdrew to the lord Peterborough's, where
we (meaning the said T. D. and Mrs. C.) continued until his
lordship (meaning the said Earl of Peterborough) had introduced
Sir Robert Payton to the Duke, which being done his lordship left
them together, as he (meaning the Earl of Peterborough) said,
and came to us, (meaning the said T. D. and Mrs. C.) where
amongst other discourse his Lordship (meaning the said Earl of
Peterborough) told me (meaning the said T. D) I had a great
opportunity to make my fortune, what I would myself, if I (again
meaning the said T. D.) would but follow the advice of his master
the Duke of York, who as his lordship said, would certainly be my
king in a very short time, adding that I (meaning the said T. D.)*

H 2

must

must be resolute in my undertakings, for, said he (meaning the said Earl of Peterborough) *the Duke* (meaning the said Duke of York) *much affects resolution, but mortally hates the timorous man, then I* (meaning the said T. D.) *answered his lordship* (meaning the said Earl of Peterborough) *that I* (meaning the said T. D.) *valued not my life, provided to lose it, would be serviceable to the Duke's interest, at which expression he* (meaning the said Earl of Peterborough) *seemed fully satisfied, and from that time called me* (meaning the said T. D.) *Captain Willoughby, and at our* (meaning the said T. D. and Mrs. C.) *coming away his lordship* (meaning the said Earl of Peterborough) *gave particular order to his servants, that at what time soever, day or night, either Mrs. Cellier or myself,* (meaning the said T. D.) *should come to speak with his lordship, we should be forthwith admitted, and then we* (meaning the said T. D. and Mrs. C.) *parted. Some short time after I* (meaning the said T. D.) *went to wait on his lordship* (meaning * P. 51. the said Earl of Peterborough) *from the lady Powis * at midnight, to desire him* (meaning the said Earl of Peterborough) *to move the Duke* (meaning the said Duke of York) *to get me* (meaning the said T. D.) *with all expedition to the king for then I was ready. About four days after this, his lordship sent for me, and took me* (meaning the said T. D.) *to the Duke* (meaning the said Duke of York) *again who was in his closet at Whitehall, and the Duke* (meaning the said Duke of York) *told me* (meaning the said T. D.) *I must prepare myself to wait on the king, and give his majesty a more particular account of the Presbyterian plot, than what the little book made mention of, which book the Duke* (meaning the said Duke of York) *said he had given to the king, and that he* (meaning the said Duke of York) *had so ordered the matter, that I* (meaning the said T. D.) *should be furnished with money to enable me in the prosecution thereof, but his highness* (meaning the said Duke of York) *charged me to consider well my story before I* (meaning the said T. D.) *waited on the king; then the Duke* (meaning the said Duke of York) *told me* (meaning the said T. D.) *I had gained by my diligence a good reputation among the catholicks, and that I* (meaning the said T. D.) *should highly merit by my services to that cause, adding that I* (meaning the said T. D.) *should in a short time see the catholick religion flourish in these kingdoms, and heresy torn up by the roots, and that he* (meaning the said duke of York) *had heard of the proposal which had been made me* (meaning the said T. D.) *by the Lords Powis and Arundell, about taking off the king,* (meaning our most serene lord the king) *and of my refusal, and also what I* (meaning the said T. D.) *had accepted, touching my lord Shaftsbury, and of all my transactions in the Presbyterian plot, saying in these words, viz. if you* (meaning the said T. D.) *value the religion you profess and my interest,* (meaning the interest of the said Duke of York) *as you say you do, and your future happiness, take my advice* (meaning the advice of the said Duke of York) *and depend*

upon

upon my honour and interest for your advancement; you look like a man of courage and wit, and therefore less discourse may serve with you (meaning the said T. D.) *than another, so that if you will but move by the measures which I* (meaning the said Duke of York) *will give you* (meaning the said T. D.) *you shall not only escape with safety, but be rewarded according to the greatness of your actions. To all this I* (meaning the said T. D.) *replied, I* (meaning the said T. D.) *would stand and fall in defence of the catholick religion, and his highness's service,* (meaning the service of the said Duke of York) *and was not a little concerned for my refusal to kill the king,* (meaning our most serene lord the king) *whom I* (meaning the said T. D.) *was then satisfied by my ghostly father, stood condemned as an heretick, but this I* (meaning the said T. D.) *did offer, that if his highness* (meaning the said Duke of York) *would command me* (meaning the said T. D.) *to the attempt, I would not fail either to accomplish it or to lose my life, upon which the Duke* (meaning the said Duke of York) *gave me twenty guineas, and said if I* (meaning the said T. D.) *would be but vigorous in what* I *(meaning the said T. D.) had undertaken* P. 52. *already, he* (meaning the said Duke of York) *would so order it that my life should not be in the least danger, adding in these words, viz. we are not to have men taken in such daring actions, but to have them make an effectual dispatch and be gone, upon which I* (meaning the said T. D.) *took my leave. Some short time after this, when I* (meaning the said T. D.) *was ready to convey the letters into Colonel Mansel's chamber, I* (meaning the said T. D.) *went to the Earl of Peterborough, who brought me to the Duke,* (meaning the said Duke of York) *to whom I told how I* (meaning the said T. D.) *was ready to fix the letters in the Colonel's chamber, to which his highness* (meaning the said Duke of York) *answered, I* (meaning the said T. D.) *must make haste, that I* (meaning the said T. D.) *might be impowered to make a general search of the like nature, for said the Duke* (meaning the said Duke of York) *in these words, viz. since I* (meaning the said Duke of York) *saw you* (meaning the said T. D.) *last, the lady Lewis has informed me* (meaning the said Duke of York) *that there are abundance of letters and witnesses ready, so that it is now high time to begin, by this time there was some great man came to wait on the Duke, so I withdrew. About four days after this, when I* (meaning the said T. D.) *had been pressing earnestly with Mr. Secretary Coventry for a warrant, and could not prevail, I* (meaning the said T. D.) *went to the lord Peterborough, and did desire his lordship to make application to the Duke,* (meaning the said Duke of York) *to use some means for a warrant, to which his lordship* (meaning the said Earl of Peterborough) *answered, it was my fault that there was not a warrant granted and that the Duke* (meaning the said Duke of York) *was sensible of my neglecting to make an affidavit, so that now he* (meaning the said Duke of York) *did begin to doubt my courage, Thomas Dangerfield"*

In

In manifest contempt of the laws of this kingdom of England, to the evil example of all other persons in the like case offending, and against the peace of the said lord the now king, &c. whereupon the said attorney-general of the said lord the now king, for the said lord the king, prays the consideration, &c. And now to wit, on the Friday next after the morrow of the Holy Trinity in this same term, before the lord the king at Westminster, comes the said William Williams, by Simon Harcourt, his attorney, and having heard the information aforesaid, saith, that he doth not apprehend, that the lord the now king, to the information aforesaid, in the court of the said lord the king, will or ought to be answered, because he saith, that the matter in the said information mentioned, to him the said William Williams, in the form aforesaid charged, ought to be heard and determined in parliament, and not in the court of the lord the now king here, and the said William Williams further saith, that by the law and custom of the parliament of this kingdom of England, the speaker of the House of Commons in parliament assembled, for the time being, (during the sitting of parliament) according to the duty of his office, as a minister of the said house, ought and * always hath been accustomed to speak, sign and publish such proceedings of the said House of Commons, and in such manner and form as he by the said commons so assembled hath been ordered to speak, sign and publish; and that every speaking, signing and publishing of any proceeding of the said House of Commons, by the aforesaid speaker, by the order of the said commons done in the form aforesaid, according to the law and custom of parliament, are the acts and deeds of the said commons so in parliament assembled, and always have been accepted and taken as their speaking, signing and publishing, and not as the proper acts or deeds of such speaker; and that such speaker for such speaking, signing or publishing by him, by the order of the said commons in parliament assembled, done during the sitting of parliament, ought not to answer in any other court or place whatsoever, except only in the parliament. And the said W. W. further saith, that a certain parliament of the lord Charles the 2d, late king, &c. by him the late king, in the due manner, summoned to begin at Westminster aforesaid, on the 17th day of October, in the 31st year of the reign of the said late king, by different prorogations was continued, to wit, at Westminster aforesaid, until the 21st day of October, in the 32d year of the reign of the said late king, on which 21st day of October, that parliament at Westminster aforesaid was held, and there from that day until the 10th day of January, in the 32d year aforesaid, of the said late king did continue sitting; and that the said W. W. before the said 17th day of October, on the 31st aforesaid year, &c. to wit, on the 10th day of
October,

Plea to the jurisdiction, that being speaker of the House of Commons, he caused it to be printed by the order of the said House.

*** P. 53.**

A parliament summoned the 31 Char. 2d.

October, in the 31ft year aforefaid, &c. was in the due man- *Defendant elected and returned a member for faid parliament.*
ner elected at the city of Weft Chefter, in the county of the
faid city, one of the citizens for the faid city of Weft Chefter,
to ferve in the faid parliament, and afterwards to wit, on the
faid 17th day of October, in the 31ft year of the reign of
the late king aforefaid, at Weftminfter aforefaid, the faid
William Williams fo elected in the due manner, was returned
one of the citizens to ferve in the faid parliament, for the faid
city of Weft Chefter, as by the return thereof in the court of
Chancery at Weftminfter aforefaid, remaining of record more
fully appears, and during the whole time of the faid parliament the faid W. W. was and remained one of the commons
in the faid parliament, and that the faid W. W. at the faid
feffion of parliament, held by prorogation as aforefaid, at
Weftminfter aforefaid, on the 21ft day of October, in the 32d *And was elected speaker for the commons.*
year, &c. aforefaid, at Weftminfter aforefaid, in the due man-
ner was elected and appointed fpeaker for the commons in the
faid parliament affembled, and the faid W. W. fo continued
fpeaker for the commons in the faid parliament affembled, until
the diffolution of the faid parliament, and that in the faid
feffion of the parliament aforefaid, at the opening of the faid
feffion to wit, on the 21ft day of October aforefaid, at Weftminfter aforefaid, the faid lord the late king addreffed the lords
and commons then in the faid parliament affembled, to profecute the further examination of the Plot, with ftrict and impartial inquiry, and to them then and there faid that he did not
think that he or they were fafe until that matter fhould be
finifhed. And the faid W. W. further faith that in the faid
feffion of the parliament aforefaid, which at Weftminfter
aforefaid, did continue until the 10th day of January, in the
* 32d year, &c. aforefaid, both houfes of the faid parliament, * **P. 54.**
in the profecution of the direction of the faid late king, made
ftrict and impartial inquiry of the aforementioned plot, of and
concerning the faid late king; and upon the faid inquiry in the
faid feffion of the parliament aforefaid, the faid Thomas Dan- *Information upon oath.*
gerfield, gent. in the information aforefaid above fpecified
upon oath, the faid libel entitled " *The information of Thomas
Dangerfield, gent.*" as his true information of the plot aforefaid, did exhibit and deliver as well to the lords of parliament
(in the faid parliament in their houfe at Weftminfter aforefaid
affembled) which there was and is recorded, as by the record
thereof, among the records of parliament, remaining more
fully appears, as to the commons of the kingdom of England,
in the fame parliament in their houfe at Weftminfter aforefaid
affembled, at the bar of the faid houfe with his proper hands
did exhibit and deliver, and after the faid exhibition and delivery thereof to the faid commons as aforefaid, to wit, at the
faid feffion of the parliament aforefaid, the faid commons of *Ordered to be printed.*
this kingdom of England, in the faid parliament in their houfe
aforefaid,

aforesaid, at Westminster aforesaid assembled, did order that the said information of the said Thomas Dangerfield, among the other informations before that time given in at the bar of the said house touching the said plot should be printed, (being first perused and signed by the speaker of the said commons) and that the said speaker should nominate and appoint persons to print the information aforesaid, whereupon the said W. W. (the said W. W. during the whole session of parliament afore-said, being one of the commons in the parliament assembled, and speaker of the said House of Commons, as aforesaid) in prosecution of the order aforesaid, as speaker of the House of Commons aforesaid, afterwards and during the same session of the parliament aforesaid, to wit, on the 10th day of November, in the 32d year of the reign of the said lord the late king aforesaid, at the said parish of St. Martin in the fields, in the county of Middlesex aforesaid; the said information of the said Thomas Dangerfield, exhibited to the said commons of this kingdom of England as aforesaid, did peruse, and did sign, by putting thereto the name of William Williams, speaker of the House of Commons aforesaid, and then and there appoint-ed Thomas Newcombe and Henry Hills, (then printers of the said lord the late king) to print the said information of the said Thomas Dangerfield, according to the said order of the said commons, and the duty of his office; and thereupon the said information of the said Thomas Dangerfield, afterwards and during the said session of parliament aforesaid, to wit, on the 10th day of November, in the 32d year of the reign of the said lord the late king aforesaid, was printed by the said Thomas Newcombe and Henry Hills, according to the order aforesaid, to wit, at the said parish of St. Martin in the fields, which putting thereto of the name of William Williams, speaker of the House of Commons aforesaid, and appointing of the said Thomas Newcombe and Henry Hills, to print the said infor-mation of the said Thomas Dangerfield, according to the order of the said commons, in the said session of the parliament aforesaid assembled, as aforesaid, by him the said W. W. in the form aforesaid done, are the same causing and appoint-ing of the printing and publishing of the libel * aforesaid, in the said information of the said attorney-general of the said lord the king mentioned, whereof the said William Williams, by the said information is above charged, without this that the said W. W. is guilty of the premisses specified in the said information of the said attorney-general of the lord the king, upon the said 9th day of November, in the said information specified, or at any time after the said session of the parlia-ment aforesaid, or before the said session, or otherwise; or in any other manner than as the said William Williams above by pleading hath alledged, and this he is ready to verify, wherefore because that the matter aforesaid, was done by the

said

* P. 55.

Traverse. That he is not guilty on the day in the infor mation, or at any time before or after the said session of Parlia-ment.

said William Williams, as speaker of the House of Commons in parliament assembled, by order of the said Commons, in their house assembled, and sitting that parliament, and not otherwise, and not in any other manner, or at any other time, the said William Williams prays judgment if the lord the now king, to the information aforesaid, in the court of the said lord the now king here, will or ought to be answered.

To this the attorney-general demurs, and the defendant joined in demurrer, but without argument judgment was entered for the king, and the defendant fined 10,000l. it is reported in 2 Shower 471.

Rex *against* Barnadiston.

Hilary, 35 *and* 36 Charles 2d.   *Roll* 43.

Middlesex,
To wit. THAT, whereas a certain diabolical and traiter-ous plot and insurrection of divers seditious and evil-disposed persons, to kill and murder our lord Charles the 2d, the now king of England, and to subvert the laws and the government of this kingdom of England as now by the laws settled and established, had been discovered. And also whereas one William Russel, esquire, and divers other persons for that plot and treason by the due process of law, had been tried, convicted, and attainted, and for the same had been executed; and one Algernon Sidney, esquire, in like manner was tried and convicted of the plot and treason aforesaid: And whereas, upon the trials of the said W. R. and A. S. William lord Howard of Esrick was produced witness on behalf of the said lord the king to prove the treason and plot aforesaid: One Samuel Barnadiston, late of London, baronet, being a seditious and pernicious man, of turbulent and unquiet mind and conversation, falsely, unlawfully, wickedly, maliciously, and seditiously devising, practising and intending to bring and put the said lord the now king, and his rule and government, and also the publick administration of justice in this kingdom of England into hatred, scandal and contempt with his subjects, and to move, stir up, and put discord and sedition between the said lord the king and his liege subjects, and also among the said subjects, and also to disquiet, molest and * disturb the peace of the said lord the king, and the tranquility of this kingdom of England, and to conceal the plot and treason aforesaid, and to vilify, scandalize and deter the evidence for the said lord the king

Information for composing and publishing three seditious Libels.

* P. 56.

I
king

king in that behalf: and to fulfil, perfect and bring to effect, his moft wicked, diabolical and deteftable devices, practifes and intentions, on the 20th day of September, in the 35th year of the reign of our lord Charles the 2d, &c. at the parifh of St. Michael, Cornhill, London, with force and arms, &c. falfely unlawfully, unjuftly, malicioufly, corruptly and feditioufly did make, compofe and write, and did caufe to be made, compofed, written and publifhed, a certain falfe, fcandalous and feditious libel, bearing date the 29th day of November, in the year of our Lord, 1683, in which libel among other things were contained, thefe falfe, feigned, malicious, fcandalous, libellous and feditious Englifh fentences following, to wit,—" *Sir, The return of the duke of Monmouth to Whitehall, and his being received into extraordinary favour by his majefty, hath made a ftrange alteration of affairs at court, for thofe that before fpoke of him very indecently, now court, cringe, and creep to him. His Grace complained to the king of the fcandalous mifreprefentation that was made of him in the Monday Gazette, upon which the Gazetteer was called to account for it, who alledged for himfelf, that a perfon of great quality fent him in writing the words therein recited, commanding him to put them in the Gazette. Yefterday being the laft day of the term, all the prifoners that were in the tower upon the fham Prefbyterian plot* (meaning the plot and treafon aforefaid) *were difcharged upon bail. Mr. Braddon who profecuted the murder of the Earl of Effex* [the information put in againft him in the King's-bench, by mr. Attorney, for fubornation, &c.] *was not profecuted, and his bail was difcharged; and the paffing fentence upon the author of Julian the apoftate, and the printer of the late lord Ruffel's fpeech, were paffed over in filence. Great applications were made to his majefty for the pardoning mr. Sidney in the tower,* (meaning the faid Algernon Sidney convicted as aforefaid) *which is believed will be attained, and that he will be banifhed. The lord Howard,* (meaning the faid William Howard) *appears defpicable in the eyes of all men: He is under a guard at Whitehall, and* [as believed] *will be fent to the tower, for that the duke of Monmouth,* (meaning James duke of Monmouth) *will accufe him concerning the teftimony he hath given,* &c. (meaning the evidence upon the trial and conviction of the faid W. R. and A. S. by the faid lord Howard, given as aforefaid). *The Papifts and Tories are quite down in the mouth; their pride is abated, themfelves and their plot confounded, but their malice is not affuaged. 'Tis generally faid the earl of Effex was murdered. The brave lord Ruffel,* (meaning the faid William Ruffel, for the confpiring aforefaid, convicted, attainted and executed as aforefaid) *is afrefh lamented. The Plot,* (meaning the plot and treafon aforefaid) *is loft here; except you in the country can find it out among the addreffors or abhorrers. This fudden turn is an amazement to all men, and muft produce fome ftrange event, which a little time will fhew.*" * And to fulfil, perfect, and bring to effect his moft wicked contrivances and intentions aforefaid,
the

the said S. B. baronet, afterwards, to wit, on the 20th day
of December, in the 35th year of the reign of the said lord
the now king, at the parish of St. Michael, Cornhill, London,
aforesaid, falsely, unlawfully, corruptly, wickedly, maliciously,
and seditiously did make, compose and write, and did cause to
be made, composed, written and published, a certain other false,
scandalous, libellous and seditious libel, bearing date the 1st day
of Decm. in the year of our Lord, 1683, in which libel among
other things were contained these false, feigned, scandalous, malicious, libellous, and seditious English sentences, following.—
" *Dear, Sir, I am to answer your's of the 27th and 29th past, and
truly I cannot but with great sorrow lament the loss of our good
friend, honest Sir John Wright, but with patience we must submit
to the Almighty, who can as well raise up instruments to do his work,
as change hearts, of which we have so great an instance in the times
of the duke of Monmouth,* (meaning the said James duke of Monmouth) *that no age or history can parallel. I am thoroughly satisfied that what was printed in the Monday Gazette is utterly false,
and you will see it so shortly declared. The king is never pleased but
when he is with him; hath commanded all the privy-council to wait
on him, and happy is he that hath most of his favour. His pardon
was sealed and delivered him last Wednesday. It's said he will be
restored to be master of the horse, and be called into the council-table,
and to all his other places; and it is reported he will be made cap-
tain-general of all the forces, and lord high-admiral; and he treats
all his old friends that daily visit him with civilities. They are satisfied with his integrity, and if God spares his life doubt not but he
will be an instrument of much good to the king and kingdom. He
said publickly that he knew my Lrd Russel,* (meaning the said William Russel, for the plot and treason aforesaid, tried, convicted and executed) *was as loyal a subject as any in England, and
that his majesty believed the same; Now I intend shortly to wait on
him myself; it would make you laugh to see how strangely our high-
tories and clergy are mortified, their countenances speak it; were my
lord S. to be moved for now, it would be readily granted. Sir George*
(meaning Sir George Jeffrys, knight and baronet, then and as
yet chief justice of the lord the king, assigned to hold pleas in
the court of the said lord the king, before the king himself,)
is grown very humble. It is said mr. Sidney, (meaning the said
A. S.) *is reprieved for forty days, which bids well.*" And to
fulfil, perfect and bring to effect his most wicked and detestable contrivances and intentions aforesaid, the said J. B.
bart. afterwards to wit, on the said 20th day of December, in
the 35th year of the reign, &c. aforesaid, at the parish of St.
Michael's, Cornhill, London, aforesaid, falsely, unlawfully,
corruptly, wickedly, maliciously and seditiously did make,
compose and write, and did cause to be made, composed,
written and published a certain other false, scandalous, libellous and seditious libel, bearing date the 1st day of December,

in

in the year of our Lord 1683, in which libel among other things were contained, these false, feigned, scandalous, malicious, * P. 58. cious, libellous and seditious English * sentences following, to wit. " *The late charge here in public affairs is great aad strange, that we are like men in a dream, can hardly believe we see, and fear we are not fit for so great a mercy as the present juncture seems to promise. The sham Protestant plot* (meaning the plot and treason aforesaid) *is quite lost and confounded ; the earl of Macclesfield is bringing actions of scandalum mangatum against all the Grand-jurymen that indicted him at the last assizes, and the several gentlemen that were indicted in Cheshire and Northamptonshire, will bring their several actions at law against them.*"————And further to fulfil, perfect and bring to effect his most wicked and detestable contrivances and intentions aforesaid, the said S. B. baronet, afterwards to wit, on the 20th day of December, in the 35th year of the reign, &c. at the parish of St. Michael, Cornhill, London, aforesaid, falsely, unlawfully, unjustly, corruptly and seditiously did make, compose and write, and caused to be made, composed, written and published, a certain other false, scandalous, libellous and seditious libel, bearing date the 4th day of December, in the year of our Lord 1683, in which libel among other things were contained, these false, feigned, scandalous, malicious, libellous and seditious English sentences following, to wit, " *Contrary to most mens expectations, a warrant is signed at last, for beheading mr. Sidney,* (meaning the said A. S.) *at tower-hill, next Friday ; great endeavours have been used to obtain his pardon, but the contrary party have carried it, which much dasheth our hopes, but God still governs.*" With intention to stir up, move and procure sedition, ill-will and discord between the said lord the king, and the subjects of the said lord the king of this kingdom of England, and also between the said subjects themselves, to the evil and pernicious example of all others in like case offending, and against the peace of the said lord the now king, his crown and dignity, &c.

The trial of the defendant on this information, is in the State Trials, vol. 3. 313 to 322.

The King *against* Colmer.

3*d. Sedition,* by Words.

To wit. THAT John Colmer, late of Chideock, in the county of Dorset, gentleman, not having the fear of God in his heart, but being moved and seduced by the instigation of the devil, and not weighing the duty of his allegiance, and entirely withdrawing the cordial love which every true and faithful subject of the said lord the king, towards the said lord the king, his supreme and natural lord should and of right ought to bear, and devising, and intending to disturb the peace and public tranquility of this kingdom of England, and to move sedition within this kingdom, and also to bring the said lord the king into hatred and* scandal with his subjects, on the 7th day of November, in the 30th year of the reign of our lord Charles the 2d, king, &c. with force and arms, &c. at Chideock, in the county aforesaid, then and there having a discourse with one Thomas Payne, then and there a constable of Chideock aforesaid, in the county aforesaid, and with Richard Luce, clerk, (the said Thomas Payne being authorized by certain deputy lieutenants of the county aforesaid, to search for arms in the houses of suspected papists) he the said J. C. in the hearing and in the presence of them the said Thomas and Richard, and of divers other liege subjects of the said lord the now king, then and there being present, advisedly, seditiously, maliciously and contemptuously, openly and publickly, with a loud voice did speak, utter, declare and pronounce these express, seditious, malicious and contemptuous English words following, to wit, " *You* (meaning the said Thomas Payne) *have searched the first and second time for arms, and you may search the third and fourth time, and not find what you look for, and yet we* (meaning himself and other papists) *may have arms enough to do your business.*" To the great contempt of the said lord the now king, to the evil example of all others in the like case offending, and against the peace of the said lord the now king, his crown and dignity, &c.

Information for seditious words spoke to one who came to search for arms of suspected papists.

* P. 59.

Th

The King *against* Snow.

Hilary, 1st of James 2d.   *Roll.* 46.

Information for seditious words.

To wit. THAT William Snow, late of Westminster, in the county of Middlesex, gentleman, being a pernicious and seditious man, of impious, unquiet and turbulent disposition, devising, practising, and falsely, wickedly, maliciously and seditiously intending the most serene lord Charles the 2d, the now king of England, &c. his natural lord, and also James duke of York and Albany, the only brother of the said lord the now king, and the justices, the judges, and also the common justice of this kingdom of England, and the government thereof, by the said lord the king, to bring and draw into the greatest contempt, hatred and disregard with all the liege subjects of the said lord the now king, and to disquiet, molest and disturb the public tranquility and happy state of this kingdom of England ; and that the said W. S. to fulfil, perfect and bring to effect his most wicked, detestable, diabolical and seditious devices, practices and intentions, on the 21st day of November, in the 30th year of the reign, &c. at the parish of St. Stephen, Coleman-street, London, in the presence, and in the hearing of divers of the liege subjects of the said lord the king, then and there being present, having a discourse concerning the said lord the now king, and the said James duke of York and Albany, and also of the rule and government of the said lord the now king, of this his kingdom of England, he the said W. S. then and there falsely, unlawfully, unjustly, wickedly, maliciously and * seditiously did speak, assert, publish, pronounce, and with a loud voice did declare, " *That if the Duke of Monmouth (meaning James Duke of Monmouth) had not obeyed the warrant and messenger, the differences then stirred up among divers evil-disposed and seditious persons, within this kingdom of England, would in a short time have been decided, because there then were a thousand persons in the city of London, and elsewhere, ready to assist him the Duke of Monmouth ; and that they (meaning the W. W. and divers evil-disposed and seditious persons, within this kingdom of England) were certain that the government of this kingdom, could not stand until Christmas, because the Londoners, and the eastern and western protestants were ready, and*

* P. 60.

that

that divers hundreds then belonged to club meetings within the city of London, and in the parts thereto circumjacent ; and that they (meaning divers factious and seditious persons within this kingdom of England) *at the then last parliament were determined to stick to, and that there were clubs through the whole kingdom of England for those purposes."* And the said attorney-general of the said lord the king, for the said lord the king further gives the court here to understand and to be informed that the said William Snow, then and there, to wit, on the said 21st day of November, in the 35th year, &c. aforesaid, at the parish of St. Stephen, Coleman-street, London, aforesaid, in the presence, and in the hearing of divers of the liege subjects of the said lord the king then and there being present, falsely, wickedly, maliciously and seditiously did say, assert and publish, and with a loud voice did declare, " *That the lord the now king was a papist in his heart, and that Stephen College* (who then lately before for certain high treasons, in the lawful manner was attainted and executed] *did undeservedly die, and that the prosecutors of the said S. C. the judges and jury before whom, and by whom the said S. C. was tried, convicted and attainted for that cause, should be taken off, for what they had done ;. and that the said lord the now king, and the said James Duke of York and Albany were combined in the burning of London,"* (meaning the late great burning of the city of London) to the evil and pernicious example of all others in the like case offending, and against the peace of the said lord the now king, his crown and dignity, &c. whereupon, &c.

---

* *The* King *against* Edes.   * P. 61.

Trinity, 1st James 2d. *Roll* 25.

Suffex, **T**HAT Henry Edes, late of Chichester, in the
To wit,   county of Suffex, doctor in divinity, being a pernicious, factious and seditious man, and a person of a depraved mind, of impious, unquiet, turbulent and seditious disposition and conversation, and devising, practising and falsely, maliciously and most wickedly intending to disquiet, molest and disturb the peace and the publick tranquility of this kingdom of England, and to bring and draw the most serene lord Charles the 2d late king of England, and his royal Majesty, and also his crown and dignity, and the government and rule of this kingdom of
England

Information for speaking in commendation of a seditious book.

England by law eſtabliſhed, into the greateſt hatred, contempt and diſregard, and to fulfil, perfect, and bring to effect his moſt wicked, deteſtable and diabolical contrivances, devices and intentions aforeſaid, he the ſaid H. E. on the 5th day of Sept. in the 36th year of the reign of the ſaid lord Charles the 2d, late king of England, at Chicheſter aforeſaid, in the county of Suſſex aforeſaid, having a diſcourſe with divers liege and faithful ſubjects of the ſaid lord the late king, of and concerning a certain unlawful, ſeditious and libellous book, printed of and concerning the king, parliament and government of this kingdom of England, entitled, "*A treatiſe of Monarchy*," he the ſaid Henry Eles then and there falſely, unlawfully, unjuſtly, wickedly, maliciouſly and ſeditiouſly in the preſence and hearing of divers liege ſubjects of the ſaid late lord the king, then and there being preſent, of the ſaid falſe, ſeditious and libellous book, falſely, unlawfully, unjuſtly, wickedly and ſeditiouſly did ſay, aſſert, publiſh and affirm for truth that the ſaid book, entitled a treatiſe of Monarchy, was the beſt book of the kind that ever was written, and that the contents of the ſaid book were true, and that the ſaid book was not anſwerable. And the ſaid attorney general of the ſaid lord the now king, for the ſaid lord the king further gives the court here to underſtand and be informed that in the ſaid falſe, libellous and ſeditious book, among other things were contained theſe words following, to wit, "*This is my aſſertion, the two eſtates in parliament* (meaning the lords and commons of this kingdom of England, in parliament aſſembled) *may lawfully by force of arms, reſiſt any perſons or number of perſons adviſing or aſſiſting the king,* (meaning the ſaid late lord the king of this kingdom of England, and the ſucceſſors of the ſaid lord the king) *in the performance of a command illegal and deſtructive to themſelves or the public.*" And that in another place of the ſaid falſe, libellous and ſeditious book, among other things were contained theſe other falſe, libellous and ſeditious Engliſh ſentences, to wit, "*Becauſe it is a power put into the two eſtates,* (meaning the lords and commons of this kingdom of England, in parliament aſſembled) *by the very reaſon of their inſtitution, and therefore they* (meaning the lords and commons of the * parliament of this kingdom of England) *not only may but alſo ought to uſe it for public ſafety, yea they* (meaning the lords and commons of this kingdom of England, in parliament aſſembled) *ſhould betray the very truſt repoſed in them by the fundamentals of the kingdom,* (meaning this kingdom of England) *if they ſhould not. An authority legiſlative they have ; now to make laws and to preſerve laws are acts of the ſame power, yea if three powers* (meaning the kings of this kingdom of England, and the lords ſpiritual and temporal, and the commons of the ſame aſſembled) *jointly have intereſt in making laws, ſurely either of theſe ſeverally have and ought to uſe that power in preſerving them.*"

And

* P. 62.

And that in another place in the said false, libellous and seditious book, among other things were contain'd these other false, seditious and libellous sentences in these English words, to wit, " *The two houses* (meaning the houses of Lords and Commons of this kingdom of England in parliament assembled) *in virtue of the legislative authority in part residing in them are invested in the preservation of laws and government as well as the king* (meaning the said late lord the king, and the other kings of this kingdom of England) *and in case the king should misemploy that power of arms to strengthen subverting instruments, or in case the laws and government be in apparent danger, the king refusing to use the sword to that end of preservation to which it was committed to him, I say in this case the two estates* (meaning the Lords and Commons of this kingdom of England in parliament assembled) *may by extraordinary and temporary ordinances assume those arms wherewith the king is entrusted and perform the king's trust, and though such ordinances of theirs be not formally legal, yet it is eminently legal, justified by the very intent of the Architects of the government, when for those uses they committed these arms to the king, and no doubt they may command the strength of the kingdom, to save the being of the kingdom, for none can reasonably imagine the architectonical Powers, when they committed the power of government, and arms to one to preserve the frame they had composed, did thereby intend to disable any much less the two estates from preserving it in case the king should fail to do it, in this last need, and thus doing the king's work, it ought to be interpreted as done by his will, because as the law is his will, so that the law should be preserved in his will, which he expressed when he undertook the government, 'tis his deliberate will and ought to be done though at any time he oppose by an after will, for that is his sudden will.*" And the said attorney-general of the said lord the now king, for the said lord the king further gives the court here to understand and to be informed, that in another place in the said false, malicious, scandalous and seditious book, among other things were contained these other false, scandalous, seditious and defamatory sentences in these English words following, to wit, " *Affirmatively I conceive three cases when the other estates may lawfully assume the force of the kingdom, the king* (meaning the lord the late king and the other successors of the said late king) *not joining or dissenting though the same be by law committed to* * *him. First, when there is an invasion actually made or imminently feared by a foreign power. Secondly, when by an intestine faction, the laws and frame of government are secretly undermined or openly assaulted; in both these cases, the being of the government being endangered their trust binds as to assist the king in securing, so to secure it by themselves the king refusing in extreme necessities; the liberty of voices cannot take place, neither ought a negative voice to hinder in this exigency, there being no freedom of deliberation and choice when the question is about the last end, their* (meaning the

* P. 63.

K

lords

lords and commons of this kingdom of England in parliament assembled) *assuming the sword (in these cases) is for the king, whose being (as king) depends on the being of the kingdom, and being interpretatively his act, is no disparagement of his prerogative, thirdly, in case the fundamental rights, of either of the three estates be invaded by one or both the rest, the wronged may lawfully assume force, because else it were not free, but dependant on the pleasure of the other.* And the said attorney-general of the said lord the now king, for the said lord the king further gives the court here to understand and be informed that the said Henry Edes, afterwards to wit, on the said 5th day of September, in the 36th year of the reign of the said lord the king as aforesaid, at Chichester aforesaid, in the county of Suffex aforesaid, falfely, unlawfully, unjustly, wickedly, maliciously and seditiously in the presence and hearing of divers liege subjects of the said lord the late king, then and there being present, did say, assert, affirm, publish, and with a loud voice did declare, " *That the French king is in great power with his army, and that we* (meaning the people of this kingdom of England) *are in great danger of being invaded, but if the lord the king* (meaning the lord Charles the 2d, late king of England) *would rouse the army of antient soldiers,* (meaning the soldiers of Oliver Cromwell late then before a traiterous usurper of this kingdom of England) *then that we* (meaning the subjects of this kingdom of England) *would be safe: and I* (meaning him the said Henry Edes) *will lay a wager of an hundred pounds, that the French king next intends to invade and conquer us,"* (meaning the subjects of the said kingdom of England). To the evil example of all others in like case offending, and against the peace as well of the said late lord the king, as of the lord the now king their crowns and dignities. Whereupon the said coroner and attorney, &c. &c.

The defendant on a trial at bar, was convicted on this information, and after motion in arrest of judgment, the court gave judgment for the king. The case is reported 2 Shower 468.

---

* P. 64. 　　　　* The King *against* Sorocold.

Easter, the 2d of James II.

<table>
<tr><td>Information for seditious words.</td><td>London,
To wit. }</td><td>THAT William Sorocold, late of London, gentleman, not having the fear of God before his eyes, but being moved and seduced by the instigation</td></tr>
</table>

of

of the devil, on the 21st day of January, in the   year of the reign of our lord Charles the 2d, &c. at London, to wit, in the parish, &c. in the ward of Farringdon without, within London aforesaid, falsely, maliciously and seditiously contriving and devising, to move and stir up discord between the said lord the king, and his liege subjects within this kingdom of England, and to move the said lord the king to displeasure and suspicion towards the parliament of this kingdom of England, of and concerning the said lord the now king, then and there falsely, maliciously and seditiously in the presence and hearing of divers subjects of the said lord the king, did say, " *That before the 24th of next June, if the king* (meaning the said lord the king) *would permit the parliament* (meaning the parliament of this kingdom of England) *to sit, that he the said William Scroecold did not doubt to see the head of the king* (meaning the head of the said lord the king) *divided as far from his body* (meaning the body of the said lord the king) *as the head of his father* (meaning the head of Charles the iii, late king of England, of blessed memory, the father of the said lord the now king) *ever was, for there are twenty-five articles against him,*" (again meaning the said lord the king). In contempt of the said lord the king. and of his laws, to the evil and pernicious example of all others in the like case offending, and against the peace of the said lord the now king his crown and dignity, and whereupon the said attorney, &c.

The King *against* Wetwang.

Trinity, 3d James II.   *Roll.* 17.

Middlesex,
To wit. } THAT Joseph Wetwang, late of the parish of St. Martin, in the fields, in the county of Middlesex, gentleman, being a pernicious and seditious man, and a person of a depraved, impious and unquiet mind, and of seditious disposition and conversation, and devising, practising, and falsely, maliciously, turbulently and seditiously intending the peace and public tranquility of the said lord the now king, and of this kingdom of England, to disquiet, molest, and disturb, and to bring and draw our most serene lord James the 2d, now king of England, into the greatest hatred, contempt and scandal, with all the liege and faithful subjects of this kingdom of England, and also the * colonels, captains, lieutenants,

* P. 65

Information for seditious words. Stubbs 641

lieutenants, and other military officers and soldiers of the said lord the king, to scandalize and vilify, and that the said Joseph Wetwang, to fulfil, perfect, and bring to effect his most wicked and detestable devices, practices and intentions aforesaid, on the 10th day of May, in the 3d year of the reign, &c. at the parish of St. Martin in the field, in the county, &c. [having a discourse then and there concerning the said lord the now king, and concerning the regiment of guards of the said lord the king, and of their business] in the presence, and in the hearing of divers liege subjects of the said lord the king, then and there present, falsely, maliciously, unlawfully, wickedly and seditiously, of the said lord the now king, and of his colonels and officers, did say, assert, affirm and publish, and with a loud voice did declare, these false, feigned, malicious, seditious and opprobrious English words and falsehoods following, to wit, "*The colonels and the rest of the officers* (meaning the colonels, and the officers in the regiment of guards of the said lord the king) *are a company of rogues and villains, for that their business is to uphold their master,* (meaning the said lord the now king) *who* (meaning the said lord the king) *is a villain and a rogue, and never kept his word in any thing he* (meaning the said lord the king) *said.*" And the said Joseph Wetwang in further prosecution of his malice against the said lord the king, before had, afterwards to wit, on the same day and year, at, &c. falsely, maliciously, diabolically, seditiously and most wickedly, in the presence, and in the hearing of divers other liege and faithful subjects of the said lord the now king, then and there present, did say, utter, and with a loud voice did pronounce, assert and affirm, "*That the said lord the now king was a villain and a rogue, and never kept his word in any thing that he said.*" To the great scandal, dishonour and shame of the said lord the now king, the colonels, captains, and the other officers, and soldiers, of the guards of the said lord the king, to the evil example of all others, &c. and against the peace, &c.

The King *against* Harris.

Easter, 36 Charles *the* 2d.

<table>
<tr><td>Information " for sedi-
tious words,
spoken up-
on hanging
up the kings
picture.</td><td>Berks,
To wit,</td><td>THAT Edward Harris, late of the town of New Windsor, in the county of Berks, gent, being a person of an evil-disposed and deprayed mind, and also of unquiet, seditious and turbulent disposition, and devising, practising, and falsely, maliciously and seditiously intending most
 wickedly </td></tr>
</table>

wickedly to draw and bring the most serene prince the lord Charles the 2d, king, &c. his supreme, &c. natural lord, into the greatest hatred, contempt, ridicule, and scandal with all the liege subjects of the said lord the now king, and to expose the said lord the king as a mock and block, and to diminish his imperial dignity among his subjects, and to fulfil, perfect, and bring to effect his most wicked, detestable and diabolical intentions aforesaid, the said E. H. on the   day of   in the year, &c. at, &c. in the county, &c. having a discourse with divers subjects of the said lord the now king, concerning the said lord the now king and a picture of the said lord the now king, impiously, maliciously, factiously, seditiously, and in derision of the said lord the now king did say, pronoun, and with a loud voice did declare these malicious, scandalous, and opprobrious words following, to wit, *I*, [meaning him the said E. H] *will go and see that comical fellow*, [meaning in derision the said lord the now king] *drawn up*; and that the said E. H. afterwards, to wit, on the same day and year, at the said town of New Windsor, in the said county of Berks, upon a certain other discourse, with divers other liege and faithful subjects of the said lord the king then and there had of and concerning the said lord the now king, and of the said picture of the said lord the now king in the presence and hearing of divers persons then and there present and hearing, of the said lord the now king, and of the picture aforesaid, maliciously, impiously and in derision of the said lord the now king did say, pronounce, and with a loud voice did publish and declare, " *That he* (the said E. H.) *did not care if he* (the said E. H.) *went and saw that comical fellow* (meaning in derision the said lord the now king) *drawn up*," against the duty of his allegiance, in great contempt of the said lord the now king, and to the evil example of all others in the like case offending, and against the peace, &c. &c.

* P. 66.

The King *against* Harvey.

Trinity, 3*d* James 2*d*.

Lincoln,   } THAT Thomas Harvey, late of Spalding, in the
To wit,   } county of Lincoln, bricklayer, being a pernicious and seditious person, of depraved mind and imagination, and devising, and falsely, maliciously, and seditiously intending, the peace and public tranquility of the said lord the king and of his subjects of this kingdom of England, to disquiet, molest and disturb, and to move and provoke insurrection and rebelli-

Information for affirming that the duke of Monmouth was alive after his execution for treason,

" the words
spoken in
difcourfe
with ano-
ther."

on within this kingdom of England, and to create falfe opinions and fufpicions among the people and fubjects of the faid lord the king, concerning James, late duke of Monmouth, lately convicted, attainted, and executed, and who fuffered the punifhment of death for high-treafon againft the faid lord the now king, and to caufe the faid fubjects to be of opinion, and to believe, that the faid James, late duke of Monmouth was alive, and in full life after his execution aforefaid, and after the fuffering of the punifhment of death, with intention and purpofe to withdraw the cordial love, due fidelity and allegiance of divers fubjects of the faid lord the king from the faid lord the king, and to caufe the faid liege fubjects of the faid lord the king, to leave and defert the faid lord the now king; and that the faid Thomas Harvey to fulfil, perfect and bring to effect his moft wicked devices, and diabolical * intentions aforefaid, on the 31ft of March, in the 3d year, &c, after the death of the faid duke of Monmouth, at Spalding, aforefaid, in the county aforefaid, having a difcourfe with one James O—. gent. and divers other fubjects of the faid lord the now king, being then and there collected of and concerning the faid James late duke of Monmouth, convicted, attainted, and executed for high-treafon as is aforefaid, he the faid T. H. then and there in the prefence and hearing of the faid J. O. and of divers liege fubjects of the faid lord the now king then and there prefent, concerning the faid James late duke of Monmouth, attainted and executed for high-treafon as is aforefaid, falfely advifedly, malicioufly, and feditioufly, did fay, affert, publifh and declare, " *That the faid James duke of Monmouth then was alive and living, and that then there were none but fools who believed that he (the late duke of Monmouth) was dead,*" and the faid J. O. [then and there anfwering the faid T. H.] then and there did fay to the faid T. H. "*. That if he the faid T. H. held at that rate, that he would reflect upon the faid lord the king, and the privy-council of the faid lord the now king,*" whereupon the faid T. H. of his further malice, to the faid J. O. falfely, feditioufly, turbulently, and factioufly replying this in the prefence of divers fubjects then and there prefent, did fay, anfwer, and with a loud voice did publifh, concerning the faid late duke of Monmouth, that " *he the faid duke of Monmouth was alive, and in this life, and that all were fools who believed to the contrary.*" Againft the duty of his allegiance, in contempt of the faid lord the now king, and of his laws, and to the evil and pernicious example, &c. &c.

* P. 67.

The King *against* Watson.

Hilary, the 36th Charles II.

London,
To wit.

THAT Randolph Watson, late of the parish, &c. being a factious, irreligious, pernicious, and seditious man, and devising, practising, and falsely, maliciously, seditiously and unlawfully intending the book of the common prayer, rightly, lawfully and piously established and appointed by the laws and statutes of this kingdom of England, into the greatest hatred, contempt and scandal, with all the liege subjects of the said lord the king, to bring and draw, and to fulfil, perfect, and bring to effect his most wicked, detestable and diabolical intentions aforesaid, the said Randolph Watson then and there in derogation, depravation and contempt of the said book of common prayer, wickedly, diabolically, maliciously and seditiously in plain English words, did declare, say and publish as follows, " *The common prayer of the church are innovations, it is too early now to have the organs, if I had thought of it there was fidlers at Thomas Chandler's,* (meaning the house of one Thomas Chandler, situate in * the parish afore- * P. 68 said) *I would have brought them down that you* (meaning the subjects of the said lord the king then present) *might have musick with your prayers,* (meaning the common prayers in the book of common prayer aforesaid contained) *you that are so hot in zeal, that can be warm by the prayers of the church, may go and warm yourselves by them,* (meaning the common prayers aforesaid) *for they could never warm me,* (meaning him the said Randolph Watson) *I* (meaning him the said R. W.) *dare aver that neither the laws of God or man can command or require it* (meaning the use of the prayers in the said book of common prayer mentioned and contained) *of us; those that will have a may-pole, shall have a may-pole, and those that will have no may-pole, shall have no may-pole.*" In manifest contempt of the laws of this kingdom of England, to the evil example of all others in the like case offending, and against the peace, &c.

Information for contemptuous words against the common Prayer, and organs in church.

Indictments

Indictments for scandalizing Magistrates, and others.

1. By Libels.   2. By Words.

1. By Libels.

<table>
<tr><td>

Information
for publish-
ing a scan-
dalous libel
on a private
person, in
the form of
a letter.

</td><td>

Surry,
To wit.

</td><td>

BE it remembered that Thomas Fanshaw, knight, coroner and attorney of the lord the king, in the court of the said lord the king, before the king himself, who for the said lord the king in this behalf prosecutes, in his pro-

</td></tr>
</table>

per person comes here into the court of the said lord the king, before the king himself at Westminster, on Monday next after the octave of St. Hilary, in this same term, and for the said lord the king gives the court here to understand and to be informed, that G. S. late of, &c. in the county of Surry, yeoman, being a person of evil name, fame. and of impious conversation, on the   day, &c. in the 21st year of the reign of the lord Charles the 2d, king, &c. and on divers other days and times before, at, &c. devising, intending and practising to deprive one H. R. esquire, of his good name, fame and credit, and to bring the said H. R. into the greatest hatred, scandal, contempt and infamy, as well with the said lord the king as with all the liege subjects of the said lord the king of this kingdom of England, and to fulfil and perfect his said devices, intentions and practices, the said G. S. on the said day of, &c. in the 21st year of the reign of the lord the now king aforesaid, at S. aforesaid, in the said county of Surry, a certain false, malicious, scandalous and libellous writing, against the said H. R. falsely, maliciously and scandalously did frame and make, and in the name of the said G. S. then and there did cause to be written and published under the form of a * letter directed to the said H. R. the tenor of which writing follows in these English words and figures follow-ing, to wit, " *These for, &c.* " (reciting the whole writing ver-batim & literatim) and that the said G. S. with intention to scandalize the said H. R. and bring him into contempt, the said false, malicious, scandalous and libellous writing, so framed and made as aforesaid, afterwards to wit, on the said day and year aforesaid, and at divers others days and times then before, at, &c. to divers subjects of the said lord the king

* P. 69.

then

then and there present, falsely, maliciously and scandalously did deliver and caused to be delivered, and did publish, to the great scandal, infamy, and great damage of him the said H. R. and to the evil and pernicious example of all others in the like case offending, and against the peace of the said lord the king, his crown and dignity, &c. Whereupon the said coroner and attorney of the said lord the king, for the said lord the king prays the consideration of the court here in the premisses, and that due process of law may be awarded against the said G. S. in this behalf, to make him answer to the said lord the king, of and concerning the premisses, &c. whereupon the sheriff of the county of Surry is commanded that he do not omit, &c. but that he cause him to come, &c. to answer, &c.

Not-guilty pleaded, venire facias awarded.

The King *against* Newton.

Hilary, the 1st of James the 2d.   *Roll* 125.

York, } TO be informed that Hugh Cholmley, baronet, on
To wit. } the 31st day of July, in the 30th year of the reign of the lord Charles the 2d, late king of England, &c and long before and continually after until the 5th day of February, in the 37th year of the reign of the said late lord the king, was lord of the manor of Whitby, in the county of York, and one of the justices of the said lord the late king, assigned to preserve the peace of the said lord the late king, in the north riding of the county of York aforesaid, and also one of the deputy lieutenants of the said lord the late king, in the north riding aforesaid, in the county aforesaid, and that the said Hugh Cholmley on the 31st day of July, in the 36th year aforesaid, at Whitby, in the county aforesaid, by his certain writing, under his hand and seal, bearing date the said 31st day of July, in the 36th year aforesaid, did authorize one Christopher Wise to be one of his game-keepers within the manor aforesaid, and the said Hugh Cholmley, among other things by the said writing did command the said Christopher to take and seize all grey-hounds which were used within the manor aforesaid, by any person prohibited by the statute made in the 22d and 23d years of the said lord the late king, and that the said Christopher Wise so being as aforesaid, one of the game-keepers within the manor aforesaid, afterwards to wit,

(margin:) Information for fixing a scandalous libel, on Whitby-bridge, in Yorkshire, reflecting upon Sir H. C. lord of the manor of Whitby, justice of peace, and deputy lieutenant of the same county, for hanging a grey-hound taken within his manor.

L   on

on the day and year, &c. at W. within the manor aforesaid, by virtue of the writing aforesaid, did seize a certain grey-hound of one Isaac Newton, gent. [commonly called Captain Newton] and the said dog to the mansion-house * of the said H. Cholmley, in Whitby aforesaid, [commonly called Whitby-abby] did lead, and the said dog then and there did hang: And that the said I. N. of W. aforesaid, in the county aforesaid, gentleman, well-knowing the premisses aforesaid, but being a person of evil and wicked conversation, and a malicious slanderer of persons of good and honest name, reputation and conversation, and a common fighter, and provoker, and challenger to fight, and disturber of the peace of the lord the king, and contriving and maliciously intending, the said H. C. to scandalize, defame and to bring into hatred and contempt, on the day and year, &c. at W. aforesaid, in the county aforesaid, a certain false, malicious, scandalous and defamatory libel in writing, of and concerning the said H. C. falsely, unlawfully and maliciously in and upon a certain bridge, commonly called Whitby-bridge, at Whitby aforesaid, did fix and publish, the tenor of which false, malicious, scandalous and defamatory libel, follows, to wit, "*He that sent for Captain Newton's grey-hound, to Whitby-abby, and since caused him to be hanged, is a base cowardly rascal, and was not worthy of the honour to be topman to such a dog. Whitby men beware of those people who one day may have no more esteem for you than they now have for dogs. You are advised by your assured friend, Isaac Newton.*" In contempt of the laws of this kingdom of England, to the great scandal, disgrace and infamy of the said H. C. to the evil example of all others in the like case offending, and against the peace as well of the said lord the late king, as of the lord the now king, their crowns and dignities. Whereupon the said attorney, &c.

P. 70.

The King *against* Oakover.

Hilary, the 2d and 3d of James the 2d.

Information for writing a scandalous letter, by way of challenge, and publishing the same, and giving out that he ex-

Middlesex, THAT Humphrey Oakover, late of, &c. and To wit. others, &c. and each and every of them being persons of evil fame, name, and dishonest conversation, and common fighters, and duellers, and challengers, and instigaters to fight, and disturbers of the peace of the said lord the now king, and devising, practising, conspiring and intending, as much as in them lay, not only to deceive and defraud one R. R. baronet, of divers sums of money, but also to disquiet

and

and moleſt the happy ſtate and condition of the ſaid R. R. baronet, and him to bring and draw into the greateſt hatred, contempt and ſcandal with the ſaid lord the now king, and with all the liege ſubjects of the ſaid lord the king of this kingdom of England, and to fulfil, perfect, and bring to effect their moſt wicked conſpiracies, devices, practices and intentions aforeſaid, they the ſaid H. O. and others, on the day and year, &c. at, &c. demanded of the ſaid R. R. one thouſand pounds, which they then pretended to be due to them, or one of them, ſrom and by the ſaid R. R. which when the ſaid R. R. then denied to be due, or to pay the ſame, they the ſaid H. O. and others, then and there did declare, * and publiſh that the ſaid R. R. ſhould pay to them, or one of them, the ſaid thouſand pounds, or that he ſhould fight them the ſaid H. O. and others, &c. and afterwards to wit, on the day, &c. in the year, &c. aforeſaid, they the ſaid H. O. and others, in further proſecution of their conſpiracies, devices and practices aforeſaid, a certain malicious writing, did frame and make, and did cauſe to be framed and made, and then and there did cauſe to be written and publiſhed under the name of the ſaid H. O. and under the form of a letter directed to the ſaid R. R. baronet, &c. (with intention to incite and move the ſaid R. R. bart. to fight the duel aforeſaid, with the ſaid H. O. ſo that the ſaid H. O. might kill and murder the ſaid R. R. baronet) in theſe Engliſh words following, to wit, &c. *Sir, I do*, &c. (as in the letter). And that the ſaid H. O. and others, with intention to provoke the ſaid R. R. to fight with the ſaid H. O. and to ſcandalize and diſquiet the ſaid R. R. and to bring him into contempt, the ſaid malicious writing afterwards to wit, on the day and year aforeſaid, at, &c. to the ſaid R. R. did ſend, and did cauſe to be delivered, and alſo to divers ſubjects of the ſaid lord the king, then and there maliciouſly and ſcandalouſly did publiſh, and cauſed to be publiſhed; and the ſaid coroner and attorney of the ſaid lord the king, for the ſaid lord the king further gives the court here to underſtand, and to be informed, that afterwards to wit, on the day and year &c. at, &c. the ſaid H. O. did publiſh and declare, " *That he the ſaid H. O. did expect of the ſaid R. R. baronet, one thouſand pieces of gold, called guineas, or that the ſaid R. R. with his friend, would meet the ſaid H. O. and if the ſaid R. R. would not meet the ſaid H. O. that he the ſaid H. O. would expoſe the ſaid R. R. in all the coffee-houſes in town, at Whitehall, and the ſaid H. O. then and there did declare, that he the ſaid H. O. would ſet upon the ſaid R. R. whereſoever the ſaid H. O. could meet the ſaid R. R.*" And the ſaid H. O. and others, other wrongs then and there with force and arms to the ſaid R. R. did, to the great ſcandal, infamy, great damage and diſparagement of the ſaid R. R. in contempt of the ſaid lord the now king, and of his laws, to the evil example, &c. and againſt the peace, &c.

L 2

The

* pected 1000 guineas of the perſon, or that he ſhould rect him to fight, and if he did not, that he would expoſe him in all the coffee-houſes, and would ſet upon him whereover he met him.

P. 71.

The King *against* Jackett.

Michaelmas, 1ft James II.

Information for two scandalous libels on the Earl of Feversham.

Middlesex, To wit. THAT Helen Jackett, late of the parish of St. Martin, in the fields, in the county of Middlesex, spinster, otherwise called Helen Lloyd, the wife of John Lloyd, late of the parish aforesaid, in the county aforesaid, esq. otherwise called Helen Lloyd, of the parish aforesaid, in the county aforesaid widow, being a person of a depraved mind, and of impious, unquiet and turbulent disposition and conversation, and devising, practising, and falsely, maliciously, wickedly and turbulently intending (as much as in her lay) to disquiet, molest and disturb the happy state and tranquility of the most noble Lewis, Earl of Feversham, * one of the peers of this kingdom of England, and other liege and faithful subjects of the said lord the king, to the said attorney-general as yet unknown, and to bring and draw the said Lewis, Earl of Feversham into the greatest hatred, contempt, scandal and disgrace with the said lord the now king, and with all the liege and faithful subjects of the said lord the now king of this his kingdom of England; and to fulfil, perfect, and bring to effect her most wicked, detestable and diabolical devices, practices and intentions aforesaid, she the said Helen Jackett, on the 14th day of April, in the 1ft year, &c with force and arms, &c. at the parish of St. Martin in the fields, in the county of Middlesex, falsely, maliciously, unlawfully, unjustly, wickedly, scandalously and libellously did make, compose, write and publish, and did cause to be written and published, a certain false, libellous and defamatory letter, of and concerning the said Lewis Earl of Feversham, in which false, scandalous, libellous and defamatory letter, among other things were contained, these false, scandalous, defamatory English sentences following, to wit, " *This for the Earl of Feversham, &c.*" And the said attorney-general of the said lord the now king, for the said lord the king further gives the court here to understand and to be informed, that the said Helen Jackett in further prosecution of her most wicked and detestable devices and practices aforesaid, she the said H. Jackett afterwards to wit, on the 22d day of October, in the first year, &c. aforesaid, with force and arms, &c. at, &c. falsely, maliciously, unlawfully, unjustly, wickedly,

scandalously

* P. 72.

scandalously and libellously did make, compose, write and publish, and cause to be made, composed, written and published, a certain other false, libellous, scandalous, and defamatory letter, of and concerning the said Lewis, Earl of Feversham, subscribed with the name Helen Vaughan, and directed to the said Lewis, Earl of Feversham, the tenor of which other letter is as follows, " *this for the Earl of Feversham, &c.*" To the great contempt, scandal, infamy and disparagement of the said Lewis, Earl of Feversham, to the evil and pernicious example, &c. and against the peace, &c.

---

* The King *against* Barbone.

* P. 73.

Michaelmas, the 36th of Charles the 2d.

2. By Words.

Middlesex, } THAT Nicholas Barbone, late of, &c. R. A. late of, &c. and others, &c. with divers other
To wit. malefactors and disturbers of the peace of the said lord the now king, to the number of one hundred persons, to the jurors aforesaid as yet unknown, on the day and year, &c. as rioters, routers, disturbers of the peace of the said lord the now king, to disturb the peace of the said lord the now king, at, &c. with force and arms, &c. unlawfully, riotously and routously did assemble and collect themselves, and so being then and there assembled and collected, a certain gate of the said lord the king, commonly called King's-gate, Holbourn, the fore part thereof being at that time, with a certain bolt fastened to one post, and the hinder part of the gate aforesaid, being at that time hanging upon hooks in another post, fixed in the parish aforesaid, then and there violently, unlawfully, riotously, routously and injuriously did lift off the hooks aforesaid, and then and there the gate aforesaid, forcibly, unlawfully, riotously, routously and injuriously did throw and set open ; and the jurors aforesaid further say upon their oath aforesaid, that Edward Guise, esquire, then and as yet, one of the justices of the said lord the king, assigned to preserve the peace in the county aforesaid, and also, &c. then and there being present, with one W. C. then and as yet one of the constables of the said lord the king, within the parish aforesaid, &c. to make his best endeavour to suppress the riot aforesaid, and to preserve the peace of the said lord the king, the said S. F. one of the rioters aforesaid, so riotously and routously assembled with the other rioters aforesaid, not ignorant of the

premisses,

Indictment for contemptuous words, spoken of a justice of the peace:

premisses, but devising, and maliciously and contemptuously intending, as much as in him lay, to take away and contemn the authority of the said Edward Guise, and of all the other justices of the said lord the king, within the county aforesaid, and to bring the said justice into contempt and hatred with the liege subjects of the said lord the king, these opprobrious and contemptuous English words following, concerning the said justice of the said lord the king, in the presence and hearing of divers liege subjects of the said lord the king, then and there did say, pronounce, and with a loud voice did publish, to wit, " *There shall be no more justices long*;" and the jurors aforesaid, upon their oath aforesaid, further say that the said N. B, and others, &c. as aforesaid, riotously, routously and unlawfully assembled, not weighing the duty of their allegiance, but devising and maliciously intending, not only to disturb the peace of the said lord the king, and the public tranquility of this kingdom of England, but also as much as in them lay, to ＊ P. 75. ＊ bring and draw the said lord the king, into hatred, scandal, disaffection, dishonour and contempt with all his faithful subjects ; on the day aforesaid, in the year aforesaid, at the parish aforesaid, &c. of their wicked minds, maliciously, scandalously, contemptuously and advisedly, in the presence and hearing of divers liege subjects of the said lord the now king, then and there present did speak, publish and utter, of the said lord the now king, these opprobrious, contemptuous, scandalous, seditious English words following, to wit, " *that the king himself*, (meaning the said lord the now king) *is but a trespasser here*," against the duty of their allegiance, in great contempt, scandal, dishonour, derogation and infamy of the Royal Majesty of the said lord the now king, and in great contempt and derogation of the authority of the said justice, to the great disquiet, terror and fear of all the liege subjects of the said lord the king, then and there dwelling and residing, to the evil, pernicious and bad example of all others in the like case offending, and against the peace of the said lord the now king, his crown and dignity, &c.

The King *against* Price.

Michaelmas, the 36th Charles the 2d.

Information for scandalous words spoken of a justice of peace.

The town and county of Haverford West, To wit. } **T**HAT James Price, late of, &c. in the county, &c. being a person of evil disposition, and a malicious brawler and slanderer of persons of good and honest conversation

tion and reputation, and also devising and maliciously intending one A. L. then one of the justices of the said lord the king, assigned to preserve the peace in the county aforesaid, and also to hear and determine divers felonies, trespasses, and other misdeeds in the said county perpetrated, to bring and draw into the greatest hatred, contempt and scandal, among the liege subjects of the said lord the king, on the day and year, &c. at, &c. in the county, &c. falsely, maliciously, scandalously, and of his most wicked intention, these false, feigned, odious and scandalous English words following, of and concerning the said A. L. openly and publickly in the presence and hearing of divers liege subjects of the said lord the king, then and there present, † to wit, " *thou* (meaning the said A.L.) *art a bribing justice of the peace.*" Whereupon the said A. then and there did question the said James, in these English words following, to wit, " *What do you* (meaning the said James) *mean by that?*" to which question of the said A. the said J. then and there did answer in these English words, to wit, " *thou* (meaning the said A.) *hast received bribes to my knowledge,* (meaning the knowledge of him the said J.) *and I* (meaning the said J.) *will prove it.*" To the great contempt, scandal, reproach and disgrace of the said A. L. to the evil example of all others, &c. against the peace, &c. Whereupon the said attorney, &c.

† Did say, publish, pronounce and declare, (seem to be wanting here, they are not in the original).

- - - - -

The King *against* Nosworthy. • P. 75.

Easter, 36th Charles the 2d.

Wilts, } THAT on Wednesday, next after three weeks of
To wit. } Easter, in the 33d year of the reign of our lord Charles 2d, of England, &c. now king, &c. in the court of the said lord the king, before the king himself here, one Edward Fitzharris, late of the parish of St. Martin, in the fields, in the county of Middlesex, gentleman, by the oath of twelve jurors, good and lawful men of the said county, in the due manner was indicted for high treason, in traiterously compassing, imagining and intending the death and final destruction of the said lord the king, and to change, alter and entirely subvert the antient government of this kingdom of England, and to depose and deprive him the said lord the now king, of his title, honour and royal name, and of the imperial crown of this kingdom of England, and to move and levy war, and rebellion, against the said lord the king, within this kingdom of England, and that afterwards to wit, on the Wednesday next

Information for reflecting words spoken of Sir Francis Pemberton, chief justice of the King's Bench, and the rest of the judges of that court, for giving judgment against Edward Fitzharri, indicted for High-Treason, where-after one month of Easter, in the 33d year of the reign of the said lord the now king aforesaid, in the said court here, came the said Edward Fitzharris, in his proper person, and being demanded of the premisses above charged against him, how he would acquit himself, thereof, said that he ought not to be compelled to answer to the indictment aforesaid, because he said that before the indictment aforesaid, by the jurors aforesaid, in the form aforesaid found, to wit, at a parliament of the lord the now king, begun and held at Oxford, in the county of Oxford, on the   day of, &c. and in the   year, &c. he the said E. F. by the knights, citizens and burgesses in the said parliament assembled, in the name of themselves, and of all the commons of England, according to the law and custom of parliament, of high-treason, before the lords and peers of this kingdom of England, in the same parliament assembled, was impeached, and that the said impeachment at that time did remain and exist in its full force and effect, as by the record thereof, among the records of parliament remaining did more fully appear; and the said E. F. then and there further said, that the high-treason in the indictment aforesaid, by the jurors aforesaid, in the form aforesaid found, specified and mentioned, and the high-treason, whereof he the said E. F. in the parliament aforesaid, then as aforesaid was and stood impeached, were one and the same treason, and not another nor different, and that he the said E. F. in the indictment aforesaid named, and the said E. F. in the impeachment named, was one and the same person, and not another, nor different, and that this he was ready to verify, &c. whereupon he the said E. F. prayed judgment, if the said court here would any further proceed against him upon the indictment aforesaid, &c. and Robert Sawyer, knight, then and as yet attorney-general of the said lord the now king, who for the said lord the king, in that behalf prosecuted, for the said lord the king, said that the plea aforesaid, by the said E. F. in the manner and form aforesaid above pleaded, and the matter therein contained

* P. 76. were not sufficient in law to *: preclude the said court here from proceeding upon the indictment aforesaid, and that this he was ready to verify as the said court should consider, whereupon he prayed judgment, and that the said E. F. to that indictment should answer. And the said E. F. did say that the plea aforesaid, by him the said E. F. in the manner and form aforesaid above pleaded, and the matter in the same contained, were good and sufficient in law to preclude the said court from proceeding upon the indictment aforesaid, which plea and the matter in the same contained, the said E. F. was ready to verify and prove, as the said court here should consider, whereupon as before, he prayed judgment if the said court would proceed further upon the indictment aforesaid, &c. and that afterwards to wit, on the Saturday next after one month of

Easter,

Easter, in the 33d year of the reign of the said lord the now king aforesaid, upon the seeing, reading and hearing a l and singular of the premisses for this, because that it seemed to the said court here, that the plea of the said E. F. in the manner and form aforesaid above pleaded, and the matter in the same plea contained, were not sufficient in law to preclude the said court of the said lord the king here, from proceeding on the indictment aforesaid, it was considered that the said E. F. to the indictment aforesaid should answer. And that upon the said judgment, Francis Pemberton, knight, at the said time chief justice of the said lord the king, assigned to hold pleas before the king himself, Thomas Jones, knight, and Thomas Raymond, knt. at that time two other justices of the said lord the king, assigned to hold pleas before the king himself, then and there judicially sat in the said court here, and then and there declared, that the plea of the said E. F. in the manner and form aforesaid above pleaded, and the matter in the same contained, were not sufficient in law to preclude the said court of the said lord the king here, from proceeding upon the the indictment aforesaid, and that the said E. F. ought to answer to the indictment aforesaid, and thereupon the said E. F. being forthwith demanded of the premisses, by the indictment aforesaid above charged to him, how he would acquit himself thereof, said that he was not guilty thereof, and thereof for good and evil, put himself upon the country. And that afterwards to wit, in the term of the Holy Trinity, in the 33d year, &c. aforesaid, in the said court here, the said E. F. by a certain jury of the country thereupon taken, between the said lord the king and the said E. F. in the due manner was tried for the high-treason aforesaid, and upon that trial then and there, of the high-treason aforesaid, in the due manner was convicted, and thereupon by the judgment of the said court was attainted, and that the said Francis Pemberton, Thomas Jones and Thomas Raymond, then as aforesaid justices of the said lord the king, assigned to hold pleas before the king himself, judicially sat in the said court here, in the terms of Easter and of the Holy Trinity, at the arraignment, trial, conviction and attainder of the said E. F. of the high-treason aforesaid. And that one Edward Nosworthy, late of London, esquire, well knowing the premisses, and being a pernicious and seditious man, and devising, and maliciously intending to disturb the peace and public tranquility of this kingdom of England, and the said Francis Pemberton, Thomas Jones and Thomas Raymond, to * scandalize and bring into hatred and contempt, on the 1st day of September, in the 33d year, &c. aforesaid, at New-Sarum, in the county of Wilts, having a discourse with F. I. and H. H. gentlemen, of and concerning the trial and execution of the said E. F. for the treason aforesaid, in the presence and hearing of divers liege subjects of the said

* P. 77.

M

lord

lord the king, falfely, malicioufly, fubtily, fcandaloufly and feditioufly did fay, affert, publifh and proclaim that, " *He* (meaning the faid E. N.) *did hope that the next parliament would hang all the judges who gave it for the law to try E. F.*" (meaning the faid E. F.) In contempt of the faid lord the now king, and of his laws, to the great fcandal and difhonour of the faid Francis Pemberton, Thomas Jones and Thomas Raymond, to the evil and pernicious example, &c. againft the peace, &c. whereupon the faid attorney, &c.

The King *againft* J. C.

Hilary, the 36th of Charles the 2d.   *Roll* 103.

<table>
<tr><td>Information for fcandalous words on the court of Admiralty.</td><td>

London,
To wit.

THAT on the 19th day of October, in the year, &c. a certain caufe was depending in judgment, in the fupreme court of the faid lord the king, of the admiralty of England, within the inn of the Lords Advocates, fituate near Paul's Wharf, London, before the venerable and excellent lord Richard Lloyd, knt. doctor of laws, furrogate of the honourable man, the lord Leoline Jenkins, knight, doctor of laws, lieutenant general and commiffary in the fupreme court of the admiralty of England aforefaid, and of the faid court, judge and prefident, lawfully conftituted on the part of Richard Peake, proprietor of one half part of a certain hoy or fmack, called the Providence of London, of which John Whitfield then was late mafter, and of her tackle and apparel, againft the other half part of the faid hoy or fmack, and her tackle and apparel belonging to the faid J. W. and againft the faid J. W. in particular, and all others in general, then having or pretending to have his title or intereft in the faid half part of the faid hoy or fmack, called the Providence of London aforefaid, and further the faid attorney general of the faid lord the now king, for the faid lord the king further gives the court here to underftand and to be informed, that afterwards to wit, on the day and year aforefaid, &c. in the court of admiralty, in the caufe aforefaid, it was in fuch fort proceeded, that in the faid court of the faid lord the king, before the judge aforefaid, it was decreed that the hoy or fmack aforefaid, and her tackle and apparel fhould be reduced into a true, full and perfect inventory, and faithfully and juftly fhould be appraifed and valued according to the true value of
the

</td></tr>
</table>

the same. And that afterwards to wit, on the day and year aforesaid, &c. a certain precept of the said lord the king, upon the decree aforesaid, under the seal of t'e said court, in the lawful manner * issued out of the said supreme court of ad- * P. 78
miralty, directed to one William Joynes, gentleman, then marshal of the said court, by which precept, reciting the decree aforesaid, in the said court of admiralty, given as aforesaid, the said lord the king commanded the said marshal or his deputy, that they should not omit, but the said hoy or smack, and her tackle and apparel, should reduce into a true, full and perfect inventory in writing, and by five or four good and lawful men, having better knowledge chosen by the said marshal or his deputy, faithfully and justly, according to the true values of the same, should appraise and value, or should cause to be valued and appraised, and the said appraisement subscribed with their hands, or with the hand of one of them, and with the hands of the said appraisers, to the said lord the king, or to the judge of the court of admiralty aforesaid, or to his surrogate into that court, immediately after the execution of the presents duly should transmit, which precept afterwards to wit, on the day and year, &c at, &c. was delivered to one R. S. constituted in the due manner deputy of the said W. J. then marshal, to be executed in the due form of law, and that the said R. S. with certain W. T. and others, &c. good and lawful men, having better knowledge, and elected appraisers in that behalf, by the said R. S. did enter the said hoy or smack, being then and there upon the river Thames, within the parish and county aforesaid, to make a true and perfect inventory of the said hoy or smack, and of the tackle and apparel thereof, and to appraise and value the true value of the same, according to the effect of the decree and precept aforesaid, and that one J. C. late of the parish, &c. well-knowing the premisses aforesaid, but being a pernicious and seditious man, and devising, practising and intending to disquiet, molest and disturb the peace of the said lord the now king, and the public tranquility of this kingdom of England, and to bring and draw the said court of admiralty, and the officers and ministers of the said court into the greatest hatred, contempt and disregard with the said lord the now king, and with the faithful subjects of the said lord the now king, and to fulfil, perfect and bring to effect his most wicked and detestable devices, practices and intentions aforesaid, he the said J. C. then and there to wit, on the said day and year, &c. aforesaid, at, &c. falsely, unlawfully, unjustly, maliciously and corruptly, in the presence and hearing of divers subjects of the said lord the king, then and there present, § did say, assert, and with a loud voice, did publish and declare of the said court of admiralty, and also of the officers and ministers of the said court, and to and of the said R. S. and others, &c. being in the execution of the said

precept

§ " These false, feigned, scandalous and malicious English words following," seem to be wanting here, and are not in the original.

precept as aforesaid, "*That they the said R. S. and others, &c. were rogues, robbers and pirates, and that they the said R. S. and others, &c. came to the hoy or smack aforesaid, to rob.*" And then and there the said J. C. did speak to the servants of the said J. C. then present, and did command them, "*That they should draw their knives, and should ‡ slay those rogues;* (meaning the said R. S. and the others, &c. being in the execution of the precept aforesaid) *and that the court of admiralty was a roguish court, and a cheating court, and that all who belonged to that court were rogues and * fools,*" (meaning the judges and other officers of the court of admiralty aforesaid). To the great contempt, scandal, disparagement and infamy of the said court of admiralty, and of the officers and ministers of the said court, to the evil and pernicious example, &c. and against the peace. &c.

‡ The precedent is with blanks here, but the sense * P. 79. shews it was some such thing, J. C. commanded his servants.

The King *against* Vavasour.

Easter, the 36th Charles II.

Information for the like.

Middlesex,
To wit. } THAT a certain cause was and as yet is depending in judgment, in the supreme court of the lord the king, of the admiralty of England, within the inn of the Lords Advocates, within the parish, &c. before the venerable and excellent man, the lord Richard Lloyd, kt. doctor of laws, surrogate of the honourable man, Leoline Jenkins, knt. doctor of laws, lieutenant-general and commissary in the supreme court of admiralty of England aforesaid, and of the said court judge and president lawfully constituted, on the part of J. W. and R. his wife, executrix of the last will and testament of one W. D. deceased, against one-third part of the ship, called the William and Jane, of which ship, Giles Daniel was master, and the tackle and apparel belonging to her, and against the said Giles in particular, and all others in general, pretending title or interest in the said one-third part of the said ship, and also against one R. C. for his interest in two parts of the said ship, and of the tackle and apparel belonging to the said ship, in three parts to be divided, and that in the said court, in the cause aforesaid, before the said judge, it was in such sort proceeded, that it was decreed by the said court, that the said R. C. should have the possession of the said ship delivered to him by the marshal of the said court, and that afterwards to wit, on the day and year, &c.

at,

at, &c. a certain discourse was had and moved, between one M. Vavasour, and divers other subjects of the said lord the king, of and concerning the ship aforesaid, and the decree and proceedings in the court of admiralty aforesaid, in the cause aforesaid; and that the said M. Vavasour of London, gentleman, being a person of evil conversation, and a common disturber of the peace of the said lord the king, and falsely, wickedly, unlawfully and unjustly intending, not only the said Leoline Jenkins, knt. doctor of laws, then and as yet judge of the said court of the lord the king of the admiralty of England, but also the jurisdiction and authority of the said court of the said lord the king, of the admiralty of England, especially to scandalize, and to bring into hatred and contempt among the subjects of the said lord the king, then and there in the presence and hearing of divers subjects of the said lord the now king, falsely and maliciously did say and assert, and with a loud voice did publish these false, malicious, scandalous, and opprobrious English words following, to wit, " *Let the admiralty court, and Sir Leoline Jenkins* (meaning the said court of admiralty of England, and the said Leoline Jenkins, knt. judge of the said court) *kiss my arse*, (meaning the posteriors of the said M. V.) *I* (meaning the said M. V.) *care not a turd for them*, * (meaning the said court of admiralty of England, and * P. 80. the said Leoline Jenkins, judge of the said court) *they* (meaning the said court of admiralty of England, and the said Leoline Jenkins, knt. judge of the said court) *have nothing to do with the ship*," (meaning the said ship William and Jane). To the great scandal and infamy of the said Leoline Jenkins, judge of the said court of admiralty aforesaid, and of the jurisdiction of the said court, in great contempt of the said lord the now king, and of his laws, to the evil example, &c.

The King *against* Forth.

Easter, 36 Charles *the 2d.*

Middlesex, } THAT in the term of St. Michael, in the 35th
To wit. } year of the reign of the lord Charles the 2d, king, &c. in the court of the said lord the king, before the king himself, (the said court being then held at Westminster, in the county of Middlesex) one Algernon Sidney, late of the parish of St. Martin in the fields, in the county of Middlesex, esquire,

Information for reflecting on the jury which found Algernon Sidney, esquire, guilty of high-treason

esquire, for certain high-treasons touching the person of the said lord the king, in the lawful manner was indicted, and afterwards to wit, in the said term of St. Michael, in the year aforesaid, at Westminster aforesaid, in the said county of Middlesex, in the said court of the said lord the now king, the said Algernon Sidney, by a certain jury of the county, between the said lord the king and the said Algernon Sidney taken, for the high-treasons aforesaid, in the due manner was tried, and afterwards convicted and attainted as by the record and proceedings thereof in the said court more fully appears. And that Alex. Forth, late of the parish of St. Martin in the fields, in the county of Middlesex, joiner, well knowing the premisses, and being a person of evil name, fame and of unquiet conversation and disposition, and devising, practising and most wickedly intending to disquiet, molest and disturb the peace and public tranquility of this kingdom of England, and to bring and draw the trial aforesaid with the verdict thereon, for the said lord the king against the said Algernon Sidney given, and the due course of law in that behalf, had as aforesaid, into the hatred, contempt and scandal with all the liege subjects of the said lord the king, and to persuade and cause the subjects of the said lord the king to believe, that the trial aforesaid was unduly had, and that the said Algernon Sidney did undeservedly die, he the said Alexander Forth afterwards to wit, on the 29th day of November, in the 35th year, &c. aforesaid, at Westminster, in the county aforesaid, to fulfil, perfect and bring to effect his most wicked devices and intentions aforesaid, to one George Clisby, gent. upon a certain discourse of and concerning the verdict, trial and jury aforesaid, with the said G. C. had, in the presence and hearing of divers liege subjects of the said lord the now king, then and there present, falsely, unlawfully, unjustly, wickedly and seditiously of the jury aforesaid, which gave the verdict aforesaid, against the said Algernon Sidney for the high-treason aforesaid, did say, affirm, and with a loud voice did * declare as follows in these English words following to wit, " *God damn all that is like your loggerhead jury, that brought in a verdict* (meaning the verdict aforesaid, against the said Algernon Sidney for the said high-treason aforesaid) *which they had no evidence for."* And the said attorney-general of the said lord the now king, for the said lord the king gives the court here to understand and to be informed, that the said Alexander Forth afterwards to wit, on the 1st day of December, in the 35th year, &c. aforesaid, at Westminster, in the county aforesaid, of his further malice, and to fulfil, perfect and bring to effect, his most wicked devices and intentions aforesaid, upon a certain other discourse of and concerning the verdict aforesaid, given against the said Algernon Sidney, for the high-treason aforesaid, and of and concerning the jury aforesaid, with the said George Clisby then and

* P. 81.

there

there had, in the presence and hearing of divers liege subjects of the said lord the king then and there present, falsely, unlawfully, unjustly, wickedly and seditiously of the jury aforesaid, which gave the verdict aforesaid, against the said Algernon Sidney for the high-treason aforesaid, did say, utter, affirm, and with a loud voice did declare, " *That the jury which gave their verdict aforesaid, that the said Algernon Sidney was guilty of the high-treason aforesaid, against the said lord the now king, were a loggerheaded jury, and gave their verdict aforesaid, for which they had no evidence.*" In contempt of the said lord the now king, and of his laws, to the evil and pernicious example, &c. and against the peace, &c. whereupon the said attorney, &c.

The King *against* Hoskins.

Hilary, the 34th and 35th of Charles II.

To wit. } THAT Peter Hoskins, of Iverton, in the county of Dorset, aforesaid, gentleman, being a person of unquiet and turbulent spirit, not weighing the duty of his allegiance, and entirely withdrawing the cordial love, and true, due and natural obedience which every true and faithful subject of the said lord the king, towards the said lord the king his supreme and natural lord, should and of right ought to bear; and devising and intending the most noble lord the Earl of Bristol, Thomas Strangeways, esquire, Robert Coker, esq. George Rivee, esquire, George Fulford, esquire, William Strode, esq. Edward Meller, esquire, and divers other faithful and liege subjects of the said lord the king, who lately had signed a certain address to the said lord the king, giving thanks to the said lord the king, for a certain declaration of the said lord the king, lately published by the order of his majesty, to satisfy all his subjects, of and concerning the dissolution of several parliaments by the said lord the king lately called and assembled; to scandalize and them into hatred and scandal with the subjects of the said lord the king, endeavouring to bring, on the 17th day of October, in the 33d * year, &c. with force and arms, &c. at Wooland in the county aforesaid, then and there having

Information for reflecting on the Earl of Bristol, and others, for addressing the king.

* P. 82.

ing

ing a discourse with one Robert Coker, jun. and Benjamin Coker, gent. of and concerning several addresses to the said lord the king presented, he the said Peter Hoskins then and there in the presence of the said Robert Coker, jun. and Benjamin Coker, gent. and of other subjects of the said lord the king, then and there present, openly and publickly with a loud voice maliciously, contemptuously, scandalously, seditiously and slanderously of the said addressors did say, publish, pronounce and declare in these English words following, to wit, " *That none but fools and rogues* (meaning the addressors aforesaid) *did address.*" In great contempt of the said lord the king, to the evil example, &c. and against the peace, &c.

The defendant was found guilty, and fined one hundred marks.

Indictments for Conspiracies.

The King *against* Turner *and others.*

Trinity, 26th of Charles the 2d.

To wit, } **T**HAT Randolph Turner of Framlingham, in the county of Suffolk, yeoman, Elizabeth Turner, wife of the said Randolph Turner, Richard Butcher, late of the parish aforesaid, in the county aforesaid, yeoman, and Francis Carlowe, late of the parish aforesaid, in the county aforesaid, being persons of evil name and fame and dishonest conversation, on the 2d day of February, in the 26th year, &c. at Framlingham, in the county aforesaid, together among themselves, unlawfully did conspire and combine, the good name, fame, credit and reputation of one George Green, without any cause to stain, destroy, deprive and defile, and falsely, maliciously, and for the sake of wicked gain, to charge the said George Green with the crime of adultery with the said Elizabeth Turner, the wife of the said Randolph Turner, and to bring and draw him the said George Green into the greatest hatred, scandal, infamy and reproach, and into the greatest confusion, trouble and anxiety of mind, and also to obtain and extort into their hands great sums of money from the said George Green, by unlawful cozening ways and means. And the said attorney-general of the said lord the king, for the said lord the king further gives the court here to understand and be informed that they the said Randolph Turner, Elizabeth Turner, Richard Butcher and Francis Carlowe, in execution of the premisses, and according to their conspiracy, combination and * agreement aforesaid, afterwards to wit, on the 2d day of February, in the 26th year, &c. and at divers other days and times, as well before as after, at Framlingham aforesaid, in the county aforesaid, and in divers other places in the said county falsely, unlawfully, maliciously, diabolically and for the sake of wicked gain, in the hearing of many of the liege subjects

Information for conspiring to charge a person with being the father of a child born by another man's wife.

* P. 83.

N of

of the said lord the king, worthy of belief, severally did charge and accuse the said George Green, that he the said George Green then lately before had carnal knowledge of the body of the said Elizabeth Turner, and had carnally known the said Elizabeth Turner, and that he the said George Green was the reputed father of a certain spurious child, born of the body of the said Elizabeth Turner, to the great damage, scandal, infamy and reproach of the said George Green, to the evil example, &c. and against the peace, &c.

The King *against* Crispe, and others.

Michaelmas, the 33d of Charles the 2d.

Information for entering into an unlawful conspiracy and combination to engross and monopolize all the vitriol in London.

London, To wit. } TO be informed that John Crispe, late of London, esquire, John Knap, of London, waxchandler, Francis Chamberlin, of London, apothecary, and Thomas Sandford, of London, salter, on the 1st day of October, the 33d year, &c. and for a long time before and continually afterwards, until the day of the exhibition of this information, at the parish of St. Michael, Cornhill, London, using and each of them using the art and mystery of a salter, and then and there being, and each of them being a common buyer and seller of vitriol; they the said J. C. J. K. F. C. and T. S. then and there falsely, unlawfully, unjustly, wickedly and deceitfully did devise and conspire among themselves for their private gain to acquire, obtain and engross into their hands and possession all the vitriol made and manufactured, or then afterwards to be made, for the space of divers years then to come, by the workers and proprietors of the vitriol works in and about the city of London, to make a monopoly thereof, and to encrease and make at their pleasure and will the price of such vitriol, being a commodity very necessary and requisite for the dying of cloth, and for other necessary uses, and to fulfil, perfect, and bring to effect their most wicked devices, practices, conspiracies and intentions aforesaid, they the said J. C. J. K. F. C. and T. S. afterwards to wit, on the said 1st day of Oct. the 33d year, &c. aforesaid, at the parish of St. Michael, Cornhill, London, aforesaid, falsely, unlawfully, unjustly, fraudulently and deceitfully did conspire, combine and agree, and a certain deceitful, bad and unlawful bargain, contract and agreement with

the

the poffeffors and proprietors of the vitriol works, in and about
the city of London, and with divers other perfons to the faid
attorney-general of the faid lord of the now king as yet unknown, hen and there againft the laws and ftatutes of this
kingdom of England, did make, and to obftruct and impede
the free and open * buying and felling among the liege fubjects   * P. 84.
of the faid lord the now king of all the vitriol by the faid poffeffors and proprietors of the vitriol works aforefaid, before
that time made and remaining in their hands or afterwards for
the fpace of divers years then as yet to come, to be made, they
the faid J. C. J. K. F. C. and T. S. did bind in divers contracts
the faid proprietors and poffeffors of the vitriol works aforefaid, in and about the city of London aforefaid, that they the
poffeffors and proprietors of the vitriol works aforefaid, fhould
not fell or deliver during the time aforefaid, any vitriol to any
perfon or perfons whatfoever, except only to them the faid J. C.
J. K. F. C. and T. S. to the intent that they the faid J. C.
J. K. F. C. and T. S. afterwards might utter and fell the vitriol
aforefaid at exceffive and greater prices than are reafonable; and
in further profecution and execution of the wicked and unjuft
confpiracy and agreement aforefaid, they the faid J. C. J. K.
F. C. and T. S afterwards to wit, on the faid 1ft day of October, in the 33d year, &c. aforefaid, and at divers other days
and times as well after as before, at the parifh of St. Michael,
Cornhill, London, aforefaid, falfely, unlawfully and unjuftly, under pretence and colour of fuch contract and agreement, great
quantities of vitriol into their hands and poffeffion did take,
obtain and engrofs, and the vitriol aforefaid fo by them bought,
immediately after the buying thereof, then and there, at great
and exceffive rates and prices to wit, for 8l. 10s. 0d. per ton,
did fell and utter, and each and every of them did fell and utter to divers other fubjects of the faid lord the king, who were
neceffarily compelled to buy from the faid J. C. J. K. F. C
and T. S. that vitriol to fupply their neceffary ufes at fuch exceffive rate, becaufe that they could not buy vitriol from any
other perfon, whereas in fact fuch vitriol before the unlawful
confpiracy aforefaid, was fold and was ufed to be fold at 5l.
per ton only, and not more. And the faid attorney-general of
the faid lord the now king, further gives the court here to underftand and to be informed, that they the faid J. C. J. K. F. C.
and T. S. in further profecution and execution of their unjuft
and unlawful confpiracy and agreement aforefaid, afterwards to
wit, on the 10th day of October, in the 33d year, &c. aforefaid,
at the parifh of St. Michael, Cornhill, London, aforefaid, and
at divers other days and times, as well before as after, with
force and arms, &c. unlawfully, unjuftly and under pretence
and colour of the faid contract and agreement, divers quantities
of vitriol from divers liege fubjects of the faid lord the king,

N.
did

did cause and procure, to be taken and seized, and to be detained from the proprietors of the same, because that the said proprietors of the said vitriol had not bought or obtained the said vitriol, according to the tenor and effect of the unlawful contract and agreement aforesaid, in contempt of the said lord the now king, and of his laws, to the excessive encreasing of the rates and prices of vitriol, and to the destruction and subversion of divers trades, to the great damage, injury and oppression of all the liege subjects of the said lord the king, to the evil example, &c. against the peace, &c. whereupon the said attorney-general, &c.

---

* P. 85.   * *The* King *against* Freeman.

Hilary, 36th Charles II.

Middlesex, } **T**HAT Jane Freeman, late of, &c. and others,
To wit.   }   &c. being persons of evil name and fame, and
of dishonest conversation, on the day and year, &c. contriving, devising and intending one N. M. gentleman, to deceive and defraud of his monies, and also without any cause to stain, destroy, deprive and defile the good name, fame, credit and reputation of the said N. M. and the said N. M. into the greatest hatred, scandal, infamy, reproach and dishonour to bring, and to cause and procure to be brought ; on the said day and year, &c. at, &c. unlawfully, diabolically, wickedly and maliciously among themselves did conspire and combine to accuse and charge the said N. M. that he the said N. M. most wickedly, unlawfully and diabolically, and against the order of nature, had attempted and endeavoured to have a venereal affair with the said Jane Freeman ; and that the said N. M. violently in and upon the said Jane Freeman, had made an assault with intention with her the said Jane Freeman that detestable, horrible and sodomitical crime, called buggery, among christians not to be named, before the time aforesaid, wickedly, feloniously and diabolically to commit and perpetrate, and to perform, perfect, and make their malicious, unlawful, most wicked and diabolical purpose aforesaid, more certain and undoubted

they

Information for conspiring falsely to charge one, and for charging him with an attempt of Buggery.

they the said Jane Freeman and others, &c. aforesaid, on the day and year, &c. aforesaid, at, &c. in the county, &c. according to the conspiracy aforesaid, so as aforesaid between them had, the said N. M. then and there, with the said crime and assault, falsely, diabolically, wickedly and maliciously did charge and accuse, whereas in truth and in fact, the said N. M. was never guilty of nor did commit any such crime as aforesaid, nor any crime whatsoever of the like nature, to the great trouble of the mind, and also to the great damage, injury and expence of the said N. M. in contempt of the said lord the now king, and of his laws, to the evil example, &c.

Indictments for Cheats, Deceits, &c.

The King *against* Record, and others.

Easter, 27th Charles the 2d.

<table>
<tr>
<td>

Information for cheating
* P. 86.
a person of
divers sums
of money,
on false
pretences.

</td>
<td>

To wit.   }

</td>
<td>

THAT Charles Record, late of, &c. Anne Smith, late of, &c. otherwise called Frances Markham, &c. and George Fearne, late of, &c. being persons of evil name, fame, and of * dishonest conversation, common cheats and deceivers, of the liege subjects of the said lord the king, and that the said C. R. A. S otherwise called F. M. and G. F. conspiring, devising, practising, and falsely, unlawfully,

</td>
</tr>
</table>

fraudulently and deceitfully intending, the lady Dorothea Seymour, spinster, of divers sums of money, falsely, unlawfully, fraudulently and deceitfully to deceive and defraud, and to fulfil and perfect their most wicked conspiracies, devices, practices and intentions aforesaid, on the 20th day of January, in the 26th of the reign of the lord Charles the 2d, &c. at the parish of St. Giles in the fields, in the county of Middlesex aforesaid, she the said A. S. otherwise called F. M. otherwise called F. B. falsely, unlawfully, fraudulently and deceitfully did assert, affirm and pretend to the said lady D. S. that the said A. S. otherwise, &c. at that time was a maid and unmarried. And that the said A. S. otherwise, &c. then and there by the name of A. S. spinster, into the service of the lady D. S. and into the house of the said lady D. S. situate in the parish of St. Giles in the fields, in the county of Middlesex, was admitted as the servant of the said D. S. and that the said A. S. otherwise called, &c. afterwards to wit, on the said 20th day of January, in the 26th year, &c. aforesaid, at the parish aforesaid, in the county aforesaid, falsely, unlawfully, fraudulently and deceitfully did pretend, assert and affirm to the said lady D. S. that the said C. R. was the cousin of her the said A S. otherwise called, &c. and that he the said C. R. then had an estate in reversion, to the value of one thousand five hundred pounds per annum; and that

the

the said A. S. otherwise called, &c. afterwards to wit, on the said 20th day of January, in the 26th year, &c. aforesaid, at the parish of St. Giles in the fields, in the county of Middlesex aforesaid, her the said lady D. S. did greatly persuade and solicit to receive the said C. R. into the service and house of the said lady D. S. upon which solicitations and persuasions of the said A. S. otherwise called, &c. the said C. R. into the service and house of the said lady D. S. was received and admitted, and that the said C. R. A. S. otherwise called, &c. and G. F. afterwards to wit, on the said 20th day of January, 26th year, &c. aforesaid, at the parish of St. Giles in the fields, in the county of Middlesex aforesaid, to fulfil and perfect their most wicked conspiracies, devices, practices and intentions, then and there falsely, unlawfully, fraudulently and deceitfully to the said lady D. S. did affirm and pretend, and each and every of them to the said lady D. S. did affirm and pretend, that the said C. R. for one thousand pounds, by the said C. R. then afterwards to be paid, could buy and acquire the place and office of a colonel in the service of the states of Holland, of the value of eight hundred pounds by the year, and that the said C. R. then and there immediately could buy and acquire the said place and office of a colonel, from one ——— Wayne, and that the said C. R. and the said A. S. otherwise called, &c. then and there falsely, unlawfully, fraudulently and * deceitfully did pretend,   *** P. 87.** affirm and assert to the said lady D. S. that if she the said lady D. S. would pay and deposit the sum of one thousand pounds for the buying and acquiring the office and place of a colonel aforesaid, for the natural life of the said C. R. she the said lady D. S. should receive the sum of two hundred pounds by the year, during the natural life of the said C. R. and if the said C. R. in the office and place aforesaid, should die or be removed, that then she the said lady D. S. should have one hundred and sixty pound by the year, to her the said lady D. S. for the space of five years, after the death or removal of the said C. R. and further the said C. R. A. S. otherwise called, &c. and G. F. in further prosecution of their wicked conspiracies, deceits, devices, practices and intentions aforesaid, afterwards to wit, on the said 20th day of January, in the 26th year, &c. aforesaid, at the parish aforesaid, in the county aforesaid, falsely, unlawfully, fraudulently and deceitfully did pretend, affirm and assert, and each and every of them falsely, unlawfully, fraudulently and deceitfully did pretend, affirm and assert to the said lady D. S. that at that time there was a pleasant house, and fit for the habitation of the said C. R. nigh to the Hague in Holland, with orchard and garden, &c. to the value of five hundred pounds by the year, and that the said C. R. could have the said house, orchard and garden aforesaid, for eight hundred pounds, and the said C. R. A. S. otherwise called,

&c.

&c. and G. F. afterwards to wit, on the said 20th day of January, in the 26th year, &c. aforesaid, at the parish aforesaid, in the county aforesaid, to fulfil and perfect their most wicked conspiracies, contrivances, practices and intentions, then and there falsely, unlawfully, fraudulently and deceitfully the said lady D. S. did persuade and incite to pay and deposit into the hands of the said C. R. the sum of four hundred pounds, towards the buying and acquiring of the house, orchard and garden aforesaid, (they the said C. R. A. S. otherwise called, &c. and G. F. then and there falsely, unlawfully, fraudulently and deceitfully pretending and affirming to the said lady D. S. that she the said lady D. S. should have the said house, orchard and garden aforesaid, in mortgage to her the said lady D. S. as a security for the said sum of four hundred pounds). And the said coroner and attorney of the said lord the now king, for the said lord the king further saith, that the said C. R. A. S. otherwise called, &c and G. F. afterwards to wit, on the said 20th day of January, 26th year, &c. aforesaid, at the parish of St. Giles in the fields aforesaid, in the county of Middlesex aforesaid, by their most wicked conspiracies, practices and persuasions aforesaid, among them had as aforesaid, falsely, unlawfully, fraudulently and deceitfully the sum of three hundred pounds, and another sum of forty pounds, and another sum of five hundred pounds, from her the said lady D. S. did receive and have and to the proper use of them, the said C. R. A. S. otherwise called, &c. and G. F. did convert and dispose, to the great deception, defrauding and impoverishment of the said lady D. S. to the evil example, &c. and against the peace, &c. whereupon the said coroner and attorney, &c.

---

* P. 88.

* The King against Norton and others.

Information for a notorious cheat, in first cheating a parson of divers sums, under false pretences, and afterward attempting to poison him.

To wit. } **T**HAT one Lucas Norton, late of the parish of St. Martin in the Fields, in the county of Middlesex, gent. otherwise called Lucas Norton of Whitehall, in the county of Middlesex, aforesaid. esq; Bridget Gaunt, of the parish of St. Clement Danes, in the county of Middlesex aforesaid, widow, William Bromley, late of the same, yeoman, and Henry Lewis, late of the same, yeoman; on the 1st day of February, in the twenty-seventh year of the reign of the lord Charles the 2d, the now king of England, &c. were,

were, and for divers years now laſt paſt, have been perſons of evil name and fame, and of diſhoneſt converſation, common cheats and deceivers of the liege ſubjects of the ſaid lord the now king, and that the ſaid L. N. B. G. W. B. and H. L. conſpiring, deviſing, and practiſing, and falſely, unlawfully, fraudulently, and deceitfully intending one Richard Biggs, gent. of divers ſums of money falſely, unlawfully, fraudulently and deceitfully to deceive and defraud, and to fulfil and perfect their moſt wicked devices, practices and intentions aforeſaid, afterwards, to wit, on the ſaid 1ſt day of February, in the twenty-ſeventh year, &c. aforeſaid, at the pariſh of St. Martin in the Fields, county of Middleſex aforeſaid, ſhe the ſaid B. G. fraudulently and deceitfully did aſſert, affirm, and pretend to the ſaid R. B. that if the ſaid R. B. did want any office or place, that he the ſaid R. B. ſhould repair to the ſaid L. N. and that the ſaid B. G. then and there falſely, unlawfully, fraudulently, and deceitfully further did pretend and affirm that the ſaid L. N. was a man of reputation, and that the ſaid B. G. afterwards, to wit, on the 1ſt day of February, in the twenty-ſeventh-year, &c. aforeſaid, at the pariſh of St. Martin in the Fields, in the county of Middleſex aforeſaid, unlawfully, fraudulently and deceitfully did perſuade the ſaid R. B. to go to the ſaid L. N. upon which perſuaſion the ſaid R. B. afterwards, to wit, on the 1ſt day, &c in the twenty-ſeventh year, &c. aforeſaid, at, &c. in, &c. did go to the ſaid L. N. and that to fulfil and perfect their moſt wicked conſpiracies, intentions, devices and practices aforeſaid, the ſaid L. N. afterwards, to wit, on the ſaid 1ſt day, &c. the twenty-ſeventh year, &c. aforeſaid, at, &c. in, &c. falſely, unlawfully, fraudulently and deceitfully, did pretend, aſſert, and affirm to the ſaid R B. that he the ſaid L. N. would find for the ſaid R. B. ſome benefice or parſonage of great value, and then and there unlawfully, fraudulently and deceitfully did ſolicit and perſuade the ſaid R. B. to take upon himſelf Holy Orders, by which ſolicitations and perſuaſions of the ſaid L. N. the ſaid R. B. afterwards, to wit, on the ſaid 1ſt day, &c. in the twenty-ſeventh year, &c. at, &c. in, &c. did take upon himſelf Holy Orders, and * into the order of a Deacon was inſtituted and admitted ; and the ſaid coroner and attorney of the ſaid lord the king, for the ſaid lord the king further ſaith, and to the court here ſhews, that the ſaid L. N. B. G. W. B. and H. L. to fulfil and perfect their moſt wicked devices, conſpiracies, intentions and practices aforeſaid, afterwards, to wit, on the ſaid 1ſt day, &c. in the twenty-ſeventh year, &c. at, &c. in, &c. to the ſaid R. B. did affirm and pretend, and each and every of them to the ſaid R. B. did affirm and pretend, that a certain benefice or parſonage in the county of Northampton, of the yearly value of four hundred and forty four pounds was vacant, and that the benefice was in the gift of the lord the king, and that the

* P. 89.

O

ſaid

said L. N. then and there falsely, unlawfully, fradulently and deceitfully to the said R. B. did affirm and pretend, that the said lord the now king had given and relinquished the difpofiti-on of the benefice aforefaid to the lord Arlington (meaning Henry lord Arlington) and that the said lord Arlington had re-linquished the difpofition of that benefice to the said L. N. and that the said L N. then and there falsely, unlawfully, fraudulently and deceitfully, did pretend and affert, to the said R. B. that if the said R. B. would pay to the said L. N. the fum of fix hundred pounds for his labour and expences in and about the acquiring the benefice aforefaid, and for the difcharg-ing of a certain fequeftration before that time laid upon the benefice aforefaid, and in and about the obtaining and perfect-ing of letters patent of the said lord the now king, for the be-nefice aforefaid, he the said L. N. the said letters patent of the said lord the now king, fealed under the great feal of Eng-land, to enjoy the said benefice or parfonage, in the said coun-ty of Northampton, of the yearly value of four hundred and forty four pounds, to the said R. B. on a certain day then to come would obtain, procure and deliver, and that in further profecution of their moft wicked confpiracies, contrivances, practices and intentions aforefaid, the said L. N. afterwards, to wit, on the said 1ft day of, &c. in the 27th year, &c. at, &c. in, &c. aforefaid, falsely, unlawfully, deceitfully, and fraudu-lently did affert, affirm and pretend to the said R. B. that there was one Elizabeth Sands (a maiden, unmarried) in the ward-fhip of her guardian, one Mr. Turner, which Elizabeth Sands was the coufin of the said L. N. and that the said Elizabeth Sands had the fum of fix thoufand pounds in money, and alfo an eftate real in lands to the value of 200l. by the year, and that if the said R. B. would pay and lay down the fum of 600l. to the said L. N. and alfo the fum of one thoufand pieces of gold called guineas, to the wife of the said Mr. T. the said R. B. fhould have the said Elizabeth Sands in marriage, and the said L. N. B. G. W. B. and H. L. in further profecution of their moft wicked confpiracies, deceits, devices, and intenti-ons aforefaid, afterwards, to wit, on the said 1ft day of, &c. in the 27th year, &c. in, &c. at, &c. falsely, unlawfully, frau-dulently and deceitfully did pretend, affirm and affert, and each and every of them then and there did pretend, affirm and affert, that one Charles Moley had informed one of the chaplains of
P. 90. the Archbifhop of * Canterbury, of the purchafing of the said benefice or parfonage, in the county of Northampton, and that the Archbifhop of Canterbury had iffued procefs againft the said R. B. for fimony, and that a certain fine of 200l. was laid upon the said R. B. for the fimony aforefaid, by the said lord the now king; and that the said R. B. could not fecure and preferve harmlefs his eftate, and alfo the profits of the bene-fice or parfonage aforefaid, from the fine aforefaid, unlefs the

said

said R. B. would depofit, truft, and conceal his eftate in the hands of the faid L. N. and that the faid L. N. afterwards, to wit, on the 1ft day, &c. in the 27th year, &c. in, &c. aforefaid, did perfuade and folicit the faid R. B. to depofit and truft his eftate and monies into the hands of the faid L. N. upon which folicitations and perfuafions of the faid L. N. the faid R. B. then and there did depofit and truft his eftate and monies to the value of 1800l. in the hands of the faid L. N. (the faid L. N. then and there falfely, unlawfully and deceitfully affirming to the faid R. B. that he the faid L. N. would fecure the eftate and monies aforefaid, for the faid R. B.) And the Coroner and Attorney of the faid lord the king, for the faid lord the king further faith, that the faid L. N. B. G W. B. and H. L. afterwards, to wit, on the faid 1ft day, &c. in the 27th year, &c. at, &c. in, &c. aforefaid, by their moft wicked confpiracies, devices, practices and perfuafions aforefaid, among them had as aforefaid, unlawfully, fraudulently, unjuftly and deceitfully, the fum of 600l. and another fum of 500l. and another fum, to wit, the fum of 1200l. from the faid R. B. did receive and have, and to their proper ufe did convert and difpofe, and each and every of them did convert and difpofe, and alfo one writing obligatory under the hand and feal of the faid R. B. of the penalty of 1200l. conditioned for the payment of 600l. and the faid L. N. and others, &c. by their practices, confpiracies and perfuafions aforefaid, falfely, unlawfully, unjuftly, fraudulently and deceitfully then and there, the faid feveral fums from him the faid R. B. did receive, have and enjoy; and in further profecution of their intentions, practices, devices and confpiracies aforefaid, he the faid L. N. diabolically intending the death of the faid R. B. afterwards, to wit, on the faid 1ft day, &c. in the 37th year of, &c. at the parifh of St. Martin in the Fields aforefaid, in the faid county of Middlefex, wilfully and of his malice aforethought, a certain poifon called arfenick into a certain drink then and there prepared for the drinking of him the faid R. B. then and there privately did put and mingle, and then and there did perfuade the faid R. B. to take and drink the faid drink, by reafon of which perfuafion, the faid R. B. afterwards, to wit, on the faid 1ft day of, &c. in the 27th year, &c. at the parifh of St. Clement Danes, in the county of Middlefex aforefaid, the drink aforefaid, with the poifon aforefaid, mixed as aforefaid, not knowing or fufpecting that the faid drink was mixed with poifon, did take and drink, whereupon the faid R. B. immediately after the taking of the poifon aforefaid, did languifh and remain in danger of his *life, for the fpace of three months then next following, to the great damage of the faid R. B. to the evil example, &c. and againft the peace, &c. &c.

* P. 91.

The

The King *against* Wilcox.

London,
To wit. }

Information
for cheating
a perfon of
goods, under
pretence of
buying
them.

THAT Stephen Wilcox, late of London, yeoman, Hugh Bookey, of, &c. Sufannah. Bookey, of London, fpinfter, otherwife called Sufannah Bookey, the wife of the faid Hugh Bookey, and Jofeph Harrifon, late of London, yeoman, being perfons of difhoneft converfation, and not intending to obtain their living by honeft labour, according to the laws of this kingdom of England, but compaffing and daily devifing how by unlawful means they might obtain and acquire into their hands and poffeffion the goods and chattels of the honeft liege fubjects of the faid lord the king, for the maintenance of their unthrifty courfe of living, on the 23d day of July, in the 31ft year of the reign of the lord Charles the 2d, the now king, &c. with force and arms, &c. at London, to wit, in the parifh of All-Saints, Lombard-ftreet, in the ward of Bifhopfgate, London aforefaid, they the faid Stephen Wilcox, by the name of Thomas Brown, Hugh Bookey, and Sufannah Bookey, under colour and pretence of buying from one John Dutton of Stoke-Nayland, in the county of Suffolk, ftay-maker, 650 yards of cloth, called ftuff, of the value of fifteen pounds, fixteen fhillings, of the goods and chattels of the faid J. D. the faid 650 yards of cloth, called ftuff, out of the hands and cuftody of the faid J. D. into the hands and poffeffion of them the faid S. W. by the name of T. B. H. B. and S. B. then and there falfely, unlawfully, fraudulently and deceitfully did obtain and acquire, and the faid J. D. of the faid 650 yards of cloth, called ftuff, then and there falfely, unlawfully, fraudulently and deceitfully did deceive and defraud, to the great damage and manifeft deceit of the faid J. D. In contempt of the faid lord the king, and of his laws, to the evil example, &c. and againft the peace, &c.

The

The King *against* Arnope.

Michaelmas, the 36th Charles 2d.   *Roll* 17.

——— } GIVES the court here to underſtand and to be informed, that John Arnope, late of the pariſh of St. Martin in the fields, in the county of Middleſex, gent. Nathaniel Oldfield, late of the pariſh aforeſaid, in the county aforeſaid, gent. George Ward, late of the pariſh aforeſaid, in the county aforeſaid, gent. and William Oldfield, late of the pariſh aforeſaid, in the county aforeſaid, gentleman, being perſons * of diſhoneſt converſation, and common gameſters, with falſe dice and cards, and falſe play, and perſons of evil name and fame, and diſhoneſt converſation, and common cheats and deceivers of the liege ſubjects of the ſaid lord the king, to maintain their unthriſty courſe of living, on the 1ſt day of February, in the 35th year of the reign of the lord Charles the 2d. king, &c at the pariſh of St. Martin in the fields, in the county of Middleſex, and deviſing, practiſing and falſely and fraudulently and deceitfully intending, one Arthur Squibb with cards and falſe play, craſtily, ſubtily, falſely, unlawfully, unjuſtly, fraudulently and deceitfully to deceive and defraud, and divers ſums of money from the ſaid Arthur Squibb, with the cards aforeſaid, and falſe play, craftily and ſubtilly, falſely, fraudulently and deceitfully to acquire and obtain, the ſaid A. S. then and there to play at cards with the ſaid J. A. N. O. G. W. and W. O. at a certain unlawful game, called whiſt, for divers ſums of money, then and there falſely, unlawfully, unjuſtly, fraudulently and deceitfully did ſolicit, ſtir up, provoke and procure, by which ſolicitations, ſtirrings up, provocations and procurements of the ſaid J. A. N. O. G. W. and W. O. he the ſaid A. S. then and there with the ſaid J. A. N. O. G. W. and W. O. at the ſaid unlawful game, called whiſt, did play for divers ſums of money, and that the ſaid J. A. N. O. G. W. and W. O. at the ſaid unlawful game, called whiſt, then and there with falſe cards, and falſe play, the ſum of eighty pounds, of the lawful money of England, of the monies of the ſaid A. S. from the ſaid A. S. then and there, with force and arms, ſubtilly, falſely, unlawfully, unjuſtly, fraudulently and deceitfully into the hands and poſſeſſion of them the ſaid J. A. N. O. G. W. and W. O. did acquire, have, obtain and carry away; and the ſaid coroner and attorney of the ſaid

lord

Information
for a cheat
with falſe
cards, at the
game of
whiſt. and
with falſe
dice, at the
game called
paſſage
* P. 92.

lord the king, for the said lord the king gives the court here to understand and to be informed, that the said J. A. N. O. G. W. and W. O. afterwards to wit, on the said 1st day of February, in the 35th year, &c. at the parish aforesaid, in the county aforesaid, to fulfil, perfect and bring to effect their most wicked practices, devices and intentions aforesaid subtilly, falsely, unlawfully, unjustly, fraudulently and deceitfully, the said A. S. then and there, to play at dice with the said J. A. N. O. G. W. and W. O. at a certain unlawful game, called " *Passage*," for divers sums of money, falsely, subtilly, unlawfully, fraudulently and deceitfully did solicit, stir up, provoke and procure, by which solicitations, stirrings up, provocations and procurements of them the said J. A. N. O. G. W. and W. S. he the said A. S. then and there at the said unlawful game, called " *Passage*," with the said J. A. N. O. G. W. and W. O. for divers sums of money did play, and that the said J. A. N. O. G. W. and W O. at the said unlawful game called Passage with the said A. S. did play, and that the said J. A. N. O. G. W. and W. O. then and there, with false dice, and by unlawful slurring or throwing of the dice aforesaid, and with other false play, the sum of eighty pounds of the lawful money of England, of the monies of the said A. S. from the said A. S. then and * there, falsely, subtilly, unlawfully, fraudulently and deceitfully, into the hands and possession of them the said J. A. N. O. G. W. and W. O. did acquire, have and obtain, and each and every of them did have and obtain, to the manifest deceit, damage, impoverishment and ruin of the said A. S. to the evil example of all others, &c. against the peace, &c. Whereupon the said coroner, &c.

* P. 93.

The King *against* Betsworth, *and others.*

Michaelmas, the 2d of James the 2d.

<table>
<tr><td>Information
for the like,
with false
dice, at the
game of
hazard.</td><td>To wit. } THAT Arthur Betsworth, of, &c. and J. C. of, &c. being common gamesters, with cards, false dice, and false play, and persons of evil name and fame, and dishonest conversation, and common cheats and deceivers of the liege subjects of the said lord the king, of their goods, chattels, and monies, to maintain their wicked course of living, on the day and year, &c. and divers other days and times then before, at, &c. devising and fraudulently intending one Jasper Mottershead,</td></tr>
</table>

Mottershead, with false dice, and false play, unlawfully, falsely and subtilly to deceive and defraud, and divers sums of money of him the said J. M. with false dice and false play, unlawfully, craftily and deceitfully to acquire and obtain, him the said J. M. then and at divers other days and times then before, there in the parish aforesaid, to play at dice with the said A. B. and J. C. at a certain game called hazard, and at the divers other games, for divers sums of money, then and there, and at divers other days and times aforesaid, falsely, unlawfully and deceitfully did solicit, stir up, provoke and procure, by which solicitations, stirrings up, provocations and procurements of the said A. B. and J. C. he the said J. M. then and there, and at divers other days and times then before, there in the parish aforesaid, &c. at the said game, and at divers other games, with the said A. B. and J. C. for divers sums of money of the said J. M. did play, and that they the said A. B. and J. C. at the play aforesaid, called hazard, and at divers other games at dice, with the said J. M. then and at the divers other days and times aforesaid, with false dice and false play, the sum of two hundred and fifty pounds in money numbered, of the monies of the said J. M. from the said J. M. then and there, and at divers other days and times, subtilly, fraudulently, falsely and deceitfully into the hands and possession of the said A. B. and J. C. did acquire and obtain, and the said J. M. of the said sum of money, then and there falsely, unlawfully and fraudulently did deceive and defraud; to the manifest deceit, impoverishment, and great damage of the said J. M. in great contempt, &c. to the evil example, &c. and against the peace, &c.

---

* The King against Taydler, and others.   * P. 94.

To wit. } THAT John Taydler, of the parish of Mabe, in the county of Cornwall, gent. Thomas Taydler, of the same, gent. Avis Taydler, wife of T. T. of the same, gent. Guideon Traymane, of the same, yeoman, Robert Pellow, of the same, yeoman, being persons of evil name and fame, and dishonest conversation, and common frequenters of unlawful conventicles, and devising, practising, and falsely, unlawfully and deceitfully intending one Gertrude Crowgy, widow, and Gertrude Crowgy, her daughter, to deceive and defraud of certain tenements of the clear yearly value of seventy pounds, lying in Mabe and Constanton, in

Information for a cheat, by drawing a conveyance to them selves, of some leasehold estates, of two women and persuading them to the execute it,

<table>
<tr><td style="vertical-align:top; width:25%">

pretending it was only in truſt for women, and afterwards claiming and poſſeſſing the eſtates to the defendants own proper uſes.

</td><td style="vertical-align:top">

the county aforeſaid, whereof they the ſaid G. C. and G. C as executrixes of the laſt will and teſtament of one Richard Crowgy, were poſſeſſed for ſeveral terms of years, as yet to come, and unexpired, and to fulfil and perfect their moſt wicked contrivances, practices and intentions aforeſaid, they the ſaid J. T. A. T. T. T. G. T. and R. P. on the 21ſt day of December, in the 33d year of the reign of our lord Charles the 2d, king, &c. at M. aforeſaid, in the county aforeſaid, falſely, fraudulently, unlawfully, ſubtilly and deceitfully, and without the knowledge or conſent of them the ſaid G. C. widow, and G. C. her daughter, did make and procure a certain writing to be drawn, written and prepared, the tenor of which is in the form which follows, to wit, " *This indenture made the 21ſt day of December, anno Domini 1681, in the 33d year of the reign of our ſovereign lord Charles the 2d, by the grace of God, king of England, Scotland, France and Ireland, defender of the faith, &c. Between Gertrude Crowgy, of the pariſh of Mabe, in the county aforeſaid, widow, of the one part, and John Taydler, of the pariſh of Mabe, gent. and Thomas Taydler, of the pariſh of Mabe aforeſaid, of the other party, Witneſſeth, that the ſaid G. C. for the conſideration of the natural love and affection which ſhe hath and doth bear unto the ſaid John Taydler, and T. T. hath given, granted and aſſigned, ſet over and confirmed, and by theſe preſents doth give, grant, aſſign, ſet over and confirm, unto the ſaid J. T. and T. T. all that her moiety and Halfendale of all thoſe her meſſuages, lands and tenements, with the appurtenances, called Chinoweth and Tronoweth, within the pariſh of Mabe aforeſaid, Tregliſh with Wartha, in the pariſh of Conſtanton, in the ſaid county, together with all the right, eſtate, title, claim and demand of her the ſaid G. C. of, in or to the ſame or any part thereof, (except as in the ſeveral leaſes is excepted) to have and to hold all and ſingular, the ſaid aſſigned premiſſes, with the appurtenances (except before excepted) unto the ſaid J. T. and T. T. their executors, adminiſtrators and aſſigns, for and during all the reſidue of the ſaid term or number of years yet to come and unexpired, of and in the ſeveral and reſpective leaſes aforeſaid; they the ſaid J. T. and T. yielding and paying unto the landlord and landlords of the ſeveral and reſpective premiſſes, the rent, duties and ſervices from henceforth, due and payable for the ſame; and the ſaid G. C. doth for herſelf, her heirs, executors and adminiſtrators, and for every of them, covenant, grant and promiſe to and with the ſaid J. T. and T. T. their executors, adminiſtrators and aſſigns, and to and with every of them, that they the ſaid J. T. and T. T. their executors, adminiſtrators and aſſigns, ſhall and may quietly and peaceably have, hold, occupy and enjoy all and ſingular, the ſaid premiſſes, (except before excepted) in manner and form aforeſaid, and during the ſeveral terms aforeſaid, and that without the lawful let, trouble, charge or incumbrance of her the ſaid G. C. her executors, adminiſtrators or aſſigns, or any or either of them. In wit*

</td></tr>
</table>

* P. 95.

neſs

ness whereof, the parties abovesaid, to these presents interchangeably their hands and seals have put, the day and the year first above written." And that afterwards to wit, on the said 21 day of December, in the 33d year, &c. aforesaid, at C. aforesaid, in the co. aforesaid, where the said G. C. widow, at that time lay languishing at the point of death, they the said J. T. A. T. T. T. G. T. and R. P. falsely did affirm, and fraudulently, unlawfully, subtily and deceitfully did declare, alledge and pretend to the said G. C. widow, and G. C. her daughter, (being then and there women) that the writing aforesaid, was written only in trust, to preserve the tenements aforesaid, for the use and benefit of the said G. C. the daughter, and with that intention were then necessary to be made and sealed, and thereupon they the said J. T A. T. T. T. G. T. and R. P. then and there, by such false, feigned, subtil and deceitful pretences, assertions, persuasions and affirmations, falsely, fraudulently, unlawfully, subtily and deceitfully did incite and persuade the said G. C. widow, to seal and deliver the said false, feigned and deceitful writing above-mentioned and recited, and that thereupon the said G. C. widow, being as aforesaid, languishing and sick, and not able to dispose of her estate, and not knowing or suspecting fraud, covin or deceit in the premisses, but giving credit to and seduced by the false allegations, informations and persuasions of them the said J. T. A. T. T. T. G. T. and R. P. the the said G. C. then and there the said false and deceitful writing, so as aforesaid, falsely, subtily and deceitfully caused and procured to be written and prepared in the place of a writing, in trust to preserve the tenements aforesaid, for the use and benefit of the said G. C. the daughter, by the procurement of them the said J T. A. T. T. T. G. T. and R. P. did seal and deliver as her deed, (the the said G. C. widow, then lying languishing at the point of death, and not fit to dispose of her estate) and thereupon they the said J. T. A. T. T. T. G. T. and R. P. then and there, the writing aforesaid, so as aforesaid, falsely, fraudulently and deceitfully, by the deceitful ways and means aforesaid, and under the pretence of securing the estate aforesaid, for the said G. C. the daughter, from the said G. C. widow, falsely, unlawfully, fraudulently and deceitfully had and obtained, as a true writing made upon good consideration, to the said J. T. and T. T. by the said G. C. widow, for the proper use and benefit of the said J. T. and T. T. and not in trust for the said G. C. the daughter, then and there, falsely, fraudulently, unlawfully, subtily and deceitfully did publish, and each and every of them did publish; and the said J. T. and T. T. by the practice, fraud and covin then and there had between them, and the said A. T. G. T. and R. P. did claim the tenements aforesaid, by colour of the said false and deceitful writing, to the proper use of the said J. T. and T. T. and then into the tenements aforesaid did enter, and the issues and profits

P. 96.

P   *thereof,*

thereof, continually from thence hitherto, have and received and had and to the proper use of them the said J.T. and T.T. have converted and disposed to the great deceit, damage and impoverishment of the said G. C. widow, and G. C. her daughter, to the evil example, &c. and against the peace, &c. whereupon the said attorney-general of the said lord the now king, &c.

The King *against* Baker.

Information for fraudulently getting into his hands hisownbond for 200l. to one Howland, and obliterating part thereof

To wit. } THAT Thomas Baker, of Streatham, in the county of Surry, clerk, on the 9th day of May, in the 36th year of the reign of the lord Charles the 2d, late king of England, &c. at S. aforesaid, in the county aforesaid, by his writing obligatory, bearing date the 8th day of May, in the year of our Lord 1682, and in the 34th year of the reign of said late lord the king, lawfully signed and sealed, under the hand and seal of the said T. B. did bind himself to John Howland, of S. aforesaid, esquire, in two hundred pounds, of the good and lawful money of England, to be paid to the said John Howland, or his certain attorney, or his executors, administrators and assigns, to which payment well and faithfully to be made, he the said T.B. did bind himself, his heirs, executors and administrators firmly by the presents aforesaid ; and the said coroner and attorney of the said lord the king, for the said lord the king further gives the court here to understand and to be informed, that the said T. B. afterwards to wit, on the said 9th day of May, in the 36th year, &c. aforesaid, well-knowing the premisses aforesaid, at S. in the county of Surry, contriving and intending him the said I. H. in that behalf, to deceive and defraud, and the writing obligatory aforesaid, to cause to be of no force and effect, falsely, unlawfully, subtily and deceitfully the writing obligatory aforesaid, into the hands and possession of the said T. B. with force and arms did obtain, and then and there with force and arms, &c. falsely, unlawfully, unjustly, fraudulently and deceitfully, without the permission and against the will of the said I. H. the writing obligatory aforesaid, greatly did obliterate ; and then and there, with force and arms, falsely, unlawfully, unjustly, craftily, subtily, fraudulently and deceitfully, these words following to wit, "*My heirs, executors and administrators*," from the writing obligatory aforesaid, did put out, blot out and obliterate to the great deception, prejudice and injury of the said I. H. to the evil and pernicious example, &c. and against the peace, &c. whereupon the said coroner and attorney of the said lord the now king, &c.

The

* The King *against* Allibone.   * P. 97.

Michaelmas, the 1ft of James the 2d. *Roll.* 82.

Middlesex,⟩ THAT Henry Allibone, of London, yeoman,
To wit. ⟨   and others, being, and each and every of
them being persons of evil name and fame, and of dishonest
conversation, and common deceivers of the liege subjects of
the said lord the now king, and that the said Henry Allibone,
and others, &c. on the 11th day of July, in the 1ft year of the
reign of our lord James the 2d, king, &c. unlawfully, malici
oufly and deceitfully did devife and confpire, and each and
every of them did devife and confpire, one Thomas Hilliard
greatly to deceive, and the said T. H. to marry with one Bridget Thickneffe, a widow, poor and indigent, and alfo divers
penal obligations for the payment of divers fums of money to
the said H. A. and others, falfely and unjuftly from the said T.
H. to procure and to fulfil and perfect their said feveral moft
wicked confpiracies and devices aforefaid, they the said
H. A. and others, (on the said day and year, &c.) at the parifh
aforefaid, in the county aforefaid, falfely, unlawfully, fraudulently and deceitfully did fay and affirm to the said T. H. and
each and every of them did fay and affirm to the said T. H.
that the said B. T. was a perfon of great fortune, to the value
of one thoufand pounds in money numbered, and that the said
B. T. was feized in fee-fimple, of and in lands and tenements
to the yearly value of 200*l.* above and befides divers diamonds
and filver veffels of great value, which the said B. then had,
and the said H. A. and others, then and there, unjuftly and deceitfully did folicit and perfuade, and each and every of them
did folicit and perfuade the said T. H. to make his application
to the said B. T. in order to conclude a marriage, and the said
H. A. the fooner to bring to effect and perfect their devices
aforefaid, he the said H. A. then and there appointed the
said T. to meet him the said H. at the manfion-houfe of one
E. B. (being in the parifh aforefaid, and in the county aforefaid) to have then and there an interview with the said B. T.
in which place the said T. H. on the said day and year, &c.
met the said H. A. and the said H. A. and others, in further
profecution of their confpiracies and devices aforefaid, then
and there took upon themfelves, to inftruct and direct the
said T. H. by what means he the said T. H. fhould apply

P 2   himfelf

Information.
for a cheat,
in perfuad-
ing one
Hilliard to
marry a
woman
much in
debt, and
and obtain-
ing from
him diver
bonds for
the pay-
ment of
money to
the defend-
ant and
others.

himself to the said B. T. and might obtain her consent to marriage, and immediately the said T. H. then and there was introduced into the company of the said B. T. whereupon the said T. giving credit to the false assertions and affirmations aforesaid, of the said H. A. and others, and by their unlawful and deceitful solicitations, was persuaded then and there immediately to marry and take to wife the said B. T. and thereupon the said H. A. and others, &c. immediately then and there most wickedly and deceitfully did solicit, persuade and procure and each and every of them did solicit, persuade and procure the said T. H. for and in consideration of the premisses, to * P. 98. seal and deliver a certain penal * obligation of one hundred pounds, for the payment of 50l. to the said H. A. which H. A. never before that time to the said T. H. was seen or known; and to seal and deliver a certain other obligation penal of the like sum of 100l. for the payment of 50l. to the said I. B. the husband of the said E. B. and also to seal and deliver one other penal obligation of 60l. for the payment of 30l. to the said H. A. which several obligations so as aforesaid made, were made, had and procured, for the cause aforesaid, and by false and unlawful ways and means, and not for any debt due to the said H. A. and others, or to any of them, &c. and the said coroner and attorney of the said lord the king, for the said lord the king further gives the court here to understand and to be informed, that the said B. T. at the time aforesaid, was a poor and very indigent person, and had not any lands or tenements, or other wealth, as the said H. A. and others, &c. severally did affirm as aforesaid, but she the said B. T. was indebted to divers persons, in divers great sums of money, which said devices, conspiracies, deceits, solicitations and procurements aforesaid, of the said H. A. and others, are to the great damage, grief, impoverishment and final ruin of him the said T. B. to the evil example, &c. and against the peace, &c. whereupon, &c.

The King *against* Hunt, and others.

To wit, } THAT Raphael Hunt, an infant of the age of 13 years, son and heir of John Hunt, of, &c. was seized, and as yet is seized of divers lands, tenements and hereditaments, situate, lying and being in the several parishes of &c. to the value of 150l. by the year and more, and that the
said

said R. H. on the said day and year, &c. had and was possessed
of divers goods and chattels, and sums of money to the value
of 220l. and more, and that John Hunt, of, &c. and others,
on the said day and year, &c. at, &c. in the county aforesaid,
well-knowing the premisses aforesaid, but contriving, practising,
devising, and among themselves conspiring and intending the
said R. H. in the peaceable possession and enjoyment of his
estate, to disturb, and to obstruct him the said R. H. in obtaining a proper marriage for himself, or a suitable sum of money
in marriage, and to fulfil and perfect their most wicked contrivances, practices, conspiracies and intentions aforesaid, afterwards to wit, on the said day and year aforesaid, and at divers
other days and times as well after as before, at, &c. in the
county, &c. they the said J. H. and others, &c. falsely, unjustly,
unlawfully, fraudulently and deceitfully among themselves, did
conspire, contrive and agree to propose and procure a marriage
between the said R. H. an infant, and one E. H. at that time
being unmarried, and to fulfil and perfect their most wicked
contrivances, practices, intentions and conspiracies aforesaid,
they the said J. H and others, on the said day and year, &c.
and at divers other days and times, as well before as after, at,
&c. in prosecution of their false and * deceitful conspiracies,
contrivances and agreements aforesaid, and falsely, unlawfully
fraudulently and deceitfully to induce the said E. H. to take
the said R. H. to her husband, afterwards to wit, on the said
day and year, &c. at, &c. falsely, unlawfully, unjustly, fraudulently and deceitfully did affirm and insinuate, and each and
every of did affirm and insinuate to the said E. H. that the said
R. H. then had a great estate in lands to the value of 200l. by
the year and more, and also a great personal estate in goods,
chattels and sums of money, and to fulfil and perfect their
most wicked contrivances, practices, conspiracies and intentions aforesaid, they threatened, and each and every of them
threatened the said E. H. the daughter of the said J. H. then
and there to punish, chastise and transport, if she the E. H.
would deny to take the said R. H. to her husband, and that the
said J. H. and others, to fulfil and perfect their most wicked
contrivances, practices, conspiracies and intentions aforesaid,
and to procure the said R. H. to marry the said E. H. the
daughter of the said J. H. and to induce the said R. H. to take
the said E. H. to his wife, afterwards to wit, on the said day
and year, &c. at, &c. in the county, &c. falsely, unlawfully,
unjustly, fraudulently and deceitfully to the said R. H. an infant, did affirm and insinuate, and each and every of them did
affirm and insinuate, that the said E. H. the daughter of the
said J. H. would have a great portion to the value of 600l.
and more, if he the said R. H. would take the said E. H. to
his wife, and if he the said R. H. to marry with the said E. H.
the daughter of the said J. H. then and there would refuse and

deny,

* P. 99.

nings to
marry one
of the de-
fendants
daughters.

deny, then that he the faid R. H. into dark places to the friends and relations of the faid R. H. entirely unknown, then immediately fhould be fent and kept, and the faid coroner, &c. further gives, &c. that the faid J. H. and others, to fulfil and perfect their unlawful, wicked contrivances, practices and intentions aforefaid, afterwards to wit, on the faid day and year, &c. at, &c. falfely, unlawfully, fraudulently and deceitfully did caufe and procure the faid R. H. and E. H. to be joined in matrimony, and to be married together, and each and every of them, then and there did caufe and procure the faid R. H. and the faid E. H. falfely, unlawfully, unjuftly, fraudulently and deceitfully to be joined in matrimony, and to be married together, to the great difpleafure of almighty God, in contempt, &c. to the great damage, prejudice, ruin, difparagement and impoverifhment of the faid R. H. to the final forrow and grief of the friends and relations of the faid R. H. to the evil, &c. and againft the peace, &c.

The King againft T. T. and others.

Hilary, 2d and 3d of James the 2d.   Roll 101.

Information for marrying an infant by deceitful and indirect practices, to a fcandalous woman.
*P. 100.

THAT one James Silverlock, gentleman, fon and heir of R. S. efquire, on the day and year, &c. being a perfon then feized in his demefne, as of fee of lands and tenements of great value, to wit, of lands and tenements of the yearly value of 200l. in his poffeffion, and in other lands and * tenements in reverfion, after the eftate which Catherine, now wife of W. K. efquire, the mother of the faid J. S. then had and now has determinable upon her life, of the yearly value of 30l. and fo being feized, and then being an infant within the age of 21 years, and in the guardianfhip of the faid W. K. and C. neverthelefs one T. T. late of, &c. and others, being perfons of evil name, fame and of difhoneft converfation, contriving, confpiring, and moft wickedly intending and devifing to deceive and defraud the faid J. S. and to marry him to one E. M. a perfon of evil name, and of difhoneft converfation, and of no eftate or fortune, without any confent or approbation of any of the friends or relations of the faid J. S. on the faid day and

and year aforesaid, at the parish aforesaid, &c. falsely, unlawfully, fraudulently and deceitfully did affirm to the said J. S. that the said E. M. was a woman of good, honest and laudable conversation, and that she had a good estate and fortune, to wit, one thousand pounds in money, and lands and tenements of the value of 200l. by the year, and to perfect their fraudulent intentions, combinations and contrivances aforesaid, and to withhold him the said J. S. from all converse with any of his friends and relations, or from having due consideration of and concerning the premisses, they the said T. T. and others, &c. him the said J. S. in their company, or in the company of one of them, in feasting, and in carrying and removing the said James Silverlock from one place to another, for the space of three successive days did detain, to wit, at the parish, &c. in the county, &c. until that he the said J. S. being an infant as aforesaid, by false and unlawful ways and means aforesaid, by the said T. T. and others, &c. afterwards to wit, on the said day and year, &c. at, &c. at the eleventh hour of the night of the said day, there was procured to marry, and then and there did marry the said E. M. then and a long time before being not only a woman of evil and dishonest conversation, but also poor and indigent, and of no estate or fortune, and then for the whole time aforesaid, being known to the said T.T. and others, and to every of them to be a woman of evil and dishonest conversation, and to be poor and indigent, and of no estate or fortune. To the great displeasure of almighty God, to the final sorrow, great damage and grief, as well of the said J. S. as of the said W. K. and C. his wife, to the evil example, &c. and against the peace, &c. whereupon the said coroner and attorney, &c.

The King *against* Saunders *and others.*

Michaelmas, the 2d of James the 2d. *Roll* 98.

To wit. } THAT Andrew Saunders and T. B. of, &c. being persons of evil fame and dishonest conversation, devising and intending, and each of them devising and intending one R. L. of divers sums of money, falsely, unlawfully and fraudulently to deceive and defraud, and to fulfil, perfect and bring to effect their devices and intentions aforesaid, they the said

Information for cheating a person, by a forged letter.

*P. 101. said A. S. and T. B. on the day and · year, &c. at, &c. falsely, unlawfully, unjustly, fraudulently, knowingly and deceitfully did make, compose, write and forge, or did cause to be made, composed, written and forged, and each of them then and there with force and arms, &c. falsely, unlawfully, unjustly, fraudulently, knowingly and deceitfully did make, compose, write and forge, or cause to be made, composed, written and forged, a certain false, feigned, counterfeit and forged letter, in the name of one J L. the wife of the said R. L. (the said A. and T. then well-knowing that one M. W. was the brother of the said J.) bearing date the said day and year aforesaid, to the said M. W. directed and subscribed, the tenor of which letter and subscription follows in these words, " *This for Mr. Wind-ham, &c.*" and the said A. S. and T. B. afterwards to wit, on the day and year, &c. at, &c. with force and arms, falsely, unlawfully, knowingly, fraudulently and deceitfully, the said false, feigned, counterfeit and forged letter, as a true letter written by the said J. L. and by the said J. L. written and subscribed, to the said M. W. did deliver, and cause to be delivered, and then and there, the said false, feigned, counterfeit and forged letter, with force and arms, &c. unlawfully, unjustly and deceitfully did publish, and cause to be published, and each of them then and there did publish, and cause to be published, the said A. S. and T. B. then and there well knowing, and each of them well-knowing that the letter aforesaid, was false, feigned, counterfeit and forged; and that the said A. S. and T. B. then and there to wit, on the day and year, &c. aforesaid, at, &c. by pretext and colour of the said false, feigned, counterfeit and forged letter so as aforesaid, to the said M. delivered the sum of 6l. 6s. 8d. in money numbered, of and from the said M. W. falsely, unlawfully, unjustly and deceitfully into the hands and possession of the said A. S. and T. B. did acquire and obtain, and the said M. W. then and there of the said sum of 6l. 6s. 8d. falsely, unlawfully, unjustly, knowingly and fraudulently did deceive and defraud to the great imposition of the said M. W. in contempt, &c. to the evil example, &c. and against the peace, &c.

The King *against* Blackbourne.

Michaelmas, the 36th of Charles the 2d.

Indictment against a married woman, for pretending

To wit, } **T**HAT on the 6th day of May, in the thirty-fourth year of the reign of our lord Charles the 2d; now king of England, &c; Peter Daniell, knight, and
Samuel

Samuel Dafhwood, efq; at that time fheriff of the county of
Middlefex, by virtue of a certain precept, out of the court of
the faid lord the king, before the king himfelf (the faid court
then being held at Weftminfter, in the county of Middlefex)
iffuing to the faid fheriff directed, made his certain warrant
under the feal of his office to one N. T. and other bailiffs of
the hundred of Offulfton, in the county, &c. in the fame warrant named, to take J. C. widow, in the precept aforefaid
named, fo that the faid fheriff fhould have the body of the
faid J. C. before the faid lord the king at Weftminfter, on the
Monday, &c. then next * coming, to anfwer W. S. of a plea of
trefpafs, and alfo to a bill of the faid W. againft the faid J.
for fifty pounds, upon promifes according to the cuftom of the
court aforefaid, which N. T. then bailiff of the faid fheriff in
the warrant aforefaid fpecified, by virtue of the warrant aforefaid, to the faid N. T. and others, by the faid fheriff in the form
aforefaid, made and directed, afterwards and before the return
of the precept aforefaid, to wit, on the day and year, &c. at,
&c. the body of the faid J. C. took and arrefted, and her the
faid J. by virtue of the warrant aforefaid, in his cuftody and of
the faid fheriff, then and there had and detained ; and that one
I. B. wife of R. B. late of, &c. in the county, &c. well-knowing the premiffes aforefaid, devifing, practifing and intending
the faid W. S. of the faid fifty pounds, craftily and fubtily,
fraudulently, falfely and deceitfully to deceive and defraud, and
to fulfil, perfect and bring to effect, her moft wicked devices,
practices and intentions aforefaid ; fhe the faid I. B. afterwards
to wit, on the faid day and year, &c. at, &c. in the county,
&c. with force and arms, &c. falfely, unlawfully, unjuftly,
fraudulently and deceitfully did fay, affert and affirm for truth,
to the faid N. T. and the other bailiffs of the fkeriff of the
county of Middlefex, in whofe cuftody the faid J. C. then and
there was and appeared à prifoner, that fhe the faid I. B. was
a widow, and unmarried, and that the faid I. B. then and there
with force and arms, &c. unlawfully, unjuftly, falfely, fraudulently and deceitfully to the faid N. T. and the other bailiffs of
the faid fheriff of the county of Middlefex, did offer herfelf
to become bail for the faid J. C. in the action aforefaid, at the
fuit of the faid W. S. and that the faid I. B. then and there,
with force and arms, &c. unlawfully, unjuftly, craftily, falfely,
fraudulently and deceitfully to fulfil, perfect, and bring to effect, her moft wicked devices, practices and intentions aforefaid, by the name of I. B. of the parifh, &c. widow, did
become bound, to the faid P. D. and S. D. then fheriff of the
county of Middlefex aforefaid, for the appearance of the faid
J. C. widow, to the action aforefaid, at the fuit of the faid W.
S. fo as aforefaid profecuted, and that the faid I. B then and
there, with force and arms, &c. unlawfully, unjuftly, falfely,
fraudulently and deceitfully by the name of I. B. of, &c. in the

county

Q

*herfelf to
be a widow,
and as a
widow exe-
cuting a
bail-bond
to the fhe-
riff, for one
arrefted on
a writ for
fifty pounds

*P. 102.

county, &c. did become bound and acknowledged herself to be indebted to the said P. D. and S. D. then sheriff of the county of Middlesex, in the sum of one hundred pounds, upon condition that the said I. C. should appear in the court of the said lord the king, before the king himself at Westminster, on the Monday, &c. to answer to the said W. S. of a plea of trespass, and also to a bill of the said W. against the said J. for fifty pounds, upon promises, as by the obligation aforesaid, of the said I. B. so as aforesaid, made and acknowledged to the said sheriff of the county of Middlesex more fully appears ; whereas, in truth and in fact, the said I. B. then and there was not a widow, but a married woman, to wit, at Westminster aforesaid, to the great damage, deceit and injury of the said P. D. knt. S. D. esquire, and N. T. to the evil example, &c. and against the peace, &c.

---

*P. 103.

* The King *against* Edwards.

Easter, the 35th Charles II.

Information for cheating the king of his customs, by counterfeiting the almager's seal, and sealing cloth therewith, and delivering the same so sealed.

To wit. } THAT John Edwards, of, &c. and others, &c. being persons of evil name, fame and dishonest conversation, on the day and year, &c. at, &c. contriving and falsely, fraudulently and deceitfully intending the said lord the king, of the profit of the subsidy of cloth of the said lord the king, to deceive and defraud, then and there, with force and arms, &c. unlawfully, unjustly, falsely, fraudulently and deceitfully, a certain seal to the likeness and similitude of the seal of the almager and collector of the subsidy, did make and forge, and cause to be made and forged, and then and there, with force and arms, &c. falsely, unlawfully, unjustly, fraudulently and deceitfully, and for the sake of wicked gain, without any legal warrant or authority, thirty pieces of woollen cloth, called serge, of the goods and chattels of a certain person unknown, with the said false and counterfeit seal, did seal, and caused to be sealed ; and that the said John Edwards, and others, &c. the said thirty pieces of woollen cloth, called serge, so as aforesaid, by them with the said false and forged seal, sealed, then and there, with force and arms, &c. unlawfully, unjustly, falsely, fraudulently and deceitfully, to divers persons unknown, did deliver as thirty pieces of woollen cloth, by the

collector

collector of the subsidies of the said lord the king, in the lawful manner sealed, with intention that the said thirty pieces of woollen cloth, without any further sealing should be sold and exposed to sale, to the great deceit and damage of the said lord the king, and of divers subjects of the said lord the king, to the evil example, &c. and against the peace, &c.

The King *against* Poulson.

Trinity, 36th Charles 2d.

To wit. } **T**HAT one Randolph Poulson, late of the parish of St. Margaret's, Westminster, in the county of Middlesex, gentleman, being indebted to one Elizabeth Littleton, widow, in the sum of one hundred pounds, and more, the said R. falsely and deceitfully, and with intention to deceive and defraud the said Elizabeth of 89l. part of the said 100l. affirmed that one W. S. of, &c. was indebted to the said R. in 89l. of the like money of England, and the said R. falsely and deceitfully, and with intention to defraud the said Elizabeth, on the 5th day of July, in the   year, &c. at, &c. did make and give to the said E. L. widow, a certain bill of exchange in writing, under the hand of the said R. P. for the payment of the sum of 89l. and directed to the said W. S. which bill of exchange follows in these * words, "*Mr. Southton, pay to Madam Littleton, the sum of eighty-nine pounds, lawful money of England, at or upon the 29th day of September, 1673, and this order shall be your discharge for the same, London, the 5th July, 1673, Randolph Poulson.*" And afterwards the said R. P. unlawfully, wickedly and unjustly intending and contriving, on the same day and year aforesaid, her the said E. L. of the said 89l. to deceive and defraud, did forge, make, write and counterfeit a certain other writing in the nature of an acceptance of the said bill of exchange, which writing follows in these words, "*I accept this bill, and promise to pay the same at the time prefixed, according to the contents of this bill above written, W. S. S. H. and M. R. witnesses;*" which writing last mentioned, he the said R. P. afterwards to wit, on the same day and year, &c. at, &c. did publish, and as a true writing under the hand of the said W. S. to the said E. L. did deliver, (whereas in truth, the said writing last mentioned, never was written under the hand of the said

W. S.)

Information for giving one Littleton, a widow, a bill of exchange on one who was not indebted to him, with a forged acceptance thereon.

W. S.) with intention to deceive and defraud the said E. L. of the said 89l. [he the said R. P. then and there, well-knowing that the said writing last mentioned and recited, was knowingly, subtilly and falsely made and forged] in contempt, &c. to the great deceit and fraud of the said E. L. to the evil example, &c. and against the peace, &c.

The King *against* Wansborough.

Michaelmas, the 2d of James the 2d.

Information for cheating a person of 3 periwigs on a false affirmation, that a gentleman in the country had desired the defendant to get and send him three periwigs.

To wit. } **THAT** William Wansborough, of the parish of St. Martin in the fields, in the county of Middlesex, furrier, being a person of evil name, fame and dishonest conversation, and not intending to obtain his living by honest labour, according to the laws of this kingdom of England, but contriving, devising and intending by unlawful means the goods and chattels of the honest liege subjects of the lord the now king, into his hands and possession, falsely, fraudulently and deceitfully to obtain and acquire to maintain his unlawful course of living, on the 29th day of October, in the 2d year of the reign of the lord James the 2d, king, &c. then knowing that one Thomas Ward had in his possession three periwigs, of the value of 6l. on the said 29th day of October, in the 2d year, &c. aforesaid, at the parish of St. Martin in the fields, in the county of Middlesex, falsely and deceitfully did pretend, affirm and assert to the said T. W. that a gentleman in the country did require him the said W. W. to procure, and to him (meaning the said pretended gentleman) send three periwigs; and then and there, upon the said pretext, falsely and deceitfully did require the said T. W. to deliver the said 3 * periwigs, of the goods and chattels of the said T. W. to him the said W. W. for the pretended gentleman aforesaid, with intention unlawfully to defraud the said T. W. of the goods and chattels aforesaid, and that the said W. W. by colour and pretence of the said false and deceitful affirmation aforesaid, afterwards to wit, on the day and year last aforesaid, at the parish of St. Martin in the fields, in the county of Middlesex aforesaid,

*P. 105.

the

the said three periwigs of the goods and chattels of the said T. W. unlawfully and deceitfully did obtain and acquire, and himself then to places to the said T. W. unknown, with the goods aforesaid, secretly did retreat and fly, whereas in fact, no person for the purpose as aforesaid, did send to the said W. W. for any such goods, and so the said W. W. the said T. W. by the false affirmation aforesaid, of the goods and chattels aforesaid, then and there, unlawfully and deceitfully did defraud, and the goods and chattels aforesaid, to the proper use of him the said W. W. then and there did convert and dispose to the manifest deceit of the said T. W. to the evil example, &c. and against the peace, &c.

The King *against* Chamberlain.

Hilary, the 34th and 35th of Charles II.

To wit. } THAT Nathaniel Chamberlain, late of, &c. clock-maker, knowing that all things made of gold, and exposed to sale, and to be sold within this kingdom of England, ought to be made wholly of good and true gold, agreeing with the standard of the said lord the king, nevertheless the said N. C. being a person of dishonest disposition, and contriving and fraudulently intending the liege subjects of the said lord the now king, falsely, unlawfully, deceitfully, craftily and subtily to deceive and defraud, and to subvert the laws of this kingdom of England, on the 5th day in the year, &c. at, &c. in the parish, &c. one gold box-case of a watch, one gold pendant and ring affixed to the same watch, together weighing twelve penny-weights of a pound weight of gold, of more impure gold than ought to be, to wit, of gold not agreeing with the standard aforesaid, (being five penny-weights in every twelve penny-weights of a pound weight, thereof more base than gold agreeing with the standard aforesaid) with force and arms, &c. falsely, fraudulently and knowingly did make and forge, and cause to be made and forged, and the said gold box-case of a watch, with the gold pendant and ring to the same case affixed, so falsely and fraudulently made and forged, afterwards to wit, on the said day and year, &c.

Information against a clock-maker, for selling a case to a watch, and other things thereto belonging, made of base gold, pretending the same to be made of pure standard gold.

at,

at, &c. as a thing wholly made of gold, with force and arms, &c. falfely, unlawfully, fraudulently and knowingly, to a certain perfon, to the jurors aforefaid as yet unknown, did expofe to fale, and did fell in contempt of the laws, &c. to the great damage and manifeft deceit of the perfon aforefaid, to the jurors aforefaid unknown, to the evil example, &c. and againft the peace, &c.

---

*P. 106.

* The King *againft* Bonny.

Michaelmas, the 36th Charles 2d. *Roll* 48.

Information againft a goldfmith, for felling buttons made of bafe filver.

To wit. } THAT Francis Bonny, of the parifh, &c. goldfmith, who for feven years now laft paft, and more, hath exercifed the art of a goldfmith, at the parifh, &c. and many veffels and other things made of filver, under colour of his art aforefaid, there hath caufed to be made, and to divers liege fubjects of the faid lord the now king, hath expofed to fale, and hath fold, and that the faid F. B. well-knowing that all veffels and other things made of filver, by the men of the myftery of a goldfmith, to be expofed to fale, and to be fold within the parifh, &c. and elfewhere, within this kingdom of England, ought to be made wholly of good and true filver agreeing with the ftandard of the Exchequer, of the faid lord the king, nevertheless the faid F. B. being a perfon of evil and difhoneft difpofition and contriving, wickedly and fraudulently intending the liege fubjects of the faid lord the now king, falfely, unlawfully, deceitfully, craftily and fubtily to deceive and defraud, and the laws of this kingdom of England to fubvert, on the day and year, &c. and at divers other days and times then before, at, &c. nine dozen of filver buttons, and two pair of filver cuff buttons, together weighing ten ounces and more, of impure and more bafe filver than ought to be, to wit, of filver not agreeing with the ftandard of the Exchequer aforefaid, (being two fhillings and three pence in every ounce more bafe than filver agreeing with the ftandard aforefaid) with force and arms, &c. falfely, unlawfully, fraudulently and knowingly to divers liege fubjects of the faid lord the now king, to the faid attorney general of the faid lord the now king as yet unknown, then and there, as things wholly made of filver, of good and true filver, agreeing with the ftandard aforefaid, did expofe to fale, and did fell in contempt of the faid lord the now king, and of his laws, to the evil example, &c. and againft the peace, &c.

The

The King *against* Worrell.

To wit, } THAT by the ufe and cuftom of dyers, in and about the city of London and elfewhere with-in this kingdom of England, for the fpace of forty years now laft paft and more, all woollen cloth called Bays, well, fufficiently and in a workman-like manner prepared, and grounded with woad for black colour with madder, commonly called Madder-black, always have been woaded at leaft to the fourth ftall and degree of woad ; and that for the whole time aforefaid, all woollen cloth called Bays fo as aforefaid, well, fufficiently, and in a workman-like * manner prepared and grounded with woad, for black colour, with madder, common-ly called madder-lack, woaded to the fourth ftall and degree of woad, always by the Seal-mafter of the wardens and fraternity of the myftery of Dyers of the city of London, with a certain feal, for that purpofe in a lawful manner appointed, ufed and approved, were fealed before that they were fold, uttered or ex-pofed to fale, and that alfo for the whole time aforefaid, all the dyers in and about the city of London aforefaid, and elfe-where within the kingdom of England have been ufed and ac-cuftomed upon one end of every piece of woollen-cloth called Bays, fo as aforefaid woaded, and according to the art, well and fufficiently dyed a black colour with madder, for the colour called Madder-black, and not upon any other piece of woollen cloth called Bays dyed a black colour, to make and print the mark and fign of a Red Rofe in and upon the end of every fuch piece of woollen cloth called Bays. by which mark or fign in and upon the end of every fuch piece of woollen cloth called Bays, dyed a black colour with madder, for the colour called Madder-black, as aforefaid, the buyer of every fuch piece of woollen cloth called Bays, would underftand and would be cer-tain that the fame were well, fufficiently and according to the art dyed a black colour with madder for the colour called Mad-der-black, and in and for the fame in like manner would pay ; and that one Thomas Worrel of the parifh of St. Saviour, Southwark, in the county of Surry, dyer, wellknowing the premiffes, on the 1ft day of April, in the 25th year of the reign of the lord Charles the 2d, king, &c. and continually after-wards until the day of the exhibition of this information, at the

Information againft a dyer, for felling bays not duly dyed, with a counter-feit feal, and with a falfe mark.

* P. 107.

parifh

parish aforesaid, in the county aforesaid, did exercise, use and employ the art, mystery and manual occupation of a dyer; and that the said Thomas Worrel within the time aforesaid, at the parish and county aforesaid, wellknowing the premisses as aforesaid, but contriving, practising, and falsely, fraudulently and deceitfully intending the subjects of the said lord the king of this kingdom of England, and others as well within this kingdom of England as elsewhere, to deceive and defraud, and to fulfil, perfect, and bring to effect his most wicked contrivances, practices and intentions aforesaid, he the said T. W. then and there, to wit, between the said 1st day of April, in the 25th year, &c. aforesaid, and the day of the exhibition of this information, at the parish aforesaid, in the county aforesaid, &c. with force and arms, &c. falsely, unlawfully, unjustly, fraudulently, unworkmanly, and insufficiently woaded a thousand pieces of woollen cloth called Bays, for black colour with madder, commonly called Madder-black; and the said thousand pieces of woollen cloth, called Bays, and each and every piece thereof, woaded only to the 1st, 2d, and 3d, stall and degree and not more, which stall and degree of woad is too light and insufficient for black colour with madder, commonly called Madder-black; and that the said T. W. then and there, to wit, between the said 1st day of April, in the 25th year, &c. aforesaid, and the day of the exhibition of this

*P.108. information, * at the parish aforesaid, in the county aforesaid, with force and arms, &c. falsely, unlawfully, unjustly, fraudulently and deceitfully, the said thousand pieces of woollen cloth called Bays, and every piece thereof, so as aforesaid by him the said T. W. too lightly and insufficiently, to the first, second, and third stall and degree woaded, and not more for black colour with madder, commonly called Madder-black, with a false, feigned, and counterfeit seal, to the likeness and similitude of the seal by the fraternity of Dyers aforesaid used, for the sealing of woollen cloth called Bays, well, sufficiently, and in a workmanlike-manner woaded, to the fourth stall and degree of woad, and prepared and grounded with woad for black colour with madder, commonly called Madder-black, did seal and did cause to be sealed; and that the said T. W. then and there, between the said 1st day of April, in the 25th year, &c. and the day of the exhibition of this information, with force and arms, &c. at the parish aforesaid, in the county aforesaid, falsely, unlawfully, unjustly, fraudulently and deceitfully, upon the several ends of the said thousand pieces of woollen cloth called Bays, dyed a black colour, by him the said T. W. and also upon the ends of two hundred other pieces of woollen cloth called Bays, of a black colour as aforesaid, did make and print, and did cause to be made and printed, he mark and sign of a red rose, and the said thousand pieces of woollen cloth called Bays, and every piece thereof, so as afore-

said

said by the said T. W. with the sign and mark of a red rose signed and marked, and with the false seal aforesaid, by him the said T. W. sealed, and the said 200 pieces of woollen cloth called Bays, and every piece thereof, so as aforesaid by him the said T. W. with the sign and mark of the red rose aforesaid, by him the said T. W. so as aforesaid, signed and marked, for one thousand two hundred pieces of woollen cloth called Bays, of a black colour, with madder for the colour, commonly called Madder-black, well, sufficiently, and in a workmanlike manner dyed, to divers subjects of the said lord the king, and to others, as well within this kingdom, as elsewhere, to the said attorney-general of the said lord the king as yet unknown, did sell, utter and deliver, with intention that the said one thousand two hundred pieces of woollen cloth, called bays, so as aforesaid, by him the said T. W. with the sign and mark of a red-rose, signed and marked, for one thousand two hundred pieces of woollen cloth, called bays, well and sufficiently, and in all parts dyed of a black colour with madder, commonly called madder-black, should be sold, uttered and delivered to divers subjects of the said lord the king, and to others, whereas in truth, the said one thousand two hundred pieces of woollen cloth, called bays, and every piece thereof, were not maddered in all parts of them, but were maddered only upon the several ends of the said pieces of woollen cloth, called bays, where the said mark and sign of a red rose was printed and placed, to the great deceit, prejudice, damage and injury of divers subjects of the said lord the king, to the evil example, &c. against the peace, &c.

---

* The King and Albyn *against* Farmer.   * P. 109.

To wit. THAT one Benjamin Albyn, of London, merchant, trading in the buying of woollen cloth, by him to be transported into parts beyond the seas, and there to be sold, according to the custom of merchants, on the 25th day of November, in the 34th year of the reign of our lord Charles the 2d, king, &c. at London to wit, in the parish of the blessed Mary of the arches, in the ward of Cheap, did buy of one Henry Farmer of London, packer, 30 pieces of Spanish woollen cloth, at the rate and price, and of the value of eleven pounds ten shillings for every piece; and that the said Benjamin Albyn after the buying of the same, a certain leaden seal, the

A merchant had bought of the defendant 30 pieces of Spanish cloth, and stampt them with his own stamp, and left them with the property defendant.

R

who counterfeited the stamp, and delivered other pieces of less value stampt with the counterfeit stamp to the merchant, and so cheated him.

property of the said Benjamin, with a certain iron instrument called a stamp, stamped, and by the said Benjamin in such case used, upon one end of every such piece of the said thirty pieces of cloth, then and there did place and affix, and did cause to be placed and affixed, and the said thirty pieces of cloth in the custody and possession of the said H. F. did leave, with intention, that the said H. F. might procure the said thirty pieces of cloth, to be dyed into several colours for the said Benjamin, and that the said H. F. being a person of evil name and fame, and of dishonest conversation, well-knowing the premisses aforesaid, but devising, and falsely, fraudulently and deceitfully intending the said B. A. to deceive and defraud, and to cause the said B. A. to take and have other pieces of woollen cloth by him not bought, but of less value, in the place of the cloth by him as aforesaid bought, and to fulfil, perfect and bring to effect his most wicked devices, practices and intentions aforesaid; he the said H. F. on the said 25th day of November, in the 34th year, &c. aforesaid, at London aforesaid, in the parish and ward aforesaid, with force and arms, &c. the marks aforesaid, called seals, the property of the said B. A. upon twenty-five pieces of the said cloth so as aforesaid affixed, falsely, unlawfully, unjustly, fraudulently and deceitfully, and without the knowledge of the said Benjamin, then and there, did rip and tear off, and then and there with force and arms, &c. a certain false and counterfeit iron instrument, called a stamp, to the likeness of the iron instrument called a stamp of the said Benjamin, did cause and procure to be forged and made, and with the said instrument afterwards to wit, on the said 25th day of November, in the 34th year, &c. aforesaid, at London aforesaid, in the parish and ward aforesaid, with force and arms, &c. twenty-five other pieces of woollen cloth of less value to wit, each piece thereof of the value of seven pounds ten shillings and no more, upon every of them the said twenty-five pieces of cloth with a false, feigned and counterfeit leaden seal, to the likeness and similitude of the proper seal of the said Benjamin, and as the seal of the said Benjamin [which false seal the said H. F. then and there had caused and procured to be made and forged for the purpose aforesaid] falsely, *P. 110.* fraudulently and deceitfully then and there with force and * arms, did stamp, and did cause to be stamped, and then and there, with force and arms, &c. falsely, unlawfully, unjustly, fraudulently and deceitfully upon the end of every of the said 25 pieces of cloth last mentioned, the said false, feigned and counterfeit seal did place, and did cause to be placed, and by reason thereof, the said 25 pieces of cloth, and every piece thereof last mentioned, sealed with the false seal, in the place of the said 25 pieces of cloth, by the said Benjamin so as aforesaid from the said Henry bought, to the said Benjamin then and there falsely, unlawfully, fraudulently and deceitfully

fully

fully did deliver and impose, and so the said H. F. him the said B. A. of the said 25 pieces of cloth first mentioned, then and there with force and arms, &c. falsely, unlawfully and unjustly did deceive and defraud, to the great deceit, damage, prejudice and injury of the said B. A. to the evil example, &c. against the peace, &c. whereupon the said coroner and attorney, &c.

The King *against* Williams.

Easter, 36 Charles *the 2d.*

Middlesex, THAT Thomas Williams, late of, &c. on the To wit. day and year, &c. then and as yet the servant of Jonathan Ambrose, gold-melter, of the lord the king in the gold melting-house, in the mint of the lord the king within the tower of London, the said Thomas Williams then being a person of wicked mind, and of impious, corrupt and deceitful conversation, and devising, practising and falsely, fraudulently and deceitfully intending, the said lord the now king, and the subjects of the said lord the king, by unlawful ways and means to deceive and defraud, and the pure lawful money of this kingdom of England, called guinea pieces of gold, with corrupt and base metal, to vitiate, spoil and to render base and corrupt, and to fulfil, perfect and bring to effect his most wicked and detestable devices, practices and intentions, the said Thomas Williams afterwards to wit, on the said day and year, &c. at the parish of St. Catharine, near to the tower of London, in the county of Middlesex aforesaid, with force and arms, &c. falsely, unlawfully, unjustly, fraudulently and deceitfully, one piece of copper, containing eighteen grains weight, into a parcel of gold, called gold fissel, and according to the standard of the lord the king, prepared for melting, and then lying in a certain ladle, did throw and place, with intention to melt the said parcel of gold with the said piece of copper, and the said parcel of gold so be melted with the said piece of copper mixed, into certain pieces of gold, called guinea pieces of gold, to make and coin, to the great deceit and damage of the said lord the king, and the subjects of the said lord the king, to the evil example, &c. and against the peace, &c.

[Marginal note: Information against a moneyer, for throwing copper into the melting-pot in the tower of London, among the gold for coining guineas, intending thereby to cheat the king, and the people.*]*

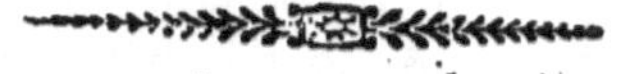

* *Indictments for Extortion.*

The King *against* Broughton.

Trinity, 24th Charles II.

Information against the defendant, keeper of the gate-house, at Westminster, for several extortions in her office.

Middlesex,
To wit. } TO be informed that Mary Broughton, of the parish of St. Margaret, Westminster, in the county of Middlesex, widow, on the first day of May, in the 22d year of the reign of the lord Charles the 2d, and continually afterwards to the day of the exhibition of this information, was and as yet is keeper of the prison of the lord the king, of the gate-house Westminster, in the county of Middlesex, and the office of keeper of the prison aforesaid, at the parish aforesaid, in the county aforesaid, for the whole time aforesaid, hath undertaken, exercised and had, and as yet doth undertake, exercise and have, nevertheless the said Mary Broughton, not regarding the duty of her office aforesaid, and the trust in her reposed entirely perverting, and devising and intending the liege subjects of the said lord the king, for the private gain of her the said M. B. to oppress, impoverish and greatly to distress, and the due execution of justice, as much as in her lay to retard and pervert, at the parish of St. Margaret, Westminster, in the county of Middlesex aforesaid, between the said 1st day of May, in the 22d year, &c. aforesaid, and the day of the exhibition of this information, under colour of her office of keeper of the goal aforesaid, unlawfully, unjustly, and extortively did exact, receive and have, and into the hands and possession of her the said M. B. did obtain, from one Edward Owen, the sum of two shillings and four pence, for the charging of one Alexander Home, esquire, then a prisoner in the prison of the gate-house, Westminster aforesaid, in the custody of the said M. B. with an action for 200l. prosecuted at the suit of the said Edward Owen. And that also the said M. B. within the time aforesaid, to wit, between the said 1st day of May, in the 22d year, &c. aforesaid, and the day of the exhibition of this information, at the parish of St. Margaret, Westminster aforesaid, in the county of Middlesex aforesaid,

1st Charge.

2d Charge.

under

under colour of her office of keeper of the goal aforesaid, unlawfully, unjustly and extorsively did exact, receive and have,
and into the hands and possession of her the said M. B. did
obtain, from one Philip Hanbury, the sum of two shillings and
four pence, for the charging the said Alexander Home, esquire,
then a prisoner in the prison of the gate-house aforesaid, in
the custody of the said M. B. with an action prosecuted at the
suit of the said P. H. for 10l. And that also the said M. B. 3d Charge.
within the time aforesaid, to wit, between the said 1st day of
May, in the 22d year, &c. aforesaid, and the day of the exhibition of this information, at the parish of St. Margaret, Westminster aforesaid, in the said county of Middlesex, under colour of her office of keeper of the goal of the lord the king,
of the gate-house, Westminste, aforesaid, in the said county
of Middlesex, unlawfully, unjustly and extorsively did receive
and have, and into the hands and possession of her the said M.
B. did obtain from one William * Crofs, the sum of two *P. 112.
shillings and four-pence for the charging of the said Alexander
Home, esquire, then a prisoner in the prison aforesaid, in the
custody of the said M. B. with an action prosecuted at the suit
of the said W. C. for 60l. And that also the said M. B. 4th Charge.
within the time aforesaid, to wit, between the said 1st day of
May, in the 22d year, &c. aforesaid, and the day of the exhibition of this information, at the parish of St. Margaret,
Westminster, aforesaid, in the said county of Middlesex, under
colour of her office of keeper of the goal of the said lord the
king, of the gate-house Westminster aforesaid, in the said
county of Middlesex, unlawfully, unjustly and extorsively did
exact, receive and have, and into the hands and possession of
her the said M. B. did obtain, from one Mary Higgins the sum
of two shillings and four-pence for the charging of the said
Alexander Home, then a prisoner in the prison aforesaid, in the
custody of the said M. B. with an action prosecuted at the suit
of the said M. H. for 10l. 10s. And that also the said M. B. 5th Charge.
within the time aforesaid, to wit, between the said 1st day of
May, in the 22d year, &c. aforesaid, and the day of the exhibition of this information, at the parish of St. Margaret,
Westminster aforesaid, in the said county of Middlesex, under
colour of her office of keeper of the goal of the said lord the
king, of the gate-house, Westminster, in the said county of
Middlesex, unlawfully, unjustly and extorsively did exact, receive and have, and into the hands and possession of her the
said M. B. did obtain from one Henry Kemp, the sum of two
shillings and four-pence, for the charging of the said Alexander
Home, esquire, then a prisoner in the prison aforesaid, in the
custody of the said M. B. with an action prosecuted at the suit
of the said H. K. for 150l. And that also the said M. B. 6th Charge.
within the time aforesaid, to wit, between the said 1st day of
May, in the 22d year, &c. aforesaid, and the day of the exhibition

bition of this information, at the parish of St. Margaret, Westminster aforesaid, in the said county of Middlesex, under colour of her office of keeper of the goal of the said lord the king, of the gate-house Westminster aforesaid, in the said county of Middlesex, unlawfully, unjustly and extorsively did exact, receive and have, and into the hands and possession of her the said M. B. did obtain, from one Thomas Kemp, the sum of two shillings and four-pence, for the charging of the said Alexander Home, esquire, then a prisoner in the prison aforesaid, in the custody of the said M. B. with an action pro-

7th Charge. secuted at the suit of the said T. K. for 25l. And that also the said M. B. within the time aforesaid, to wit, between the said 1st day of May in the said 22d year, &c. aforesaid, and the day of the exhibition of this information, at the parish of St. Margaret, Westminster aforesaid, in the said county of Middlesex, under colour of her office of keeper of the goal of the said lord the king, of the gate-house Westminster aforesaid, in the said county of Middlesex, unlawfully, unjustly and extorsively did exact, receive and have, and into the hands and possession of her the said M. B. did obtain from one J. Godfrey, the sum of two shillings and four-pence, for the charging of one Alexander Home, otherwise called Hume, esq. then a prisoner in the prison aforesaid, in the custody of the said M. B. with an

8th Charge. action prosecuted at the suit of the said J. G. for 32l. And that also the said M. B. within the time aforesaid, to wit, between the said 1st day of May, in the 22d year, &c. aforesaid, and the day of the exhibition of this information, at the parish of St. Margaret, Westminster, aforesaid, in the said county of Middlesex, under colour of her office of keeper of the goal of the said lord * the king, of the gate-house Westminster

*P. 113. aforesaid, in the said county of Middlesex, unlawfully, unjustly and extorsively did exact, receive and have, and into the hands and possession of her the said M. B. did obtain from one John Deale, the sum of two shillings and four-pence, for the charging of Alexander Home, then a prisoner in the prison aforesaid, in the custody of the said M. B. with an action pro-

9th Charge. secuted at the suit of the said J. D. for 40l. And that the said M. B. within the time aforesaid, to wit, between the said 1st day of May, in the 22d year, &c. aforesaid, and the day of the exhibition of this information, to wit, upon the 27th day of March, in the 24th year of the reign of the said lord Charles the 2d, of England, &c. king, &c. at the parish of St. Margaret, Westminster aforesaid, in the said county of Middlesex, under colour of her office of keeper of the goal of the said lord the king, of the gate-house Westminster aforesaid, in the county of Middlesex aforesaid, unlawfully, unjustly and extorsively did exact, receive and have, and into the hands and possession of her the said M. B. did obtain from one J. H. then a prisoner in the goal aforesaid, and in the custody of the said M. B. the

sum

fum of twenty fhillings, upon pretence of her fee, upon the
difcharge of the faid J. H. from the faid prifon, out of the
cuftody of her the faid M. B. whereas in truth, no fuch fum
was due to the faid M. B. upon the difcharge of the faid J. H.
And that the faid M B. within the time aforefaid, to wit, be- 10thCharge
tween the faid 1ft day of May, in the 22d year, &c. aforefaid,
and the day of the exhibition of this information, to wit, on
the 20th day of May, in the 24th year, &c. at the parifh of
St. Margaret, Weftminfter, in the county of Middlefex, under
colour of her office of keeper of the goal of the faid lord the
king, of the gate-houfe Weftminfter aforefaid, in the faid
county of Middlefex, unlawfully, unjuftly and extorfively did
exact, receive and have, and into the hands and poffeffion of
her the faid M. B. did obtain from one H. M. of, &c. yeoman,
two pieces of gold, commonly called guinea pieces of gold,
each piece thereof being the legal money of England, and of
the value of twenty fhillings, for eafe and favour, and for un-
loofing and fetting at large, one B. D. from irons, then a prifoner in the faid prifon, in the cuftody of the M. B. detained,
for felony and murder, by him the faid B. D. late before that
time fuppofed to have been committed. And that the faid M. 11thCharge
B. within the time aforefaid, to wit, between the faid 1ft day of
May, in the 22d year, &c. aforefaid, and the day of the exhibition of this information, to wit, upon the 20th day of May,
in the 24th year, &c. at the parifh of St. Margaret, Weftminfter aforefaid, in the faid county of Middlefex, under colour
of her office of keeper of the goal of the faid lord the king,
of the gate-houfe, Weftminfter aforefaid, unlawfully, unjuftly,
and extorfively did exact, receive and have, and into the hands
and poffeffion of her the faid M. B. did obtain from one W. E.
a prifoner within the prifon aforefaid, in the cuftody of the
faid M. B. detained, for felony and murder by him the faid W.
E. late before that time fuppofed to be committed, two pieces
of gold, commonly called guinea pieces of gold, each piece
thereof being the legal money of England, and of the value
of twenty fhillings, for eafe and favour fhewn to the faid W. E.
in not confining the faid W. E. in irons, being in the prifon
aforefaid, in the cuftody of the faid M. B. for the caufe aforefaid. And that the faid M. B. within the time aforefaid, to 12thCharge
wit, between the faid 1ft day of May, in the 22d * year, &c. *P. 114.
aforefaid, and the day of the exhibition of this information,
at the parifh of St. Margaret, Weftminfter, in the faid county
of Middlefex, under colour of her office of keeper of the goal
of the faid lord the king, of the gate-houfe, Weftminfter
aforefaid, in the faid county of Middlefex, unlawfully, unjuftly
and extorfively did exact, receive and have from one Philip
Peers, gent. the fum of 4l. 8s. 8d. upon the difcharge of the
faid P. P. from the faid prifon, out of the cuftody of the faid
M. B. whereas in truth, no fuch fum was due to the faid
M. B.

13th Charge M. B. upon such discharge. And that the said M. B. within the time aforesaid, to wit, between the said 1st day of May, in the 22d year, &c. aforesaid, and the day of the exhibition of this information, at the parish of St. Margaret, Westminster aforesaid, in the said county of Middlesex, under colour of her office of keeper of the goal of the said lord the king, of the gate-house, Westminster aforesaid, in the said county of Middlesex, unlawfully, unjustly and extorsively did exact, receive and have, from one J. Smith, of, &c. yeoman, the sum of twenty-three shillings of the lawful money of England, for discharging the said J. S. from the prison aforesaid; and from one Richard Meade, of, &c. yeoman, the sum of twenty-two shillings, of the lawful money of England, for discharging the said R. M. from the prison aforesaid; and from William Deane, of, &c. the sum of fourteen shillings, of the lawful money of England, for discharging the said W. D. from the prison aforesaid; and from one J. Morris, of, &c. yeoman, the sum of twenty-two shillings, of the lawful money of England, for discharging the said J. M. from the prison aforesaid, which J. S. R. M. W. D. W. D. and J. M. then were prisoners in the prison of the gate-house, Westminster aforesaid, in the said county of Middlesex, under the custody of the said M. B. to whose custody the said J. S. R. M. W. D. and J. M. by one William Sherpe, otherwise Sharpe, then one of the constables of the parish of St. Margaret, Westminster aforesaid, in the said county of Middlesex, were then late before committed for divers trespasses and offences, by the said J. S. R. M. W. D. and J. M. severally by night supposed to have been committed, and that upon the payment of the said several sums of money, respectively by the said J. S. R. M. W. D. and J. M. to the said M B. as aforesaid, she the said M. B. then and there to wit, within the time aforesaid, at the parish of St. Margaret, Westminster, in the said county of Middlesex, the said J. S. R. M. W. D. and J. M. from the said prison, out of the custody of the said M. B. without any lawful warrant, unlawfully, unjustly, and against the trust reposed in her, did discharge and permit to go at large wheresoever they would. And that also

14th Charge whereas one J. Tinsley, esquire, and one T. Kemish, esquire, within the time aforesaid, to wit, between the said 1st day of May, in the 22d year, &c. and the day of the exhibition of this information, to wit, on the said 1st day of September, in the 23d year of the reign, &c. in the night of the same day, in the parish of St. Martin in the fields, in the county of Middlesex aforesaid, were taken and apprehended by one Thomas Hoskins, then constable of the said parish, and then and there being in his watch, as malefactors, night-walkers and suspicious persons, and by the said constable then were brought to the prison of the gate-house aforesaid, and then and there were committed and delivered into the custody of the said M. B. in
that

that prison, by her to be safely kept, until the said persons so taken and committed in convenient time, on the next following day might be brought before some justice assigned to preserve the peace of the said lord the king, to be * examined and dealt *P. 115. with according to law, and she the said M. B. the said J. T. and T. K. in the said prison, in her custody then and there had and detained, and did undertake to keep them in the form aforesaid, nevertheless the said M. B. afterwards, and before that the said J. T. and T. K. were or could be brought before any justice of the peace, &c. to wit, on the 2d day of September, in the 23d year, &c. aforesaid, at the parish of St. Margaret, Westminster, in the said county of Middlesex, of her own proper head and purpose, wilfully, unlawfully and without any lawful warrant or authority, the said J. T. and T. K. from the prison aforesaid, out of her custody did discharge and dismiss, whereby the said malefactors escaped with impunity ;   And that the said M. B. 15thCharge within the time aforesaid, to wit, between the said 1st day of May, in the 22d year, &c. aforesaid, and the day of the exhibition of this information, to wit, upon the 17th day of May, in the 24th year of the reign, &c. at the parish of St. Margaret, Westminster aforesaid, in the said county of Middlesex aforesaid, unlawfully, unjustly and extorsively did exact, receive and have from one G. D. of, &c. gent. the sum of six-pence of the lawful money of England, upon pretence of her fee for permitting the said G. D. to enter into the goal of the prison of the gate-house, Westminster aforesaid, to discourse with one B. D. then a prisoner in the prison of the gate-house, Westminster aforesaid, in the said county of Middlesex, in the custody of the said M. B. detained for felony and murder, by him the said B. D. late before that time supposed to have been done and committed, whereas in truth, no such sum of money was due to the said M. B. in that behalf. And that the said M. B. within the time aforesaid, to wit, between the said 16thCharge 1st day of May, in the 22d year, &c. aforesaid, and the day of the exhibition of this information, at the parish of St. Margaret, Westminster aforesaid, in the said county of Middlesex, unlawfully, unjustly and extorsively did exact, receive and have from one F. C. of the parish of St. Margaret, Westminster aforesaid, in the said county of Middlesex, yeoman, and M. C. the wife of the said F. C. lately called M. H. the sum of forty-eight shillings and four-pence, lawful money of England, for pretence of the fee of the said M. B. upon the discharge of the said M. C. then a prisoner in the prison of the gate-house, Westminster aforesaid, in the said county of Middlesex, and in the custody of the said M. B. whereas in truth, no such sum was due to the said M. B. upon the discharge of the said M. C. And that the said M. B. within the time aforesaid, to wit, be- 17thCharge tween the said 1st day of May, in the 22d year, &c. aforesaid, and the day of the exhibition of this information, to wit, upon

S

the

the 21ſt day of May, in the 23d year, &c. the ſaid M. C. then à priſoner in the cuſtody of the ſaid M. B. for debt, out of the place commonly uſed for the common goal of the gate-houſe aforeſaid, in which priſoners for debt were uſually placed and confined, did take, and her the ſaid M. C. into a certain dungeon, within the priſon of the gate houſe aforeſaid, under the cuſtody of the ſaid M. B. unlawfully and maliciouſly did put, and her in the ſaid dungeon for the ſpace of ten weeks, then next following, without any bed or other accommodation for the natural convenience or ſupport of the ſaid M C. did confine and detain, and for this ſole cauſe, becauſe that the ſaid M. C. and her huſband aforeſaid, being poor and indigent, could not ſatisfy the ſaid M. B. for the divers other ſums of money which ſhe the ſaid M. * B. unlawfully, unjuſtly and exto-ſively did require and was willing to extort from them, and not for any other cauſe whatſoever. And whereas alſo at divers ſeveral times within the time aforeſaid, to wit, between the ſaid 1ſt day of May, in the 22d year, &c. aforeſaid, and the day of the exhibition of this information, at the pariſh of St. Margaret, Weſtminſter aforeſaid, in the county of Middleſex aforeſaid, divers pious and honeſt liege ſubjects of the ſaid lord the now king, of their pious and charitable diſpoſitions, and in commiſeration of the miſerable ſtate of the poor and indigent priſoners being in the priſon of the gate houſe, in the cuſtody of the ſaid M. B. gave and ſent bread, food and fleſh in ſeveral quantities, and alſo divers ſums of money, in money numbered, as alms for the relief and ſupport of the poor and indigent priſoners aforeſaid, being in the priſon aforeſaid, in the cuſtody of the ſaid M. B. ſo as aforeſaid, and the ſeveral alms aforeſaid, to the ſaid M. B. being as aforeſaid, the keeper of the ſaid priſon, in the priſon aforeſaid, at the pariſh of S. Margaret, Weſtminſter aforeſaid, in the ſaid county of Middleſex, from time to time were delivered, by her to be given and diſtributed to the poor priſoners aforeſaid, being in the priſon aforeſaid, under her cuſtody aforeſaid, from time to time ſo as aforeſaid, according to the pious intention of ſuch perſons aforeſaid, who ſo gave and ſent ſuch alms, nevertheleſs ſhe the ſaid M. B. from time to time as often as ſuch alms were ſo given and ſent, at the pariſh of St. Margaret, Weſtminſter, in the county aforeſaid, the greateſt part of the ſaid alms ſo given and ſent, of her great and unjuſt avarice, and for her moſt wicked gain, to her own proper uſe and benefit did convert and diſpoſe, and the ſaid poor priſoners of the ſame moſt wickedly did defraud, and the ſaid poor priſoners ſo in the priſon aforeſaid, under the cuſtody of the ſaid M. B. being in the mean time in the greateſt danger of periſhing by hunger, to the great and intolerable oppreſſion of the poor priſoners aforeſaid, and to the moſt wicked abuſe of the pious intentions of ſuch ſeveral perſons who ſo gave and ſent ſuch alms. And that the ſaid M. B. within the

time

time aforesaid, being as aforesaid, keeper of the goal of the said lord the king, of the gate-house, Westminster aforesaid, in the said county of Middlesex, at the parish of St. Margaret, Westminster aforesaid, in the said county of Middlesex, under colour of her office of keeper of the prison aforesaid, unlawfully, unjustly and extorsively did exact, have and receive divers other sums of money, from divers liege subjects of the said lord the king, for divers other things and causes, before that time unknown and unheard of, and the said sums of money, so by her the said M. B. as aforesaid received, to her own proper use there did convert and dispose; And very many other and like *enormities and* damages, oppressions, extortions, exactions, enormities and grievances, the said M. B. under colour of her office of keeper of the goal of the gate-house, Westminster aforesaid, in the said county of Middlesex, within the time aforesaid, at the parish of St. Margaret, Westminster aforesaid, in the said county of Middlesex, to divers liege subjects of the said lord the king, unlawfully, unjustly and maliciously, and for the sake of wicked gain, did commit and perpetrate against the laws and customs of this kingdom of England, and against the due execution of her office of keeper of the goal of the gate-house, Westminster aforesaid, to the great scandal, reproach, dishonour, contempt and hindrance of justice, to the great damage, grievance, oppression, impoverishment, injury and ruin of very *many of the liege subjects of the said lord the now king, to the evil example of all others in the like case offending, and against the peace of the said lord the now king, his crown and dignity, &c. Whereupon the said coroner and attorney of the said lord the now, for the said lord the king, prays the consideration of the court here in the premisses, and the due process of law, against the said M. B. in this behalf to be awarded to make her answer to the said lord the king, of and concerning the premisses, &c. whereupon the sheriff of the county aforesaid, is commanded that he do not omit, &c. but that he cause her to come to answer, &c. And now, to wit, on the Friday next after the morrow of the Holy Trinity, in this same term, before the lord the king at Westminster, comes the said M. B. by J. W. her attorney, and having heard the information aforesaid, saith that she is not guilty thereof, and of this puts herself upon the country; and Thomas Fanshaw, knt. coroner and attorney of the said lord the king, in the court of the lord the king, before the king himself, who in this behalf prosecutes, doth the like, &c. therefore let a jury come thereupon before the said lord the king, from the day of the Holy Trinity, in three weeks, wheresoever, &c. who neither, &c. to recognize, &c. because as well, &c. the same day is given as well to the said T. F. knt. who prosecutes, &c. as to the said M. B. &c. at which three weeks of the Holy Trinity, before the said lord the king at Westminster, come as well the said T. F. knt. who

S 2

prosecutes,

Marginal notes:

General Charge.

* P. 117.

Process prayed.

Venire to answer.

Not Guilty.

Venire fac' jurat' awarded.

prosecutes, &c. as the said M. B. by her attorney aforesaid, and the sheriff returns the names of twelve jurors, of whom none, &c. therefore the sheriff of the county aforesaid, is commanded that he do not omit, &c. but that he distrain them by all their lands, &c. and that of their issues, &c. and that he have their bodies before the said lord the king, from the day of St. Michael, in three weeks, wheresoever, &c. or before the beloved and faithful of the said lord the king, Matthew Hale, chief justice of the said lord the king, assigned to hold pleas before the king himself, if first on Thursday the 27th day of June, at Westminster, in the great hall of the pleas, there by the form of the statute, &c.

Distringas awarded.

Defendant was found guilty.

The dean and chapter of Westminster hereupon, make a suggestion, that they are seized in fee of the office, and that the defendant held of them only for a term of years, and therefore they pray an amoveas manu, and that they may dispose of the office.

* P. 118.

England, to wit. Be it remembered, that on Thursday next after fifteen days of St. Martin, in the term of St. Michael, in the 24th year of the reign of the lord Charles the 2d, the now king, &c. before the said lord the king at Westminster, comes John Bishop of Rochester, dean, and the chapter of the Collegiate Church of St. Peter, Westminster, by P. W. their attorney, to demand, claim, prosecute and defend, all and singular, their rights, liberties and privileges; and say that the lord James, late king of England, by his letters patent, sealed with his great seal of England, and to the court of the said lord the now king here shewn, bearing date at Westminster, the 3d day of August, in the 2d year of his reign, of England, reciting that whereas the lady Elizabeth, late queen of England, by her letters patent, bearing date at Westminster, the 21st day of May, in the 2d year of her reign, had created, erected, founded ordained, made, constituted and established the site of the late monastary of St. Peter, Westminster, and the place and church of the same, to be one Collegiate Church, of one dean, a priest, and twelve prebendaries priests, there to serve almighty God; and that the said dean and twelve prebendaries, then might and should be of themselves in * fact and in name, one body corporate, and should have perpetual succession, and that the deans and prebendaries thereof, and their successors for ever should be called and named the dean and chapter of the Collegiate Church of St. Peter, Westminster, the said late lord the king James, of his special grace, and of his certain knowledge and mere motion for himself, his heirs and successors, did give and grant to the said dean and chapter of the Collegiate Church of St. Peter, Westminster, and to their successors (among other things) to have the prison and the arresting, and imprisonment of all men arrested within the city and liberties of Westminster, as freely, fully and entirely, and in as ample a manner and form as the last abbot of the late

monastery

monaſtery of St. Peter's, Weſtminſter, had in the premiſſes, to have, hold and enjoy, to the ſaid dean and chapter, and to their ſucceſſors, to the uſe and behoof of the ſaid dean and chapter and their ſucceſſors for ever, as by the ſaid letters patent (among other things) more fully appears ; by virtue of which the ſaid dean and chapter were ſeized of the liberty of having the priſon and the arreſting and impriſonment of all men arreſted within the city and liberties of Weſtminſter aforeſaid, as of fee and right in the right of their church aforeſaid, and ſo being ſeized thereof, John Earle, doctor in divinity, dean and the chapter of the Collegiate Church of St. Peter, Weſtminſter aforeſaid, afterwards to wit, on the 5th day of October, in the 13th year of the reign of the ſaid lord the now king, at Weſtminſter, in the county of Middleſex aforeſaid, by their certain indenture then and there made, and with the common ſeal of the ſaid dean and chapter, ſealed, between the ſaid dean and chapter of the one part, and one Edward Broughton, of Weſtminſter, knt. and baronet, and Dame Mary, his wife, of the other part, one part of which indenture aforeſaid, the ſaid dean and chapter bring here into court, did demiſe, grant, and to farm let, to the ſaid Edward, and Mary his wife, (among other things) the office of keeper of their priſon aforeſaid, together with all fees, profits, advantages, commodities, caſualties, benefits and emoluments to the ſame office belonging, or in any manner appertaining, to have, hold, enjoy, exerciſe and poſſeſs the ſaid office of keeper of the ſaid priſon, and of all the priſoners in the ſame, and all fees, profits, commodities, advantages, caſualties, benefits and emoluments to the ſame office belonging, (among other things) to the ſaid Edward and Mary, their executors, adminiſtrators and aſſigns, from the making of the ſaid indenture, until the full end and term of forty years, from thence next following, and fully to be compleated and ended, as by the ſaid indenture (among other things) more fully appears, by virtue of which the ſaid E. and M. were poſſeſſed of the ſaid office, with the appurtenances for the term of years as aforeſaid, to them as aforeſaid granted, and ſo being thereof poſſeſſed, the ſaid E. B. afterwards to wit, in the 18th year of the reign of the lord the now king, at Weſtminſter aforeſaid, in the county of Middleſex aforeſaid, died, poſſeſſed of the office aforeſaid, and the ſaid Mary ſurvived him and kept herſelf therein, and was thereof ſole poſſeſſed for the reſidue of the term aforeſaid, ſo as aforeſaid granted, by the right of ſurvivorſhip, and ſo being thereof poſſeſſed, the ſaid Mary for divers offences and miſdeeds, by the ſaid Mary perpetrated in the execution of her office aforeſaid, whereof ſhe the ſaid * Mary, in the ſaid court of the ſaid lord the king here is convicted, hath forfeited the office aforeſaid, with the appurtenances, as by the record thereof, in the ſaid court of the ſaid lord the king here remaining more fully appears,

* P. 119.

appears, and for that cause the said dean and chapter pray and claim liberty to have and difpofe the said office, with the appurtenances, and all fees, profits, commodities, advantages, cafualties, benefits and emoluments, to the fame office belonging, and pray that the hands of the said lord the now king from the said liberty may be removed, and an allowance of the said liberty, according to the grant fo as aforefaid, to them made, with this, that they will verify, that the laft abbot of the monaftery of Weftminfter aforefaid, and all his predeceffors from the time that, &c. have had, and have been accuftomed to have, and have enjoyed the liberty of having the prifon, &c. within the city and liberties of Weftminfter, and this, &c.

Judgment of the court thereon.

Whereupon all and fingular the premiffes being feen, and by the court here underftood, it is confidered that the said Mary, pay to the lord the king, one hundred marks for her fine laid upon her, by reafon of the premiffes, and that the said Mary be taken to fatisfy the lord the king for the said fine, and that the office of keeper of the prifon aforefaid, be feized into the hands of the lord the king, until the court here fhall determine to who or to whom that office of right belongs, or until that the court here further thereupon fhall ordain, the right of every perfon being faved, &c. and the said Mary prefent here in court, is committed to the marfhal, fafely to be kept, until that, &c. and it is ordered by the court here, that the fheriff of Middlefex, receive the prifoners being in the said prifon, into his cuftody, and that he anfwer for them, until that the court here upon the premiffes fhall further order.

This cafe is reported in 2 Lev. 71.   1 Keb. 241.   2 Keb. 345, 3 Keb. 32, 89, 92, 106, 151.   Raym. 216.

The

The King *against* Johnson.

Trinity, the 24th of Charles the 2d.

Huntingdon, } TO be informed, that Nicholas Johnson of S.
To wit.   } in the county of Huntingdon, esq: on the
1st day of May, in the 15th year of the reign of our lord Charles
the 2d, &c. and continually afterwards until the day of the ex
hibition of this information, was, and as yet is, one of the justices of the said lord the king, assigned to preserve the peace
in the county aforesaid; nevertheless, the said N. J. not regarding the duty of his office, of one of the justices of the peace
for the county aforesaid, and entirely perverting the trust reposed in him, and contriving and intending the liege subjects
of the said lord the king, for the private gain of him the said
N. J. to oppress, impoverish and greatly to distress, and the
due execution of justice as much as in him lay, to hinder and
destroy, between the said 1st day of May, in the 15th year a-
foresaid, and the said day of the exhibition of this information, at S. aforesaid, in the county aforesaid, under colour of
his office of one of the justices of the peace of the county aforesaid, a certain sum of money, to wit, ten shillings in money *
numbered, for not returning a certain recognizance before him,
within the time aforesaid, taken for the appearance of one
George Jackson, at a certain general session of the peace of the
lord the king, for the county aforesaid, to be held next after
the taking of the recognizance aforesaid, from the said G. J.
unlawfully, unjustly, and extorsively did exact, receive, and
have, and although the said next general session of the peace,
for the county aforesaid, after the taking of the recognizance
aforesaid, and to which the recognizance aforesaid ought to have
been returned, was held at the town of Huntingdon, in the
county aforesaid, on Tuesday the 24th day of April, in the
18th year of the reign of the lord Charles the 2d, &c. before
Francis Compton, kt. John Hewit, baronet, and others their
fellow-justices of the said lord the king, assigned to preserve
the peace in the county aforesaid, and also to hear and determine divers felonies, trespasses, and other misdeeds, in the
county aforesaid perpetrated, the said N. J. the said recognizance

An Infor-
mation
against a
justice of
peace for
extorting
fees for
discharging
recogni-
zances, by
him taken
for the ap-
pearance of
persons at
the sessions
of the
peace, and
for not re-
turning the
said Recog-
*P. 120.
nizances at
the sessions.

zance to the faid general feffion of the peace, before the faid juftices as of right, and according to the law and cuftom of this kingdom of England he ought, did not return againft the duties of his office, to the great hindrance of juftice, to the evil and pernicious example, &c. and againft the peace, &c. And that alfo the faid N. J. within the time aforefaid, to wit, between the faid firft day of May, in the fifteenth year aforefaid, and the day of the exhibition of this information, at S. aforefaid, in the county aforefaid, being as aforefaid, one of the juftices of the faid lord the king, affigned to preferve the peace in the county aforefaid, under colour of his office of one of the juftices of the peace of the county aforefaid, a certain other fum of money to the faid coroner and attorney as yet unknown, of the goods and monies of one Thomas Downeham, for not returning a certain other recognizance in like manner, before the faid N. J. within the time aforefaid, taken for the appearance of the faid T. D. at a certain general goal delivery of the lord the king, of his county of Huntingdon aforefaid, to be held next after the taking of the faid laft mentioned recognizance, from the faid Thomas Downeham, unlawfully, unjuftly, and extorfively did exact, receive and have; and although the faid next general goal delivery, of the faid lord the king, to be held for the county aforefaid, at the town of Huntingdon aforefaid, in the county aforefaid, and to which the recognizance aforefaid ought to have been returned, on the third day of September, in the nineteenth year of the reign of the lord Charles the 2d, &c. was held before W. W. knt. then one of the juftices of the faid lord the king, affigned to hold pleas before the king himfelf and W. M. knt. then and as yet another juftice of the faid lord the king, affigned to hold pleas before the king himfelf, juftices of the faid lord the king, affigned to deliver his goal of the county of Huntingdon aforefaid, of the prifoners being therein, and alfo to hear and determine divers felonies, trefpaffes, and other mifdeeds in the faid county perpetrated; the faid N. J. the faid recognizance, to the faid general goal delivery, before the faid juftices laft named, did not return as of right and according to the law and cuftom of this kingdom of England he ought, againft the duty of his office, to the great damage of the faid T. D. to the great hindrance of juftice, to the evil example, &c. and againft the peace, &c. * And that the faid N. J. within the time aforefaid, to wit, between the faid 1ft day of May, in the 15th year, &c. and the day of the exhibition of this information, at S. aforefaid, in the county aforefaid, being as aforefaid, one of the juftices of the faid lord the king, to preferve the peace, in the county aforefaid, under colour of his office aforefaid, a certain other fum of money, to the coroner and attorney of our faid lord the king, as yet unknown, for not returning certain other recognizances before him, within the time aforefaid, in like manner taken, for

the

the appearance of H. S. J. C. and K. A. severally, at a certain session of the peace of the lord the king, for the county aforesaid, to be held next after the taking of the several recognizances last aforesaid mentioned, from the said H. S. J. C. and K. A. unlawfully, unjustly, and extorsively did exact, have and receive, and although the said next general session of the peace of the lord the king, last mentioned, for the county aforesaid, and to which the said several recognizances last aforesaid ought to have been returned, was held at the town of Huntingdon aforesaid, in the county aforesaid, on the 13th day of July, 21st year, &c. before F. G. knight. and T. B. baronet, and others their fellow-justices of the said lord the king, assigned to preserve the peace in the county aforesaid, and also to hear and determine divers felonies, trespasses, and other misdeeds in the county aforesaid perpetrated; the said N. J. the said several recognizances last mentioned, to the said general session of the peace, in like manner last mentioned, did not return, as of right and according to the law and custom of England he ought, against the duty of his office, to the great damage and prejudice of the said H. S. J. C. and K. A. to the great hindrance of justice, to the evil example, &c. and against the peace, &c. and that also, the said N. J. within the time a- 4th Charge. foresaid, to wit, between the said 1st day of May, in the 15th year, &c. aforesaid, and the day of the exhibition of this information, at S. aforesaid, in the county aforesaid, being as aforesaid one of the justices of the said lord the king, assigned to preserve the peace in the county aforesaid, under colour of his office aforesaid, a certain other sum of money to the coroner and attorney of our said lord the king as yet unknown, for not returning a certain other recognizance before him, within the time aforesaid in like manner taken, for the appearance of one Anne Ellis, at a certain other session of the peace of the said lord the king, for the county aforesaid, to be held next after the taking of the recognizance aforesaid last mentioned, from the said A. F. unlawfully, unjustly, and extorsively did exact, receive and have, and although the next general session of the peace for the county aforesaid, last mentioned, and to which the recognizance aforesaid last mentioned, ought to have been returned, was held at the town of Huntingdon, in the county aforesaid, on the 14th day of January, in the 19th year, &c. before I. H. bart. J. B. knt. and others their fellow-justices of the said lord the king, assigned to preserve the peace in the county aforesaid. and also to hear and determine divers felonies, trespasses and other misdeeds, in the county aforesaid perpetrated; the said N. J. the said recognizance to the said general session of the peace last mentioned, before the justices last named, did not return as of right and according to the law and custom of England he ought, against the duty of his office, to the great damage and injury of the said A. E. to the great hin-

T   drance

drance of juſtice, to the evil and pernicious example, &c. and **P. 122.** againſt the peace of the ſaid * lord the king, &c. And that 5th Charge. alſo the ſaid N. J. within the time aforeſaid, to wit, between the 1ſt day of May, in the 15th year, &c. aforeſaid, and the day of the exhibition of this information, at S. aforeſaid, in the county aforeſaid, being as aforeſaid, one of the juſtices of the ſaid lord the king, aſſigned to preſerve the peace in the county aforeſaid, under colour of his office aforeſaid, a certain other ſum of money, to the ſaid coroner and attorney of the ſaid lord the king as yet unknown, for not returning a certain other recognizance, before him within the time aforeſaid, taken for the appearance of one T. Smith, at a certain other ſeſſion of the peace, for the county aforeſaid, to be held next after the taking of the recognizance aforeſaid laſt mentioned, from the ſaid T. S. unlawfully, unjuſtly, and extorſively did exact, receive, and have, and although the next general ſeſſion of the peace of the ſaid lord the king, for the county aforeſaid laſt mentioned, and to which the recognizance aforeſaid laſt mentioned, ought to have been returned, was held at the town of Huntingdon, in the county aforeſaid, on the 12th day of January, in the 20th year, &c. before J. B. baronet, J. H. knt. and others their fellow-juſtices of the ſaid lord the now king, aſſigned to preſerve the peace in the county aforeſaid, and alſo to hear and determine divers felonies, treſpaſſes and other miſdeeds in the county aforeſaid perpetrated, the ſaid N. J. the ſaid recognizance laſt mentioned, to the ſaid general ſeſſion of the peace laſt mentioned, before the ſaid juſtices laſt named, did not return, as of right and according to the law and cuſtom of England he ought; againſt the duty of his office, to the great damage and prejudice of the ſaid J. S. to the great hindrance of juſtice, to the evil and pernicious example, &c. and againſt 6th Charge. the peace, &c. And that the ſaid N. J. within the time aforeſaid, to wit, between the ſaid 1ſt day of May, in the 15th year, &c. aforeſaid, and the day of the exhibition of this information, at S. aforeſaid, in the county aforeſaid, being as aforeſaid one of the juſtices of the peace of the ſaid lord the king, for the county aforeſaid, under colour of his office aforeſaid, a certain other ſum of money to the coroner and attorney of the ſaid lord the king as yet unknown, for not returning a certain other recognizance before him within the time aforeſaid, in like manner taken, for the appearance of one M. P. and Chriſtopher H. the younger, at a certain other ſeſſion of the peace of the ſaid lord the king, for the county aforeſaid, to be held next after the taking of the recognizance aforeſaid laſt mentioned, from the ſaid M. P. and C. H. unlawfully, unjuſtly and extorſively, did exact, have, and receive, and although the next ſeſſion of the peace of the ſaid lord the king, for the county aforeſaid, to which the recognizance aforeſaid laſt mentioned, ought to have been returned, was held at the town of Huntingdon aforeſaid, in the county aforefaid, on the 13th day of July, in the 21ft year, &c. before F. M. knt. and T. B. baronet, and others their fellow-juftices of the faid lord the king, affigned to preferve the peace in the county aforefaid, and alfo to hear and determine divers felonies, trefpaffes, and other mifdeeds in the county aforefaid perpetrated, the faid N. J. the faid recognizance laft mentioned, to the faid feffion of the peace laft mentioned did not return, as of right and according to the law and cuftom of England he ought, againft the duty of his office, to the great damage and injury of the faid M. P. and C. H. the younger, to the great obftruction of juftice, to the evil and pernicious example, &c. and againft the peace of the faid lord the now king, his * crown and dignity, &c. and many other damages, oppreffions, enormicies and grievances the faid N. J. under colour of his office aforefaid, within the time aforefaid, at S. aforefaid, in the county aforefaid, to divers liege fubjects of the faid lord the king, unlawfully, unjuftly, malicioufly, and injurioufly, and for the fake of wicked gain, did commit, do and perpetrate, againft the laws, ftatutes and cuftoms of this kingdom of England, againft the duty of his office of one of the juftices of the faid lord the king, for the county aforefaid, to the great fcandal, reproach, difhonour, contempt, and hindrance of the juftice of the faid lord the now king, within this kingdom of England, to the great damage, grievance, oppreffion, impoverifhment, injury and ruin of very many of the liege fubjects of the faid lord the now king, in great contempt of the faid lord the now king and of his laws, to the evil and pernicious example of all others in the like cafe offending, and againft the peace of our faid lord the now king, his crown and dignity, &c. Whereupon the faid coroner and attorney of the faid lord the now king, for the faid lord the now king, prays the confideration of the court here in the premiffes and the due procefs of law, againft the faid N. J. in this behalf, to be awarded, to make him anfwer to the faid lord the now king, of and concerning the premiffes, &c. Whereupon the fheriff of the county is commanded, that he do not omit, &c. but that he caufe him to come to anfwer, &c. And afterwards, to wit, on the Friday next after the morrow of the Holy Trinity, in this fame term, before the lord the king, at Weftminfter, comes the faid N. J. by J. W. his attorney, and having heard the information, faith, that he doth not apprehend that the faid lord the now king, will or ought any further to impeach or trouble him the faid N. J. becaufe of the premiffes in the information aforefaid fpecified, becaufe he faith, that the faid information, and the matter therein contained, are not fufficient in law, to which he hath no neceffity, neither is he bound by the law of the land in any manner to anfwer, and for the infufficiency thereof, prays judgment, and that he may be difmiffed of and

*P. 123.

7th and general Charge.

Procefs prayed.

Venire to anfwer.

Demurrer.

T 2

from

Joinder. from the premisses, by the court here, &c. And Thomas
Fanshaw, knt. coroner and attorney of the said lord the king,
in the court of the said lord the king, before the king himself, who for the said lord the king in this behalf prosecutes,
for the said lord the king saith, that the information aforesaid,
and the matter therein contained, are good and sufficient in law
to compel the said N. J. to answer to the said information.

The King and Stone *against* Newman *and another*.

Hilary, 32d Elizabeth. *Roll* 1427.

Information
against the
sheriff of
the city of
Gloucester,
for extorti-
on, in tak-
ing unjust
fees for
executing a
Capias ad
Satisfacien-
*P. 124.
dum, stat.
the 29th of
Elizabeth.
C. 4.

City of *Gloucester,*   BE it remembered, that on the 12th day
    To wit.   of February, in this same term, comes
here into court, one Jasper Stone, in his proper person, and
as well for the lady the queen, as for himself gives the court
here to understand and to be informed, that whereas by a certain act made by the parliament of the lady the now queen,
held at Westminster, in the county of Middlesex, on the 15th
day of February, in the 29th year of her reign, among other
things, by the authority of the said parliament, it was enacted
" *That it should not be lawful from the 1st day of May then next
following, to or for any sheriff, under-sheriff, bailiff of* * *franchises
or libertys, nor for any of their or either of their officers, ministers, servants, bailiffs or deputies, nor for any of them, by reason or colour of
their or either of their office or offices, to have, receive or take
of any person or persons whatsoever, directly or indirectly, for
the serving and executing of any extent or execution upon the body,
lands, goods or chattels of any person or persons whatsoever, more or
other consideration or recompence than in the said act was and should
be limited and appointed to be lawful to be had, received and taken,
that is to say,* 12d. *of and for every twenty shillings, where the sum
should not exceed one hundred pounds, and six-pence of and for every
twenty shillings being over and above the said sum of one hundred
pounds, which he or they should so levy or extend and deliver in execution, or for which they should take the body in execution, by virtue
and force of any such extent or execution whatsoever, under the pain
and penalty that all and every the sheriff, under-sheriff, bailiff of franchises or libertys, their and every of their ministers, servants,*
officers,

officers, bailiffs or deputies, who at any time after the said 1st day of May then next ensuing, directly or indirectly should do to the contrary should lose and forfeit to the party aggrieved, treble damages, and should forfeit the sum of forty pounds, of good and lawful money of England, for every time that he, they, or any of them should do to the contrary, one moiety to go to the said lady the queen, her heirs and successors, and the other moiety thereof, to the party or parties which should prosecute for the same, by any plaint, action, suit, bill or information, wherein no essoign, wager of law, or protection should be allowed, as by the said act among other things more fully appears.'' And the said Jasper further saith, that after the said 1st day of May, in the act aforesaid specified, one Richard Hands and John Newman, from the 6th day of October, in the 30th year of the reign of the lady the now queen, for the space of one whole year next following were sheriff of the city of Gloucester aforesaid, and that within the space of the said year, to wit, on the 12th day of February, in the 31st year of the reign of the said lady the now queen, one Edward Alye, a certain writ of the said lady the queen, of capias ad satisfaciendum, at Westminster, in the county of Middlesex, out of the court of the said lady the queen, of the bench here, obtained and prosecuted to the said R. H. and J. N. then sheriff directed, returnable here, from the day of Easter, in fifteen days next following, for execution to be had as well of a certain debt of one hundred and sixty pounds, as of forty-six shillings, for damages, by the said Edward against the said Jasper, in the court of the bench here then lately recovered, which said writ afterwards to wit, on the 14th day of April, in the 31st year aforesaid, at the city of Gloucester aforesaid, to the said Richard Hands and John Newman then being sheriff of the county aforesaid, by the said Edward to take the body of the said Jasper, by virtue of the writ aforesaid, was delivered, whereupon the said R. H. and J. N. afterwards to wit, on the 17th day of April, in the 31st year aforesaid, then being sheriff of the city aforesaid, at the said city the body of the said Jasper Stone, by virtue of the writ aforesaid, did take and arrest, and in execution for the debt and damages * afore- *P. 125. said, at the said city of Gloucester, in the county of the said city aforesaid, in the prison of the lady the queen, under the custody of the said R. H. and J. N. then sheriff, did keep, and the said R. H. and J. N. not regarding the statute aforesaid, nor in any manner fearing the penalty in the same contained; seven pounds for the serving and executing the execution aforesaid, upon the body of the said Jasper, in the form aforesaid, of one Elizabeth Stone, afterwards to wit, on the 18th day of April, in the 31st year aforesaid, at the said city of Gloucester, in the county of that city, under colour of their office aforesaid, did have and receive; which seven pounds, by the said then sheriff from the said Elizabeth, for executing the execution

execution aforesaid, had and received, exceeds the rate of twelve pence for every twenty shillings, where the sum to be levied, doth not exceed one hundred pounds, and of six-pence for every twenty shillings, so being to be levied over and above the sum of one hundred pounds, against the form and effect of the statute aforesaid, whereby the said Richard Hands and John Newman have forfeited forty pounds. Whereupon the said Jasper who as well for the said lady the queen as for himself in this behalf prosecutes, prays one moiety according to the form of the statute aforesaid, and as well for the said lady the queen as for himself, prays the consideration of the court in the premisses, and that due process of law may be awarded against the said R. H. and J. N. in this behalf, to make them to answer as well to the said lady the queen, as to the said Jasper, who, &c. in the premisses, &c. and it is granted to him, &c. Pledges to prosecute John Doe and Richard Doe; whereupon the said Richard Hands and John Newman are commanded, that laying aside all pretences and excuses, in their proper persons, they be before the justices here, on Friday next after one month of Easter, to answer to the said lady the queen, and the said Jasper, who, &c. in the premisses, &c. and that this in no wise either of them omit under the pain of one hundred pounds, &c. At which day here come as well the said Jasper, who, &c. by William Aylesbury his attorney, as the said R. H. and J. N. by William Evans their attorney, for this purpose, by the favour of the court specially admitted, and the said R. and J. defend the force and injury, when, &c. and pray oyer of the information aforesaid, and it is read to them, &c. which being read and heard the said R. H. and J. N. pray leave to imparl thereto, here until the Friday next after the morrow of the Holy Trinity, and they have, &c. the same day is given to the said Jasper, who, &c. here, &c. At which day here come as well the said Jasper, who, &c. as the said R. H. and J. N. by their attornies aforesaid, and thereupon the said R. H. and J. N. further pray leave to imparl thereto, here until the Saturday next after the octave of St. Michael, and they have, &c. the same day is given to the said Jasper, who, &c. here, &c. At which day here come as well the said Jasper, who, &c. as the said R. H. and J. N. by their attornies aforesaid, and thereupon the said R. and J. further pray leave to imparl thereto, here until the Saturday next after the octave of St. Hilary, and they have, &c. the same day is given to the said Jasper, who, &c. here, &c. At which day here come as well the said Jasper, who, &c. as the said R. and J. by their attornies aforesaid; and thereupon the said R. and J. further pray leave to imparl thereto, until the Wednesday next after fifteen days of Easter, and they have, &c. and the same day is given to the said Jasper, who, &c. And now at this day to wit, on the said Wednesday next after fifteen days from the day of Easter,

Marginal notes:
- Process prayed.
- Venire to answer awarded to the sheriff, the defendants.
- 1st Imparlance.
- 2d Imparlance.
- 3d Imparlance.
- 4th Imparlance.

Easter, here come as well the said * Jasper, who, &c. as the *P. 126.
said R. and J. by their attornies aforesaid, and thereupon the
said Jasper, who, &c. prays that the said R. and J. to the premisses in the information aforesaid contained, may answer, &c.
whereupon the said R. and J. as before, defend the force and
injury, when, &c. And they say that the said Jasper, who, &c.
ought not to have his action aforesaid against them, because Plea. That
protesting that the said R. and J. under colour of their office in the act
aforesaid, have not had or received from the said Elizabeth there is a
Stone, the said seven pounds nor one-penny thereof for serv- proviso
ing and executing the execution aforesaid, in the manner and that the
form as in the information aforesaid is above specified; for plea said act
say that in the said act of parliament aforesaid, in the said in- should not
formation above specified, it is provided that the act aforesaid, extend to
nor any thing in the said act contained, should not extend to cities and
any fee, to be had or received for any execution within any towns cor-
city or town corporate, any thing in the said act mentioned to porate.
the contrary thereof notwithstanding; and this they are ready
to verify, wherefore they pray judgment if the said Jasper ought
to have his action aforesaid, against them, &c. with this that
the said R. H and J. N. will verify, that the said city
of Gloucester at the time of the making of the said act of
parliament, was and as yet is a city, &c.

And the said Jasper, who, &c. saith, that the said plea of Demurrer.
the said R H. and J. N. above in bar to the information aforesaid pleaded, is not sufficient in law to preclude the said Jasper
from having and maintaining his information aforesaid, for the
said lady the queen, and for himself, or to discharge the said R.
and J. of the premisses in the said information contained, and
that the said Jasper, who, &c. for the said lady the queen as for
himself, to that plea in the manner and form aforesaid pleaded,
hath no necessity, neither is he bound by the law of the land to
answer; and this he is ready to verify, wherefore for want of
a sufficient answer in this behalf, the said Jasper, who, &c.
for the said lady the queen as for himself, prays judgment,
and that the said R. H. and J. N. of the premisses in the information aforesaid contained, may be convicted, &c. and for
causes of demurrer in law thereupon, the said Jasper, who, &c. Special
according to the form of the statute, &c. to the court here causes of
shews that by the said information it fully appears, that the Demurrer.
execution aforesaid, was made by virtue of a writ of the lady
the queen, to the said late sheriff directed, upon a judgment
given before the justices of the lady the queen at Westminster,
and the provision aforesaid, doth not extend but to executions
to be made upon judgments, given in the courts within cities
and towns corporate, and not to executions to be made within
cities and towns corporate, by virtue of the writ or writs of the
lady the queen, issuing from or out of any of the courts of the
lady

lady the queen at Westminster, upon judgments given in the same courts at Westminster, and also for this, that the said R. and J. say that the said Jasper, who, &c. ought not to have his action aforesaid, against them, whereas they ought to say, that the lady the queen, and the said Jasper, who, &c. ought not to have their action aforesaid, against them, &c.

Joinder.

And the said Richard Hands and John Newman, because that they, sufficient matter in law to preclude the said Jasper, who as well for the said lady the queen, as for himself

***P. 127.** in this behalf prosecutes, from having and maintaining against them his * information aforesaid, for the said lady the queen, and for himself, and also to discharge them the said R. and J. of the premisses in the information aforesaid contained, above by pleading have alledged which they are ready to verify, and which matter the said Jasper, who, &c, for the said lady the queen, as for himself, doth not deny, nor to the same in any wise answer, but that averment to admit altogether

Curia advisare. hath refused, as before pray judgment, and that they discharged of the premisses, by the court here may be dismissed. And because that the justices here will advise themselves of and concerning the premisses, before that they give judgment thereupon, day is given to the parties aforesaid, here until the Friday next after the morrow of the Holy Trinity, to hear their judgment thereupon, because that the said justices here thereof, not as yet,&c. At which day come as well the said Jasper, who, &c. as the said R. H. and J. N. by their attornies aforesaid, and because the justices here will advise themselves further of and concerning the premisses, before that they give judgment thereupon, day is further given to the parties here, until the Saturday next after the octave of St. Michael, to hear their judgment thereupon, because that the said justices here thereof

Judgment for the defendants. not as yet, &c. At which day here come as well the said Jasper, who, &c. as the said Richard Hands and John Newman by their attornies aforesaid, and thereupon the premisses being seen, and by the justices here fully understood, it seems to the said justices here that the said plea of the said R. and J. above in bar to the information aforesaid pleaded, is sufficient in law to preclude the said Jasper from having and maintaining his information aforesaid, for the said lady the queen, and for himself, as the said R. and J. above have alledged. Therefore it is considered that the said Jasper take nothing by his information aforesaid, but for his false plaint be in mercy, and that the said R. and J. may go thence without day, &c. also it is considered that the said R. and J. recover against the said Jasper, ninety shillings for their costs and charges in that behalf sustained, according to the form of the statute, &c. by the court here adjudged, &c.

This case is reported Croke Eliz. 264. *Vide* Cr. El. 335. Cr. Ch. 286. Pop. 173. 2 Cro. 103. Sir William Jones 307.

Indictments

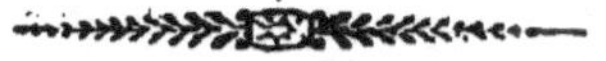

Indictments for Forgery.

The King *against* Rutter.

Hilary, the 24th and 25th of Charles II.

Devon, } **T**O be informed, that Edward Rutter, late of
To wit. } Cherwell, in the county of Devon aforesaid,
gentleman, in the 23d year of the reign of the lord Charles
the 2d, king, &c. at Cherwell, in the county of Devon aforesaid, a certain writing in parchment, supposed to be a writ
of the said lord the * king, in the form of a writ of the
said lord the king, out of the court of the said lord the king,
before the king himself issuing, and to the sheriff of Devon directed, knowingly, falsely and fraudulently did write and counterfeit, or did cause to be written and counterfeited, the tenor
of which writing follows in these words, " *Charles the 2d, by
the grace of God, of England, Scotland, France and Ireland,
king, defender of the faith, &c. to the sheriff of Devon, greeting,
whereas we lately commanded our sheriff of Middlesex, that he
should take John Chauncey, Samuel Corbett, —— Jeffreys, and
—— Cussans, widow, if they might be found in his bailiwick, and
them safely keep, so that he should have their bodies before us, at
Westminster, on the Monday next after fifteen days of Easter, to
answer to Edward Rutter, esquire, of a plea of trespass, and also
to a bill of the said Edward, against the said John Chauncey for
80l against the said S. for 150l. and against the said Jeffreys, according to the custom of our court before us to be exhibited, and our said
sheriff of Middlesex at that day returned to us, that the said J. C. ——
Jeffreys and Cussans are not found in his bailiwick, whereupon on behalf of the said E. in our court before us it is sufficiently attested, that the
said J. C. —— Jeffreys and —— Cussans, run up and down, and secrete
themselves in your county; therefore we command you that you take
them if they may be found in your bailiwick, and them safely keep,
so that you may have their bodies before us at Westminster, on Monday next after fifteen days of the Holy Trinity, to answer to the said*

Information
for forging
a writ of
latitat, and
delivering
it to the
*P. 128.
sheriff, to
be execu-
ted.
1st Count,
" *forging.*"

U

Edward

2d Count,
'*publishing*'

Edward of the plea and bill aforesaid, and have there then this writ, witness Matthew Hale, knt. at Westminster the 5th day of June, in the 23d year of our reign. Henly." And that the said Edward Rutter afterwards, to wit, on the said 5th day of June, in the 23d year aforesaid, at Cherwell aforesaid, in the county aforesaid, knowing the writing aforesaid, to be a false and forged writing, and by him according to the form of a writ issuing out of the court of the said lord the king, before the king himself, falsely and fraudulently written and counterfeited, the said writing as a true writ issuing out of the court of the said lord the king, before the king himself, did publish, and then to the sheriff of Devon aforesaid, did cause to be delivered, in contempt of the said lord the now king, and of his said court, to the damage of his people, to the abuse and manifest subversion of his laws, to the great damage and injury of the said J. C. to the evil and pernicious example, &c. and against the peace, &c. whereupon the said coroner and attorney, &c.

The King *against* Champion.

Michaelmas, 35th Charles II.

Information for forging and publishing a writ of fieri facias.

*P. 129.

1st Count, "*forging*."

Cornwall, } TO be informed, that Peter Champion, of Col
To wit. }   lombe, in the county of Cornwall, gentlemen, being a person of depraved and wicked mind, on the 20th day of May, in the 34th year, &c. with force and arms, &c. at St. Collombe aforesaid, of his own proper imagination, a certain false, feigned, forged and counterfeit writing, in the form of a writ of the said lord the king of * fieri facias out of the court here, issuing under the seal of the said court, bearing date at Westminster, the 13th day of February, in the 34th year, &c. aforesaid, and to the sheriff of the county of Cornwall directed, that he should cause to be made of the goods and chattels of T. Halfe, in the bailiwick of the said sheriff, one hundred pounds, which John Cowling in the court here recovered against the said T. H. for debt, as also fifty shillings, which he sustained as well by the occasion of the detention of that debt, as for his costs and charges by him about the said suit in that behalf expended; and that he should have that money before the said lord the king here, on the Monday next after the morrow of the Ascension of our Lord, in the year aforesaid,

said, to render to the said J. C. for the debt and damages aforesaid, falsely, unlawfully, knowingly, subtily, fraudulenly and
deceitfully did make, compose and write, and did cause to be
made, composed and written, the tenor of which false, feigned,
counterfeit and forged writing follows, to wit, " " *Charles the
2d, by the grace of God of England, Scotland, France and Ireland,
king, defender of the faith, &c. to the sheriff of Cornwall greeting,
we command you that of the goods and chattels of Thomas Halse in
your bailiwick, you cause to be made, one hundred pounds which John
Cowling in our court before us at Westminster, recovered against him
for debt, and also fifty shillings, which to the said J. C. lately in
our said court before us were adjudged, for his damages which he
sustained, as well by the occasion of the detention of that debt as for
his costs and charges by him about that suit in that behalf expended,
whereof he is convicted as appears to us of record, and have that
money before us at Westminster, on the Monday next after the morrow of the Ascension of our Lord, to render to the said J. C. for
his debt and damages aforesaid, and have there then this writ, witness F. Pemberton, knt."* at Westminster, in the 34th year of our
reign.* And that the said P. C. afterwards to wit, on the said
20th day of May, in the 34th year aforesaid, at St. Collombe
aforesaid, in the county aforesaid, the said false, feigned,
counterfeit and forged writing, so as aforesaid by him made,
composed, written and forged, and caused to be made, composed, written and forged, as a true writ of the lord the king
of fieri facias, issuing lawfully out of the court here, falsely,
unlawfully, knowingly, deceitfully, subtily and fraudulenly
did publish, and did cause to be published, (the said Peter
Champion then and there well-knowing the writing aforesaid
to be false, feigned, forged and counterfeit) to the great deceit
of the court here, in contempt of the said lord the now king
and of his laws, and against the peace, &c. whereupon the said
coroner and attorney, &c.

The King *against* Ferrers.

Trinity, 17th Charles 2d.

To wit. } T HAT Henry Ferrers, late of Budderfly Clin-
    'ton, in the county of Warwick, esquire,
the 30th day of March, in the 8th year, &c. was indebted to
one Julius Billers, of the city of Coventry, in the county of

*P. 130.
of the per-
fon to
whom the
defendant
owed mo-
ney.

1ft Count,
"forging."

2d Count,
'publishing'

the faid city merchant, in the fum of feven * pounds of the lawful money of England, for divers merchandizes by him the faid Julius Billers to the faid H. F. then before fold and delivered, and that the faid H. F. afterwards to wit, on the 30th day of April, in the 8th year, &c. aforefaid, at the city of Coventry aforefaid, in the county of the faid city, falfely, fubtily and deceitfully, devifing and intending the faid I. B. of the faid fum of feven pounds to deceive and defraud on the faid 30th day of April, at the city of Coventry afore-faid, falfely, knowingly, fubtily, fraudulently and deceitfully, a certain writing in the form of an acquittance, in the name of William Suell, the fervant of the faid I. B. did make, forge and counterfeit, fuppofing and purporting by the faid writing, that the faid William Suell the fervant of the faid I. B. had, had and received from the faid H. F. the faid fum of feven pounds for the ufe of the faid I. B. and him the faid H. F. of the faid fum had acquitted and difcharged. And the jurors aforefaid upon their oath aforefaid further fay, that the faid H. F. afterwards to wit, on the 1ft day of May, in the 8th year aforefaid, at the city of C. aforefaid, falfely, knowingly, fubtily and deceitfully did publifh the faid falfe and counterfeit writing, fo by him the faid H. F. in the manner and form afore-faid, falfely, knowingly, fubtily and deceitfully made and forged, as the true writing of acquittance of the faid William Suell then fervant of the faid I. B. whereas in truth the faid William Suell never had or received the faid fum of feven pounds of the faid H. F. and whereas in truth the faid Willi-am Suell never made or gave any acquittance to the faid H. F. for the faid fum of feven pounds, to the great damage of the faid I. B. in contempt of the laws of this kingdom of Eng-land, to the evil and pernicious example of all others in the like cafe offending, and againft the peace of the faid lord the king, his crown and dignity.

The defendant was found guilty, and fined one hundred pounds. reported Sid. 278.

King *againft* Newman.

An infor-
mation a-
gainft a
man, for
rafing and
expunging

To wit.   THAT within the manor of Penryn, in the county of Cornwall, there is and from the time where-of, the memory of man is not to the contrary, there was a

certain

certain court of the lord the king, of record held at the manor aforefaid, before the fteward of the faid manor, for the time being, from three weeks to three weeks, for all actions perfonal arifing within the faid manor, and that in the faid court there is and for the whole time aforefaid, there was a certain book, called the fteward's book, kept within the court aforefaid, in which book all actions and plaints in the faid court levyed, and the procefs, appearance, judgment and execution thereupon for the whole time aforefaid, were entered and have been accuftomed to be entered, and that at the faid court of of the faid lord the king, held at Capell St. Leonard, within the manor aforefaid, and within the jurifdiction of the faid court, before James Robins, gent. fteward, of the court of the manor aforefaid, judge of the faid court, on the 18th day of October, in the 12th year of the reign of the lord Charles the 2d, by the grace of God of * England, &c. king, &c. came one Philip Lillicrapp, and then in the faid court levied his certain plaint againft one Robert Newcoll in a plea of trefpafs upon the cafe. And that upon that plaint the faid Robert Newcoll by procefs in the due manner, iffuing out of the faid court was arrefted, which plaint and procefs thereupon in the faid book called the fteward's book, according to the cuftom aforefaid, was entered in thefe words following to wit, " *Peter Lillicrup plaintiff, againft Robert Newcoll, in a plea of trefpafs upon the cafe, arrefted by John Cooke, and delivered on the bail of George Jewel.*" And that one John Newman of Penryn in the county of Cornwall aforefaid, gentleman, after the entry of the plaint aforefaid, and the procefs thereupon made, to wit, on the 1ft day of May, in the 12th year, &c. at Glafney, in the county aforefaid, falfely, unlawfully and deceitfully contriving and intending the faid Robert Newcoll in his perfonal eftate, greatly to impoverifh, and him the faid R. to diftrefs and opprefs, the entry of the plaint aforefaid, and the procefs thereupon fo as aforefaid, in the faid book called the fteward's book entered, falfely, unlawfully, fraudulently and deceitfully then and there did erafe, expunge and entirely obliterate, and the faid John afterwards to wit, on the day and year laft aforefaid, at Glafney aforefaid, in the county aforefaid, in the faid book called the fteward's book, in another folio of the faid book, (in which other folio, plaints in the court aforefaid, held on the 26th day of September, in the 12th year of the reign of the faid lord the now king aforefaid, levied, and procefs thereupon were entered) falfely, unlawfully, fraudulently and deceitfully did forge, write, enter and infert, and did caufe to be forged, written, entered and inferted, in the ufual manner and form of the entry of plaints, procefs and judgment thereupon, thefe words and figures following to wit, *Peter Lillicrapp plaintiff, againft Robert Newcoll, in a plea of trefpafs upon the cafe, and capias awarded on the 18th of October 1660; defendant was*

out of the book of a fteward of a court of record, a plaint there entered, and for forging another plaint againft the fame perfon and procefs, and proceedings thereupon.

* P. 131.

*was arrested by John Cook, and delivered on the bail of George Jewel, and declaration, and called for default of appearance, and writ of damages, with subpœna by Tonken, the 10th of January, another writ of damages, 31st January 1660, damages assessed at 10l. 3s. 4d. and 3s. 4d. for costs, whereupon judgment and execution against defendant and bail for 12l. 2s. 4d." which words and figures so forged, written, entered and inserted in the said other folio of the book aforesaid, according to the custom of the said court used from the whole time aforesaid, evidently and manifestly remain as evidence, that another plaint was levied by the said Peter Lillicrapp against the said Robert Newcoll, in the said court of the lord the king of record, of a plea of trespass on the case, on the said 20th day of September, in the 12th year, &c. and that the said R. by the process of that court was taken and arrested, and that the said R. in the said court had found the said G. J. his mainpernor, and that upon the said plaint in the said court it was in such manner proceeded, that the said P. in the said court of the said lord the king of record, by the custom of the said court had recovered against the said R. his damages to the said sum of 10l. 3s. 4d. and 3s. 4d. for his costs. And thereupon in the said court, execution out of the said court did issue against the * said R. and his mainpernor aforesaid, for 12l. 2s. 4d. whereas in truth, any such plaint, as by the said J. N. as aforesaid was entered, by the said Peter in the said court of record, never was levied, nor did any process out of the said court thereupon ever lawfully issue, nor did the said Robert ever find the said Jewel his mainpernor on the said plaint; and whereas in truth, the said Peter in the said court of the said lord the king of record, by the custom of the said court never did recover, against the said R. his damages to the said sum of 10l. 3s. 4d. and to 3s. 4d. for his costs, to the great damage, vexation, impoverishment and ruin of the said R. N. to the evil example, &c. and against the peace, &c. whereupon, &c.

*P. 132.

The King *against* Wordell.

Michaelmas, 30th Charles II.

An Information on the statute for forging and publishing a

To wit. } THAT whereas one Samuel Kirke, citizen and sadler of London, in the term of St. Hilary, in the 35th year, &c. in the court of the said lord the king, before the king himself, then being at Westminster, in the

county

county of Middlesex, by the judgment of the said court had
recovered against John Wordell, late of Tottenham High-
Cross, in the county of Middlesex, malster, 340l. for his damages, which he had sustained as well by occasion of a certain
trespass upon the case, to the said S. by the said J. W. then
late before done, as for his costs and charges by him, about
that suit in that behalf expended, by the said court to the
said Samuel adjudged; whereof he J. W. is convicted, as by
the record of the judgment aforesaid, in the said court remaining manifestly appears, and that he the said J. W. being a
person of dishonest disposition, and falsely, subtily and deceitfully devising and intending by art, deceit, fraud and subtily to deceive and defraud the said S. K. of the said sum of
money in the form aforesaid recovered, he the said J. W. after
the judgment aforesaid obtained, to wit, on the 8th day of February, in the 36th year, &c. at London aforesaid, to wit, at the parish of the blessed Mary of the arches, in the ward of Cheap,
London, of his own proper head and imagination, knowingly,
subtily, falsely and deceitfully did forge and counterfeit, and
did cause to be forged and counterfeited, a certain writing,
sealed, subscribed with the name of the said Samuel Kirke, in
which writing it is recited, contained and supposed, that the
said S. K. in the term of St. Hilary, in the 34th and 35th years,
&c. had obtained in the court of the said lord the king, before
the king himself at Westminster, one verdict and judgment
thereupon, against the said J. W. for 340l. for his damages,
costs and charges, and that for and in consideration of the sum
of fifty pounds of the lawful money of England, to the said S.
K. by the said J. W. paid, he the said S. K. by the * said writing did declare, that he was fully and absolutely satisfied of and
for all and every sum and sums of money to the said S. due,
by or upon the judgment aforesaid, and that the said Samuel
Kirke had authorized Godfrey Woodward, Edward Shaller and
Charelton Beaumont, gentlemen, attornies of the court of the
said lord the king, before the king himself, to acknowledge
satisfaction upon the record of the said judgment. And that
the said J. W. afterwards to wit, on the 10th day of February, in the 36th year, &c. aforesaid, at London aforesaid, to
wit, at the parish of the blessed Mary of the arches, in the ward
of Cheap aforesaid, knowingly, subtily and falsely did publish
the said false, counterfeit and forged writing sealed, and with the
name of the said S. K. thereto subscribed, so as aforesaid by
him the said J. W. in the manner and form aforesaid, falsely,
knowingly, subtily and deceitfully counterfeited and forged,
and caused to be made and forged, as the true deed of the said
S. K. by him sealed and subscribed, whereas in truth and in
fact, the said J. W. never paid to the said S. the said fifty
pounds, or one penny thereof, and whereas in truth and in fact
the said writing was not nor is the deed of the said S. K.

but

* P. 133.

warrant of
attorney,
for ack-
nowledging
satisfaction
on a judg-
ment ob-
tained a-
gainst the
defendant.

but by the said I. W. falsely, knowingly and subtily, counterfeited and forged, craftily and subtily to deceive and defraud the said S. K. of the money aforesaid, upon the judgment aforesaid, in the form aforesaid recovered, and to discharge and acquit the said J. W. from the payment and satisfaction of the money aforesaid, to the great damage of the said S. K. in manifest contempt of the laws of this kingdom of England, to the evil example, &c. and against the peace, &c. and against the form of the statute in such case made and provided ; whereupon the said coroner and attorney of the said lord the king, for the said lord the king prays the consideration of the court here in the premisses, and the due process of law against the said J. W. in this behalf to be awarded, to make him to answer to the said lord the king of and concerning the premisses, &c. whereupon the sheriffs of the city of London aforesaid, are commanded that they cause him to come to answer,&c. And now to wit, on the Thursday next after three weeks of St. Michael, in this same term, before the lord king at Westminster, comes the said John Wotdell, by Benedict Brown his attorney, and having heard the information aforesaid, saith, that he is not guilty thereof, and of this he puts himself upon the country, and the said Samuel Astrey, knt. coroner and attorney of the said lord the king, in the court of the said lord the king, before the king himself, who for the said lord the king in this behalf prosecutes, doth the like, &c. therefore let a jury come thereupon, before the said lord the king, on the octave of St. Martin, wheresoever, &c. by whom, &c. and at who neither, &c. to recognize, &c. because as well, &c. the same day is given as well to the said Samuel Astry, knt. who prosecutes, &c. at which octave of St. Martin, before the said lord the king at Westminster, come as well the said Samuel Astry, knt. who prosecutes, &c. as the said J. W. by his attorney aforesaid, and the sheriffs of the city of London aforesaid, return the names of twelve jurors of whom none, &c. therefore the sheriffs of the city of London aforesaid, are commanded that they distrain them by all their lands, &c. and that of the issues, &c. and that they have their bodies before the said lord the king, at the octave of St. Hilary, wheresoever, &c. or before the beloved and faithful of the said lord the * king, George Jeffreys, knt. and baronet, chief justice of the said lord the king, assigned to hold pleas before the king himself, if first on Monday the 1st day of December, he shall come to the Guild-hall of the city of London aforesaid, by the form of the statute, &c. for default of jurors, &c. therefore let the sheriffs have their bodies, &c. to recognize in the form aforesaid, &c. the same day is given as well to the said Samuel Astry, knt. who prosecutes, &c. as to the said J. W. &c. at which octave of St. Hilary, before the lord the king at Westminster, come as well the said Samuel Astry, knt. who

prosecutes,

Venire awarded.

Not guilty pleaded.

Venire facias jur' awarded.

Distringas awarded.

*P. 134.

profecutes, &c. as the faid J.W. by his attorney aforefaid. And the faid chief juftice before whom, &c. hath fent here his record before him had in thefe words. Afterwards, on the day and place within mentioned, before the within named George Jeffreys, knt. and bart. the within mentioned chief juftice of the faid lord the king, S. Gee, gent. being affociated to him by the form of the ftatute, &c. come as well the within named Samuel Aftry, knt. who profecutes, &c. as the within named J. W. by his attorney within mentioned; and the jurors of the faid jury whereof mention is within made, being called, certain of them to wit, T. H. J. W. &c. come, and are fworn upon that jury, and becaufe the reft of the jurors of that jury do not appear, therefore others of the bye-ftanders chofen for this purpofe, by the fheriffs of the city of London, at the requeft of the attorney-general of the faid lord the now king, and by the command of the faid chief Juftice, are anew appointed, whofe names are affiled in the panel within written, according to the form of the ftatute, in fuch cafe made and provided, which jurors fo anew appointed, to wit, P. G. I. B. &c. come, and are fworn upon that jury; and thereupon publifh proclamation for our lord the king being made as the cuftom is, that if there was any one who could inform the faid chief juftice or the ferjeant at law of the faid lord the king, or the attorney-general of the faid lord the king, or the jurors aforefaid of the matter within contained, he fhould come and fhould be heard, and thereupon Thomas Jones, efquire, one of the counfel of the faid lord the king, on behalf of the faid lord the king, offers himfelf to do this, whereupon the court here proceeded to the taking of the jury aforefaid, as well by the jurors aforefaid firft impanelled, as by the other jurors aforefaid now appearing, who elected, tried and fworn to fpeak the truth of and concerning the matters within contained, fay upon their oath, that the faid J. W. is guilty of the premiffes in the information, in the within written record fpecified, in the manner and form as by the information aforefaid within is fuppofed againft him, whereupon all and fingular the premiffes being feen, and by the court here fully underftood, it is confidered, that the faid J. W. pay to the faid S. K. the party aggrieved, the fum of 300l. being double the cofts and charges expended and fuftained, by reafon of the forgery aforefaid, and that the faid J. W. is committed to the marfhal of this court in execution, until he pays the fum aforefaid, and that the faid J. W. fhall ftand in and upon the pillory, at the Royal Exchange, at Cornhill, London, on the Thurfday next after three weeks of Eafter next coming, between the eleventh hour before mid-day, and the fecond hour after mid-day of the faid day, for the fpace of one hour, and that one of his ears then and there fhall be cut off by the common executioner of the city of London, and that the marfhal of this court fhall deliver

Poftea.

Tales.

Proclamation.

Verdict Guilty.

Judgment to pay the party grieved double coft, to ftand in the pillory, and have one ear cut off, and to be imprifoned for one year without bail or mainprize.

X

*P. 135.

liver the faid J. W. to the fheriffs of London, to execute the judgment aforefaid, and that after the execution of the judgment aforefaid, the fheriffs of London fhall redeliver the * faid J. W. to the faid marfhal of this court fafely to be kept for the fpace of one year, without bail or mainprife, and that the faid John Wordell is committed, &c.

The King *againft* Ivy.

Trinity, 36th Charles II.   *Roll* 48.

Information againft dameTheodofia Ivy, for forging and publifhing two indentures.

To wit, } THAT Theodofia Bryan, of &c.otherwife called Dame Theodofia Ivy, of, &c. widow, on the day and year, &c. with force and arms, &c. at Weftminfter in the county of Middlefex, of her own proper head and imagination, fubtily, falfely and fraudulently did make and forge, and did caufe to be made and forged, a certain falfe deed, containing the matter following to wit, " *this indenture made the 12th day of November, in the 2d and 3d year of the reign of our*

1ft Count, forging.

lord and lady Philip and Mary, by the grace of God, king and queen of England, Spain, France and Ireland, defenders of the faith, arch-dukes of Auftria, dukes of Burgundy, Milan and Brabant, counts of Flanders, Hafburgh and Tyrol, between Marcellus Hall, of Radcliffe, miller, on the one part, and Richard Roper, citizen and falter of London, of the other part, witneffeth, &c." as by the faid falfe and counterfeit deed more fully appears ; and that tne faid Theodofia Bryan, otherwife called Dame T.

2d Count, publifhing.

Ivy, afterwards to wit, on the day and year, &c. at, &c. knowingly, fubtily and falfely the faid falfe and forged deed did publifh, and did caufe to be publifhed, as the true deed of the faid Marcellus Hall, fealed and delivered by the faid M. H. whereas in truth, the faid T. B. otherwife called Dame T. I. then and there well did know and underftand the faid deed, to be falfe, forged and counterfeit, and that it was not the deed of the faid M. H. nor by him fealed and delivered ; and further the faid coroner and attorney of the faid lord the king,for the faid lord the king gives the court here to underftand and to be informed, that the faid T. B. otherwife, &c. &c. afterwards to wit, on the day and year, &c. aforefaid, with force and arms, &c. of her own proper head and imagination,

3d Count, forging.

knowingly, fubtily, falfely and fraudulently did make and forge, and did caufe to be made and forged, a certain other falfe deed,

containing

containing the matter following, to wit, " *This indenture made,
&c. &c.*" as by the said last mentioned false and counterfeit
deed, more fully appears ; and the said T. B. otherwise, &c. 4th Count,
&c.   Afterwards to wit, on the day and year aforesaid, &c. at, publishing.
&c. knowingly, subtily and falsely the said false and forged
deed last mentioned, did publish, and did cause to be published
as the true deed of the said M. H. sealed and delivered by the
said M. H. whereas in truth, the said T. B. otherwise, &c.
then and there did well know and understand that the said
last mentioned deed was false, forged and counterfeit, and that
it was not the deed of the said M. H. nor by him sealed and
delivered, to the great damage of the said G. B. in contempt
of the said lord the now king, and of his laws, to the evil and
pernicious example of all others in the like case offending,
and against the peace of the said lord the now king, his
crown and dignity, &c. &c.

*P. 136. *Indictments, 1. *for Perjury.* 2. *for Subornation of Perjury.*

The King *against* Cross.

Hilary, 25 and 26 Charles the 2d.

Information against a clerk of a market, for perjury, in giving evidence on the trial of an Information for buying of malt by unlawful meafure.

Information recited.

Middlesex, To wit. } TO be informed, that in the term of Eafter, in the 25th year of the reign of our lord Charles the 2d, by the Grace of God, of England, Scotland, France, and Ireland, king, defender of the faith, &c. in the court of the said lord the king, before the king himfelf, (the said court being then held at Weftminfter, in the county of Middlefex) he, the said Heneage Finch, knt. and baronet, then, and yet, attorney-general of our said lord the king, who for our said lord the king then profecuted, in his proper perfon came there into the court of the said lord the king, before the king himfelf at Weft-minfter, and then and there gave the said court to underftand, and to be informed, that Thomas Bide, of the parifh of St. Leonard Shoreditch, in the county aforefaid, knt. and John Fofter of the fame, efquire, between the 26th day of March, in the 25th year of the reign of our lord Charles, &c. and the day of the exhibition of the said information, at the parifh aforefaid, in the county aforefaid, unlawfully and unjuftly bought and each of them bought, and by bargain into the hands of them the said T. B. and J.F. acquired, by a meafure not fealed, nor agreeing with the ftandard, or meafure called the ftandard, marked in the Exchequer of the said lord the king, called Win-chefter meafure, containing eight gallons, to wit, by a certain meafure called a Vat, containing fixty and four gallons at the leaft, and by other unlawful meafures two thoufand quarters of unground malt, every quarter thereof of the value of twenty fhillings, to the great deceit of the fubjects of the said lord the now king, and againft the peace of the said lord the now king, his crown and dignity, &c. and alfo againft the ftatute in fuch cafe made and provided; with this, that the said attorney-general of the said lord the now king, for the said lord the now

king,

king, would verify, that malt, at the time of the offence aforesaid committed, and also from the whole time whereof the memory of man is not to the contrary, was usually sold by the bushel, as well at the parish aforesaid, as in all the rest of this kingdom of England, whereupon the said attorney-general of the said lord the now king, for the said lord the now king, then prayed the consideration of the court in the premisses, and the due process of law to be awarded against them, the said T. B. and J. F. in that behalf, to make them to answer, &c. whereupon the sheriff of the county aforesaid, was commanded, that he should not omit, &c. but should cause them to come to answer, &c. And afterwards, to wit, on the Friday next after the morrow of the Holy Trinity, in the 25th year of the reign of the said ⸳ lord the now king, &c. aforesaid, before the said lord *P. 137 the king, at Westminster came the said Thomas Bide, knt. and John Foster, esq; by Jasper Waterhouse, their attorney, and having heard the information aforesaid, said that they were not guilty thereof, and of that then put themselves upon the Country ; and the said Heneage Finch, knt. and baronet, attorney-general of the said lord the now king, who for the said lord the now king in that behalf prosecuted, did the like, &c. in which cause it was in such manner proceeded, that afterwards, to wit, on the Thursday next after the end of the said term of the Holy Trinity, to wit, on the 19th day of June, in the 25th year, &c. aforesaid, at Westminster aforesaid, in the county aforesaid, the issue aforesaid, so as aforesaid joined, before Matthew Hale, knt. chief justice of the said lord the king assigned to hold pleas before the king himself, by the due course of law, was tried by a certain jury of the country, upon which trial of the issue aforesaid, so as aforesaid joined, by the jurors of the said jury, before the said Matthew Hale, kt. then and as yet chief justice of the said lord the king, assigned to hold pleas before the king himself, on the said Thursday, the 19th day of June, in the 25th year, &c. aforesaid, at Westminster aforesaid, in the said county of Middlesex, one William Cross the elder, of the parish of Ware, in the county of Hertford, gentleman, was produced as a witness on the behalf of the said T. B. and J. F. defendants in the cause aforesaid, and then and there was sworn   Oath upon the Holy Gospel of God, to speak the truth, the whole truth, and nothing but the truth, of and concerning the premisses aforesaid, so as aforesaid put in issue to the jurors of the jury aforesaid, sworn to try the issue aforesaid. And the said William Cross the elder, then and there before the said chief justice of the said lord the king falsely, wilfully and corruptly did say, depose, swear, and give in evidence upon his oath, to the jury aforesaid, to try the issue aforesaid, so as aforesaid joined,—" *That he was clerk of the market of the town of Ware*, Perjury. *in the county of Hertford, and that all corn bushels at Ware*, (meaning the town of Ware in the county of Hertford) *and belonging* *to the town of Ware, during the space of one year, and the half of one year before that time* (meaning the said 19th day of June, in the 25th year, &c. aforesaid) *in the presence of him the said William Crofs the elder, were cut, and truly sized and gaged, and that the bushels aforesaid* (meaning the bushels within the town of Ware in the county of Hertford) *then* (meaning the said 19th day of June, in the 25th year, &c. aforesaid) *were agreeable to the Standard in the Exchequer of the said lord the king, called Winchefter meafure*;" whereas in truth and in fact the corn bushels at Ware in the co. of Hertford, during the fpace of one year and the half of one year before the trial aforesaid, or during at any fpace of that time, in the prefence of him the faid W. C. the elder, were not cut, nor truly fized and gaged; and whereas in truth and in fact the bushels aforefaid, on the faid 19th day of June, in the 25th year aforefaid, were not agreeable to the ftandard in the Exchequer of the faid lord the king, called Winchefter meafure. And fo the faid W. C. the elder, on the faid 19th day of June, in the 25th year, &c. aforefaid, at Weftminfter aforefaid, in the faid * co. of Middlefex, before the faid chief jufticeof the faid lord the king, affigned to hold pleas before the king himfelf, in the caufe aforefaid, by his own proper act and confent, falfely, wilfully, and corruptly did commit wilful and corrupt perjury, to the great difpleafure of Almighty God, to the evil example of all others in the like cafe offending, and againft the peace of the faid lord the now king, his crown and dignity, &c. Whereupon the faid attorney-general of the faid lord the now king, prays the confideration of the court here in the premiffes, and that due procefs of law may be awarded againft him, the faid W. C. the elder, to make him to anfwer, &c. Whereupon the fheriff of the county aforefaid is commanded that he do not omit, &c. but that he caufe him to come to anfwer, &c. And now, to wit, on the Friday next after the Octave of St. Hilary, in this fame term, before the lord the king, at Weftminfter, comes the faid William Crofs the elder, by Jafper Waterhoufe his attorney, and having heard the information aforefaid, faith, that he is not guilty thereof, and of this puts himfelf upon his country. And Francis North, knt. attorney-general of the lord the now king, who for the faid lord the now king in this behalf profecutes doth the like, &c. therefore let a jury come thereupon, before the faid lord the king, at the Octave of the Purification of the bleffed Virgin Mary, wherefoever, &c. who neither, &c. to recognize, &c. becaufe as well, &c. the fame day is given as well to the faid Francis North knt. who profecutes, &c. as to the faid William Crofs the elder, &c. At which Octave of the Purification of the bleffed Virgin Mary, before the faid lord the king at Weftminfter come as well the faid Francis North, knt. who profecutes, &c. as the faid William Crofs the elder, by his attorney aforefaid, and the fheriff returns the names of twelve jurors, of whom none, &c.

Whereupon

Whereupon the sheriff of the county aforesaid is commanded that he do not omit, &c. but that he distrain them by all their lands, &c. and that of the issues, &c. and that he have their bodies before the said lord the king, from the day of Easter in 15 days, wheresoever, &c. or before the beloved and faithful of the lord the king, Matthew Hale, knt. chief justice of the said lord the king, assigned to hold pleas before the king himself, if he shall first come on the Friday next after the end of this term, at Westminster, into the great hall of the pleas there, according to the form of the statute, &c. for default of the jurors, &c. therefore let the sheriff have the bodies, &c. to recognize in the form aforesaid, &c. the same day is given as well to the said Francis North, knt. who prosecutes, &c. as to the said William Crofs the elder, &c.

The King *against* Jole, and others.

To wit. } TO be informed that in the term of Easter, in the 24th year of the reign of our lord Charles the 2d, king of England, &c. in the court of the said lord the king, before the king himself, at Westminster, in the county of Middlesex, he the said Thomas Fanshaw, kt. then and as yet coroner and attorney of the said lord the now king, before the king himself, brought here into the court of the said lord the now king, before the king himself, then there, a certain information against R. P. late of Jacobstowe, in the county of Cornwall, gent. and by the said information then and there gave the * court here to understand and to be informed, that in the term of St. Michael, in the 23d year of the reign of our lord Charles the 2d, the now king, &c. a certain complaint was exhibited before the justices of the court of our lord the king, of the bench at Westminster, against one Robert Pearce, then being one of the attornies of the said court among other things, for maliciously prosecuting an outlawry against one William Strout, and one Thomas Trevethick, whereby the said William had sustained much damage and expence, and for the taking of a certain bill, from one Thomas Strout and his brother, fons of the said William Strout, for the payment of 5l. ; whereupon the said Robert Pearce, late of Jacobstowe, in the county of Cornwall, gent.

An information against three persons for perjury, in giving evidence on a trial on an information against a person for perjury, in *P. 139. an affidavit sworn before one of the justices of the court of Common Pleas.

by

by the name of Robert Pearce, gent. on the 30th day of May, in the 23d year of the reign of our lord Charles the 2d, of England, &c. king, &c. and the year of our Lord 1671, at Westminster, in the county of Middlesex, in his proper person came before Thomas Tyrril, knight, then one of the justices of the said lord the king of the bench, and then and there took his corporal oath upon the Holy Gospel of God, before the said Thomas Tyrril, (he the said Thomas Tyrril then and there having sufficient power and authority to administer the said oath to the said Robert Pearce :) and that the said Robert Pearce upon his oath aforesaid, then and there before the said Thomas Tyrril by his own proper act and consent, falsely, wilfully and corruptly upon his corporal oath, deposed and swore in writing as follows, to wit, " *Robert Pearce, gent. one of the attorneys of the court of Common Pleas, maketh oath that he being about 17 years since retained by one Thomas Trevethick and William Strout, to prosecute and defend divers suits in law for them, in the beginning of March 1658, as this deponent findeth by his books of accompt, he did deliver them bills of costs, and on the 29th of the same month, being then 1659, there were all accompts perfected between them, and the said Trevethick and Strout became bound to this deponent in one penal bill of 40l. for the payment of 20l and upwards, at a certain day afterwards ; and the said Strout, the same time or a little before, became bound to the said deponent in two other bills, which were forfeited about twelve months after, and are still in force, and this deponent being kept out of his money upwards of four years, in Trinity and Michaelmas term 1660, did sue forth an original capias alias and pluries against the said Trevethick and Strout, upon one of his said bills, and the said obligors then keeping house, or so absenting themselves that they could not be arrested, this deponent did run the same to the exigent, and in Easter 1661, as he finds by his books, they were outlawed, and in Trinity vacation then following, upon a special capias utlagatum, there was an inquisition taken and certified into the Exchequer, but this deponent did never stir or move in it afterwards ; and this deponent further saith, that he had not one penny of the said money, of the said Trevethick or Strout, but confesseth that one Mr. Christopher Leach, on the 23d day of October 1662, did pay unto this deponent the most part of the money mentioned in the said * first bill, and did then give his own bill for 3l. residue of the said money, which is as yet not satisfied, as by the same doth appear, but how the name of Robert in some of the offices was made William this deponent knoweth not, and this deponent likewise saith, that at the time the said Mr. Leach paid him part of the said money, he gave him a note to one Mr. Franklyn, in the outlawry-office, that he should consent to the reversal of the outlawry, and advised the said Mr. Leach to discharge the said seizure, otherwise it would come forth in charge for many years after ; who replied, that he had received 5l. for the doing of it, to whom this deponent answered, he did believe it would cost 8l. and after that for five or six years it was*

still

ftill in charge, only the name and parish altered, and thereupon the sheriff did forbear to levy any money, until about the 15th of October 1668, the sheriff or his bailiff having taken their goods, it was agreed on between the bailiff and Strout, that there should be a bond given to the sheriff's use, to discharge him, and thereupon this deponent two or three days after the taking of the said goods, upon the request of the bailiffs and Strout, went into an house where they were making strict enquiry for the under sheriff's clerk's name, whose christian name this deponent could not certainly tell; and then th y often and sundry times desired that the bond might be in his name, and that they should speedily bring money for to procure a discharge for the sheriff, and take off the seizure, but this deponent utterly refused to take any bill in his name, but promised if they should find money sufficient to take off the security, and so left them; and after this deponent was gone out within one hour after, the bailiff took a bill, in his this deponents name, for 5l. to be paid the 21st day of December following, and about six weeks after that time, John Strout came to the deponent's house, and brought 10s. for this deponent's man, to search how things stood, and discharge the sheriff, which he accordingly did, by retaining Mr. Bernard, and giving him five shillings and other money to his clerk; and the sheriff, as this deponent hath been informed, was by him discharged for the preceding year, and that if Strout had brought more money the seizure had been discharged; and this deponent doth utterly deny that he did at any time threaten or expect to have any part of their estate, only before the money was paid, he doth not well remember, the said Strout and Trevethick keeping house, or absenting themselves for other debts, whether or no he did say he should take a lease out of the Exchequer; but since the payment of the said money, this deponent did never put them to any charge, neither did they suffer a penny damage, either by means of him, or any other by his this deponent's privity and procurement; and this deponent further faith, that he hath by himself and others, tendered the said bills of 5l. to the said John Strout, which he refused to take, Robert Pearce." As by the oath aforesaid, of the said Robert Pearce in writing remaining, of record, in the court of the said lord the king, of the bench at Westminster, in the county of Middlesex aforesaid, more fully appears, whereas in truth and in fact, the bailiffs aforesaid, did not take the* bill *P. 145. Averments in the recited information. aforesaid, in the oath aforesaid mentioned, for the payment of 5l. as aforesaid, in the name of the said R. P, after the departure of the said Robert from the house aforesaid, but he the said R. in his own proper name, in the house aforesaid, took the bill aforesaid. And whereas in truth and in fact, the said Robert Pearce threatened to have part of the estate of the said William Strout, and whereas in truth and in fact, after the payment of the said sum of money, (to wit, meaning the said sum of money, by the said Christopher Leach above as aforesaid, paid to the said Robert Pearce, on the 23d day of October, in the year of our Lord 1662) the said William Strout by the said

Y

Robert

Robert did suftain many expences, and by the procurement or affent of the faid Robert Pearce was damaged to the value of two hundred pounds and more. And fo the faid Robert Pearce on the 30th day of May, in the 23d year of the reign of the lord Charles the 2d, now king of England, &c. aforefaid, at Weftminfter aforefaid, in the faid county of Middlefex, before the faid Thomas Tyrrill, then one of the juftices of the faid lord the king, of the bench as aforefaid, then having fufficient power and authority to adminifter the oath aforefaid, to the faid Robert Pearce, falfely, wilfully and corruptly, by his own proper act and confent, in the manner and form aforefaid, committed wilful and corrupt perjury, to the great difpleafure of Almighty God, in contempt of the faid lord the now king, and of his laws, to the evil and pernicious example of all others in the like cafe offending, and againft the peace of the faid lord the now king, his crown and dignity, &c. whereupon the faid coroner and attorney of the faid lord the king, for the faid lord the king then prayed the confideration of the court here, in the premiffes, and that due procefs of law fhould be awarded againft the faid Robert Pearce, to make him to anfwer to the faid lord the king, of and concerning the premiffes, &c. as by the information aforefaid, in the court of the faid lord the king, before the king himfelf, here in the court remaining of record more fully appears; and further the faid coroner and attorney of the faid lord the king, gives the court here to underftand and to be informed, that afterwards to wit, on the Wednefday next after three weeks of St. Michael, in the 24th year of the reign of the faid lord the now king, before the faid lord the king at Weftminfter, came the faid Robert Pearce, by Jafper Waterhoufe his attorney, and having heard the information aforefaid, faid that he was not guilty thereof, and of that then put himfelf upon the country; and the faid Thomas Fanfhaw, knt. coroner and attorney of the faid lord the king, in the court of the faid lord the king, before the king himfelf, who for the faid lord the king in that behalf profecuted, did the like, &c. In which caufe it was in fuchwife proceeded in the court aforefaid, that the iffue aforefaid, fo as aforefaid joined afterwards to wit, on the Friday next after the octave of St. Martin, to wit, on Friday the 22d day of November, in the 24th year of the reign of the faid lord the now king, before Matthew Hale, knt. chief juftice of the faid lord the king, affigned to hold pleas before the king himfelf, at Weftminfter, in the county of Middlefex, in the due manner was tried by a certain jury of the country thereon, in the caufe aforefaid taken, upon which trial of the iffue aforefaid, fo as aforefaid joined, before the faid chief juftice laft mentioned, one Thomas Jole of Launcefton, in the county of Cornwall, carpenter, and John Baker, of Jacobftowe, in the county of Cornwall aforefaid, * carpenter, and John Pearne,

of

of Jacobstowe aforesaid, carpenter, then and there were produced witnesses on the behalf of the said Robert Pearce defendant, in the cause aforesaid, and then and there before the said chief justice last mentioned, were sworn, and each and every of them was sworn upon the Holy Gospel of God, to speak the truth, the whole truth, and nothing but the truth, of and concerning the premisses, in the manner and form afore- *Oath.* said, put in issue as aforesaid, and so being sworn, he the said Thomas Jole not having the fear of God before his eyes, but being moved and seduced by the instigation of the devil, then and there to wit, on the said 22d day of November, in the 24th year aforesaid, at Westminster aforesaid, in the said county of Middlesex, before the said chief justice upon his oath aforesaid, and upon the issue aforesaid, in the manner and form aforesaid joined, falsely, wilfully and corruptly did say depose, swear *Perjury by* and give in evidence to the jurors of the jury aforesaid, " *That* Thomas *John Strout and William Strout did deliver the writing obligatory* Jole. *for five pounds,* (meaning the writing obligatory in the information aforesaid mentioned) *to John Pearne, to the use of the under-sheriff,* (meaning to the use of John Littleton, then subsheriff of the county of Cornwall) *and that Mr. Pearce,* (meaning the said Robert Pearce the defendant in the cause aforesaid) *at the time of the sealing and delivery of the writing obligatory aforesaid, was not in the house,* (meaning the mansion-house of the said Thomas Jole) *but in the church,* (meaning the parochial church of Jacobstowe, in the county of Cornwall aforesaid) *and that then* (meaning the time of the sealing and delivery of the writing obligatory aforesaid) *there were only six persons in the said house, to wit, John Strout, William Strout, two bailiffs and two witnesses,* " (meaning the two witnesses who subscribed the writing obligatory aforesaid). Whereas in truth and in fact, the said John Strout and William Strout did not deliver the *Averments* writing obligatory for five pounds, to John Pearne to the use *of perjury.* of the sub-sheriff: and whereas in truth and in fact, the said Mr. Pearce at the time of the sealing and delivery of the writing obligatory aforesaid, was in the house of the said Thomas Jole, and not in the church: and whereas in truth and in fact, at the time of the sealing of the obligation aforesaid, there were more than six persons in the said house, as the said Thomas Jole falsely, wilfully and corruptly did say, depose, swear, and upon his oath affirm, and give in evidence to the jury aforesaid. And that the said John Baker, on the said 22d day *Perjury by* of November, in the 24th year of the reign of the said lord John Baker the now king aforesaid, at Westminster aforesaid, in the said county of Middlesex, before the said chief justice and the jury aforesaid, falsely, wilfully and corruptly did say, depose, swear, and upon his oath affirm, and give in evidence to the jury aforesaid, sworn to try the issue aforesaid, " *That the writing obligatory* (meaning the writing obligatory in the information aforesaid mentioned)

mentioned) *was delivered to John Pearne,* (meaning the said John Pearne) *to the use of the sub-sheriff,* (meaning to the use of John Littleton, sub-sheriff of the county of Cornwall aforesaid) *and that the writing obligatory aforesaid, was in the name of Mr. Pearce,* (meaning the said Robert Pearce, the defendant in the cause aforesaid) *and that at the time of the sealing and delivery of the writing obligatory aforesaid, the said Mr. Pearce* (meaning *P. 143. the said Robert Pearce) *was in the* summer-house, (meaning a certain gallery at the mansion-house of the said Thomas Jole)." Whereas in truth and in fact, the writing obligatory aforesaid, was not delivered to the said John Pearne, to the use of the sub-sheriff, and whereas in truth and in fact, at the time of the sealing and delivery of the writing obligatory aforesaid, the said Robert Pearce was not in the summer-house, as the said John Baker, falsely, wilfully and corruptly did say, depose, swear and upon his oath affirm, and give in evidence to the jury aforesaid. And the said John Pearne, on the said 22d day of November, in the 24th year of the reign of the said lord the king aforesaid, at Westminster aforesaid, in the said county of Middlesex, before the said chief justice and the jury aforesaid, falsely, wilfully and corruptly did say, depose, swear, and upon his oath affirm and give in evidence to the jury aforesaid, sworn to try the issue aforesaid, " *That the writing obligatory* (meaning the writing obligatory in the information aforesaid mentioned) *was sealed and delivered to himself, to the use of the sub-sheriff,* (meaning to the use of John Littleton, then sub-sheriff of the county of Cornwall) *and that the writing obligatory aforesaid, was in the name of Mr. Pearce,* (meaning in the name of the said Robert Pearce, defendant in the information aforesaid)." Whereas in truth and in fact, the writing obligatory aforesaid, was not sealed or delivered to the said John Pearne, to the use of the sub-sheriff, as the said John Pearne, falsely, wilfully and corruptly did say, depose, swear, and upon his oath affirm, and give in evidence to the jury aforesaid. And so the said Thomas Jole, John Baker and John Pearne, on the 22d day of November, in the 24th year of the reign of the said lord the now king aforesaid, before the said chief justice, at Westminster aforesaid, in the said county of Middlesex, falsely, maliciously, wilfully and corruptly, did commit wilful and corrupt perjury, and each and every of them, falsely, maliciously, wilfully and corruptly, did commit wilful and corrupt perjury, to the great displeasure of Almighty God, &c.

The

P. 143.

Averments of perjury.

Perjury by John Pearne.

Averments of perjury.

General conclusion.

The King *against* Hanson.

To wit. } THAT whereas heretofore to wit, in the term of Easter last past, in the court of the said lord the king, before the king himself, the said court then being held at Westminster, in the said county of Middlesex, a certain issue was joined and recorded in the said court, between one Hamlet Borer, gent. by the name, &c. plaintiff, and one John Bingham, by the name, &c. defendant, in a plea of trespass upon the case. which issue afterwards to wit, on Wednesday the 30th day of May, in the 18th year of the reign of the said lord the now king, before John Keylynge, knt. chief justice of the said lord the king, assigned to hold pleas before the king himself, at Westminster, in the great hall of the pleas there, by the form of the statute, &c. in the due manner came to be tried, by a jury of the said country, then and there sworn and charged to try the issue aforesaid; one John Hanson, late of, &c. in the county aforesaid, on the said 30th day of May, in the * 18th year of the reign of the said lord the now king, at Westminster aforesaid, came before the said chief justice, and not having the fear of God before his eyes, nor fearing to commit the crime of perjury, but contriving and diabolically intending, not only to weaken, but also to prevent the public justice of this kingdom of England, and unjustly to injure and aggrieve him the said John Bingham, and to overturn the truth; he the said John Hanson, on the 30th day of May, in the 18th year aforesaid, at Westminster aforesaid, in the said county of Middlesex, then and there † being sworn upon the Holy Gospels of God, to speak the truth to the said jury, then and there upon his oath aforesaid, falsely, corruptly, wilfully and maliciously did say, depose and give in evidence to the same jury, "*That he the said J. H. in the year of our lord 1661, at the mansion-house of one John Trenchard, esquire, situate at Fox-hall, in the county of Surry, delivered to the said John Bingham an account in writing, which account the said J. B. then and there received, and said to the said John Hanson, that he the said John Bingham would consider thereof;*" and the said J. H. then and there, upon his oath aforesaid, before the said chief justice further did say, depose, and falsely, corruptly, maliciously and injuriously did give in evidence to the said jury, "*That the said John Bingham afterwards, to wit, in the year of our Lord 1661 aforesaid,*

Information for perjury, in giving evidence on the trial of an issue at Nisi Prius, before chief justice Kelynge.

*P. 144.

Oath.

† The precedent doth not say concerning what.

Perjury.

aforesaid, at the said manfion-house of the said John Trenchard aforesaid, acknowledged the account aforesaid, and that he upon that account owed to the said Hamlet, the sum of 84l. 5s. 4d. and·that he promised to pay the same." Whereas in truth and in fact, the

Affignments of perjury.

said John Bingham was not at any time within the year of our Lord 1661, at the said manfion-house of the said John Trenchard, at Fox-hall aforesaid, nor had the said difcourfe with the said John Hanfon concerning the premiffes, nor received the account aforefaid, from the said John Hanfon, nor said to the said John Hanfon, that he the said John Bingham would confider thereof, nor acknowledged the said account, and that he the said John Bingham owed to the said Hamlet the said sum of 84l. 5s. 4d. as the said John Hanfon falfely did say and depofe, to the evil example of all others in the like cafe offending, to the fubverfion of the good government of this kingdom of England, and againft the peace, &c.

The King *againft* C. T.

Information for the like, on trial of an iffue at the affizes.

To wit. } TO be informed, that whereas in the term of St. Michael, in the 22d year of the reign of our lord Charles the 2d, by the grace of God of England, &c. king, &c. in the court of the said lord the king, before the king himfelf, the said court then being at Weftminfter, in the said county of Middlefex, one W. L. had impleaded one J. C. the elder, J. C. the younger, and T. W. of, &c. for this that they the said J. C. the elder, J. C. the younger, and T. W. on

*P. 145.

the   day   in the * 20th year of the reign of the said lord the now king, with force and arms, &c. the clofes of the said W. called the wafte and plot of ground, at the parifh of, &c. in the county of Devon, broke and entered, and the grafs of the said W. to the value of 40l. in the clofes aforefaid lately growing, with their feet, by walking trod down and confumed, and alfo other grafs of the said W. to the value, &c. in the clofes aforefaid, in like manner growing, with certain cattle, to wit, horfes, oxen, cows, hogs and fheep, eat up, trod down and confumed, and alfo then and there the foil of the clofes aforefaid, dug up and fubverted, and alfo in and upon the foil of the clofes aforefaid, planted trees, to wit, twenty oak and afh trees, (the trefpaffes aforefaid, as to the eating up, treading down and confuming of the other grafs aforefaid, with the cattle aforefaid, from the said   day   in the year, &c.

&c. aforesaid, until the   day   in the 22d year of the
reign of the said lord the now king, at sundry days and times
continuing) and also him the said W. for the whole time aforesaid, from the possession and occupation of the closes aforesaid,
kept and held out, whereby the said W. lost and was deprived
of all the profit and benefit of the closes aforesaid, for the
whole time aforesaid, and other outrages to him did, against
the peace of the said lord the now king, and to the damage of
the said W. of 20l. and thereupon he produced his suit, &c.
and that afterwards to wit, on the Monday next after the
octave of St. Hilary, in the 22d year of the reign of the said
lord the now king aforesaid, to which day the said J. J. and T.
had leave to imparl thereto, and then to answer, &c. before the
said lord the king, came as well the said W. by G. E. his attorney, as the said J. J. and T. by their attorney and the said
J. J. and T. defended the force and injury, and said that
they were not guilty thereof, and of this put themselves
upon the country, and the said W. did the like, &c.—
upon which issue so as aforesaid joined, it was in such wise
proceeded between the parties, that afterwards to wit, at the
assizes holden for the county of Devon aforesaid, at the city of
Exeter, in the said county of Devon, on Wednesday the 5th
of April, in the 22d year, &c. before R. R. knt. one of the
justices of the said lord the king, assigned to hold pleas before
the king himself, and L. S. esquire, to the said R. R. and
I. V. knt. chief justice of the said lord the king of the bench,
justices of the said lord the king, assigned to take assizes in the Si non om-
county of Devon aforesaid, by the form of the statute, &c. nes.
for that time associated, the presence of the said I. V. not being expected, by virtue of a writ of the said lord the king of
si non omnes, &c. a trial in the due manner was had, upon
which trial one C. T. of, &c. in the county of Devon aforesaid
yeoman, then and there was produced as a witness on behalf
of W. L. plaintiff in the cause aforesaid, and then and there Oath.
was sworn upon the Holy Gospel of God, to speak the truth
of and concerning the premisses in the said issue, and that the
said C. T. so being sworn as aforesaid, not having the fear of
God before his eyes, but being wholly moved and seduced by
the instigation of the devil, then and there by his own proper act
and consent, upon his oath aforesaid, falsely, maliciously, wilfully and corruptly did say, depose, swear and give in evidence
to the jurors then and there impanelled, elected, tried and sworn
to try the issue aforesaid, in the manner aforesaid joined, " *That* *P. 146.*
*for the time * that he the said C. T. farmed the plot of ground,* Perjury.
(meaning the said plot of ground in the declaration aforesaid
mentioned) *from the defendant's* (meaning the said I. C. the
elder, I. C. the younger, and T. W. the said defendants in the
said cause mentioned) *he th said C. T. made no use of the said
ground, nor kept or depastured any horses, oxen or sheep upon the said*
pl.

<table>
<tr><td>Affignment of perjury.</td><td>

plot of ground;" whereas in truth and in fact, he the faid C. T. for fome time to wit, for the fpace of half one year, in which the faid C. T. farmed the aforefaid plot of ground, from the faid defendants J. C. the elder, J. C. the younger, and T. W. made ufe of the faid plot of ground; and whereas in truth and in fact, he the faid C. T. kept and depaftured fome horfes, oxen

</td></tr>
<tr><td>Conclufion.</td><td>

and fheep upon the faid plot of ground. And fo the faid C. T. on the faid Wednefday the 5th day of April, in the 22d year of the reign, &c. aforefaid, before the faid juftices at the affizes aforefaid, at the city of Exeter aforefaid, ⸱ the faid county, by his own proper act and confent in the manner and form aforefaid, by his oath aforefaid, falfely, malicioufly and corruptly did commit wilful and corrupt perjury, to the great difpleafure of Almighty God, to the evil and pernicious example of all others in the like cafe offending, and againft the peace of the faid lord the king, his crown and dignity. Whereupon the faid coroner and attorney, &c.

</td></tr>
</table>

King *againft* Trotter.

<table>
<tr><td>

Indictment for wilful perjury, in giving evidence on a trial at the bar of the court of Common Pleas on an ejectment, and for which he was committed to the Fleet by the court of Common Pleas.

</td><td>

Middlefex, } THE Jurors for the lord the king, upon their
To wit.   } oath prefent, that Henry Trotter, late of Grimfton-law, in the county of Northumberland, yeoman, on the 30th day of Oct. in the eighth year of the reign of our lord William the 3d, of England, &c. now king, in the court of the faid lord the king, of the bench at Weftminfter, before George Treby, knt. and his brethren juftices of the faid lord the king, of the bench aforefaid, being then and there produced as a witnefs, and by the court aforefaid upon the holy Gofpel of God, in the due form of law fworn, to teftify the truth in a certain action, between Anthony Dawfon, plaintiff, and Charles Howard, late of Ford, in the county of Northumberland, efq; William Nelfon, late of the parifh of St. John-lee, otherwife St. John Lees, in the county aforefaid, gent. Edward Hudfpetch, late of the parifh of St. John-lee, otherwife St. John Lees, in the county aforefaid, yeoman, John Chicken, late of the parifh of St. John-lee, otherwife St. John Lees, in the county aforefaid, yeoman, John Heron, late of the parifh of St. John-lee, otherwife St. John Lees, in the county aforefaid, yeoman, defendants in a plea of trefpafs and ejectment of a farm, then in the faid court depending, and then and there in the faid court, before the juftices aforefaid, in the due courfe of law brought to

</td></tr>
</table>

b2

be tried by a jury of the country, he the said Henry Trotter, then and there, in the said court, before the justices aforesaid, upon his oath aforesaid, then and there by the court aforesaid, to the said Henry Trotter in due form of law administered, falsely, wilfully and corruptly did swear, and to the jurors of the jury aforesaid, then and there in the due manner sworn and charged, to try the issue * between the said parties, in the plea aforesaid joined, did give in evidence, and did depose, " *That a certain writing then and there in the court aforesaid, before the justices aforesaid produced, and to the jurors last-mentioned, shewn in evidence, purporting to be the last will and testament of Thomas Errington, lately deceased, and by the said Thomas Errington to be signed and sealed, and by the said Henry Trotter, and one William Mills and Thomas Story to be attested, was not the last will and testament of the said Thomas Errington, lately deceased, and that the said Thomas Errington lately deceased did not, sign nor seal the writing aforesaid, nor did he publish that writing to be the last will and testament of him, the said Thomas Errington, lately deceased, but that one Mrs. Errington, then Mrs. Wilson, or the said William Mills did subscribe the name of the said Thomas Errington thereto, and that the said Mrs. Errington, then Mrs. Wilson, after the death of the said Thomas Errington, did cause a certain boy whose name was Thomas Errington to seal the said writing.*"—*Whereas in truth and in fact, the said writing, so as aforesaid shewn in evidence, was the last will and testament of the said Thomas Errington, lately deceased, and the said Thomas Errington lately deceased, in his lifetime did sign and seal that writing, and did publish the said writing to be the last will and testament of him the said Thomas Errington lately deceased, to wit, at Westminster, aforesaid, in the county of Middlesex; and whereas, in truth and in fact neither the said Mrs. Errington, then Mrs. Wilson, nor the said William Mills did subscribe the name of the said Thomas Errington thereto; and whereas in truth and in fact, the said Mrs. Errington, then Mrs. Wilson, at any time whatsoever did not cause any person whatsoever to seal the said writing; and so the said Henry Trotter, on the said 30th day of October, in the 8th year aforesaid, at Westminster, in the county of Middlesex aforesaid, in the court of the bench aforesaid, before the said justices, there in the manner and form aforesaid, corruptly, wilfully and maliciously, did commit false, corrupt and wilful Perjury, against the peace, &c.

*P. 147.

Perjury.

Assignments of perjury.

Conclusion.

This indictment was found by the Grand-jury, in the court of the King's-bench, and the defendant confessed the perjury, and was set in the pillory, by judgment and rule of the court.

Z

The

Indictments for Perjury.

The King *against* Trotter.

Saturday next after the Octave of St. Martin, in the Eighth Year of William the 3d, King, &c.

The rule of the court.

Confession and judgment thereon.
*P. 148.

Henry Trotter was brought here into court, under the custody of the Warden of the Fleet, upon a writ of Habeas Corpus ad Subjiciendum, &c. It is ordered that the writ aforesaid and the return thereto be filed, and being charged to answer the indictment against him for perjury, he confesseth here in court, that he is guilty of the perjury in the indictment * aforesaid mentioned, and thereupon his confession is recorded by the court, and so being thereof convicted by his own proper confession, it is ordered that he pay to the lord the king the sum of twenty pounds, for his fine, for the occasion aforesaid, and he is committed to the Marshal in execution, safely to be kept, until he shall pay the fine; and that he shall stand in and upon the pillory, on the Tuesday next, in the court yard of the palace, at Westminster, with a paper upon his head, denoting his offence, between the 11th hour before mid-day of the said day, and the 2d hour after mid-day of the said day, for the space of 1 hour, and also that he shall stand in and upon the pillory, on the Wednesday next, at Charing-Cross, with the said paper upon his head, between the hours aforesaid, for the space aforesaid, and that the said Marshal shall deliver the defendant to the Sheriff of Middlesex, to execute the judgment aforesaid, and after the execution of the said judgment, the said sheriff shall redeliver him to the said Marshal, safely to keep until he shall pay the fine, and that also he shall stand in and upon the pillory, on the Friday next, nigh to the gate of the Inner-temple, in Fleet-street, London, with the like paper upon his head, between the said hours, for the space aforesaid, and that the said marshal deliver the defendant to the sheriffs of London, to execute the judgment aforesaid, and after the execution of the said judgment, the sheriffs shall redeliver the defendant to the said marshal safely to be kept, until he shall pay the fine. By the Court.

The King *against* Stone.

Indictment for perjury in a deposition, before a master in Chancery,

Middlesex, }   THE Jurors, &c. that on the 29th day of July,
To wit. }   in the 23d year of the reign of the said lord the now king, there was a certain suit then depending in the court of Chancery of the said lord the now king, at Westmin-

Rener, in the county of Middlesex aforesaid, by English petition, between Robert Atkyns, knight of the Bath, and Richard Atkyns, esq; and that thereupon one Robert Stone, of the parish of St. Martin in the Fields, in the county of Middlesex aforesaid, mealman, on the said twenty-ninth day of July, and 23d year aforesaid, came before Mundeford Bramston, knt. then being one of the masters of the court of Chancery, of the lord the now king, at Westminster aforesaid, and then and there the said Robert Stone not having the fear of God before his eyes, but being moved and seduced by the instigation of the devil, before the said Mundeford Bramston then and as yet one of the masters of the said court of Chancery, having full and sufficient power and authority to administer an oath to the said Robert Stone in that behalf, upon the Holy Gospel of God in the due form of law was sworn, and took his corporal oath, and the said Robert Stone, then and there upon his oath aforesaid, before the said M. B. then being one of the masters of the said court of Chancery as aforesaid, and having full and sufficient power and authority to administer an oath to the said Robert Stone in that behalf as aforesaid, falsely, wilfully and corruptly did say, swear and depose, " *that on Saturday then being the said twenty-ninth day of July, he met the said Richard Atkins in the Inner-temple, and the said Robert Stone having the writ of execution of an order to serve * him out of the honourable court of Chancery, at the suit of the said Robert Atkyns, the said Robert Stone did shew to the said Richard Atkyns the said writ, under seal, and did offer to deliver to him a copy of the said writ, and serve him therewith, but the said Richard Atkyns swore a desperate oath that if the said Robert Stone would come near him the said Richard, to serve him therewith, he the said Richard Atkyns, him the said Robert Stone would run through, or would be the death of him; and that the servant of the said Richard Atkyns then being present with his said master aforesaid, swore many desperate oaths, that if he the said Robert Stone would approach to him, he would run the said Robert Stone through, and also swore that if he ever met the said Robert he would be his death; and the said Robert further did depose, that upon the Thursday then last, he was at the Chamber in the Middle-temple, where the said Richard Atkyns did lodge, and that the said Richard Atkyns then was in the said Chamber, and spoke to one James Johnson, who was with the said Robert Stone, and the said James Johnson did deliver to the servant of the said Richard Atkyns a copy of the said writ of execution; and one Mary Jackson, who then was with the said Robert Stone, did shew to the servant of the said Richard Atkyns, the said writ under seal; and as soon as she had shewn the said writ under seal, the said servant laid his hand upon his sword, and pursued the said Robert three pair of stairs, swearing that he would be the death of him, the said Robert Stone,"* whereas in truth and in fact, the said Robert Stone did not shew

Z 2

concerning the service of a writ of execution of an order of that court, in a cause between Sir Robert Atkyns, afterwards lord chief baron of the Exchequer, and Richard Atkyns, esquire.

Perjury,

* P. 149,

Assignment of perjury.

to the said Richard Atkyns any writ of execution under seal, at the suit of the said Robert Atkyns, nor did he offer to shew any such writ, or to deliver to the said Richard any copy of any such writ, or to serve him therewith; and whereas in truth and in fact, the said Richard Atkyns did not swear that if the said Robert Stone would come near him, he the said Richard him the said Robert would run through, nor did he swear that if he should ever meet the said Robert Stone, he would be his death, as the said Robert Stone upon his oath aforesaid, before the said Mundeford Bramston, falsely, wilfully and corruptly did say, depose and swear. And so the jurors aforesaid, now here sworn to enquire for the said lord the king and for the body of the county aforesaid, upon their oath aforesaid, say that the said Robert Stone on the said 29th day of July, in the 23d year, &c. aforesaid, at Westminster aforesaid, in the county aforesaid, before the said Mundeford Bramston then being one of the masters of the said court of Chancery, who then and there had full power and authority to administer the said oath to the said Robert Stone, falsely, wilfully and corruptly did commit false, wilful and corrupt perjury, to the great displeasure of Almighty God, in contempt of the said lord the king and of his laws, to the great damage of the said Richard Atkyns, to the evil and pernicious example of all others in the like case offending, and against the peace, &c.

Conclusion.

---

* The King *against* Boucher, and others.

Hilary, 26th and 27th Charles II.

Information against three defendants for perjury, in a deposition, before a justice of the peace, that a person was present at an unlawful conventicle, whereby the person was fined.

To wit. } THAT Henry Boucher, of, &c. in the county of Somerset, labourer, Ed. Cornelius, the younger, of Winefield, in the county of Wilts, labourer, and Tho. Love, of Winefield, in the said county of Wilts, labourer, on the 28th day of May, in the 20th year of the reign of our lord Charles the 2d, of England, &c. contriving and intending one Mary Swath, widow, greatly to oppress and distress, on the said 28th day of May, in the 20th year, &c. aforesaid, at Cutteridge, within the parish of Northbradly, in the county of Wilts aforesaid, in their proper persons came before William Trenchard, esquire, one of the justices of the said lord the king, assigned to preserve the peace of the said lord the king, in the said county of Wilts aforesaid, and then and there did take their

corporal

corporal oaths upon the holy Gospel of God, before the said Oaths.
William Trenchard, (the said William Trenchard then and there
having full and sufficient power and authority to administer the
said oaths to the said H. B. E. C. and E. L.) and that the said
H. B. E. C. and E. L. upon their oaths aforesaid so taken, not
having the fear of God before their eyes, but being moved and
seduced by the instigation of the devil, then and there by their
several acts and their own proper consents, falsely, maliciously,
wilfully and corruptly upon their oaths aforesaid, did say, depose and swear, and each and every of them, by his own proper act and consent upon his oath aforesaid, falsely, maliciously, wilfully and corruptly did say, depose and swear that the
said Mary Swath was present at an unlawful assembly at Brook Perjury.
in the parish of Westbury, in the barn and close of Thomas
Edwards, on the 17th day of May, in the 26th year aforesaid,
under colour and pretence of the exercise of religion, in another manner than according to the practice of the church of
England, by reason of which the said William Trenchard for
that offence did impose upon the said Mary Swath the fine of
5l. and 5s. Whereas in truth and in fact the said Mary Swath, Assignment
was not present at an unlawful assembly at B. in the parish of perjury.
W. in the barn and close of Thomas Edwards, on the 17th
day of May, in the 26th year, &c. aforesaid, under colour and
pretence of the exercise of religion, in another manner than
according to the practice of the church of England, as the said
H. B. E. C. and E. L. by their several acts, and their own
proper consents, falsely, maliciously, wilfully and corruptly, Conclusion.
upon their oaths aforesaid did say, depose and swear, and so
they the said H. B. E. C. and E. L. on the said 28th day of
May, in the 26th year, &c. aforesaid, at C. aforesaid, at the
parish of N. aforesaid, in the said county, before the said W.
T. one of the justices as aforesaid, then and there having sufficient power and authority, to administer the oaths aforesaid,
to the said H. B. E. C. and E. L. in that behalf, falsely, maliciously, wilfully and corruptly, by their several acts and * by *P. 151.
their own proper consents, in the manner and form aforesaid,
did commit wilful and corrupt perjury, and each and every of
them by his act and by his own proper consent, falsely, maliciously, wilfully and corruptly in the manner and form aforesaid, did commit wilful and corrupt perjury, to the great displeasure of Almighty God, to the great damage of the said
Mary Swath, in contempt of the laws of this kingdom of
England, to the evil and pernicious example of all others in
the like case offending, and against the peace of the said lord
the now king, his crown and dignity. Whereupon the said Process
attorney-general of the said lord the now king, for the said prays.
lord the king, prays the consideration of the court here in the
premisses, and that the due process of law against the said
H. B.

Venire to answer awarded.

H. B. E. C. and E. L. may be awarded in this behalf, to make them to answer to the said lord the king, of and touching the premisses, &c. Whereupon the sheriff of the county is commanded, that he do not omit, &c. but that he cause them to come to answer, &c. And now, to wit, on the Saturday next after the octave of St. Hilary, in this same term, before the lord the king at Westminster, come the said H. B. E. C. and E. L. by W. E. their attorney, and having heard the informa-

Not guilty

tion aforesaid, severally say that they are not guilty thereof, and of this put themselves upon the country, and William Jones, knt. attorney-general of the said lord the king, who for the said lord the king in this behalf now prosecutes, doth

Venire facias juratores, awarded.

the like, &c. Therefore let a jury come thereupon before the said lord the king, from the day of Easter in 15 days, wheresoever, &c. and who neither, &c. to recognize, &c. because as well, &c. the same day is given as well to the said William Jones who prosecutes, &c. as to the said H. B. E. C. and E. L. at which fifteen days of Easter, before the said lord the

' Vicecomes non misit breve.'

king,' at Westminster come, as well the said William Jones, who prosecutes, &c. as the said H. B. E. C. and E. L. by W. E. their attorney aforesaid; and the sheriff hath not sent the writ thereupon, therefore as before let a jury come thereupon, before the said lord the king, on the morrow of the Holy Trinity, wheresoever, &c. and who, &c. to recognize, &c. because as well, &c. the same day is given as well to the said William Jones, who prosecutes, &c. as to the said H. B. E. C. and E. L. &c. At which morrow of the Holy Trinity, before the said lord the king at Westminster, come as well the said William Jones who prosecutes, &c. as the said H. B. E. C. and E. L. by their attorney aforesaid, and the sheriff returns the names of 24 jurors, of whom none, &c. Therefore he

Distringas awarded.

is commanded that he do not omit, but that he distrain them by all their lands, &c. and that of the issues, &c. and that he have their bodies before the said lord the king, from the day of St. Michael, in three weeks, wheresoever, &c. or before the justices of the said lord the king, assigned to take assizes in the county of Wilts aforesaid, &c.

The King *against* Brooks.

Indictment for perjury, in an answer in Chancery.

Caption.

To wit. } **B**E it remembered, that at the general quarter sessions of the peace of the lord the king, held for the city of London, at the Guildhall of the said city, and within the said city, to wit, on Wednesday the 11th day

of

of January, in the 17th year of the reign of our lord Charles the 2d, of England, &c. king, &c. before John Lawrence, kt. mayor of the city of London, Thomas Adams, knt. and bart. &c. and others, their fellow justices of the said lord the king, assigned to preserve the peace in the said city, and also to hear and determine divers felonies, * trespasses, and other misdeeds in the said city perpetrated, the said session of the peace of the said lord the king was adjourned by the said justices of the said lord the king there, until the Friday next, to wit, the 13th day of the said month of January, in the year aforesaid, at the 7th hour before mid-day of the said day, at Justice-hall, in the old Baily, in the parish of St. Sepulchre, in the ward of Farringdon, without, London aforesaid, to be held before the said justices and othesr their fellows justices of the said lord the king, &c. and to do further as the court shall consider, &c. And thereupon by a certain inquisition taken, at the said general quarter sessions of the peace of the said lord the king, held for the city of London, by the adjournment aforesaid, at Justice-hall aforesaid, in the parish and ward aforesaid, on the said Friday the 13th day of January aforesaid, in the year aforesaid, before the said J. L. knt. mayor of the city of London, T. A. knt. and baronet, R. B. knt. &c. aldermen of the said city, and William Wylde, knt. and bart. one of the said lord the king's serjeants at law, and recorder of the said city, and others their fellows, justices of the said lord the king, assigned to preserve the peace in the said city, and also to hear and determine divers felonies, trespasses and other misdeeds within the said city perpetrated, by the oath of Francis Perkins, W. S. P. G. (and 14 others) good and lawful men of the city of London aforesaid, then and there sworn and charged to enquire for the said lord the king and body of the said city, it is presented that the following bill is true, " *London to wit, the jurers for the said lord the king upon their oath present, that whereas Nathaniel Sharp of London, haberdasher, on the 22d day of April, in the 14th year of the reign of our lord Charles the 2d, by the grace of God of England, &c. king, &c. did exhibit his bill of complaint in the court of Chancery, of the said lord the king, the said court then being held at Westminster, in the county of Middle-sex, against one Nathaniel Brooks of London, stationer, which bill of complaint was directed to the most noble Edward, Earl of Clarendon, lord chancellor of England, and the said Nathaniel Sharp, in and by his said bill did set forth, that he the said N. S. being indebted about the year 1655, was compelled by extreme losses, and otherwise to call his creditors together, and thereon to make a composition with his said creditors; and the said Nathaniel Sharp, by the insinuation and advice of the said Nathaniel Brooks (to whom the said N. S. was in no manner indebted) was persuaded that the said N. B. should appear as a creditor of the said N. S. for 40l. among the other creditors of the said N. S. and that the said N. S. should*

feal

* P. 152.

Adjournment to Justice-hall in the Old Baily.

Bill of indictment found.

Bill filed in the court of Chancery.

seal an obligation to the said N. B. bearing date about the 28th day of February, in the year of our Lord 1655, in which obligation one John Fowler of London, fishmonger, should be named, to be bound to the said N. B. in the penalty of 40l. and that the said obligation should be sealed by the said N. B. and J. F. upon trust only, and for the intention that the said N. B. should appear as a creditor of the said N. S. for 40l. among the other creditors of the said N. S. And that upon such perfuasions of the said N. B. the said N. S. did believe that he had sealed such an obligation for 40l. altho' he did not know

***P. 153.** *or believe that the said J. F. ⸰ had ever sealed the same, and that the said N. B. afterwards did seal and deliver as his act and deed, a general release of all obligations, bills, complaints, and demands whatsoever; and whereas the said N. S. in and by his bill of complaint aforesaid, among other things did pray, that the said N. B. might set forth, declare, and discover upon the corporal oath of the said N. B. whether the said obligation, bearing date the said 28th day of February, in the year of our Lord 1665, in the penalty of 40l. pretended to be sealed by the said N. S. and J. F was not sealed to give colour that the said N. B. was a creditor of the said N. S. and who are the witnesses to the said obligation; and whether they did deliver the said obligation as the act and deed of them, the said N. S. and J. F. and for what reason and consideration the said N. S. did seal the same, and what money or other lawful consideration, the said N. S. had for the same; and when, where, how, by who, or whom, before who, or whom the said N. S. did receive the same; and whether the said N. B. after the sealing of the said obligation, did not seal and deliver as his act and deed, before two witnesses, to the said N. S. a certain general release, bearing date after the said obligation, and by which release, the said N. S. was released and acquitted, by the said N. B. of and from all obligations, bills, complaints and demands whatsoever, from the beginning of the world to the day of the date of the said release; as by the* said bill remaining of record in the said court of Chancery among other things more fully appears. And that the said N. B. of London, stationer, afterwards, to wit, on the 5th day of May, in the 14th year, &c. aforesaid, at London, to wit, in the parish of St. Dunstan, in the west, in the ward of Farringdon without, London aforesaid, came before Nathaniel Hubbert, knt. then one of the masters of the said court of Chancery, and then and there, before the said N. H. did exhibit in writing, the answer of the said N. B. to the said bill of complaint aforesaid, and the said N. B. being then and there

Oath. sworn in the due form of law, upon the Holy Gospel of God, before the said N. H. then one of the masters of the said court of Chancery, and then having sufficient authority to administer an oath to the said N. B. the said N. B. then and there, upon his oath before the said N. H. knt. then one of the masters of the said court of Chancery, did swear, that so much of the answer of the said N. B. so as aforesaid before the said N. H. exhibited, as concerned the proper acts and deeds of the said N.

B. he

B. he the said N. B. knew to be true, and that so much of the said answer as concerned the acts and deeds of any other person, he the said N. B. believed to be true. And that the said N. B. not having the fear of God before his eyes, but being moved and seduced by the instigation of the devil, and disregarding the laws of this kingdom of England, nor in any manner fearing the penalty in the same contained, and holding his oath aforesaid, as nothing, then and there upon his oath aforesaid, in his said answer to the bill of complaint aforesaid, falsely, wilfully, and corruptly among other things did answer, say and swear, in writing, in these English * words following, " *That the complain-ant* (meaning the said N. S.) *being indebted to the defendant* (mean-ing the said N. B.) *for money lent at several times unto him* (mean-ing the said N. S.) *by this defendant* (meaning the said N. B.) *and being likewise indebted to him* (meaning the said N. B.) *in 8l. for books sold unto him,* (meaning the said N. S.) *and for his lodg-ing, washing and diet ; and this deponent* (meaning the said N. B.) *having laid out several sums of money for him* (meaning the said N. S.) *in attending on the execution of a commission of bankruptcy sued out against him* (meaning the said N. B.) *the commissioners in the said commission having sat several times upon it ; and this defendant* (meaning the said N. B.) *having laid out several sums of money for him* (meaning the said N. B.) *both before and after the said commission was sued out in prosecuting a composition with his creditors* (meaning the creditors of the said N. S.) *and this defendant* (meaning the said N. B.) *having taken great pains, and deserved much therein, in all amounting to 19l. 12s. at least, and the complainant* (meaning the said N. S) *being very sensible thereof, did upon the 28th day of February, 1655, he* (meaning the said N. S) *then lodging at this defendant's house* (meaning the house of the said N. B.) *of his own accord came unto this defendant* (meaning the said N. B.) *in his said house* (meaning the house of the said N. B,) *with John Fowler* (meaning the said J. Fowler) *his brother-in-law, and then and there acknowledging the said debt, did for the full satisfaction there-of, together with the said J. F.* (meaning the said J. F.) *as his surety, enter into a bond to this defendant* (meaning the said N. B.) *and which obligation* (meaning the said obligation) *the complain-ant* (meaning the said N. S.) *wrote with his own hand, of the pe-nalty of 40l. bearing date the said 28th day of February, in the year aforesaid* (meaning the said 28th day of February, in the year of our Lord, 1655) *and sealed both by the said complainant* (meaning the said N. S.) *and the said John Fowler, conditioned for the pay-ment of 19l. 12s. to this defendant* (meaning the said N. B.) *up-on the 28th day of August then next following* (meaning the 28th day of August, in the year of our lord, 1656). *and this defen-dant* (meaning the said N. B.) *denieth that the said bond was en-tered into or sealed upon any of the persuasions, allegations, reasons and purposes or intents, in the bill scandalously alledged, or that it was entered into, or sealed upon, or for any other reason, and pur-

Perjury.

*P. 154.

A a

pose

pose or intent, than this defendant (meaning the said N. B.) *hath before set forth; and particularly this defendant* (meaning the said N. B.) *denieth that the said bond was sealed, or to be sealed by the complainant* (meaning the said N. S.) *and the said J. Fowler* (meaning the said J. Fowler,) *or either of them* (meaning the said N. S. and J. F.) *in trust, or that this defendant* (meaning the said N. B.) *might appear a creditor to the complainant, or to colour this defendant's* (meaning the said N. B.) *being a creditor to him* (meaning the said N. S.) *and saith, that the complainant* (meaning the said N. S.) *did set his hand and seal* (meaning the hand and seal of the said N. S.) *and the said John Fowler, only his seal* (meaning * the seal of the said J. F.) *to the said bond, and both the complainants* (meaning the said N. S. and the said John Fowler) *did after the ensealing of the said bond, deliver the same as their act and deed* (meaning the act and deed of the said N. S. and J. F.) *and this defendant* (meaning the said N. B.) *denieth that he this defendant* (meaning the said N. B.) *did after the sealing of the said bond, seal or deliver any release,"* as by the said answer of the said N. B. to the said bill of complaint in the said court of Chancery remaining of record more fully appears. Whereas in truth and in fact, the said N. S. at the time of the date of the said obligation, in the bill of the said N. S. and in the answer of the said N. B. mentioned, to wit, on the said 28th day of February, in the year of our Lord, 1655, was not indebted to the said N. B. in any sum of money for the lodging, washing, and diet of the said N. S. before the date of the said obligation, nor did the said N. B. lay out any sum of money for the said N. S. in any attendance upon the execution of any commission of bankruptcy sued out against the said N. S. and whereas in truth and in fact, no commission of bankruptcy was sued out against the said N. S. before the date of the said obligation ; and whereas in truth and in fact, the said N. S. on the said 28th day of February, in the year of our lord 1655, did not lodge at the house of the said N. B. and whereas in truth and in fact, the said obligation was sealed by the said N. S. upon trust, and only for the intention, that the said N. B. should appear as a creditor of the said N. S. and to give colour that the said N. B. was a creditor of the said N. S. and whereas in truth and in fact, the said J. F. did never seal and deliver as his deed, the said obligation in the bill and answer aforesaid mentioned ; and whereas in truth and in fact, the said N. B. after the sealing of the said obligation, did seal and deliver to the said N. B. a release of the said obligation. And so the said jurors now here sworn to enquire for the said lord the king, and for the body of the city of London aforesaid, upon their oath say, that the said N. B. on the said 5th day of May, in the 14th year aforesaid, at the parish aforesaid, in the ward aforesaid, in his answer aforesaid, to the bill of complaint aforesaid, in the manner and form aforesaid, falsely, wilfully, and corruptly did

commit

*P. 155.

Assignment of perjury.

commit wilful and corrupt perjury, in contempt of the said lord the now king, and of his laws, to the evil example of all others in the like case offending, and against the peace of the said lord the now king his crown and dignity.

Will.

The King *against* Sotherton *and others.*

To wit, } TO be informed that one Elizabeth Sotherton, in the court of Chancery of the lord the king, the said court then being at Westminster, in the county of Middlesex, did exhibit a certain English bill of complaint, against one Edward Wood, Catharine Rawdon, Elenor Ramford and Robert Ramford, of and concerning a certain messuage or tenement with the appurtenances, situate in the parish of St. Magdalen * Bermondsey in Southwark, by one John Sotherton, then deceased, late the husband of the said E. S. the said plaintiff, then before supposed to be taken from the said Edward Wood and the said defendants, and by a certain deed of the said Edward indented, for and in consideration of a competent sum of money to the said Edward Wood, supposed to be paid by the said J. Sotherton, late the husband of the said E. the said plaintiff, and also at and under a great annual rent, supposed to be demised to the said John Sotherton, his executors and administrators, for a certain long term of years, in the said deed expressed, and then at the time of the commencing of the said suit between the said parties, not expired; and also of and concerning the said Eliz. Sotherton the said plaintiff, being arrested by the said Edward Wood, by virtue of a certain process, out of the court of the marshal, or out of the palace court at Westminster, for certain supposed arrears of rent, supposed and pretended to be due and payable to the said Edward Wood for the premisses, to which bill of complaint the said defendants in the court of Chancery of the said lord the king, did exhibit a certain answer in writing, and thereupon it was in such wise proceeded between the said parties, according to the course and custom of the said court in such cases, that the said Elizabeth Sotherton (on the day and year. &c.) did exhibit interrogatories in the said court of Chancery, to be administered to the witnesses produced, on the behalf of the said E. S. of which interrogatories, the tenor of the second interrogatory follows in

Information for perjury, in depositions upon interrogatories in a cause depending in Chancery. *P. 156.

A a 2

these

these words, (Likewise do you know, &c.) whereupon after-wards, one Augustin Sotherton, of the parish of St. M. B. afore-said, in the county of Surry, dyer, and Thomas Davies, of, &c. labourer, were produced as witnesses, on behalf of the said Elizabeth, in the said cause, and the said Augustin, so as afore-said, being produced a witness, on the part of the said E. in the said cause, the said A. afterwards, to wit, on the day and year, &c. came before Walter Littleton, knt. then one of the mas-ters of the said court of Chancery, and then having a sufficient authority to administer an oath, to the said A. S. in that be-half, and was sworn upon the holy Gospel of God, in the due form of law ; and the said A. S. then and there upon his oath, before the said W. L. knt. then one of the masters of the said court of Chancery, did swear that he the said A. would make true answer to all such questions as should be demanded of him, of and concerning the said interrogatory, and that he would depose the truth, the whole truth, and nothing but the truth, without favour or affection to either of the parties, and there-upon the said A. then and there, of and upon the said interro-gatory, being examined he the said A. upon his said oath, falsely, wilfully and corruptly then and there did say, depose, swear, and did answer to the said second interrogatory, in these words as follows, " *To the second interrogatory this deponent saith, that; &c,* whereas in truth and in fact, &c. and so the said A. on the day and year, &c. in the said court of Chancery, before the king himself, at Westminster, in the said county of Middlesex, falsely, wilfully and corruptly did commit wilful and corrupt perjury, in contempt of the said lord the now king, and of his laws, to the great damage of the said E. W. to the evil and pernicious example of all others in the like case offending, and against the peace of the said lord the now king, his crown and dignity.

Oath. (margin)
Perjury. (margin)
Assignment of perjury. (margin)
Conclusion. (margin)

---

* *The King against* Saxon.   *P. 157.

Hilary, the 1st and 2d of *James II.*   *Roll* 5.

To wit, } TO be informed that by a certain inquisition taken at Chester, in the county of Chester, on Friday the 11th day of December, in the 1st year of the reign of our lord James the 2d, by the grace of God of England, &c. king, &c. before Edward Lutwyche, kt. one of the said lord the king's serjeants at law, and justice of Chester, John Warre, esq; another justice of Chester, Philip Egerton, knt. and Peter Shakerly, knt. assigned by letters patent of the said lord the king, made to them and others, and to any three or more of them, to enquire by the oath of good and lawful men of the county of Chester, by whom the truth of the matter might be better known, and by other ways, methods, and means, by which they might or could know better, as well within liberties as without, more fully the truth of certain treasons, misprisions of treasons, insurrections, rebellions, counterfeitings, clippings, washings, false coinings, and other falsities of the monies of this kingdom of England, and of other kingdoms or dominions whatsoever ; and of certain murders, felonies, manslaughters, killings, burglaries, rapes of women, meetings, conventicles, unlawful uttering of words, combinations, misprisions, confederacies, false allegations, trespasses, riots, routs, retentions, escapes, contempts, falsities, negligencies, concealments, maintenances, oppressions, champarties, deceits, and other misdeeds, offences, and injuries whatsoever, and also of the accessaries of the same, within the said county of Chester, as well within liberties as without, by whomsoever, and in what manner soever, had, done, committed, or perpetrated, by whom, to whom, when, how, and in what manner, and of other articles and circumstances, the premisses, and every and any of them howsoever concerning, and the said treasons and other premisses to hear and determine, according to the law and custom of the kingdom of the said lord the now king of England, by the oath of twelve jurors, good and lawful men of the said county of Chester, then and there sworn and charged to enquire for the said lord the king,

Information
For wilful
and corrupt
perjury, up-
on the trial
of lord De-
lemere, for
high trea-
son, before
the lord high
Steward,
and theother
peers of the
realm.

Caption.

and

Recital of
Bill of In-
dictment for
high treason

and for the body of the said county of Chester, it was presented, that Henry baron of Delemere, in the county of Chester, as a
false traitor, against the most excellent and illustrious prince,
James the 2d, by the Grace of God, of England, &c. king, &c.
his natural lord, not having the fear of God in his heart, nor
weighing the duty of his allegiance, but being moved and seduced by the instigation of the devil, and entirely withdrawing the cordial love, and true, due and natural obedience which
a true and faithful subject of the said lord the king, towards
the said lord the king should, and of right ought to bear ; and
devising, practising, and as much as in him lay intending, to
disquiet, molest and disturb the peace and public tranquility of
this kingdom of England, and to stir up, move and procure war
and rebellion against the said * lord the king, within this kingdom of England, and to subvert, change and alter the government of the said lord the king of this kingdom of England, and
to depose and deprive the said lord the king of his title, honor,
and royal name, and from the imperial crown of this kingdom
of England, and to put and bring the said lord the king to death
and final destruction, on the 14th day of April, in the 1st year
of the reign, &c. aforesaid, and at divers other days and times,
as well before as after, at Mere, in the said county of Chester,
falsely, maliciously, diabolically and traiterously, with divers o-
ther false traitors and rebels to the jurors aforesaid unknown,
had conspired, compassed, imagined and intended, not only to
deprive and remove the said lord the king, his supreme and natural lord, from his royal estate, title, power, and rule of this
kingdom of England, but also to kill and bring, and put to
death the said lord the king, and to change, alter, and entirely
to subvert the antient government of this kingdom of England,
and to cause and procure, a miserable slaughter among the subjects of the said lord the king, throughout the whole kingdom of England, and to procure and abet rebellion and insurrection against the said lord the king, within this kingdom of
England, and to fulfil, perfect and bring to effect his said most
wicked, detestable, and diabolical, treasons, and traiterous
compassings, imaginations and purposes, he the said Henry,
baron of Delemere, as a false traitor, then and there, to wit,
on the said 14th day of April, in the 1st year aforesaid, and
at divers other days and times, as well before as after, at Mere,
aforesaid, in the county aforesaid, falsely, unlawfully, wickedly, and traiterously, with Charles Gerard, esq; and with other
false traitors to the jurors aforesaid unknown, assembled, met,
consulted, and agreed to raise and procure divers great sums of
money, and great numbers of armed men, to make and levy
war and rebellion against the said king, within this kingdom of
England, and the city of Chester in the county of the said city,
and the castle of the said lord the king of Chester, at Chester,
in the said county of Chester, and all the magazines then being

in

in the said castle, to enter, take, seize, surprize, and into their possession and power to obtain ; and the jurors aforesaid, upon their said oath further did then say, that the said Henry, baron of Delemere afterwards, to wit, on the 27th day of May, in the 1st year, &c. aforesaid, falsely, unlawfully, wickedly, and traiterously had travelled from the city of London, to Mere aforesaid, in the county of Chester aforesaid, to fulfil and perfect his treasonable purposes aforesaid, and that the said Henry, baron of Delemere afterwards, to wit, on the 4th day of June, in the 1st year, &c. aforesaid, at M. aforesaid, in the said county of Chester, in further prosecution of his said wicked, unlawful and traiterous purposes, falsely, unlawfully, wickedly and traiterously had stirred up, animated and persuaded divers liege subjects of the said lord the king, to the jurors aforesaid unknown, to join and adhere to the said Henry, baron of Delemere, and to the other false traitors to the jurors aforesaid unknown, in the said war and rebellion, and in their traiterous purposes aforesaid, against the duty of his allegiance, against the peace of the said lord the now king, his crown and dignity, and also * against the form in the statute in such case *P. 159. made and provided. And the said attorney-general of the said lord the now king, for the said lord the now king, further gives the court here to understand, and to be informed, that afterwards, to wit, on the 14th day of the month of January, in the said 1st year, &c. aforesaid, George, lord Jeffreys, baron of Wem, lord chancellor of England, and for that time steward of England, by virtue of the letters patent of the said lord the king made in the lawful manner, and to the said George lord Jefferys, baron of Wem, then lord chancellor of England, directed the said indictment before him at Westminster, in the county of Middlesex, in the great hall of the pleas, there, on Thursday the 14th day of Jan. in the 1st year of the reign, &c. aforesaid, _Indictment_ caused to come to be determined, &c. and that afterwards, to _removed_ wit, on the said 14th day of January, in the 1st year of the reign, _before the_ &c. aforesaid, at Westminster, in the county of Middlesex, in _peers._ the great hall of the pleas there, before the said George, lord Jeffreys, baron of Wem, lord chancellor of England, and then steward of England, came the said Henry, baron of Delamere, under the custody of Thomas Cheek, esq; then lieutenant of the tower of the said lord the king, of London, by virtue of a writ of the said lord the king, of Habeas Corpus ad subjiciendum, to him directed, brought there to the bar in his proper person, and immediately being demanded of the premisses above charged against him, how he would acquit himself thereof, then said, that he was not guilty thereof, and thereof for good and evil, put himself upon the peers ; In which _Not guilty._ cause it was in such wise proceeded, that the issue aforesaid, so as aforesaid joined, to wit, on the said 14th day of _Taliter_ January, _proceditum._

January, in the 1st year of the reign, &c. aforesaid, at West-minster aforesaid, in the said county of Middlesex, in the great hall of the pelas there, before the said George, lord Jeffreys, baron of Wem, lord chancellor of England, and for that time then steward of England, in the due manner was tried by the peers, upon which trial of the issue aforesaid, so as aforesaid joined, between the said parties, one Thomas Saxon, late of Westminster, in the county of Middlesex, yeoman, was produced witness, in the said cause, on the behalf of the said lord the king, and then and there was sworn upon the Holy Gospel of God, to speak the truth, the whole truth, and nothing but the truth, of, and concerning the said premisses ; and so being sworn, the said Thomas Saxon, not having the fear of God before his eyes, but being moved and seduced by the instigation of the devil, and not regarding the laws of this kingdom of England, nor in any manner fearing the pains in the same contained, on the said 14th day of January, in the 1st year of the reign, aforesaid, before the said George, lord Jeffreys, baron of Wem, lord chancellor of England, and for that time steward of England, at Westminster aforesaid, in the said county of Middlesex, falsely, wilfully and corruptly, by his own proper act and consent, and of his own most wicked mind, upon his said oath did say, depose, swear, and did give in evidence to the peers of the said Henry, baron of Delemere, then and there in the due manner elected to try the said issue, between the said lord the king and the said Henry, baron of Delemere, then and there in the manner and form aforesaid joined, *"That in the beginning of June then last, he the said Thomas Saxon was sent for to Mere,* (meaning the mansion house of the said Henry, baron of Delemere, situate at Mere, in the county of Chester,) *where, when he the said* * *Thomas Saxon came, he was conducted into a lower room, where lord Delemere* (meaning the said Henry, baron of Delemere) *Robert Cotton, knt, and baronet,* (meaning one Robert Cotton of Combermere, in the county of Chester aforesaid, knt. and baronet) *and Mr. Offley,* (meaning one John Crew Offley, of Crew, in the county of Chester aforesaid,) esq; *were present,"* and the said Thomas Saxon then and there, at and upon the trial aforesaid, being interrogated by the said George, lord Jeffreys, baron of Wem, lord chancellor of England, and then for that time steward of England, at what time in the month of July it was when he the said Thomas Saxon was at Mere aforesaid ? He the said Thomas Saxon then and there, to wit, on the said Thursday, the 14th day of January, in the 1st year, &c. aforesaid, at Westminster aforesaid, in the said county of Middlesex, falsely, wilfully, and corruptly did say, depose, swear, answer, and upon his oath aforesaid, further did give in evidence to the said peers, of the said Henry, baron of Delemere, *"That he the said Thomas Saxon could not tell the day, because that he did not set it down in writing, but did believe that it was the 3d or 4th*

day

Defendant produced as a witness.
Oath.

Perjury.
1st Charge.

*P. 160.

day of June." And the said attorney-general of the said lord **td Charge**
the now king, further gives the court here to understand, and
to be informed, that the said Thomas Saxon, then and there
upon the said trial, falsely, unlawfully, wickedly and corruptly did say, depose, swear, and upon his said oath did give in
evidence, to the said peers, of the said Henry, baron of Delemere, " *That the said Henry, baron of Delemere, Robert Cotton, knt.
and baronet, and John Crew Offley, esq; interrogated him the said
Thomas Saxon, whether he the said Thomas Saxon would undertake
to carry a message from the said H. B. of D. R. C. knt. and bart. and
J. C. O. esq; to the duke of Monmouth* (meaning James late duke
of Monmouth, lately attainted for high treason) *which he the
said Thomas Saxon undertook to do, and there received eleven pieces of
gold, called guinea pieces of gold, and five pounds in silver, for his
journey,* (meaning the journey of the said T. S. to the said duke
of Monmouth) *and that he the said T. S. then afterwards, hired a
horse and delivered the message to the duke of Monmouth,* (meaning
the said late duke of Monmouth)," and that the said T. S. then
and there upon the said trial being interrogated by the said
George, lord Jeffreys, baron of Wem, lord chancellor of England, and then steward of England, from whom he the said T.
S. had received the said money, he the said T. S. then and there
falsely, maliciously, wickedly and corruptly did say, depose,
swear, answer, and upon his said oath further did give in evidence to the said peers, of the said Henry, baron of Delemere,
" *That he the said T. S. had received the said money from lord Delemere,*" whereas in truth and in fact, in the beginning of June,
then last past, the said T.S. was not sent for to Mere, and whereas in truth and in fact, the said T. S. was not conducted into a
lower room at Mere ; and whereas in truth and in fact, the said
lord Delemere, R. C. kt. and baronet, and Mr. Offley were not
there present ; and whereas in truth and in fact, the said lord
Delemere, R. C. knt. and bart. and Mr. Offley, did not inter-
rogate the said T. S. whether he the said T. S. would undertake
to carry a message from them to the duke of Monmouth ; and
whereas in truth and in fact, the * said T. S. did not undertake
to do it ; and whereas in truth and in fact the said T. S. never
received eleven pieces of gold called guinea pieces of gold, nor
five pounds in silver, for his journey ; and whereas in truth and
in fact, the said T. S. never received said money from the said
lord Delemere, as the said T. S. by his false and untrue testimony aforesaid, falsely, maliciously, wilfully, and corruptly,
by his own proper act and consent, upon his oath aforesaid,
did say, depose, relate and give in evidence to the peers of the
said Henry, baron of Delemere, at and upon the said trial ;—
And so the said T. S. on the said Thursday the 14th day of
January, in the 1st year of the reign, &c. aforesaid, at Westminster aforesaid, in the said county of Middlesex, before the
said George, lord Jeffreys, baron of Wem, lord chancellor of

Assign-
ments of
perju y.

*P. 161.

Conclusion.

E b   England,

England, and then steward of England, by his own proper act and consent, and of his own most wicked mind, in the manner and form aforesaid, falsely, maliciously, wilfully and corruptly, upon his oath aforesaid, did commit wilful, voluntary, and corrupt perjury, to the great displeasure of Almighty God, in manifest contempt of the laws of this kingdom of England, to the evil and pernicious example of all others in the like case offending, and against the peace of the said lord the now king, his crown and dignity; whereupon the said attorney-general of the said lord the now king, for the said lord the king, prays the consideration of the court here in the premisses, and that

Procefs prayed. due process of law may be awarded against the said T. S. in this behalf, to make him to answer to the said lord the king of, and touching the premisses, &c. And now, to wit, on the Saturday next, after the octave of St. Hilary, in this same term, before the said lord the king, at Westminster, comes the said T. S. in his proper person, under the custody of William Richardson, gent. keeper of the goal of the said lord the king of Newgate, and having heard the information aforesaid, saith, he is not

Not guilty. guilty thereof, and of this puts himself upon the country, and R. S. knt. attorney-general of the said lord the now king, who for the said lord the king in this behalf prosecutes, doth the like, therefore let a jury come thereupon, before the lord the

Venire facias award-ed. king, in the court of the said lord the king, before the king himself, at Westminster, on the Monday next after the morrow of the purification of the blessed Virgin Mary, by whom, &c. the same day is given as well to the said R. S. knt. who prosecutes, &c. as to the said T. S. at which Monday next after the morrow of the purification of the blessed Virgin Mary, before the lord the king, at Westminster come, as well the said R. S. knt. who prosecutes, &c. as the said T. S. in his proper person. And the sheriff returns the names of twelve jurors, of whom

Proclama-tion. none, &c. which jurors being called come, whereupon public proclamation being made here in the court, for the said lord the king, as the custom is, that if there be any person who for the said lord the king would inform the serjeant at law of the said lord the king, or the attorney-general of the said lord the king, or the jury aforesaid, of the matters aforesaid, that he should come forth and should be heard, and thereupon Thomas Jones, esq; one of the council of the said lord the king offered himself to do this, whereupon the court here proceeded to the taking of

Trial at Bar. the said jury, by the said jury now appearing, who being elect-ed, tried, and sworn to speak the truth of the premisses afore-

Verdict guilty. said, say upon their oath that the said T. S. is guilty of the premisses in the information aforesaid mentioned, as the said information above supposes against him, * whereupon all and

P. 162. singular the premisses being seen, and by the court here under-stood, it is considered, that the said T. S. shall stand in and upon the pillory, on Saturday the 13th day of February, in the
court.

court-yard of the palace, at Westminster, between the 10th and 12th hours of the said day, for the space of one hour, with a paper fixed on his head denoting his offence, in large letters, to wit, " *Thomas Saxon convicted upon full evidence for horrid perjury,*" and that the said T. S. shall stand in and upon the pillory at Temple-bar in Fleet-street, on Monday the 15th day of February aforesaid, between the 12th hour and the 2d hour after mid-day of the said day, for the said space, with the said paper fixed upon his head, and that the said T. S. shall be whipt by the common executioner, from the gate of the city of London, called Ludgate, unto Westminster-hall in the county of Middlesex, on Thursday the 16th day of February; and that the said T. S. shall stand in and upon the pillory at Cornhill, nigh to the Royal Exchange there, on Wednesday the 17th day of February, between the 12th hour and the 2d hour after mid-day of the said day, for the space aforesaid, with the said paper fixed on his head, and that the said T. S. shall be whipt by the said common executioner, on Friday the 19th day of Feb. aforesaid, from the gate of the city of London, called Newgate, to the gallows at Tyburn, in the county of Middlesex aforesaid, and that the sheriffs of London and Middlesex shall be aiding and assisting at the several places and times aforesaid, to execute the said judgment, and that the said T. S. pay the lord the king five hundred marks, laid upon him for a fine, for the occasion aforesaid ; and that the said T. S. is committed to the keeper of the goal of Newgate, until that he shall pay the said fine.

Judgment.

The King *against* H. P.

Trinity, 36th Charles II.

Kent,
To wit. } THAT on the 22d day of February, in the year, &c. in the court of the bishop of Rochester, in the county of Kent, before William Trumbell, doctor of laws to the reverend father in Christ, Francis, by divine permission, lord bishop of Rochester, vicar-general in spirituals and official principal lawfully constituted, certain allegations or articles of and concerning the crime of adultery, fornication or incontinency, committed and perpetrated by one G. B. of the parish, &c. in the county, &c. with one J. A. wife of G. A. at the promotion of the said G. A. were

Information for perjury, in depositions, in a cause depending in the Ecclesiastical Court.

exhibited,

exhibited, and that among other things in the 3d, 4th and 5th of the said articles, it was alledged as follows, " (3.) *Likewise we article to you the said G. that on or about the 17th day of June, in the year of our Lord 1682, &c.*" as by the allegation and article aforesaid, relation being thereto had more fully appears: in which cause it was in such manner proceeded between the said parties, that afterwards to wit, on the   day of   and in the year, &c. one H. P. of the parish, &c. and others, &c. among others were produced as witnesses on the behalf of the said G. A. to prove and testify the truth of the articles aforesaid above mentioned, in the said cause exhibited as aforesaid, and then and there were sworn, and each and every of them then and there was * sworn upon the Holy Gospel of God, to say and depose the truth, the whole truth, and nothing but the truth, to the said articles; and the said H. P. and others, &c. so being sworn, the said H. P. then and there before the said W. T. doctor of laws to the reverend father in Christ, Francis, by divine permission, lord bishop of Rochester, vicar-general in spirituals and official principal, lawfully constituted; by his own proper act and consent, and upon his oath aforesaid, falsely, maliciously, wilfully and corruptly did say, and to the said 3d article did depose among other things, " *That this deponent came, &c.*" as by the deposition of the said H. P. to the said 3d article relation being thereto had more fully appears, whereas in truth and in fact, &c. And so the said coroner and attorney of the said lord the king, for the said lord faith, that the said H. P. and others, &c. on the said day and year, &c. at, &c. in the county, &c. before the said W. T. doctor of laws to the reverend father in Christ, Francis, by divine permission, lord bishop of Rochester, vicar-general in spirituals and official principal, lawfully constituted, by their own proper acts and consents, and upon their oaths aforesaid, falsely, maliciously, wilfully and corruptly did commit wilful and corrupt perjury, and each of them by his own proper act and consent, upon his oath aforesaid, falsely, maliciously, wilfully and corruptly did commit wilful and corrupt perjury, &c. And the said coroner and attorney of the said lord the now king further shews, that in the said cause it was in such manner proceeded, that afterwards to wit, on the day and year aforesaid, certain interrogatories in writing, in the due manner were exhibited in the said court, before the said W. T. on the behalf of the said G. B. to the witnesses produced, or to be produced on the part of the said G. A. touching the matter aforesaid abovementioned, among other things to be alledged and articled, of which interrogatories, the tenor of the seventh interrogatory follows in these words, " *Likewise the said H. P. is interrogated, whether did not you on or about the month of January last, in the presence and hearing of Mr. Pordage, &c.*" as by the said interrogatory

relation

relation being thereto had more fully appears; and that the said H. P. then and there, before the said W. T. doctor of laws to the reverend father in Christ, Francis, by divine permission, lord bishop of Rochester, vicar-general in spirituals and official principal, lawfully constituted, was sworn upon the Holy Gospel of God, to answer and depose the truth, the whole truth, and nothing but the truth, to the said interrogatory, and the said H. P. then and there so being sworn, the said H. P. not having the fear of God before his eyes, but being moved and seduced by the instigation of the devil, then and there before the said W. T. doctor of laws, by his own proper act and consent, falsely, maliciously, wilfully and corruptly did say, depose, and to the said seventh interrogatory did negatively answer, (" *never declaring any such thing to the persons, &c.*") as by the deposition, &c. whereas in truth and in fact, &c. And so the said coroner and attorney of the said lord the now king saith, that the said H. P. on the day and year, &c. at, &c. before the said W. T. doctor of laws to the reverend father in Christ, Francis, by divine permission, lord bishop of Rochester, vicar-general in spirituals and official principal, lawfully constituted, by his own proper act and consent, upon his oath aforesaid, did commit wilful and corrupt perjury, * to the great displeasure of Almighty God, against the laws of this kingdom of England, to the evil and pernicious example of all others in the like case offending, and against the peace of the said lord the now king, his crown and dignity, &c. whereupon the said coroner and attorney, &c.

Oath.

Perjury.

Assignment of perjury.

Conclusion.

*P. 164.

The King *against* Hutchinson.

Easter, 36th Charles *the* 2d.

London, } **T**HAT on the day, and in the year, &c. a certain
To wit. } process, containing a citation in writing, concerning a certain decree issued out of the consistorial court of the reverend father in Christ, Henry, by divine permission, lord bishop of London, under the seal of his office directed to all and singular the clerks and curates whomsoever in and throughout his whole diocese of London, wheresoever constituted, by which process reciting that, whereas the reverend father in Christ, Thomas, by divine permission, lord bishop of Lincoln

Information for perjury, in an affidavit in a cause in the spiritual court, concerning the service of a process of that court.

or

or his vicar-general in spirituals, or his lawful surrogate, rightly and duly proceeding, one T. I. of, &c. in the county, &c. and in the diocese of London, administrator of the goods, rights and credits of J. I. late of, &c. and of the diocese of Lincoln aforesaid intestate, which were not administered by S. I. his relict and administratrix of his goods, rights and credits, then also deceased, had oftentimes diligently sought by the mandatary lawfully authorised, to cite him personally to the effect within written, who had nevertheless so absconded, that he could not be personally cited, as it was before him in that behalf alledged, at the petition of the party, John Huffey, of H. &c. uncle to the said S. I. lately deceased, and residuary legatee in the testament or last will of the said S. I. widow deceased, and administrator with the said will annexed of the goods, rights and credits of the said deceased, had decreed that he should be cited and summoned to judgment, at the day, hour and place, and to the effect in the said process underwritten, and in the manner and form in the same within described, because that the said T. I. hath dwelt out of the diocese of Lincoln, and within his diocese of London, so that he could not be cited by his ordinary authority to the effect under written, therefore, had requested Henry, by divine permission, bishop of London, since that the said bishop of London was willing in the aid of justice, to cite by his authority, the said T. J. to the effect underwritten, therefore the said Henry, lord bishop of London, to all and singular the clerks and curates in and throughout the diocese of London, wheresoever constituted, jointly and severally by the process aforesaid, did give in charge, and firmly enjoining did command that they should peremptorily cite or cause to be cited, the said T. J. personally, if he could be so cited, and there was a free access for them so to cite him, otherwise publickly by affixing the presents upon the gates or outward doors of the parochial church of, &c. or of the house of his usual residence, where *P. 165. he dwelt or was accustomed to dwell, the said present * writing being for some time put there, and a true copy of the said process being there left, and by other ways, methods and means, by which that might be lawfully better and more effectually done, so that such citation might most likely come to his knowledge, that he should appear before the said reverend father the lord bishop of London, or his vicar aforesaid, or his surrogate, or some other competent judge in that behalf, in the cathedral church of St. Mary of Lincoln, in the consistorial place there, on the   day of   in the   year, &c. next ensuing, between the eighth and twelfth hours before mid-day, at the usual hours of hearing causes, and doing justice there, to exhibit the letters of administration, as well of the goods, rights and credits of the said S. J. deceased, as

of

of the goods, rights and credits of the said J. J. deceased, by the said S. J. his relict, unadministered to the said T. J. howsoever committed and granted, and to give bond with good and sufficient sureties for the faithful administration of the goods, rights and credits as well of the said S. J. as of the said J. J. deceased, otherwise to shew and propound good and lawful cause if he had, or knew any thing to say for himself, why the said divers letters of administration should not be revoked and quashed, and new letters of administration of the goods, rights and credits as well of the said S. J. lately deceased, as of the said J. J. deceased, unadministered by the said S. J. his relict, to the said J. H. the uncle of the said S. J. lately deceased, and residuary legatee named in the testament or last will of the said S. J. widow deceased, and administrator with the said will annexed in the due form of law should not be respectively committed and granted, and further at the promotion of the said J. H. to do and receive that which was just in that behalf; and the said lord bishop of London, to his said clerks and curates in and throughout his diocese of London aforesaid, by the said process firmly enjoining, did command that they should peremptorily intimate, or should cause to be intimated to the said T. J. that if he at the said day, hours and place, to the effect aforesaid should not appear, or appearing should not shew sufficient cause to the contrary, the said reverend father or his vicar-general in spirituals, or his surrogate, or some other competent judge in that behalf, did intend to proceed, and would proceed to the revocation and quashing of the said divers letters of administration, as well of the goods, rights and credits of the said S. J. lately deceased, as of the goods, rights and credits of the said J. J. deceased, unadministered by the said S. J. and his relict deceased, howsoever granted, and also to the committing and granting of new letters of administration, as well of the goods, rights and credits of the said S. J. deceased, as of the goods, rights and credits of the said J. J. deceased, by the said J. J. widow, unadministered as aforesaid, to the said J. H. the absence or rather the contumacy of the said T. J. in anywise notwithstanding, and what they should do in the premisses, they should duly certify to the said bishop of London, his vicar, or his surrogate, or some other competent judge in that behalf, together with the process aforesaid. And the said coroner and attorney of the said lord the now king, for the said lord the king further gives the court here to understand and to be informed that one W. * H. of, &c. *P. 166 on the   day of   and in the   year, &c. at, &c. in his proper person came before T. E. knt. and doctor of laws to the said reverend father in Christ, Henry, by divine permission, lord bishop of London, then and as yet vicar-general in spirituals, and then official principal lawfully constituted, and then and there of and concerning the serving the process aforesaid,

upon

upon the said T. J. personally, and the delivering to the said T. J. a true copy of the same, did take his corporal oath upon the Holy Gospel of God, before the said T. E. doctor of laws, then being vicar-general in spirituals and official principal, lawfully constituted as aforesaid, [the said T. E. then having full power and authority to administer the oath aforesaid, to the said W. H. in that behalf] and that the said W. H. so being sworn, then and there, not having the fear of God before his eyes, but being moved and seduced by the instigation of the devil, and lightly regarding the laws of this kingdom of England, nor in anywise fearing the penalties in the same contained, then and there to wit, on the said day and year, &c. at, &c. before the said T. E. knt. doctor of laws, vicar-general in spirituals and official principal as aforesaid, of his own most wicked mind, by his own proper act and consent, falsely, maliciously, wickedly, wilfully and corruptly did say, depose, swear, and upon his oath, upon the process aforesaid, then and there did make affidavit in writing, as follows in these English words following to wit, " *This decree* (meaning the process aforesaid) *was personally served upon the within named T. J.* (meaning the said T. J. in the said process as aforesaid named) *in the parish of, &c.*" as by the said oath of the said W. H. in writing remaining, affiled in the office of the register of the said bishop of Lincoln more fully appears ; whereas in truth and in fact the said process nor decree was not personally served upon the said T. J. in the said parish, &c. as the said W. H. in and by his false oath aforesaid, by his own proper act and consent, falsely, maliciously, wilfully and corruptly in the form aforesaid, did say, depose, swear and affirm. And so the said coroner and attorney of the said lord the now king, for the said lord the king faith, that the said W. H. on the said day and year, &c. at, &c. before the said T. E. knt. doctor of laws, then vicar-general in spirituals and official principal as aforesaid, [the said T. E. then having sufficient power and authority to administer the said oath to the said W. H. in that behalf] of his own most wicked mind, by his own proper act and consent, falsely, maliciously, wickedly and corruptly upon his oath aforesaid, in the manner and form aforesaid, did commit wilful and corrupt perjury, to the great displeasure of Almighty God, to the evil example of all others in the like case offending, and against the peace, &c. whereupon, &c.

Oath.

Assignments of perjury.

Conclusion.

---

*The King *against* Hawkins.*   *P. 167.

To wit. } TO be informed, that John Hawkins, of, &c. gent. on the 28th day of May, in the 27th year of the reign of the lord Charles the 2d, &c. late king, &c. by virtue of a writ of dedimus poteftatem, iffuing out of the court of the Chancery of the faid lord the king, to him and to others directed, bearing date the 22d day of May, in the 27th year, &c. aforefaid, to receive the acknowledgment of a certain fine of John Thompfon, upon a writ of covenant depending before the juftices of the faid lord the late king of the bench, between Richard Winterbottom and Elizabeth his wife, complainants, and the faid John Thompfon, deforciant, of one meffuage, one barn, one ftable, one garden, one orchard and common of pafture for all cattle, with the appurtenances in I. otherwife E. in the county of H. to levy a fine thereof between them, before the faid juftices of the faid bench, according to the law and cuftom of England, and plainly and openly to return the acknowledgment of the faid fine, before the faid juftices of the faid bench under their feals, that the faid fine might be levied between the faid parties of the faid premiffes, before the faid juftices, according to the law and cuftom aforefaid, and that the faid J. H. on the   day of, &c. in the 27th year of the reign of the faid Charles the 2d, late king, &c. aforefaid, at Serjeant's-inn, in the parifh of St. Dunftan in the weft, London, before H. W. knight, then one of the juftices of the faid lord the king of the bench, being fworn upon the Holy Gofpel of God, to fpeak the truth, and nothing but the truth, in and concerning the premiffes, he the faid J. H. then and there by his own proper act and confent falfely, wilfully and corruptly did fay, fwear, and affirm upon his oath, " *That the faid fine was executed in the due manner;*"— whereas in truth and in fact, the faid J. T. always from the time of his nativity was an idiot, and not capable to levy the faid fine, and the faid fine was not executed in the due manner. And fo the faid coroner and attorney of the faid lord the now king, for the faid lord the king faith, that the faid J. H. on the faid   day of   in the 27th year of the reign of the

Information againft a commiffioner named in a writ of dedimus poteftatem, for taking a fine, for perjury in an affidavit of the due caption of the fine, whereas the perfon who acknowledged it was an idiot.

Oath.

Perjury.

Affignment of perjury.

   faid

said lord Charles the 2d, late king of England, &c. at Serjeant's-inn, in Chancery-lane, in the said parish of St. Dunstan in the west, London aforesaid, before the said H. W. knt. then one of the justices of the said lord the late king of the bench, (the said H. W. then having sufficient power and authority to administer the said oath to the said J. H.) falsely, maliciously, wilfully and corruptly did commit wilful and corrupt perjury, to the great displeasure of Almighty God, in contempt of the laws of this kingdom of England, to the evil and pernicious example of all others, &c. and against the peace, &c. whereupon the said coroner and attorney, &c.

2. For

* 2. *For Subornation of Perjury.* *P. 163.

The King *against* Margerum.

Hilary, 3d. James II.

Surrey, } THAT John Margerum, late of, &c. in the coun-
To wit, } ty, &c. being a person of evil name and fame,
and of dishonest conversation, and not having the fear of God
before his eyes, but being moved and seduced by the devil, and
devising, and falsely, unlawfully, unjustly, fraudulently, and deceitfully intending to bring and draw one Francis White into
great anxiety of mind, and into hatred, contempt and scandal
with the said lord the king, and with the people of this kingdom of England ; and also to cause the said Francis White to
be accused, impleaded, indicted and convicted of the speaking,
publishing and uttering of divers scandalous and opprobrious
words by him the said Francis White, against George, lord Jeffreys, baron of Wem, lord chancellor of England, and late
chief justice, assigned to hold pleas before the king himself,
and also that the said J. M. to fulfil, perfect, and bring to effect
his said devices, practices, and intentions, on the day and year,
&c. with force and arms, &c. at, &c. in the county, &c. falsely, wickedly and diabolically did solicit, labour and endeavour
to procure, suborn, and cause one R. A. and others, for divers
great sums of money, by him the said J. M. to the said R. A.
then and there promised, contrary to the truth, falsely, unlawfully and diabolically to swear, and upon his oath to give in
evidence, that the said Francis White did say, publish and utter, these false, feigned, scandalous, opprobrious, and defamatory English words following, of the said George, lord Jeffreys,
baron of Wem, lord chancellor of England, and late chief
justice of the said lord the king, assigned to hold pleas before
the king himself, to wit, " *God damn Jeffreys,* (meaning the
said George, lord Jeffreys, now lord chancellor of England,

Information
for endea-
vouring to
suborn one to
swearfalsely
that T. W.
had spoken
reflecting
words of
lord chan-
cellor Jef-
freys.

 and

and then chief justice of the said lord the king, assigned to hold pleas before the king himself) *he* (again meaning the said George, lord Jeffreys, &c.) *is a rogue for serving Oates so,* (meaning one T. O. who in the said court of the said lord the king, before the king himself, in the due manner was indicted and convicted of certain horrible and wilful perjuries, and had stood in and upon the pillory, in several places in and about the city of London and county of Middlesex, and had been whipped from Newgate to the gallows at Tyburn.") And the coroner and attorney of the said lord the king, for the said lord the king further gives the court here to understand and to be informed, that the said J. M. to induce and cause the said R. A. to swear, and upon his oath to give in evidence, and prove against the said F. W. the scandalous * and opprobrious words aforementioned, then and there falsely, unlawfully, wickedly and diabolically did promise to give the said R. A. the sum of 20l. to the great damage, disquiet and disgrace of the said F. W. to the evil example, &c. and against the peace of our said lord the king his crown and dignity, &c.

21 Court.

**P. 169.*

The King *against* Tasborough, and others.

To wit. } HERETOFORE to wit, on the day, &c. last past, before the lord the king at Westminster, by the oath of twelve jurors, good and lawful men of the said county, sworn and charged to enquire for the said lord the king, and for the body of the said county it is presented, that whereas one Thomas White otherwise Whitebread, clerk, John Fenwick, clerk, William Harcourt otherwise Harrison, clerk, John Cavan, clerk, Anthony Turner, clerk, and Jacob Cocker, false traitors, against our most serene lord Charles the 2d, by the grace of God of England, &c. on the 13th day of June, in the 31st year of the reign of the said lord the now king, at the delivery of the goal of the said lord the now king of Newgate, held by adjournment for the said county, at Justice-hall, in the old Baily, in the suburbs of the city of London, before the justices then and there assigned to deliver said goal, stood indicted for compassing the death and final destruction of the said lord the king, and for other high treasons in the same indictment specified, and afterwards at the said session, the said T. W. otherwise &c. J. F. W. H. otherwise &c. J. C. and A. T. by a jury of the county, then and there

there, in the due manner, were thereof tried and convicted, and by the judgment of the court, then and there in the due manner were attainted, as appears by the record thereof, to the jurors aforesaid shewn in evidence; and whereas also one Richard Langhorn, esquire, afterwards to wit, at the delivery of the goal of the said lord the king, held by adjournment for the city of London, at Justice-hall aforesaid, before the justices then and there assigned to deliver the goal aforesaid, on the 14th day of June, in the 31st year, &c. aforesaid, in the lawful manner stood indicted for compassing the death and final destruction of the said lord the king, and for other high treasons in the same indictment specified, and afterwards thereupon at the said session was tried by a jury of the country, and then and there by the judgment of the court was attainted, as appears by the record thereof, to the jurors aforesaid, in like manner shewn in evidence; and whereas also one Stephen Dugdale, upon the several trials of the said indictments was produced and sworn as a witness on the behalf of the said lord the now king, and then and there in the lawful manner did give material evidence against the said T. W. W. H. J. G. A. T. and R. L. to prove them guilty of the matter in the said indictment specified; one John Tasburgh, late of, &c. gent. otherwise called John Tisburgh, of, &c. gent. and Anne Price, of, &c. spinster, well knowing the said premisses, and being persons diabolically affected towards our most serene lord Charles the 2d, now of England, &c. king, &c. their * supreme and natural lord, and devising and as much as in them lay, intending to disturb the peace and the public tranquility of this kingdom of England, and to prevent and stifle the further discovery of the said treasons, and as much as in them lay to elude the due course of justice, and to cause and procure that it might be believed, that the persons so as aforesaid attainted, were not attainted justly, they the said J. T. and A. P. before the trial of the said W. H. to wit, on the said 13th day of June, in the 31st year, &c. at the parish of St. Andrew Holborn, in the county of Middlesex, falsely, unlawfully, and corruptly, and against the duty of their allegiance did solicit, suborn and endeavour to persuade, and each of them then and there did solicit, suborn and endeavour to persuade the said Stephen Dugdale, that he the said Stephen Dugdale was not a witness, and that he could not give evidence against the said W. H. otherwise, &c. upon the trial of the said W. H. otherwise, &c. for the treasons aforesaid, and that the said J. T. and A. P. after the said trial to wit, on the 14th day of October, in the 31st year, &c. aforesaid, at the parish of St. Andrew Holborn, in the county of Middlesex, falsely, unlawfully, unjustly, advisedly, and against the duty of their allegiance, did solicit, suborn and endeavour to persuade, and

promising him rewards to sign it.

P. 170.

1st Count, persuading the witness that he could not give evidence.

2d Count, promising the witness, after the trial, sums of money to retract his evidence

each and to with-

draw him-
felf into
parts un-
known.

each of them then and there falfely, unlawfully, unjuftly, advifedly, did folicit, fuborn and endeavour to perfuade the faid
S. D. that he the faid Stephen Dugdale fhould retract and deny
the whole evidence, which he the faid S. D. had given as aforefaid, againft the faid traitors, they the faid J. T. and A. P. then
and there falfely, unlawfully, unjuftly, advifedly and corruptly
promifing, and each of them promifing to the faid S. D. great
fums of money and goods if he the faid S. D. would retract and
deny the whole evidence given by him the faid S. D. againft the
faid traitors as aforefaid, and would withdraw and abfent himfelf the faid S. D. to places unknown, and beyond the feas.
And that the faid J. T. and A. P. to fulfil and perfect their
moft wicked devices, practices and intentions aforefaid, afterwards to wit, on the 14th day of October, in the 31ft year, &c.

3d Count,
producing
to the wit-
nefs a paper
purporting
to be a re-
traction of
his evidence

aforefaid, at the parifh of St. Andrew Holborn, in the faid
county of Middlefex, falfely, unlawfully, unjuftly, advifedly
and corruptly, againft the duty of their allegiance did produce
and fhow, and each of them then and there did fhew to the faid
S. D. a certain note in writing, the tenor of which note follows
in thefe Englifh words following, to wit, "*Being touched with a
remorfe of confcience and hearty forrow for the great ill I did in
coming in a witnefs againft the catholicks, and there fpeaking things
which in my own confcience I knew to be very far from the truth, I
think myfelf bound in duty both to God and man, and for the fafety
of my own foul, to make a true declaration how I was drawn into
this wicked action, but being very well fatisfied that I fhall create
myfelf very many powerful enemies, on this account, I have retired
myfelf to a place of fafety, where I will with my own hand difcover
the great wrong that hath been done the catholicks, and I hope it may
gain belief; and likewife I proteft before Almighty God, that I have
no motive to induce me to this confeffion, but a true * repentance for
the mifchiefs I have done, and hope Almighty God will forgive me."

*P.171.
4th Count,
Endeavour-
ing to per-
fuade him
to fign it.

And that the faid J. T. and A. P. afterwards to wit, on the
faid 14th day of October, in the 31ft year, &c. aforefaid, at
the parifh of St. Andrew Holborn aforefaid, in the county of
Middlefex aforefaid, falfely, unlawfully, unjuftly, advifedly,
corruptly, and againft the duty of their allegiance, did folicit
and endeavour to perfuade, and each of them then and there
did folicit and endeavour to perfuade the faid S. D. to fign and
fubfcribe the faid note in writing, fo as aforefaid produced and
fhewn to the faid S. D. and then and there, falfely, unlawfully,
unjuftly, advifedly and corruptly did promife, and each of them
then and there did promife that if he the faid S. D. would fign
and fubfcribe the faid note in writing, that then he the faid
S. D. fhould have and receive a great fum of money, to the
evil and pernicious example of all others in the like cafe offending, and againft the peace, &c. &c.

The

The King and the Duke of Buckingham *against* Hickley, and others.

Hilary, 32d Charles II.   *Roll* 46.

To wit, } **THAT** Maurice Hickley, late of the parish of St. Martin in the fields, in the county of Middlesex, gent. otherwise called Maurice Higgins, late of the parish aforesaid, in the county aforesaid, gent. Robert Smith, of, &c. gent. otherwise called Robert Jones, of, &c. gent. John Hayley, of the parish aforesaid, in the county aforesaid, gent. Thomas Curtis, of the parish aforesaid, in the county aforesaid, gent. Thomas Blood, of the parish of St. Margaret, Westminster, in the said county, gent. Edward Christian, late of the parish of St. Martin in the fields, in the county of Middlesex, esquire, Arthur O'Brien, of the parish of St. Martin in the fields, in the county of Middlesex, gent. Philip Le Mar, late of the parish of St. Martin in the fields, in the county of Middlesex, gent. Jane Bradly, late of the parish of St. Martin in the fields, in the county of Middlesex, widow, on the 17th day of March, in the 30th year, &c. with force and arms, &c. at the parish of St. Martin in the fields, in the county of Middlesex, falsely, unlawfully, unjustly, wickedly, diabolically and corruptly, by unlawful ways and means, among themselves did practise, conspire, intend and devise the most noble George, Duke of Buckingham, then and as yet one of the peers and lords of this kingdom of England, not only to despoil and deprive of his honour, esteem and reputation, but also to take away and destroy the life and estate of the said Duke, and to cause the said George, Duke of Buckingham, to be taken, arrested and condemned to death, for the detestable crime and offence of sodomy and buggery, by him the said George, Duke of Buckingham supposed to be committed with one Sarah Harwood, and with divers other persons, against the order of nature, and also for the felonious killing or transporting into parts beyond the seas of the said S. H. to stifle and take away her evidence of and concerning the crimes and offences

Indictment for subornation of perjury, in endeavouring to persuade persons to swear against the Duke of Buckingham, that he was guilty of buggery.

*P.172. fences of sodomy and buggery aforesaid, * and that the said
M. H. otherwise, &c. R. S. otherwise, &c. J. H. T. C. T. B.
E. C. A. O. P. L. M. and J. B. to fulfil and perfect their most
wicked devices, conspiracies and diabolical intentions aforesaid, afterwards and at divers days and times between the said
17th day of March, in the 30th year, &c. aforesaid, and the
day of the taking of this inquisition, at the parish, &c. falsely,
unlawfully, unjustly, maliciously, wickedly and diabolically
did solicit, labour and endeavour to persuade, procure, suborn
and cause one Philemon Coddan and Samuel Ryther, then or
late servants of the said G. D. of B. for divers great sums of
money, promotions and preferments, against all truth, falsely,
unlawfully, unjustly, wickedly and diabolically to swear, and
to say in evidence upon their oaths, upon the trial of the said
G. duke of B. for the crimes and offences aforesaid, that the
said crimes and offences aforementioned, were committed by
the said G. duke of B. And to induce and cause them the said
P. C. and S. R. to swear, and to say in evidence, and to prove
against him the said G. duke of B. the crimes and offences
aforesaid, they the said M. H. otherwise, &c. R. S. otherwise,
&c. J. H. T. C. T. B. E. C. A. O. P. L. M. and J. B.
within the time aforesaid, to wit, between the said 17th day of
March, in the 30th year, &c. aforesaid, and the day of the
taking of this inquisition, at the said parish of St. Martin in
the fields, in the said county of Middlesex, them the said. P. C.
and S. R. with wine, entertainments, and with other allurements, unlawfully, unjustly, falsely, corruptly and diabolically, in prosecution of their conspiracies aforesaid, did compass and lay hold of, and then and there to wit, within the said
time, in the parish, &c. aforesaid, falsely, unlawfully, unjustly,
wickedly, diabolically, and in prosecution of their said conspiracies did expend divers great sums of money upon the said
P. C. and S. R. in the whole amounting to the sum of 150l.
and during their entertainments, and drinking of wine, and
allurements, as well as otherwise then and there to wit, within
the time aforesaid, in the parish and county aforesaid, unlawfully, unjustly and corruptly, and in prosecution of their said
conspiracies, divers great advantages and promotions, to the
said P. C. and S. R. did promise, and each and every of them
did promise, if they the said P. C. and S. R. in the manner and
form aforesaid, would swear and prove the crimes and offences
aforesaid, to be perpetrated by him the said G. duke of B.

2d Count. And the jurors aforesaid, upon their oath aforesaid, further say
and present that the said M. H. otherwise, &c. R. S. otherwise, &c. J. H. T. C. T. B. F. C. A. O. P. L. M. and J. B.
afterwards to wit, between the said 17th day of March, in the
30th year, &c. aforesaid, and the taking of this inquisition, at
the parish of St. Martin in the fields, &c. falsely, unlawfully,
unjustly,

unjuſtly, corruptly, diabolically and in proſecution of their ſaid conſpiracies, did give, put and pay into the hands of the ſaid **P. C.** divers ſums of money, in the whole amounting to the ſum of 40l. of the lawful money of England, for and towards the maintenance and incitement of the ſaid **P. C.** to do, compaſs and perfect their moſt wicked, unlawful and diabolical devices, practiſes and intentions aforeſaid, and that the ſaid **M. H.** otherwiſe, &c. **R. S.** otherwiſe, &c. **J. H. T. C. T. B. E. C. A. O. P. L'M.** and **J. B.** afterwards to wit, within the time aforeſaid, in the pariſh, &c. aforeſaid, falſely, unlawfully, unjuſtly, wickedly, corruptly and diabolically in the proſecution of their conſpiracies aforeſaid, upon themſelves did aſſume, and to the ſaid **P. C.** faithfully did promiſe, that he the ſaid **P. C.** ſhould have the friendſhip and reſpect of * certain peers, and of men of great power and rank, and alſo that he ſhould have a place or office in and about the buſineſs *P. 173. of the cuſtoms of the ſaid lord the now king, called the place or office of a land-waiter, of the yearly value of 20cl. and 40l. in money, and a certain maintenance during life, if he the ſaid **P. C.** would ſwear and ſay in evidence that the crimes and offences aforeſaid, in the manner and form aforeſaid, were perpetrated by the ſaid **G.** duke of **B.** And the jury aforeſaid 3d Count. upon their oath aforeſaid, further ſay and preſent, that the ſaid **M. H.** otherwiſe, &c. **R. S.** otherwiſe, &c. **J. H. T. C. T. B. E. C. A. O. P. L'M.** and **J. B.** afterwards to wit, within the time aforeſaid; to wit, between the ſaid 17th day of March, in the 30th year, &c. aforeſaid, and the day of the taking of this inquiſition, at the pariſh, &c. falſely, unlawfully, unjuſtly, corruptly and diabolically, in proſecution of their ſaid conſpiracies, did give, depoſit and pay into the hands of the ſaid **S. R.** divers other ſums of money, in the whole amounting to 50l. for and towards the maintenance and incitement of the ſaid **S. R.** to do and compaſs their unlawful and moſt wicked devices aforeſaid, and that the ſaid **M. H.** otherwiſe, &c. **R. S.** otherwiſe, &c. **J. H. T. C. T. B. E. C. A. O. P. L'M.** and **J. B.** afterwards to wit, within the time aforeſaid, to wit, between the ſaid 17th day of March, in the 30th year, &c. aforeſaid, and the day of the taking of this inquiſition, at the pariſh of St. Martin in the fields, in the ſaid county of Middleſex, falſely, unlawfully, unjuſtly, corruptly and diabolically, and in proſecution of their ſaid conſpiracies upon themſelves did aſſume, &c. and to the ſaid **S. R.** did faithfully promiſe, that he the ſaid **S. R.** ſhould have the friendſhip of certain peers, and of men of great eſtate and degree, and alſo ſhould have a place or office in and about the buſineſs of the cuſtoms of the ſaid lord the now king, and alſo ſhould have money to redeem his eſtate, being conveyed in mortgage by him the ſaid **S. R.** for above the ſum of 300l. and alſo 300l. more in money numbered, if he the ſaid **S. R.** in the manner and form aforeſaid,

·Dd

ſaid,

said, would swear and say in evidence against him the said G. duke of B. that the crimes and offences aforesaid were committed by him the said G. duke of B. And the jurors aforesaid upon their oath aforesaid, further say that the said M. H. R. S. J. H. T. B. E. C. A. O. P. L'M. and J. B. afterwards to wit, within the time aforesaid, to wit, between the said 17th day of March, in the 30th year aforesaid, and the day of the taking of this inquisition, at the parish, &c. aforesaid, falsely, unlawfully, unjustly, wickedly, corruptly, diabolically, and in prosecution of the said conspiracies, and in order to fix and secure them the said P. C. and R. S. to perform and execute their malicious devices, practises and conspiracies aforesaid, did make, compose and write, and did cause to be made, composed and written, a certain false and scandalous writing in paper, the tenor of which writing, follows in these English words and figures following to wit, " *Whereas Samuel Ryther and Philip Geddam, gent. in St. Martin's parish in the fields, do hereby confess and declare that Sarah Harwood, of the city of London, gentlewoman, did confess before us, that the lord duke of Buckingham was, with his privy members as far in both her private parts as he could go, with forcible entrance, stopping her breath, and that the said lord duke of Buckingham, hath since conveyed the said Sarah Harwood out of the way, by which means the king lost his evidence, and do further * declare, that since that time the said duke did order the said Sarah to be murdered, and since that time is murdered or sold beyond sea, and do further declare that the said duke hath committed said sin of sodomy with several more, which we are ready to prove when we are required as the king's evidence, witness our hands, this 12th day of January, 1679-80.*" And although all and singular the matters in the said writing contained, were and as yet are altogether false and scandalous, and against all truth, nevertheless the said M. H. &c. afterwards to wit, within the said time to wit, between the said 17th day of March, in the 30th year, &c. aforesaid, and the taking of this inquisition, at the parish, &c. aforesaid, falsely, unlawfully, unjustly, wickedly, corruptly and diabolically, and in prosecution of their said conspiracies against the said G. duke of B. his life, estate and honour, then and there the said writing in the said paper, to the said S. R. did produce, shew and present, and each and every of them then and there, falsely, unlawfully, unjustly, wickedly, corruptly and diabolically, in prosecution of their conspiracies aforesaid, did produce, shew and present the said note to the said S. R. and then and there falsely, unlawfully, wickedly, corruptly and diabolically in prosecution of their conspiracies aforesaid, a certain purse of gold, in which were then contained three hundred pieces of gold of the value of 300l. to the said S. R. did present, and to the said S. R. did promise to give, and each and every of them then and there did promise to give if he the said S. R. would sign and subscribe the

said

said writing with his name and proper hand writing, which to do the said S. K. then and there entirely did refuse, which device, conspiracy, subornation and unlawful, and diabolical practise of the said M. H. otherwise, &c. R. S. &c. J. H. T. C. T. B. E. C. A. O. P. L'M. and J. B. are to the great danger of the life, and to the destruction of the said G. duke of B. to the manifest perversion of the laws of this kingdom of England, to the evil example, &c. and against the peace, &c. &c.

The King *against* Hilton *and* Browne.

Middlesex, } **T**HE jurors, &c. that after the 10th day of
To wit. } May, in the year of our Lord 1673, to wit, on the 22d day of August, in the 2d year of the reign of our lord James the 2d, the now king, &c. in the mansion-house of one Susannah Herne, widow, situate in the parish of St. Michael, Queen-hithe, London, a certain unlawful conventicle was held, where were five persons present, every of them being above the age of 16 years, and natural subjects of this kingdom of England, over and above those of the family of the said Susannah Herne, under colour of the exercise of religion, in another manner than according to the liturgy and practise of the church of England, against the form and effect of the statute, in such cause thereupon lately made and provided. And that George Hilton, late of, &c. and John Brown, late of, &c. being men of evil name, fame and conversation, well knowing that one Mary Parker, wife of T. Parker, of the parish, &c. was not present at the said conventicle, * nor could upon her oath depose any information upon her knowledge of the said conventicle; and devising and intending to procure the said Mary Parker to commit wilful and corrupt perjury, afterwards and within three months, after the conventicle aforesaid, so as aforesaid had, to wit. on the 24th day of August, in the 2d year, &c. aforesaid, at the parish of St. Giles, without Cripplegate, in the said county of Middlesex aforesaid, with force and arms, &c. falsely, maliciously, wickedly and unlawfully did move and incite the said M. P. by corrupt and wicked persuasion to commit and perpetrate wilful and corrupt perjury, and then and there falsely, maliciously and unlawfully did persuade, incite, suborn and counsel the said M. P. to go before one of the justices of the said lord the king, assigned to preserve the peace within the city of London, and to make oath before the said justice, of the truth of the existence of the said conventicle, and further to persuade and procure the said M. P. to make the said false oath, they the said

* P. 175.

Indictment for subornation of perjury.

D d 2 G. H.

G. H. and J. B. then and there did say and inform the said M. P. that the said M. P. to prove the said conventicle, might swear by the maiden name of the said M. P being Mary Winston, and that then she the said Mary would not be discovered; and further to procure the said Mary to commit the said perjury, they the said G. and J. then and there informed, and for the truth affirmed, that upon the proof and conviction of the said conventicles, thirty pounds of the lawful money of England, would be levied upon the said Susannah Herne, the mistress of the said house where the said conventicle was held, and that ten pounds thereof would be divided among the informers of the said conventicle, to wit, among the said G. H. J. B. and the said Mary, to the great damage and disquiet of the said Mary, to the evil example, &c. and against the peace, &c.

The defendants were tried upon this indictment, at Hicks's-hall, and found guilty, and judgment for fine and pillory was given against them, whereupon a writ of error was brought, and judgment reversed in B. R. for want of the words, prohorum & legalium hominum, *in the caption of the indictment; the case is reported* 3 Mod. 122.

The King *against* Brooks.

Trinity, 36th Charles II.

Information for embracery, for persuading one who *P. 176. was summoned as a juror, to appear and give his verdict in favour of the defendant in the issue, and to influence the rest of the jury to at, &c. do the like.

County of Worcester, To wit.

THAT Anthony Brooks, of the parish, &c. on the day and year, &c. then knowing that a certain jury of the said county of W. was impanelled and returned to try the said issue, joined in the court of the said lord the king of the common bench, * at Westminster, in the county of Middlesex, between P. S. plaintiff, and R. F. defendant, in a plea of trespass upon the case; and then knowing that a trial was to be had upon the said issue, on the said   day of   and in the year aforesaid, before, &c. then justices of the said lord the king, assigned to take assizes for the county of Worcester aforesaid, the said Anthony Brooks, then being a common embracer of jurors, and devising, and wickedly and unlawfully intending to hinder the due and lawful trial of the said issue, by the jurors aforesaid impanelled and returned to try the said issue, on the said day and year, &c. then at, &c. in the county, &c. unlawfully, wickedly and unjustly, on behalf of the said R. F. defendant in the said cause, did solicit and persuade one B. S. of, &c. one of the jurors of the

said

said jury, impanelled and returned for the trial of the said issue, at the trial aforesaid, upon the jury aforesaid, to appear and attend in favour of the said R. F. (the said Anthony Brooks then well knowing that the said B. S. was one of the jurors returned and impanelled to try the said issue) and then and there did say and utter to the said B. S. one of the jurors aforesaid, divers words and discourses by way of commendation, on behalf of the said R. F. the defendant, and then and there did say and utter to the said B. S. divers words and discourses, by way of dispraise of the said P. S. the plaintiff; and that the said Anthony Brooks, then and there unlawfully and corruptly, did move and desire the said B. S. to solicit and persuade the other jurors impanelled and returned to try the said issue, to give a verdict for the said R. F. the defendant in the said cause, And that the jurors of the said jury, sworn for the trial of the said issue, by reason of the speaking of the said words and discourses by way of commendation, on the behalf of the said R. F. the defendant, did give their verdict for the said R. F. the defendant, in great contempt of the said lord the king and of his laws, to the manifest perversion and destruction of justice, to the great damage and injury of the said P. S. to the evil example, &c. and against the peace, &c.

Indictments for maintenance of Suits.

The King *against* Langrish.

Indictment for maintaining a defendant in a suit in Chancery, by furnishing money to counsel, agents, &c.

***P. 177.**

To wit. } THAT whereas in the term of St. Michael, in the year of our Lord, 1655, one William Walker, of Charter-house, Heydon, in the county of Somerset, esquire, did exhibit his bill of complaint in the high court of Chancery, the said court then being held at Westminster, in the county of Middlesex, against Theodore Langrish, Joyse his wife, and Robert May and others, and among other things in and by the said bill did pray remedy and relief, of and concerning a certain statute of the penalty of 2800l. in and by the said bill supposed to be before that time acknowledged by one Clement Walker, esquire, deceased, the * father of the said William Walker, to one Christopher May, deceased, upon which statute it was by the said bill alledged, that the said Joyse, as the administratrix of one Robert May, deceased, the father of the said Joyse had claimed and demanded the sum of 600l. although the said sum of 600l. was fully satisfied and paid, as by the bill aforesaid, affiled in the said high court of Chancery more fully appears ; and whereas also the said Theodore Langrish, and Joyse his wife, in the said court of Chancery, held at Westminster aforesaid, in the said county of Middlesex, did put in their answers to the said bill, and in and by their said answers did deny that they or either of them had received any part of the said 600l. as by the said answers of the said T. and J. his wife, affiled in the said court of Chancery more fully appears. And whereas also the said cause between the said parties in the said high court of Chancery did depend, undetermined from the said term of St. Michael, in the year of our Lord 1655, until the term of St. Michael, in the 17th year of the reign of our lord Charles the 2d, &c. And whereas also the said Theodore Langrish, on the 1st day of May, in the year of Lord 1660, at Westminster aforesaid died, one Thomas Langrish, late of London, &c. disregarding the laws and statutes of this kingdom of England, nor in any manner fearing the penalties in the same contained, on the 3d day of June,

June, in the 17th year, &c. aforesaid, and at divers other days and times, as well before as after, (the said suit in the said court of Chancery being undismissed and undetermined) at London aforesaid, to wit, in the parish of St. Dunstan in the west, in the ward of Farringdon without London aforesaid, and at divers other places within the city of London aforesaid, the said suit between the said parties, on behalf of the said Joyse Langrishe, against the said William Walker, unlawfully and unjustly did maintain, and then and there, and on the said other days and times as well before as after, (the said suit between the parties aforesaid, remaining undismissed and undetermined in the said court of Chancery) divers sums of money, of the proper money of the said T. L. in and for the maintenance of the said suit, on behalf of the said J. L. against the said W. W. to divers serjeants at law, apprentices of the law, attorneys, clerks, solicitors, and to other officers belonging to the law, unlawfully, unjustly, and for the sake of vexation, did expend, pay and deliver, to the manifest prejudice of justice, to the evil example, &c. and against the peace, &c. and also against the form of the statute in such case made and provided.

The King *against* Price.

To wit. } THAT one Lyson Price, late of the parish of Wanriddan, in the county of Glamorgan, on the 10th day of April, in the 20th year, &c. and for the space of one whole year then next following, a certain plea depending in the court of the said lord the king of his Exchequer, before the barons of the said Exchequer, at Westminster, in the county of Middlesex, between one Charles Llewellyn, plaintiff, and one David Jenkins, defendant, of a plea of trespass and ejectment of a * farm of one hundred acres of land, fifty acres of meadow, sixty acres of pasture, and sixty acres of furze and brush-wood, with the appurtenances in W. aforesaid, in the said county of Glamorgan, on behalf of the said Daniel Jenkins, at Westminster aforesaid, unlawfully did maintain; in contempt of the said lord the now king, and of his laws, to the great damage of the said C. L. to the evil and pernicious example, &c. and against the form of divers statutes, in such case made and provided, and also against the peace

Information for the maintenance of a suit in the Exchequer and another in the Chancery. *" drawn by S.aunders."* *P. 178.

peace of the said lord the now king, his crown and dignity.

2d Count. And the said Thomas Fanshaw, knt. cororer and attorney of our said lord the now king, in the court of the said lord the king, before the king himself, who for the said lord the king in this behalf prosecutes, further gives the court here to understand and to be informed, that the said Lyson Price afterwards to wit, on the   day of   in the year, &c. a certain suit by English bill, depending in the said court of Chancery of the said lord the now king, at Westmirster, in the county of Middlesex, between the said D. Jenkins and one W. Jenkins, plaintiffs, and one Edward Lloyd, defendant, of and concerning the title of the said tenements, on the behalf of them the said D. J. and W. J. at Westminster aforesaid, in like manner unlawfully did maintain, in contempt of the said lord the now king, and of his laws, to the great damage of the said E. L. to the evil and pernicious example of all others in the like case offending, and against the form of the statute in such case lately made and provided, and also against the peace of the said lord the now king, his crown and dignity, &c. whereupon, &c.

" Edmund Saunders."

Indictments for Riots, Routs and unlawful Assemblies.

The King *against* Sherley, *and others.*

Easter, 34th Charles *the* 2d.

Middlesex,
To wit. } **T**HAT Thomas Sherley, late of the parish of St. Clement Danes, in the county of Middlesex, gent. and others, &c. with divers other persons unknown, disturbers of the peace of the said lord the now king, on the 22d day of April, in the 34th year, &c. with force and arms, &c. riotously, routously and unlawfully, at the parish, &c. in the county, &c. did assemble, collect and gather themselves together, to disturb the peace of the said lord the now king, and so being assembled, collected and gathered together, then and there with force and arms, &c. riotously, routously and unlawfully, the mansion-house of one Dame Elizabeth Long, widow, situate in the parish and county aforesaid, did break and enter, and then and there with force and arms, &c. riotously, routously and unlawfully the door of the chamber of the said Dame Elizabeth Long, widow, did break; and then and there with force and arms, &c. riotously, routously and unlawfully into the chamber of the said D. E. L. widow, with drawn swords did enter, and did make an entry; and her the said Dame E. Long, did put in great peril of her life, and other outrages to the said Elizabeth Long, and to one Jane Coats then and there did, and that the said Edward Sherley, then and there by the suggestion and incitement of the said T. S. and others, &c. and in their presence and hearing, and also in the hearing of divers liege subjects of the said lord the now king, then and there present, maliciously, opprobriously, and in a threatening manner did say, assert, publish, and with a loud voice declare of, to and concerning the said Dame Elizabeth Long, as follows in these English words following, to wit, " *Damn me,* (meaning himself the said E. S.) *you* (meaning the said Dame Elizabeth Long) *are a bitch, you* (meaning the said Dame Elizabeth Long) *are an ugly old witch, you* (again meaning the said Dame Elizabeth Long) *look like a witch, I* (meaning himself the said E. S.)

Information against several persons breaking and entering the dwelling house of lady Long, and breaking open her chamber door, and there giving abusive language.

*P. 179.

believe

believe you (meaning the said Dame Elizabeth Long) *are one, and that you* (again meaning the said Dame Elizabeth Long) *can ride on a stick up the chimney, you* (meaning the said Dame Elizabeth Long, and one Jane Coats, spinster, sister to the said Dame Elizabeth Long, then in like manner present) *are a couple of old bawds, here is a guinea for you,* (meaning the said Dame Elizabeth Long, and the said Jane Coats) *help me* (meaning himself the said E. S.) *to a whore, I* (again meaning himself the said E. S.) *am sure you* (meaning the said Dame Elizabeth Long, and the said Jane Coats) *can do it."* To the great terror, disquiet and discomposure of the said Dame E. Long and the same Jane Coats, to the evil example of all others in the like case offending, and against the peace of the said lord the now king, his crown and dignity, &c. whereupon, &c.

The King *against* Wakeman, *and others.*

Trinity, 35th Charles II. *Roll* 4.

<table>
<tr><td>

Information against several persons, for taking upon themselves without legal authority to be justices of the peace for a borough, and in a riotous manner, holding sessions of the peace for the said borough.

*P. 180.

</td><td>

To wit,} **T**HAT the borough of Barnstaple, on the 23d day of April, in the 35th year, &c. and long before, was and yet is, an antient borough incorporate, by the name of the mayor, aldermen and burgesses of the borough and parish of Barnstaple, in the county of D. and that William Wakeman, of B. aforesaid, in the said county gentleman, Richard Salisbury of B. aforesaid, in the said county gentleman, and John Stephens, otherwise Gregory, of B. aforesaid, in the said county, gent. falsely, unlawfully, and maliciously conspiring, devising and designing among themselves, to disturb and subvert the good, lawful and settled rule and government of the borough and parish aforesaid, and also, to usurp and assume to themselves, the rule and authority of the said borough and parish aforesaid, and also to have and exercise the power and authority of justices to preserve the peace of the said lord the king within the borough and parish aforesaid, and also to hear and determine divers trespasses and other misdeeds perpetrated within the borough and parish aforesaid, they the said **W. W. R. S.** and **J. S.** otherwise **G.** on the said 23d of April in the 35th *year, &c. aforesaid, with force and arms, &c. at the borough and parish aforesaid, without any commission, warrant or lawful authority, given by the said lord the king or by his predecessors, did usurp, take upon themselves and execute, and each and every of them then and there did usurp, take upon himself, and

</td></tr>
</table>

execute

execute the power and jurisdiction of a justice, to preserve the peace within the borough and parish aforesaid, and then and there with force and arms, &c. unlawfully, riotously, routously and turbulently did assemble and gather themselves together, to disturb the peace of the said lord the now king, and so being assembled and gathered together, a certain court of the session of the peace for the borough and parish aforesaid, without any warrant or lawful authority, unlawfully, riotously, routously and turbulently, then and there did hold, and as the court of session of the peace for the borough and parish aforesaid, then and there did exercise; and one Charles Standish before that time bound by recognisance to appear at the next session of the peace for the borough and parish aforesaid, then and there from the said recognisance did discharge and entirely release, in contempt of the said lord the king, and of his laws, to the evil and pernicious example of all others in the like case offending, and against the peace of the said lord the now king, his crown and dignity, &c. whereupon, &c.

The King *against* W. M.

Easter, 1st James the 2d.

Stafford,
To wit. THAT whereas on the day and year, &c. at the borough of Newcastle under the line, in the county of Stafford, W. C. esquire, at that time mayor of the said borough, and the aldermen and common-council of the said borough, were assembled in the Guildhall of the said borough, there to do the business of the said borough, nevertheless one W. M. of, &c. together with divers other malefactors and disturbers of the peace of the said lord the now king, to the number of five hundred persons, whose names are as yet unknown to the attorney general of the said lord the now king, well knowing the premisses, but being evil-disposed persons, and devising and intending to disquiet and disturb the peace of the said lord the now king, and to hinder and obstruct the said mayor, aldermen and common-council of the said borough, there to do their business as aforesaid, with force and arms, &c. at, &c. unlawfully, riotously, routously and tumultuously did assemble and gather themselves together, to disturb the peace of the said lord the now king, and they as aforesaid then and there, with force and arms, &c. unlawfully, riotously, routously and tumultuously being assembled and gathered together, the

said

said Guildhall there, being the guildhall and freehold of the said mayor, aldermen, bailiffs and burgeffes of Newcaftle under the line aforefaid, then and there with force and arms, &c. unlawfully, riotoufly, routoufly and tumultuoufly did break and enter; and for the fpace of one hour, by making a great noife, riot, difturbance, clamour and tumult, did fo difturb and hinder the mayor, aldermen and common-council aforefaid,

***P. 181.** then and there being, and then doing, and tranfacting * certain bufinefs of and concerning the faid borough, that they the faid mayor, aldermen and common-council for the fpace aforefaid, could not proceed to go through their bufinefs as aforefaid, in contempt of the faid lord the now king, and of his laws, to the manifeft difturbance and violation of the peace of the faid lord the now king, to the evil example, &c.

The King *againft* Wilts.

Eafter, the 1ft *James* II.

Indictment or riotoufly breaking into a dwelling houfe, on pretence of an execution.

To wit } **T**HAT Thomas Wilts, &c. and five other malefactors, to the jurors aforefaid unknown, on the day and year, &c. did devife, and among themfelves wickedly did confpire and intend falfely, unlawfully, wickedly and deceitfully to deprive, deceive and defraud one Elizabeth Palmer, widow, of her goods and chattels, and her the faid Elizabeth Palmer, from her manfion-houfe, with force and arms, &c. fuddenly and forcibly to certain places unknown, againft the will, and without the confent of the faid E. P. to carry away, and her the faid E. P. in the faid places unknown, falfely, unlawfully, unjuftly, and againft the will and without the confent of the faid E. P. to imprifon, the faid T. W. and the five other malefactors, to the jurors aforefaid unknown, for the better performance and execution of the faid evil intentions of the faid T. W. &c. and of the faid five malefactors, to the jurors aforefaid unknown, fo as aforefaid among themfelves before had, afterwards to wit, on the faid day and year, &c. at, &c. as rioters, routours, and difturbers of the peace of the faid lord the now king, with force and arms, &c. at, &c. unlawfully, riotoufly, routoufly did affemble and gather themfelves together, to difturb the peace of the faid lord the king, and fo then and there being affembled and gathered together, the faid Thomas Wilts, and the faid five malefactors, to the jurors aforefaid unknown, afterwards to wit, on the faid day and year, &c. at, &c. the manfion-houfe of her the faid E. P. there fituate, then and there unlawfully, riotoufly,

oufly,

oufly and routoufly did break and enter, and the door of the chamber of the faid E. P. in which the faid E. P. then in the faid manfion-houfe was, (the faid door of the faid chamber then being fhut and locked) they the faid five perfons to the jurors aforefaid unknown, then and there unlawfully, riotoufly and routoufly did endeavour and attempt to open, under pretence that they the faid malefactors to the jurors aforefaid unknown, then and there had an execution againft the faid E. P. for 10,000l. and that the faid five malefactors, to the jurors aforefaid unknown, afterwards to wit, on the day and year, &c. at, &c. in and upon one F. H. fpinfter, the fervant of the faid E. P. then and there being in the faid manfion-houfe, and then and there being in the peace of God, and of the faid lord the king, with a certain drawn fword, then and there riotoufly and routoufly did make an affault, and her the faid F. H. then and there in great peril of her life, unlawfully, riotoufly and routoufly did put, and other outrages to the faid E. P. and F. H. unlawfully, riotoufly and routoufly did, to the great damage, &c. and againft the peace, &c.

---

* The King *againft* Pilkington, *and others.*   *P. 182.

Trinity, 34th, and *Hilary*, 34th and 35th Charles II. *Roll.*

London,
To wit. } THAT on the 24th day of June, in the 34th year of the reign of our lord Charles the 2d, the now king, &c. at the Guildhall of the city of London, a certain court of affembly of the citizens and freemen of the city of London, commonly called a common hall, by John Moore, knight, then and as yet mayor of the city of London, fummoned and called before the faid John Moore, knt. mayor of the city of London aforefaid, in the due manner was held, as well for the due election of fheriffs of the faid city, for the execution of the office of Sheriffs of the faid city, for one whole year next enfuing, after the eve of the feaft of St. Michael the Archangel, then and as yet next to come, as for the election of divers other officers of the faid city, and that then and there in the faid court, it was begun to take poll of the electors then and there prefent, for the manifeftation of the election of the perfons to ferve in the office of fheriffs of the faid city, for the year aforefaid. And that the faid John Moore, knight, mayor of the faid city, afterwards to wit, on the

Information for a riot at an election of fheriffs, for the city of London.

faid

said 24th day of June, in the 34th year, &c. aforesaid, at the Guildhall of the city of London aforesaid, in the parish of St. Michael Bassishaw, London aforesaid, in the lawful manner did make and cause to be made, proclamation for the adjournment of the court, so as aforesaid held; and then and there the said John Moore, knt. mayor of the said city, in the lawful manner the said court did adjourn to the Tuesday next ensuing, then to be held at the Guildhall of the city of London aforesaid; and then and there after the adjournment so as aforesaid made, he the said John Moore, knt. mayor of the city, did make and cause to be made, public proclamation for the departure of all persons there assembled for the occasion aforesaid. And the said attorney-general of the said lord the now king, for the said lord the king further gives the court here to understand and to be informed, that Thomas Pilkington, late of London, esquire, and Samuel Shute, late of London, esquire, (then sheriffs of the city of London aforesaid) and Henry Cornish, late of London, esquire, Ford, lord Grey, of Warke, Thomas Gould, late of London, knight, John Shorter, late of London, knight, Thomas Player, late of London, knight, William Guliton, late of London, knight, Slingsby Bethel, late of London, esquire, —— Nelthorpe, late of London, esquire, John Ayliffe, late of London, esquire, John Ellis, late of London, esquire, Francis Jenks, late of London, mercer, Robert Barker, late of London, gent. John Deagle, late of London, clothier, Richard Freeman, late of London, cheesemonger, Benjamin Smith, late of London, gent. Richard Goodenough, late of London, gent. R. Hay, late of London, merchant, Lucy Knightly, late of London, gent. John Wickham, late of London, gent. Samuel Swynnock, late of London, merchant, Joshua Brooks, late of London, gent. Joseph *P. 183. Jekyll, late of London, * gent. Dorman Newman, late of L. gent. T. Rawlinson, late of L. gent. T. Carpenter, late of L. gent. T. Charleton, late of L. gent. John Jekyll, the younger, late of L. gent. Benjamin Alsop, late of L. gent. M. Meriton, late of L. gent. Charles Bateman, late of L. gent. John Trenchard, late of L. esquire, Simon Miller, late of L. gent. Jervas Ryfield, late of L. gent. W. Feachy, late of L. gent. and Richard Farringdon, late of L. esquire, well-knowing the premisses aforesaid, but being evil-disposed persons, and devising and intending to disquiet, molest and disturb the peace of said lord the now king, and the public tranquility of this kingdom of England, they the said T. Pilkington, S. Shute, under colour of their office of sheriffs of London aforesaid, and the said Henry Cornish, Ford, lord Grey, T. Gould, knt. J. Shorter, knt. &c. afterwards, and after the said adjournment to wit, on the said 24th day of June, in the 34th year, &c. aforesaid, at the parish of St. Michael Bassishaw, London aforesaid, in the Guildhall aforesaid, there

with

with force and arms, &c. riotoully, routoully, unlawfully and feditioully with many other evil-difpofed perfons, and difturbers of the peace of the faid lord the now king, to the number of one thoufand perfons, to the attorney-general of the faid lord the now king as yet unknown, did affemble, unite and gather themfelves together, to difturb the peace of the faid lord the now king, and fo being affembled, united and gathered together, then and there with force and arms, &c. riotoully, routoully and unlawfully in and upon the faid John Moore, kt. mayor of the faid city, then and there being in the peace of God, and of our faid lord the king, did make an affault and affray, and him the faid John Moore, knt. then and there did ftrike, wound and ill-treat, fo that of his life it was greatly defpaired; and after the adjournment aforefaid, and the proclamation fo as aforefaid made, by the faid John Moore, knt. mayor of the faid city, they the faid T. Pilkington and Samuel Shute then and there under colour of their office of fheriffs of the city of London aforefaid, and the faid Henry Cornifh, Ford, lord Grey, T. Gould, knt. and J. Shorter, knt. &c. with divers other perfons to the faid attorney-general of the faid lord the now king as yet unknown, them the faid T. P. and S. S. unlawfully and feditioully aiding and affifting, with force and arms, riotoully, routoully and unlawfully there did continue to take the poll of the perfons fo then and there unlawfully affembled, as if and as though the faid perfons were lawfully affembled, for the election of fheriffs of the faid city; and that the faid T. Pilkington, S. Shute, H. Cornifh, Ford, lord Grey, T. Gold, knt. J. Shorter, knt. &c. then and there unlawfully, tumultuoully and feditioully did affirm, and each and every of them did affirm and fay, and with a loud voice to the faid evil-difpofed perfons did affirm, that the faid John Moore, knt. mayor of the city of London aforefaid, unjuftly and unlawfully had affumed upon himfelf liberty to adjourn the faid court, which to him the faid John Moore did not appertain; and that the faid T. Pilkington, S. Shute, H. Cornifh, Ford, lord Grey, T. Gould, knt. and John Shorter, knt. &c. then and there the evil difpofed perfons as aforefaid unlawfully affembled and gathered together, with force and arms, &c. riotoully, routoully, unlawfully and feditioully for the fpace of three hours did excite, * move, perfuade and pro-   ***P. 184.** cure to difturb the peace of the faid lord the king, and to commit the faid riot; and then and there for the whole time aforefaid, in the Guildhall of London aforefaid, in the parifh and ward aforefaid, with force and arms, &c. riotoully, routoully, unlawfully, tumultuoully and feditioully did make and ftir up, and caufe to be made, great difturbance, clamour, riot, and terrible and unufual noife, in contempt of the faid lord the now king, and of his laws, to the manifeft difturbance and violation of his peace, to the great danger of provoking and

moving,

moving of tumult, and the sheadling of much blood there, to the great terror, disquiet and fear of all the liege subjects of the said lord the now king, to the evil example of all others in the like case offending, and against the peace of the said lord the now king his crown and dignity, &c. Whereupon the said attorney-general of the said lord the now king, prays the confideration of the court here in the premisses, and that due procefs of law may be awarded against them the said T. Pilkington, S. Shute, Ford, lord Grey, T. Gould, knt. and J. Shorter, knt. &c. in this behalf, to make them to answer to the said lord the king, of and touching the premisses, &c. Whereupon the sheriffs of the city of London are commanded that they cause them to come to answer, &c. and now to wit, on the Wednesday next after three weeks, from the day of the Holy Trinity, before the lord the king at Westminster, come the said T. Pilkington, J. Shute and Richard Goodenough, by Benedict Brown, their attorney, and having heard the information aforesaid, they severally say that they are not guilty thereof, and of this put themselves severally upon the country; and the said Robert Sawyer, knt. attorney-general of the said lord the now king, who for the lord the king in this behalf profecutes, doth the like, &c. and thereupon the said attorney-general of the said lord the now king, faith, and to the court here shews, that T. Pilkington and S. Shute, efqrs. two of the defendants aforesaid, at present are sheriffs of the city of London aforesaid, nevertheless he the said attorney-general of the said lord the now king, prays the writ of venire faciatis the said lord the king, to be directed to the said sheriffs of London, that they cause to come before the king, twelve, &c. to try the issues aforesaid, between the said lord the king, and the said parties above in the form aforesaid joined, and because the said defendants do not gainsay this, therefore the sheriffs of the city of London, are commanded that they cause to come before the said lord the king, from the day of St. Michael in three weeks, wheresoever, &c. twelve, &c. by whom, &c. and who, &c. to recognize, &c. because as well, &c. the same day is given as well to the said Robert Sawyer, knt. who profecutes as to the said T. P. S. S. and R. G. At which three weeks of St. Michael, before the said lord the king, come as well the said Robert Sawyer, knt. who profecutes, &c. as the said T. P. S. S. and R. G. by their attorney aforesaid, and the sheriffs of London have not sent the writ thereupon, therefore as before let a jury come thereupon, before the said lord the king, at the octave of St. Hilary, wheresoever, &c. by whom, &c. and who, &c. to recognize, because as well, &c. the same day is given as well to the said Robert Sawyer, knt. who profecutes as to the said T. P. S. S. and R. G. at which octave of St. Hilary, before the said lord the king at Westminster, come as well the said Robert Sawyer, knt. who profecutes, &c. as the

said

said T. P. S. S. and R. G. by their attorney aforesaid, and
Ford, lord Grey, H. Cornish, T. Gold, knt. J. Shorter, knt.
and T. Player, * knt. &c. in like manner come by B. B. their * P. 185.
attorney, and having heard the information aforesaid, severally
say that they are not guilty thereof, and of this in like manner
severally put themselves upon the country; and the said Robert
Sawyer, knt. attorney-general of the said lord the now king,
who for the said lord the now king in this behalf prosecutes,
doth the like, and therefore as before, let a jury come the e- Venire
upon before the lord the king, at the octave of the purification awarded.
of the blessed Virgin Mary, wheresoever, &c. by whom, &c.
who neither, &c. to recognize, &c. because as well, &c. the
same day is given as well to the said Robert Sawyer, knt. who
prosecutes, &c. as to the said T. P. S. S. R. G. Ford, lord
Grey, &c. at which octave of the purification of the blessed
Virgin Mary, come as well the said R. Sawyer, knt. who prosecutes, &c. as the said T. P. S. S. R. G. Ford, lord Grey,
H. C. T. G. knt. &c. by their attorney aforesaid; and the Return of
sheriffs of the city of London, return the names of twelve the veniro.
jurors, of whom none, &c. therefore the sheriffs are commanded, that they distrain them by all their lands, &c. and that of Distringas
the issues, &c. and that he may have their bodies before the awarded.
said lord the king, from the day of Easter in five weeks, wheresoever, &c. or before the beloved and faithful of the lord the
king, Edward Saunders, knt. chief justice of the said lord the
king, assigned to hold pleas before the king himself, if he shall
first come on Tuesday next after one month of Easter, at the
Guildhall of the city of London, according to the form of
the statute, &c. for the default of jurors, &c. therefore let
the sheriffs have their bodies, &c. to recognize in the form
aforesaid, &c. the same day is given as well to the said Robert
Sawyer, knt. who prosecutes, &c. as to the said T. P. S. S.
R. G. Ford, lord Grey, H. C. T. G. knt. &c. at which five
weeks of Easter in this term, before the lord the king, at
Westminster, come as well the said R. S. knt. who prosecutes,
&c. as the said T. P. S. S. R. G. F. lord Grey, H. C. &c.
by their attorney aforesaid, and the said chief justice before
whom, &c. hath sent here his record before him had in these
words. Afterwards, at the day and place within contained before Postea.
the within named Edward Saunders, knt. the chief justice of
the said lord the king within written, Edward Watts, gent.
being associated to him by the form of the statute, come as
well the within named Robert Sawyer, knt. attorney-general
of the said lord the now king, who prosecutes, &c. as the said
T. P. S. S. R. G. F. lord G. H. C. &c. by their attorney
within written, and the jurors of the jury whereof mention
is within made being called, come and are sworn upon that
jury. And thereupon public proclamation for our lord the Proclama-
king being made as is the custom, that if there was any one tion.
F f who

who would inform the said chief justice of the said lord the king, or the serjeant at law of the said lord the king, or the attorney-general of the said lord the king, or the jury aforesaid, concerning the matters within contained, that he should come forth and should be heard, and thereupon George Jeffreys, knight and baronet, on behalf of the said lord the king, offered himself to do this, whereupon it was proceeded by the court here to the taking of the jury aforesaid, by the said jury now appearing, who being elected, tried and sworn to speak the truth concerning the matters within contained, say upon their oath aforesaid, that the said T. Gould, knt. J. Brooks, W. Miller, T. Charleton, D. Newman, J. Jekyl, the younger, B. Alsop, M. Meriton, J. Trenchard and J. Byfield, are not guilty, nor is any of them guilty of the premisses in the * information in the said record mentioned, as within by pleading they have alledged. And the jury aforesaid upon their oath aforesaid further say, that the said Thomas Pilkington, S. Shute, Ford, lord Grey, T. Player, knt. S. Bethel, esquire, F. Jenks, J. Deagle, R. Freeman, R. Goodenough, R. Hay, J. Wickham, S. Symmock and J. Jekyl, the elder, are guilty, and each and every of them is guilty of the premisses in the information within written mentioned, as by the said information within, against them is supposed, therefore, &c.

Verdict.

***P. 186.**

The trial of the defendants upon this information, before the lord chief justice Saunders, is in the State Trials, vol. 3. fol. 78.—And Sir Bartholomew Shower in the 2d vol. of his reports, fol. 262. says " That there was a challenge to the array, because no knight was returned in the pannel, as then ought to have been, (the lord Grey being a peer of the realm) and that the chief justice was of opinion that it was a good cause of challenge, but it appears by the trial that the challenge was over-ruled, for that it could not be pleaded at nisi prius.

The King *against* Strode.

Michaelmas, 32d Charles II.

Middlesex, } **T**HAT one Essex Strode, late of the parish of
To wit. St. Margaret, Westminster, in the county of Middlesex, esquire, Ferdinand Burleigh, late of the parish aforesaid, in the county aforesaid, gent. (and several others particularly

particularly named) together with divers other malefactors to the said attorney-general of the said lord the king, as yet unknown, on the 8th day of July, in the 32d year of the reign of the lord Charles the 2d, by the grace of God, of England, &c. king, &c. at the parish of St. Martin in the fields, in the county of Middlesex aforesaid, with force and arms, &c. unlawfully, riotously and routously did assemble, unite and gather themselves together, to disturb the peace of the said lord the now king, and then and there so being assembled and collected, with force and arms, &c. riotously, routously and unlawfully the doors of the mansion-house of the most noble Lewis Joseph Turnett, count of Portengue in Piedmont, in parts beyond the seas, envoy extraordinary sent from his royal highness the Duke of Savoy, to our said lord Charles the 2d, of England, &c. king defender of the faith, &c. did break down, and the said house, the doors being so broken down, with force and arms, &c. unlawfully, riotously and routously did break and enter, and the goods and houshold furniture of the said Lewis Joseph Turnett, count of Portengue, being envoy as aforesaid, then and there found, with force and arms, &c. riotously, routously and unlawfully did take and carry away, and him the said Lewis Joseph Turnett, count of P. being envoy as aforesaid, for a long time to wit, from the 8th * day of July, in the 32d * P. 187, year, &c. aforesaid, until the 11th day of the same month of July, with force and arms, &c. unlawfully, riotously and routously from the possession of the said house did expel and keep out; and other wrongs to him did, to the evil example of all others in the like case offending, and against the peace of the said lord the now king his crown and dignity, &c. whereupon, &c.

There was a trial at bar on this information, and the defendant would have justified the entering the house, and taking the goods there as the goods of one Doughty, who being convicted of murder, had thereby forfeited them to the dean and chapter of Westminster, (the defendant Strode being high-bailiff of Westminster) but the court over ruled the evidence as insufficient, and held this to be a riot. This case is reported, 2 Shower 149.

Indictments for Assaults and Woundings.

The King *against* Goftwick, *and others.*

Trinity, 3d. James II.

<table>
<tr><td valign="top" width="180">

Informat'on
for confpir-
ing to beat
and wound
a man, and
for tharpur-
pofe fending
for him un-
der a feign-
ed name, to
come to a
tavern, and
way-laying
him, and
in his com-
ing, griev-
oufly beat-
ing and
wounding
him.

</td><td>

London, ⎫ **T**HAT William Goftwick, late of Willington,
To wit. ⎭ in the county of Bedford, knight and baronet,
and others, &c. being and each and every of them being per-
fons of evil name, fame and of wicked difpofition, and devi-
fing, and malicioufly intending, and among themfelves con-
fpiring, compaffing and devifing one S. V. gent. by way-laying
to beat, wound and ill-treat, on the 1ft day of Sept. in the
year, &c. at, &c. the fooner to fulfil, perfect and bring to
effect their moft wicked intentions, compaffings and devices
aforefaid; they the M. B. and J. R. by the direction and confent
of the faid W. G. and others, and in profecution of their faid
confpiracy, did fend under a feigned name for the faid S. V.
to a certain tavern, known by the name of the Green Dragon
tavern, fituate in Fleet-ftreet, London, in the parifh of, &c.
and him the faid S. V. then and there did way-lay; and that
the faid M. B. and others, &c. afterwards to wit, on the day
and year, &c. with force and arms, &c. at the parifh, &c. by
the procurement and incitement of the faid W. G. and G. C.
they the faid M. B. and others, &c. then and there by way-lay-
ing, in and upon the faid S. V. in the peace of God and of
the faid lord the king, then and there being, with force and
arms, &c. did make an affault and affray; and him the faid S.
then and there, with force and arms, &c. moft grievoufly and
dangeroufly did beat, wound and ill-treat, fo that of his life
it was greatly defpaired; and the faid coroner and attorney of
the faid lord the now king, further gives the court here to un-
derftand and to be informed, that the faid S. V. of the beating,
wounding and ill-treating aforefaid, from the day and year
aforefaid, until the day of the exhibition of this information,

</td></tr>
</table>

P. 188. at the * parifh, &c. did languifh, and languifhing did live, and

was

was in great peril of his life, and that the said W. G. and others, &c. other wrongs to him the said S. V. then and there with force and arms did, to the great damage of the said S. V. and against the peace of the said lord the now king, &c. &c.

The King *against* the Earl of Devonshire.

Easter, 3d *James* II.

Middlesex,
To wit, } **T**HAT William Earl of Devonshire, late of the parish of St. Martin in the fields, in the county of Middlesex, on the 24th day of April, in the 3d year of the reign of our lord James the 2d, by the grace of God of England, &c. king, defender of the faith, &c. with force and arms, &c. at the city of Westminster, in the county of Middlesex, within the palace of the said lord the king there, to wit, within the court of the said lord the king, commonly called Whitehall, (the said lord the king then and there in his said palace, in his royal person being, continuing and abiding) one Thomas Colepeppar, esquire, in the peace of God, and of the said lord the now king, then and there being did provoke and challenge to fight, with him the said William Earl of Devonshire, with intention to kill and murder the said Thomas Colepeppar. And that the said William, Earl of Devonshire, afterwards to wit, on the said day and year, &c. aforesaid, at the city of Westminster aforesaid, in the said county of Middlesex, within the said palace of the said lord the king, to wit, within the said court, commonly called Whitehall, (the said lord the king then and there in the said palace, in his royal person as aforesaid, being, continuing and abiding) with force and arms, &c. in and upon the said Thomas Colepeppar, in the peace of God and of the said lord the now king, then and there in the said palace being did make an assault, and him the said Thomas Colepeppar then and there, with force and arms, &c. maliciously did strike, beat and ill-treat, so that of his life it was greatly despaired, and other wrongs to the said Thomas Colepeppar, then and there, with force and arms, &c. did, to the great damage of the said Thomas Colepeppar, to the manifest contempt of the said lord the now king, and of his laws, and against the peace of the said lord the now king, his crown and dignity, &c.

Information for challenging Mr. Colepeppar in the king's palace, and assaulting and wounding him.

And

Indictments for Affaults and Woundings.

And now to wit, on the Monday next after the morrow of
the Afcenfion of our Lord, in this fame term before the lord
the king, at Weftminfter, come as well Thomas Powis, knt.
folicitor-general of the faid lord the now king, who for the
faid lord the king in this behalf profecutes, in his proper perfon, as the faid William, Earl of Devonfhire in his proper
perfon, and the faid William, Earl of Devonfhire faith, that
that he on the 19th day of May, in the 1ft year of the reign of
the lord the now king, and long before, and continually from
thence hitherto afterwards, was and as yet is Earl of Devonfhire, one of the nobles, lords and peers of this kingdom of
England, * and that at the prefent parliament of the faid lord
the now king, begun and held at Weftminfter, in the county of
Middlefex, on the faid 19th day of May, in the 1ft year of the
reign of the faid lord the now king aforefaid, and there by feveral prorogations continued until the 28th day of April, in
the 3d year of the reign of the faid lord the now king, and
then at Weftminfter aforefaid affembled, and from that day
further prorogued to the 22d day of November then next
coming, the faid Earl by the fummons of the faid lord the
now king, did come, attend and continue as one of the peers
of this kingdom; and the faid Earl further faith, that according to the law and cuftom of parliament, ufed and approved
from the time whereof the memory of man is not to the contrary, all peers of this kingdom of England coming to the
parliament of the lord the king, by the fummons of the faid
king, by any court inferior to the faid court of parliament,
during the time of the fitting of fuch parliament, or within
the ufual time of privilege of fuch parliament next before or
next after any prorogation of fuch parliament made, by reafon
or pretence of any trefpafs, contempt, mifbehaviour, or other
caufe or matter whatfoever, (treafon, felony, or refufal to find
fecurity for good behaviour towards the faid lord the king, and
all his people only excepted) ought not nor have been accuftomed for the whole time aforefaid, to be arrefted, imprifoned, troubled or difquieted, or to any fuch trefpafs, contempt,
mifbehaviour, or other caufe or matter whatfoever (except as
aforefaid) be compelled to anfwer, and this he is ready to verify, wherefore, becaufe the faid information was exhibited
againft him the faid Earl, within the ufual time of the privilege of the faid parliament, to wit, within forty days next after
the laft prorogation of this prefent parliament which are not
yet expired, the faid Earl prays judgment if the court here will
or ought to hold cognizance of the faid plea, now within the
ufual time of the privilege of the faid parliament, &c.

And the faid Thomas Powis, knt. folicitor-general of the
faid lord the now king, who for the faid lord the king in this
behalf

behalf profecutes, for the faid lord the king faith, that the faid plea by the faid William, Earl of Devonfhire, in the manner and form aforefaid above pleaded, and the matter in the fame contained are not fufficient in law to preclude the court of the faid lord the king here from proceeding upon the faid information, and this he is ready to verify as the court here fhall confider, wherefore he prays judgment, and that the faid William Earl of Devonfhire may further anfwer to the faid information, &c.

And the faid William, Earl of Devonfhire faith, that the plea aforefaid, by him the faid William, Earl of Devonfhire, in the manner and form aforefaid pleaded, and the matter in the fame contained, are good and fufficient in law to preclude the court of the faid lord the king here, from proceeding upon the faid information, which plea and the matter in the fame contained, the faid William, Earl of Devonfhire is ready to verify and prove as the court here fhall confider, wherefore as before, he prays judgment, if the court of the lord the king, here, upon the faid information will any further proceed; and thereupon all and fingular the premiffes being read and heard becaufe that it feems to the court here, that the faid plea of the faid Earl of Devonfhire, in the manner and form aforefaid above pleaded, and the matter * in the fame plea contained, are not fufficient in law to preclude the court of the faid lord the now king here, from proceeding upon the faid information, therefore it is faid to the faid William, Earl of Devonfhire, that he the faid William, Earl of Devonfhire do further anfwer to the faid information.

Joinder.

Judgment.

*P. 190.

Refpondeat oufter.

On the 15th of May 1689, the Houfe of Lords declared, " *That the court of King's-Bench in over-ruling the Earl of Devonfhire's plea of Privilege of Parliament, and forcing him to plead over in chief, it being within the ufual time of privilege, did thereby commit a manifeft breach of privilege, &c,*" *Vide* Rapin's Hiftory of England, vol. 13. page 245.

The King *againft* Colepeppar.

The palace of the lord the king, at Weftminfter, in the county of Middlefex, to wit. BE it remembered, that at the general feffion to hear and determine all treafons, mifprifions of treafon, murders, killings, bloodfheds, and other malicious ftrikings by reafon whereof blood fhould be fhed againft the peace of the faid lord the king,

Indictment againft Mr. Colepeppar, at the feffions held fortheking's houfhold, within by virtue of

Indictments for Assaults and Woundings.

the statute of H. 8.) for assaulting, striking and wounding the earl of Devonshire, where y his blood was shed.

within the houshold of the said lord the king, held for the said lord the king, within the palace of the said lord the king, at Westminster, in the county of Middlesex, to wit, on Monday the 20th day of July, in the 1st year of the reign of our lord James, by the grace of God, of England, &c. king, defender of the faith, &c. before James, duke of Ormond, steward of the houshold of the said lord the king, according to the form of the statute in such case made and provided, by the oath of Michael Arnold, Richard Dalton, &c. inferior officers of the houshold of the said lord the king, whose names are inrolled in the rolls of the counting house of the lord the king's houshold, then and there sworn and charged to enquire for the said lord the king, according to the form of the statute in this behalf, within the said palace, it is presented as follows, to wit, the palace of the lord the king, at Westminster, in the county of Middlesex, to wit, the jurors for the lord the king upon their oath present, that T. Colepepper, late of, &c. esquire, on the 9th day of July, in the 1st year of the reign of our lord James, by the grace of God, of England, &c. king, &c. with force and arms, &c. within the palace of the said lord the king at Westminster, in the county of Middlesex, (the said lord the king, then and there, in his said palace, in his royal person being, continuing and abiding) in and upon the most noble William, earl of Devonshire, then and within the said palace being, did make an assault, and him the said William, earl of Devonshire, then and within the said palace, maliciously did strike and wound, by reason of which the blood of the said William, earl of Devonshire, then within the said palace was shed; to the great damage of the said William, earl of Devonshire, to the manifest contempt of the said lord the now king, and of his laws, against the peace of the said lord the now king his crown and dignity, and also against the form of the statute in such case made and provided, &c. &c.

* *Indictments for forcible Entries, and* *P. 191. *Procejs thereon.*

The King *against* Hayton.

Surrey, } BE it remembered, that on the 19th day of the
To wit. } month of July, in the 34th year of the reign
of our lord Charles the 2d, by the grace of God, of England, &c. king, &c. one Peter Effington of the parish of St. Bottolph Aldgate, citizen and goldsmith of London, on the behalf of Moses Winkworth, citizen and glover of London, complained to me, William Pyers, esq. one of the justices of the said lord the king, assigned to preserve the peace in the said county; that Robert Hayton, in the parish of Wansworth, in the county of Surry aforesaid, and certain others unknown, disturbers of the peace of the said lord the king, into a certain mill with the appurtenances of the said Moses Winkworth, at Wimbleton Mills, in the parish of Wimbleton, in the said county of Surrey, with a strong hand did enter, and upon the peaceable possession of the said M. W. thereof, with a strong hand into the said mill did enter, and with an armed power, as yet do hold, and thereupon prayed that remedy should be given by me to the said M. W. in that behalf, which complaints and petitions being heard, I the said W. P. immediately in my own person approached to the said mill, and in the said mill I then found the said R. Hayton, and certain others, to wit, A. R. F. R. and J. C. holding the said mill, with force and arms, and with a strong hand, and with an armed power to wit, with staves, and swords, and bludgeons, and with other arms, offensive and defensive, against the form of the statute in such case made and provided, and thereupon I the said W. P. then and there did arrest the said R. H. A. R. F. B. and J. C. and have caused them to be brought to the next gaol of the said lord the king, at the borough of Southwark, in the said county of Surrey, as being convicted of the said with-holding by a strong hand, by my view and record, there to remain until they shall pay to the said lord the king, the fines for their said trespasses. Given at the bridge-house within the borough of Southwark, under my hand and seal, the day and year aforesaid first written.

Record of a force upon view of a justice of the peace.

By virtue of the statutes of the 15th R. ch. 2. c. 2. 8 H. 6. c. 9. 31 El. c. 11 and 21 J. 1. 6. 15.

G 2   The

The King *against* Hampson.

Information for a forcible entry on the tenant for years.
*P. 192.

To wit. THAT Dennis Hampson, late of London, esquire, and others, on the 14th day of June, in the 23d year of the reign of our lord Charles the 2d, by the grace of God, of England, &c. king, &c. with force and * arms, at the parish of Taplowe aforesaid, in the said county of Bucks, unlawfully, riotously and routously did assemble and gather themselves together, to disturb the peace of the said lord the now king, and they so as aforesaid, then and there with force and arms, &c. being riotously and unlawfully assembled and gathered together, into one messuage and 400 acres of land, with the appurtenances situate, lying and being in the said parish of Taplowe, in the said county, and then being in the peaceable possession of one Richard King, the younger, for a term of divers years then to come, with force and arms aforesaid, riotously, routously, unlawfully and unjustly, and with a strong hand did enter and make an entry, and him the said R. K. the younger, (his term aforesaid not then nor as yet being expired) thereout, then and there with force and arms, riotously, routously, unlawfully and unjustly, and with strong hand did expel, eject and amove, and him the said Richard King so thereout expelled, ejected and amoved, from the said 14th day of June, in the 23d year, &c. aforesaid, to the day of the exhibition of this information, with force and arms, &c. riotously, routously, unlawfully and unjustly, and with strong hand thereout did hold and as yet do hold, to the great damage of the said Richard King, and against the peace of the said lord the now king his crown and dignity, &c. whereupon, &c.

The King *against* Edwards *and* wife.

Inquisition for a forcible entry into a freehold.

Devonshire, To wit. HERETOFORE to wit, on Thursday the 15th day of March, in the year of our Lord 1648, by a certain inquisition for the keepers of the liberty of England, by the authority of parliament, taken at the Goal-garden,

den, nigh to the city of Exeter, in the said county, before John
Wilde, chief baron of the public Exchequer, Henry Wal-
dron, esquire, Henry Fry, esquire, and others their fellows
keepers of the peace, and justices assigned to preserve the
peace in the said county, and also to hear and determine divers
felonies, trespasses, and other misdeeds in the said county perpetrated, by the oath of twelve jurors it is presented, that
Robert Edwards, late of Errington, in the said county yeoman,
and Catherine Edwards, the wife of the said Robert, with
many others unknown, to the number of three persons armed
and arrayed in a warlike manner, on the 10th day of February,
in the 20th year of the reign of the lord Charles, late king of
England, &c. with force and arms, &c. at Keeton, in the parish of Errington aforesaid, in the county aforesaid, into one
messuage with the appurtenances, five acres of land, one acre
of meadow, five acres of pasture, with the appurtenances, in
the parish of Errington, in the county aforesaid, then being
the freehold of one William Rogers, and then in the tenure and
occupation of one Hugh Flasham, unlawfully, and with strong
hand did enter and did make an entry, and him the said W.
Rogers with force and arms, &c. aforesaid, unlawfully, with
strong hand, and without judgment, then and there did dif-
seize, and him the said H. Flasham from his possession thereof,
then and there with force and arms aforesaid, and with strong
hand did expel and eject, and him the said W. R. so thereof
disseized, and him the said H. F. so therefrom expelled and
ejected from the said 10th day of February, in the 20th year of
the reign of the said late king, &c. aforesaid, to the day of the
taking of this *information, from the said messuage and the other   *P. 193.
premisses with the appurtenances, with force and arms aforesaid, unlawfully and with strong hand aforesaid, did keep out,
and as yet do keep out, in contempt of the said late king, and
as well against the peace of the said lord the king, as against
the public peace, &c. and also against the form of the statute,
in such case made and provided, &c. Whereupon the sheriff   Venire to
is commanded that he do not omit, &c. but that he cause them   answer
to come to answer, &c. And now to wit, on the Friday next   awarded.
after the morrow of the Holy Trinity, in this same term,
before the keepers of the liberty of England by the authority   Plea in bar
of parliament, in the upper bench at Westminster, come the said   of restitu-
said R. Edwards, and Catherine Edwards his wife, by Peter   tion.
Goffright their attorney, and having heard the indictment
aforesaid, protesting that they the said Robert and Catherine,   Protestation
into the said messuage with the appurtenances, and into the five
acres of land, &c. in the said indictment specified, with force
and arms, and with strong hand did not enter, nevertheless for
plea for the preventing and quashing of a writ of restitution
against them, upon that indictment to be adjudged, they the
said R. and C. his wife, say, that long before the said day, in

Gg 2

which

which the indictment aforesaid, so as aforesaid was found, one William Rogers, cousin of the said William Rogers in the indictment aforesaid above named, on the 10th day of August, in the 8th year of the reign of the lord Charles, late king of England, &c. was seized of and in the said messuage with the appurtenances, and of and in the said five acres of land, one acre of meadow, five acres of pasture, with the appurtenances in his demesne as of fee, and so being seized thereof, to wit, on the said 10th day of August, in the 8th year, &c. aforesaid, at Keeton, in the parish of Errington aforesaid, in the said county, did grant and to farm let, to the said Robert and his assigns, the said tenements with the appurtenances, to have from the time of demise aforesaid, for the term of 99 years from thence next following, if the said Catherine, wife of the said Robert, and J. Edwards and T Edwards, sons of the said Robert or any of them should so long happen to live, and by virtue of which demise, the said Robert afterwards to wit, on the said 10th day of August, in the 8th year, &c. aforesaid, into the tenements with the appurtenances did enter, and was and as yet is thereof possessed, and was in the quiet possession of the said tenements with the said appurtenances, for the space of three whole years together, next before the day in which the indictment aforesaid, was found as aforesaid, his term aforesaid not as yet being ended and determined, and this the said R. and C are ready to verify as the court, &c. Whereupon they pray judgment, and that restitution according to the form of the statute in such case made and provided, may be altogether quashed in this behalf, with this that they the said R. and C. are ready to verify, that the said J. and T. as yet are alive and in full life, to wit. at Keeton aforesaid, in the parish of Errington aforesaid, in the county aforesaid, &c.

Replication Protestando that the ancestor was nor seized, nor made the lease.

*P. 194.

And the said William Rogers and Hugh Flasham say that they by anything by the said R. E. and C. his wife pleaded for the preventing and quashing of the said writ of restitution, against them the said R. E and C. his wife, and each of them upon the indictment aforesaid to be adjudged, ought not to be precluded, because protesting they say that the said W. Rogers, the cousin aforesaid, on the 10th day of August, in the 8th year aforesaid, was not seized of and in the said messuage with the said appurtenances, and of and in the said five acres of land, one acre of meadow, and five acres of pasture, with the appurtenances aforesaid, in his demesne as of fee, nor on the said 10th day of August, in the 8th year aforesaid, at Keeton aforesaid, in the parish of E. aforesaid, in the county aforesaid, did he grant and to farm let, to the said R. E. and his assigns, the said tenements with the appurtenances to have from the time of the said demise, for the said term of 99 years then next coming, if the said C. the wife of the said

Robert,

Robert, and one J. E. and T. E. the sons of the said Robert should so long happen to live, or if any of them should so long happen to live, as the said R. and C. above by pleading have alledged. But replying, they the said W. R. H. F. say that the said R. E. was not possessed, nor was in the quiet possession of the said one messuage, with the appurtenances aforesaid, and of the said five acres of land, one acre of meadow, and five acres of pasture, with the appurtenances aforesaid, in the indictment aforesaid above specified, for the space of three years together next before the said day, in which the said indictment was found as aforesaid, in the manner and form as the said R. E. and C. above by pleading have alledged, and this the said W. R. and H. F. are ready to verify as the court, &c. Wherefore they pray judgment, and that the said writ of restitution may be adjudged against them the said R. E. and C. and each of them, according to the form of the statute in such case made and provided. And the said R. E. and C. as before say, that he the said R. was possessed, and was in quiet possession of the said one messuage, with the appurtenances, and of the said five acres of land, one acre of meadow, and five acres of pasture, with the appurtenances aforesaid, in the said indictment above specified, for the said space of three years together next before the day in which the said indictment was found as aforesaid, in the manner and form as they the said R. E. and C. above, by pleading have alledged, and this they the said R. E. and C. pray may be enquired of by the country. And the said W. R. and H. F. do the like, &c therefore let a jury come thereupon before the lords the keepers, &c.

Replication

Rejoinder.

Issue.

Indictment for an Escape and Rescue.

The King *against* Blake, *and others.*

Michaelmas, 1st *James* II.

For contriving the escape of a man in the custody of a messenger for treasonable practises, by dressing him in woman's clothes, whereby he escaped from the messenger

**P. 195.*

Middlesex, To wit. } **T**HAT Thomas Atterbury, one of the messengers in ordinary, of the chamber of the lord the king, on the day and year, &c. at, &c. by virtue of a warrant in writing, under the hand and seal of the most noble Robert, Earl of Sunderland, baron S. of W. then one of the privy-council of the lord the now king, and principal secretary of state, to the said Thomas Atterbury in that behalf directed, the body of one Daniel Blake, of, &c. took, and him the said D. B. then and there to wit, on the said day and year, &c. in the house of the said T. A. situate in the parish, &c. in his custody, by virtue of the warrant aforesaid detained, for the occasion of certain dangerous and traiterous practises in the warrant aforesaid specified and contained, one E. B. of &c. and M.B. of, &c. well knowing the premisses, but devising, practising, confederating, and among themselves fraudulently and * deceitfully intending to hinder and obstruct the due course of law, and to cause the said D. B. from the due pain and punishment in that behalf to escape, and go at large, and to fulfil, perfect and bring to effect their most wicked devices, practises and intentions aforesaid, they the said E. B. and M. B. on the day and year, &c. aforesaid, came to the said house of the said T. A. situate in the said parish, &c. and then and there with force and arms, falsely, unlawfully, unjustly, fraudulently, subtily and deceitfully him the said D. B. in women's garments did dress and disfigure, and each of them him the said D. B. then and there in women's garments did dress and disfigure, and that the said E. B. and M. B. then and there, with force and arms, falsely, unlawfully, unjustly, fraudulently, subtily and deceitfully the said D. B. so as aforesaid, in the garments aforesaid dressed and disfigured, from the custody of the said T. A. did take, carry away and rescue, and each of them did take, carry away and rescue, and did cause and each of them did cause and procure the said D. B. to escape and go at large wheresoever he would, against the will of the said T. A. to the evil example, &c. and against the peace, &c.

Indictments and Informations, 1. For Nuisances, 2. For not Repairing Highways.

The King *against* Brooks.

To wit, } THAT John Bowles, late of, &c. merchant, on the 1st day of February, in the 30th year of the reign of our lord Charles the 2d, by the grace of God, of England, &c. king, &c. and continually afterwards, until the day taking of this inquisition, with force and arms,&c. at parish, &c. a certain glafs-house there situate, lately before that time, by a certain person to the jurors aforesaid unknown erected,upon the west part of a certain publick street,called Stoney-street, in the parish and county aforesaid, nigh adjacent to the mansion houses of divers of the liege subjects of the said lord the king there situate, unlawfully and unjustly did continue,and as yet doth continue. And that the said J. B. for the whole time aforesaid, with force and arms, &c. at the parish aforesaid, in the county aforesaid, in the said glafs-house of the said J. B. unlawfully and unjustly did make, have and keep, and did cause to be made and kept as well by night as by day, great, terrible and large fires of sea coals, and of other noxious things, by reason of which great quantities of fire, and of putrified smoke from the said fire, then and there within the time aforesaid, as well by night as by day, have arisen and do arife, so that the air there is rendered very insalubrious, to the great danger of burning the mansion-houses of divers liege subjects of the said lord the king, adjacent to and joining the said glafs-house of the said J. B. to the common nuisance of all the liege subjects of the said * lord the king, going, labouring and passing in by and through the said street with their horses, coaches and carriages, and to the common nuisance of all others nigh thereto inhabiting and refiding, &c. and against the peace, &c. &c.

Indictment for a nuisance by keeping a glafs-house.

*P. 196.

The

The King *against* H. P.

Information for a nuisance by encroaching on the highway.

Kent, To wit, } T HAT one H. P. late of London, carpenter, on the 1st day of October, in the 27th year of the reign of our lord Charles the 2d, by the grace of God, of England, &c. king, &c. with force and arms, &c. at, &c. in and upon the king's common highway, in a certain place there, commonly called Challock, leading from Challock to Chareing, in the county aforesaid, by a certain structure or edifice there, containing in length twenty feet, and in breadth eight feet, before that time erected and built by the said H. unlawfully and unjustly hath incroached and as yet doth incroach, and the structure or edifice aforesaid, so as aforesaid, before that time erected and built by the said H. from the said day and year, &c. to the day of the exhibition of this information at Challock aforesaid, in the said county, with force and arms, &c. unlawfully and unjustly hath continued, and as yet doth continue, by reason of which the king's common highway aforesaid, hath become greatly confined and straitened so that the liege subjects of the said lord the king in and through the said king's common highway, cannot go, pass, ride and labour with their horses, coaches and carriages, as they ought and have been accustomed, to the great and common nuisance of all the liege subjects of the said lord the king, going, passing, riding and labouring in and through the king's common highway aforesaid, and against the peace of the said lord the now king his crown and dignity, whereupon the said attorney, &c. &c.

The King *against* Baxter.

Hilary, 1st James the 2d.

Information for an incroachment on the river Thames.

Middlesex, To wit. } T HAT Nicholas Baxter, late of, &c. in the county, &c. in the year, &c. with force and arms, &c. at the parish, &c. in the said county, three several

parts

parts of the foil and ground of the river Thames there, to wit, one of the said parts containing in length thereof twenty feet, and in breadth thereof ten feet, the second of the said parts containing in length thereof thirty feet, and in breadth thereof four feet, and the third of the said parts containing in length thereof thirty feet, and in breadth thereof twenty-four feet, for the erecting and building of three wharfs, in and * upon the foil and ground of the river Thames, unlawfully *P. 197. and unjustly did inclose and incroach, and the said parts of the foil and ground of the said river Thames, (then and from the time whereof the memory of man is not to the contrary, being the king's common highway, for all liege subjects of the said lord the king, with their boats, hoys, and other vessels in through and upon the river Thames aforesaid, about their necessary business, with their goods, chattels and merchandize to pass, row, sail and labour at their pleasure) there so as aforesaid by him the said N. B. inclosed and incroached with the said wharfs, from the said 7th day of February, in the year, &c. aforesaid, to the day of the exhibition of this information aforesaid, at the parish aforesaid, in the county aforesaid, wilfully, unlawfully and unjustly he the said N. B. did keep, maintain and continue, and as yet doth keep, maintain and continue, to the great damage and common nuisance, obstruction, impediment and danger of all the said liege subjects of the said lord the king, in through and over the said parts of the river Thames aforesaid, and king's common highway aforesaid, with their boats, hoys, and other vessels about their necessary business, with their goods, chattels and merchandize, going, rowing, failing and labouring, to the evil example, &c. and against the peace, &c. &c.

The King *against* Harvey.

Essex,
To wit. ⟩ THAT one Richard Harvey, late of Stratford Langton, in the parish, &c. on the 1st day of March, in the 26th year of the reign of our lord Charles the 2d, by the grace of God, of England, &c. king, &c. and at divers other days and times as well before as after, with force and arms, &c. at, &c. as well in and upon the king's common highway, as in and upon the common foot way there leading from Stratford Langton aforesaid, to the village of Epping, in the said county of Essex, divers great pieces of timber did lay and place, and did cause to be laid and placed. And the

Hh   said

said great pieces of timber so as aforesaid laid and placed, from the said 1st day of March, in the said 2*th year, &c. aforesaid, to the day of the exhibition of this information, as well in and upon the king's common highway aforesaid, as in and upon the common foot way aforesaid, did permit and as yet doth permit to be, lie and remain, to the great common nuisance of all the liege subjects of the said lord the king, as well in and by the king's common highway aforesaid, as in and by the common foot way aforesaid, going, passing, riding and labouring, against the peace of the said lord the now king, his crown and dignity, &c. whereupon, &c.

----

*P. 198.

* The King *against* Cole.

Hilary, 35th Charles II.

Information for a nuisance in keeping of a soap-boiler's house, and boiling soap there.

Middlesex, } THAT John Cole, late of the parish of St.
To wit. } Martin in the fields, in the county of Middlesex, soap-boiler, on the day and year, &c. at, &c. at the parish, &c. in a certain place there, nigh to a certain street, called the Haymarket, and to a certain other street, called James's-street, situate in the parish, &c. in the county, &c. and also nigh to the mansion houses of divers honourable persons, and of other liege subjects of the said lord the now king there situate, did make, place, build and erect, and did cause to be made, placed, built and erected a certain soap-boiler's house, furnace, and boiling vessel, for the boiling of soap, and for the melting of putrid tallow, fat, grease, and of other noisome, bad-smelling, pestilential things, and that the said John Cole afterwards to wit, on the day and year, &c. aforesaid, and at divers other days and times as well before as after, at, &c. as well in the night as in the day, with force and arms, &c. unlawfully and unjustly in the furnace aforesaid, under the boiling vessel aforesaid, did make and cause to be made mighty and great fires of sea coal, which fires of sea coal, great quantities of unwholesome and insalubrious smoak for the whole time aforesaid, did emit and daily do emit, and that the said John Cole afterwards to wit, on the day and year, &c. and at divers other days and times as well before as after, with force and arms, &c. at, &c. unlawfully and unjustly with the mighty and great fires so as aforesaid made in the said furnace,

i9

great quantities of putrid tallow, fat, greafe, foap, and other noifome and bad-fmelling peftilential things, in the boiling veffel aforefaid, did melt and boil, by the reafon of which the air there is rendered very infalubrious, and was and is greatly filled and infected with many offenfive, dangerous and unwholefome fmells, to the common nuifance of all the liege fubjects of the faid lord the now king, going, paffing, riding, and labouring, in, by or through the faid ftreets, and the king's highways nigh thereto adjacent, and alfo of divers honourable perfons, and other liege fubjects of the faid lord the now king nigh thereto inhabiting, refiding and dwelling, and againft the peace of the faid lord the now king, his crown and dignity, &c. whereupon, &c. &c.

*P. 199. *Indictments for not repairing Highways.*

The King *against* Fanshaw.

Michaelmas, 29th Charles II.

Record upon a Writ of error upon a conviction for not repairing a common bridge, which the defendant was by tenure bound to repair.

Essex, To wit. } THE lord the king hath sent to his justices, assigned by his letters patent, to enquire by the oath of good and lawful men of the county of Essex, by whom the truth of the matter might be the better known and enquired into, or by other ways, methods and means by which they might or could know better, as well within liberties as without, more fully the truth of certain treasons, misprisions of treasons, insurrections, rebellions, counterfeitings, clippings, washings, false coinings and other falsities of the monies of this kingdom of England, and of other kingdoms or dominions whatsoever, and of certain murders, felonies, manslaughters, killings, burglaries, rapes of women, unlawful meetings and conventicles, unlawful uttering of words, misprisions combinations, false allegations, trespasses, riots, routs, retentions, escapes, contempts, falsities, negligences, concealments, maintenances, oppressions, champarties, deceits, and all other misdeeds, offences and injuries whatsoever, and also of the accessaries of the same, within the county aforesaid, as well within liberties as without, by whomsoever and howsoever had, done, committed or perpetrated, and by whom, or to whom, when, how and in what manner, and of all other articles and circumstances the premisses, and every or any of them howsoever concerning, and for that time to hear and determine the said treasons and the other premisses, according to the laws and customs of his kingdom of England, and to every of them his writ close in these words, to wit, Charles the 2d, by the grace of God, of England, Scotland, France and Ireland king, defender of the faith, &c. to our justices assigned by our letters patent, to enquire by the oath of good and lawful men of our county of Essex, by whom the truth of the matter

Writ of error.

might

might be the better known and enquired into, or by other ways, methods and means, by which they might or could know better, as well within liberties as without, more fully the truth of certain treasons, misprisions of treasons, insurrections, rebellions, counterfeitings, clippings, washings, false coinings, and other falsities of the monies of this our kingdom of England, and of other kingdoms and dominions whatsoever, and of certain murders, felonies, manslaughters, killings, burglaries, rapes of women, unlawful assemblies and conventicles, unlawful uttering of words, combinations, misprisions, confederacies, false allegations, trespasses, riots, routs, retentions, escapes, contempts, falsities, negligences, concealments, maintenances, oppressions, champarties, deceits, and all other misdeeds, offences, and injuries whatsoever, and also of the accessaries of the same, within the said county, as well within liberties as without, by whomsoever and howsoever had, done, * perpetrated or committed, and by whom or to whom, where, *P. 200. how and what manner, and of all other articles and circumstances, the premisses, and every or any of them howsoever concerning; and for that time to hear and determine the said treasons and the other premisses, according to the laws and customs of this our kingdom of England, and to every of them greeting. Because in the record and process, and also in the giving of judgment of a certain indictment made, against Thomas Fanshaw, late of Barking, in the county of Essex, knight, for certain trespasses, contempts and nuisances whereof he is indicted, and thereupon by a certain jury of the country, between us and the said Thomas Fanshaw taken, is convicted, as it is said manifest error hath intervened, to the great damage of the said T. F. as from his complaint we have received information, we willing that the error, if any there be, in due manner be corrected, and that full and speedy justice be done to the said T. F. in this behalf command you that if judgment be thereupon given, then that you or one of you send to us the record and process aforesaid, with all things touching the same, under your seals, or the seal of one of you, distinctly and openly, and this writ, so that we may have them from the day of St. Michael in three weeks, wheresoever we shall then be in England, that inspecting the record and process aforesaid, we may further cause to be done thereupon, for correcting that error, that which of right, and according to the law and custom of our kingdom of England shall be to be done. Witness ourself at Westminster, the 14th day of July, in the 29th year of our reign.

The record and process of a certain indictment with all things touching the same, whereof mention is made in this writ, I have caused to be sent before the lord the king at Westminster, at the day and place in this writ contained, as by this writ I am commanded. The answer of
Edward

Edward Thurland, knt, one of the barons of the Exchequer of the said lord the king, and one of the justices within written.

The record. *Essex,* to wit, Heretofore by a certain inquisition taken for the lord the king, at Chelmsford, in the county of Essex aforesaid, on Monday the 3d day of April, in the 2cth year of the reign of our lord Charles the 2d, by the grace of God of England, &c. king, &c. before Matthew Hale, kt. chief justice of the said lord the king, assigned to hold pleas before the king himself, Thomas Twysden, knight and baronet, one of the justices of the said lord the king, assigned to hold pleas before the king himself, and William Hicks, baronet, and others, their fellows justices of the said lord the king, assigned by letters patent of the said lord the king, under the great seal, made to them, to others, and to any three or more of them, whereof one of them the said Matthew Hale and Thomas Twysden, the said lord the king would have to be one, to enquire by the oath of good and lawful men of the county aforesaid, by whom the truth of the matter might be the better known and enquired into, and by other ways, methods and means by which they might or could know better, as well within

*P. 201. * liberties as without, more fully the truth of certain treasons, misprisions of treasons, insurrections, rebellions, counterfeitings, clippings, washings, false coinings, and other falsities of the monies of this kingdom of England, and of other kingdoms and dominions whatsoever, and also of certain murders, felonies, manslaughters, killings, burglaries, rapes of women, unlawful assemblies and conventicles, unlawful uttering of words, combinations, misprisions, confederacies, false allegations, trespasses, riots, routs, retentions, escapes, contempts, falsities, negligences, concealments, maintenances, oppressions, champarties, deceits, and other misdeeds, offences and injuries whatsoever, and also the accessaries of the same, in the said county as well within liberties as without, by whomsoever and howsoever had done, perpetrated and committed, and by whom, to whom, where, how and in what manner, and of other articles and circumstances, the premisses and every or any of them howsoever concerning; and for that time to hear and determine the said treasons and the other premisses, according to the law and custom of England, by the oath of T. Wynch, of D. esquire, and others, good and lawful men of the said county, then and there sworn and charged to enquire for the said lord the king, and for the body of the said county it is presented, that a certain common bridge, commonly called Daggenham Beam, lying and being in the parish of Daggenham, in the county of Essex aforesaid, in the king's common highway there, leading from Daggenham aforesaid, in the county aforesaid, to the town of Raynham in the said county, always and from the time whereof, the memory of man is not to the contrary, being

the

the king's common highway for all the liege subjects of the said
lord the king and his ancestors, with their horses, carts and
carriages, to go, pass, ride and labour upon, at their will and
pleasure, on the 11th day of March, in the 26th year of the
reign of our lord Charles the 2d, of England, &c. king, &c.
was and as yet is in great decay and ruin, so that the liege subjects of the said lord the now king, in and upon and over the
said bridge, with their horses, carts and carriages could not, nor
cannot go, pass, ride and labour as they ought, and have been
accustomed to do, to the great damage and nuisance of all the
liege subjects of the said lord the king, by upon and over the said
bridge, going, passing, riding and labouring, and against the
peace of the said lord the now king his crown and dignity, &c.
And that Norton Knatchbull, late of Barking, in the county
aforesaid, bart. and Thomas Fanshaw, late of Barking aforesaid, in the county aforesaid, knight, by reason of the tenure
of certain lands lying in the parish of Barking aforesaid, and
elsewhere, in the said county of Essex, late the lands of the
abbess of the abbey of Barking aforesaid, the said common
bridge ought to make, repair and amend, as often as and
whensoever there hath been need, and they have not done,
&c. Whereupon the sheriff was commanded by the writ of
the said lord the king, to the sheriff of the said county directed, that he should not omit by reason of any liberty in
his bailiwick, but that he should cause the said Norton
Knatchbull and Thomas Fanshaw, to come to answer, &c. before the justices of the said lord the king, assigned to enquire
of all felonies, trespasses, and other misdeeds, offences and
injuries whatsoever, and also to hear and determine the * said
felonies, and other the premisses in the said county perpetrated.
And afterwards to wit, at the session of Oyer and Terminer,
held for the county aforesaid, on Monday the 10th day of June,
in the 28th year of the reign of the said lord the now king, at
Chelmsford, in the county aforesaid, before T. Jones, knight,
one of the justices of the said lord the king, assigned to hold
pleas before the king himself, William Hicks, baronet, and
John Brampston, knight of the bath, and others their fellows,
justices of the said lord the king, assigned by letters patent of
the said lord the king, under his great seal of England, made
to them and to others, and to any three or more of them, of
whom the said lord the king would have that the said Thomas
Jones should be one, to enquire by the oath of good and lawful men of the county aforesaid, by whom the truth of the
matter might be the better known and enquired into, and by
other ways, methods and means, by which they could or might
know better, more fully the truth of certain treasons, misprisions of treason, insurrections, rebellions, counterfeitings,
clippings, washings, false coinings, and other falsities of the
monies of this kingdom of England, and of other kingdoms
and

Venire to
answer
awarded.

*P. 202.

and dominions whatsoever, and of certain murders, felonies, manslaughters, killings, burglaries, rapes of women, unlawful meetings and conventicles, unlawful uttering of words, combinations, misprisions, confederacies, false allegations, trespasses, riots, routs, retentions, escapes, contempts, falsities, negligences, concealments, maintenances, oppressions, champarties, deceits, and other misdeeds, offences and injuries whatsoever and also the accessaries of the same, within the said county, as well within liberties as without, by whomsoever and howsoever had, done, committed and perpetrated, and by whom, to whom, when, how, and in what manner, and of the other articles and circumstances the premisses, and every or any of them howsoever concerning, and to hear and determine for that time the said treasons and the other premisses, according to the law and custom of this kingdom of England, cometh the said Thomas Fanshaw in his proper person, and having had oyer of the said indictment, saith, that he by reason of the tenure of the said land, in the said indictment specified, ought not to make, repair and amend the said bridge, and of this he puts himself upon the country, and John Smith, gent. who for the said lord the king in this behalf prosecutes doth the like, &c. And the said Thomas Fanshaw further saith, that the said bridge is within the parish of Daggenham aforesaid, in the county aforesaid, and that the inhabitants of the said parish of Daggenham, of common right ought to make, repair and amend the said bridge, and for the not repairing of the same now here in like manner are indicted, and are the parties who prosecute the said indictment against the said T. F. and for that cause the said T. F. prays the writ of venire facias of the said lord the king, to be directed to the sheriff of the said county, that he cause to come before the justices of the said lord the king, assigned to enquire of all felonies, trespasses, and other offences, misdeeds and injuries whatsoever, and also to hear and determine the said felonies, and other the premisses in the said county perpetrated, at the next session of oyer and terminer, to be held for the said county, twelve, &c. of the vicinage of Brentwood, in the said county, which is the vill and vicinage in the said county, next adjacent to the said parish of * Daggenham, in the said county, to try the issue aforesaid, in the form aforesaid above joined; therefore by the direction of the court, and of the aforesaid justices last named, and by the consent of the said John Smith, who prosecutes, &c. the sheriff of the county aforesaid is commanded that he do not omit, &c. but that he cause to come before the justices of the said lord the king, assigned to enquire of all felonies, trespasses, and other misdeeds, injuries and offences whatsoever, and also to hear and determine the said felonies, and other the premisses in the said county perpetrated, at the next session of oyer and terminer for the county aforesaid to be held, twelve, &c. of the vicinage

of

* P. 203.

of Brentwood aforesaid, by whom, &c. who neither, &c. to recognize, &c. because as well, &c. the same day is given as well to the said John Smith, gent. who prosecutes as to the said T. F. At which next session of oyer and terminer held for the said county, to wit, at the session of oyer and terminer held for the said county, on Monday the 12th day of March, in the 29th year of the reign of our Lord, Charles 2d, &c. before Hugh Windham, knt. one of the justices of the bench of the said lord the king, Andrew Jenner, baronet, and Thomas Lee, esquire, and others their fellows justices of the said lord the king, assigned by the letters patent of the said lord the king, under the great seal of this kingdom of England, made to them and to others, and to any three or more of them, of whom the said lord the king would have that the said Hugh Windham should be one, to enquire by the oath of good and lawful men of the said county, by whom the truth of the matter might be the better known and enquired into, and by other ways, methods and means by which they could or might know better, as well within liberties as without, more fully the truth of certain treasons, misprisions of treason, insurrections, rebellions, counterfeitings, clippings, washings, false coinings, and other falsities of the monies of this kingdom of England, and of other kingdoms and dominions whatsoever, and of certain murders, felonies, manslaughters, killings, burglaries, rapes of women, unlawful assemblies and conventicles, unlawful uttering of words, combinations, confederacies, false allegations, riots, routs, retentions, escapes, contempts, falsities, negligences, concealments, maintenances, oppressions, champarties, deceits, and other misdeeds, offences and injuries whatsoever, and also the accessaries of the same, in the said county, as well within liberties as without, by whomsoever and howsoever, had, done, committed and perpetrated, and by whom, to whom, when, how and in what manner; and for that time to hear and determine the said treasons, and the other premisses, according to the laws and customs of this kingdom of England, come as well the said John Smith, who prosecutes, &c. as the said T. F. in his proper person; and the ju- *Jury appear.* rors of the said jury by John Morecroft, then sheriff of the said county for this purpose impanelled, to wit, Edward Goulding, &c. being called, come, and whereupon here in court pub- *Proclamation.* lic proclamation being made for the lord the king, as the custom is, that if there be any one who would inform the said justices last named, or the serjeant at law of the said lord the king, or the attorney-general of the said lord the king, concerning the premisses, that he should come forth and should be heard   And thereupon Francis Brampton, serjeant at law, who for the lord the king in this behalf prosecutes, offered himself to do this, whereupon it was proceeded to the taking of the said * jury, by the said jury now appearing, who being elected, **P. 204.*

I i

tried,

Verdict for the king.

Judgment.

Defendant surrenders himself to the marshal.

Errors affigned.

tried and fworn to fpeak the truth of and concerning the premiffes, lay upon their oath, that the faid Thomas Fanfhaw, by reafon of the tenure of the faid lands, lying in the parifh of Barking aforefaid, and elfewhere in the faid county of Effex, late the lands of the abbefs of the abbey of Barking aforefaid, ought to make, repair and amend the faid common bridge, as often as, and whenfoever there fhould be need, and that he hath not done it, in the manner and form as by the indictment aforefaid is fuppofed againft him. Whereupon all and fingular the premiffes being feen and by the court here fully underftood, it is confidered by the court here, that the faid T. F. pay to the faid lord the king, twenty pounds for his fine, by the court here upon him laid, for and by occafion of the trefpafs, offence and nuifance aforefaid, whereof he is in the form aforefaid convicted, and that the faid T. F. be taken to fatisfy the faid lord the king for the faid fine. And now to wit, on Monday next after the octave of St. Martin, in this fame term, before the lord the king at Weftminfter, comes the faid T. F. in his proper perfon, and furrenders himfelf prifoner to the marfhal of the marfhalfea of the lord the king before the king himfelf, for the occafion aforefaid, who is committed to the faid marfhal, &c. And forthwith faith, that on the record and proceedings aforefaid, and alfo in the rendition of the judgment aforefaid, there is manifeft error in this to wit, becaufe that it doth not appear in and by the faid indictment, againft the faid N. K. baronet, and him the faid T. F. that they the faid N. K. and T. F. ought to make, repair and amend the bridge in the faid indictment mentioned, as often as and whenever there hath been need, by reafon of the tenure of the lands in the faid indictment fpecified, as all thofe whofe eftate they the faid N. and T. now have in thofe lands, have been accuftomed from the time whereof the memory of man is not to the contrary, to make, repair and amend the faid bridge, as by the law of the land ought to be. Alfo there is manifeft error in this, becaufe that the faid jury impanelled and fworn to try the iffue aforefaid, upon the indictment aforefaid, fo as aforefaid joined, did give their verdict, that the faid T. F. by reafon of the tenure of the faid lands lying and being in the faid parifh of Barking and elfewhere, in the faid county of Effex, late the lands of the abbefs of the abbey of Barking aforefaid, ought to make, repair and amend the faid bridge, as often as and whenever there fhould be need, in the manner and form as by the faid indictment above is fuppofed againft him, whereas by that indictment it is found that the faid N. K. and T. F. ought to make, repair and amend the faid bridge, as often as, and whenever there fhould be need, by reafon of the tenure of the faid lands, therefore in that there is manifeft error. Whereupon the faid T. F. prays judgment, and that the judgment aforefaid, for the errors aforefaid, and others

being

being and found in the record and proceedings aforesaid, may be reversed and entirely annulled; and that he the said T. F. may be restored to all things which he hath lost by occasion of the said judgment, and that the court here may proceed to the examination of the record and proceedings aforesaid. And because that the court of the said lord the king here are not yet advised to give their judgment of and upon the premisses, day is given thereupon to the said T. F. in the state as now, &c. until the 15th day of St. Martin wheresoever, &c. to hear their judgment thereupon, &c. and thereupon the said T. F. is delivered on bail to John Fanshaw, of Parsloes, in the county of Essex, esquire, and to Thomas ————, of the parish of St. Dunstan in the * west, London, sadler, until the said term * P. 203. and so from day to day until that, &c. to prosecute the writ of error with effect, to wit, each of the pledges of the said T. F. under the pain of twenty pounds, and himself under the pain of forty pounds, which, &c.

This case is reported 1 Ventris 331, *and in* 3 Keble 855, *but it does not appear whether the judgment was reversed or affirmed.*

The King *against* the Inhabitants of the County of Essex.

Trinity, the 30th of Charles the II.

Essex,
To wit. } THAT from the time whereof the memory of man is not the contrary, there was and yet is a certain common stone bridge, commonly called Daggenham-bridge, otherwise Daggenham-beam, situate, lying and being in the several parishes of Horn church and Daggenham in the said county, in the king's common highway leading from the parish of Raynham, in the county aforesaid, to the parish of Daggenham aforesaid, in the county aforesaid, and so towards the city of London, for all the liege subjects of the said lord the now king, and of his predecessors late kings and queens of this kingdom of England, with their horses, coaches, carts and carriages, to go, return, pass, ride and labour without any impediment at any time of the year, which bridge on the 1st day of May, in the 29th year of the reign of our lord Charles the

in affirmation
or not re-
pairing a
common
bridge,
which
ought to
be repaired
by the
whole
county

                    2d,

2d. by the grace of God, of England, &c. king, &c. at the several parishes of Horn-church and Daggenham aforesaid, in the county aforesaid, was and yet is very ruinous, dangerous, broken, and in such decay for want of repairing and amending the same, so that the liege subjects of the said lord the king, over, beyond and upon the said bridge without great danger of their lives, and the loss of their limbs and goods, cannot go, return, pass, ride and labour with their horses, coaches, carts and carriages as they ought, and have been accustomed and for the whole time aforesaid have been used and accustomed, to the great and common nuisance of all the liege subjects of the said lord the king, over beyond and upon the said bridge, with their horses, coaches, carts and carriages, going, returning, riding, passing and labouring, and against the peace of the said lord the now king his crown and dignity, &c. And that it cannot be known that any hundred, riding, wapentake, city borough, town or parish, or particular person or body corporate ought to make, build, repair and amend the said bridge; nor can it in any manner be made to appear that the said bridge was ever heretofore made, rebuilt, repaired or amended by any hundred, riding, wapentake, city, borough, town or parish, or particular person or body corporate; and that the inhabitants of the whole county of Essex, ought to make, rebuild, repair and amend th said bridge, according to the form of the † statute in such case made and provided. * Nevertheless they the said inhabitants of the said county have not rebuilt or repaired the said bridge as they ought to have done, but have permitted and as yet do permit the said bridge altogether to be and remain ruinous and unrepaired from the said 1st day of May, in the year aforesaid hitherto, to the great damage and common nuisance of all the liege subjects of the said lord the now king. Whereupon the said coroner and attorney of the said lord the now king, for the said lord the king, prays the consideration of the court here in the premisses, and the due process of law to be awarded against the said inhabitants of the said county in this behalf, to make them to answer to the said lord the king, of and touching the premisses, &c. Whereupon the sheriff of the said county is commanded that he do not omit, &c. but that he cause the said inhabitants of the said county of Essex, to come to answer, &c. And now to wit, on the Wednesday next after three weeks of the Holy Trinity, before the lord the king at Westminster, come Charles Argoll and John Stephens, gentlemen, two inhabitants of the said county of Essex, in the name of all the inhabitants of the said county of Essex, by Philip Ward their attorney, and having heard the information aforesaid, say that the said inhabitants of the said county of Essex, ought not to be charged for the repairing and amending of the said bridge, because they say that heretofore to wit, by a certain inquisition taken for the

said

† 22 Hen.
8. c. 5. f. 2,
3.
* P. 206.

Process
prayed.

Venire to
answer
awarded.

Plea by two
inhabitants
in the name
of all the
rest, f the
prefert-
ment ver-
dict and

faid lord the king, at Chelmsford, in the county of Effex aforefaid, on Monday the 3d day of Auguft, in the 26th year of the reign of our lord Charles the 2d, by the grace of God, of England, &c. king, &c. before Matthew Hale, knt. then chief juftice of the faid lord the king, affigned to hold pleas before the king himfelf, Thomas Twyfden, knight and baronet, then and as yet one of the juftices of the faid lord the king, affigned to hold pleas before the king himfelf, and William Hicks, baronet, and others their fellows juftices of the faid lord the king, affigned by letters patent, &c. *"And fo plead the next preceding record of the indictment found at the affixes, againft Sir Thomas Fanfhaw, for not repairing the faid bridge, and the conviction and judgment thereon,"* as by the record and proceedings thereupon, which the faid lord the now king hath lately made to come before him to be corrected for error in the court of the faid lord the now king, before the king himfelf here remaining at Weftminfter manifeftly appeareth. And further the faid C. Argoll and J. Stephens, two inhabitants of the faid county of Effex, in the name of all the inhabitants of the faid county, fay and will verify, that the faid bridge in the faid record and judgment mentioned, and the bridge in the faid information mentioned and expreffed, is one and the fame bridge, and not another nor different, and that the faid judgment as yet ftands and remains in all its full force, vigour and effect, unreverfed and without being annulled. And this the faid C A. and J. S. two inhabitants of the faid county of Effex, in the name of all the inhabitants of the faid county, are ready to verify, wherefore they pray judgment, and that the faid inhabitants of the faid county of Effex by the court here may be difmiffed and difcharged of the faid premiffes in the faid information contained.

judgment againft the profecutor, that he ought to repair.

Edmund Saunders.

* And Samuel Aftry, knt. now coroner and attorney of the lord the king, in the court of the faid lord the king, before the king himfelf, who for the faid lord the king in this behalf profecutes, having heard the plea of the faid Charles Argoll and John Stephens, two of the inhabitants of the faid county, in the manner and form aforefaid above pleaded, for the faid lord king faith, that the faid plea and the matter in the fame contained, are not fufficient in law, &c. *and fo demurs in law and the defendants join in demurrer.*

**P. 207. Demurrer.*

In this cafe judgment was given for the king, becaufe the bridge in the information, and the bridge in the plea, are not the fame bridge; the one is laid to be in one parifh, and the other in two parifhes. This cafe is reported in Raymond 384.

The

The King *against* the Inhabitants of Stains and Egham.

Easter, 36th Charles II.

Information for not repairing a public bridge.

Surrey,   } THAT from the time whereof the memory
To wit.   } of man is not to the contrary, there was and as yet ought to be a certain common and public wooden bridge, called Stains-bridge, lying over the river Thames, in the several counties of Middlesex and Surrey, in the king's highway leading from the market town of Stains, in the county of Middlesex, to the town of Egham, in the county of Surrey, and one part of the said bridge was and did lye in the parish of Stains, in the said county of Middlesex, and the other part of the said bridge was and did lye in the parish of Egham, in the said county of Surrey, for all the liege subjects of the said lord the king, with their horses, coaches, carts and carriages to go, return, pass, ride and labour over and upon, for the whole time aforesaid, at all times of the year, and without any impediment. And that the said bridge from the 1st day of S. in the year, &c. and continually afterwards until the day of the exhibition of this information, at the several parishes of Stains, in the county of Middlesex, and of Egham, in the county of Surrey, was and as yet is totally broken and demolished, and in so great decay that the liege subjects of the said lord the king, with their horses, coaches, carts and carriages, over and upon the said bridge, cannot go, return, pass, ride and labour as they have been used and accustomed, to the great damage and common nuisance of all the liege subjects of the said lord the king, in, over and upon the said bridge, going, returning, passing, riding and labouring ; and the said attorney-general of the said lord the king, for the said lord the king further saith, that the said bridge is no within any liberty, city or town corporate, and that it cannot be known that any hundred, riding, wapentake, city, borough, town or parish, or certain person, or body corporate, of right ought to make and repair the said bridge ; and that the inhabitants of the county of Middlesex ought to make, repair and amend the said part of the said bridge, so as aforesaid lying and being in the parish of Stains,

in

in the county of Middlesex, as often as and whenever need hath been. And that the inhabitants of the county of * Surrey aforesaid, ought to make, repair and amend the said part of the said bridge, so as aforesaid lying and being in the parish of Egham, in the said county of Surrey, as often as and whenever need hath been, according to the form of the † statute in such made and provided. Nevertheless the inhabitants of the said county of Middlesex, and of the said county of Surrey, have not made nor repaired the said bridge, but have permitted as yet do permit the said bridge, from the 1st day of September, in the year, &c. to the day of the exhibition of this information, at the parish of S. in the county of Middlesex, and at the parish of E. in the county of Surrey, to remain very much broken, ruinous, and in great decay, and also totally demolithed, to the common nuisance of all the liege subjects of the said lord the king, in, upon, over and beyond the said bridge, in the king's highway aforesaid, going, passing, riding and labouring, and against the peace of the said lord the king his crown and dignity, &c. whereupon the said attorney, &c. &c.

*P. 208.

† 22 H. 8. c. 5. f. 2, 3.

The King *against* the Inhabitants of the County of the City of Norwich.

Norfolk, } THAT a certain common and public bridge, To wit. } commonly called Lakenham-bridge, lying and being at Lakenham, in the county of the city of Norwich, in the king's highway there, on the 1st day of March, in the 22d year of the reign of our lord Charles the 2d, by the grace of God, of England, &c. king, &c. was and as yet is very ruinous, broken, dangerous, noxious, and in such decay, for want of repairing and amending the same, so that the liege subjects of the said lord the now king, over, upon and beyond the said bridge, cannot go, return, pass and labour as they ought and have been accustomed without great danger of their lives, and the loss of their limbs and goods, to the great and common nuisance of all the liege subjects of the said lord the king, over, upon and beyond the said bridge, going, returning, passing and labouring, and against the peace of the said lord the now king his crown and dignity, and that the inhabitants of the whole county of the city of Norwich, ought to repair and amend the said bridge as often as and whenever need hath been, &c.

Indictment for not repairing a public bridge.

*P. 209. * *Indictments for divers Mifdemeanors.*

1. Againſt the Common Law.　2. Againſt Statutes.

1. Againſt the Common Law.

The King *againſt* Montague, and others.

Eaſter, 1ſt *James* II.　*Roll* 19.

Information for enticing a man's wife to elope from him, and to live with one of the defendants in adultery.

To wit. } THAT William Montague, late of the pariſh of St. Giles in the fields, in the county of Middlefex, efquire, Dorothea Danvers, late of the city of Chichcſter, in the county of Suffex, fpinſter, and Godfrey Kneller, late of Weſt-Deane, in the ſaid county of Suffex, gentleman, being peiſons of evil name, fame, and of moſt wicked and diſhoneſt converfation and reputation, and deviſing, practiſing, and among themſelves moſt wickedly, bafely and diabolically combining and intending, and each and every of them deviſing, practiſing and intending not only the happy ſtate, quiet and peaceable tranquility of John Lewknor, of Weſt-Deane aforefaid, in the ſaid county of Suffex, efquire, and of Jane his wife, by unlawful, impure, wicked and diabolical ways and means, to difquiet, defpoil, infringe and moleſt, but alfo the perſon of the ſaid John Lewknor, to ruin and entirely deſtroy; and that the ſaid W. Montague, D. D. and G. K. to fulfil, perfect and bring to effect their moſt wicked, deteſtable and diabolical devices, practiſes and intentions aforefaid, on the 20th day of April, in the 1ſt year of the reign of our lord James the 2d, the now king, &c. at the pariſh of Weſt-Deane, in the ſaid county of Suffex, with force and arms, &c. unlawfully, unjuſtly, wickedly, infamouſly, moſt vilely and diabolically did ſtir up, tempt and folicit, and each and every of them, then and there did ſtir up, tempt and folicit the ſaid Jane Lewknor, then and as yet the wife of the ſaid

John

Indictments for Misdemeanors.

John Lewknor, to defert the faid John Lewknor her hufband, and to elope from the faid John Lewknor, and to commit adultery, and to live in adultery with the faid W. M. And 2d Count. the faid attorney-general of the faid lord the new king, for the faid lord the king further gives the court here to underftand and to be informed, that the faid W. M. D. D. and G. K. to fulfil, perfect and bring to effect their moft wicked and diabolical devices, practifes and intentions aforefaid, on the faid 20th day of April, in the year afrefaid, at the parifh of Weft-Deane, in the faid county of Suffex, with force and arms, &c. falfely, unlawfully, wickedly and corruptly did take, carry away and convey, and did caufe, and each and every of them then and there did caufe to be taken, carried away and conveyed, from the houfe of the faid J. L. and out of the cuftody of the faid J. L. and againft the will of the faid J. L. to certain places to the faid J. L. unknown, and for the ufe and benefit of the faid W. M. divers goods and chattels and fums of money of the faid J. L. to wit, one box made of olive wood, of the value of five pounds of the lawful money of * England, one hundred pieces of gold, called guinea pieces * P. 210. of gold, every piece thereof of the value of twenty fhillings, of the like money, twenty other pieces of gold, called guinea pieces of gold, every piece thereof of the value of five pounds of the like money, one hundred other pieces of gold, called half guinea pieces of gold, every piece thereof of the value of ten fhillings of the like money, twenty other pieces of gold, called old broad pieces of gold, every piece thereof of the value of twenty fhillings of the like money, and one box made of gold, of the value of fix pounds of the like money. And the faid attorney-general of the faid lord the king, fur- 3d Count. ther gives the court here to underftand and to be informed, that the faid W. M. further to fulfil, perfect and bring to effect his moft wicked, impure, vile, infamous and diabolical intentions aforefaid, on the 20th day of April, in the laft year aforefaid, with force and arms, &c. at the parifh of W. aforefaid, in the faid county of Suffex, falfely, unlawfully, unjuftly, wickedly, vilely, infamoufly and diabolically did make, compofe, write and publifh, and did caufe to be made, compofed, written and publifhed a certain falfe, impure, corrupt, profane, vile, infamous and diabolical letter in writing, to the faid J. the wife of the faid J. L. bearing date the 26th day of February, 1604, which letter was directed then and there as follows, to wit, *" Thefe for Madam Lewknor, of Weft Deane in Suffex,* (meaning the faid wife of the faid John Lewknor, then abiding at Weft Deane aforefaid, in the faid county of Suffex) *humbly prefent,* (the tenor of which letter follows, to wit) Thurfday noon, being the 26th of Feb. 84-5.—*My dear foul, thou only preferver of my life! oh thou divine being! how can I pay duty enough to thee for all thy immenfe goodnefs to me thy poor flave?*

K k

No,

No, I am never able to requite dearest thee if I should continue this thousand years, and yet if thou makest good thy dear promisses, I shall go near to live a good part of them. I have now no further doubt but that thou art resolved to save me, therefore it is no matter how soon thy tyrant knows I cannot live without thee, for thou art mine, and I shall die if I am much longer absent from thee : Dearest angel dost wish thyself with me? ah thou may'st have me whenever thou pleasest, Oh don't let me want what we both so much desire, if it be thy blest will, for nothing can be physic to cure my dying body but thy divine presence ; 'tis fine work these fellows Richard and Moody intend to make, my villain Mudley shall pay dear for his inquisitiveness, and being such a traitor to his master, but assure thyself it is only guessing, for I examined the boy, who protests he never saw nor knew he had a letter, or to whom directed ; but I'll defer his punishment till I hear more from thee. Mrs. Savory may easily hinder them from finding out the plates, by sending them out of the house, and then she may say she hath them not. The esquire came here on Friday last, when I was at London ; my mother Eve begged of him but to stay till I came home, which would be at night ; no not he, for he said he had sworn never to lie in the house more, but declared he would spend 100l. in opposing my coming in for parliament man, he went away in a great rage, and told my mother he had a ridiculing letter from an unknown hand, who told him all that had passed in his absence. I fear all for thee, nothing for myself, for he is the pittyfullest of men where he cannot domineer. By the love thou bearest me, suffer him not to strike nor abuse thy divine person, without giving me speedy notice of it, I claim this justice of thee, thou being my better part, and know I shall die with grief as well as absence, if I should live in dread of his beating thee, and thou not advertise me of it ; I hope thou wilt not do so cruel a thing to thy faithful lover. No doubt but his worship brought home his delicate humour to thee on Saturday night, he spent most of that day at Midhurst, making all he could against me ; he, together with his myrmidons, spread abroad that I was not at the charge of getting them their charter, and great many such silly nonsensical lies, he being, thou knowest, good at them. I sent Charles to the burghers on Monday, and he is not yet returned, so can send thee no account what lord Montague, the town and Mr. Alcock says, for I writ to them all ; I hear that some of the burghers stickle very much for me ; I will get it if possible, only if it be but to disturb my destroyer. Dearest, there is no fear of his taking my letters to thee, if our dear friend but let her trusty maid be at the post-house on Fridays, as soon as the letters come in ; because he can have no way at coming at them, but to get the post-master to give him or his agents any letter directed to our friend, till he finds one ; but if she takes this course, it is impossible for him to intercept a letter, therefore pray discourse it with her. Then for thy blest ones to me, never fear their being opened, send a packet if thou pleasest, there's no danger. I wonder not at all at the insolency of Richardson thy tyrant, and my destroyer intends to make all

P. 211.

se

*so to thee that he can; but, blessing on thy dear heart, his reign is but short. And since my life depends upon thy divine promise, let me once more, before I send this scribble, beseech thee upon my bended knees, to remember that I tell thee I cannot promise to secure my life to thee long, if I continue thus deprived of thee; and my destroyer is contriving all the ways he can invent to keep me from thee, he knows it will kill me, and that he knows will be the safest way to be rid of me: 'Tis only by thee and from thee I can receive my life, and thou my divinity, can'st frustrate his and all their cruelties to me; and since it is so, I fear nothing. And I pray and praise thee every day, by whose blest promises and mercy I live, and my days will not be long enough to express to dear thee my gratitude for thy saving me, thy poor slave; but while I breath thou shalt see me attend thee with the purest love, the vastest obedience, and the greatest reverence, that can or ever was paid by man. Ah, dearest life! what can I * return thee for all thy benefits bestowed upon me, thy poor creature, only a heart brimfull of love and admiration of thee, the which will continue for ever, being I am thine and only thine, thou hast been pleased to accept of so mean a gift, for which be pleased to accept of the most humble thanks and eternal adoration of thy most dutiful and affectionate husband. On Monday night, Ned Thurland and three men coming from London all very drunk, one Simon the best of them fell into our gravel-pit and was drowned, the night being very dark, and it being about the hour of twelve; this comes of drunkenness. Thy dear sister is to be married on Shrove-tuesday, and at night to be laid upon her back as flat as a pancake, and no doubt will give and receive a curious time on't. Charles is just come in, and brings me an account what opposition there is against me, made by my lord, the esquire, and Sir William Morley; but finds all that were bailiffs, and above thirty are for me: I intend to come down once amongst them, and try how far it will go; next week I tell thee more. God Almighty keep me in thy blest favour, and it is no matter what becomes of this affair.* *P. 210. And the said attorney-general of the said lord the king, for the said lord the king further gives the court here to understand and to be informed, that the said W. M. further to conceal and the sooner to fulfil, perfect and bring to effect his most wicked devices and intentions and diabolical purposes aforesaid, afterwards to wit, on the said 26th day of April, in the 1st year, &c. aforesaid, at the said parish of West-Deane, in the said county of Sussex, with force and arms, &c. falsely, unlawfully, unjustly, wickedly and diabolically did make, compose, write and publish, and did cause to be made, composed, written and published, a certain other corrupt and diabolical letter, bearing date the said 26th day of February, the tenor of which last mentioned letter follows to wit, "*These for Mrs. Danvers, at Mr. Anderson's house in Chichester, in Sussex, with care and speed, present, February, 26th D. V. For fear any letter should be intercepted, I beg of you every Friday, be pleased to send any one you can trust to the post-house as it is come in, and when* 4th Count.

K k 2

the

the mail is opened, let them take your letter, for we are afraid the esquire should send somebody to take it, which this way will prevent, which is all at present from your most obliged faithful servant, W. M." And that the said William Montague, then and there to wit, on the said 20th day of April, in the 1st year, &c. aforesaid, at the parish of West-Deane aforesaid, in the county of Suffex, in further prosecution of his most wicked devices and intentions aforesaid, with force and arms, &c. unlawfully, unjustly, wickedly and diabolically the said first mentioned letter, directed as aforesaid, to the said Madam Lewknor, in the said last mentioned letter, directed as aforesaid, to the said Mrs. Danvers did place and inclose, and did cause to be placed and inclosed, with intention that the said first mentioned letter might be delivered to the said Jane Lewknor, then and as yet being as aforesaid, the wife of the said John Lewknor, in contempt of the laws of this kingdom of England, to the great displeasure of Almighty God, to the final sorrow, great *P. 213.* damage, affliction and * discomfort of the said John Lewknor, to the evil and pernicious example of all others in the like case offending, and against the peace of the said lord the now king his crown and dignity, &c. whereupon the said attorney-general, &c.

The King *against* Dingley.

Michaelmas, 2d James II.

Information &c.   To wit. } THAT Thomas Dingley, late of, &c. and Sarah his wife, being persons of evil name, fame and conversation, and of wicked and dishonest reputation, and well knowing that one Jane Fane, the wife of Roden Fane, esquire, ... estate, by articles of agreement, ... res and conveyances at law, upon the ... J. in certain trustees of the said ... of of the said J. from time to ... disposed of by the said J. and ... among themselves most wickedly com- ... each and every of them devising, ... to make a prey of the said J. and also ... state, to them the said T. D. and S. and ... ways and means, to bring the said R. F.

into

into hatred and contempt with the said J. his wife, and afterwards to fulfil, perfect and bring to effect their most wicked and detestable devices, practises and intentions, on the day and year, &c. and at divers other places in the said county, &c. with force and arms, &c. unlawfully, unjustly, wickedly and diabolically did stir up, tempt and solicit, and each and every of them did stir up, tempt and solicit the said J. F. then and as yet the wife of the said R. F. to go away from the said R. F. her husband, and to desert the said R. F. her husband, and to live in secret places, unknown to the said R. F. by which unlawful, unjust and wicked stirrings up, temptations and solicitations of the said T. D. and S. his wife, the the said J. F. the wife of the said R. F. unlawfully and unjustly, wickedly and diabolically at the parish of St. Ann, Westminster, in the county of Middlesex aforesaid, did desert and elope from the said R. F. her husband, against the will of the said R. F. into certain places, to the said coroner and to the said R. F. as yet unknown, and that the said T. D and S his wife, divers great sums of money from the said J. F. did obtain, and did convert and dispose to their own proper use, in manifest contempt of the laws of this kingdom of England, to the great displeasure of Almighty God, to the final sorrow, great damage, discomfort and affliction of the said R. F. to the evil and pernicious example, &c. and against the peace, &c. whereupon the said coroner, &c.

---

* The King *against* Aleway.

Easter, 35th Charles II.

Bucks,
To wit. } THAT Thomas Aleway, late of Great Marlow, in the county of Bucks, barber-chirurgeon, being a person of evil name, fame and reputation, and of wicked conversation, and devising and intending by unlawful, impure and diabolical ways and means to despoil, infringe and disturb the peace and quiet of one Owen Blower, late of the same, malster, he the said T. A. not having the fear of God before his eyes, but being moved and seduced by the instigation of the devil, on the 1st day of June, in the 25th year of the reign of the lord Charles the 2d, the now king of England, &c. at Great Marlow aforesaid, in the county of Bucks aforesaid, wickedly, vilely, infamously and diabolically did

tempt,

Information
for the live,
and living
with her in
adultery.

tempt, ftir up and folicit one Ann, then and as yet the wife of the faid O. to defert the faid O. her hufband, and to elope from the faid O. and to commit adultery, and to live in adultery with the faid T. A. And the faid coroner and attorney of the faid lord the king, for the faid lord the king further faith, that the faid T. A. in further profecution of his moft wicked devices and intentions, then and there to wit, between the faid 1ft day of June, in the 25th year of the reign of the faid lord the now king aforefaid, and the day of the exhibition of this-information, at the parifh of Gleat Marlow, in the faid county of Bucks, unlawfully, unjuftly, wickedly and diabolically did folicit, ftir up, perfuade and procure the faid A. B. then and as yet the wife of the faid O. B. from the faid O. B. her hufband, without the leave and againft the will of the faid O. B. to fly, depart and elope, and with the faid T. A. to remain and cohabit in divers fecret places, to the faid coroner and attorney, and to the faid O. B. entirely unknown, by which unlawful, wicked and diabolical folicitations, perfuafions, ftirrings up and procurements of the faid T. A. fhe the faid A. B. the wife of the faid O. B. then and there did elope, and withdraw and abfent herfelf from the faid O. B. and from the company, dwelling and fociety of the faid O. B. her hufband, without his leave, and againft the will of the faid O. B. and with the faid T. A. in divers fecret and wicked places for the fpace of eight years and more did remain and cohabit, and with him the faid T. A. did live in adultery. And that the faid T. A. then and there within the time aforefaid, unlawfully, wickedly and diabolically without the leave and againft the will of the faid O. B. the hufband of the faid A. B. did receive, maintain and abett the faid A. B. fo being departed, withdrawn and eloped from the faid O. B. her hufband, without the leave and againft the will of the faid O. B. her hufband; and the faid T. A. then and there alfo had carnal knowledge of the body of the faid A. B. the wife of the faid O. B. and with the faid A. B. then and there unlawfully, unjuftly, wickedly and diabolically did commit the crime of fornication and adultery, and with the faid A. B. did live in adultery, to the great difpleafure of Almighty God, to the great damage and difcomfort of the faid O. B. to the evil example of all others in the like cafe offending, and * againft the peace of the faid lord the now king his crown and dignity, whereupon the faid coroner and attorney, &c. &c.

The

The King *against* Lord Grey.

Michaelmas, 34th Charles II.   *Roll.*

To wit. } THAT Ford, lord Grey, of Wark, R. C. late of, &c. gentleman, A. C. wife of the said R. C. D. J. F. J. wife of the said D. J. and R. J with divers other evil-disposed persons, to the said attorney-general of the said lord the king as yet unknown, on the 20th day of August, in the 34th year of the reign of our lord Charles the 2d, the now king of England, &c. and at divers other days and times as well before as after, at the parish of Epsom, in the county of Surrey, falsely, unlawfully, unjustly and most wickedly by unlawful and impure ways and means, conspiring, devising, practising and intending the final ruin and destruction of the lady Henrietta Berkley, then a maiden unmarried, within the age of 18 years, and one of the daughters of the most noble George, earl Berkley, (she the said lady Henrietta Berkley, then and there being under the wardship, government and education of her father, the said most noble George, earl Berkley) they the said Ford, lord Grey, R. C. &c. and divers other persons unknown, then and there falsely, unlawfully, unjustly and diabolically to fulfil, perfect and bring to effect their most wicked, detestable and diabolical intentions aforesaid, did tempt, incite and solicit, and each and every of them then and there did tempt, incite and solicit the said lady H. B. to desert the said most noble G. earl B. the father of the said lady H. B. and to commit whoredom, fornication and adultery, and in whoredom, fornication and adultery with the said Ford lord Grey, against all laws human and divine, impiously, wickedly, vilely and scandalously to live and cohabit, (the said F. lord G. then and long before, and as yet being the husband of the lady Mary, one other daughter of the said most noble George, earl Berkley, and sister of the said lady H. B.) And that the said F. lord G. R. C. &c. and the other persons unknown, with force and arms, &c. unlawfully, unjustly without the leave, and against the will of the said most noble George, earl Berkley, in prosecution of their most wicked conspiracies aforesaid, her the said lady H. B. there about the hour of twelve in the night of the said 20th day of August, in the year
aforesaid,

Information
for enticing
his wife's
sister from
her father's
house, and
living in
adultery
with her.

aforesaid, at the parish of E. in the county of S aforesaid, out of the mansion house of the said most noble George, earl B. there situate and being, and out of the wardship and government of the said G. earl B. did take, lead and carry away. And did cause and procure, and each and every of them did cause and procure the said lady H. B. from the said 20th day of August, in the year aforesaid, and continually afterwards until the day of the exhibition of this information, at the parish of E. aforesaid, in the county aforesaid, and in divers secret places there with the said Fod, lord Grey, unlawfully, wickedly and scandalously to live, cohabit and remain, to the great displeasure of Almighty God, to the ruin and destruction of the said lady H. B. and to the affliction and discomfort of her friends, to the evil and pernicious example, &c. and against the peace, &c. whereupon, &c.

The trial of this case is in the State Trials, vol. 3. fol. 52.

P. 216.

* The King *against* Allen, *and* another.

Indictment for kidnapping and carrying a maiden into parts beyond sea, into slavery.

To wit. } THAT John Allen, late of, &c. and Thomas Parker, late of, &c. on the 10th day of September, in the 22d year of the reign of our lord Charles the 2d, by the grace of God, of England, &c. king, &c. with force and arms, &c. at London aforesaid, to wit, in the parish of St. Andrew, Holborn, in the ward of Farringdon without London aforesaid, in and upon one Grace Luther, spinster, the daughter of one Anne Vincent, in the peace of God and of the said lord the king, then and there being, unlawfully and wickedly did make an assault, and her the said Grace Luther then and there unlawfully and violently did beat, wound and ill-treat, and the said G. L. then and there, with force and arms, &c. against the will as well of the said G. L. as of the said A. V. her mother aforesaid, unlawfully, violently and wickedly did take, lead, carry away and carry off, and the said G. L. against the will as well of the said G. L. as the said A. V. into foreign parts and parts beyond the seas, called Virginia, then and there unlawfully, violently and for the sake of wicked gain, did lead, carry away, and transport, and did cause to be led, carried away and transported; and her the
said

said G. L. there in Virginia aforesaid, in most miserable slavery, continually afterwards until the taking of this inquisition, unlawfully, violently, cruelly, and for the sake of wicked gain, did keep and detain, and did cause to be kept and detained, to the great damage and final destruction of the said G. L. to the great sorrow, grief and discomfort of the said A. V. the mother of the said G. L. to the evil and pernicious example of all others in the like case offending, and against the peace of the said lord the now king his crown and dignity, &c.

The King *against* Bayly, *and others.*

Michaelmas, 36th Charles II.   *Roll*

To wit. } THAT Abraham Bayly, of the parish of Stebonheath, otherwise Stepney, in the county of Middlesex, esquire; William Haveland, otherwise Haverland, of the parish, &c. yeoman, T. A. of the parish, &c. gentleman, and T. Hutchins, of the parish, &c. yeoman, being and each and every of them being persons greedy of great gain, not regarding, and each and every of them not regarding by what ways, methods and means they could acquire gain, lucre and profit for themselves; although to the damage and injury of others, on the 10th day of August, in the 36th year of the reign of our lord Charles the 2d, the now king of England, &c. with force and arms, &c. at, &c. one John Winch, the son of Richard Winch, into a certain vessel, commonly called the Jeffrys, then being in the river Thames, against the will of the said R. Winch, and Alice his wife, his parents, and also of the friends of the said * John Winch, craftily, subtily, unlawfully and unjustly did convey and seduce, and did cause to be conveyed and seduced, and each and every of them then and there did convey and seduce, and did cause to be conveyed and seduced, with intention him the said J. W. into parts beyond the seas, called Virginia, to convey and transport, and in the said parts beyond the seas, to sell and detain, for the wicked gain and profit of them the said A. B. W. H. T. A. and T. H. to the great damage and injury of the said J. W. and also of the parents and friends of the said J. W. to the evil and pernicious example of all others in the like case offending, and against the peace of the said lord the now king his crown and dignity, &c. whereupon the said coroner, &c.

Information for kidnapping a young man, with intent to carry him beyond seas, and there to sell him.

*P. 217.

L l

'The

The King *against* King.

To wit. } THAT Robert King, of the borough of Wincanton, in the county of Somerset, yeoman, on the 8th day of October, in the 24th year of the reign of our lord Charles the 2d, the now king of England, &c. and long before and always afterwards, until the day of the exhibition of this information, was inhabiting and residing within the hundred of Norton Ferris, in the county of Somerset. And that the said Robert King, on the said 8th day of October, in the 24th year, &c. aforesaid, in the court-leet of the hundred of Norton Ferris, then held at Wincanton aforesaid, in the county aforesaid, for the hundred aforesaid, within the hundred, in the county aforesaid, lawfully and in the due manner was elected into the office of constable for the hundred aforesaid, in the county aforesaid, for one year then next following, to do and execute all and singular the things which belong to the said office of constable; and that the said Robert King, afterwards to wit, on the 9th day of December, in the 24th year, &c. aforesaid, at the borough of Wincanton aforesaid, in the said county of Somerset had notice thereof, and then and there was required to appear before the steward of the court-leet of the hundred of Norton Ferris, at Wincanton aforesaid, in the said county, on the said 9th day of December, in the 24th year, &c. aforesaid, to take his oath for the due execution of his office of constable aforesaid, according to the duty of his office, nevertheless he the said Robert King not regarding his duty in this behalf, but devising and intending totally to neglect and omit the due execution of the office of constable aforesaid, after his due election aforesaid to the office aforesaid, to wit, on the said 9th day of December, in the 24th year, &c. aforesaid, and continually afterwards until the day of the exhibition of this information, although often requested at Wincanton aforesaid, within the hundred of Norton Ferris aforesaid, in the county of Somerset, to take his said oath for the due execution of the office of constable aforesaid, and to execute the said office, his oath aforesaid to take, and his office aforesaid to execute, wilfully, obstinately and contemptuously, entirely hath refused and denied, and as yet doth refuse and deny, against the duty of his

said

said office, in manifest contempt of the said lord the now king, and of his laws, to the evil and pernicious example of all others in the like case offending, and against the peace of *P. 218. the said lord the now king his crown and dignity, &c. whereupon the said coroner, &c.

And now to wit, on the Thursday next after the octave of St. Hilary, in this same term, before the lord the king at Westminster, comes the said Robert King, by William Mathews his attorney, and having heard the said information, saith, that he doth not apprehend that the said lord the now king will impeach or trouble him the said Robert, because of the premises in the information aforesaid specified, because protesting that the information aforesaid, and the matter in the same contained, are not good and sufficient in law, to which he hath no necessity neither is he bound by the law of the land to answer, for plea the said Robert saith, that the borough of Wincanton aforesaid, is an antient borough, situate and lying within the hundred of Norton Ferris aforesaid, within which borough there is and from the whole time whereof the memory of man is not to the contrary, there hath been a court-leet and view of frankpledge held for the borough aforesaid, at that borough, before the steward of the lord of the said borough for the time being, twice in the year, to wit, once within one month after the feast of Easter, and again within one month after the feast of St. Michael the Archangel, of all the inhabitants and residents within the said borough, at which court for the said borough, all the inhabitants and residents within the said borough, for the whole time aforesaid, have appeared and done their suit, and have been used and accustomed to appear and do their suit, and not at the said leet of the said hundred, and that from the whole time aforesaid, two men annually, of the inhabitants and residents within the said borough, at the said court-leet and view of frankpledge of the said borough, have been elected and appointed, and have been accustomed to be elected and appointed, and as yet are and of right ought to be elected and appointed for executing the office of constable within the said borough: and that by reason thereof the inhabitants and residents within the said borough, for the said whole time, whereof the memory of man is not to the contrary, always have been exempted, acquitted and discharged from appearing and doing their suit at the court-leet of the said hundred, and from all election and execution of the office of constable of the said hundred. And the said Robert further saith, that he on the said 8th day of October, in the 24th year, &c. aforesaid, was and as yet is a resident and inhabitant within the said borough of Wincanton, and always did appear and do his suit at the said court-leet of that borough, and not at the court-leet of the said hundred. And that the said Robert

plea, that the defendant is an inhabitant of a borough, and therefore is liable to be chosen constable for the said borough, and therefore is discharged from executing the office of constable of the hundred.

so being a resident and inhabitant within the said borough, on the said 8th day of October, in the 24th year aforesaid, was elected in fact into the office of constable for the said hundred, in the said court-leet of the said hundred, but the said Robert after the said election to take oath for the due execution of the office of constable for the said hundred, for the cause aforesaid did refuse and deny, as it was lawful for him to do, and this the said Robert is ready to verify, wherefore he prays judgment, &c. &c.

The attorney-general demurs.

This case is reported 3 Keble 197, 230, 251, *no Judgment: but the court seemed inclined to give judgment for the king.*

---

*P.219.

*. The King *against* Caslin.

Michaelmas, 29th Charles II.

Indictment for the like offence.

Somerset,
To wit. } HERETOFORE to wit, on Tuesday to wit, the 9th day of January, in the 28th year of the reign of our lord Charles the 2d, by the grace of God of England, &c. king, &c. at a general session of the peace of the lord the king, held for his county of Somerset, at the city of Wells, in the said county, before Robert Hunt, esquire, the reverend father in Christ, Peter Bishop of Bath and Wells, and others their fellows justices of the said lord the king, assigned to preserve the peace in the said county, and also to hear and determine divers felonies, trespasses, and other misdeeds in the said county perpetrated, by the oath of 12 jurors, good and lawful men of the said county, impanelled, sworn and charged to enquire for the said lord the king, and for the body of the said county, it was presented, that at the court of the view of frank-pledge of George Speke, esquire, held for the hundred of Abdick, in the said county of Somerset, on Thursday to wit, the 12th day of October, within one month of St. Michael, in the 28th year, &c. aforesaid, at Ilton in the said county, within the jurisdiction of the said court, before John Chase, gentleman, then and as yet steward of the said court, one John Caslin of Horton, within the parish of Ilmister, in the said county, yeoman, being a fit and proper person, then and there abiding and inhabiting within the said hundred, in the due manner was nominated, appointed and elected to be constable of the said hundred, for one whole year following, of which election the said J. C. afterwards to wit, on the 15th day of October, in the year aforesaid, had notice; nevertheless the said

J. C.

J. C. not ignorant of the premisses, afterwards to wit, on the said 15th day of October, in the year aforesaid and always afterwards unto the taking of this inquisition at H. aforesaid, in the parish of I. aforesaid, in the county aforesaid, obstinately, contemptuously and unlawfully did refuse and deny to take upon himself the said office of constable of the hundred of A. aforesaid, upon the election and notice aforesaid, and then and there hath omitted and neglected to take the oath of constable of the said hundred, to the great obstruction of the execution of justice, the evil example of all others in the like case offending, and against the peace of the said lord the now king his crown and dignity, &c. Which indictment the lord the king hath caused to come before him for certain causes to be determined, &c. Whereupon the sheriff of the county aforesaid is commanded that he do not omit, &c. but that he cause him to come to answer, &c. And now to wit, on the Tuesday next after three weeks from the day of St. Michael, in this same term, before the lord the king at Westminster, comes the said J. C. by W. E. his attorney, and having heard the indictment aforesaid, saith, that he doth not apprehend that he ought to be impeached or troubled by any of the premisses in the indictment aforesaid specified, because saying that the said indictment and the matter in the same contained are not sufficient in law, to which he hath nor is he bound by the law of the land to answer, and the said J. C. saith, that the said parish of Il-mister is a parish situate, lying and being within the hundred of Abdick aforesaid, within which parish there is and is from the time whereof the memory of man is not to the contrary, there hath been a court-leet and view of frank pledge, held for the said parish at the said parish, before the steward of that court for the time being twice in the year, to wit, once within one month of Easter, and again within one month of St. Michael the Archangel, of all the inhabitants and residents within the said parish; at which court held for the said parish, all the inhabitants and residents within the said parish for the whole time aforesaid have appeared and have done their suit, and have been used and accustomed, and ought to appear and do their suit, and not at the said court of the view of frank-pledge of the hundred aforesaid, and that from the whole time aforesaid, two men of the inhabitants and residents with the said parish at the said court of view of frank-pledge, held for the said parish annually have been elected and chosen, and as yet are, and ought of right to be elected and chosen for executing the office of constable within the said parish, and that according to the custom used and approved of within the said hundred for the whole time aforesaid, to wit, at Ilmister aforesaid, the inhabitants and residents within the said parish, always have been used and accustomed, and ought to be acquitted and exonerated from

Indictment removed by Certiorari.

Protestation +P. 220.

Plea that defendant is an inhabitant within the parish of Il-mister, and liable to be chosen constable there.

from all election and execution of the office of constable for the hundred aforesaid. And the said J. C. further saith, that he on the said 12th day of October, in the 28th year, &c. aforesaid, was and as yet is seized of one tenement within the parish aforesaid, and on the said 12th day of October, and long before was and yet is a resident and inhabitant within the parish of Ilmister aforesaid, &c. And on the said 12th day of October, in the 28th year, &c. aforesaid, and long before was, and yet is liable to be charged with and chosen into the office of constable for the said parish, in the said court of view of frankpledge for the said parish, and this the said J. C. is ready to verify, &c. Wherefore he prays judgment, &c. with this that the said J. C. will verify that within the hundred aforesaid, and without the said parish of Ilmister aforesaid, on the said 12th day of October, in the 28th year, &c. aforesaid, there were and yet are residing and inhabiting divers fit and proper persons to execute the office of constable of the said hundred who never executed the said office, to wit, Ambrose Hare of C. within the hundred aforesaid, and Thomas Yard of S. within the hundred aforesaid.

---

* The King *against* Bettesworth.

Michaelmas, 30th Charles II.

Indictment for refusing to execute the office of high constable in a hundred,

Surrey, THAT at the general quarter sessions of the peace *To wit.* of the said lord the king, held in and for the county aforesaid, at Guilford in the said county, to wit, on the 11th day of July, in the 28th year, &c. before A. O. esq. A. B. bart. and others their fellows justices of the said lord the king, assigned to preserve the peace in the said county, and also to hear and determine divers felonies, trespasses, and other misdeeds, committed and perpetrated in the said county; one W. B. late of, &c. yeoman, then and long before being an inhabitant and resident within the parish aforesaid, in the hundred aforesaid, in the county aforesaid, and a fit and proper man to execute the office of high constable within the hundred aforesaid, in the due manner was elected to be one of the high constables of the hundred aforesaid, in the room of one J. B. whereof the said W. B. afterwards to wit, on the 20th day of July, in the 28th year, &c. aforesaid, and at divers other days and times afterwards at T. aforesaid, in the county aforesaid, had lawful notice, nevertheless the said W. B. not regarding his duty in this behalf, but devising and intending as much as in him lay, totally to obstruct and hinder the due execution

of

of justice, from the said 20th day of July, in the 28th year aforesaid, to the day of the taking of this inquisition, at the parish aforesaid, in the county aforesaid, wilfully, obstinately and contemptuously entirely hath refused to take upon himself and to execute the said office of high constable aforesaid, against his duty aforesaid, to the manifest contempt and obstruction of justice, to the evil example of all others in the like case offending, and against the peace of the said lord the now king, his crown and dignity, &c. Whereupon the sheriff of the said county was commanded by the said court first above mentioned, that he do not omit, &c. but that he cause the said W. B. to come, so that he be before the justices of the said lord the king, assigned to preserve the peace in the said county, and also to hear and determine divers felonies, &c. at the next general quarter sessions of the peace of the said lord the king, to be held for the said county. And afterwards to wit, at the next general quarter session of the peace of the said lord the king, held for the said county, at G. in the said county, on Tuesday, in one week next after, &c. to wit. on the 10th day of July, in the 29th year, &c. before R. H. esquire, A. G. esquire, and others, their fellows justices of the said lord the king, assigned to preserve the peace in the said county, and also to hear and determine divers felonies, &c. comes the sheriff of the said county, and returns his writ, to wit, that the said W. B. had nothing in his bailiwick by which he could be attached, whereupon the sheriff of the said county is commanded by the court here that he do not omit, &c. but that he should take the said W. B. if, &c. and him safely should keep so that he should have his body before the justices of the said lord the king, assigned to preserve the peace of the said lord the king, within the said county, and also to hear and determine divers felonies, &c. at the next general quarter session of the peace of the said lord the king, to be held for the * said county. Whereupon afterwards to wit, at the general quarter session of the peace of the said lord the king, held for the county aforesaid, at G. in the said county, on the day, &c. to wit, on the 2d day of October, in the 29th year, &c. before A. B. baronet, &c. and others their fellows justices of the said lord the king, assigned to preserve the peace in the said county, and also to hear and determine divers felonies, &c. comes the said W. B. and having heard the indictment aforesaid, saith, that he is not guilty thereof, and of this puts himself upon the country, and E. S. gentleman, clerk of the peace of the county aforesaid, who for the said lord the king in this behalf prosecuteth, doth the like, &c. Therefore the sheriff is commanded by the said court that he do not omit, &c. but that he cause to come before the justices of the said lord the king, assigned to preserve the peace of the said lord the king in the said county, and also to hear and determine divers felonies, &c. at the next general quarter

sessions

sessions of the peace to be held for the said county, twelve good and lawful men of the neighbourhood of the parish of T. in the county aforesaid, by whom, &c. and who neither, &c. to recognize, &c. because as well, &c. The same day is given as well to the said E. S. who prosecutes as to the said W. B. &c. And afterwards to wit, at the general quarter session of the peace of the said lord the king held for the county aforesaid, at G. in the said county, on ————, &c. to wit, on the 15th day of January, in the 29th year, &c. aforesaid, before S. H. esquire, R. K. knight, and others their fellows justices of the said lord the king, assigned to preserve the peace in the said county, and also to hear and determine divers felonies, &c. come as well the said E. S. who for the lord the king in this behalf prose-

Non misit breve. cutes, as the said W. B. in their proper persons, and the sheriff hath not thereupon sent the writ, therefore as before the sheriff of the county aforesaid, is commanded by the court here that he do not omit, &c. but that he cause to come before the justices of the said lord the king, assigned to preserve the peace of the said lord the king, in the said county, and also to hear and determine divers felonies, &c. at the next general quarter session of the peace of the said lord the king, to be held for the said county, twelve good and lawful men of the parish of T. aforesaid, in the county aforesaid, by whom, &c. and who neither, &c. to recognize, &c. because as well, &c. The same day is given as well to the said E. S. who prosecutes as to the said W. B. And afterwards to wit, at the next general quarter session of the peace of the said lord the king held for the county aforesaid, at R. in the said county, on the day to wit, on the 9th day, &c. of April, in the 30th year of the reign, &c. before E. T. knight, one of the barons of the Exchequer, of the said lord the king, A. B. baronet, and others their fellows justices of the said lord the king, assigned to preserve the peace of the said lord the king, the in county aforesaid, and also to hear and determine divers felonies, &c. come as well the said E. S. who prosecutes, &c. as the said W. B. in their proper persons; and the jurors of the said jury by the said sheriff for this purpose impanelled and returned, to wit, R. R. J. H. &c. being called, come, who being elected, tried and sworn to speak the truth of and concerning the premisses

Special verdict that the defend-
***P. 223.**
ant is a freeholder of the ma-
nor of W.
within the hundred,
held in ancient demesne, and aforesaid, say upon their oath, *"that the manor of W. in the*
" county of Surrey, is of the ancient demesne of the crown of
" England, and that the parish of T. in the indictment aforesaid
" mentioned, is within the said manor of W. and that the said manor
*" of W. is within the hundred of G. and the jurors further * say*
" upon their oath, that the said W. B. at the said general quarter
" session of the peace of the said lord the king, held for the county
" of Surrey aforesaid, at G. in the said county of Surrey, on the
" day, &c. to wit, on the 11th day of July, in the 28th year, &c.
" Before A. O. esquire, A. B. baronet, and others their fellows
" justices

Indictments for Misdemeanors.

Justices of the said lord the king, assigned to preserve the peace in whether
the said county, &c. also to hear and determine divers felonies, &c. such
in the due manner was elected to be one of the high constables of tenants are
the hundred of G. aforesaid, as in the said indictment is above men- liable to the
tioned. And the jurors aforesaid, upon their oath aforesaid, further office of
say, that the said W. B. before and at the time of his election afore- high con-
said, into the office aforesaid, and continually afterwards during the stable the
time in the indictment aforesaid mentioned, was resident within the jury doubt.
*said parish of T. aforesaid, &c. tenant of the said manor of W.
and that the said W. B. had legal notice of the said election, as
by the said indictment is above mentioned. And that he the said W.
B. at the time of his election aforesaid and continually afterwards
during the time in the indictment aforesaid mentioned, was a fit and
proper man to execute the office of high constable within the said
hundred; and he the said W. B. did refuse to take upon himself
and to execute the office of high constable of G. aforesaid,
because that he was as aforesaid, tenant of the manor of W. aforesaid, being of the antient demesne of the crown of England, but
whether the tenant of lands within the said manor of the antient demesne of the crown of England, be liable to be charged to execute
the office of high constable of the hundred of G. aforesaid, or not
the said jurors are wholly ignorant, and pray thereupon the advice
and consideration of the court, and if it shall seem to the court that
the tenant of lands within the said manor of the antient demesne
of the crown of England, be liable to be charged to execute the
office of high constable of the said hundred, then the said jurors
say upon their oath aforesaid, that the said W. B. is guilty of the
premisses in the said indictment above specified, in the manner and form
as by the said indictment above is supposed against him, and if upon
the whole matter aforesaid, by the jurors aforesaid, in the form
aforesaid, found it shall seem to the court here, that the tenant of
lands within the said manor of the antient demesne of the crown of
England, is not liable to be charged to execute the office of high constable of the said hundred, then the said jurors say upon their oath
aforesaid, that the said W. B. is not guilty of the premisses in the
said indictment above specified, in the manner and form as by the
said indictment above is supposed against him."* And because the Curia advi-
court will advise of and concerning the premisses, before that fur- sari vult.
ther, &c. day is given as well to the said B. S. who for the
lord the king in this behalf prosecutes, as to the said W. B.
in the same state in which now until the next general quarter
sessions of the peace of the said lord the now king, to be
held for the said county, &c. &c.

*This record was removed into the King's Bench and after several
arguments judgment was given for the king; it is reported 2 Shower 75 and in 1 Ventris 344.*

M m

The

#P. 224.

The King against Spencer and others.

Session of
the peace in
London,
the 12th
Nov. 21.
Charles 2d.
Indictment
against tw
common
barretors.

London, THE jurors, &c. That Edward Spencer late of
To wit, London, poulterer, and William Dalton, late of
London, yeoman, on the 10th day of August, in the 21st year
of the reign of our lord Charles the 2d, by the grace of God
of England, &c. king, &c. and at divers other days and times
as well before as after, at London to wit, in the parish of St.
Catherine, Creed-church, otherwise Christ-Church, in the ward
of Aldgate, London aforesaid, and at divers other places in the
said city, were and as yet are common barretors, and each and
every of them was and as yet is a common barretor, and daily
disturber of the peace of the said lord the now king, and also
a common brawler, quarreller, fighter, defamer, and sower of
sedition, strife and discord among his neighbours, and other
liege subjects of the said lord the king, so that they the said E.
S. and W. D. then and at the several days and times aforesaid,
at the parish and ward aforesaid, and at other places in the city
of London, did move and stir up, and each and every of them
did move and stir up, divers seditions, disputes, quarrels,
actions, suits, controversies and fightings, among divers liege
subjects of the said lord the king, to the great expence, grief,
disturbance, damage, cost, ruin and impoverishment of their
neighbours, and of other liege subjects of the said lord the
king, to the great disturbance of the peace of the said lord the
king, to the evil example of all others in the like case offending, and against the peace of the said lord the now king, his
crown and dignity, &c. &c.

The King against Ledlingham.

Information
against a
landlord,
for oppres-
sing his te-
nants with

To wit, THAT whereas one Warwick Ledlingham, late
of the parish of Otterye St. Mary, in the
county of Devon, esquire, for the space of divers years now
last past, hath been and as yet is lord of the manor of OtteryeSt.
Mary,

Mary, and whereas also within the manor and parish of Otterye causeless and unreasonable distresses, and vexatious suits. aforesaid, there are very many subjects of the said lord the now king, who hold their lands and tenements within the manor aforesaid, of the lord of the said manor to them and to their heirs for ever, as well in free socage as by copy of the court roll of the said manor, according to the custom of the said manor, and also other subjects of the said lord the king, within the said manor and parish of Otterye inhabiting, the said W. L. being a person of evil, malicious and turbulent mind and disposition, and maliciously, wickedly and unjustly devising and intending not only the tenants of the said manor, and the other subjects of the said lord the king there inhabiting, greatly to harrass, disquiet and oppress, but also the said tenants and the said other subjects of the said lord the king, there inhabiting in their possessions, maliciously to disturb and disquiet, and from their tenements aforesaid, unlawfully to expel and amove, and divers sums of money from the said tenants, and from the said other * subjects of the said lord the king unlawfully and P. 225. unjustly to extort, on the 23d day of October, in the 19th year of the reign of our lord Charles the 2d, &c. and at divers other days and times as well before as after, at O. in the said county of Devon, the said tenants and the other subjects of the said lord the king there inhabiting, by excessive and unlawful distresses, and driving away of their cattle, unlawfully and injuriously did harrass, disquiet, oppress and persecute, and did procure to be harrassed, disquieted, oppressed and persecuted, and divers sums of money from the said tenants, and the other subjects of the said lord the king there inhabiting did exact and extort, and divers other causeless actions and suits against the said tenants, and divers other subjects of the said lord the king, unlawfully, maliciously and injuriously did stir up, move and procure. And also that the said W. L. then and there was and yet is a common disturber of the peace of the said lord the now king, and a common oppressor of the said tenants and of his neighbours, and a sower and procurer of strife and discord among his neighbours, to the great damage, loss, grievance and disturbance of the tenants and subjects aforesaid, to the abuse and great contempt of the laws of this kingdom of England, to the evil and pernicious example of all others in the like case offending, and against the peace of the said lord the now king, his crown and dignity, whereupon the said, &c. &c.

The defendant was found guilty; and it was several times moved in arrest of Judgment, whether an information lay or not, and at length the court adjudged that no information lay, but the remedy is by action on the statute of Marlbridge. It is reported in 1 Mod. 71, 288. 1 Ventris 97, 104. Raymond 193, 205. 1 Lev. 299. 2 Keble 687, 697.

The

The King against Doyley.

Trinity, 30th Charles II.

Information for blasphemy.

To wit, THAT Thomas Doyley, late of the parish of St. Peter, in the county of Middlesex, gentleman, not having the fear of God in his heart, but being moved and seduced by the instigation of the devil, and devising and intending to defame and vilify the true and christian religion, received and publicly professed in this kingdom of England, and to blaspheme God and our Lord Jesus Christ, the saviour of the world, and the Holy Ghost, on the 1st day of February, in the 27th year, &c. at the parish aforesaid, in the county aforesaid, having and holding in his hands a certain cup of wine, unlawfully, most wickedly and in a blasphemous manner, in the presence and hearing of divers liege subjects of the said lord the king, worthy of belief, did say, pronounce, and with a loud voice did publish these profane and blasphemous English words following to wit, " *Here's a health to Father, Son and* " *Holy Ghost,*" (meaning Almighty God, Jesus Christ, the saviour of the world, and the Holy Ghost) and immediately thereupon, then and there did drink up the said * wine, out of the said cup, to the great dishonour of Almighty God, in great contempt and dishonour of the Holy Trinity, to the great scandal of the profession of the true christian religion, to the evil and pernicious example of all others in the like case offending, and against the peace of the said lord the now king, his crown and dignity, &c. whereupon, &c. &c.

*P. 226.

The King against Taylor.

Michaelmas, 27th Charles 2d.

Information for the like.

To wit, THAT John Taylor, late of the parish of St. Clement Danes, in the county of Middlesex, yeoman, not having the fear of God in his heart, but being moved and seduced by the instigation of the devil, and devising and intending to defame and vilify the true and christian religion, received and professed in this kingdom of England, and also to blaspheme God and our Lord Jesus Christ, the saviour of

the

the world, on the 26th day of April, in the 27th year, &c. in the parish of the Holy Trinity, in the town of Guilford, in the county of Surrey, then being of sound memory, these false, blasphemous and most wicked English words of and concerning the christian religion, and our Lord Jesus Christ, in the presence and hearing of divers liege subjects of the said lord the king worthy of belief, falsely, maliciously, advisedly, wickedly, and in a blasphemous manner, did say, pronounce, and with a loud voice did publish to wit, " *Christ* (meaning our Lord Jesus Christ, the only begotten son of Almighty God) *is a whore-master, and religion* (meaning the christian religion) *is a cheat, and profession* (meaning the profession of the christian religion) *is a cloak, and they* (meaning the said christian religion, and the profession of the said religion) *are both cheats, and all the earth is mine,* (meaning his the said J. T.) *and I am a king's son, my father sent me* (meaning him the said J. T.) *hither, and made me* (again meaning the said J. T.) *a fisherman to take vipers, and I* (meaning himself the said J. T.) *neither fear God, devil, nor man, and I* (meaning himself the said J. T.) *am a younger brother to Christ,* (meaning our Lord Jesus Christ) *an angel of God* (meaning an angel of the Almighty God) *and no man fears God but an hypocrite, Christ* (meaning our Lord Jesus Christ) *is a bastard, God damn and confound all your gods, Christ* (meaning our Lord Jesus Christ) *is the whore's* (meaning the blessed virgin Mary, mother of our Lord Jesus Christ) *master,*" to the great dishonour of Almighty God, to the great contempt and dishonour of our Lord Jesus Christ, to the great scandal of the profession of the true christian religion, to the destruction of christian government and society, in manifest contempt of the Holy Trinity, and in blasphemy of the Godhead of our Lord Jesus Christ, to the evil and pernicious example of all others in the like case offending, and against the peace, &c. whereupon the said attorney, &c. &c.

* And now to wit, on the Monday next after fifteen days of St. Martin, in this same term, before the lord the king, at Westminster, comes the said J. T. in his proper person, under the custody of Joseph Sheldon, mayor of the city of London, and of the community of the citizens of the said city, and of the governors of the possessions, rents and hospital of St. Mary of Bethlem, situate without Bishopsgate, London, into whose custody before that time for the said cause he was committed and detained, by virtue of a writ of habeas corpus ad subjiciendum to them directed, in his proper person, and is committed to the marshal, &c. and having heard the information aforesaid, saith, that he is not guilty thereof, and of this puts himself upon the country, &c. and William Jones, knt. &c. doth the like, &c. therefore let a jury come thereupon, &c. at which Monday next after the morrow of the purification of

the

*P. 227.

Habeas corpus to Bethlem, to remove defendant.

Plea not guilty.

the blessed virgin Mary, before the lord the king at Westminster, come as well the said W. Jones, who prosecutes, &c. as the said J. T. in his proper person under the custody of the marshal of the marshalsea of the lord the king to whose custody for the cause aforesaid he was committed as aforesaid; and the jurors of the said jury for this purpose chosen come

Verdict, Guilty.

likewise, who being elected, tried and sworn to speak the truth concerning the said premisses, say upon their oath, that the said J. T. is guilty of the premisses in the information aforesaid above specified, whereupon all and singular the premisses

Judgment.

being seen and by the court here understood, it is considered, that the said J. T. do pay to the lord the king, 1000*l.* for his fine, for the blasphemy in the information aforesaid contained, whereof he is convicted, and that he find security for his good behaviour during his life, and that he shall stand in the pillory in the court yard of the palace of Westminster, for the space of one hour, with a paper affixed upon his head, with these words in writing in large letters, to wit, " *For* " *blasphemous words, tending to the subversion of all government.*" And that the said J. T. shall stand in the pillory, in the market town of Guilford, in the county of Surrey, in the open market place, at the time of market, for the space of one hour, with the like paper affixed upon his head, with the said words in writing, in large letters; and that the defendant present here in court, is committed to the marshal of this court, safely to be kept until that, &c.

This case is reported 3 Keble 607, 621.

The King *against* J. C. *and others.*

Information for coining halfpence, and uttering them in payment.

To wit, THAT J. C. of the parish of S. in the county of H. labourer, R. M. of, &c. inn-keeper, and W. C. of the same victualler, assuming and each and every of them assuming upon himself the royal prerogative and authority, and devising and intending the said lord the king and all his people falsly, unlawfully and deceitfully to deceive and defraud between the day, &c. and the day of the exhibition of this information at the parish, &c. in the county, &c. Three hundred pieces of brass and copper, with certain letters and other marks and signs, to the said attorney general of the said lord the now king as yet unknown, unlawfully, unjustly and deceitfully and for the sake of wicked gain, without any law-

P. 228. ful * warrant or authority, did forge, coin and cause to be stamped, and each and every of them did forge, coin and cause

to

to be stamped, and did cause to be forged, coined and stamped, with intention to utter and expose the said three hundred pieces of brass and copper, and every piece thereof, in exchange, payment and traffick, to the said subjects of the said lord the king, for and in the name and as the half part of one penny, of the lawful money of England, commonly called an halfpenny. And the said J. C. R. M. and W. C. afterwards to wit, within the said time, at the parish aforesaid, in the county aforesaid, the said three hundred pieces of brass and copper, and every piece thereof, by them the said J. C. R. M. and W. C. so as aforesaid unlawfully, unjustly, deceitfully and for the sake of wicked gain, made, forged, coined and stamped, and caused to be forged and stamped, for and in the name and as the half part of one penny, of the lawful money of England, commonly called an halfpenny, to divers other persons to the said attorney general of the said lord the king as yet unknown, unlawfully, unjustly, and for the sake of wicked gain, did utter and expose, and each and every of them did utter and expose, whereas in truth they the said J. C. R. M. and W. C. then and there well knew, and each and every of them well knew that the said three hundred pieces of brass and copper were only of the value of two shillings and not more, to the great deceit, injury and fraud, as well of the said lord the king as of all the liege subjects of the said lord the king, in contempt of the said lord the now king and of his laws, to the evil example of all others in the like case offending, and against the peace of the said lord the now king his crown and dignity, &c. whereupon the said attorney, &c.

The King against Tyack.

To wit, THAT the borough of Saltash, in the county of Cornwall, is and from the time whereof, the memory of man is not to the contrary, hath been an antient borough and the free burgesses of the said borough from the time whereof, the memory of man is not to the contrary, even to at and upon the 29th day of June, in the 27th year of the reign of the lady Elizabeth, late queen of England, &c. have been incorporated by the name of the free burgesses of the borough of Essa, otherwise Saltash, on which day the said lady Elizabeth, by her letters patent under her great seal, bearing date at Westminster, on the same day and year incorporated the free burgesses of the borough of Essa, otherwise Saltash, by the name of the mayor and free burgesses of the borough of Saltash, and so being incorporated, they the said mayor and

the corpo-
ration; for
publishing
the same,
as the deed
of the whole
corporation,
and causing
the same to
be enrolled
in Chan-
cery.

*P. 229.

free burgesses of the borough of Saltash aforesaid, on the 5th day of August, in the 34th year of the reign of the said lord the now king, were seized of divers lands, tenements, rents, customs, markets, tolls and hereditaments, as well in the borough of Saltash aforesaid, as elsewhere, within this kingdom of England, of great yearly value in their demesne as of fee, and then and always before, from the time that they as aforesaid were incorporated by the name of the mayor and free burgesses of the borough of Saltash, and the said free burgesses of the borough of Essa, otherwise Saltash aforesaid, from the whole time whereof the memory of man is not to the contrary, until the said time of incorporation by the name of the † mayor and free burgesses of the borough of Saltash, had, held and enjoyed, and have been used and accustomed and of right ought to have, hold and enjoy to themselves, and to their successors, many and divers liberties, privileges, franchises, immunities, jurisdictions and emoluments, and were lawfully possessed of goods and chattels and writings obligatory of great value for ĭthe payment of money, as of their proper goods and chattels and writings obligatory. And the said coroner and attorney of the said lord the king, for the said lord the king, gives the court here further to understand and to be informed, that one Nicholas Tyack, of the borough of Saltash aforesaid, gentleman, before the said 5th day of August, in the 34th year of the reign of the said lord the now king, was one of the free burgesses of the borough of Saltash aforesaid, and at the time of his admission to be one of the free burgesses of the said borough, the said Nicholas there, according to the custom of the said borough, upon the holy gospel of God, took his oath, that he would maintain the laws, customs and franchises of the said borough; nevertheless the said N. T. well knowing all and singular the premisses, wickedly and maliciously devising and intending to destroy the good estate and condition of the burgesses of the said borough, and to move and sow strife and discord between the said free burgesses, and them entirely to deprive of their said liberties, franchises, jurisdictions, immunities, emoluments, goods and chattels, debts, lands, tenements and hereditaments, and also entirely to dissolve the said body corporate and politick, on the 5th day of August, in the 34th year of the reign of the said lord the now king aforesaid, under colour of his office of mayor of the said borough, but against the duty of the office of mayor of the said borough, and against the form and effect of his oath aforesaid, at the borough of Saltash aforesaid, a certain chest then sealed and in which the common seal of the mayor and free burgesses of the said borough of Saltash, then was contained, and which chest, according to the custom of the said borough, ought not nor was accustomed to be opened without the consent of the free burgesses of the said borough,
with

with force and arms, &c. did break and open, and the said
common feal did take thereout, and then and there that feal,
which without the affent of the free burgeffes of the faid borough, to any writing ought not nor was accuftomed to be
put, as the common feal of the mayor and free burgeffes of
the faid borough, of his own proper mind, falfe imagination,
confpiracy and covin, without the affent and againft the will
of the free burgeffes of the faid borough, to a certain writing
or inftrument (purporting to be a grant to the faid lord the
now king and to his heirs and fucceffors, by the mayor and
free burgeffes of the borough of Saltafh aforefaid, of all
and fingular their manors, meffuages, lands, rents, tenements
and hereditaments, with their appurtenances and of all and
every their chattels as well real as perfonal, and a grant and
furrender to the faid lord the now king by the faid mayor and
free burgeffes of all their franchifes, charters, letters patent
of incorporation, powers, privileges, liberties and immunities
whatfoever) falfely and deceitfully did put, although the
mayor and certain free burgeffes of the faid borough of Saltafh, to the number of fifty perfons and more, being by much
the greater part of the free burgeffes of the faid borough, never did confent nor were willing to confent, nor had granted
that any furrender of any charter, liberty, franchife or privilege of the faid body corporate fhould be made either by the
faid N. or by any member of the * faid body corporate or by *P. 230.
any other perfon or perfons whatfoever; which writing or inftrument by him the faid N. fo as aforefaid, falfely and deceitfully with the faid common feal fealed, he the faid N. afterwards to wit, on the faid 5th day of Auguft, in the 34th
year, &c. aforefaid, falfely and malicioufly, did utter and publifh, as the deed of the mayor and free burgeffes of the borough
of Saltafh aforefaid, to wit, at S. aforefaid, and the faid deed
in the court of Chancery of the faid lord the king, at Weftminfter
in the county of Middlefex, on the twentieth day of February,
in the 35th year of the reign of the faid lord the now king,
falfely and deceitfully did procure and caufe to be acknowledged to be the deed of the faid mayor and free burgeffes, by pretence of which that writing afterwards to wit, on the 23d day
of February, in the 35th year laft aforefaid, in the faid court of
Chancery, as the deed of the mayor and free burgeffes of the
borough of Saltafh aforefaid, was enrolled of record, as by the
enrollment thereof in the faid court of Chancery of the faid
lord the king, at Weftminfter aforefaid, in the county of Middlefex, remaining of record more fully appears, and fo the faid
N. the faid writing or inftrument as if it had been the deed of
the mayor and free burgeffes of the borough of Saltafh aforefaid
fealed with their common feal, (whereas in truth and in fact Averments.
the faid N. on the faid 5th day of Auguft, in the 34th year aforefaid, was not mayor of the borough of Saltafh aforefaid,
and whereas in truth and in fact, that writing was not the

N n   deed

deed of the mayor and free burgesses of the borough of Saltath aforesaid) falsely, subtily and fraudulently, against his oath aforesaid, did seal, publish and procure to be enrolled in the manner and form aforesaid, without the assent or consent, and against the will of the mayor and free burgesses of the borough of S. aforesaid, to the deception, deceit and contempt of the said lord the now king, and of his laws, to the great damage of the mayor and free burgesses of the borough of S. aforesaid, to the great disturbance of the tranquillity of the said borough, to the evil and pernicious example of all others in the like case offending, and against the peace of the said lord the now king, his crown and dignity, &c.

The King *against* Atkins, *and others.*

Hilary, 33d and 34th of Charles the 2d. *Roll.* 90

Indictment against a recorder and several aldermen of Bristol, for meeting and chusing an alderman of the city, in the room of one deceased, and this without any summons of the mayor of Bristol.
*P. 231.

City of Bristol, to wit.
{ BE it remembered that at the general quarter session of the peace of the lord the king, held in and for the county of the city of Bristol aforesaid, in the Guild-Hall of the said city on Tuesday to wit the 4th day of October, in the 33d year of the reign of our lord Charles the second by the grace of God of England, &c. king, &c. before T. Earl, mayor of the city of Bristol aforesaid, R. Cam, knight and baronet, and others their fellows aldermen of the said city, justices of the said lord the king, assigned to preserve the peace within the county of the city aforesaid, and also to hear and determine divers felonies, trespasses and other misdeeds, in the said county perpetrated, &c. by the oath of I. M. F. B. and fifteen others good and lawful men of the county of the city aforesaid, then and there sworn and charged to enquire for the said lord the king and for the body of the county of the city aforesaid, it is * presented that the bill annexed to this schedule is true; the answer of Thomas Earl, knight, mayor of the city of Bristol, R. Cam, knight and baronet, and others their fellows aldermen of the said city, keepers of the peace and justices, &c. City of Bristol to wit, the jurors for our lord the king upon their oath say and present, that the lord Henry the 7th, of his name, heretofore king of England, on the 17th day of September, in the 15th year of his reign, by his letters patent, under his great seal of England, bearing date at Knoll, the said day and
year,

year, granted to the then mayor and citizens of the town of
Briftol (the faid city of Briftol then being a town) and to
their fucceffors, among other things, that if any of the faid
community fhould be procurers, abettors or maintainers, to
make debate and difcord upon the election of mayor or his
other officer whatfoever, of his faid town of Briftol the fuburbs and precincts of the fame, immediately by the mayor
and two aldermen of the faid town for the time being, by the
mayor of the faid town for the time being, to be nominated
and affigned, they fhould be punifhed in the due manner according to the quantity and quality of their crime, according
to the law and cuftom of his kingdom of England as by the
exemplification of the faid letters patent of the lord the king,
under his great feal, to the jurors aforefaid now fhewn in evidence more fully appears. And that according to the privileges by the lady Elizabeth, late queen of England, by her letters patent under her great feal of England, dated at Weftminfter, on the 28th day of June, in the 23d year of her
reign, after the time in which the faid late town of Briftol,
was lawfully created and erected into a city, to the mayor and
community of the faid city and their fucceffors granted, as by the
exemplification of the letters patent laft mentioned under the
great feal of the faid lady the queen, now in like manner fhewn
in evidence to the faid jury more fully appears ; there have been
or ought to have been from the time of the making of the faid
letters patent of the faid lady Elizabeth, and there are or
ought to be twelve aldermen of the faid city, of whom the recorder of the faid city for the time being, hath been and ought to
have been and now is one. And according to the faid privileges
fo as aforefaid granted, for the whole time aforefaid, after the
death of any fuch alderman the mayor and remaining furviving
aldermen of the faid city for the time being, and the major part
of them affembled at the fummons of the faid mayor, have
elected and have been accuftomed to elect one other perfon
of the prudent citizens of the faid city, into an alderman of
the faid city in the place of the alderman fo dying as aforefaid.
And by the faid privileges fo granted, the faid mayor and aldermen of the faid city for the time being, being thereto lawfully elected, and fworn to execute their feveral offices, for the
whole time aforefaid, have been and are and ought to be keepers and juftices of the faid lord the king of England for the
time being, affigned to preferve the peace in the city of Briftol aforefaid, and alfo to hear and determine divers felonies,
trefpaffes and other mifdeeds there perpetuated as long as
they refpectively remained in their offices aforefaid, and that
continually after the time of the making of the faid letters
patent of the faid lady Elizabeth, the recorder and the other aldermen of the faid city for the time being, have been and ought
to be of the privy council of the mayor of the faid city for

                                    the

＊P.232. the ＊ time being in particular cases concerning the good state and government of the said city, whensoever such mayor would summon them, and such privy council for the whole time aforesaid, hath not been accustomed nor ought not to be summoned, nor ought to transact any business pertaining to that council, unless by the summons and in the presence of such mayor. And that after the death of one John Lloyd, knight, deceased, being at the time of his death, one of the aldermen of the said city, one Robert Atkins, late of the said city, knight of the bath, then and as yet recorder of the said city, John Knight, late of the said city, knight, John Lawford, late of the said city, esquire, and Joseph Creswick, late of the said city, esquire, all then being aldermen of the said city, and who all then were free burgesses of the said city, to maintain factions in the said city, and to make debate and discord upon the election of an alderman of the said city, and officer of the king, there in the place of the said alderman, so as aforesaid deceased, on the 8th day of March, in the 33d year of the reign of the said lord the now king, unduly, unjustly, wickedly and without the example of former times, at Bristol aforesaid, to wit, at the parish and ward of St. Adonai, within the city aforesaid, in the county of the said city, among themselves altogether, and mutually did conspire to hold a privy council of the aldermen of the said city, and in the said council to elect and create one of the citizens of the said city, into an alderman of the said city, in the place of the said I. L. alderman, deceased, without the summons and in the absence and against the will of Richard Hart, knight, then being mayor of the said city, and to fulfil and perfect their unjust and wicked conspiracy aforesaid, they the said R. A. I. K. I. L. and I. C. afterwards to wit, on the said day and year last mentioned, into the common house and place of audience of the mayor and community of the said city, commonly called the Tolsey, and into the council chamber of the mayor and community of the said city, commonly called the council house, parcel of the house aforesaid, situate in the parish and ward aforesaid, with force and arms, &c. did enter, and then and there riotously and routously did assemble themselves to execute their said evil purposes, and afterwards to wit, on the said day and year and place last aforesaid mentioned, they the said R. A. I. K. I. L. and I. C. together with other aldermen of the said city, not knowing the said purposes of the said conspirators, in fact did hold a privy council of the aldermen of the said city, and then and there in fact and as much as in them lay, did elect and create one T. Day, then being a citizen of the said city, into an alderman of the said city, into the place of the said John Lloyd, then as aforesaid deceased, without any summons, by the said R. Hart, then mayor of the said city, made to them to assemble, and in the
                                                                        absence

absence and against the will of the said mayor; and the said conspirators then and there in the absence and against the will of the said mayor, the said election in the common book in which the acts of the mayor and aldermen of the said city, done in the said privy council are commonly written, did cause to be written and entered, as an order of the privy council aforesaid, whereby great discord among the community of the said city, and the * mayor and aldermen of the said city then being and the other officers of the said lord the now king in the city aforesaid, hath arisen to the great disgrace and dishonour of the good government of the said city, against the form of the letters patent above before recited, against the tenor of the several oaths by the said conspirators respectively taken, as burgesses, aldermen and recorder of the said city, and against the peace of the said lord the now king, his crown and dignity, &c.

*P. 233.

This indictment was against Sir Robert Atkyns, afterwards lord chief baron of the Exchequer: all the defendants were upon the trial, found guilty, and Sir Robert himself, with great learning and ingenuity, moved in arrest of judgment, and upon his argument, judgment was arrested. It is at large reported in 3 Mod. 3. and 2 Show. 236.

The King *against* Deeds.

Easter, the 1st of James the 2d. *Roll* 121.

Kent,
To wit, } THAT whereas on the 15th day of February, in the 1st year of the reign of our lord James the 2d, now king of England, &c. in night of the said day at Stade, in the county of Kent, within the liberty and precincts of the town and port of Hythe there, certain malefactors, to the said attorney-general of the said lord the now king as yet unknown, had prepared and there had great quantity of English wool, to be transported into parts beyond the seas, and then and there upon the sea-shore had prepared and attempted to put the said wool into certain boats, there lying, to be transported into the said parts beyond the seas, against the laws and statutes in such case made and provided. And whereas also one John Walker, then and there being an officer, lawfully authorized to prevent the said transportation, and James Marsh and John Lecandle, in his aid then and there as much as in them

Information against a coroner, for returning an inquisition of murder, against several into the court of King's-Bench; whereof they were acquitted on trial there, whereas in fact, the

said inquisi-
tion was
not found
by any jury. them lay, endeavoured to prevent the transportation aforesaid, and thereupon one Robert Desborow, and many other persons to the number of twenty, to the said attorney-general as yet unknown, assembled themselves, and then and there with blunderbusses, swords and knives, riotously and in a warlike manner, in and upon the said J. W. J. M. and J. L. so as aforesaid, endeavouring to prevent the transportation of the said wool, did make an assault, and him the said James, then and there did strike and wound, and thereupon it so happened that the said R. Desborow, in fighting and endeavouring with the other persons unknown, on his side to transport the said wool, and the said James Marsh, in opposing the said transportation, he the said R D then and there by the said J. M. was slain. And whereas also Julius Deeds, esquire, then was mayor of the town and port of Hythe aforesaid, and coroner of the said lord the king, within the said town and port, and the liberties and precincts of the same, and also justice of the peace of the said lord the king within the said town and port, and the liberties and precincts of the same, he the said J. D. being a person of evil * name, fame and dishonest conversation, and a great maintainer and assister of persons to transport English wool into parts beyond the seas, against the laws and statutes aforesaid, and not having the fear of God before his eyes, but being moved and seduced by the instigation of the devil, and devising, and falsely, unlawfully and unjustly, wickedly and corruptly intending to deter men from preventing the transportation of wool, and to deprive the said J. M. of the testimony and evidence of the said J. W. and J. L. of and concerning the death of the said R. D. to be had on behalf of the said J. M. and in like manner to cause him the said J. M. to lose his life by the process of law, and to cause them the said J. W. and J. L. to be imprisoned and tried for the murder and death of the said R. D. he the said J. D. the sooner to fulfil, perfect and bring to effect his most wicked devices, practices and intentions aforesaid, on the 27th day of February, in the 1st year of the reign of our lord James the 2d, by the grace of God, of England, &c. king, &c. with force and arms, &c. at the town and port of H. aforesaid, in the county of K. aforesaid, did cause them the said J. W. J. M. and J. L. to be arrested and to be detained in prison in safe and close custody, for the felony and murder of the said R. D. before that time by them supposed to be committed and perpetrated, and then and there a certain writing indented, purporting to be an inquisition taken at the town and port of Hythe aforesaid, in the said county of Kent, on Friday to wit, the 27th day of February, in the 1st year of the reign of our said lord James the 2d, &c. before him the said J. D. esquire, mayor of the town and port of H. aforesaid, and coroner of the said lord the king, with the said town and port of H. and the liberties and precincts of the same, upon

the

* P. 234.

the view of the body of the said R. D. of H. aforesaid, wool-comber, then and there lying dead, by the oath J. L. E. T. and ten other good and lawful men of the town and port of H. aforesaid, sworn and charged to enquire how and by what means the said R. D. came to his death, of his own proper head and imagination, knowingly, subtily, falsely and fraudulently, and against the duty of his office, did make and cause to be made; the tenor of which follows, to wit, *Hythe*, to wit, Inquisition. An inquisition indented, taken at the town and port of Hythe, in the county of Kent, on Friday to wit, the 27th day of February, in the 1st year of the reign of our lord James the 2d, king, &c. and in the year of our Lord 1684, before J. D. esquire, mayor of the town and port of H. aforesaid, and coroner of the said lord the king, within the said town and port, and the liberties and precincts of the same, according to the usage and custom of town and port aforesaid, from the time whereof, &c. on the view of the body of R. D. of the said town of H. woolcomber, then and there being lying dead, upon the oath of J. T. E. L. and ten others, good and lawful men of the town and port of H. aforesaid, sworn to enquire how and by what means the said R. D. came to his death, who say upon their oath aforesaid, that James Marsh, of the town and port of Dover, in the county aforesaid, gentleman, John Walker, of D. aforesaid, gentleman, and John Lecandie, of D. aforesaid, innholder, with divers other persons to the jurors aforesaid unknown, not having the fear of God before their eyes, but being moved and seduced by the instigation of the devil, on the 25th day of this present month of February, about the eleventh hour, in the night of the same day, nigh to a certain place called Old Stake, within the * liberties of the *P. 235. town and port of H. aforesaid, with force and arms, to wit, with swords, bayonets, guns and pistols, in and upon the said R. D. in the peace of God, and of our said lord the king then and there being, did make an assault and affray, and that the said James, a certain pistol of the value of five shillings, charged with gun-powder, and one leaden bullet, which he the said James Marsh in his right hand then and there had and held, in and upon him the said R. D. then and there feloniously, wilfully, and of his malice aforethought, did discharge, and him the said R. D. then and there, with the leaden bullet aforesaid, so shot forth by him the said J. M. out of the pistol aforesaid, did strike, giving to the said R. D. then and there, with the leaden bullet aforesaid, so as aforesaid shot forth, one mortal wound in his belly, and through his bowels and liver penetrating of the breadth of one inch and an half, and of the depth of ten inches, of which mortal wound, he the said R. D. did languish, from the 25th day of February, in the 1st year aforesaid, until this present 27th day of February, on which said 27th day of February, about the second hour of the morning

of

of the said day, he the said R. D. of the mortal wound aforesaid, at H. aforesaid, in the county aforesaid died, and that the said J W. J. L. and divers other persons unknown, on the said 25th day of February, about the eleventh hour of the night of the said day, nigh to the place called the Old Stake, within the liberty of the town and port of H. aforesaid, feloniously, and of their malice aforethought, were present with swords, bayonets, guns and pistols, then and there abetting, procuring, comforting and maintaining the said James Marsh, feloniously to commit and perpetrate the felony and murder aforesaid, in the manner and form aforesaid, against the peace of the said lord the now king his crown and dignity, &c. And so the jurors aforesaid, upon their oath aforesaid, say that the said J. M. J. W. J. L. and the said several persons unknown, him the said R. D. in the manner and form aforesaid, feloniously, wilfully, and of their malice aforethought, did kill and murder against the peace of the said lord the king, his crown and dignity; and moreover the jurors aforesaid, say upon their oath aforesaid, that the said J. M. J. W. J. L. and the said several persons unknown, had not or any of them had, at the time of the felony and murder aforesaid, committed and perpetrated, any goods or chattels, lands or tenements, to their knowledge within the liberty of the town and port of H. aforesaid, and that the said several persons unknown, immediately after the felony and murder aforesaid, was committed and perpetrated fled, against the peace of the said lord the now king his crown and dignity. In witness whereof, as well the said mayor and coroner hath set to this inquisition, his hand and the seal of his office of mayor of the town and port of H. as the said jurors have set their hands and seals, dated the day and year aforesaid, J. D. mayor and coroner, J. I. E. T. and ten others; and afterwards to wit, on the 6th day of May, in the 1st year aforesaid, the said writing indented, purporting to be an inquisition [written in the Latin tongue, in the manner and form aforesaid] as the true inquisition of the jury aforesaid, upon their oath aforesaid, before the said J. D. upon view of the body, in the due and lawful manner found and taken, in further prosecution of his malicious and wicked devices and intentions aforesaid, he the said J. D. * falsely, and against the duty of his office, wickedly and fraudulently to the subversion of the law and justice of this kingdom of England, into the court here before the king himself, to wit, at Westminster, in the county of Middlesex, did deliver of record, to be proceeded upon in the due form of law, and thereupon it was in such manner proceeded, that afterwards to wit, in this present term, as well the said J. M. as the said J. W. and J. L. upon the writing indented aforesaid, as a true inquisition taken in the due manner, at the bar of the said court here, in the due manner were tried, and of the said murder were acquitted,

P. 236.

Talliter Processum.

quitted, as by the record thereof in the court here remaining, affiled of record more fully appeareth. Whereas in truth and in fact the jurors aforesaid, in the writing indented aforesaid mentioned, or any other jurors never did find upon their oath the said inquisition, or that they the said J. W. and J. L. or either of them, were present abetting, procuring, comforting and maintaining the said J. M. to commit and perpetrate the felony and murder aforesaid, in the writing indented aforesaid mentioned, to the great damage, and injury of them the said J. M. J. W. and J. L. to the evil and pernicious example of all others in the like case offending, and against the peace of the said lord the now king his crown and dignity, &c. whereupon the said attorney-general, &c.

Averments.

The King against Crofs.

Easter, 1st James II. Roll 122.

Somerfet, to wit. } THAT John Crofs, late of Trull, in the county of Somerset, gentleman, on the 22nd day of March, in the 32nd year of the reign of the lord Charles the 2d, the late king, &c. was one of the coroners of the said late lord the king, in and for the said county, and the office of one of the coroners of the said lord the king, and for the said county, continually afterwards hitherto hath taken upon himself had and exercised, and as yet doth have and exercise, and that during the time that the said John Crofs was one of the coroners, in and for the said county, to wit, on the said 21st day of March, in the 32nd year of the reign of our late lord Charles the 2nd, &c. aforesaid, at E—— in the said county of Somerset, one John Pearle, of E—— aforesaid, yeoman, being of found mind, wilfully, feloniously, and as a felon, of himself then and there did kill and murder himself, against the peace of the lord the king his crown and dignity. And that thereupon afterwards to wit, on the said 21st day of March, in the 32nd year of the reign of our said lord Charles the 2nd, late king, &c. aforesaid, at E—— aforesaid, in the said county, one Hugh Brockford, J. L. the elder, J. L. the younger. J. F. &c. as the manner and custom is, upon the view of the body of the said J. P. were sworn, and charged before the said J. C. one of the coroners of the said lord the late king in and for the county aforesaid, then and there being, to enquire of the death of the said J. P. then and there lying dead, and that the said J. C. on the said 21st day of March, in the 32nd

Information against a coroner, for persuading a jury after full evidence of a persons being felo de se, to find that he was non compos mentis.

O o
year

year aforesaid, at E—— aforesaid, in the said county, not regarding the duty of his office of one of the coroners of the said lord the late king, but devising, and fraudulently intending to stifle and conceal the truth of the premisses, and to obstruct, prevent and hinder as much as in him lay the due course of *P. 237. course of law, and to conceal the said felony and murder, and with the intention that the said lord the late king might totally lose the whole profits and advantages, which he ought to have in such case, and also to deprive, deceive and defraud the said lord the late king, of the goods and chattels, which were the said J. P's. at the time of his death, he the said J. C. then and there falsly, unlawfully and unjustly, and against the duty of his office, did say and assert to the said jury then and there impanelled sworn and charged to enquire of the death of the said J. P. *" that the said J. P. at the time that " he slew himself was mad, and not of sound understanding."* And thereupon the said J. C. then and there falsly, unlawfully, unduly and unjustly by deceitful and subtil ways and means, and false allegations, persuasions and practises by him the said J. C. on the jurors aforesaid used and practised, then and there falsly, unlawfully, unduly and unjustly, and against the duty of his office in the premisses, for bribes by him the said J. C. then and there in that behalf had and received, and against the full and manifest evidence to the jurors aforesaid, then and there given, did cause and procure upon the inquisition, in that behalf taken, by the oath of the said jurors, before him the said J. C. then being one of the coroners of the said lord the late king, for the said county, that it should be found *" That the said John Pearse, at E——* *" aforesaid, in a barn belonging to the house of the said J. P. about* *" the hour of ten before mid day, being alone, then and there not* *" being of sound understanding, with one rope of the value* *" of four pence, which he then and there in his hands had* *" and held [one end about his own neck, then and there did put,* *" and the other end about a certain beam] himself with the* *" said rope then did hang and suffocate, and so the said J. P.* *" not being of sound mind, came to his death."* Whereas in truth and in fact the said J. P. wilfully and feloniously himself did kill and murder, and was of sound mind at the time that he perpetrated the felony and murder aforesaid, by reason of which premisses, the said lord the late king hath totally lost the entire advantages and profits which he ought to have had in such case; and the said coroner and attorney of the said lord the now king further gives the court here to understand and to be informed, that the said John Cross, on the said 21st day of March, in the 32d year of the reign of the lord Charles the 2d, the late king, &c. being as aforesaid one of the coroners of the said lord the late king, for the county aforesaid, with force and arms, &c. at E——

&c.

&c. unlawfully, unjustly and extorsively did exact, receive
and have from Joan Pearse, the widow of the said John
Pearse, over and above the sum of 13s. 4d. to wit, the sum
of 5l. of the lawful money of England, for the fee of the
said J. C. as one of the coroners of the said lord the late
king, of the said county, for taking the said inquisition upon
the view of the body of the said John Pearse, against the
duty of his said office, to the evil example of all others in
the like case offending, to the hindrance of Justice, and
against the peace of the said lord the late king his crown
and dignity, and also against the form of the statute in such
case made and provided, &c. whereupon the said coroner
and attorney, &c.

<h2 style="text-align:center">* The King against Voysey.   *P. 238.</h2>

Cornwall,
to wit.
THAT one Benjamin Stevens, on the 14th day
of August, in the 3d year of the reign of our
lord James, by the grace of God, of England, &c. king, &c.
at Gluvias, in the said county, was slain, against the peace
of the said lord the now king, his crown and dignity, and
that thereupon afterwards to wit, on the 15th day of August,
in the 3d year aforesaid, at G. aforesaid, notice of the death
of the said Benjamin, and of the body of the said Benjamin,
then and there lying dead, was given to one George Collins,
gentleman, and then and there being one of the coroners of
the said lord the king, in and for the county of Cornwall
aforesaid, and then and there having legal authority within the
county and parish aforesaid, to do and execute those things
which appertain to the office of a coroner, in that behalf, with
intention that the said coroner, according to the duty of his
office, and the course of law, might enquire concerning the
death of the said Benjamin, then and there lying dead, and
might take and transmit of record an inquisition thereof, according to the law of the land and the duty of his office;
and that one Thomas Voysey, late of Gluvias aforesaid, not
being one of the coroners of the said lord the king, in the
said county, but being a person illiterate and entirely unfit to
execute those things which appertain to the office of a coroner,
in the said county, not ignorant of the premisses, but maliciously contriving, and unjustly, wickedly and corruptly design-
ing and devising, that no coroner in the said case might take an
inquisition upon view of the body of the said Benjamin, according to the duty of his office and the law of the land, he

[Margin note:] Information against a person for usurping the office of coroner, and summoning and swearing a jury to enquire of the death of a person slain.

O o 2   the

the said T. V. on the said 15th day of August, in the 3d year aforesaid, at Gluvias aforesaid, unlawfully and unduly without any lawful warrant or authority thereon, did usurp, and take upon himself to execute those things which to the office of one of the coroners of the said lord the king, in and for the said county, appertain to be done in the premisses. And the said T. V. then and there of his own proper head and imagination, without any lawful warrant or lawful authority thereupon, suddenly after the death of the said Benjamin, knowingly, subtily and unduly did cause and procure 16 several persons upon the view of the body of the said B. then and there, to take their several oaths, as the custom is, before the said T. V. that they would enquire how and by what means the said B. came to his death, and the said T. V. then and there unlawfully did administer and cause to be administered to the said 16 persons, the oath used in such case, whereas in

Averment. truth and in fact the said T. V. had not any power or authority to administer such oath to the said persons in such case, whereby the body of the said Benjamin was removed and buried ; and the said coroner or any other coroner of the said county, could not nor can as yet inquire in the due manner, upon view of the body of the said B. within the said county, according to the law of this kingdom of England, nor was any inquisition ever had, taken or recorded how or by what means the said B. came to his death, as according to the law

P. 239. of the land of this kingdom of England, in * such case ought to be done, in contempt of the said lord the now king, and of his laws, to the evil and pernicious example of all others in the like case offending, and against the peace, &c. &c.

The King against Parry.

Trinity, 2d James II.

Salop, THAT Anthony Parry, late of Lan St. Kathe-

Information for removing a seat in church, and disturbing the parson in reading divine service on a Sunday.

To wit, rine, in the county of Carnarvon, yeoman, being a pernicious and irreligious man, on the 9th day of May, in the 2d year of the reign of our lord James, by the grace of God, of England, &c. king, &c being the Lord's-day, called Sunday, with force and arms, &c. at the parish aforesaid, in the county aforesaid, in the parochial church there, at the time of the celebration of divine service, the bench of one Anne Jones, widow, there being from its antient place, un-

lawfully

lawfully and unjustly did take and remove, and also one *Evan Roberts*, clerk, then curate of the said parochial church, in the execution of his office in reading divine service, then and there being, then and there with force and arms, &c. unlawfully, unjustly and irreverently did disturb and obstruct, in contempt of the laws of this kingdom of *England*, to the evil example of all others in the like case offending, and against the peace of the said lord the now king his crown and dignity, &c.

The King against Hynde.

London,
To wit.

THAT one *John Hynde*, late of *London*, goldsmith, using and exercising the art of merchandize, by way of bargaining, exchange, barter and chovisance, and seeking his manner of living by buying and selling, on the 7th day of *November*, in the 1st year of the reign of our lord *James* the 2d, of *England*, &c. king, &c. at *London*, to wit, in the parish of St. *Michael Baffishaw*, in the ward of *Baffishaw*, *London*, aforesaid, was and as yet is a bankrupt, within the several statutes against bankrupts lately made, with intention to defraud and obstruct *S. Dashwood*, kt. *S. P.* and others, his creditors, of their just debts, due and belonging to the said creditors, and the jurors aforesaid, upon their oath aforesaid, further say, that afterwards to wit, on the said day and year aforesaid, the said *John Hynde*, so as aforesaid being a bankrupt, a certain commission of the said lord the king, issued out of the court of *Chancery*, of the said lord the king at *Westminster*, in the county of *Middlesex*, made under his great seal of *England*, directed to *T. Gooding*, *W. B.* esquires, *P. G.* &c. * by which commission, the said lord the king did grant to the said *T. G.* &c, and to four or three of them, of whom the said lord the king willed, that the said *T. G.* or *W. B.* should be one, to do and to execute all and all manner of things whatsoever, as well for the satisfaction and payment of the said creditors, as for all other intentions and purposes whatsoever, according to the ordinances and provisions of the statutes aforesaid; and the jurors aforesaid, further say upon their oath, that the said *T. G. W. B.* and *J. V.* three of the commissioners in the said commission named, afterwards to wit, on the 20th day of *March*, in the second year, &c. at the parish of St. *George*, *Southwark* aforesaid, in the county of *Surrey*, did meet to examine the said *J. Hynde*, of and upon the premisses in the commission and statutes aforesaid specified and that he the said *J. H.* then and there at the parish of St'
George

Indictment against a bankrupt, for refusing to answer the commissioners questions upon his examination before them.

*P. 240.

George aforesaid, in the county of S. aforesaid, being present, before the said commissioners last named, and then and there being duly examined and required by the said commissioners, to make known to the said commissioners what accidental losses he the said J. H. had sustained, by which he became unable to pay his debts, he the said J. H. being a person of dishonest disposition, and devising and fraudulently intending not only the said S. D. J. P. &c. the creditors of the said J. H. but also all the other creditors of the said J. H. (whose names to the jurors aforesaid, are yet unknown) of their just debts to deceive and defraud, he the said J. H. aforesaid to wit, on the said 20th day of March, in the 2d year, &c. aforesaid, at the parish aforesaid, in the county aforesaid, falsely, unlawfully and fraudulently, did say and answer to the said commissioners, that he the said J. H. could not give the said commissioners any account thereof (they the said commissioners last named, then having full power and authority to examine the said John Hynde in that behalf) but then and there falsely and deceitfully did refuse, and totally neglect to give any account concerning the said premisses, to the said commissioners, in contempt of the said lord the now king, and of his laws, to the great obstruction of the execution of the said statutes, to the deceiving and defrauding the said creditors of great sums of money, due to the said creditors, to the evil and pernicious example, &c. and against the peace, &c.

The King against Pick.

Hilary, the 36th of Charles the 2d.

<table>
<tr><td valign="top">Indictment for setting a mastiff dog on a man, who bit and wounded him on his left leg.
*P. 241.</td><td>

Middlesex, THAT Robert Pick, late of the parish, &c. in
To wit. the county, &c. on the day and year, &c. with force and arms, &c. at, &c. in and upon one John Messenger, in the peace of God and of the said lord the now king, then and there being, did make an assault, and that the said R. P. then and there having with him a certain mastiff dog, the said mastiff dog, in and upon the said J. M. did incite, by reason of which incitement, the said mastiff dog, * in and upon the said J. M. then and there did seize, and the said J. M. in the left leg of the said J. M. then and there did grievously bite and wound, by reason of which grievous biting and wounding of the said J. M. in his left leg aforesaid, he the said J. M. from the said day and year, &c. to the day of the taking of this inquisition, at the parish aforesaid, in the county aforesaid, did languish, and languishing did live, and as yet is in great peril of his life, and other wrongs to the said J. M. then and there did, to the great damage of the said J. M. and against the peace of the said lord the now king his crown and dignity, &c.

</td></tr>
</table>

The

The King *against* Milner.

Michaelmas, the 1st of James the 2d.

London, THAT Jonathan Milner, late of the parish, &c. being a person greedy of gain, of wicked mind and dishonest conversation, and devising, practising and falsely, fraudulently and deceitfully intending to deceive and defraud the apprentices, young men, and other liege and faithful subjects of this kingdom of England, of their monies, goods and chattels, by a certain false, deceitful and unlawful game, with dice, called raffling, for silver money, goods and chattels, and divers great sums of money, from divers subjects of the said lord the king unknown, to acquire and obtain at the said unlawful game with dice, in the shop of the said J. M. situate within the parish, &c. he the said J. M. to fulfil, perfect and bring to effect his most wicked devices, practises and intentions aforesaid, on the 24th day of August, in the 1st year of the reign of our lord James the 2d, and for the space of fourteen days then next ensuing, with force and arms, &c. falsely, unlawfully, unjustly, wickedly, fraudulently and deceitfully, for the proper advantage and gain of the said J. M. unlawfully and wickedly did maintain, continue and keep a certain unlawful, publick and open gaming house, for the said game, called raffling, and in the said shop, the said game called raffling, with dice, for silver money, goods and chattels, with force and arms, &c. during the whole time aforesaid, falsely, deceitfully and unlawfully, did maintain, exercise and continue, to wit, at, &c. and there within the time aforesaid, falsely, unlawfully, unjustly, wickedly, fraudulently and deceitfully did seduce, cause and procure divers apprentices and poor persons unknown, to play at the said unlawful game, called raffling, and to lose divers goods of great value and sums of money at the said game, with dice, to the great deceit, ruin, fraud and impoverishment of the apprentices and poor persons aforesaid, and of other liege subjects of the said lord the king, frequenting and going to the said gaming shop of the said J. M. at unlawful times, as well in the night as in the day, in manifest contempt of the laws of this kingdom of England, to the evil and pernicious example, &c. and against the peace, &c.

to wit.

Information for keeping a common raffling shop.

The

* The King against Harsant.

Hilary, 2d and 3d James 2d.

Information against an empirick, for exercising the faculty of a physician and surgeon without licence.

Suffolk, THAT John Harsant, of, &c. being an illiterate to wit. man, and unlearned and unskilled in the art or faculty of medicine and surgery, and devising and intending by divers unlawful means, falsely, unlawfully, craftily and wickedly to deceive and defraud the liege and faithful subjects of the said lord the king, of their goods, chattels and monies, to maintain his dishonest course of living, on the day and year, &c. and continually afterwards, until the day of the exhibition of this information, to wit, for the space of ten whole months and more, with force and arms, &c. at, &c. in the county, &c. and in divers other places in the said county, falsely, unlawfully, impudently, and for the sake of wicked gain, did assume upon himself, to execute, exercise and occupy the art, faculty and science of a physician and surgeon, and then and there falsely and impudently did publish that he was a physician and surgeon, and as a physician and surgeon did give, administer and apply improper, noxious, insalubrious and most dangerous medicines, as good and salubrious medicines to divers subjects of the said lord the king, afflicted with various infirmities, diseases and wounds, in the county, &c. to wit, in the parish, &c. in the county, &c. and in divers other places in the said county, (the said J. H. never being admitted, approved or allowed by the bishop of Norwich, in whose diocese the said J. H. for the whole time aforesaid did dwell, and for the same time did act and practise as a physician and surgeon, or in the absence of the said bishop from his diocese, by the vicar general of the said bishop, to exercise the said faculty) to the great damage, injury and manifest deceit of very many liege subjects of the said lord the king, to the evil and pernicious example, &c. and against the peace, &c.

The

The King *against* Lewis *and others.*

Trinity, 4th James 2d.

Eex, THAT several rivers and waters commonly named
To wit. and called by the several names of Burnham,
otherwise Wallfleet-pont, Laylingfleet, Mazyshole, Mazy-
fleet, Peldonfleet, Coanepycfleet, Baslethansfleet Ryesands,
Manning-tree-water, Southfleet, running and flowing in the
county of Essex, are and from the time whereof, the memory
of man is not to the contrary, have been common rivers and
navigable waters, and arms of the sea in which the salt water
daily ebbs and flows, by its own course, and the vessels of
this kingdom of England may and can sail, and in * which
rivers and waters, oysters and other fish from time to time
for the whole time aforesaid, have been used and accustomed
to grow, encrease, propagate and multiply, and the subjects
of this kingdom of England there coming and willing to
fish with lawful nets of whatsoever kind, and with dredges
for oysters and other fish of whatsoever kind, at seasonable
times, of common right have been used, accustomed, ought
and may freely fish, and that John Lewis, the younger, of
Burnham, in the county of Essex, fisherman, John London
of the same, fisherman, Richard Rowe of S. aforesaid, in
the county aforesaid, fisherman, Dionysius Ignator, of P. in
the county aforesaid, fisherman, and others, not ignorant of
the premisses, but knowing them well, and being malicious
and evil disposed persons, and seeking their living although
by the injury of others, and maliciously, unjustly, unlawfully
and unduly contriving, devising and intending to ruin, destroy
and despoil the oysters, and the increase, propagation and
multiplication of oysters, and also the spits of oysters,
from time to time growing, renewing and increasing in the
rivers or waters of the sea aforesaid, and to deprive, frustrate and hinder the subjects of the said lord the king there
coming and willing to fish for the profit, advantage and
benefit of fishing for and catching oysters, which they there
at seasonable times have been used and accustomed to have
and enjoy, and ought to use have and enjoy, they the said
J. L. the younger, and others, on the 1st day of December,
in the 2d year of the reign of our lord James the 2d, the
now king of England, &c. and at divers other days and times

Information
for destroy-
ing a great
quantity of
small oys-
ters, and
of spat and
culch by
dredging in
the arms of
the sea,
*P. 243.
where the
oysters used
to breed.

P p
between

between the said 1st day of December, in the 2d year aforesaid, and the day of the exhibition of this information, to
wit, the 1st day of May, in the 4th year, &c. aforesaid, in
and upon the rivers or waters of the sea, aforesaid, to wit,
at Westmearsy, in the county aforesaid, in and with several
boats, wherries, and other vessels did row and sail, and
each and every of them did row and sail, and in further prosecution of their malicious and unlawful intentions aforesaid,
and for their sole and private gain, and proper advantage,
then and there in the rivers or waters aforesaid, at unseasonable times, with force and arms, unlawfully, unjustly, unduly, injuriously and for the sake of wicked gain, with
certain unlawful trammels, drag-nets, sweep-nets, engines
and instruments, did dredge and fish for oysters, and several
great quantities of very small oysters, of the length and
breadth of only one inch, then and there found and propa-
gated, to wit, 40,000 bushels of very small oysters aforesaid,
and great quantities of spats of oysters, and culch for the
preservation and setting of the spats of oysters, there, to
wit, 40,000 bushels of the spats of oysters, and 40,000
bushels of culch for the preservation and setting of the spats
of oysters, in the rivers or waters aforesaid, then and there
being and found, with force and arms, &c. unlawfully, unjustly, unduly and injuriously, at unseasonable times, in
and from the rivers or waters aforesaid, then with the said unlawful trammels, drag-nets, sweep-nets, engines and instruments, did dredge, take, ruin, destroy and carry away, and
to their own proper use did convert and dispose, and each
and every of them did dredge, take, ruin, destroy and carry
away, to the great destruction, ruin and spoliation of the
oysters, and the spats of oysters, in the rivers or * waters aforesaid, growing, increasing and coming, and to the hindrance
of the increase, propagation and multiplication of oysters,
there, to the evil example, &c. and against the peace, &c.
whereupon the said attorney, &c. &c.

P. 244.

Not guilty pleaded, and venire facias awarded.

The King *against* Glover.

Easter, 2d James 2d.

Surrey, THAT whereas on the 8th day of July, in the
To wit. 1st year of the reign of our lord James the 2nd
by the grace of God, of England, &c. king, &c. a certain
writ of the said lord the king of habeas corpus, out of the
court of the said lord the king before the king himself, at
Westminster,

Information
against the
marshal of
the king's
Bench, for
suffering a

Westminster, in the county of Middlesex, to the then sheriff of the county of Middlesex aforesaid directed, duly and lawfully issued, by which writ the sheriff of the county of Middlesex aforesaid was commanded, that he the said sheriff should have the body of one Zacheus Green, in the prison of the said lord the king, under the custody of the said sheriff detained, under safe and secure conduct, together with the day and cause of the caption and detention of the said Zacheus, before Francis Withins, knight, one of the justices of the said lord the king, assigned to hold pleas before the king himself, at his chamber situate in Serjeants-inn, Fleet street, London, immediately after the receipt of the said writ, to do and receive all and singular the things, which the said Francis Withins, knight, then and there concerning him should consider in that behalf, which writ afterwards to wit, on the 21st day of November, in the 1st year aforesaid, at Westminster aforesaid, in the said county of Middlesex, was delivered to Benjamin Thorowgood, knight, and Thomas Kinsey, knight, then being sheriff of the county of Middlesex aforesaid, in the form of law to be executed, upon which writ the said B. T. and T. K. then being sheriff of the county of Middlesex aforesaid, afterwards to wit, on the said 21st day of November, in the 1st year, &c. aforesaid, returned and certified to the said Francis Withins, knight, then being one of the justices of the said lord the king, assigned to hold pleas before the king himself, at his chamber situate in Serjeants-inn, Fleet street, London aforesaid, "That before the delivery of the said writ of the lord the "king of habeas corpus to the said sheriff directed, to wit, on "the 1st day of October, in the 1st year of the reign of the said "lord the now king, the said Zacheus Green, in the said writ "named, was taken by the said sheriff and in the prison of the "said lord the now king under the custody of the said sheriff is "detained, by virtue of a certain writ of the said lord the king "of capias utlagatum, at the suit of one Humphrey Fenners, "esquire, of a plea of trespass upon the case, returnable into the "court of the said lord the king of the bench, at Westminster, at "the octave of St. Martin, from thence next ensuing, before the "justices of the said court of the said lord the king of the bench "aforesaid." And also the said sheriff of the county of Middlesex aforesaid, then and there to the said Francis Withins, knight, then being one of the justices of the said lord the * king, assigned to hold pleas before the king himself, farther returned and certified "that the said Zacheus was taken "by him the said sheriff of the county of Middlesex aforesaid, "and in the prison of the said lord the king under the custody of "the said sheriff is detained, by virtue of a certain precept of the "said lord the king, called a bill of Middlesex, returnable before "the said lord the king at Westminster, on the Thursday next after

* P. 245.

prisoner
turned over
to him on an
habeas cor-
pus, by a
judge,
discharged
with divers
actions, to
escape out
of his
custody.

P p 2

"the

" *the octave of St. Martin, to anfwer to one John Green, Gentle-*
" *man, one of the attorneys, &c. of a plea of trefpafs upon the*
" *cafe. And that thefe were the caufes of the caption and detention*
" *of the faid Zacheus, in the prifon aforefaid, under the cuftody of*
" *the faid fheriff of the county of Middlefex aforefaid, and that*
" *the faid fheriff had the body of the faid Zacheus ready, before the*
" *faid Francis Withins, knight, one of the juftices of the faid lord*
" *the king, affigned to hold pleas before the king himfelf, accord-*
" *ing to the tenor of the faid writ of habeas corpus."* And the faid
coroner and attorney of the faid lord the king, for the faid lord
the king further gives the court here to underftand and to be informed, that the faid F. W. kt. then being as aforefaid one of
the juftices of the faid lord the king, affigned to hold pleas
before the king himfelf, afterwards to wit, on the faid 21ft
day of November, in the 1ft year aforefaid, at Serjeants-inn
aforefaid, in Fleet ftreet, London aforefaid, committed the
faid Zacheus to the cuftody of Henry Glover, of the parifh,
&c. marfhal of the marfhalfea of the lord the king, before
the king himfelf, for default of mainpeinors, charged with
the faid writ of the faid lord the king of capias utlagatum,
at the fuit of the faid Humphrey Jennens, and alfo with
the faid precept of the faid lord the king, called a bill of
Middlefex, at the fuit of the faid John Green, as is aforefaid, as by the return of the faid fheriff upon the faid writ
of the faid lord the king of habeas corpus, iffuing out of the
court of the faid lord the king, before the king himfelf, in the
due manner, and to the fame writ annexed, in the court of the
faid lord the king here, before the king himfelf, to wit, at Weftminfter aforefaid, remaining affiled relation being thereto had
more fully appears. And the faid coroner and attorney of the
faid lord the king, for the faid lord the king further gives the
court here to underftand and to be informed, that the faid Z.
by virtue of the faid commitment, by the faid F. W. knight,
then being one of the juftices of the faid lord the king, affigned to hold pleas before the king himfelf, as aforefaid, to
the faid marfhal, with the charge as is aforefaid, on the 21ft
day of November, in the 1ft year, &c. aforefaid, then was
fafe and fecure in and under the cuftody of the faid H. G.
marfhal of the marfhalfea aforefaid, then being kept and
detained a prifoner by the marfhal of the marfhalfea of the
faid lord the king, before the king himfelf, at the faid parifh
of St. George, Southwark, in the faid county of Surrey,
lawfully and by the command of the faid Francis Withins,
knight, for the default of mainpernors as is aforefaid. Nevertheleſs the faid H. G. after the commitment of the faid
Z. G. before that the faid Z. G. was delivered by the due
form of law out of the cuftody of the faid H. G. to wit,
on the 30th day of April, in the 2d year of the reign of our
lord

lord James the 2d, the now king of England, &c. at the said parish of St. George, Southwark, in the said county of Surrey, then as aforesaid, being marshal of the marshalsea of the said lord the king before the king himself, and also keeper of the prison of the marshalsea aforesaid, situate at the said parish of St. George, Southwark, in the said county of Surrey, well knowing the said Zachens to be charged with the said writ of capias utlagatum, and with the said precept, him the said Z. G. at the said parish of St. George, in Southwark, out of the custody of him the said H. G. and * also out of the prison of the marshalsea aforesaid, *P. 246. (the said writ of capias utlagatum not being reversed or annulled, or the said Humphrey Jennens, not being satisfied or in any manner contented, of his said action against the said Z. G.) unlawfully and wilfully did permit, to escape and as yet doth permit to go at large, wheresoever he will, to the evil example of all others in the like case offending, and against the peace of the said lord the now king, his crown and dignity, &c. whereupon, &c.

The King *against* Manlove.

Trinity, 36th Charles 2d.

Middlesex,
To wit. } THAT whereas heretofore to wit, in the term of St. Michael, in the 31st year of the reign of our lord Charles 2d, king, &c. in the said court of the said lord the king, before the king himself, here to wit, at Westminster aforesaid, in the county of Middlesex, then and there being held, by the said court there, it was considered, that one Thomas Cudmore, by the name of Thomas Cudmore, for certain trespasses and misdeeds by him the said Thomas Cudmore committed and perpetrated, and thereof in the due manner indicted and convicted, should pay to the said lord the king the sum of 500l. for his fine imposed upon him by occasion of the premisses, and that the said T. C. should be taken, &c. as by the record and proceedings thereof in the said court of the said lord the king, before the king himself, now to wit, at Westminster aforesaid, in the said county of Middlesex, remaining of record manifestly appeareth; afterwards to wit, on the day and year, &c. a certain writ of the said lord the king of habeas corpus cum causa, issued out of the court of the said lord the king

before the king himself, then being held at Westminster aforesaid, directed to the warden of the prison of the said lord the king, of the fleet, or his deputy there, by which writ the said warden of the said prison of the fleet, was commanded that he should have the body of the said T. C. then detained in the prison of the said lord the king, under the custody of the said warden of the said prison, together with the day and cause of the caption and detention of the said T. by whatsoever name the said T. might be called in the same, before the said lord the king, at Westminster, on the Friday after the morrow of the ascension of our Lord then next coming, to submit to and receive the things which the said court of the said lord the king, concerning the said T. C. should order in that behalf, and that the said warden should in no wise omit at his peril, and should have there then that writ; which writ of habeas corpus so as aforesaid issued and directed, afterwards and before the return thereof, to wit, on the day and year, &c. at the said prison of the fleet, situate in the parish, &c. was delivered to Richard Manlove, Esquire, then and ever since continually and hitherto being warden of the said prison of the said lord the king, of the fleet, to be executed in the due form of law, (the said T. C. then being in the due manner a prisoner in the said prison, under the custody of the said warden.) And the said attorney general of the said lord the king, for the said lord the king further gives the court here to understand and to be informed, that the said writ of habeas corpus to have the body of the said T. C. issued out of the court of the said lord the king, before the

P. 247. king himself here, and to the said warden of the said prison of the said lord the king, of the fleet, was directed and delivered with intention to remove the body of the said T. C. from the said prison of the fleet, into the said court of the said lord the king, before the king himself, now here according to the command of the said writ, so that the said T. C. by the said court might be committed a prisoner to the marshal of the marshalsea of the said lord the king, before the king himself, in execution for the said fine of 500*l.* so as aforesaid imposed upon the said T. C. there to remain until that he should fully satisfy the lord the king thereof; whereupon the said R. Manlove, being as aforesaid warden of the said prison of the fleet, not regarding the duty of his office aforesaid, but despising the said writ of the said lord the king of habeas corpus, to the said warden, for the occasion aforesaid, so as aforesaid directed and delivered, and instigated and seduced by the hope of base lucre, afterwards to wit, on the————day of in the year, &c. at, &c. him the said T. C. out of the said prison of the fleet, and out of the custody of the said warden, in which as aforesaid the said T. C. was detained, without any lawful warrant therefore, and a-

gainst

gainst the duty of his office aforesaid, wilfully and corruptly
and with the consent of the said warden did permit to escape
and go at large wheresoever he the said T. C. would
(the said lord the now king then not being paid or satisfied
of the said fine of 500*l.* or of any part thereof, imposed upon the said T. C. as aforesaid) in manifest contempt of the
said lord the now king and of his laws, and to the danger
of losing of his said fine, to the forfeiture of his office aforesaid, and to the evil example of all others in the like case
offending, and against the peace of the said lord the now
king his crown and dignity, &c.

The King *against* Lee.

Easter, 20th Charles 2d.

London, }   THAT John Lee, late of London, esquire, on
To wit. }   the 1st day of December, in the 13th year of
the reign of our lord Charles the 2d, of England, &c. king,
&c. and continually afterwards until the 1st day of January,
in the 17th year of the reign of our said lord the now king,
was the deputy of John Weld, esquire, town clerk of the
city of London, and by virtue of his office of town clerk of
the city aforesaid, ought to estreat and return into the Exchequer of the said lord the king, for the whole time aforesaid, all forfeited recognizances for not appearing at any
session of the peace and goal delivery, held for the said city,
returned to the said sessions; nevertheless the said J. L. not
regarding the duty of his office of deputy of the town clerk
of the said city, and perverting the trust in him reposed,
*and devising and intending the said lord the king of divers
sums of money, by the forfeiture of divers recognizances to
the said lord the king due, to deceive and defraud, between
the said 1st day, &c. in the year aforesaid, and the 1st day,
&c. unlawfully, extorsively and under colour of his office
aforesaid, did receive and take of and from one * H. R. and
others, who were bound to the said lord the king, in a certain
recognizance, for the appearance of L. F. at the session of
the peace and goal delivery for the city aforesaid, next after
the taking of the said recognizance to be held, a certain sum
of money to wit, 16 shillings of the lawful money of England, to defer returning and estreating the said recognizance
into the said exchequer; and of J. K. and others, and also

*Information
against the
town clerk
of London's
deputy, for
not estreat-
ing recog-
nizances
which were
forfeited at
the sessions,
but discharg-
ing them
after for-
feiture.*

*P. 248.

of

of divers other subjects of the said lord the king, whose names are yet unknown to the said attorney of the said lord the now king, several other sums of money, to defer returning and estreating into the said exchequer, divers other recognizances by them severally acknowledged before several justices of the peace of the said lord the now king, for the appearance of several other malefactors and delinquents, in the same recognizances respectively named, at the said several sessions of the peace and goal delivery, at which they ought severally to appear, all which several recognizances before mentioned, for the non appearance of the said several malefactors and delinquents, at the said several sessions of the peace and goal delivery, at which they ought severally to appear, were returned and severally were forfeited to the said lord the now king; and that the said J. L. devising and intending the said lord the now king, of the money arising to the said lord the king, from the several recognizances aforesaid, so as aforesaid forfeited, to deceive and defraud, the said several recognizances after the return of the same to the several sessions aforesaid, and after the several forfeitures of the same, did not return and estreat into the Exchequer of the said lord the now king, but the said several recognizances for his own proper gain and advantage, at the parish aforesaid, &c. between the days first aforesaid mentioned, unlawfully and unjustly did procure to be discharged, against the duty of his office, against the trust in him reposed, to the great deceit of the said lord the king, to the evil example of all others in the like case offending, and against the peace, &c. &c. &c.

The King against Lock.

Easter, 36th Charles 2d.

Sussex, To wit. } THAT on the 27th day of June, in the 35th year of the reign of our lord Charles the 2d, king of England, &c. at Westminster, in the county of Middlesex, Ford, lord Grey, for divers high treasons by him late before that time supposed to be perpetrated, was in the due manner taken, and that afterwards to wit, on the said 27th day of June, in the 35th year of the reign of our said lord the king aforesaid, Leoline Jenkins, knight, then one of the privy council of the said lord the king, and principal secretary of state of the said lord the king, at Westminster aforesaid, in the said county of Middlesex, made his certain warrant in writing, dated the said day and year, and sealed with the seal of the said Leoline Jenkins, knight, and signed and subscribed with the proper hand writing of the said Leoline Jenkins, and directed to one Thomas Cheeke, Esquire, then lieutenant of the Tower of London, by which warrant the said Leoline Jenkins, knight, then and there in the name of the said lord the king, willed and required the said Thomas Cheeke, Esquire, to receive into his custody the person of the said Ford, lord Grey, then committed for high treason, in compassing the death of the said most serene lord the king, and conspiring to levy war against the said lord the king, and that the said Thomas Cheeke, Esquire, him the said Ford, lord Grey, should safely keep, until that he should be afterwards delivered according to the due course of law, and that afterwards to wit, on the said 27th day of June, in the 35th year, &c. aforesaid, at Westminster, in the said county of Middlesex, the said warrant so as aforesaid made, signed and sealed, and also the person of the said Ford, lord Grey, were delivered to one Henry Dercham, esquire, then being one of the serjeants at arms in ordinary of the said lord the king, by virtue of which warrant the said H. Dereham, took and in his custody had and detained, the said Ford, lord Grey, and then and there the said H. Dercham, by the said Leoline Jenkins, was required him the said Ford, lord Grey, in safe custody to deliver to the said Thomas Cheeke, esquire, then lieutenant of the Tower of London, safely and securely to be kept, for the cause aforesaid above alledged, according to the tenor of the said warrant, and that the said H. D. afterwards to wit, on the day and year, &c. aforesaid, at the parish of St. Catherine, nigh to the Tower of London, in the said county of Middlesex, permitted him the said lord Grey, to escape and go at large out of his custody, wheresoever he would, and that one Robert Lock, late of Horsham, in the county of Sussex, sailor, well knowing the premisses aforesaid, afterwards to wit, on the 30th day of June, in the 35th year, &c. aforesaid, at Horsham, in the said county of Sussex, with force and arms, &c. unlawfully, unjustly and corruptly him the said Ford, lord Grey, into the custody of the said Robert Lock, did take and conceal, and the said Ford, lord Grey, then and there in a certain vessel called the Hare, under the custody of the said Robert Lock, did carry away and convey into parts beyond the seas, to wit, to Middleburgh in Flanders, to the great obstruction of justice, to the evil and pernicious example of all others

was committed for treason by the secretary of state.

*P. 249.

in the like case offending, and against the peace of the said lord the now king his crown and dignity, &c. Where-upon, &c.

The King *against* Martin.

To wit. THAT the offices of Cursitors, are antient offices, in the high court of Chancery, of the said lord the king, and of his progenitors, kings and queens of this kingdom of England, (the said court now being at Westminster, in the county of Middlesex,) for making original writs, for the subjects of the said lord the king, and of his progenitors, out of the court of Chancery aforesaid, from time to time issuing, and that it hath ap-pertained, and ought to appertain to every the cursitor and cursitors aforesaid, from the time whereof the memory of man is not to the contrary, by reason of his office, to re-ceive and pay fines upon every original writ by him made, to the said lord the king, and to his progenitors, due of right, to wit, upon every writ original upon actions upon the case, where the damages reach to one hundred pounds, ten shillings, and for every hundred pounds of damages, in such writ demanded or * charged above the sum of 100l. 10s. and that Henry Martin, late of, &c. was and as yet is one of the cursitors in the said court of Chancery, of the said lord the king, for the city of London, nevertheless the said H. M. being a person greedy of unjust gain, and devising and intending, by reason of his office, to gain and acquire sums of money, as well by deceiving and defraud-ing the said lord the now king, as his subjects, he the said H. M. afterwards to wit, on the day and year, &c. at, &c. in the county, &c. two pieces of gold coin called guineas, of the value of 43 shillings, of the lawful money of Eng-land, [40 shillings thereof, for and in the name of a fine to be paid upon an original writ, by him to be made, in an action of trespass upon the case, by the president of the college or community of the faculty of medicine, London, against John Culter, knight and baronet, for 50l. damages] from one William Ravenhill, gent. under colour of his office, did have and receive, and although the said writ was never made and sealed, nevertheless the said H. M. unjustly, fraudulently and deceitfully, the said 40 shillings, under colour of his office aforesaid, in
the

he manner and form aforesaid, for the said fine by him had and received to his own proper use, benefit and profit did detain, without any return or repayment thereof to the said W. R. or payment to any other person, or rendering any account thereof to the said lord the king, but in fraud and deceit, as well of the said lord the king, as of his subjects, the said money to his own proper use then and there did convert and dispose, against the duty of his office aforesaid, in great deceit of the said lord the king, and of his people, in manifest contempt of the laws of this kingdom of England, to the evil example, &c. &c.

The King *against* Farringdon.

Easter, 1*st* James 2d.

To wit, THAT heretofore to wit, on Monday in the week next after the feast of St. Michael the archangel, to wit, on Monday the 2d day of October, in the 34th year of the reign of our lord Charles the 2d, the late king of England, &c. at a general Quarter-sessions of the peace, of the said lord the late king, held for the county of Sussex aforesaid, at Midhurst in the said county, before R. M. knight, J. A. esquire, and others their fellow-justices of the said late lord the king, assigned to preserve the peace in the said county, and also to hear and determine divers felonies, trespasses, and other misdeeds in the said county perpetrated, &c. By the oath of 12 jurors, good and lawful men of the body of the said county, then and there sworn, and charged to enquire for the said late lord the king, and for the body of the said county, it was presented, that J. Davies, late of, &c. labourer, and R. Farringdon, late of, &c. gent. not having the fear of God before their eyes, but being moved and seduced by the instigation of the devil, on the 6th day of August, in the 34th year, &c. aforesaid, with force and arms, &c. at the parish, &c. in and upon one Richard Habin, in the peace of God, and of the said late lord the king * then and there being, feloniously, wilfully, and of their malice aforethought did make an assault, and the said J. D. with a certain staff, of the value of one penny which he the said J. D. then and there in his right-hand had and held, him the said R. H. in and upon the right part of the head of the said R. H. did strike, then and there giving to the said R. H. in and upon the said right part of the head of him the said

*Information for cutting the hair of one indicted for murder, and disguising him in an unusual habit, and keeping him in private places, and maintaining him, and supporting him, to keep him from the justice of the law

*P. 251.

R. H.

R. H. one mortal wound, of the length of one inch, and of the breadth of half one inch, and of the depth of one inch, of which mortal wound the said R. H. then and there instantly died; and that the said R. F. on the said 6th day of August, in the 34th year, &c. aforesaid, of his malice aforethought, feloniously was present, aiding, comforting, abetting and maintaining the said J. D. feloniously, wilfully, and of his malice aforethought to kill and murder the said R. H. in the form aforesaid; and so the jurors aforesaid then did say upon their oath aforesaid, that the said J. D. and R. F. feloniously, wilfully, and of their malice aforethought then and there him the said R. H. did kill and murder, against the peace of the said late lord the king, his crown and dignity; as by the indictment aforesaid, in the court of the said lord the now king, by a writ of the said lord the late king of Certiorari in the due manner returned, and there now remaining of record more fully appeareth. And the said Attorney-general of the said lord the now king, for the said lord the king, further gives the court here to understand and to be informed, that the said R. Farringdon, late of the parish of, &c. and J. B. late of, &c. and others well-knowing, and each of them well-knowing the said premisses, but being persons of evil name, fame, and of dishonest conversation, and devising, practising, and among themselves falsely, unlawfully, unjustly, wickedly, and diabolically intending as much as in them lay, to obstruct, turn aside and retard the due course of law, afterwards, to wit, on the 19th day of May, in the 35th year of the reign of the said late lord the king, at the parish, &c. falsely, unlawfully, wickedly, and diabolically among themselves did conspire, devise and practise, and each and every of them did conspire, contrive and practise, to hide, and conceal the said J. Davies from the process of the law for the said murder, and to render the process of the law against the said J. Davies, for the said murder of no effect, and to fulfil, perfect, and bring to effect their most wicked devices, practises and intentions aforesaid, they the said R. F. J. B. and others, on the said 19th day of May, in the said 35th year aforesaid, and at divers other days and times as well before as after, with force and arms, &c. at &c. and in divers other secret and unknown places, falsely, unlawfully and unjustly, wickedly, seditiously, wilfully, knowingly and diabolically the hair from the head of the said J. Davies did cut off, and did cause to be cut off, and each and every of them did cut off, and did cause to be cut off, and him the said J. Davies then and there in unusual garments did disguise, and each of them did disguise and did cause to be disguised, and him the said J. Davies so as aforesaid disguised, then and there with force and arms, &c. unlawfully, unjustly, wickedly

and

and diabolically into divers parts, and secret and obscure places,
did send and convey, and did cause and procure to be sent
and conveyed, and each and every of them did send and convey, and did cause and procure to be sent and conveyed, and
divers great sums of money to the said J. Davies, then and
there with force and arms, &c. unlawfully, unjustly, * wickedly and diabolically did send, give, and deliver, and did cause
and procure to be sent, given and delivered, and each and e-
very of them did send, give and deliver, and did cause and procure to be sent given and delivered for the supporting, maintaining comforting and concealing of the said J. D. and the
said J. D. by the said unlawful ways then and there, and at
the other days and times aforesaid did support and maintain,
and each and every of them did support and maintain in
contempt of the laws of this kingdom of England, to the
manifest obstruction of justice, to the evil and pernicious
example of all others in the like case offending, and against
the peace of our said lord the now king, his crown and dignity, &c. whereupon the said attorney, &c.

*P. 252.

The King *against* Cox.

Michaelmas, 36th Charles 2d.

Middlesex, THAT the art and mystery of frame-work-
To wit. knitters, is a new art and mystery, lately
and first invented in England by the subjects of the lord
the king, of this kingdom of England, and by the said
subjects of the said lord the king, of this kingdom of
England, for divers years now past, solely and exclusively
exercised, by which art and mystery very many subjects of
the said lord the now king, of this kingdom of England,
exercising the said art and mystery, not only have acquired
and yet do acquire for themselves a living, but also great
riches, and for the greater benefit and encouragement of
the persons using the said art and mystery, the said lord the
now king by his letters patent, bearing date at Westminster, the 19th day, &c. in the 15th year of the reign of
our said lord the king, &c. incorporated them by the
name of the master, wardens and assistants, of the society
of frame-work knitters, of the cities of London and Westminster,

Information
against a
frame-work
knitter, for
seducing se-
veral of that
art, to leave
the kingdom
and go to
France, and
teach the
French that
art.

minster, of the said lord the king, and of the kingdom of England, and of the lordship of Wales; and that Lancelot otherwise called Giles Cox, of the parish, &c. in the county, &c. frame-work knitter, being a natural subject of the said lord the now king, and a free-man of the said corporation, not ignorant of the premisses, nor in any wise weighing the duty of his allegiance, but desiring to acquire lucre and profit to himself, by the ruin and impoverishment of all the other subjects of the said lord the now king, using the said art and mystery, on the 1st day, &c. in the year, &c. one Charles Hilton, of, &c. frame-work knitter, a natural subject of the said lord the now king, and who for the space of divers years, then last past, at, &c. in the county, &c. had diligently used and exercised the said art and mystery, and by the use and exercise of the said art and mystery, had competently supported and maintained himself, his wife and the rest of his family; and also divers other natural subjects of the said lord the king, the said art and mystery, at the parish, &c. then and there using, unlawfully did solicit, entice and seduce to leave and desert their respective families, to suffer poverty, without any provision for the support of them, or of any of them, and to * pass beyond the sea with the said L. &c. and others, &c. and the said other persons, so by the said L. &c. enticed and seduced, on the said day, year and place aforesaid, he the said L. otherwise G. C. did transport, and cause to be transported, from the parish, &c. in the county, &c. to Paris, in the kingdom of France, and there them did occupy and put to labour, for the said L. C. in the art and mystery aforesaid, and also did cause and procure the said C. H. to teach and instruct divers other persons, being subjects of the French king, in the art and mystery aforesaid, and that afterwards to wit, on the day and year, &c. the said L. for a certain sum of money, to him the said L. paid, did sell and dispose him the said C. H. to a certain foreigner, being a subject of the said French king, with intention that the said C. H. might instruct other foreigners, ignorant of the said art and mystery, in the art and mystery aforesaid, whereby the said art and mystery is greatly injured in this kingdom of England, and the profits and benefits heretofore arising therefrom are totally lost and destroyed, to the great impoverishment of all the subjects of the said lord the now king, using the said art and mystery, and whereby the respective wives and families, of the said C. H. and the others so seduced and transported, have fallen into great want and

poverty,

*P. 253.

poverty, in manifest contempt of the laws of this kingdom of England, to the evil example of all others in the like case offending, and against the peace, &c. &e.

The King *against* Russell *and others.*

Michaelmas, 2d James 2d.

London, **T**HAT the lord Charles 2d, the late king of *Information*
To wit. England, by his letters patent, sealed with his *for setting*
great seal of England, bearing date at Westminster, on the 22d *up an office*
day of April, in the 17th year of the reign of the said late *for registring*
king, which are produced to the court here, for himself his *policies of assurance*
heirs and successors, gave and granted to one Allen Broderick, *upon ships,*
knight, and to his assigns the office of making, and registering *when the*
of all manner of policies of assurance, renunciation, intima- *said office*
tion, and of all other things whatsoever, which might be *was by the*
made or done upon any ship or ships, or any goods, mer- *kings letters*
chandizes or any other thing or things in the royal exchange, *patent,*
or in any other place or places, within his city of London, *granted to*
by any person or persons whatsoever, of whatsoever nation, *another.*
condition or quality he or they might be, either going out or
coming into this kingdom, or going or coming into any
other place or places whatsoever; and further the said late
king, by the said letters patent for himself, his heirs and successors, created, made, constituted, ordained and appointed,
the said Allen Broderick and his assigns, makers and registers
of all manner of policies of assurance, intimation and renunciation, and of the other premisses, to have, hold, occupy
and enjoy the making * and registering of all the aforesaid po- *P. 254.
licies of assurance and assurances, intimation, renunciation and
the other premisses, to him the said Allen Broderick and his
assigns, to be used and exercised by him, or by them, or by
his or their sufficient deputy or deputies, for and during
the natural lives of him the said Allen Broderick, and of
one William Broderick of London, Merchant, and for
the life of the survivor of them, together with such and
the like fees, sums of money, duties and benefits whatsoever,
as formerly were usually had, taken and received by Giles
Over-

Overbury, Walter Overbury, Richard Bogan and the said
Allen Broderick, or by any of them, or by any other person or persons, who at any time then before had used, had
or exercised the said office, for and concerning the said poli
cies of assurance, intimation and renunciation, and the other
premisses; and further the said late king, by his said letters
patent, for himself, his heirs and successors, ordained and
strictly commanded all persons whatsoever, as well his
subjects as strangers, who within the royal Exchange aforesaid, or in any other place or places within his city of London aforesaid, should make or cause to be made, any manner of policy of assurance, intimation, renunciation or
contract of assurance, either upon ships, goods or merchandize, or upon money taken upon the hazard or safe proceedings of any ship or ships, goods or merchandize, or
of any other thing whatsoever, touching and concerning
the same, and whereof any policy or contract should be
made as aforesaid, that, from that time, the same should
be made and registered by the said Allen Broderick, and his
assigns, during the lives of the said Allen Broderick and
William Broderick, and the life of him living the longest
of them, or by his or their deputy or deputies, whom the
said late king by the said letters patent, authorized and appointed to do and execute the same, and that every policy
of assurance, contract of assurance, or intimation, or renunciation, which after the date of the said letters patent,
should be made upon any ship or ships, goods or merchandizes, or any other the premisses, by any other person or
persons, within the royal Exchange aforesaid, or in any
other place or places within his city of London aforesaid,
and not being made and registered by the said Allen Broderick and his assigns, or by his or their deputy or deputies as
aforesaid, should be from that time void and of no effect;
and further the said late king, by his letters patent aforesaid,
for himself, his heirs and successors, did give and grant to
the said Allen Broderick, his executors, administrators and
assigns, the office of making and registering of all manner of
policies of assurance, intimation and renunciation, and of
all other things whatsoever, which should be made or done
upon any ship or ships, goods, merchandizes or other thing
or things, in the royal Exchange aforesaid, or in any other
place or places within his city of London * aforesaid, by
any person or persons whatsoever, of whatsoever nation,
condition or quality, he or they might be, either going out
or coming into this kingdom, or going or coming to any
other place or places whatsoever, and did create, make,
constitute and appoint the said Allen Broderick, his executors,

wagering
policies not
prevented
in Eng'and
until the 19
of Geo. 2d
C. 37.

*P. 255.

executors, adminiftrators and affigns, the makers and regifters of all manner of policies of affurance, intimation and renunciation, and of the other premiffes aforefaid, to have, hold, occupy and enjoy the making and regiftering of all the faid policies of affurance and affurances, intimations, and renunciations, and of the other premiffes to the faid Allen Broderick, his executors, adminiftrators and affigns, to be exercifed himfelf, or themfelves, or by his or their fufficient duputy or deputies immediately from and after the faid office fhould become vacant, by the death of the faid Allen Broderick and William Broderick, and the furvivor of them, or by the furreuder, forfeiture, or other determination of the faid ftate and intereft of the faid Allen and his affigns of and in the faid office atorefaid, above by the letters patent aforefaid, granted or mentioned to be granted to the faid Allen and his affigns, for and during the lives of the faid Allen and William, and for the life of him living the longeft of them as aforefaid, for and during the term of 31 years, from that time next following, fully to be compleated and ended, together with fuch and the like fees, fums of money, duties and benefits whatfoever, as before that time were ufually had, taken and received by the faid E. O. W. O. R. B. and the faid A. B. or by any of them, or by any other perfon or perfons whatfoever, who for any time then before had ufed, had or exercifed the faid office, of and concerning the faid policies of infurance, intimation and renunciation, and of the other premiffes. And further, the faid late king, for himfelf, his heirs and fucceffors, by the faid letters patent, did ordain and ftrictly command all manner of perfons whatfoever, as well his fubjects as foreigners, who within the royal Exchange aforefaid, or in any other place or places within the city of London aforefaid, fhould make or caufe to be made, any manner of affurance upon fhips, goods or merchandize, or upon money taken upon the hazard or fafe proceedings of any fhip or fhips, or of any goods or merchandizes, or of any other thing whatfoever, touching or concerning the fame, and whereof any contract or policy fhould be made as aforefaid, that from thenceforth the fame fhould be made and regiftered by the faid Allen, his executors, adminiftrators or affigns, or by his or their deputy or deputies, whom the faid late king, by the faid letters patent, authorifed and appointed to do and execute the fame ; and that every policy of affurance, contract of affurance, intimation or renunciation, which fhould be made during the faid term of 31 years, commencing as aforefaid upon any fhip or fhips, any goods, merchandizes, or other things, by any other perfon * or perfons, within the royal Exchange aforefaid, or in any other place or places within his city of London aforefaid, not being made and regiftered by the faid Allen Broderick, his executors, adminiftrators

* P. 256.

or affigns, or by his or their deputy or deputies as aforefaid
fhould be from thence void, and of no effect, as by the letters
patent aforefaid, more fully appears; by virtue of which
letters patent, the faid Allen Broderick, of the faid office
of the making and regiftering of all manner of the faid policies of affurance, intimation and renunciation, and of the
other premiffes, and of the entire intereft thereof granted
by the faid letters patent, was feized and poffeffed, and the
faid Allen Broderick and his affigns, and his and their deputy and deputies of the faid office, immediately after the
making of the faid letters patent, and continually afterwards,
hath and have kept a publick and convenient office for the
making and regiftering of all manner of policies of affurance,
intimation and renunciation, and of all other things whatfoever, which could be made or done upon any ship or
fhips, or any goods, merchandizes, or other thing or things,
in the royal Exchange, or in any other place or places, within the city of London, by any perfon or perfons whatfoever,
of whatfoever nation, condition or quality, he or they might
be, either going out or coming into this kingdom, or going
or coming into any other place or places whatfoever, and
hath, and have, had, ufed and exercifed, from the making
of the faid letters patent, and continually afterwards, until
the day of the exhibition of this information, the faid office
of the making and regiftering of the faid policies of affurance, intimation and renunciation, and of the other premiffes aforefaid, to wit, at London aforefaid, in the parifh of St. Bartholomew Exchange, in the ward of Broad-
ftreet, London; And the faid grant of the faid office, and the
ftate and intereft thereof granted by the faid letters patent,
as yet is and remains in its full force and vigor; the faid office by the faid letters patent granted as yet continuing, and
not being vacant, furrendered, forfeited, or in any other manner determined. And the faid Attorney-general of the faid
lord the now king, for the faid lord the king, further gives the
court here to underftand and to be informed, that Richard Ruf-
fell of London, gent. J. Browne, of, &c. S. Baxter, of, &c.
W. Jones of, &c. S. Lupton of, &c. well knowing, and each
and every of them well knowing the faid premiffes, but being
perfons greedy of gain, and devifing, practifing, and among
themfelves confpiring and intending, and each and every of
them devifing, practifing and intending to have the Royal prerogative of the lord the now king in contempt, and to dero-
gate and deminifh the fame and to make the Royal Grant a-
forefaid, in the manner and form aforefaid made, vain, void,
and of no effect; and the fooner to fulfil, perfect, and bring
to effect their moft wicked devices, practifes and intentions
aforefaid, in profecution of their faid confpiracy, he the
faid R. R. on the 12th day of March, in the 2d year of the
reign

reign of our lord James the 2d, the now king of England, &c. with force and arms, &c. at London, to wit, in the parish of St. Bartholomew Exchange, in the * ward of Broad Street, London, of his own proper injury, and without any lawful authority, a certain other publick office for the making and regiſtering of the ſaid policies of aſſurance, intimation and renunciation, and of the other premiſſes, unlawfully did erect and keep, and that office, from the ſaid 12th day, &c. in the year, &c. aforeſaid, to the day of the exhibition of this information, to wit, the 9th day of November, in the year, &c. aforeſaid, by himſelf and his ſervants, unjuſtly, and without the conſent or licence of the ſaid A. B. or his aſſigns, or his or their deputy or deputies, of his ſaid office aforeſaid, did continue and exerciſe, and within that time then and there, in his ſaid office ſo erected, unlawfully and without the conſent or licence of the ſaid A. B. or his aſſigns, or his or their deputy or deputies, of his ſaid office aforeſaid, with force and arms, &c. divers policies of aſſurance, intimation and renunciation, to wit, 500 policies of aſſurance, 10 of intimation, and 20 of renunciation, did make and regiſter, and the fees and profits for the making and regiſtering of the ſaid policies of aſſurance, intimation and renunciation, amounting to the ſum of 50l. then and there did receive and have, and the ſaid J. B. on the ſaid 12th day, &c. in the year, &c. aforeſaid, with force and arms, &c. at London aforeſaid, in the pariſh and ward aforeſaid, of his own proper injury and without any lawful warrant or authority, a certain other publick office for the making and regiſtering of the ſaid policies of aſſurance, intimation and renunciation, and of the other premiſſes aforeſaid, unlawfully did erect and keep, and that office, from the ſaid 12th day of, &c. in the year, &c. aforeſaid, by himſelf and his ſervants, there unlawfully, and without the conſent or licence of the ſaid A. B. or his aſſigns, or of his or their deputy or deputies, of his ſaid office aforeſaid, did continue and exerciſe, and within that time then and there, in his ſaid office ſo erected, unlawfully and without the licence or conſent of the ſaid A. B. or of his aſſigns, or of his or their deputy or deputies, of his ſaid office aforeſaid, with force and arms, &c. divers policies of aſſurance, intimation and renunciation, to wit, 500 policies of aſſurance, 10 of intimation, and 20 of renunciation, did make and regiſter, and the fees and profits for the making and regiſtering of the ſaid policies of aſſurance, intimation and renunciation, amounting to the ſum of 500l. then and there did receive and have; and the ſaid S. B. W. j. and S. L. (word for word as aforeſaid, &c.) in great contempt of the ſaid lord the king, and of his laws, to the great damage and injury of his royal prerogative, and alſo to the

great

great ruin and impoverishment of the said office by the said letters patent erected, and to the evil and pernicious example of all others in the like case offending, and against the peace of the said lord the now king, his crown and dignity, &c. Whereupon, &c.

---

* P. 258

* The King *against* Gundrey.

Michaelmas, 3d. James the 2d.

Information for procuring an infant to levy a fine of lands and tenements, whereof he was seized in fee, and to declare the uses to the defendant, and his heirs to the prejudice of the infant's heir at law, in case he should die without issue

Middlesex, THAT one Robert Browne, esquire, on the 13th 'To wit. day of October, in the 2d year of the reign of our lord James by the grace of God of England, &c. king, &c. at Westminster, in the county of Middlesex, was and as yet is an infant within the age of 21 years, to wit, of the age of sixteen years, and then was seized in his demesne as of fee of, and in the manor of Nether Cerne, otherwise lower Cerne, Fampton, Crookeway, Notton Thorpe, otherwise Notton-Throope, and Bettiscombe, otherwise Bettoscombe, with the appurtenances, and of and in 100 Messuages, 34 Cottages, 40 Tofts, 3 Water-mills, 2 Tucking-mills, 1 Dove-cot, 130 Gardens, 60 Orchards, 2265 acres of land, 518 acres of meadow, 1516 acres of pasture, 180 acres of wood, 960 acres of Furze and Brush-wood, with the appurtenances in Nether C. otherwise lower C. F. C. N. T. &c. in the county of Dorset, of the clear yearly value of 2000l. and of and in 12 Messuages, &c. with the appurtenances in S. C. L. in the county of Somerset, of the clear yearly value of 500l. and that one John Williams, gent. then, to wit, on the 13th day of October, in the 2d year aforesaid, at Westminster, aforesaid, in the said county of Middlesex, was and as yet is the cousin, and the person next heir to the said Robert Browne, to wit, &c. to which John Williams, and his heirs, the manors, lands and tenements aforesaid, would descend, as of right then they ought to descend in case that the said Robert Browne, should die without issue of his body lawfully begotten, before that he would arrive at his age of 21 years, and that one Thomas Gundrey, of the Middle Temple, esquire, well knowing the premisses, then and there, to wit, at Westminster, falsely, fraudulently

fraudulently unlawfully and deceitfully, contriving practising, devising and intending, him the said *John Williams*, and his heirs, in case the said R. B. should die without issue of his body lawfully begotten, before that he would arrive at his age of 21 years, of the manors, lands and tenements aforesaid, unlawfully, injuriously and unduly to deprive, deceive, defraud and disinherit, and also of the avaricious mind and disposition of the said *Thomas Gundrey*, wickedly, subtilly and unjustly, desiring and intending, all and singular, the manors, lands and tenements aforesaid, to himself and to the proper use and benefit of the said T. G. and his heirs unduly to obtain and secure, and to execute, perfect and fulfil the wicked intentions of him, the said T. G. in that behalf, he the said T. G. afterwards, to wit, on the said 13th, day of October, in the 2d year, &c. aforesaid at Westminster, aforesaid, falsely and subtilly did pretend that he was the guardian of the said R. B. and that he had the government and disposition of the said R. B. and of his lands, and falsely, unlawfully, unjustly, wickedly, unduly, deceitfully, privily and secretly, then and there did advise, stir up, and persuade, the said R. B. then being as aforesaid, seized of the manor and tenements aforesaid, and then, and as yet there being an *P. 259. infant within the age of 21 years, to acknowledge and levy to the said T. G. while the said R. B. was an infant within the age of 21 years, two several fines in the court of the said lord the king of the bench, before the then justices of the said bench, containing and comprising in the said fines all and singular the manors and tenements aforesaid, and that for the cause and to the intentions aforesaid, and for the more quick, easy, and secret taking the acknowledging and the levying of the said fines, of the said manors and tenements, the said T. G. afterwards to wit, on the said 13th day of Oct. in the 2d year, &c. aforesaid, at Westminster, aforesaid, subtilly, unlawfully, fraudulently, unduly and deceitfully, privily and secretly, and in deceit of the court of Chancery of the said lord the king did procure and obtain out of the said court of Chancery, of the said lord the king at Westminster, aforesaid, a certain writ of the said lord the king of *Dedimus Potestatem*, sealed under his great seal of England, directed to one N. W. baronet, and to F. S. R. F. and T. G. persons by the said T. G. in that behalf named and appointed, by which writ of *Dedimus Potestatem*, the said lord the now king, reciting several writs, of covenant of the said lord the king between him the said T. G. and the said R. B. of the several manors and tenements aforesaid, in the said several writs of covenant, separately and respectively mentioned and described, falsely supposed and pretended to be then depending before the justices of the said lord the king of the bench aforesaid, to levy fines thereof between them, before the justices of the said lord the king,

of

of the bench according to the law and custom of this kingdom
of England, and that the said Robert was then so weak, that
without great danger of his body he could not go to Westminster, at the days in the said writs contained to make the
acknowledgment which was required in that behalf, did
give to the said W. N. F. S. R. F. and T. G. or to two of
them the power to receive the acknowldgement which the
said R. B. was willing to make before them or two of them
concerning the premisses, and that afterwards to wit, on the
3d day of February, in the 2d year aforesaid, at Westminster,
aforesaid, he the said T. G. craftily, fraudulently, unduly,
deceitfully, privily and secretly did advise, stir up, cause and
procure the said R. B. then as aforesaid, being seized of the
manors and tenements aforesaid, and then and as yet there
being an infant within the age of 21 years, to wit, being of
the age of 16 years, to come before the said T. C. and R. F.
dependants of the said T. G. and then and there mean and
illiterate, persons, being suitable persons for such an affair to
acknowledge a certain note or abstract of the said fines of
the manors and tenements aforesaid, by him the said R. B.
to him the said T. G. so as aforesaid, craftily devised to be
levied, which note or abstract the said T. G. then and there
in that behalf for the occasion aforesaid, had caused and procured to be written and engrossed in parchment, and that
thereupon the said R. B. being an infant within the age of 21
years as aforesaid, and by the subtilties and fair speeches of
the said T. G. in that behalf being moved, stirred up and seduced by the procurement of the said T. G. afterwards to
wit, on the said 3d day of Februray now last past at Westminster, did come before the said F. F. and T. C.
dependants of the said T. G. and mean and illiterate
persons, and suitable persons for such an affair, * and then
and there did acknowledge the said note or abstract of the
said fines, of the said manors and tenements aforesaid, by him
the said R. B. while he was within age, to him the said T. G.
so as aforesaid, subtilly designed to be levied, and that thereupon the said T. G. afterwards to wit, on the said 3d day of
February, in the second year, &c. aforesaid, at Westminster
aforesaid, falsely, subtilly, deceitfully, fraudulently and unduly
did cause and procure the said note or abstract of the said fines
by him the said R. B. so as aforesaid, unduly acknowledged,
and the said acknowledgment thereof made and taken with
and upon the said writ of *Dedimus Potestatem*, to be returned,
certified and recorded in the said court of the said lord the king
of the bench aforesaid, at Westminster, with intention that
thereupon the said fines, in the said court might be recorded
and levied, of the manors and tenements aforesaid, while
the said R. B. was within the age of 21 years, and that thereupon the said T. G. afterwards to wit, in the term of St
Hilary, now last past, at Westminster aforesaid, falsely, unlawfully.

* P. 260

lawfully, fraudulently, unjustly, craftily, unduly, deceitfuly, privily and secretly, by fraud, practise and covin, and against the course and custom of the said court of the said lord the king of the bench aforesaid, and in deceit of the said court did cause and procure the said fines between him the said T. G. complainant and the said R. B. deforciant of the manors and tenements aforesaid, to be ingrossed, perfected and recorded in the said court of the said lord the king of the bench at Westminster, before the then justices of the said lord the king of the said bench, while the said R. B. was within the age of 21 years, as if the said R. B. was a person of the full age of 21 years, the said T. G. then and there craftily and fradulently concealing the true age of the said R. B. from the knowledge of the said court, and from the justices of the said court, and that by the said fines in the said court, between the said T. G. complainant, and the said R. B. deforciant, of the said manors and tenements, as aforesaid, had and levied, he the said R. B. while he was within the age of 21 years, did acknowledge the manors and tenements aforesaid, with the appurtenances, to be the right of the said T. G. as those which the said T. G. had of the gift of the said R. B. and those, he did remise and quit claim from himself and his heirs, to the said Thomas G. and his heirs for ever, and that by the said fines of the manors and tenements aforesaid, in the court aforesaid, in the form aforesaid, unduly acknowledged, levied, had, and recorded, and by the uses thereof, by the procurement of the said T. G. then and there by him the said R. B. while he was within the age of 21 years aforesaid, declared, the said John Williams, and his heirs, were, and are in danger of being disinherited, deprived, deceived and defrauded of all, and singular the manors, lands and tenements aforesaid, in case the said R. B. should happen to die without issue of his body, lawfully begotten, before the said R. B. would arrive at his age of 21 years, and the said T. G. and his heirs, would have and hold all and singular the manors, lands and tenements aforesaid, to the use of the said T. G. and his heirs for ever, in contempt of the said lord the now king and of his laws, of this kingdom of England, to the great damage and deceit of the said John Williams and his heirs, to the evil example, &c. &c. &c.

---

* The King *against* Walker.

* P. 261

Indictment against a counsellor; for betraying his clients cause and taking fees of the other side,

To wit. THE jurors, &c. present, that whereas in the term of St. Michael, in the year of our lord 1655, one William Walker, of Charter-House, haydon, in the county of Somerset, esquire, exhibited his bill of complaint in the high court of Chancery, the said court then being held at Westminster, in the county of Middlesex, against Theodore Langrish, Joyce, his wife, Robert May and others, and among other things in and by the said bill, prayed remedy and relief of and concerning a certain statute of the penalty of two thousand eight hundred pounds, in and by the said bill, supposed to be before that time acknowledged by one Clement Walker, the father of the said William Walker, to one Christopher May, deceased, upon which statute it was alledged by the said bill that the said Joyce, as the administratrix of Robert May, her father, deceased, claimed and demanded the sum of 600l. altho the said sum of 600l. was fully satisfied and paid as by the bill aforesaid, in the said high court of Chancery affiled more fully appeareth ; and whereas also the said Theodore Langrish, and Joyce his wife, in the said court of Chancery, held at Westminster aforesaid, in the said county of Middlesex, put in their answer to the said bill, and by their said answer to the said bill among other things, denied that they or either of them had received any part of the said sum of 600l. as by the said answer of the said T. Langrish, and J. his wife in the court of Chancery aforesaid affiled more fully appeareth ; and whereas also the said cause, from the said term of St. Michael, in the year of our lord 1655, unto the term of St. Michael, in the 17th year of the reign of our lord Charles the 2d, of England, &c. king, &c. in the high court of Chancery aforesaid, depended undetermined ; and whereas also, the said Theodore Langrish, on the 1st. day of May, 1668, died, and whereas also, the said William Walker, on the 16th day of May, in the 17th year, &c. aforesaid, and at divers other days and times as well before as after, (during the pendency of the said cause) at London, to wit, in the parish, &c. retained one John Walker, of London, esquire, being an apprentice of the law, to be of council with the said William Walker, in the said cause, against the said Joyce, Langrish, and Robert May, and divers sums of money, to the said John Walker, gave and paid as fees for giving good, faithful, and salutary council to the said William Waker, in the said cause, and he the said William Waker, trusting and confiding in the honesty, integrity, sincerity and candour of the said John Walker, in the said cause, he the said William Walker, declared and made known to the said John Waker, all and singular the secret matters and circumstances, touching and concerning the said cause, nevertheless the said John Walker, late of London, afterwards to wit, on the said 16th day of May, in the 17th year, &c. aforesaid, and at divers other days and times, as well before as after at London, to wit, in the parish, &c. and at other places in the city of London aforesaid, falsely, secretly, clandestinely, corruptly, subtilly, deceitfully, unjustly, wickedly

and

and for the fake of wicked gain, did receive and have of
and from the faid Joyfe Langrifh and Robert May, and of
the attornies and folicitors of the faid Joyfe Langrifh and
Robert May, divers fums of money as fees, to give council
to the faid Joyfe Langrifh and Robert May againft the faid
William Walker, his faid client in the faid caufe, and then
and there, and at the faid other days and times, as well before as after, falfely, fecretly, clandeftinely, corruptly, fubtilly, wickedly and for the fake of wicked gain, did betray,
relate and difclofe, to the faid Joyfe Langrifh and Robert
May, the fecret matters and circumftances of the faid caufe,
by the faid William Walker, on behalf of the faid William
Walker, to the faid John Walker, trufted faithfully to be
concealed, and not to be revealed to the faid Joyfe Langrifh
and Robert May or to either of them, or to the attornies or
folicitors of the faid Joyfe Langrifh and Robert May, altho
on the 16th day of May, in the 17th year, &c. aforefaid,
and on the faid days and times as well before as after being
as aforefaid, retained of council with the faid William Walker, and having and receiving from the faid William Walker,
divers fums of money as fees to give good and faithful council
to the faid W. Walker, in the faid caufe againft the faid
Joyfe Langrifh and Robert May, and then and there and at
the faid other days and times, falfely, fubtilly and deceitfully
promifing and affirming to the faid William Walker, that
he the faid John would give to the faid William good and
faithful council in the faid caufe according to the beft experi-
ence, ftudy and learning of him the faid John in the law, and
that he would faithfully conceal the fecrets and matters of the
faid William Walker, in the faid caufe and would not reveal
them to the faid Joyfe Langrifh and Robert May, to the great
fcandal and abufe of juftice, to the manifeft injury of the
laws of this kingdom of England, to the evil example, &c.
and againft the peace of the faid lord the now king his crown
d dignity, &c.

* 2. *Agcinſt Statutes.*

Fowler *againſt* Alſop.

Trinity, 1650.

Middleſex, BE it remembered that E. A. one of the juſtices
To wit. of the common Bench here, on the 14th day
of June, in this ſame term, with his own proper hands
delivered here, a certain information before him, on the
4th day of June laſt paſt, by one B. F. who as well for
the keepers of the liberties of England, by the authority
of Parliament, as for himſelf proſecutes againſt one R. A.
exhibited, and in the court here to be enrolled, the tenor
of which information follows in theſe words, To the juſtices
of the common bench, Middleſex, to wit, Be it remembered
that Bartholomew Fowler, who as well for the keepers of
the liberties of England, by the authority of parliament,
as for himſelf, in this behalf proſecutes, cometh before
E. A. one of the juſtices of the common bench, on the
4th day of June, in the year of our Lord 1650, in his
proper perſon, and as well for the ſaid keepers, as for
himſelf, gives the ſaid juſtices to underſtand and to be
informed, that one R. Alſop, late of the pariſh of St.
Clement-danes, in the ſaid county, vintner, after the
feaſt of St. John the baptiſt, in the 33d year of the reign
of the lord Henry the 8th, late king of England, to wit,
on the 28th day of February, in the year of our Lord
1649, and continually afterwards, for the ſpace of 60 days
then next following, at the pariſh of St. C. D. in the ſaid
county, for the advantage and gain of the ſaid R. A.
did keep, have, hold and maintain, one common gaming-
houſe, for tables and cards, and for a certain other unlawful

---

Side note: Information on the 33 H. 8th. againſt a vintner for keeping unlawful games in his houſe; exhibited to a judge of the common pleas in vacation.

lawful game called billiards, otherwiſe billyards, and the ſaid unlawful games, for the whole time aforeſaid, in his manſion-houſe, ſituate in the pariſh of St. Clement-danes, aforeſaid, did permit to be held, played and gamed, againſt the form of the ſtatute of the ſaid 33d year of the ſaid lord the king Henry the 8th, in ſuch caſe made and provided, whereby the ſaid R. A. hath forfeited the ſum of 120l. of the lawful money of England, to wit, for every day of the ſaid 60 days, in which the ſaid R. A. ſo as aforeſaid the ſaid common gaming-houſe did keep and main-tain, againſt the form of the ſaid ſtatute, &c. in the whole, amounting according to that rate to the ſaid ſum of 120l. wherefore the ſaid B. F. as well for the ſaid keepers of the liberties of England, by the authority of parliament, as for himſelf prays the conſideration of the court here in the premiſſes, and that he the ſaid B. F. may have the moiety of the ſaid forfeiture, according to the form of the ſaid ſtatute, and alſo that the ſaid R. A. may come here into court, to anſwer as well to the ſaid keepers, &c. as to the ſaid B. F. who as well, &c. in and upon the premiſſes, &c.

---

* The King *againſt* Plym.

Michaelmas, 29th Charles 2d.

London, THAT John Plym, late of the pariſh of Egham,
To wit. in the county of Surrey, Yeoman, otherwiſe called John Plumbe, late of the pariſh aforeſaid, in the county aforeſaid, Yeoman, who on the 12th day of January, in the 5th year of the reign of the lady Elizabeth, late queen of England, &c. did not lawfully uſe or exerciſe any art, myſtery or manual occupation, nevertheleſs the ſaid J. P. otherwiſe J. P. afterwards, to wit, on the 1ſt day of February, in the 29th year of the reign of our lord Charles the 2d, of England, &c. king, &c. and continually afterwards, until the day of the taking of this inquiſition, to wit, for the ſpace of two whole months and more, at London, to wit, in the pariſh of St. Faith, in the ward of C. London, did ſet up, uſe and exerciſe the art, myſtery or manual occupation of a fruiterer,

Indictment againſt a fruiterer for exerciſing that trade, not having been ap-prentice to it 7 years, againſt the ſtat. 5th Eliz.

S ſ 2
       being

being an art, myſtery or occupation uſed within this kingdom of England, on the ſaid 12th day of January, in the 5th year of the reign of the ſaid lady Elizabeth, late queen, &c aforeſaid, in which art, myſtery or manual occupation of a fruiterer, he the ſaid J. P. otherwiſe J. P. was not educated for the ſpace of 7 years as an apprentice, againſt the form of the ſtatute in ſuch caſe made and provided, and againſt the peace of the ſaid lord the now king, his crown and dignity, &c. &c. &c.

To this indictment Pollexfen demurred, and the court ſeemed ſtrongly of opinion, that a fruiterer is not a trade within the ſtatute of the 5th of queen Elizabeth ; but no judgement. The caſe is reported 1 Ventris 326, 346, 2 Lev. 206, 3 Keble, 816. 843.

The King *againſt* Pyne.

Michaelmas, 27th Charles 2d.

Indictment againſt a gentleman for refuſing to receive an apprentice, bound to him by the overſeers of the poor and church wardens, with the conſent of 2 juſtices of the peace purſuant to the ſtatute.
*P. 265.

Somerſet,) THAT George Powel, Robert Sheppard, To wit.) Michael Potter and William Laſcombe, on the 27th day of October, in the 26th year of the reign of our lord Charles the 2d, of England, &c. king, &c. then and as yet being overſeers of the poor of the pariſh of North-currey, in the county of Somerſet, Arthur Weaver and John Smith, on the day and year aforeſaid, then being church wardens of the pariſh of North-currey aforeſaid, in the county aforeſaid, in the due manner nominated and appointed, with the conſent of Robert Hawles and Edward Court, Eſquires, two of the juſtices of the ſaid lord the king, aſſigned to preſerve the peace in the ſaid county, and alſo to hear and determine divers felonies, treſpaſſes and other * miſdeeds, in the ſaid county perpetrated, one of them being and inhabiting nigh the pariſh of N. C. aforeſaid, in the ſaid county, according to the form of the ſtatute in that behalf made and provided, by indenture bearing date the ſaid day and year, did bind one Joan Randall, Spinſter, one of the poor of the pariſh of N. C. aforeſaid, apprentice to one John Pyne, of Currey mallet, in the ſaid county, eſquire, in reſpect of a certain

tenement

tenement and farm, of him the ſaid J. P. at North Curréy
aforeſaid, in the ſaid county, and afterwards to wit, on
the 27th day of October, in the year aforeſaid, in the due
form of law, did deliver the ſaid Joan Randall, to the
ſaid John Pyne, with one part of the ſaid indenture, nevertheleſs the ſaid John Pyne, not being ignorant of the
ſaid premiſſes, afterwards to wit, on the ſaid 27th day of
October, in the year aforeſaid, and always afterwards,
until the taking of this inquiſition, then and as yet being an
occupier of the tenement and farm aforeſaid, with force and
arms, &c. at N. C. aforeſaid, unlawfully and contemp-
tuouſly, then and there, entirely hath refuſed and denied
to receive the ſaid J. R. as his apprentice, or in any man-
nér to provide for her, although thereto he was often re-
queſted in the due manner; in contempt of the ſaid lord
the now king, againſt the peace of the ſaid lord the now
king, his crown and dignity, &c. againſt the form of the ſtatute, in ſuch caſe thereupon lately made and provided, &c. &c.

*After conference between all the judges of England, (who
declared their opinion, that the overſeers could not force an apprentice on any one who did not perſonally occupy huſbandry)
this indictment was quaſhed. It is reported 3d Keble, 516, 625,
636, 686, 854, and Shower, 193.*

The King *againſt* Baxter.

To wit. BE it remembered that at the aſſizes holden for the
county of Surrey, at Kingſton, upon Thames, in
the ſaid county, on Thurſday, the 28th day of July, in the
35 year of the reign of our lord Charles the 2d by the grace
of God of England, &c. king, &c. before Francis Pemberton, knight, chief juſtice of the ſaid lord king of the
bench, and Edward Atkyns, knight, one of the barons of
the Exchequer of the ſaid lord the king, juſtices of our ſaid
lord the king, aſſigned to take aſſizes in the ſaid county
of Surrey, by the form of the ſtatute, &c. by the oath
of Chriſtopher Buckle of B. knight, and 16 others, good
and lawful men of the ſaid county, then and there ſworn
and charged to enquire for the ſaid lord the king and
for the body of the ſaid county, it is preſented that

*Information
for taking a
young wo-
man out of
the cuſtody
of her guar-
dian, againſt
the ſtatute,
4 and 5, Phil.
and Mary,
c. 8.*

Nicholas

Nicholas Baxter of Haſcombe in the county of Surrey, Black-ſmith, E. L. of &c. A. L. of &c. J. B. of &c. E. B. of &c. and J. C. of &c. on the 29th day of January, in the 34 year of the reign of our lord Charles the 2d of England, &c. king, &c. being and each and every of them being above the age of 14 years, to wit, of the age of 21 years, afterwards to wit, on the ſaid 29th day of January, in the 34th year, aforeſaid, with force and arms, &c. at the pariſh of Bramley in the county of Surrey, aforeſaid, in and upon one Ann Still-
* P. 266 well, a maiden * unmarried, then being within the age of ſix-teen years, to wit, of the age of eleven years and nine months, and daughter and heir of one James Stillwell, deceaſed, who hath left to the ſaid Ann, lands and tenements in the ſaid county, of the clear yearly value of 100l. above repriſals, did make an aſſault, (ſhe the ſaid A. S. then and there being in the poſſeſſion of one R. E. her grand father,) and her the ſaid A. S. then and there, out of and from the poſſeſſion and againſt the will of the ſaid R. E. the grand father of the ſaid A. S. who then and there, by lawful ways and means, had the diſpoſition, wardſhip, education and governance, of the ſaid A. S. unlawfully did take and convey away, with in-tention to marry the ſaid A. S. to the ſaid N. B. and her the ſaid A. S. from the ſaid 29th day of January, in the 34th year, aforeſaid, to the 31ſt day of the ſaid month of January, in the 35th year, &c. at the pariſh of B. aforeſaid, and elſewhere, in the ſaid county, with force and arms, &c. out of and from the poſſeſſion and againſt the will of the ſaid R. E. the grand father, of the ſaid A. S. unlawfully and unjuſtly, did detain, in contempt of the ſaid lord the king and of his laws, to the great affliction of the ſaid R. E. againſt the form of the ſtatute, in ſuch caſe made and provided, and againſt the peace of the ſaid lord the now king, his crown and dignity, &c. whereupon the ſheriff of the ſaid county, is commanded that he do not omit, &c. but that he cauſe them to come to anſwer &c. And now to wit, at the ſaid aſſizes held for the ſaid county at Kingſton, upon Thames, aforeſaid, in the county aforeſaid, on the ſaid Thurſday, the 26th day of July, in the 35th year, &c. aforeſaid, before the ſaid juſtices, come the ſaid N. B. &c. according to certain recogniſances by them, and by their bail in this behalf before acknowledged, in their proper perſons, and having heard the indictment aforeſaid, ſeverally ſay, that they are not guilty thereof, and of this ſeverally put them-ſelves upon the country, and Eldred Lancelot Lee, eſquire, clerk of the aſſizes for the ſaid county, who for the ſaid lord the king in this behalf proſecutes, doth the like, and therefore, by the conſent of the ſaid N. B. &c. let a jury come there-upon immediately, &c. and the jurors of that jury by Anthony Rawlins, eſquire, ſheriff of the ſaid county, for this purpoſe impanelled,

Venire a-warded a-gainſt defen-dants who appear upon their recognizance and plead not guilty.

By conſent of defen-dants, Venire fac. jur. awarded returnable immediately and there-upon, they are found guilty.

impanelled, to wit, W. Y. and eleven others, being called, come who being elected tried and ſworn to ſpeak the truth of and concerning the premiſſes, ſay upon their oath, that the ſaid N. B. E. L. A. L. J. B. E. B. and J. C. are guilty and each and every of them is guilty of the treſpaſs and contempt aforeſaid, in the indictment ſpecified to them above ſeverally charged in the manner and form as by the ſaid indictment, above againſt them is ſuppoſed, whereupon all and ſingular the premiſſes, being ſeen and by the court here fully under-ſtood, it is conſidered by the court, here that the ſaid N. B. E. L. A. L. J. B. E. B. and J. C. ſhall have and undergo the impriſonment of their bodies, and each and every of them ſhall have and undergo the impriſoment of his and her body for the ſpace of two whole years, without bail and mainprize according to the form of the ſtatute, in ſuch caſe made and provided by occaſion of the treſpaſs, contempt and offence aforeſaid, whereof as aforeſaid, they are convicted and each and every of them is convicted, and that they be taken, and that each and every of them be taken, &c. and the ſaid N. B. E. L. A. L. J. B. E. B. and J. C. preſent here in court are committed, and each and every of them is com-mitted to the goal of the ſaid lord the king of the ſaid county, there to remain under the cuſtody of the ſheriff of the county aforeſaid, in the ſaid goal ſafely to be kept for the ſpace of two whole years, without bail or mainprize according to the form of the ſtatute aforeſaid, for the treſpaſſes, contempts and offences aforeſaid, &c. &c.

Judgement of impriſon-ment for 2 years with-out bail or mainprize

commit-ment by the court.

---

* P. 267

* The King againſt Fenton and others,

Trinity, 27th Charles 2d.

Eſſex, To wit. THAT William Fenton, of the pariſh of Halſtead, in the county aforeſaid, yeoman, W. R. of &c. J. C. of &c. J. F. of &c. N. H. of &c. and J. A. of &c. on the 10th day of March, in the 26th year of the reign of our lord Charles 2d, by the grace of God of England, &c. king, &c. were and each and every of them was of the age of 16 years and more, from the ſaid 10th day of March, in the year

Information againſt 6 de-fendants for not coming to church, &c. upon the ſtatutes 23 & 29 Eliz.

year aforeſaid, did not repair, nor did any of them repair to his or their parochial church or churches, nor to any other church, chapel, or uſual place of public prayer, nor were they nor was any of them there at the time of publick prayer, at any time within the ſpace of eleven whole months, next following the ſaid 10th day of March, in the year aforeſaid, but they have forborne, and each and every of them hath forborne to go to the ſame from the ſaid 10th day of March, in the year aforeſaid, for the ſaid ſpace of eleven months, from thence next enſuing, without any reaſonable cauſe, to wit, at Halſtead, aforeſaid, againſt the form of the ſtatute in ſuch caſe made and provided, and alſo againſt the peace of the ſaid lord the now king, his crown and dignity, &c. whereupon the ſaid co-

Venire a-
warded.

roner and attorney of the ſaid lord the king, for the ſaid lord the king, prays the conſideration, &c. whereupon the ſheriff of the ſaid county, is commanded that he do not omit, &c. but that he cauſe them to come to anſwer, &c. And now to wit, on the Friday next after the morrow, of the Holy Trinity, in this ſame term, before the lord the king at Weſtminſter, come the ſaid W. F. W. R. J. F. N. H. and J. A. by P. W. their attorney, and pray oyer of the ſaid

Five defen-
dants appear
and plead
that they
did not for-
bear, &c.

information, and it is read to them, which being had and by them heard and underſtood they the ſaid W. W. J. N. and J. complain that they are grievouſly vexed and diſquieted, under colour of the ſaid information, and this not juſtly, becauſe they ſay that they the ſaid W. W. J. N. and J. have not forborne, nor hath any of them forborne to go to their or his pariſh church, or uſual place of publick prayer for the ſpace of the ſaid eleven months, in the ſaid information above mentioned or for the ſpace of any one month thereof, againſt the form of the ſaid ſtatute, as by the ſaid information above is ſuppoſed, and this they are ready to verify, as the court, &c. wherefore they pray judgement, and that they from the premiſſes by the court here may be diſmiſſed, &c. And T. Fanſhawe, knight, coroner and attorney, of the ſaid lord the king, in the court of the ſaid lord the king, before the king himſelf, who for the ſaid lord the king in this behalf proſecutes, having heard the ſaid plea by the ſaid W. F. W. R. J. F. N. H. and J. A. in the manner and form aforeſaid, above pleaded, ſaith that the ſaid lord the king, by any thing

Replication
as to three
defendants.

by the ſaid W. W. J. N. and J. above by pleading alledged, ought not to be precluded from the information aforeſaid, againſt them, becauſe he ſaith that they ſaid W. F. W. R.

* P. 268

and J. F. at the pariſh of H. aforeſaid, have forborne and each and every of them hath forborne to go to their or his parochial church or churches, and to any other church, chapel or uſual place of publick prayer, for the ſpace of the ſaid eleven months in the ſaid information, above mentioned, or of ſome one month thereof, againſt the form of the ſaid ſtatute, as by the ſaid information above, againſt them is ſuppoſed,

ed,

ed, and this the said coroner and attorney, of the said lord the king, prays may be enquired of by the country: and the said W. F. W. R. and J. F. do the like. Therefore let a jury come thereupon from the day of the Holy Trinity, in three weeks, before the said lord the king, wheresoever, &c. and who neither, &c. by whom, &c. to recognise, &c. because as well, &c. the same day is given as well to the said T. Fanshaw, knight, who prosecutes, &c. as to the said W. R. W. F. and J. F. &c. at which three weeks from the day of the Holy Trinity, before the said lord the king at Westminster, come as well the said T. Fanshaw, knight, who prosecutes, &c. as the said W. F. W. R. and J. F. by their attorney, aforesaid, and the sheriff, returns the names of 12 jurors, of whom none, &c. Therefore the sheriff of the said county is commanded that he do not omit, &c. but that he distrain them by all their lands and tenements, &c. and that of the issues, &c. and that he have their bodies before the said lord the king, from the day of St. Michael, in three weeks wheresoever, &c. or before the justices of the said lord the king, assigned to take assizes in the said county of Essex, if first on Monday the 12th day of July, at Chelmsford, in the said county, &c. &c.

Information against six, five appear and plead, the coroner and attorney, replies only to three, without any continuance as to the other two, this held no discontinuance, because the offences are several, and a Nolle prosequi as to the other two salves all, (which may be entered at any time Quod nota) and afterwards the party conformed before doctor Stillingfleet, and this held as well as if done before the bishop of the diocess, he approving it afterwards. This case is reported, 3 Keble, 527, 535, 545, 573, 610.

(marginal notes: Venire facias · Distringas. · nisi prius*)*

The King *against* Smith.

Michaelmas, 26th Charles 2d.

Surry.
To wit. } THAT John Smith, of Trinity Minories, in the parish of Aldgate without, in the county of Middlesex, Mealman, on the 10th day of July, in the 35th year of the reign of our lord Charles the 2d, of England, &c. king, &c. at the town of Farnham, in the county of Surrey,

(marginal note: Information for buying unground corn by a bushel not being Winchester mea-*)*

T t   unlawfully

fure againſt the form of the ſtatute.

unlawfully and unjuſtly did buy corn, to wit, 5 quarters of unground wheat, of the value of nine pounds by a certain buſhel, not agreeing with the ſtandard, marked in the Exchequer of the lord the king, commonly called Wincheſter meaſure, containing eight gallons to the buſhel, in great deceit of the ſubjects of the ſaid lord the king, againſt the form of

\# P. 269 the ſtatute * made and provided, and alſo againſt the peace of the ſaid lord the now king his crown and dignity, &c. with this that the ſaid coroner and attorney, of the ſaid lord the king will verify that wheat on the 10th day of July, in the year aforeſaid, and alſo from the time whereof the memory of man is not to the contrary, was uſed to be bought, and yet is bought, by the buſhel as well in the pariſh afore-ſaid, as in all the reſt of this kingdom of England, whereupon the ſaid coroner, &c. &c.

The King *againſt* Farmer.

Michaelmas, 26th Charles 2d.

Information for uſury.

Surrey, **T**HAT Thomas Farmer, late of the pariſh of St.
To wit. George, Southwark in the county of Surrey, aforeſaid, gent. on the 1ſt day of July, in the 26th year of the reign of our lord Charles the 2d, by the grace of God of England, &c. king, &c. at the pariſh, &c. aforeſaid, in the ſaid county of Surrey, unlawfully and unjuſtly, did take, have and receive by deceitful ways and means and by covin of one Mark Hinch, the ſum of 80 ſhillings, of the lawful money of England, of the monies of the ſaid M. H. to wit, 20 ſhillings for every quarter of one year for the forbearance and giving day of payment of the ſum of 6l. of the monies of the ſaid T. F. by him the ſaid T. F. lent and forbore to the ſaid M. H. from the 1ſt day of July, in the 25th year of the reign of our ſaid lord Charles the 2d king, &c. until the ſaid 1ſt day of July, in the year aforeſaid, being over the ſum and above the rate of 6l. for the loan and forbearance of 100l. for one year, againſt the form of the ſtatute, in ſuch caſe made and provided, and againſt the peace of the ſaid lord the now king his crown and dignity, &c. whereupon, &c. &c.

Traverſes,

Traverses, Pleadings and other Proceedings on Indictments and Informations.

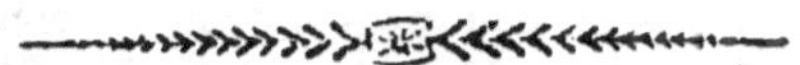

A. B. at the Suit of the *Lord the King.*

To wit. AND now to wit, on the Monday next after the octave of St. Hilary, in this same term before the lord the king at Westminster, comes the said A. B. by W. J. his attorney, and having heard the indictment aforesaid, saith that he doth not apprehend that the said lord the now king will any further impeach or trouble him for the occasion of the premisses, because he saith that the said W. B. * on the said time when, &c. at the said parish of St. Dunstan, in the county aforesaid, with force and arms, &c. in and upon the said A. in the peace of God, and of the said lord the king, then and there being, did make an assault and affray, and him the said A. then and there would have beaten, wounded and ill treated, unless he the said A. immediately in that behalf had defended himself against the said W. whereupon the said A. then and there, himself, then and there against the said W. did defend, and if any damage happened to the said W. it was from the proper assault of the said W. and in the defence of the said A. which is the same assault, affray, beating, wounding, and ill treating, in the indictment aforesaid specified, and this he is ready to verify, whereupon he prays judgment if he ought any further to be impeached, or troubled by occasion of the premisses.

Quære if this can be pleaded to an indictment. vide cases 2d and 3d Ann 172, where it is said by Holt, chief justice, that it cannot be pleaded, but may be given in evidence, and that thereupon the party must be acquitted.

To wit. AND having heard the indictment aforesaid, saith that he doth not apprehend that the said lord the now king will or ought impeach or trouble him the said J.

Son assault demesne pleaded to an indict- ment for as- sault and battery.

* P. 270.

Special de- murrer to an indict- ment for

that it doth not appear by the indictment on what certain day, year & place the offence was committed.

any further concerning the premisses, becaufe he faith that the indictment aforefaid is not fufficient in law to compel the faid J. to anfwer to that indictment, and that by the law of the land, no procefs ought to be made againft the faid J. upon the faid indictment, for this becaufe that it doth not appear by the faid indictment in certain on what certain day, year and place the faid offence in the indictment aforefaid, by the faid D. fuppofed to be done, was committed, as by the law of the land, ought to be made, wherefore for the infufficiency of the fame he prays judgment, and that he by the court here may be difmiffed of and from the premiffes, &c. whereupon all and fingular the premiffes being feen and by the court here fully underftood, &c.

Judgment for the defendant.

The King *againft* Butler.

Plea to an inquifition —"that the defendant delivered a deodand, found by the inquifition to be in his hands, to the royal patentee."

* P. 271.

To wit. AND the faid J. Butler, cometh by J. H. his attorney, and having had oyer of the information aforefaid, faith that he doth not apprehend that the faid lord the king, will impeach him for occafion of the premiffes, becaufe he faith, that before the death of the faid J. J. the faid lady Elizabeth, late queen of England, by her letters patent made under her great feal of England, bearing date at Greenwich, the 25th day of July, in the 39th year of her reign, which the faid J. B. brings here into court, granted to William Pagett, then efquire, afterwards lord William Pagett, all deodands within the manor of Longden aforefaid, to have and to hold to the faid Wm. Pagett, * and his heirs, by virtue of which grant the faid William was feized of the faid franchife, of having and taking to his own proper ufe all deodands within the manor aforefaid, as of fee and right, and fo being feized thereof, the faid W. P. afterwards to wit, on the 1ft day of March, in the 3d year of the reign of the lord Charles the 1ft late king of England, at L. aforefaid, died, fo feized thereof, after whofe death the faid franchifes defcended to the faid Wm. lord P. in the inquifition aforefaid, named as the fon and heir of the faid W. P. deceafed, whereby the faid William lord P. the fon was and as yet is feized of

all

all the ſaid franchiſes of having and taking to his own proper uſe all deodands within the ſaid manor, whereupon the ſaid J. B. after the taking of the ſaid inquiſition to wit, on the 1ſt day of May, in the 20th year aforeſaid, at the manor aforeſaid, the ſaid oak to the ſaid William lord P. the ſon did deliver and the ſaid William lord P. the ſon, the ſaid oak then and there from the ſaid J. B. had and received, and this he is ready to verify, whereupon he prays judgment and that he of and from the premiſſes by the court here may be diſmiſſed, &c. &c.

E. S.

The King *againſt* D.

AND the ſaid D. cometh by J. his attorney, and having heard the indictment aforeſaid, ſaith, he doth not apprehend that the ſaid lord the king, will impeach him for occaſion of the premiſſes, becauſe he ſaith that the ſaid aſſault, beating and wounding and ill treating, were done out of the juriſdiction of the juſtices of the peace, &c. to wit, at Lambeth in the county of Surrey aforeſaid, without this that the ſaid aſſault, &c. was done within the juriſdiction of the ſaid juſtices of the peace, &c. as by the ſaid indictment above is ſuppoſed, and this he is ready to verify, wherefore he prays judgment, and that he of and from the premiſſes by the court here, may be diſmiſſed, &c.

Edward Saunders.

Quære of this plea, for it ſeems only to amount to the general iſſue.

Plea to an indictment at the ſeſſions of the peace that the fact was committed out of the juriſdiction of the juſtices of the peace.

The Queen *againſt* Arundell.

Trinity, 30th Elizabeth.

Middleſex, ⎫ THAT he cauſe to come 12, &c. of the neighTo wit. ⎬ bourhood of the city of Weſtminſter, in the county aforeſaid, and who are in no wiſe of kin to John Arundell, late of Quarnack, in the county of Cornwall, eſquire, otherwiſe called, &c. to recogniſe, &c. if the ſaid John Arundell,

Venire facias awarded, de viceneto Civitatis Weſtm'

Arundell, is guilty of a certain feloney and murder, whereof he is indicted or not, becauſe, &c. the ſame day is given to the ſaid J. Arundell, * under the cuſtody of the marſhall in the meantime committed, &c. At which day the ſheriff returns the writ with the panel of whom none, &c. therefore, &c.

*P. 272

Diſtringas awarded. that he diſtrain the jurors, &c. on the Saturday, after 15 days of the Holy Trinity, &c. at which day comes the ſaid J. Arundell, under the cuſtody of the ſaid marſhall, and the jurors being called come, who being elected, tried, ſworn and charged to ſpeak the truth of and concerning the premiſſes, ſay upon their oath, that the ſaid J. A. is guilty of the felony and murder aforeſaid, and that he had no goods and chattels,

Curia adviſare. &c. and he is recommitted to the ſaid marſhall, &c. and thereupon the court will adviſe to the octave of St. Michael, &c. at which day the ſaid continuance by the writ of the lady the

Writ of adjournment. Queen, of common adjournment was adjourned, from the day of St. Michael, for one month, before the lady the Queen, &c. at which day, becauſe that the writ of venire facias was

Verdict quaſhed. awarded to the city of Weſtminſter, whereas it ought to be awarded to the pariſh of St. Margaret, Weſtminſter, in the county aforeſaid, for the trial of the iſſue in that behalf joined, therefore judgment is given that the verdict aforeſaid, in the form aforeſaid, given, be taken and held for nothing ; and that the ſaid J. A. of that verdict may go thence without day, &c. whereupon Edward Coke, eſquire, attorney general of the ſaid lady the Queen, for the ſaid lady the Queen prays an-

Venire de novo. other writ of venire facias, anew for the trial of the ſaid iſſue of the neighbourhood of the pariſh of St. Margaret, Weſtminſter, aforeſaid, in the county aforeſaid, and it is granted to him, &c. therefore, &c. that the ſheriff cauſe to come anew on the Tueſday next after the morrow of the purifica-

Some of the jury appear, others make default. tion, &c. at which day, &c. and the ſheriff of, &c. returns the writ with the panel, &c. therefore, &c. that he diſtrain, &c. on the Monday next after the octave of the purification, &c. At which day the jurors being called, certain of them come, and certain of them do not come as appears by the pa-

Challenge. nel, and certain of thoſe jurors appearing are ſworn upon that jury, and certain of them in like manner appearing, becauſe that they by the ſaid John Arundell, are peremptorily challenged, are entirely withdrawn from the ſaid panel, as

Remanet. appears in the ſaid panel, &c. whereby that jury at that day for the default of jurors remains to be taken, &c. therefore,

Diſtringas awarded with 20 ſuch, &c. &c. that he diſtrain, &c. on Monday after 3 weeks of Eaſter, &c. and that he add 20 ſuch as thoſe removed, &c. the ſame day is given to the ſaid John Arundell, under the cuſtody of the ſaid marſhall, in the mean time committed, &c. at which day comes the ſaid J. Arundell, in his proper perſon under the cuſtody of the ſaid marſhall, and the jurors of the ſaid

Jury appear. jury being called in like manner come, who being elected, tried

and

and sworn to speak the truth of and concerning the premisses, say upon their oath that the said John Arundell is not guilty of the felony and murder aforesaid, to him above charged, and that he never fled for the occasion of the same. But the said jurors further say upon their oath, that the said J. A. is guilty of the felony and manslaughter, &c. and that he hath no goods nor chattels, lands nor tenements, &c. therefore it is considered that the said J. A. as to the felony and murder aforesaid, go quit thereof, &c. whereupon for divers causes the court of the said lady the queen, then specially moving the said J. A. is recommitted to the marshall, &c. and afterwards to wit, on Friday, after fifteen days of the Holy Trinity, comes the said John Arundell, under the custody of the said marshall, in his proper person, and as to the felony and manslaughter aforesaid, hath pleaded the act of parliament of general pardon of the 35th year of the said lady the queen, and prays the allowance thereof, &c. and Edward Coke, esquire, attorney general of the said lady the queen, who for the said lady the queen, prosecutes for the said lady the queen, * saith that the said J. A. ought not to have or enjoy the benefit of the said pardon, because he saith that he the said J. A. on the last day of the session of the said parliament, was in the prison of the marshall of the marshalsea of the lady the queen, before the queen herself by the command of T. Heneage, knight, then and as yet being one of the privy council of the said lady the queen, to wit, at the borough of Southwark, in the county of Surrey. And therefore at the prayer of the said John Arundell, day is given as well to the said John Arundell, as to the said attorney general who prosecutes, &c. upon the said plea until the octave of St. Michael, before the said lady the queen, wheresoever, &c. in the state in which now, &c. under the custody of the said marshall in the mean time committed, &c. at which day before the lady the queen at Westminster, come as well the said Edward Coke, esquire, who prosecutes, &c. as the said J. A. under the custody of the marshall in his proper person, and saith that the said lady the queen, ought not to preclude or prevent him the said John from the benefit of the general pardon aforesaid, by him as aforesaid, prayed, because he saith that he on the said last day of the session of the parliament aforsaid, was not in the prison of the marshall of the marshalsea of the said lady the queen, before the queen herself, by the command of the said T. Heneage, knight, to wit, at the borough of Southwark in the co. of Surrey, aforesaid, in the manner and form as the said attorney general, by replying hath alledged; and of this he puts himself upon the country, and the said attorney general of the said lady the queen who, &c. doth the like, &c. therefore let the sheriff of the county of Surrey cause to come, &c. in fifteen days of St. Martin, &c. at which day, &c. the sheriff

And find defendant not guilty of the murder, but guilty of manslaughter.

Defendant prays the benefit of the act of general pardon of the 35 Eliz.

* P. 273

The attorney general replies that he ought not to have the benefit of it because he was a prisoner of the king's bench prison the last day of the session of parliament by the command of a privy counsellor.

The defendant rejoyns that he was not a prisoner prout, issue joyned thereon and venire awarded.

 riff returns the writ with the panell, &c. therefore that he diſtrain, &c. fifteen days of St. Hilary, &c. the ſame day is given as well to the ſaid attorney general who proſecutes, &c. as to the ſaid J. A. under the cuſtody of the ſaid marſhall again committed, &c.

See 6th Coke 14, a. where this caſe is reported.

The King *againſt* Lord Lovelace.

Trinity, 4th James 2d.

 Berks, } **T**O be informed that John, lord Lovelace, ba-
To wit. } ron of Hurley, in the pariſh of Hurley, in the county of Berks, being a perſon ill affected to the ſaid lord the king, and to his government, within this kingdom of England, and deviſing, practiſing, and unlawfully, ma-liciouſly, factiouſly and ſeditiouſly, intending to diſquiet, moleſt and diſturb the peace and public tranquility of this kingdom of England, and to bring and draw our moſt ſerene lord the now king, and his rule and government of this kingdom of England, into hatred and contempt, and to create falſe opinions and ſuſpicions among the people and ſubjects of the ſaid lord the king, of and concerning the government and rule of the ſaid lord the king, and of the royal power and undoubted prerogative of the ſaid lord the king, within this kingdom of England ; and that the ſaid John, lord Lovelace, to fulfil, perfect and bring to effect his moſt wicked devices and intentions aforeſaid, on the   day of   in the   year, &c. at, &c. in the county of Berks aforeſaid, with force and arms, &c. the

 execution of a * certain warrant in writing, under the hadns and ſeals of Francis Perkins, eſquire, and of Richard Perkins, eſquire, then and as yet juſtices of the ſaid lord the now king, aſſigned to preſerve the peace of the ſaid lord the king, in and for the county of Berks aforeſaid, and alſo to hear and determine divers felonies, treſ-paſſes and other miſdeeds, in the ſaid county perpetrated, duly made, bearing date the 28th day of January, in the 4th year aforeſaid, to the then conſtables and tything-
me

men of the parifh of Ufton, in the county of Berks aforefaid, and to any one of them, and alfo to the church-wardens
and overfeers of the parifh of Hurley, in the county of
Berks aforefaid, and to all and fingular the feveral and
refpective inhabitants of the faid parifhes, in the county of
Berks aforefaid, and to each and every of them directed,
for the fettlement of one William R. then late an inhabitant
of the faid parifh of Hurley, and of Catherine, the wife
of the faid William, and of a male child of the faid William and Catherine, within the faid parifh of Hurley, in
the county of Berks aforefaid, unlawfully, unjuftly, contemptuoufly, malicioufly, factioufly and feditioufly, did oppofe and hinder, and then and at divers other times, between
the faid time and the 11th day of February, next following
with force and arms, one William Grove, then and as yet
being church-warden of the parifh of Hurley aforefaid,
and —— Rowe, then and as yet being an inhabitant within
the parifh of Hurley aforefaid, and divers other inhabitants
and parifhioners of the faid parifh, in the faid parifh then
and as yet dwelling, and there keeping and maintaining
manfion houfes, did hinder and obftruct, to obey the faid
warrant; and the faid William Grove, and divers other
inhabitants and parifhioners of the faid parifh, then and
there did ftir up, animate and abet, to oppofe and refift the
faid warrant, and the execution thereof; and that the faid
John, lord Lovelace, the further to fulfil, perfect and bring
to effect his malicious and feditious purpofes and intentions
aforefaid, upon a certain difcourfe, of and concerning the
faid warrant and the execution thereof, and of and concerning the faid juftices of the peace, of the faid lord the king
as aforefaid, and of the authority of the faid juftices of the
peace, of the faid lord the now king as aforefaid, on the
30th day of January, in the 4th year aforefaid, at the
parifh of Hurley, in the county of Berks aforefaid, in the
prefence and hearing of the faid officers, and of divers other
fubjects of the faid lord the now king, then and there being
prefent, falfely, malicioufly and unlawfully, contemptuoufly
and feditioufly did fay, utter, declare, affirm and with a
loud voice did publifh, " *that he* (meaning the faid John,
lord Lovelace, baron of Hurley,) *did no more value the faid
warrant than the dirt of his fhoes, and that the faid warrant ought
not to be obeyed.*" And the faid John lord Lovelace, then
and there, to the faid William Grove, church-warden of
the parifh of Hurley aforefaid, then and there being prefent
as aforefaid, further did fay and affert, "*that if he the faid*
" *William Grove would difobey, and not obey the faid warrant,*
" *that he the faid lord Lovelace, him the faid William Grove,*
" *then being church-warden of the parifh of Hurley aforefaid,*

U u

" and

*P. 275.

" *and the other inhabitants within the parish of Hurley aforesaid,* " *in the county of* * *Berks aforesaid, would save harmless, altho' it* " *should cost him the said lord Lovelace 500l.*" to the derogation, great damage, diminution and injury of the said lord the now king, and of his royal prerogative, in contempt of . the said lord the now king, and of his laws, and of the power and authority of the said Francis Perkins and Richard Perkins, justices of the peace of the said lord the now king, under the said lord the now king derived, in diminution and derision of the authority and power of the said lord the now king, to the evil example of all others in the like case offending, and against the peace of the said lord the now king, his crown and dignity, &c. Whereupon the said attorney-general, &c.

And now, to wit, on the Friday next after the morrow of the Holy Trinity, in this same term, before the lord the king, at Westminster, comes the said John lord Lovelace, by Robert Seyliard his attorney, and having heard the information aforesaid, complains that he, under colour of the premises in the information aforesaid mentioned, is greatly vexed and disquieted, and this not justly; Because, protesting that the information aforesaid, and the matter in the same contained, are not good and sufficient in law, to which information aforesaid, he hath no necessity, neither is he bound by the law of the land to answer in any manner; for plea nevertheless, as to the coming with force and arms, and to whatever is against the peace, or in contempt of the said lord the now king and of his laws, or to the derogation, damage, diminution or prejudice of the said lord the king, or of his royal prerogative, or to the diminution or derision of the authority or power of the said lord the now king, and also as to all other the premisses in the information aforesaid specified, charged against him, except the opposing, hindering and obstructing of the said warrant and the execution thereof, and the speaking, declaring and publishing the words in the said information mentioned by him, the said John lord Lovelace, above supposed to be done, he the said John Lovelace saith that he is not guilty thereof, as by the said information above is supposed, and of this he puts himself upon the country. And as to the opposing, hindering, and obstructing the said warrant, and the execution thereof, and the speaking, declaring and publishing the words in the information aforesaid mentioned, by him the said John lord Lovelace above, supposed to be done, he the said John lord Lovelace saith, that the said lord the now king ought not to impeach, or trouble him by occasion thereof, because he saith, that after the making of a certain act, made and provided in a parliament of the lord Charles the 2d, late king of England, by prorogation held at Westminster in the county of Middlesex, on the 4th day of

February,

Defendant justifies that the justices of the peace were not qualified, not having taken the oaths, &c. pursuant to act of parliament.

not guilty as to vi and armis, &c.

February, in the 25th year of his reign, intitled an act to prevent dangers which may happen, from Popish Recufants, and long after the term of Eafter, 1673, in the faid flatute mentioned, the faid F. Perkins and R. Perkins in the information aforefaid above named, by a commiffion of the faid lord the now king, fealed under his Great Seal of England, bearing date at Weftminfter, the 17th day of February, in the 3d year of the reign of the faid lord the now king, were (among other perfons in the faid commiffion named) jointly and feparately conftituted and affigned juftices of the faid lord the now king, to preferve the peace in the faid county, which F. Perkins and R. Perkins afterwards, and for eleven months and more before the making of the faid warrant in the faid information above **P. 276.** fpecified, to wit, on the 24th day of February, in the 3d year of the reign of the faid lord the now king aforefaid, in the parifh of Hurley aforefaid, in the faid county of Berks, in the due manner were fworn, and each of them then and there in the due manner was fworn, well and faithfully to execute the office of juftice of the peace, in the faid county of Berks. And thereupon they the faid F. Perkins and R. Perkins, then and there by virtue of the faid commiffion, were admitted to exercife the office of juftices of the faid lord the now king, to preferve the peace of the faid lord the now king, in the faid county of Berks. And each of them then and there was admitted to execute the office of one of the juftices of the faid lord the now king, to preferve the peace of the faid lord the king in the faid county. And that office, then and there did take upon themfelves, and each of them did take upon himfelf, by virtue of the faid commiffion, and in the exercife of that office in fact, from thence until the time of the making of the faid warrant, to wit, to the 28th day of January, in the 4th year aforefaid, did continue, and each of them did continue, to wit, at the parifh of Hurley aforefaid, in the county aforefaid; and that the faid office of Juftice of the faid lord the king, in and for the county of Berks aforefaid, is a civil office, and an office of truft, under the faid lord the now king, and concerns the public juftice within this kingdom of England. And the faid John lord Lovelace protefting, that the faid F. Perkins and R. Perkins, being Popifh recufants, and each of them being Popifh recufants, at any time after their faid admiffion into the office of juftice of the peace aforefaid, have not received, nor hath either of them received the facrament of the Lord's-fupper, or have taken or performed, nor hath either of them taken or performed the oaths of fupremacy and allegiance, according to the form and effect of the faid ftatute, in fuch cafe made and provided, in fact, and for plea, the faid John Lord Lovelace further faith, that after the admiffion of the faid F. and R. into the faid office of

U u 2

juftices

justices of the peace of the said lord the king for the said county, and before the making of the said warrant, to wit, on the 5th day of April, in the 3d year of the reign of the said lord the now king, the Quarter session of the peace, for the said county, was held at Newbery in the said county, and that the said F. Perkins at any time after the making aforesaid of the commission aforesaid, of the lord the now king, nor after his admission aforesaid, into the office of justice of the peace of the said lord the now king, did not make and subscribe the declaration specified in the statute aforesaid, in such case made and provided, and by the said statute appointed to be made and subscribed according to the form and effect of the said statute. And that the said R. Perkins, at any time after the making aforesaid, of the commission aforesaid, of the said lord the king, nor after his admission aforesaid, into the said office of justice of the peace, of the said lord the now king, did not make and subscribe the declaration in the said statute mentioned, and by the said statute appointed to be made and subscribed, according to the form and effect of the said statute, but they the said F. P. and R. P. so to do entirely have neglected, and each of them hath neglected, against the form of the said statute, before the making of the said warrant, in the said information mentioned, whereby by force of the said statute, they the said F. P. and R. P. before the making of the said warrant, in the information aforesaid mentioned, became in fact disqualified and incapable in law, * and each of them became disqualified and incapable in law, to all intents and purposes, to be or continue justices of the said lord the king, to preserve the peace in and for the said county, and so did continue and were, and each of them did continue and was disqualified and incapable at the time of the making of the said warrant in the information aforesaid mentioned, and at the time of the making of the said warrant, then were not, nor was either of them justices or justice of the said lord the king, to preserve the peace of the said lord the king, in the said county, and so the warrant aforesaid, by them so as aforesaid made, never was valid, but was altogether void and of no effect in law, and for nought ought entirely to be had and held. And the said John lord Lovelace further saith, that he at the time of the making of the said warrant and long before, and from that time continually afterwards, hitherto was a parishioner and inhabitant of the said parish of Hurley, in the said county of Berks, and chargeable and charged towards the support of the poor of the said parish, and the other charges to be sustained by the parishioners of the said parish; and that if the said W. R. and Catherine his wife, and their

said

*P. 277.

said male child, in the information aforesaid named, by pretence of the said warrant, should be settled in the said parish of Hurley, a charge unjustly would fall upon the said John Lord Lovelace, and upon the other parishioners of the said parish of Hurley, for the support of the said W. R. Catherine his wife, and of the said male child, [they being poor and in want,] by reason whereof he the said John lord Lovelace, on the said 30th day of January, in the 4th year of the reign of our said lord the now king aforesaid, at the parish of Hurley, having a discourse with the said William Grove, then church-warden of the said parish of Hurley, and with —— Row, and with divers other inhabitants and parishioners of the said parish of Hurley, concerning the premisses, and the said constables and tything-men of the said parish of Ufton, requiring and urging them under pretence of the said warrant, to receive and settle the said W. R. and Catherine his wife, and the male child aforesaid, in the said parish of Hurley, he the said John lord Lovelace, to free and save himself and the other parishioners of the said parish of Hurley, from the charge which would arise to them by the unjust settlement of the said W. R. and Catherine, and of their male child aforesaid, within the parish of Hurley aforesaid, under pretence of the said warrant so being invalid and void, then and there did oppose and hinder the execution of the said warrant as being invalid and void, and made by persons who were not justices of the peace, and then and there did say, that the said warrant ought not to be obeyed, and did give advice to the said William Grove, and to the said other inhabitants and parishioners of the parish of Hurley aforesaid, not to obey the said warrant, and then and there did say to the said William Grove, and to the other inhabitants and parishioners aforesaid, that he did no more value the said warrant than the dirt of his shoes, and that if the said William Grove would disobey and not obey the said warrant, that he the said John lord Lovelace would save harmless, the said William Grove and the other parishioners of the said parish of Hurley, although it should cost him 500l. as it was well lawful for him, which are the said opposing, hindering and obstructing of the said warrant and the execution of the same, and the * speaking, declaring and publishing of the words in the information aforesaid mentioned, to him by the information aforesaid above charged, without this, that the said John lord Lovelace is guilty of the said premisses, to him by the said information above charged, otherwise, or in any other manner than he above by pleading hath alledged, all and singular which things the said John Lord Lovelace is ready to verify, wherefore he doth not apprehend that

*P. 278.

Traverse.

the

the faid lord the now king, will or ought to impeach or trouble him the faid John lord Lovelace for occafion thereof, and he prays judgment, and that he as to the faid premiffes, by the court here may be difmiffed, &c. &c. &c. &c.

Attainders

The King *against* Gerrard.

HEREtofore to wit, on the day, &c. laſt paſt before the lord the king at Weſtminſter, by the oath of 12 jurors good and lawful men of the ſaid county, then and there ſworn and charged to enquire for the ſaid lord the king and for the body of the ſaid county, it is preſented that Charles Gerrard, late of the pariſh of St. Martin, in the fields in the county of Middleſex, eſquire, as a falſe traitor againſt the moſt illuſtrious and moſt excellent lord Charles the 2d, late king of England, &c. his natural lord, not having the fear of God in his heart, nor weighing the duty of allegiance, but being moved and ſeduced by the inſtigation of the devil, and entirely withdrawing the cordial love, and true due and natural obedience which a true and faithful ſubject of the ſaid late lord the king, towards the ſaid late lord the king ſhould bear and of right was bound to bear, and deviſing, practiſing and as much as in him lay, intending to diſquiet, moleſt and diſturb the peace and public tranquillity of this kingdom of England, and to ſtir up, move and procure war, rebellion and inſurrection againſt the ſaid late lord the king, within this kingdom of England, and to ſubvert, change and alter the government of the ſaid late lord the king of this kingdom of England, and the ſaid late lord the king from his title, honour and royal name, and from the imperial crown of this kingdom of England, to depoſe and deprive, and the ſaid late lord the king to bring and put to death and final deſtruction, on the 30th day of March, in the 35th year of the reign of the ſaid lord Charles the 2d, late king of England, &c. and at divers other days and times as well before as after, at the pariſh of *St.* Martin, in the fields in the county of Middleſex, falſely, maliciouſly, diabolically and traiterouſly, with divers other falſe rebels and traitors to the jurors aforeſaid, unknown did conſpire, compaſs, imagine, and intend * the ſaid late lord the king then his ſupreme and natural lord not only from his royal ſtate, title, power

Indictment
for high
treaſon, by
conſpiring to
depoſe and
murder the
king.

P. 279.

power and government of his kingdom of England, to deprive
and depose, but also the said lord the king to kill, and to
bring and put to death, and to change alter and entirely subvert the antient government of this kingdom of England, and
to cause and procure a miserable slaughter among the subjects
of the said late lord the king, throughout his whole kingdom
of England, and to procure and abet war, insurrection and rebellion against the said late lord the king within this kingdom
of England, and to fulfil, perfect and bring to effect the said
most wicked, detestable and diabolical treasons and traitorous
compassings, imaginations and purposes, he the said Charles
Gerrard as a false traitor, then and there, to wit on the said
30th day of March in the 36th year of the reign of the said
late king aforesaid, and at divers other days as well before as
after at the parish, &c. in the said county of Middlesex,
falsely, unlawfully, wickedly and traiterously with James
duke of Monmouth and with divers other false traitors to
the jurors aforesaid unknown, did assemble, meet and consult, to raise and procure divers great sums of money, and
great numbers of armed men, to levy and make war and
rebellion against the said lord the late king, within this kingdom of England, and to take and seize the castle of the said
late lord the king of Chester, against the duty of the allegiance, and against the peace as well of the said late lord the king
as of the said lord the now king, their crowns and dignities,
&c. and also against the form of the statute in such case made
and provided, &c. whereupon the sheriff of the said county
is commanded that he do not omit, &c. but that he take him
to answer, &c. And now to wit on the Saturday next after the
morrow of St. Martin, in this same term, before the lord the
king at Westminster, comes the said C. G. under the custody
of Thomas Cheeke, esquire, lieutenant of the Tower of
London, by virtue of the writ of the lord the king of habeas
corpus ad subjiciendum, &c. into whose custody before for
the cause aforesaid, he was committed to the bar here brought
in his proper person, who is committed to the said lieutenant,
&c. and forthwith being demanded of the premises above
charged against him, how he will acquit himself thereof,
saith that he is not guilty thereof, and thereof of good and
evil puts himself upon the country; therefore let a jury come
thereupon before the said lord the king at Westminster, on
the Thursday next after fifteen days of St Martin next ensuing,
by whom, &c. and who neither, &c. to recognise, &c. because as well, &c. the same day is given to the said Charles
Gerrard, &c. under the custody aforesaid, of the lieutenant
of the Tower of London aforesaid, &c. and in the mean time
is committed safely to be kept until, &c. At which day be-
foi e

fore the lord the king at Westminster, comes the said Charles Gerrard under the custody aforesaid, of the lieutenant of the Tower of London aforesaid, to the bar here brought in his proper person, and the jurors of the said jury for this purpose by the sheriff of the said county impanelled, being called come, who being elected, tried and sworn to speak the truth of and concerning the premisses, say upon their oath that the said Charles Gerrard is guilty of the high treason aforesaid, **Verdict guilty.** in the said indictment specified in the manner and form as by the said indictment above against him is supposed, and that the said Charles Gerrard at the time of the perpetration of the high treason aforesaid, or at any time afterwards * had no ***P. 280.** goods or chattels, lands or tenements to the knowledge of the said jurors; and the said Charles Gerrard, being demanded if he had or knew any thing to say for himself, wherefore the court here should not proceed to judgment and execution against him, upon the verdict aforesaid, saith nothing except as before he hath said, whereupon immediately the attorney general of the said lord the now king according to the **Judgment and execution prayed.** due form of law, prays against him the said Charles Gerrard, judgment and execution to be had upon the verdict aforesaid, for the said lord the king. Whereupon all and singular the premisses being seen and by the court here fully understood, it is considered that the said C. G. be brought by the said **Judgment.** lieutenant of the Tower of London to the prison of the said lord the king of the Tower aforesaid, and from thence that he be drawn to the place of execution, &c. &c.

The King *against* Morley.

Michaelmas, 24th Charles 2d.

City of York } ————HERETOFORE to wit, on Tuesday **Indictment**
To wit. } to wit, the 7th day of August, in the year **for a murder** of our Lord 1649, at the assizes and general goal delivery **by shooting the deceased** held at the Guild-hall of the city of York, in the county of the said city of York, before J. Pulleston, one of the

X x   justices

justices of the common bench, and Francis Thorp, one of the barons of the public Exchequer, William Allenton, knight, and others their fellows justices and commissioners assigned as well to hear and examine and to deliver the goal there, as to enquire by the oath of good and lawful men within the said city, by whom the truth of the matter might be the better known, and by other ways, methods and means, by which they might and could know better, as well within liberties as without, of certain treasons, misprisions of treason, insurrections, rebellions, murders, killings, felonies, burglaries, &c. in the county of the said city perpetrated, &c. and to hear and determine, &c. by the oath of P. L. and eleven others, good and lawful men of the county of the said city, impanelled, sworn and charged to enquire for the keepers of the liberties of England, by the authority of parliament, and for the body of the county of the said city, it is presented as follows, to wit, The jurors

Indictment.

for the keepers of the liberties of England, by the authority of parliament, upon their oath present, that Cuthbert Morley, late of, &c. gentleman, on the 15th day of May, in the year of our Lord 1649, not having the fear of God before his eyes, but being moved and seduced by the instigation of the devil, with force and arms, &c. at the city of York, in the county of the said city, in and upon one Richard Harrison then and there, in the peace of God and in the public peace being, feloniously, wilfully and of his malice aforethought, did make an assault, and then and there a certain pistol, of the value of 12 pence, charged with bullets and gun-powder, which he the said Cuthbert in his hands then and there had and held, did discharge, and him the said R. Harrison, in and upon the right part of his side or shoulder, feloniously, wilfully and of his malice afore-

* P. 281 in & super dextram partem lateris five humeri sui.

thought did strike, and * then and there, did give to the said R. H. with the said pistol, in the manner and form aforesaid charged, in and upon the said right part of his side or shoulder aforesaid, one mortal wound, of the length of one inch and of the depth of six inches, of which mortal wound the said R. H. did languish and languishing did live, from the said 15th day of May, in the year aforesaid, until the 26th day of the month of May, in the year aforesaid, upon which 26th day of May in the year aforesaid, he the said R. H. at the city of York aforesaid, in the county aforesaid, of the said

Conclusion.

mortal wound died. And so the said C. M. him the said R. H. on the said 15th day of May in the year aforesaid, at the city of York aforesaid, in the county aforesaid, in the manner and form aforesaid, feloniously, wilfully, and of his malice aforethought did kill and murder against the the public peace, &c. whereupon the sheriffs of the county of the city of York,

are

are commanded that they do not omit, because of any liberty
of the county there, but that they take the said C. M. if he
can be found in their bailiwick, and him safely keep, so that
they may have his body before the justices, at the next general
goal-delivery, to be held in the county of the said city, to answer to the said keepers of the liberties of England, by the
authority of parliament, of the felony and murder aforesaid; at
which day to wit, at the next general goal-delivery held at the
city of York, in the county of the said city, on the 25th day
of March, in the year of our Lord, 1650, before Francis
Thorpe one of the barons of the Exchequer, T. Widerington
and others, their fellow-justices, and commissioners assigned as
well to hear and examine, and deliver the goal there, as to
enquire by the oath of, &c. of certain treasons, misprisions of
treasons, insurrections, rebellions, murders, killings, felonies, *Return non*
&c. in the said county perpetrated, &c. and to hear and de- *est inventu-,*
termine, &c. the sheriffs of the said city return the said precept *alias capias*
to them in the form aforesaid directed, and further testify, *awarded.*
that the said C. M. is not found in their bailiwick. Whereupon the said sheriffs of the said city are commanded as before
they were commanded, that they do not omit, because of any
liberty of their city, but that they take the said C. M. if he
can be found in their bailiwick and him safely keep, so that
they may have his body before the justices, at the next general goal-delivery, held at the city of York, in the county of
the said city, to answer to the keepers of the liberties of England, by the authority of parliament, of the felony and murder aforesaid, and the said writ, &c. At which day, to wit,
at the assizes and general goal-delivery, held at the city of
York, in the county of the said city, on the 30th day of July,
in the year of our Lord, 1650. before Francis Thorpe, one
of the barons of the publick Exchequer, Peter Warburton,
one of the justices of the Common-bench, W. A. and others
their fellows-justices and commissioners, assigned as well to
hear and examine, and to deliver the goal there, as to enquire
by the oath, &c. of certain treasons, misprisions of treasons, insurrections, rebellions, murders, killings and felonies in the
said city perpetrated, &c. and to hear and determine, &c. *Non mise-*
the sheriffs of the city of York aforesaid, have not sent the *rum breve,*
said writ thereupon, therefore the sheriffs of the said city are *Pluries.*
commanded, as they often were commanded, that they do not
omit because of any liberty of their city, but that they take
the said C. M. if he may be found in their bailiwick, and him
safely keep, so that they may have his body before the justices
at the next general * goal delivery to be held in the said city, ** P. 282*
to answer to the keepers of the liberties of England, by the
authority of parliament, of the felony and murder aforesaid,
and the said writ, &c. At which day, to wit, at the general
goal-delivery, held at the city of York, in the county of the

                    said

said city, on the 12th day of March, in the year of our Lord, 1650, before F. Thorpe, one of the barons of the public Exchequer, J. Parker, serjeant at law, and others their fellows justices and commissioners assigned as well to hear and examine, and to deliver the goal there, as to enquire by the oath, &c. of certain treasons, misprisions of treasons, insurrections, rebellions, murders, killings, felonies, &c. C. B. and G. R. sheriffs of the said city of York return the said precept to them, in the form aforesaid directed; and further testify, that the

Non inventus est.

said C. M. is not found in their bailiwick; Whereupon the said sheriffs are commanded that they do not omit, because of any liberty of their city, but that they cause the said C. M. to be called from county to county, until that according to

Exigent awarded.

the law and custom of England he shall be outlawed if he do not appear; and if he shall appear, then that they take him and safely, &c. so that they may have his body before the justices, at the next general goal-delivery to be held in the said city, to answer to the said keepers of the liberties of England, by the authority of parliament, of the felony and murder aforesaid; at which day, to wit, at the next general goal-delivery, held at the Guild-hall of the city of York, in the county of the same city, on the 22d day of July, in the year of our Lord, 1651, before F. T. one of the barons of the public Exchequer, J——, serjeant at law and others, justices and commissioners as well to hear and examine, and the goal there to deliver, as to enquire by the oaths, &c. of certain treasons, misprisions of treasons, insurrections, rebellions,

Return of the exigent.

murders, killings, felonies, robberies, &c. C. B. and G. P. sheriffs of the city of York aforesaid, returned the said prescript to them, in form aforesaid directed, thus indorsed, that is to say, At our county of the city of York, held at the city of York, in the county of the said city, on Monday, to wit, the 31st day of March, in the year of our Lord, 1651, C. M.

1st Exact.

within named, was the first time called and did not appear; and at our county of the said city there held, on the 28th day of April in the year of our Lord, 1651, the said C. M.

2d

was the second time called and did not appear; and at our county of the city there held, the 26th day of May, in the year of our Lord, 1651, the said C. M. was the third time

3d

called and did not appear; and at the county of the said city there held, the 28th day of June, in the year aforesaid, the said C. M. was a fourth time called and did not appear; and

4th

at our county of the said city there held, the 21st day of July, in the year aforesaid, the said C. M. was the fifth time

5th

called and did not appear. Therefore by the judgment of the coroners of the county of the city of York, the said C. M. is out-lawed. Which record the lord the now king, for certain

Defendant out-lawed.

causes

caufes afterwards hath caufed to come before him, &c. whereupon the fheriffs of city of York aforefaid, are commanded
that they take him if, &c. to ftand right in court, &c. And
now to wit, on the Tuefday next after 15 days of St. Martin
in this fame term, before the lord * the king at Weftminfter,
comes Mary Morley, daughter and heir of the faid C. M. who
is within the age of 21 years, by Philip Ward her guardian,
by the court of the lord the now king here fpecially admitted,
and forthwith produces here in court a certain writ of the faid
lord the now king clofe, to his juftices here directed, which
follows in thefe words ; Charles the fecond by the grace of
God, &c. to our juftices affigned to hold pleas before us,
greeting, becaufe in the record and proceedings, and alfo in
the pronouncing of the outlawry againft C. M. deceafed, for
a certain felony and murder, whereof he is indicted, and thereupon is outlawed, in the county of the city of York pronounced, and before us returned, as it is faid manifeft error
hath intervened, to the great damage of Mary Morley, daughter and heir of the faid C. M. as from her complaint we have
underftood ; we willing that the error, if any hath been, in
the due manner be corrected, and that full and fpeedy juftice
be done the faid Mary in this behalf, command you, that if
the the faid outlawry is returned before us, as it is faid, then
the record and the faid proceedings now remaining before us
as it is faid being infpected, and thofe being fummoned before
you, whom you fhall think fit to fummon in this behalf, you
further caufe to be done therein, for the annulling of the faid
outlawry, that which of right and according to the law and
cuftom of our kingdom of England fhall be to be done, witnefs Ourfelf, &c. And thereupon the faid M. M. daughter
and heir of the faid C. by her guardian aforefaid faith, that
in the record and proceedings aforefaid, there is manifeft error in this, to wit, that it doth not appear by the indictment
in the record aforefaid fpecified, in what part of the body of
the faid R. Harrifon, he the faid R. Harrifon was wounded
as ought ; and alfo, there is manifeft error in this, to wit, becaufe in the indictment aforefaid, in the record aforefaid fpecified, it is expreffed that the faid C. M. on the 15th day of
May, in the year of our Lord, 1649, at the city of York aforefaid, felonioufly, wilfully, and of his malice aforethought,
him the faid R. H. did kill and murder, and neverthelefs, in
the record aforefaid it plainly appears, that he the faid R. H.
died on the 26th day of May, in the year aforefaid ; and alfo
there is a manifeft error in this, to wit, becaufe the faid writ
of the lord the king of capias with proclamation, was not directed to the fheriff of the county of York, in which county
of York the faid C. M. dwelt at the time of the felony and
murder aforefaid, as appears by the record, as it ought to
be, and in this there is a manifeft error, wherefore the
faid

Capias ad
ftandum
recte.

*P. 285.
The daugh-
ter and heir
of the out-
law appears
and produces
a writ of er-
ror to the
judges of
B. R.

Errors af-
figned.

faid M. M. by her guardian aforefaid prays judgment, and that the outlawry aforefaid, for the errors aforefaid and others in the record and proceedings aforefaid found, may be reverfed, annulled and entirely held for nought; and that fhe to the Common Law of the kingdom of England, and to all things which fhe hath loft, by reafon of the faid outlawry may be reftored ; and that the court here may proceed to the examination of the record and proceedings aforefaid, &c. and becaufe that it feems neceffary and expedient to the court here, before the court do proceed in this behalf, that as well the tenants of the lands and tenements, which were of the faid C. M. on the faid 15th day of May, in the year of our Lord, 1649, aforefaid, on which day the felony and murder aforefaid was committed, or at any time after, as the lords of whom the faid lands and tenements mediately and immediately may be holden, fhould be forewarned to be before the lord the king, to hear the record and proceedings aforefaid, if they fhall think fit. Therefore the fheriffs of the city of York, and the fheriff of the county of York, are commanded that they do not omit, &c. but that by * good and lawful men of their faid feveral bailiwicks, they give notice as well to the tenants of the lands and tenements which were of the faid C. M. on the faid 15th day of May, in the year of our Lord 1649 aforefaid, or at any time afterwards, as to the lords of whom the faid lands and tenements mediately and immediately are holden, that they be before the lord the king at the octave of St. Hilary, wherefoever, &c. to hear the record and proceedings aforefaid, &c. the fame day is given to the faid M. M. by her guardian aforefaid, &c. at which octave of St. Hilary, before the lord the king, at Weftminfter, comes the faid M. M. by her guardian aforefaid, and T. W. and R. H. fheriffs of the county of the city of York, return here into court the faid writ of the lord the king, of fcire facias, to them as aforefaid directed, under this form, To the moft ferene lord the king, we moft humbly certify, that there are not any tenants, nor is there any tenant of any lands or tenements, which were of the within named C. M. on the 15th day of May, in the year of our Lord 1649, on which day the felony and murder within mentioned, is fuppofed to be committed, or at any time afterwards, nor are there any lords, nor is there any lord of whom any lands and tenements of the faid C. M. mediately or immediately are holden in our bailwick, to whom we could give notice as within we are commanded, the anfwer of T. W. and R. H. efquires, fheriffs. And at the fame day J. R. fheriff of the county of York, returns here into court the faid writ of the lord the king, of fcire facias, to him as aforefaid directed, under this form, To the within written lord the king, I certify that there are

not

Marginal notes:

Scire facias to the fheriff of the county and the fheriffs of the city of York, to fummon the ter-tenants and lords mediate and immediate.

* P. 284

Return by the fheriffs of the city that there are none &c

The like return by the

not any tenants, nor is there any tenant, of any lands and sheriff of the county.
tenements, which were of the within named C. M. on the
15th day of May, in the year of our Lord 1649, the within
mentioned time of the fuppofed felony and murder within
written, or at any time afterwards, nor are there any lords
nor is there any lord, of whom any lands or tenements of
the faid C. M. mediately or immediately are holden, in my
bailiwick, to whom I could give notice as within I am
commanded. The anfwer of J. R. efquire, fheriff.

*Whether this attainder was reverfed non conftat, but there are
fome notes of the proceedings in this cafe, 3 Keble, 29, 31, 125,
whereby it appears the opinion of the court was, that the wound
laid to be in et fuper dextram partem lateris five humeri fui, was
uncertain. Secondly, that the laying, that the deceafed was fhot
the 15th of May, and languifhed till the 26th. and then died, et fic
Morley murdered him that the 15th was naught, and the beft way is
to fay generally et fic, &c. quod Morley modo et forma pradict'
murdered him.*

Vide Hales, Pl. Cor. 207.

*Stubbs 345, Dogherty 296, lay the conlufion in that manner and
fee the next precedent.*

---

* The King *againft* Doughty, *and another.* *P. 285.

Middlefex,
To wit. **B**E it remembered that at the general quarter Caption.
feffion of the peace of the lord the king
held for the county of Middlefex, at Hicks-Hall in St. John
ftreet in the faid county on Monday to wit, the 5th day of
July, in the 32d year of the reign of our lord Charles the 2d, Indictment at a feffion of the peace for Middlefex, held the 5th day July 32 Ch. 2 for murder with a rapier.
&c. Before William earl Craven, N. F. and others their fel-
lows juftices of the faid lord the king affigned to preferve the
peace in the faid county and alfo affigned to hear and determine
divers felonies, trefpaffes and other mifdeeds in the faid county
perpetrated, by the oath of S. P. and 16 others, good and
lawful men of the faid county then and there fworn and
charged to enquire for the faid lord the king and for the body
of the county aforefaid, it is prefented in the manner and form
following to wit. Middlefex to wit, the jurors for the lord
the king upon their oath prefent that Philip Doughty late of
the parifh of St. Margaret, Weftminfter in the county of
Middlefex, efquire, and Anthony Hamilton late of the parifh
aforefaid in the county aforefaid, efquire, not having the fear
of

of God before their eyes, but being moved and seduced by the instigation of the devil, on the 23d day of April in the 32d year of the reign of the lord Charles the 2d by the grace of God, &c. with force and arms, &c. at the parish, &c. in the county, &c. in and upon one Richard Capps, in the peace of God and of the said lord the now king, then and there being, feloniously, wilfully and of their malice aforethought did make an assault, and that the said P. D. with a certain rapier made of iron and steel of the value of 5 shillings, which he the said P. D. in his right hand then and there had and held drawn, him the said R. Capps then and there being in and upon the left side of him the said R. Capps, nigh to the left pap of him the said R. Capps, feloniously, wilfully and of his malice aforethought did strike and thrust, giving to the said R. Capps then and there with the drawn rapier aforesaid, in and upon the left side of him the said R. C. nigh to the said left pap of him the said R. C. one mortal wound of the breadth of half one inch and of the depth of six inches, of which mortal wound he the said R. C. from the said 23d day of April in the year aforesaid, until the 11th day of June, from that time next ensuing in the year aforesaid, at the parish aforesaid and county aforesaid, and at the parish of St. Martin in the fields, in the county aforesaid, did languish and languishing did live, on which 11th day of June aforesaid, he the said R. Capps, at the said parish of St. Martin in the fields in the county of Middlesex aforesaid, of the mortal wound aforesaid died; and that the said A. Hamilton, feloniously, wickedly and of his malice aforethought was present, abetting, assisting, comforting and maintaining the said P. D. him the said R. C. to kill and murder, in the manner and form aforesaid, and so the jurors aforesaid say upon their oath aforesaid that the said P. D. and A. H. him the said R. C. in the manner and form aforesaid, feloniously, wilfully and of their malice aforethought did kill and murder, against the peace of the said lord the now king his crown and dignity, &c. whereupon the sheriff of the county of Middlesex is commanded that he do not omit, &c. but that he take them, * to answer, &c. which indictment the said justices of the said lord the king, afterwards to wit, at the delivery of the goal of the said lord the king of Newgate held for the said county at Justice Hall in the old Baily in the suburbs of the city of London on Wednesday to wit, the 7th day of July in the 32d year aforesaid, before R. Clayton knight, mayor of the city of London, T. A. knight, and baronet, and others their fellows justices of the said lord the king assigned to deliver his goal of Newgate of the prisoners being therein by their own proper hands did deliver here in court of record in the form of the law to be determined, and thereupon at the said delivery of the goal of the said lord the king held for the said county at Justice Hall aforesaid, on the said Wednesday the 7th day of July in the year aforesaid, before the said justices last

named

named come the faid **P. D.** and **A. H.** under the cuftody of **J. R.** knight, and **S. L.** knight, fheriff of the faid county, into whofe cuftody for the faid caufe before they were committed brought here to the bar in their proper perfons, who are committed to the faid fheriff, and forthwith being feverally demanded of the felony aforefaid and of the murder aforefaid, in the indictment aforefaid, above fpecified, how they will acquit, themfelves thereof, they the faid **P. D.** and **A. H.** feverally fay that they are not guilty thereof, and thereof for good and evil feverally put themfelves upon the country, therefore immediately let a jury come thereupon before the juftices laft named here, &c. who neither, &c. to recognize, &c. And the jurors of that jury by the faid fheriff for that purpofe impaneled to wit, **X. P. W. P.** and ten others being called come, who being elected tried and fworn to fpeak the truth of and upon the premifes, fay upon their oath that the faid **P. D.** is guilty of the felony and murder aforefaid, in the indictment aforefaid, above fpecified in the manner and form as by the faid indictment above againft him is fuppofed, and that the faid **P. D.** hath no goods or chattels, lands or tenements to the knowledge of the faid jurors, and that the faid **A. H.** is not guilty of the felony and murder aforefaid, in the indictment aforefaid, above fpecified, as he the faid **A. H.** for himfelf above by pleading hath alledged, nor hath he ever fled for that occafion; and thereupon immediately the faid **P. D.** is afked if he hath or knoweth any thing to fay for himfelf, why the court here fhould not proceed to judgment and execution againft him upon the faid verdict, who faith nothing except as before he hath faid, whereupon all and fingular the premifes being feen and by the court here underftood, it is confidered by the court here that the faid **P. D.** be hanged by his neck until that, &c. and that the **A. H.** be thereof quit, and that he go thereof without day. And now to wit, on the Monday next after the morrow of the afcenfion of our Lord, in this fame term before the lord the king at Weftminfter, comes the faid **P. D.** in his proper perfon, who is committed to the marfhal, &c. and forthwith faith that in the record and procefs aforefaid, there is error in this to wit, that whereas it is fuppofed that the faid indictment was taken, at the general quarter feffion of the peace of the county of Middlefex, and the faid general quarter feffion of the peace appears to be held on the 5th day of July, before the feaft of the tranflation of St. Thomas the martyr, which always is and falls upon the 7th day of July, whereas the general quarter feffion of the peace ought to be held in the firft week after the faid feftival, therefore in that there is manifeft error, alfo there is error in this, that it doth not appear by the faid record

Defendants plead not guilty.

Venire facias.

Doughty found guilty

Hamilton not guilty.

Judgment.

Affignment of errors in B. R.

that any iſſue was joined between the ſaid lord the king and the ſaid P. and nevertheleſs the * ſaid P. is tried and convicted without any iſſue being joined thereupon, and ſo in that there is manifeſt error; alſo there is manifeſt error in this, becauſe that by the writ of precept in the ſaid record mentioned the ſheriff is commanded that he cauſe to come 12, &c. who neither to the ſaid lord the king nor him the ſaid P. are in any wiſe of kin, whereas this word "*neither*" ought to have been omitted, and ſo in that in like manner there is manifeſt error, and this he is ready to verify, wherefore he prays judgment, and that the judgment and attainder aforeſaid, for the errors aforeſaid, and for others in the record and proceſs aforeſaid, appearing may be reverſed, annulled and entirely held nought, and that he the ſaid P. may be reſtored to the common law and to all things which he hath loſt by occaſion of the ſaid attainder, and that he as well of the ſaid conviction and attainder as of the ſaid indictment may be diſmiſſed by the court here, and that the court here may proceed to the examination of the record and proceſs aforeſaid. And becauſe that it ſeems neceſſary and expedient to the court here, before the court here ſhall proceed in that behalf that as well the tenants of the ſaid lands and tenements which were of the ſaid P. D. on the ſaid 23d day of April in the 32d year aforeſaid, or at any time after as the lords of whom the ſaid lands and tenements mediately or immediately are holden, ſhould be forewarned to be before the lord the king to hear the record and proceſs aforeſaid, if they ſhall think fit, therefore the ſheriff of the ſaid county of Middleſex is commanded that he do not omit, &c. but that by good and lawful men of his bailiwick he give notice to the tenants of the lands and tenements which were of the ſaid P. D. on the ſaid 23d day of April, in the 32d year aforeſaid, or at any time afterwards, as alſo to the lords of whom the ſaid lands and tenements mediately or immediately are holden, that they be before the lord the king on the morrow of the Holy Trinity whereſoever, &c. to hear the record and proceſs aforeſaid, and the ſame day is given to the ſaid P. D. here, &c. and thereupon by the ſpecial favour of the court the ſaid P. D. is delivered in bail to T. L. of the pariſh, &c. eſquire, and to A. M. of W. eſquire, untill, &c. to wit, the ſaid T. L. and A. M. under the penalty of 500l. each and the ſaid P. D. under the penalty of 1000l. which, &c. at which morrow of the ſaid Holy Trinity before the lord the king at Weſtminſter, comes the ſaid P. D. in his proper perſon according to the form of his recogniſance aforeſaid, in this behalf before acknowledged, and S. B. eſquire, and H. C. eſquire, ſheriff of the county aforeſaid, return that there

are

* P. 287.

Scire facias to the tertenants and lords mediate and immediate

Doughty bailed.

are not any tenants, nor is there any tenant of lands and tenements which were of the within named P. D. on the 23d day
of April, in the 32d year aforesaid, within written nor at
any time afterwards, in his bailiwick, to whom he could give
notice, and thereupon the said P. D. as before prays judgment
and that the conviction and attainder aforesaid, for the said
errors, and others in the record of conviction and attainder
being found may be reversed and annulled, and entirely held
for nought, and that he may be restored to the common law and
to all things which he hath lost by occasion of the judgment,
and attainder aforesaid, and that he of the judgment and attainder aforesaid, may by the court here be discharged and
dismissed, &c. &c.

Sheriff re-
turns no ter-
tenants.

---

* The King *against* Stone.   *P. 238.

To wit. **T**HE lord the king hath sent to his justices assigned
to deliver his goal of the county of Somerset, of
the prisoners being therein, and also to the keepers of his
peace and to his justices assigned to hear and determine divers
felonies, trespasses and other misdeeds in the said county perpetrated, his writ close in these words to wit, Charles the second by the grace of God, &c. to our justices assigned to deliver our goal in the county of Somerset of the prisoners being
therein and also to the keepers of the peace in the said county
and to our justices assigned to hear and determine divers felonies, trespasses and other misdeeds in the said county perpetrated, greeting, because in the record and process of conviction of
Peter Stone and Ed. Ivy, for felony and robbery whereof they
are indicted, and by a certain jury, of the country are convicted, as
it is said, manifest error hath intervened to the great damage of
the said Peter and Edward, as we have understood from their
complaint, we willing that the error if any there hath been in
the due manner by corrected and that full and speedy justice be
done to the said P. and E. in this behalf, command you that
if judgment be given thereupon, then that you send the record
and process aforesaid, with all things touching the same, to
us, under your seals distinctly and openly, and this writ, so

Writ of er-
ror directed
to the jus-
tices of the
peace and
the justices
of goal de-
livery of the
county of
Somerset.

Y y 2   that

that we may have them on the octave of St. Hilary, wheresoever we shall then be England, that the record and procefs aforefaid, being infpected we may further caufe to be done thereupon for correcting the error that which of right and according to the law and cuftom of our kingdom of England, fhall be to be done, witnefs ourfelf the 9th day of January, in the 33d year of our reign. The anfwer of the within written *The return.* juftices. The execution of this writ appears in a certain fche-*The record.* dule to this writ annexed, F. North. The record and procefs whereof mention is within made follows in thefe words, to *Caption.* wit, Somerfet to wit. Be it remembered that at the general delivery of the goal of the lord the king of his county of Somerfet, of the prifoners being therein, held at the city of Wells in and for the faid county on the Saturday to wit, the 9th day of Auguft, in the 14th year of the reign of our lord Charles the 2d, &c. before R. Fofter, knight, chief juftice of the faid lord the king, affigned to hold pleas before the king himfelf and J. Archer, ferjeant at law, juftices of the faid lord the king, affigned to deliver his goal of the county of Somerfet, of the prifoners being therein, and to preferve the peace in the faid county, and alfo affigned to hear and determine divers felonies, trefpaffes and other mifdeeds in the faid county perpetrated. by the oath of H. W. efquire, J. H. efquire, and 15 others good and lawful men of the county of Somerfet aforefaid, impaneled, fworn and charged to enquire for the faid lord the king and for the body of the county *Indictment* aforefaid, it is prefented that Peter Stone of W. in the county *againft* of S. aforefaid, glazier, on the 28th day of March, in the *Stone for* 14th year of the reign of our lord Charles 2d, &c. with force *affaulting* and arms, &c. at Houlfton in the faid county in the kings *and putting* high way there, in and upon Edward Ivy and Joan Plympton *in fear Ivy* widow, in the peace of God and of the faid lord the king, *and Plymp-* then and there being, then and there * did make an affault *P. 289* and affray, and themthe faid E. I. and J. P. in bodily fear of *ton and ta-* their lives did put, and thirty pounds in monies numbered of *ing from* the goods and chattels and monies of the faid J. P. in the *Ivy 50. of* king's high way, then there found; from the perfon of the *the money* faid J. E. then and there felonioufly and violently did fteal, *of Plympton* take and carry away againft the peace of the faid lord the now king his crown and dignity, &c. and afterwards to wit, on the 9th day of Auguft in the 14th year aforefaid, at the faid general delivery of the goal of the lord the king of the faid county held at the city of Wells, in the faid county before R. F. and J. A. the juftices aforefaid, the faid P. S. by G. S. efquire, then and there fheriff of the county aforefaid, was brought to the bar in his proper perfon, and forthwith *Plead not* being demanded of the premifes above charged againft him, *guilty.* how he will acquit himfelf thereof faith that he is not guilty
thereof,

thereof, and thereof for good and evil puts himself upon the county, and S. W. esquire, who for the lord the king in this behalf prosecutes doth the like, &c. whereupon the sheriff of the county aforesaid. was commanded that he cause to come immediately 12, &c. of the neighbourhood of Houllton, aforesaid, in the county aforesaid, and who neither, &c. to recognize, &c. and thereupon H. A. W. B. and 10 others, jurors by the said sheriff for this purpose impaneled being called come, who being elected, tried and sworn to speak the truth of and concerning the premises say upon their oath aforesaid, that the said P. S. is guilty of the premises in the indictment aforesaid, above against him charged, in the manner and form as by the said indictment above against him is supposed, and that he the said P. S at the time of the commission of the felony and robbery in the indictment aforesaid, specified or any time afterwards, had no goods or chattels, lands or tenements to the knowledge of the said jurors, and thereupon the said P. S. being asked by the justices aforesaid, if he hath or knoweth any thing to say for himself, wherefore the court and justices here, &c. ought not to proceed to judgment and execution of and upon the premises against him the said P. S. which P. S. saith nothing further except as before he hath said, therefore it is considered by the said justices and the court here that the said P. S. be hanged by his neck until that, &c. And afterwards to wit, at the same general delivery of the goal of the lord the king, of his said county of Somerset, held at the city of Wells aforesaid, in and for the said county on the said 9th day of August, in the 14th year aforesaid, before the said justices, by the oath of good and lawful men of the said county of Somerset, before that time impannelled, sworn and charged to enquire for the said lord the king and for the body of the said county it is also presented, that P. Stone of W. in the county aforesaid, glazier, on the 28th day of March in the 14th year of the reign of our lord Charles the 2d, &c. with force and arms, &c. at H. in the said county in the king's highway there in and upon Edward Ivy and Joan Plympton widow, in the peace of God and of the said lord the now king, then and there being, feloniously did make an assault, and them the said E. I. and J. P. in bodily fear of their lives did put, and 30l. in monies numbered of the goods and chattels and monies of the said J. P. in the king's highway there found from the person of the said E. I. then & there feloniously and violently did steal, take and carry away against the peace of the said lord the now king his crown and dignity, &c. And the jurors aforesaid, upon their oath aforesaid, further present, that E. I. of W. in the county aforesaid, gent. before the felony and robbery aforesaid, in the form aforesaid, committed and perpetrated to wit, on the 27th day of March, in the 14th year
aforesaid

Venire facias awarded.

Verdict guilty.

Judgment of execution

Another indictment preferred against Stone at the same sessions of goal delivery for the same robbery as principal.

And against Edward Ivy as accessary before the fact.

aforesaid, at W. aforesaid, in the said county * him the said P. S. feloniously to commit the felony and robbery aforesaid, in the manner and form aforesaid, with force and arms, &c. feloniously did stir up, move, abet, counsel and procure; and the said E. I. after the felony and robbery aforesaid, in the manner and form aforesaid, so committed and perpetrated, to wit, on the said 28th day of March, in the 14th year aforesaid, he the said E. I. knowing the said P. S. the felony and robbery aforesaid, in the manner and form aforesaid, so to have committed and perpetrated, the said P. S. at W. aforesaid, in the county aforesaid, with force and arms' &c. feloniously did receive harbour, maintain and comfort against the peace of the said lord the now king his crown and dignity, &c. and afterwards to wit, on the 9th day of August, in the 14th year aforesaid, at the said general delivery of the goal of the lord the king held at the city of Wells, in and for the said county, before the said justices, the said Edward Ivy, by the said G. S. then sheriff of the county aforesaid, in like manner was brought to the bar in his proper person, and forthwith being demanded of the premisses above charged against him, how he will acquit himself thereof, saith, that he is not guilty thereof, and thereof for good and evil puts himself upon the country, and the said S. W. who for the lord the king in this behalf prosecutes, doth the like, &c. whereupon the sheriff of the said county was commanded, that he cause to come before the said justices immediately, 12, &c. of of the neighbourhood of H. aforesaid, in the county aforesaid, and who neither, &c. to recognise, &c. and thereupon J. C. T. C. and 10 other jurors by the said sheriff for this purpose impanelled, being called come, who being elected tried and sworn to speak the truth of and concerning the premisses say upon their oath, that the said E. I. is guilty of the premisses in the indictment aforesaid above to him charged, in the manner and form as by the said indictment above against him is supposed, and that he the said E. I. at the time of the committing of the said felony and robbery in the said indictment specified, or at any time afterwards, had no goods or chattels, lands or tenements to the knowledge of the said jurors; and thereupon the said E. I. being asked by the said justices, if he hath or knoweth any thing to say, wherefore the court and justices here, &c. should not proceed to judgement, and to execution of and upon the premisses, against him the said E. I. which E. I. then saith nothing farther, except as before he hath said; therefore it is considered by the said justices of the court here, that the said E. Ivy be hanged by the neck until that, &c. And afterwards, to wit on the said

9th

P. 290

And as accessary after the fact.

Ivy pleads not guilty.

Verdict that Ivy is guilty

Judgment.

9th day of Auguft, in the 14th year aforefaid, at the faid general delivery of the goal, of the lord the king, of the county
aforefaid, held at the city of Wells aforefaid, in the county
aforefaid, before the faid juftices, the execution of the faid
judgment upon the faid P. Stone and E. Ivy, by the fpecial
warrant or mandate of the lord the king was refpited until
that, &c. And afterwards the faid P. S. and E. I. by letters
patent of the lord the king, made under the great feal of Erg-
land were pardoned, and at the general delivery of the
goal of the lord the king, of his county of Somerfet, of
the prifoners being therein held at the city of Bath, in and
for the faid county, on Wednefday to wit, the 24th day of
Auguft, in the 16th year of the reign of our lord Charles
the 2d, &c. before Matthew Hale, knight, chief baron of
the Exchequer of the faid lord the king, and John Archer,
knight, one of the Juftices of the faid lord the king of
the bench, being juftices of the faid lord the king, affigned
to deliver his goal of his county of Somerfet, of the prifoners being therein, and to preferve the peace in the faid
county, and alfo affigned to hear and determine divers
felonies, trefpaffes and other mifdeeds in the faid county,
they the faid P. S. and E. I. being afked and each of them
being afked by the juftices aforefaid, if they have or know
any thing to fay for themfelves, or if either of them hath
or knoweth any thing to fay for himfelf, wherefore the
court and juftices here, &c. fhould not proceed to judgment
upon the premifes againft them, the faid P. S. and E. I.
and each of them, they the faid P. S. and E. I. feverally
pray the benefit of the faid letters patent, of the faid lord
the king, to be granted to them in this behalf, and it is granted to them, &c. And now to wit, on the Saturday next
after one month of Eafter, before the lord the king at
Weftminfter, comes the faid Edward Ivy, in his proper
perfon, who is committed to the marfhal, &c. and immediately faith, that in the record and procefs aforefaid, and
alfo in the giving of the judgment aforefaid, there is manifeft error in this, to wit, That it doth not appear by the
faid record, that the faid Joan Plympton, at the time of
the perpetration of the felony and robbery aforefaid, was
put in bodily fear of her life, but that the faid Joan Plympton,
was put in bodily fear of her life, and the words "*then and
there*" are omitted, therefore in that there is manifeft
error, alfo there is error in this, to wit, That in the
writ of venire facias juratores, the' fheriff of the county
of Somerfet, *was* commanded that he caufe to come
12, &c. whereas it ought to be *is* commanded,
—and who neither to the faid lord the king, nor to the faid
Edward

Execution of
both refpit-
ted.

Letters pa-
tent of par-
don for both

P. 291.

And they
plead their
pardon at
the affizes.

Affignment
of error.

Edward Ivy are in any wise of kin, whereas this word "*neither*," ought to have been omitted; and in that there is manifest error; therefore he prays, that the judgment aforesaid, for the errors aforesaid, and others in the record and procefs aforesaid being found, may be reversed, annulled, and be entirely held for nought; and that he may be restored to the Common Law of this kingdom of England, and to all things which he hath lost by occasion of the said judgment; and that the court here may proceed to the examination of the record and procefs aforesaid, &c. And because the court of the said lord the king here are not yet advised to give their judgment of and upon the premisses; day thereupon is given to the said E. I in the state in which now, &c. until Monday in five weeks of Easter, and so from day to day, until, &c. before the said lord the king wheresoever, &c. to hear their judgment thereon, &c. And thereupon by the special favour of the court, the said E. I. is delivered on bail to J. Robins of, &c. and W. Stowe of, &c. until Monday in five weeks of Easter, and so from day to day until, &c. to prosecute his writ of error with effect, to wit, each of the bail under the penalty of 200*l*, which, &c. And because it seems to the court here necessary and expedient before the court here may proceed in this behalf, that as well the tenants of the lands and tenements which were of the said E. I. on the said 28th day of March, in the 14th year of the reign of our lord, &c. or at any time after as the lords of whom the said lands and tenements mediately or immediately are holden, should be forewarned to be before the lord the king, to hear the record and procefs aforesaid if they shall think fit, therefore the sheriff of the county of Somerset is commanded that he do not omit, &c. but that by good and lawful men of his bailiwick, he give notice to the tenants of the lands and tenements which were of the said E. I. on the said 28th day of March, in the 14th year aforesaid, or at any time afterwards, as also to the lords of whom the said lands and tenements mediately or immediately may be holden, that they be before the lord the king at Westminster, on the morrow of the Holy Trinity, wheresoever, &c. to hear the record and procefs aforesaid, if, &c. At which morrow of the Holy Trinity, before the lord the king at Westminster, T. Warr, esquire, then sheriff of the county of Somerset, returns that he by J. Pitman and J. Porter, good and lawful men of his bailiwick, hath given notice to William * Ivy, John King, Francis Ditty and John White otherwise Forsty, tenants of one Messuage, called the Winchoop, 40 acres of land, twenty acres of Meadow, and 40 acres of Pasture, with the appurtenances, situate, lying and being in the parish of W. in the county of Somerset, which were the lands and tenements of the

said

Side notes:

Curia nondum advisatur.

Ivy bailed.

Scire facias to the ter-tenants and lords.

Sheriff returns 4 tenants warned.

* P. 292.

said E. I. within named, and of which the said E. on the day
of the giving of the judgment and afterwards was seized in
his demesne as of fee, that they be before the lord the king
within written at the day and place within contained, to hear
the record in the form within written, and further to do and
receive as the said writ in itself commands and requires. And
now to wit, on the Tuesday after the morrow St. Martin, in
this same term before the lord the king at Westminster, come
the said J. K. F. D. J. W. otherwise F. and W. J. by B.
B. their attorney, and having heard the record and the said
writ of scire facias, the said J. K. faith that he is not, nor on
the day of the issuing of the said writ of scire facias in this
behalf, or at any time after, was tenant of the freehold or freeholds aforesaid; in the said return mentioned, nor of any part
thereof, and this he is ready to verify, wherefore, &c. and the
said F. D. faith, that he is not, nor on the day of the issuing
of the said writ of scire facias in this behalf, or at any time
afterwards was tenant of the freehold or freeholds in the return aforesaid mentioned, nor of any part thereof, and this he
is ready to verify, &c. wherefore, &c. and the said J. W.
otherwise F. faith that he is not, nor on the day of the issuing
of the said writ of scire facias in this behalf or at any time
afterwards was tenant of the freehold or freeholds aforesaid,
in the return aforesaid, mentioned nor of any part thereof and
this he is ready to verify, &c. wherefore, &c. and the said W.
Ivy prays oyer of the said writ of scire facias, and it is read to
him in these words, to wit, Charles the 2d by the grace of
God, &c. to the sheriff of Somerset greeting, because in the
record and process and also in the giving of judgment against
Edward Ivy of W. in your county gentleman, for a certain
felony and robbery on the 7th day of March in the 14th year
of our reign supposed to be committed by one Peter Stone,
whereof the said Edw. as accessary is convicted and attainted,
manifest error hath intervened to the great damage of the said
Edw. Ivy, as by inspecting of the record and process aforesaid,
before us remaining evidently appears, we willing that the
error if any there hath been in the due manner be corrected,
and that full and speedy justice be done to the said E. in this
behalf, command you that you do not omit because of any liberty in your bailiwick, but that by good and lawful men of
your said bailiwick, you give notice severally as well to the
tenants of the lands and tenements which were of the said E.
on the said 18th day of March, in the 14th year aforesaid, or
ever afterwards, as to the lords of whom the said lands and
tenements mediately and immediately are holden, that they be
before us on the morrow of the holy Trinity, wheresoever we
shall then be in England, to hear the record and process if
they shall think fit, and further to do and receive what our

Z z   court

court in that behalf fhall confider, and that you have there then the names of thofe by whom you fo fhall give notice, and this writ; witnefs F. Pemberton, &c. And he prays alfo oyer of the return of the faid writ, and it is read to him in thefe words, to wit, By virtue of this writ to me directed by J. Pitman and J. Potter, good and lawful men of my bailiwick, I have given notice to W. Ivy, J. King, F. Ditty and J. White, otherwife Forlty, * tenants of one meffuage, called the Winchoop, 40 acres of meadow and 40 acres of pafture with the appurtenances fituate, lying and being in the parifh of W. in the county of Somerfet, which were the lands and tenements of the within named Edward Ivy, and of which the faid Edward, on the day of the giving of the faid judgment, and afterwards was feized in his demefue as of fee, that they be before the lord the king within written, at the day and place within contained, to hear the record in the form aforefaid within written, and further to do and receive as that writ in itfelf commands and requires; Which being read and heard, the faid William Ivy faith, that he the faid William Ivy on the faid time of the iffuing of the faid writ of Seire Facias, to wit, on the faid 3d day of May, in the 34th year of the reign of our lord Charles the 2d. &c. was and is fole tenant of the tenements aforefaid, with the apputenances in the return aforefaid fpecified, but the faid W. I. further faith, that after the faid judgment, in the manner and form aforefaid, againft the faid Edward Ivy given, and before the fuing out of the faid writ, for the correcting of errors, to wit, on the 20th day of January, in the 16th reign of our faid lord the now king, he the faid William Ivy was feized of and in the faid meffuage and tenements aforefaid, whereof he the faid W. is returned to be tenant in his demefne as of fee; and he the faid W. I. fo being feized, he the faid E. I. in the record aforefaid named, after the faid 28th day of March, in the 14th year of the reign of the faid lord the now king aforefaid, and before the day of the fuing the faid writ, for the correcting of errors in this behalf, to wit, on the faid 20th day of January, in the 16th year of the reign of the faid lord the now king aforefaid, at W. aforefaid, in the county aforefaid, by his certain writing of releafe, which the faid William brings into court here, fealed with the feal of the faid E. the date of which is the faid day and year, did remife, releafe, and for ever quit claim to the faid W. and his heirs [the faid W. then being in full and peaceable poffeffion, and feized of the tenements aforefaid, with the appurtenances in the faid return fpecified] all the eftate, title, intereft, claim and demand whatfoever, which the faid E. I. or his heirs then had, or at any time from that time afterwards might have, claim or pretend to have of, in, or to the faid tenements, with the appurtenances; and this the faid W. I. is ready to verify, wherefore

he

Side notes:

prays Oyer of the Return

* P. 293

Wm. Ivy pleads to the Scire Facias, that after the 28th of March, in the 14th year of the king aforefaid, and before the fuing out of the writ of error, Edw. Ivy releafed the premifes to him and prays judgment, that Edw. Ivy may not be reftored, &c.

he prays judgment, and that the said E. I. may not be restored to the said tenements, in the said return of the said writ of Scire Facias mentioned, nor to any part thereof, &c. And the said Edward Ivy comes in his proper person according to his recognizance in this behalf before acknowledged, and saith, that he by any thing by the said W. I. before alledged ought not to be precluded from the restitution of the said tenements, because protesting that he the said Edward Ivy, at the time of the making of the said writing of release, was within the age of 21 years, and protesting also, that at the time of the making of the said writing, the said William Ivy was not seized of the said tenements, for plea saith, that the said plea of the said W. I. in the form aforesaid above pleaded, and the matter in the same contained, are not sufficient in law, to which he hath no necessity, neither is he bound by the law of the land in any manner to answer; wherefore for want of a sufficient plea of the said W. in this behalf, the said E. I. prays judgment, and that he to the tenements aforesaid in the return of the said writ of Scire Facias mentioned, may be restored, &c. And the said W. I. by his attorney aforesaid comes and saith, that the said plea by him, the said W. Ivy, in the manner and form aforesaid pleaded, and the matter in the same contained, are good and sufficient in law to preclude the said E. I. from having restitution of the tenements aforesaid, in the said return of the said writ of Scire Facias mentioned, and this he is ready to verify, wherefore the said W. I. prays judgment, and that the said E. I. may not be restored to the said tenements, in the said return of the writ of Scire Facias mentioned; nor to any part thereof, &c. &c. &c.

E. J. Ivy by protesting that he was an infant at the time of the release, and that Wm. Ivy was not then seiz'd, demurs to the plea.

** P. 294.*

Joinder in Demurrer.

The King *against* Holles *and others.*

Michaelmas, 10th Charles 2d.   Roll 75.

BE it remembered that Robert Heath, knight, Attorney-general of the lord the now king, who for the said lord the king, in this behalf prosecutes, in his proper person came here into the court of the said lord the king, before the king himself at Westminster, on the Wednesday next after the morrow of All Souls, in that same term, and for the said lord the king, brought here into the court of the said lord the king, before the king himself, then there,

An information in the King's-bench against Sir J. Elliot, Ben. Valentine and Denzill Holles, esqrs members of

                    a certain

a certain information againft John Elliot, late of London, knight, Benjamin Valentine, late of London, efquire, and Denzill Holles, late of London, efquire, which follows in thefe words, to wit, Be it remembered that Robert Heath, knight, Attorney-general of the lord the now king, who for the faid lord the king, in this behalf profecutes, in his proper perfon, comes here into the court of the faid lord the king, before the king himfelf, at Weftminfter, on the Wednefday next after the morrow of All Souls, in this fame term, and for the faid lord the king, gives the court here to underftand and to be informed, that whereas the faid lord the king, for divers weighty and urgent affairs, concerning the faid lord the king, and the ftate and defence of his kingdom of England, and the church of England, had ordained that his certain parliament fhould be held at his city of Weftminfter aforefaid, and whereas thereupon his certain parliament, in the due manner was begun and held at Weftminfter aforefaid, on the 17th day of March, in the 3d year of the reign of the faid lord the king, and there by divers prorogations continued until the 10th day of March, in the 4th year of the reign of the faid lord the king, on which 10th day of March, the faid parliament was diffolved, and whereas before the faid 17th day of March, in the 3d year aforefaid, to wit, on the 16th day of March, in the 3d year aforefaid, John Elliot, late of London, knight, in the due manner was elected and returned one of the knights for the county of Cornwall, to ferve in the faid parliament, and whereas alfo, Benjamin Valentine, late of London, efquire, on the faid 16th day of March, in the 3d year aforefaid, in the due manner was elected and returned one of the burgeffes for the borough of St. Germains, in the faid county of Cornwall, to ferve in the faid parliament ; and whereas alfo, Denzill Holles, late of London, efquire, on the faid 16th day of March, in the 3d year aforefaid, in the due manner was elected and returned one of the burgeffes for the borough of Dorchefter, in the county of Dorfet, to ferve in the faid parliament. And whereas, alfo, John Finch, kt. on the faid 16th day of March, in the 3d year aforefaid, in the due manner was elected and returned one of the citizens, for the city of Canterbury, to ferve in the faid parliament ; * And whereas on the faid 16th day of March, in the 3d year aforefaid, the faid John Finch at Weftminfter aforefaid, in the due manner was elected and conftituted Speaker for the commons in the faid parliament, and fo did continue Speaker for the commons until the diffolution of the faid parliament ; and that the faid John Elliot, devifing and intending as much as in him lay, difcord, ill-will, murmurrings and feditions, as well between the faid lord the king and his nobles, prelates, peers and juftices of the kingdom of England, as between the

*P. 295.

faid

said nobles, prelates, peers and justices of the said lord the king, and his other subjects, to sow, procure and stir up, and the rule and government of this kingdom of England, as well in the said lord the king as in his counsellors and servants of every kind, totally to deprive and weaken, and tumult and confusion in all states and parts of this kingdom of England, to introduce, and to the intent that the true and liege subjects of the said lord the king might withdraw their cordial love from the said lord the king: in and during the parliament aforesaid, to wit, on the 23d day of February, in the 4th year aforesaid, at Westminster aforesaid, in the commons house of parliament there, and during the sitting of the said house, the knights, citizens and burgesses then and there being assembled, and in their presence and hearing falsely, maliciously and seditiously these false, feigned, malicious and scandalous English words, with a loud voice did say and publish to wit, " *The king's privy council, all his judges, and his council learned, have conspired together to trample under their feet, the liberty of the subjects of this realm, and the privileges of |this house|,*" (meaning the privileges of the said commons house of parliament) of summoning parliament and of continuing, adjourning, proroguing and dissolving the same, belongs to the lord the king, and of right appertains to his will and good pleasure; and whereas the said lord the king, for divers weighty reasons specially moving him to this on the 2d day of March, in the 4th year aforesaid, did ordain that the said parliament should be adjourned, from the said 2d day of March, until the 10th day of the said month of March, then next ensuing; And the said lord the king on the 2d day of March in the 4th year aforesaid, at Westminster aforesaid, did command the said John Finch, then the Speaker aforesaid, that he on the said 2d day of March, to the knights, citizens and burgesses in the commons house of parliament then and there assembled, the good pleasure of the said lord the king should signify and make known, that immediately after that signification so made, the said commons house, by the said knights, citizens and burgesses, should be adjourned until the 10th day of March then next ensuing; and thereupon the said John Finch on the said 2d day of March, at Westminster aforesaid, to the knights, citizens and burgesses in the said commons house of parliament then and there assembled, during the sitting of the said house, publickly did signify and make known the said good pleasure of the said lord the king, that the said house immediately after that signification made, should be adjourned by themselves, until the said 10th day of March, and that the said John Elliot, B. Valentine, and Denzill Holles, at the time of the said signification, by the said

Speaker,

Speaker, in the form aforesaid made, were present in the
commons house aforesaid, and then and there did hear
the said signification, and the same did well understand, *
nevertheless the said J. E. B. V. and D. H. on the said
second day of March, in the fourth year aforesaid, at
Westminster aforesaid, maliciously did agree and among themselves did conspire to disturb the knights, citizens and burgesses of the said commons house of parliament, in the said
house at Westminster aforesaid, then and there assembled,
left that they according to the good pleasure of the said lord
the king, to them as aforesaid, signified should adjourn themselves; and the said J. E. according to the agreement and conspiracy aforesaid, and for the malicious purposes and intentions aforesaid, afterwards to wit, on the said 2d day of
March in the 4th year aforesaid, at Westminster aforesaid, in
the said commons house of parliament, in the presence
and hearing of the said knights, citizens and burgesses, then
and there assembled with a loud voice, falsely, maliciously
and seditiously did say and publish these false, feigned, scandalous, malicious and seditious English words following
*" The miserable condition we are in, both in matters of religion
and policy, makes me look with a tender eye, both to the person of
the king and the subject : you know how Arminianism doth undermine us, and how popery comes upon us so openfaced, as it gives a terror to the law; that particularly concerning the plantation of Jesuits
amongst us, and other things incident thereto do manifestly shew it.
And not only these men who are actors themselves, I mean the
Jesuits, but those that are their great masters and fautors, they have
the power of the law, and dare check magistrates in the execution
of their duties ; from them it comes, that we suffer their guilt, and
the fear of punishment that may befall them, brings us upon these
rocks ; there are among them some prelates of the church, the great
bishop of Winchester and his fellows, it is apparent what they have done
to cast an aspersion upon the honour and piety and goodness of the
king; these are not all, but is extended to some others, who I fear
in guilt and conscience of their own ill deserts, do join their power
with that bishop and the rest to draw his majesty into a jealousy of
the parliament, amongst them I shall not fear to name the great
lord treasurer, in whose person is I fear contracted all that which
we suffer ; if we look into religion and policy I find him building
on the ground laid by the duke of Bucks, his great master, from
him I fear came those ill councils which contracted that unhappy
conclusion of the last session of parliament, and whoever shall go
about to break parliaments, parliament shall break him ; I find that
not only in the affections of his heart but also in relation to him he
is the head of the papists, they and their priests and Jesuits have
all relation to him, and I doubt not to fix it indubitably upon him,
and so from the greatness and power of him, comes the danger of,*

our

* P. 296.

*our religion, for policy in that great question of tonnage and pound-
age, that interest that is pretended to be the king's is but the interest
of that person to undermine the policy of the government and thereby
to weaken the kingdom; it was the counsel of Hospitals, chancellor
to Charles the 9th king of France, that the way to weaken this king-*
*P. 297.
*dom was to impeach the trade * of it, and so to lay our walls waste
and open, and I doubt not but by the disquisition of a few days to
prove that his labours are to undermine us; that he invites strangers
to come in and drive our trade, or at least our merchants to trade in
strange bottoms, which is as dangerous; and this is that which imprints
this fear in his person, and makes him to misinterpret our proceedings
to his majesty, now therefore it will be fit for true Englishmen to perform their duties and shew their desire of the safety both of the
king and of the kingdom, and to resolve to defend the sincerity of
our religion, and to declare our resolutions also for the defence of
the subject, whereby we may declare ourselves to be freemen, and so
the more wealthy and able to supply his majesty on all occasions,
and that we should declare all that we have suffered, to be the effect
of new counsels to the ruin of the government of this state, and to
make a protestation against all those men whether greater or subordi-
nate, that they shall all be declared capital enemies to the king and
kingdom, that will persuade the king to take tonnage and poundage
without grant of parliament; and that if any merchants shall wil-
lingly pay those duties, without consent of parliament, they shall be declared as accessaries to the rest.*" And that the said D. H. according
to the agreement and conspiracy thereon between him and the
said J. E. and B. V. before had as aforesaid, afterwards to wit
on the said 2d day of March in the 4th year aforesaid,
at Westminster aforesaid, in the said commons house of
parliament, the knights, citizens and burgesses then and there
being assembled, in their presence and hearing with a loud
voice falsely, maliciously and seditiously did say and publish
these false, malicious, pernicious and seditious English words
following to wit, "*whosoever shall counsel the taking up of tonnage
and poundage without an act of parliament, let him be accounted a
capital enemy to the king and kingdom, and what merchant soever
shall pay tonnage and poundage without an act of parliament, let
him be accounted a betrayer of the liberties of the subject, and a capital enemy to the king and kingdom.*" And that the said B. V.
and D. H. according to the agreement and conspiracy aforesaid, thereon between them and the said J. E. before had for
the intentions and purposes aforesaid, and for the intention
that the said J. E. and D. H. the said false, malicious, scandalous and seditious words aforesaid, in the form aforesaid, and
for the intentions and purposes aforesaid, by them on the said 2d
day of March in the 4th year aforesaid, spoken and published as
aforesaid, might speak and publish, on the said 2d day of
March, after the signification aforesaid, of the said good pleasure

fure of the said lord the king, for making the adjournment of the said commons house of parliament as aforesaid, by the said speaker made, and before the speaking and publishing of any of the words aforesaid, by the said J. E. and D. H. on the said 2d day of March as aforesaid, spoken and published, he the said John Finch the speaker aforesaid, then and there being in a certain chair called the Speaker's chair in the said house, & endeavouring to go out of the said chair according to the command of the said lord the king, to him in that behalf before given, in and upon the * said John Finch, then and there in the peace of God and of the said lord the king being, with force and arms and with a strong hand and unlawfully did make an assault, and the said John Finch did ill-treat, and the said John French in the said chair against his will with strong hand and unlawfully did detain; and that afterwards on the said 2d day of March, and before the speaking and publishing of any of the words aforesaid, by the said J. E. and D. H. spoken and published on the said 2d day of March in the 4th year aforesaid, he the said J. F. the said speaker at Westminster aforesaid, in the house aforesaid, then being out of the said chair, in and upon the said J. F. and then and there in the peace of God and of the said lord the king being, did make an assault, and the said J. F. did ill-treat and violently and with strong hand, and unlawfully against his will into the said chair, did drag, thrust and force, whereby a great tumult and a dangerous commotion and confusion in the commons house aforesaid, and great terror to the said knights citizens and burgesses then and there assembled, then and there were moved and stired up, against the duty of their allegiance, in great contempt and to the manifest disherison of the said lord the king and in derogation of his person, rule and royal prerogative, and in subversion of the laws and state of this kingdom of England and to the great scandal, and dishonour of the counsellors of the privy council of the lord the king, and of the nobles, prelates and peers of this kingdom of England, and of the justice and the justices of the said lord the king, and to the disturbance and terror of the commons in the said parliament so as aforesaid assembled, and also to the evil and pernicious example of all others in the like case offending, and against the peace of the said lord the king his crown and dignity, &c. and also against the form of the statute, &c. wherefore the said attorney, &c. whereupon the sheriff was commanded that he do not omit, &c. but that he cause them to come to answer, &c.

*P. 298.

The Defendants severally plead that they were members of

And now to wit, on the Tuesday next after the octave of St. Martin, in this same term, before the lord the king, at Westminster, come the said J. E. knight, B. V. and D. H. in their proper persons, and the said J. E. having heard the said

said information, he the said J. as to the supposed trespass, contempt and offence aforesaid, in the said information mentioned, in speaking and publishing the said English words, in the information aforesaid above recited, and to the said J. by the said information, in the form aforesaid charged, saith, that he doth not apprehend that the said lord the king, of or for the said supposed trespass, contempt and offence to him the said J. so charged, in the court of the said lord the now king here, will or ought to be answered, because he saith that the supposed offence, trespass and contempt, in speaking and publishing the said English words, in the said information mentioned, and to the said J. in the form aforesaid charged, in parliament, and not in the court of the lord the now king, here ought to be heard and determined, &c. And the said John further saith, that he on the said 16th day of March, in the 3d year aforesaid, in the information aforesaid mentioned, in the due manner was elected and returned, one of the knights for the county of Cornwall, to serve in the said parliament, as in the said information is above mentioned, and that the said John at the time of the supposed offence, trespass and contempt aforesaid, in speaking and publishing the said English words, to him the said John in the form aforesaid charged, and during the whole time of the parliament aforesaid, at Westminster aforesaid, was and * remained one of the knights for the county of Cornwall, in the said parliament, and this he is ready to verify: wherefore because in the information aforesaid, it evidently and plainly appears, that the supposed trespass, contempt and offence aforesaid, in speaking and publishing the said English words, to the said John in the form aforesaid charged, and by the said information supposed to be committed, was committed in the said commons house of parliament aforesaid, in the parliament aforesaid, he the said J. prays judgment, if the said lord the now king here, of the contempt, trespass and offence aforesaid, as to the English words aforesaid, by him the said J. in the parliament aforesaid, in the form aforesaid, supposed to be spoken and published, in the court of the said lord the now king, here will or ought to be answered; and as to the entire residue of the supposed offence, trespass and contempt, in the information aforesaid mentioned, to the said J. in the form aforesaid charged, he the said J. saith that he doth not apprehend that the said lord the now king, of or for the said residue of the offence, trespass and contempt aforesaid, in the said information mentioned, to the said J. in the form aforesaid, above charged in the court of the said lord the now king here, will or ought to be answered, because he saith that the residue of

the

*parliament, that the offences were committed in parliament and ought there to be heard and determined, and not in the King's-bench.

*P. 299.

the said supposed offence, trespass and contempt, in the information aforesaid above specified, to him the said John by the said information, in the form aforesaid charged, in parliament and not in the court of the lord the now king, here ought to be heard and determined; and the said John further saith, that he on the said 16th day of March, in the 3d year aforesaid, in the information aforesaid mentioned, in the due manner was elected and returned one of the knights to serve for the county of Cornwall, in the said parliament, as by the said information is above mentioned, and that the said J. at the time of the residue of the supposed offence, trespass and contempt aforesaid, to him in the form aforesaid charged, and during the whole time of the said parliament, at Westminster aforesaid, was and remained one of the knights for the said county of Cornwall, in the said parliament, and this he is ready to verify, wherefore and because that in the said information it evidently and fully appears, that the said residue of the said supposed offence, trespass and contempt aforesaid, in the information aforesaid mentioned, to the said J. in the form aforesaid charged, by the said information supposed to be committed, was committed in the said commons house of parliament aforesaid, in the parliament aforesaid, the said John, prays judgment if the said lord the now king of the residue of the said supposed trespass, contempt and offence aforesaid, in the information aforesaid mentioned, to the said J. in the form aforesaid charged, in the said parliament, in the form aforesaid, supposed to be committed, in the court of the said lord the now king, here will or ought to be answered. &c.

Valentine's plea.

And the said Benjamin Valentine having heard the information aforesaid, he the said Benjamin saith, that he doth not apprehend that the said lord the now king, of or for the supposed offence, trespass and contempt aforesaid, in the information aforesaid mentioned, to the said B. by the said information charged, in the court of the said lord the now king here, will or ought to be answered, because he saith that the said supposed offence, trespass and contempt, in the information aforesaid mentioned, to the said B. by the said information in the form aforesaid charged, in the parliament, and not in the court of the said lord the now king here ought to be heard and determined; and the said B. further saith, that he on the said 16th day of March, in the 3d year aforesaid, in the information aforesaid * mentioned, in the due manner was elected and returned one of the burgesses for the said borough of St. Germains, in the said county of Cornwall, to serve in the said parliament, as by the said information is above mentioned, and that the said B. at the time of the supposed trespass, offence and contempt aforesaid,

*P. 300.

aforesaid,

aforesaid, to him in the form aforesaid charged, and during
the whole time of the said parliament, at Westminster aforesaid, was and remained one of the burgesses for the said
borough of St. Germains, in the said parliament, and this
he is ready to verify; wherefore and because that in the said
information, it well and evidently appears, that the supposed
offence, trespass and contempt aforesaid, in the information
aforesaid mentioned, to the said B. in the form aforesaid
charged, by the information aforesaid supposed to be committed, was committed in the said commons house of parliament aforesaid, the said B prays judgment, if the said
lord the now king of the offence, trespass and contempt
aforesaid, so to him charged and by him the said B. in the
parliament aforesaid, in the form aforesaid supposed to be
committed, in the court of the said lord the now king here,
will or ought to be answered, &c. &c.

And the said Denzill Holles having heard the information
aforesaid, he the said D. as to the supposed trespass, offence
and contempt aforesaid, in the said information mentioned,
in speaking and publishing the said English words in the
information aforesaid above recited, and to the said D. by
the information aforesaid, in the form aforesaid charged,
saith, that he doth not apprehend that the lord the now
king of or for the said supposed trespass, offence and contempt to the said D. so charged, in the court of the said lord
the now king here, will or ought to be answered, because he
saith that the said supposed offence, trespass and contempt,
in speaking and publishing the said English words in the
information aforesaid mentioned, to the said D in the form
aforesaid charged, in the parliament, and not in the court
of the said lord the now king here, ought to be heard and
determined, &c. And the said D. further saith, that he
on the said 16th day of March, in the 3d year aforesaid, in
the information aforesaid mentioned, in the due manner was
elected and returned one of the burgesses for the said borough of Dorchester, in the said county of Dorset, to serve
in the parliament aforesaid, as in the said information is
above mentioned, and that the said D. at the time of the
supposed offence, trespass and contempt aforesaid, in speaking and publishing the said English words, to the said D.
in the form aforesaid charged, and during the whole time
of the parliament aforesaid, at Westminster aforesaid, was
and remained one of the burgesses for the said borough of
Dorchester, in the said parliament, and this he is ready to
verify; wherefore and because that in the said information it
evidently and fully appears, that the supposed offence, trespass and contempt aforesaid, in speaking and publishing the

said

said English words, to the said D. in the form aforesaid charged, by the said information supposed to be committed, was committed in the said commons house of parliament, aforesaid, in the said parliament, the said D. prays judgment, if the said lord the now king of the offence, trespass and contempt aforesaid, as to the said English words aforesaid, by him the said D. in the parliament aforesaid, supposed to be spoken and published, in the court of the said lord the now king here, will or ought to be answered; and as to the entire residue of the supposed offence, trespass and contempt in the information aforesaid mentioned, * to the said D. above in the form aforesaid charged, the said D. saith, that he doth not apprehend that the said lord the now king of or for the said residue of the offence, trespass and contempt aforesaid, in the said information mentioned, to the said D. above in the form aforesaid charged, in the court of the said lord the now king here, will or ought to be answered, because he saith that the said residue of the supposed offence, trespass and contempt in the information aforesaid above specified, to the said D. by the said information in the form aforesaid charged, in the parliament, and not in the court of the said lord the now king here ought to be heard and determined; and the said D. further saith, that he on the said 16th day of March, in the 3d year aforesaid, in the information aforesaid mentioned, in the due manner was elected and returned, one of the burgesses for the said borough of Dorchester, in the said county of Dorset, to serve in the parliament aforesaid, as by the said information is above mentioned; and that he the said D. at the time of the residue of the supposed offence, trespass and contempt aforesaid, to him in the form aforesaid charged, and during the whole time of the said parliament, at Westminster aforesaid, was and remained one of the burgesses for the said borough of Dorchester in the said parliament, and this he is ready to verify; Wherefore and because, that in the said information it evidently and fully appears, that the said residue of the supposed offence, trespass and contempt aforesaid in the said information mentioned, to the said D. in the form aforesaid charged by the said information supposed to be committed, was committed in the said commons house of of parliament aforesaid, in the said parliament, the said D. prays judgment, if the said lord the now king of the said residue of the supposed offence, trespass and contempt in the information aforesaid mentioned to the said D. in the form aforesaid charged, in the said parliament, in the form aforesaid supposed to be committed in the court of the said lord the now king here, will or ought to be answered, &c.

And the said Robert Heath, knight, who prosecutes, &c.

as to the faid plea of the faid J. Elliott, for the faid lord the attorney-general to the pleas feverally.
king faith, that the faid plea of the faid J. in the form aforefaid pleaded, and the matter in the faid plea contained, are not fufficient in law, to preclude the court here from their jurifdiction, to hear and determine the offence, trefpafs and contempt in the information aforefaid mentioned to the faid J. by the faid information, in the form aforefaid charged; wherefore for want of a fufficient anfwer in this behalf, he prays judgment, and that the faid J. to the faid lord the king in the court here may anfwer of and upon the premiffes, &c.

And the faid R. Heath, knight, who profecutes, &c. as to the faid plea of the faid B. V. for the faid lord the king faith, that the faid plea of the faid B. in the form aforefaid pleaded, and the matter in the fame contained, are not fufficient in law to preclude the court here from their jurifdiction to hear and determine the offence, trefpafs and contempt aforefaid, in the faid information mentioned, to the faid B. by the faid information, in the form aforefaid charged. Wherefore, for want of a fufficient anfwer in this behalf, he prays judgment; and that the faid B. to the faid lord the king in the court here, may anfwer, of and upon the premifes, &c.———*And the like as to the plea of Denzil Holles.*

* And the faid John Elliott, knt. as before faith, that the *P. 302.* Joinder in demurrer by the defendants feverally.
faid plea by him, the faid J. in the form aforefaid pleaded, and the matter in the faid plea contained, are good and fufficient in law, to preclude the court here from their jurifdiction to hear and determine the offence, trefpafs and contempt aforefaid, in the faid information mentioned, to the faid John by the faid information in the form aforefaid charged; which plea, and the matter in the faid plea contained, the faid J. E. knt. is ready to verify; wherefore becaufe that the faid Attorney-general of the faid lord the king, for the faid lord the king, to that plea hath not anfwered, nor it in any manner hath denied, but wholly refufes to admit that averment, he prays judgment, and that he the faid John, of the offence, trefpafs and contempt aforefaid, in the information aforefaid mentioned, to the faid John, by the faid information, in the form aforefaid charged, by the court here may be difcharged, &c.————*The like joinder, word for word, by Valentine and Holles feparately.*

And becaufe the court of the lord the king here is not yet Curia non-advifadum advifatur.
advifed to give their judgment thereupon, day is given thereupon as well to the faid Robert Heath, knight, who profecutes, &c. as to the faid J. E. B. V. and D. H. in the ftate in which now, &c. until the octave of St. Hilary, before the lord the king wherefoever, &c. to hear their judgment thereon, becaufe the court not as yet, &c. at which octave of St. Hilary, before the lord the king at Weftminfter, come as

well

well the said R. H. who prosecutes, &c. as the said J. E. B. V. and D. H. in their proper persons, and the said R. H. who prosecutes, &c. for the said lord the king prays judgment, and that the said J. E. B. V. and D. H. to the said lord the king in the court here may answer, and that each of them may

Judgment that the pleas to the jurisdiction are insufficient.

answer of and upon the premises, &c. whereupon all and singular the premises being seen, read and heard, because that it seems to the court here, that the said several pleas, by the said J. E. B. V. and D. H. in the form aforesaid above pleaded, and the matter in the said several pleas contained, are not sufficient in law to preclude the court here from their jurisdiction to hear and determine the offence, trespass and contempt aforesaid, in the information aforesaid mentioned, to the said J. E. B. V. and D. H. by the said information, in the form aforesaid charged, it is said, to the said J. E. B. V.

Defendants ordered to answer over.

and D. H. that they the said J. E. B. V. and D. H. to the said lord the king, in the court here answer, and that each of them answer of and upon the premises in the information aforesaid above contained, &c. and thereupon day is given by the court, to the said J. E. B. V. and D. H. before the lord the

Day given them to answer periculis suis.

king, wheresoever, &c. until the Friday next after the octave of the purification of the blessed virgin Mary, to imparl to the said information, and then to answer at their peril. At which day before the lord the king at Westminster, come as well the said R. H. who prosecutes, &c. as the said J. E. B. V. and D. H. in their proper persons, and they the said J. E. B. V. and D. H. although they are often forewarned, and solemnly called to answer, say nothing in bar, or in discharge of the information aforesaid, whereby the said lord the king remains against them undefended ; therefore it is considered that the

Judgment

said J. E. B. V. and D. H. be taken to satisfy the lord the

***P. 303.**

king of their fines, by * occasion of the trespass and contempt

Sir John Elliot committed to the Tower of London. And Valentine and Holles to the King's bench prison.

aforesaid, & that they have their bodies imprisoned at the pleasure of the said lord the king, and that before they be delivered, that each of them find sufficient security for his good behaviour towards the said lord the king and all his people ; and that the said J. E. is committed to the lieutenant of the tower of the lord the king of London, safely to be kept, until that, &c. And that the said B. V. and D. H. are committed to the marshall of the marshalsea of the lord the king, before the king himself, safely to be kept until that, &c.

Afferment of their fines

And the fine of the said J. E. is affeered by the court for the occasion aforesaid, to 2000 l.——And the fine of the said B. V. is affeered by the court for the occasion aforesaid, to 500 l.——And the fine of the said D. H. is affeered by the court, to one thousand marks.

Afterwards

Afterwards, to wit, on the Monday next after the octave of the purification of the bleffed virgin Mary, in the 12th year of the reign of our lord Charles the now king of England, &c. before the lord the king at Weftminfter, comes John Banks, kt. attorney-general of the faid lord the now king, who for the faid lord the king now in this behalf profecutes, and for the faid lord the king, fays and acknowleges, that the faid D. H. hath paid and fatisfied the faid one thoufand marks, at the receipt of the Exchequer of the faid lord the king, to the ufe of the faid lord the king, in full fatisfaction of the faid fine, upon him the faid D. for the faid offence, in the faid information above named, by the court here, upon him laid, as fully appears by the conftat, under the hand of Edward Warder, kt. clerk of the Rolls of the receipt of the Exchequer, of the faid lord the king, here in court fhewn, and the faid attorney-general of the faid lord the king, for the faid lord the king acknowledges the faid lord the king to be thereof fatisfied. Therefore let the faid D. H. of the faid 1000 marks, go thereof quit.

Afterwards, to wit, on the Wednefday next after 15 days of Eafter, in the 16th year of the reign of the faid lord the now king of England, &c. before the lord the king at Weftminfter, came John Banks, kt. Att. gen. of the faid lord the now king, in his proper perfon, and brought into the court of the faid lord the king, before the king himfelf then there, a certain writ of the faid lord the king, of privy feal to him and to others directed, and prayed that the faid writ might be enrolled and allowed the tenor of which writ follows in thefe words, Charles, by the grace of God, king of England, Scotland, France, and Ireland, defender of the faith, &c. to the lord high-treafurer of England, chancellor, under treafurer, and barons of our Exchequer, and all other officers and minifters of the fame court for the time being, and to the chief juftice, and the reft of our juftices of our court of King's Bench, and to our attorney general, and to all other officers and minifters of the fame court for the time being, greeting. Whereas in Michaelmas term, in the tenth year of our reign, upon an information in our name exhibited in our court of King's Bench, againft Benjamin Valentine, efquire, and others, for divers offences, trefpaffes and contempts therein mentioned, the fame Benjamin Valentine, by judgment of the fame court, was fined to us in the fum of 500l. * and to be committed to our prifon of our marfhalfea during our pleafure, and that he fhould find fufficient fecurity for his good behaviour to us and our people, as by the faid information and judgment, thereupon remaining upon record in our court of King's Bench, more at large may appear; and whereas the faid B. V. hath been reftrained of his liberty fince the laft parliament for not fatisfying the faid fine fo impofed on him as aforefaid, now know

ye,

The attorney general comes into court and acknowledges that Holles has paid his fine.

Afterwards the attorney general brings into court the king's letters patents under his privy feal, whereby the king remits to Valentine his fine and all the reft of the judgment; and prays the fame may be inrolled and allowed.

*P. 304.

ye, that we of our special grace have remised, released and quit-claimed, and by these presents for us, our heirs and successors, do remise, release and quit-claim unto the said B. V. the said fine or sum of 500l. by the judgment of our said court on him the said B. V. imposed as aforesaid, and all commitment, imprisonment and other matters whatsoever adjudged or inflicted upon him by our said court, for or by reason of the trespasses, offences or contempts aforesaid, wherefore we do by these presents, will and require, as well the lord treasurer, chancellor, under treasurer and barons of our Exchequer as the justices of our court of King's Bench and the officers and ministers of the said courts respectively, to whom it shall or may appertain, that they and every of them respectively at all times hereafter do forbear and utterly surcease to make or grant forth any extents, seisures, executions, or other process whatsoever, against the said B. V. his heirs, executors or administrators, or his or their lands, tenements, hereditaments, goods or chattels, for or concerning the levying of the said fine or sum of 500l. or any part thereof, and that they take order, as well for his full and clear discharge thereof, as of and from his commitment and imprisonment as aforesaid, and these presents or the inrollment thereof, shall be unto them and every of them to whom it shall or may appertain a sufficient warrant and discharge in that behalf; and lastly we will and by these presents authorize and require our attorney general for the time being for us, and in our behalf to acknowledge satisfaction upon record, of and for the said fine of 500l. on the said B. V. by judgment of our said court so imposed as aforesaid, whereby he may be fully and absolutely acquitted and discharged thereof against us, our heirs and successors, and these presents, or the inrollment thereof, shall be to our said attorney general for the time being, a good and sufficient warrant in that behalf, given under our privy seal, at our palace of Westminster, the 7th day of March, in the 15th year of our reign; and thereupon the said J. B. knt. attorney general of the said lord the king, for the said lord the king, by virtue of the writ of privy seal aforesaid, says and acknowledges that the said lord the king is fully satisfied of the said fine of 500l. upon him the said B. V. for the offence aforesaid, in the information aforesaid mentioned, by the court here as aforesaid imposed, and prays that the said B. V. by virtue of the said writ from his imprisonment, at the suit of the said lord the king, and of the said judgment may be discharged and dismissed; whereupon all and singular the premises being seen, and by the court here understood, it is considered by the court that the said B. V. of his fine for the offence aforesaid, in the information aforesaid, * above mentioned by the court here as aforesaid imposed, be therefore quit, and that he go thence without day, and that he

The attorney-general prays and the court gives judgment that Valentine be discharged.

*P. 305.

the

the said B. V. from his imprisonment, at the suit of the lord the king, and of the judgment aforesaid, against the said B. in the form aforesaid given, be discharged and dismissed, &c. Afterwards to wit, on the twelfth day of February, in the 20th year of the reign of our lord Charles the second, the now king of England, &c. the lord the king hath sent to his beloved and faithful John Kelynge, knight, chief justice of the said lord the king, assigned to hold pleas before the king himself, his writ close in these words; Charles the second, &c. to our beloved and faithful John Kelynge, knight, our chief justice assigned to hold pleas before us, greeting. Because in the record and process, and also in the giving of judgment, upon a certain information in the court of the lord Charles, the first late king of England, our most dear father; before the said late lord the king himself exhibited by Robert Heath, knight, then attorney-general of the said late lord the king, who for the said lord the king, in that behalf, did prosecute against John Elliott, late of London, knight, B. Valentine, late of London aforesaid, esquire, and D. Holles, late of London aforesaid, esquire, for divers misdemeanors, as it is said manifest error hath intervened. to the great damage of the said D. H. now lord Holles, baron of Ifield, as we have understood by his complaint, we willing that the error, if any there hath been, in the due manner be corrected, and that full and speedy justice be done to the said D. H. now lord Holles, baron of Ifield, in this behalf, command you that if judgment be thereupon given, then that you send the record and process aforesaid, with all things touching the same, to us in our present parliament, distinctly and openly, and this writ, that inspecting the record and process aforesaid, we may further cause to be done thereon, with the assent of the lords spiritual and temporal, in the said parliament being, for correcting the error, that which of right and according to the law and custom of our kingdom of England, shall be to be done. Witness ourself at Westminster, the twelfth day of February, in the twentieth year of our reign.

Norbury.

By virtue of which writ, the said chief justice the record aforesaid, to the lord the king, in the present parliament, with his proper hands hath produced, according to the command of the said writ. And afterwards to wit, on the eighth day of March, in the 20th year of the reign of the lord Charles, the second the now king, before the king himself, in the present parliament, comes the said D. H. now lord Holles, baron of Ifield, by Samuel Astry, his attorney, and saith that in the record and process aforesaid, and also in the giving of the said judgment there is manifest error, to wit, in this that

3 B

the

[Marginal notes:]
D. Holles, now lord Holles brings a writ of error upon the said judgment returnable in parliament.

The lord chief justice delivers the record.

Errors assigned.

the words in the said information mentioned, to be spoken and published in the commons house of parliament, by the said D. H. now lord Holles, then being a burgess serving for the borough of Dorchester, in the then present parliament, ought by the law of the land to be heard and determined in the commons house of parliament, and not in the court of the lord the king ; and in this, that by the information * in the said record mentioned, the said D. H. now lord Holles is charged with speaking and publishing certain words in the commons house of parliament, and also with a trespass and assault done with force and arms upon John Finch Speaker of the commons house of parliament, to which the said D. H. now lord H. did plead two several pleas, nevertheless only one judgment was given by the court upon both, and one fine, whereas two judgments ought to have been given, and two fines ought to have been imposed ; because, if perchance the trespass and assault might or ought to be heard and determined in the court of the lord the king before the king himself ; nevertheless the speaking and publishing of whatsoever words in the commons house of parliament, by the burgesses serving in the said parliament, elsewhere than in parliament, ought not to be heard or determined, &c.

*P 306.

And Geoffry Palmer, kt. and baronet, attorney-general of the said lord the now king, who for the said lord the king in this behalf prosecutes, present in his proper person, for the said lord the king saith, that neither in the record and process aforesaid, nor in the giving of the judgment aforesaid, is there any error, and he prays, &c. And because the court of parliament is not advised to give their judgment of and upon the premises, day is given as well to the said G. P. kt. and baronet who prosecutes, &c. as to the said D. lord Holles, before the said court until Wednesday the 15th day of April then next ensuing, at Westminster in the county of Middlesex, to hear their judgment thereupon ; because the said court not as yet, &c. At which day, before the said court come as well the said G. P. who prosecutes, &c. as the said D. lord H. in their proper persons, whereupon all and singular the premises being seen, and by the said court now here fully understood, and mature deliberation being thereupon had, it is considered by the court, that the said judgment, for the said errors and others in the record and process aforesaid found, be reversed, annulled, and held as entirely void, and that the said D. lord H. be restored to all things which he the said D. lord H. hath lost by occasion of the said judgment, &c.

In nullo est erratum by the Attorney general.

Curia nondum advisatur.

Judgment of reversal.

This case is reported at large in Cro. Car. 181, 182, and 604 to 610.

The

<hr>

* The King againft Hambden

Middlefex, THE lord the king hath fent to his juftices, af-
To wit ſigned to enquire by the oath of good and
lawful men of the county of Middlefex, and by other ways,
methods and means, by which they might or could know
better, of certain treafons, mifprifions of treafons, infurrections, rebellions, counterfeitings, clippings, wafhings,
falfe coinings and other falfities of the monies of this kingdom of England, and of other kingdoms and dominions
whatfoever, and of all other offences and injuries whatfoever,
and alfo to his juftices affigned to deliver his goal of Newgate of the prifoners being therein, and alfo to the keepers
of his peace, and to his juftices affigned to hear and determine divers felonies, trefpaffes and other mifdeeds in the
faid county perpetrated, and to every of them, his writ
clofe in thefe words, to wit, James the 2d by the grace of
God, &c. To our juftices affigned to enquire by the oath
of good and lawful men of the county of Middlefex, and
by other ways, methods and means by which they might or
could know better, of certain treafons, mifprifions of treafons, infurrections, rebellions, counterfeitings, clippings,
wafhings, falfe coinings and other falfities of the monies
of this kingdom of England, and of other kingdoms and
dominions whatfoever, and of all other offences and injuries
whatfoever, and to our juftices affigned to deliver our goal
of Newgate, of the prifoners being therein; and alfo to
the keepers of our peace, and to our juftices affigned to hear
and determine divers felonies, trefpaffes and other mifdeeds
in the faid county perpetrated, and to every of them, greeting. We being willing for certain caufes, that the record of
the conviction of John Hambden, gent. for certain high
treafons, whereof before you he was indicted, and thereupon
was convicted, as it is faid, be fent by you before us, command you and every of you, that you or one of you, fend
the faid record with all things touching the fame, as fully
and compleatly as the fame now remains before you, by
whatfoever name the faid John may be named in the fame,
before us under your feals, or the feal of one of you, from

Certiorari
out of the
King's feal
directed to
the juftices
of Oyer and
Terminer,
to the
juftices of
goal deliver
ry of New-
gate, and
to the
juftices of
the peace for
the county of
Middlefex,
and every of
them, to re-
move a re-
cord of con-
viction of
JohnHamb-
den, gent.
for High
Treafon.

3 B 2

the

the day of Easter in 15 days, wheresoever we shall then be in England, together with this writ, that we may further cause to be done thereupon, that which of right and according to the law and custom of our kingdom of England, we shall see fit to be done, witness, E. Herbert, kt. &c. by the court, Astry. Which writ and record in the said writ mentioned, was returned and certified as follows, to wit: By virtue of this writ to me and to others directed, the record of the conviction of the within named John Hambden, gent. whereof mention is made in the same writ, with all things touching the same, to this writ annexed I send before the lord the king as is within commanded: The answer of Rt. Jefferys kt. mayor of the city of London, and one of the within written justices.

Middlesex, to wit, be it remembered, that at the session of Oyer and Terminer of the lord the king, held for the county of Middlesex, at Hicks-hall in St. John's-street, in the said county, on Monday, to wit, the 7th day of September, in the first year of the reign of our lord James the 2d, by the grace of God, &c. before W. Smith, baronet, J. Berry, kt. and others their fellows justices * of the said lord the king, assigned by letters patent, of the said lord the king, to the said justices before named, and to any four or more of them, made under the great seal of the said lord the king of England, to enquire by the oath of good and lawful men of the county of Middlesex aforesaid, by whom the truth of the matter might be better known, and by all other ways, methods and means by which they might or could know better, as well within liberties as without, more fully the truth of certain treasons, misprisions of treasons, insurrections, rebellions, counterfeitings, clippings, washings, false-coinings, and other falsities of the monies of this kingdom of England, and of other kingdoms and dominions whatsoever; and of certain murders, felonies, manslaughters, killings, burglaries, rapes of women, unlawful assemblies and conventicles, unlawful uttering of words, combinations, misprisions, confederacies, false allegations, trespasses, riots, routs, retentions escapes, contempts, oppressions, and of other articles and offences in the said letters patent, of the said lord the king, specified; and also the accessaries of the same, within the same county, as well within liberties as without, by whomsoever and howsoever had done, perpetrated or committed; and of all other articles and circumstances, the premises, and every or any of them howsoever concerning; and to hear and determine the said treasons and the other premises, according to the law and custom of this kingdom of England, by the oath of W. Wood, esq; and fourteen others good and lawful men of the said county, then and there sworn, and charged to enquire for the said lord the king, and for the body of the county aforesaid, it is
presented

presented in the manner and form following, to wit, Middlesex, to wit, the jurors for our lord the king upon their oath present, that John Hambden, late of the parish of St. Giles in the fields, in the county of Middlesex, gent. as a false traitor against the most illustrious and most excellent prince, the lord Charles the second, late king of England, &c. his natural lord, not having the fear of God in his heart, nor weighing the duty of his allegiance, but being moved and seduced by the instigation of the Devil, and entirely withdrawing the cordial love and true, due and natural obedience, which a true and faithful subject of the said late lord the king, towards the said late lord the king should bear, and of right was bound to bear; and devising, practising, and as much as in him lay intending to disquiet, molest and disturb the peace and public tranquility of this kingdom of England, and to stir up, move and procure war and rebellion against the said late lord the king, within this kingdom of England; and to subvert, change and alter the government of the said late lord the king, of this his kingdom of England; and to depose and deprive the said late lord the king of his title, honor and royal name, and of the imperial crown of his kingdom of England; and to bring and put the said late lord the king to death, and final destruction, on the 20th day of July, in the 35th year of the reign of the said lord Charles the 2d. late king of England, and at divers other days and times, as well before as after, at the parish of St. Giles in the Fields, in the county of Middlesex, falsely, maliciously, diabolically, and traiterously with divers other false rebels and traitors, to the jurors aforesaid unknown, did conspire, compass, imagine and intend, not only to depose and deprive the said late lord the king, then his supreme and natural lord, of his royal state, title, power and government of this kingdom of England, but also the said late lord the king, to kill, and to bring and put to death, and to change, alter and entirely subvert the antient government of this kingdom of England, and to cause and procure a miserable slaughter among the subjects of the said late lord the king, throughout his whole kingdom of England, and to procure and abet insurrection and rebellion, against the said late lord the king, within this kingdom of England, and to fulfil, perfect and bring to effect, his said most wicked, detestable and diabolical treasons, traiterous compassings, imaginations and purposes aforesaid, he the said John Hambden, as a false traitor, then and there to wit, on the 20th day of July, in the 35th year of the reign of the said late lord the king aforesaid, and at divers other days and times, as well before as after, in the parish of St. Giles, in the fields aforesaid, in the said county of Middlesex, falsely,

unlawfully,

Indictment for High Treason against Charles the 2d by conspiring to depose and kill him, and to change the government, found at Hick's hall before justices of Oyer and Terminer, the 1st year of James 2d.

unlawfully, wickedly, diabolically and traiterouſly, with
James late Duke of Monmouth, and divers other falſe traitors, to the jurors aforeſaid unknown, did aſſemble, meet,
conſult and agree to raiſe and procure, divers great ſums of
money and great numbers of armed men, traiterouſly to levy
and make war and rebellion againſt the ſaid late lord the king,
within this kingdom of England, againſt the duty of his allegiance and againſt the peace of the ſaid lord the now king,
his crown and dignity, and alſo againſt theform of the ſtatute,
in ſuch caſe made and provided, &c. whereupon the ſheriff of
the county of Middleſex is commanded that he do not omit,
&c. but that he take him to anſwer, &c. And that at the delivery of the goal, of the ſaid lord the king, of Newgate,
held for the county of Middleſex aforeſaid, at Juſtice-Hall,
in the old Baily, in the ſuburbs of the city of London, on
Wedneſday to wit, the 9th day of December, in the firſt
year of the reign of the ſaid lord James the ſecond, the now
king of England, &c. aforeſaid, before Robert Jeffrys, knt.
mayor of the city of London, Edward Herbert, knight,
chief-juſtice of the ſaid lord the king, aſſigned to hold pleas
before the king himſelf and others, their fellows, juſtices of
the ſaid lord the king, aſſigned to deliver his goal of Newgate,
of the priſoners being therein, that delivery of the goal was
adjourned, by the ſaid juſtices, of the ſaid lord the king,
laſt named here, until the morrow to wit, Thurſday, the
10th day of the ſaid month of December, in the 1ſt year
aforeſaid, to be held at the ſeventh hour before mid-day of
the ſaid day, at Juſtice Hall aforeſaid, before the ſaid juſtices
of the ſaid lord the king, laſt named, to do further as the
court there ſhould conſider, &c. and upon the ſaid Thurſday,
the tenth day of the ſaid month of December, in the 1ſt year
aforeſaid, the ſaid delivery of the goal was held by the ſaid
adjournment for the ſaid county at Juſtice-Hall aforeſaid, before the ſaid juſtices of the ſaid lord the king, laſt named,
and then and there the ſaid delivery of the goal of the ſaid
lord the king, was further adjourned by the ſaid juſtices of the
ſaid lord the king, laſt named, until the morrow to wit,
Friday, the 11th day of the ſaid month, of December, in the
1ſt year aforeſaid, to be held at the ſeventh hour before mid-
day of the ſaid day, at Juſtice-Hall aforeſaid, to do further
as the court there ſhould conſider, * &c. And on the ſaid Friday the 11th day of December, in the 1ſt year aforeſaid, the
delivery of the ſaid goal was held by the ſaid adjournment
for the ſaid county, at juſtice-Hall aforeſaid, before the ſaid
juſtices of the ſaid lord the king, laſt named, and then and
there the ſaid delivery of the goal of the ſaid lord the king,
was further adjourned by the ſaid juſtices of the ſaid lord
the

*P. 310.

the king laft named here, until Saturday to wit, the nineteenth day of the faid month of December, in the firft year aforefaid, to be held at the feventh hour before mid-day of the faid day, at Juftice-hall aforefaid, before the faid juftices of the faid lord the now king laft named, to do further as the court there fhould confider, &c. And on the faid Saturday, the 19th day of the faid month of December, in the firft year aforefaid, the delivery of the faid goal was held by the faid adjournment, for the faid county, at Juftice-hall aforefaid, before the faid juftices of the faid lord the king laft named, and then and there the faid delivery of the goal of the faid lord the king was further adjourned by the faid juftices of the faid lord the king laft named here, until Wednef-day, to wit, the thirtieth day of the faid month of December, in the firft year aforefaid, to be held at the feventh hour before mid-day of the faid day, at Juftice-hall aforefaid, before the faid juftices of the faid lord the king laft named, to do further as the court there fhould confider, &c. And on the faid Wednefday, the thirtieth day of the faid month of December, in the firft year aforefaid, the delivery of the faid goal was held by the faid adjournment, for the faid county, at Juftice-hall aforefaid, before the faid juftices of the faid lord the king laft named, and on the faid Wednefday, the 30th day of the fame month of December, in the year aforefaid, at the faid delivery of the goal of the faid lord the king then held by the faid adjournment, for the faid county, at Juftice-hall aforefaid, before the faid juftices of the faid lord the king laft named, the faid juftices of the faid lord the king as aforefaid, by the faid letters patent of the faid lord the king, made under the great feal of England, by their proper hands did deliver the faid indictment here into the court of record, to be determined in form of law, &c. and thereupon at the faid delivery of the goal of the faid lord the king of Newgate, held by the faid adjournment for the faid county, at Juftice-hall aforefaid, on the faid Wednefday the 30th day of the faid month of December, in the firft year aforefaid, before the faid juftices of the faid lord the king, affigned to deliver the faid goal of the faid lord the king of Newgate aforefaid, of the prifoners being therein, comes the faid John Hambden, under the cuftody of Benjamin Thorowgood, and J. Kenfey, knights, fheriff of the county of Middlefex aforefaid, into whofe cuftody for the caufe aforefaid, before that time he was committed, brought to the bar here in his proper perfon, who committed to the faid fheriff, &c. and forthwith being demanded of the premifes in the faid indictment fpecified to him above charged, how he will acquit himfelf thereof, he the faid John Hambden faith, that he cannot deny but that he is guilty

At the laft adjourn-ment the juftices of Oyer and Terminer deliver the indictment to the juftices of goal delivery.

Defendant arraigned at the goal de-livery.

guilty of the high treason aforefaid in the indictment aforefaid fpecified to him above charged, in the manner and form as by the faid indictment above againft him is fuppofed, and ex-

He confeffeth the indict-ment.

preffly confeffeth the faid high treafon, in the faid indictment. And forthwith the faid John Hambden is afked, if he hath or knoweth any thing to fay wherefore the court here fhould not

*P. 311.

proceed to judgment and execution againft * him, upon his conviction aforefaid, and his proper confeffion of the faid high-treafon in the faid indictment above fpecified, who faith nothing except as he hath before faid, whereupon all and

Judgment.

fingular, the premifes being feen and by the court here under-ftood, it is confidered, by the court here that the faid John Hambden, be brought to the goal of the faid lord the king, of Newgate, from whence he came, and there be put upon a hurdle, and from thence be drawn to the place of execution, and there be hanged by his neck, and be cut down alive to the ground, and that his privy members be cut off, and his bowels be taken out of his belly and be put into the fire, and be there burnt, and that his head be cut off, and that his body be divided into four parts, and that his head and quarters be put where the lord the king will affign. And now to wit, on the Wednefday next after fifteen days of Eafter, in this fame term before the lord the king, at Weftminfter, comes

Defendant appears in the King's bench by recogni-zance and is commit-ted to the marfhal and pleads the king's par-don by let-ters patent.

the faid John Hambden, according to the form of the recognizance by him and his bail in this behalf before ac-knowledged, in his proper perfon, who is committed to the marfhal, &c. and then and there, by the court of the faid lord the king here, he the faid John Hambden is afked if he hath or knoweth any thing to fay for himfelf, wherefore the court here fhould not proceed to execution upon the faid judgment, in the form aforefaid given, who forthwith faith, that the faid lord the now king, of his efpecial grace, and of his certain knowledge, and mere motion, by his letters patent, under his great feal of England, bearing date at Weftminfter, the 19th day of February, in the 2d year of the reign of the faid lord the now king, hath pardoned, remifed and releafed, and by the faid prefents, for himfelf, his heirs and fucceffors, hath pardoned, remifed and releafed to John Hambden, late of the parifh of St. Giles in the fields, in the county of Middlefex, gent. or by what other name or fir-name, or addition of name or fir-name, or place, he the faid John Hambden might be known, judged, named or called, or lately was known, judged, named or called, all and all manner of treafons, mifprifions of treafons, trefpaffes, mifdeeds, crimes and offences whatfoever, by him-felf fingly or with any other perfon, or other perfons, againft the faid lord the king, or his moft dear brother Charles, the

2d. late king of England, &c. deceaſed, before the 25th day of January laſt whenſoever, howſoever, or whereſoever done, committed, or perpetrated, altho' the ſaid John Hambden of the premiſes or any of them is, or is not indicted, arreſted, appealed, impeached, attainted, convicted, outlawed, condemned or adjudged, or whereupon he might afterwards be indicted, arreſted, appealed, impeached, attainted, convicted, outlawed, condemned, or adjudged ; and all and ſingular, indictments, judgments, condemnations, attainders, executions, fines, impriſonments, puniſhments, pains of death, corporal pains, and all other pains and penalties whatſoever, upon or againſt the ſaid John Hambden of, for, or concerning the premiſes, or any of them, had, done, given or adjudged, or afterwards to be had, done, given or adjudged ; and alſo all and ſingular outlawries againſt the ſaid J. H. by reaſon or occaſion of the premiſes, or any of them pronounced, * or afterwards to be pronounced ; and all and all manner of ſuits, plaints, fines, forfeitures, impeachments, ſeizures, proceedings, and demands whatſoever, which the ſaid lord the king againſt him by reaſon of the premiſes, or any of them had, hath, or afterwards might have, or his heirs or ſucceſſors in any manner might have, and the ſuit of his peace which to the ſaid lord the king againſt him the ſaid John Hambden appertains, or may appertain, by reaſon of the premiſes or any of them ; and his firm peace to him thereupon by the ſaid preſents did give and grant. And the ſaid J. H produces here in court the letters patent aforeſaid, teſtifying the premiſes, in theſe words.—" James, by the grace of God, &c. To all to whom our preſent letters ſhall come, greeting. Know ye that we of our eſpecial grace, and of our certain knowledge and mere motion, have pardoned, remiſed, and releaſed, and by theſe preſents for ourſelves, our heirs and ſucceſſors do pardon, remiſe, and releaſe to J. H. of the pariſh, &c. gent. or by what other name or ſurname, or addition of name or ſurname or place the ſaid J. may be known, judged, named or called, or lately was known, judged, named or called, all and all manner of treaſons, miſpriſions of treaſons, treſpaſſes, miſdeeds, crimes and offences whatſoever, by him ſingly, or with any other perſon, or any other perſons againſt us, or our moſt dear brother Charles the 2d, late king of England, &c. deceaſed, before the 25th day of January now laſt paſt, whenſoever, howſoever, or whereſoever done, committed or perpetrated, altho' the ſaid J. H. is or is not of the premiſes, or any of them indicted, arreſted, appealed, impeached, attainted, convicted, condemned, outlawed or adjudged ; or whereupon hereafter he may be indicted, arreſted, appealed, impeached, attainted, convicted, outlawed, condemned or adjudged, and all and ſingular indictments, judgments, condem-

nations,

*P. 312.

The pardon brought in-to court, ſet out in hæc verba.

bations, attainders, executions, fines, imprifonments, punifh-
ments, pains of death, corporal pains, and all other pains
and penalties whatfoever upon or againft the faid J. H, of, for,
or concerning the premifes, or any of them, had, done, given,
or adjudged or in future to be had, done, given or adjudged,
and alfo all and fingular outlawries againft the faid J. H. by
reafon or occafion of the premifes, or any of them, pronounced or hereafter to be pronounced, and all and all manner of fuits, plaints, fines, forfeitures, impeachments, judgments, proceedings and demands whatfoever, which we
by reafon of the premifes, or any of them, againft him
had, have, or hereafter may have, or our heirs or fucceffors
in any manner hereafter may have, and the fuit of our peace
which to us againft the faid J. H. appertains, or may appertain by reafon of the premifes, or any of them, and our
firm peace thereupon, we give and grant to him by thefe
prefents, willing that the faid J. H. fhall not be molefted,
troubled, difturbed or in any manner aggrieved, by the fheriffs, juftices, bailiffs or other officers, of us, our heirs or
fucceffors, by occafion of the premifes, or any of them,
willing that thefe our letters patent, as to all and fingular

§P. 313. the premifes above mentioned, may be and fhall be good,
valid, firm and effectual in law, although the crimes and
offences aforefaid, are not certainly fpecified, and that this
our pardon in all our courts and elfewhere, be interpreted
and adjudged in the moft beneficial fenfe, for the moft fure
releafing, pardoning and difcharging of the faid J. H. and
alfo that they fhall be pleaded and allowed in all our courts,
without any writ of allowance, in that behalf firft obtained,
or to be obtained, notwithftanding any defect or any defects,
in thefe letters patent contained, or any ftatute, act, ordi-
nance or provifion, proclamation or reftriction, or any other
thing, caufe or matter whatfoever, to the contrary thereof
in any wife notwithftanding. In witnefs whereof, we have
caufed thefe our letters to be made patent, witnefs ourfelf
at Weftminfter, in the 2d year of our reign." Wherefore
by virtue of the faid letters patent, the faid J. H. prays
that he of the premifes, by the court here may be difcharged,
whereupon all and fingular the premifes being feen and by
the court here underftood, it is confidered that the faid J. H.

Judgment
quod eat
fine die.
go thereof without day, &c. And afterwards, to wit, on
the Monday next after the morrow of the afcenfion of our
Lord, in this fame term, before the lord the king at Weftminfter, comes the faid J. H. in his proper perfon, and brings
here into court, a certain writ of the lord the now king clofe,

Defendant
brings a writ
of error.
examinobis.
to his juftices here directed, which follows in thefe words,
James the 2d, &c. To our juftices affigned to hold pleas
before us, greeting. Becaufe in the record and procefs, and
alfo

also in the giving of judgment of a certain indictment, before our justices, assigned to deliver our goal of Newgate, of the prisoners being therein, against J. H. of the parish. &c. in the county of Middlesex, gent. for high treasons against the person of the lord Charles the 2d, late king of England, our most dear brother, whereof before them he lately was attainted, as it is said, manifest error hath intervened, to the great damage of the said John, as we have understood from his complaint, we willing that the error, if any there hath been, in the due manner be corrected, and that full and speedy justice be done to the said John, in this behalf, command you, that if judgment be thereupon given, then that inspecting and examining the record and process aforesaid, which we have caused to come before us for certain causes, and which before us now remain as it is said, we may further cause to be done thereupon, for correcting the error that which of right and according to the law and custom of our kingdom of England, shall be to be done. Witness ourself, at Westminster, the 14th day of May, in the 2d year of our reign.

And thereupon the said J. H. saith, that in the record and process aforesaid, and also in the giving of the judgment of attainder aforesaid, there is manifest error in this, to wit, that whereas by the record aforesaid, it is mentioned, that the delivery of the goal, in the record of the judgment and attainder aforesaid mentioned, was held for the county of Middlesex, at Justice-hall in the old Baily, in the suburbs of the city of London, and it doth not appear by the said record, that Justice-hall or the old Baily, are in the county of Middlesex, therefore in that there is manifest error; also there is error in this, to wit, that the indictment aforesaid, is mentioned to be taken on the 7th day of December, in the said record mentioned, before justices of Oyer and Terminer in the said record mentioned, and by them to be delivered to justices of goal delivery in the said record specified, on the thirtieth day of December, then afterwards in the form of law to be determined, and it doth not appear by the said record of conviction, that the session * of oyer and terminer had any adjournment or continuance until the said thirtieth day of December, therefore in that there is manifest error; also there is error in this, that the words, "*with force and arms, &c.*" are omitted in the said indictment, therefore, in that there is manifest error; also there is error in this, that it appears by the said record, that the process and judgment aforesaid, are entered and recorded upon the record, of justices of oyer and terminer, and not upon the record of justices of goal delivery, therefore in that there is manifest error; also there is error in this, to wit, that it doth not appear by the

Assignment of errors.

*P. 314

3 C 2

said

said record, by what authority the justices of goal delivery, in the said record mentioned, gave the said process and judgment aforesaid, against him the said J. H. upon the said indictment, therefore in that there is manifest error ; also, there is error in this, that upon the giving of the judgment in the said record mentioned, it doth not appear who there was, who on the part of the lord the king, for the said lord the king, prayed judgment upon the conviction of the matters in the said indictment mentioned, therefore in that there is manifest error ; also there is error in this, that in the said record it is said that at the delivery of the goal of the said lord the king, of Newgate, held for the county of Middlesex, at Justice-hall in the old Baily, in the suburbs of the city of London, on Wednesday to wit, the ninth day of December, before the justices of goal delivery, in the said record mentioned that, that delivery of the goal *was* adjourned by the said justices, whereas it ought to be said *is* adjourned, and not to be expressed by way of recital in the past tense, and in another place in the said record, it is said that the said delivery of the goal *was held*, whereas it ought to be expressed, *is held*, and not that it was held, because in the past tense, it is mere recital of the holding and adjourning that court, and not the positive act of the said court of goal delivery, for the determination of that judgment, therefore in that there is manifest error ; also there is error in this, to wit, that the said judgment is given for the said lord the king, whereas it ought to be given for the defendant, therefore in that there is manifest error, and this he is ready to verif, wherefore he prays judgment, and that the judgment and attainder aforesaid, for the errors aforesaid, and others in the record and process aforesaid appearing, being found, may be reversed, annulled and held as entirely void, and that he the said John may be restored to the common law of this kingdom of England, and to all things which he hath lost by occasion of the judgment and attainder aforesaid, and that he as well of the said conviction and attainder as of the said indictment by the court here, may be dismissed and discharged, and that the court here may proceed to the examination of the record and process aforesaid, &c. and because that it is necessary, and expedient before that the court here should proceed in this behalf, that the tenants of the lands and tenements, which were of the said John, on the 20th day of July, in the 35th year of the reign, of the said lord Charles the second, late king of England, &c. on which day the high-treason aforesaid, is supposed to be committed, or at any time afterwards, should be forewarned to be before the said lord the now king, to hear the record and process aforesaid, if, &c. therefore the sheriff of the

county

county of Middlefex, is commanded, that by good and law- Scire facias
ful men of his bailiwick, he give notice, feverally to the ten- awarded.
ants of the lands and tenements, which were of the faid John
on the 2oth day of July, in the 35th year of the reign of the
faid lord Charles the fecond, late king of England aforefaid,
or at any time afterwards, that they be before the lord the
king, on the morrow of the Holy Trinity, wherefoever, &c.
to hear the record and procefs aforefaid, if, &c. the fame *   *P. 315.
day is given to the faid John Hambden, &c. and thereupon
by the fpecial favour of the court, the faid J. H. is delivered
on bail to H. A. of &c. efquire, and W. I. of &c. until
the faid term, and fo, &c.

*It does not appear by the precedent, whether the judgment was
reverfed or affirmed, nor is the report of this cafe to be found in
any of the reports of that time.*

Reftitution,

Burgeſs *againſt* Coney.

<table>
<tr><td>

Writ of Re-
ſtitution
from the
juſtices of
goal-delive-
ry after con-
viction of a
felon, to re-
ſtore the
proſecutor
to his goods,
upon the
Stat. 21 Hen.
3. c. 11.

</td><td>

Middleſex,
To wit.

</td><td>

THE lord the king hath ſent to Edward Coney, his writ in theſe words to wit, William the third by the grace of God of England, Scotland, France and Ireland king, defender of the faith, &c. to Edward Coney greeting. Whereas at this delivery of our goal of Newgate, held for the county of Middleſex, at Juſtice-hall in the old Baily, in the ſuburbs of the city of London, on Wedneſday to wit, the 9th day of December, in the 8th year of our reign, before Edward Clark, knight, mayor of the city of London, George Treby, knight, chief juſtice of the bench, and others their fellows, our juſtices aſſigned to deliver our goal of Newgate of the priſoners being therein, at the freſh proſecution of John Burgeſs the elder, one Thomas Barnes late of the pariſh of Enfield, in the county of Middleſex, labourer, is convicted of this, that he on the 28th day of Auguſt, in the 8th year of our reign, at the pariſh aforeſaid, in the county aforeſaid, three heifers of a red-pyed colour, each of them of the value of 3*l.* 5*s.* and one other heifer of a black colour of the value of 3*l.* 5*s.* of the goods and chattels, of one John Burgeſs the elder, then and there being found, then and there feloniouſly did ſteal, take and drive away, againſt our peace, our crown and dignity, as by the record thereof more fully appeareth; and whereas by the information of the ſaid John Burgeſs, we now underſtand that the ſeveral heifers, goods and chattels aforeſaid, have come to your hands, and now are in your cuſtody, we therefore being willing that that which is juſt and reaſonable be done to the ſaid John Burgeſs, command you, firmly injoining that the heifers, goods and chattels aforeſaid, or ſuch of them as ever came to or now are in your hands, you reſtore and deliver to the ſaid John Burgeſs, without delay, according to the form of the ſtatute in ſuch caſe made and provided, or that you be before our juſtices aſſigned to deliver our goal of Newgate, of the priſoners being therein at the next delivery of our goal aforeſaid, to be held for the county of Middleſex, at Juſtice-hall aforeſaid, on Friday to wit, the 15th * day of January.

</td></tr>
</table>

*P. 316.

January, now next enſuing to ſhew, wherefore you will not
or cannot do the ſame, and further to do what your court in
that behalf, further ſhall conſider, and have there then this
writ. Witneſs the ſaid E. Clark, knight, mayor of the city of
London aforeſaid, at Juſtice-hall aforeſaid, the 9th day of
December, in the 8th year of our reign; Harcourt. At which
next delivery of the goal of the lord the king of Newgate,
to wit, at the delivery of the goal of the ſaid lord the
king of Newgate held for the ſaid county of Middleſex, at Juſtice-hall in the old Baily in the ſuburbs of
the city of London, on Friday, to wit, the 15th day of
January, in the 8th year of the reign of the ſaid lord the
now king, before Edward Clarke, kt. mayor of the city of
London, Edward Ward, kt. chief baron of the Exchequer of
the lord the king and others their fellows, juſtices of the ſaid
lord the king, aſſigned to deliver the goal of the ſaid lord the
king of the priſoners being therein, comes the ſaid Ed. Coney
in his proper perſon, according to the command of the ſaid
writ of reſtitution, to him in the form aforeſaid directed,
and to him lately delivered, and prays Oyer of the ſaid
record of conviction, of the ſaid Thomas Barnes, in the ſaid
writ mentioned, and it is read to him in theſe words, to wit,
Middleſex, to wit, be it remembered, that at the general ſeſſions of the peace of the lord the king, held for the county of
Middleſex, at Hicks-hall, in St. John-ſtreet, in the ſaid county, on Monday, to wit, the 7th day of Sep. in the 8th yr. of the
reign of our lord Wm. the 3d, by the grace of God, the now
king of England, &c. before John Elwes, knt. John Offley,
eſquire, and others their fellows, juſtices of the ſaid lord the
king, aſſigned to preſerve the peace, in the ſaid county, and
alſo to hear and determine divers felonies, treſpaſſes and other
miſdeeds in the ſaid county perpetrated, by the oath of John
Baily and 19 others good and lawful men of the ſaid county,
then and there ſworn, and charged to enquire for the ſaid lord
the king, and for the body of the county aforeſaid, it is preſented, that Thomas Barnes late of the pariſh of Enfield, in
the county of Middleſex, labourer, on the 28th day of Auguſt,
in the 8th year of the reign of our lord William the 3d, by
the grace of God, now king of England, &c. with force and
arms at the pariſh aforeſaid, in the county aforeſaid, three
heifers of a red-pyed colour, every one of them of the value
of 3l. 5s. and one other heifer of a black colour, of the value of 3l. 5s. of the goods and chattels of one John Burgeſs,
the elder, then and there being found, feloniouſly did ſteal,
take and drive away againſt the peace of the ſaid lord the
now king, his crown and dignity, &c. Whereupon the ſheriff
of the ſaid county is commanded that he do not omit, &c.
but that he take him, to anſwer, &c. Which indictment, the
ſaid juſtices of the ſaid lord the king of the peace, afterwards

Defendant
prays oyer
of the re-
cord of con-
viction.
The record
at large.

wards, to wit, at the delivery of the goal of the faid lord the king of Newgate, held for the faid county, at Juftice-hall, in the Old-baily, in the fuburbs of the city of London, on Wednefday, to wit, the 9th day of December, in the 8th year of the reign of the faid lord the now king, before Edw. Clarke, kt. mayor of the city of London, George Treby, kt. chief juftice of the faid lord the king of the Bench, and others, their fellows, juftices of the faid lord the king, affigned to deliver his goal of Newgate, of the prifoners being therein, by their proper hands did deliver here in court of record, to be determined in the form of law, &c. and thereupon at the faid delivery of the goal of the faid lord the king *of Newgate aforefaid, on the faid Wednefday, the 9th day of December, in the year aforefaid, before the juftices of the faid lord the king laft named, and others their fellows aforefaid, comes the faid Thomas Barnes, under the cuftody of John Woolfe, kt. and Samuel Blewit, kt. fheriff of the county aforefaid, into whofe cuftody for the caufe aforefaid, before that time he was committed, brought here to the bar in his proper perfon, who is committed to the faid fheriff; and forthwith being demanded of the felony aforefaid in the indictment aforefaid fpecified to him above charged, how he will acquit himfelf thereof, the faid Thomas Barnes faith, that he cannot deny but that he is guilty of the felony aforefaid in the indictment aforefaid fpecified, to him above charged in the manner and form as by law the faid indictment above againft him is fuppofed, and the felony aforefaid in the faid indictment above fpecified, he exprefsly confeffeth, and forthwith the faid T. Barnes is afked by the faid court, if he hath or knoweth any thing to fay for himfelf, wherefore the court here fhould not proceed to judgment and execution againft him, upon his conviction aforefaid, by his own proper confeffion of the faid felony, in the faid indictment above fpecified; who faith that he is a clerk, and prays the benefit of clergy to be allowed to him in this behalf, and thereupon the book being delivered to him the faid Thomas Barnes, he the faid Thomas Barnes read as a clerk, whereupon all and fingular the premifes being feen, and by the court here fully underftood, it is confidered by the court here, that the faid Thomas Barnes be burnt in his left hand, and be delivered according to the form of the ftatute in fuch cafe made and provided." Which being read and heard, the faid Edward Coney protefting, that that writ of, and upon the conviction aforefaid, in the form aforefaid had, fo as aforefaid adjudged and iffuing, and the matter in the faid contained, are not fufficient in law to compel him the faid Edward Coney to reftore and deliver the faid heifers in the fame writ fpecified to the faid John Burgefs, neverthelefs for plea faith, that he the faid Edward Coney for reftitution of the faid heifers, in the faid writ fpecified, ought not to be

charged,

* P. 317.

Plea of guilty.

Plea by the defendant.

Proteftation

charged, becauſe that as to one of the four heifers, to wit, the heifer of a black colour, he ſaith that the ſaid heifer of a black colour is not in his cuſtody, nor ever was, nor ever came to the hands or poſſeſſion of the ſaid Edward, as by the ſaid writ is ſuppoſed, and this he is ready to verify ; wherefore he prays judgment, if he ought to be charged for the reſtitution of the ſaid heifer, &c. And as to the three other heifers, the reſidue of the ſaid heifers in the ſaid writ above ſpecified, he the ſaid Edward faith, that in the ſuburbs of the city of London, within the pariſh of St. Sepulchre, in the ward of Farringdon without London, in a certain place there called Smithfield, on every Monday and every Friday, in every week, there is had and held, and from the time whereof the memory of man is not to the contrary, was had and held, a certain publick and open market, called Smithfield market, for the buying and ſelling, and for the expoſing to ſale, of certain live cattle, to wit, oxen, cows, ſteers and heifers, and ſheep, by and between whatſoever perſons were willing to buy or ſell ſuch cattle, in the ſaid market, and that after the ſaid time, in which it is ſuppoſed that the ſaid heifers, by the ſaid Thomas Barnes were * ſtolen, taken and drove away, and long before the ſaid T. B. thereof ſo as aforeſaid was indicted, to wit, on Friday the ſaid 28th day of Auguſt, in the 8th year of the reign of the ſaid lord the now king aforeſaid, one John Bodely, (who was accuſtomed and very often uſed to ſell ſuch cattle, in the ſaid market, called Smithfield-market, and was well known there in that behalf,) the ſaid three heifers, the reſidue of the ſaid heifers in that market, at London, to wit, at the pariſh of St. Sepulchre, in the ward aforeſaid, in the ſaid place called Smithfield, there then held, did expoſe to ſale, and openly and publickly did offer to be ſold, and the ſaid Edward Coney in good faith, and without any knowledge or underſtanding by him then or before had, that the ſaid heifers were ſtolen, the ſaid three heifers, from the ſaid John Bodely, in the ſaid full and open market, for ſeveral reaſonable and ſufficient prices of the ſame reſpectively, between the ſaid J. Bodely and the ſaid E. Coney, thereupon agreed, amounting in the whole to a great ſum of money, to wit, to the ſum of 7l. 1s. by him the ſaid E. Coney thereupon paid, then and there did buy, and thereupon the ſaid three heifers, into his poſſeſſion, and by the delivery of the ſaid John of the ſame, to the ſaid Edward, in the ſaid open market, then and there did take and have, and ſo the ſaid Edward Coney, did become, and was poſſeſſed, lawfully, rightly and duly, of the three heifers aforeſaid, as of his own proper cattle, and this he is ready to verify, wherefore

as to one he pleads that it never came to his hands.

As to the reſidue he pleads that he bought them in market vert in Smithfield.

* P. 318.

3 D

he

he prays judgment, if he ought to be charged to reſtore or deliver the ſaid heifers to the ſaid John Burgeſs, &c.

L. Agar.

<table><tr><td>Nolle proſe-
qui as to
parcel.</td><td>And the ſaid John Burgeſs, as to the ſaid heifer of a black colour, conteſſes, that he will not any further proſecute againſt the ſaid Edward Coney, for the ſaid heifer of a black colour, therefore as to the ſaid heifer of a black colour, the ſaid Edward Coney may be thereof quit, and may go thereof without day, &c. and as to the three other</td></tr></table>

Quoad the reſidue of the plea, the plaintiff demurs.

heifers, the reſidue of the heifers aforeſaid, in the writ aforeſaid, above ſpecified, the ſaid John ſaith, that he by any thing, by the ſaid E. C. above by pleading alledged, from having reſtitution of the ſaid three heifers, the reſidue of the ſaid heifers, in the ſaid writ above ſpecified, ought not to be precluded, becauſe he ſaith, that the plea aforeſaid, by the ſaid Edward Coney, as to the ſaid three heifers laſt mentioned, in the manner and form aforeſaid, above pleaded, and the matter in the ſame contained, are not ſufficient in law, to preclude him the ſaid John, from having reſtitution of the ſaid three heifers, the reſidue of the heifers aforeſaid, in the writ aforeſaid above ſpecified, to which he the ſaid John hath no neceſſity, neither is he bound by the law of the land in any manner to anſwer, and this he is ready to verify, wherefore becauſe that the ſaid Edward Coney, in his plea aforeſaid, confeſſeth that the ſaid three heifers laſt mentioned, after that the ſaid heifers, in the manner and form above ſpecified, by the ſaid T. Barnes feloniouſly were ſtolen, taken and driven away, came to the hands of him the ſaid Edward, the ſaid John prays reſtitution to be * made to him, of the ſaid three heifers, the reſidue of the ſaid heifers in the writ aforeſaid above ſpecified, according to the command of the ſaid writ, and according to the form of the ſtatute, thereupon lately made and provided, &c.

*P 319.

Ed. Northey.

<table><tr><td>Joinder in demurrer.</td><td>And the ſaid Edward Coney, becauſe that he above hath alledged ſufficient matter in law, in his plea aforeſaid, as to the ſaid three heifers, the reſidue of the heifers aforeſaid, above pleaded, to preclude him the ſaid John Burgeſs, from having reſtitution of the ſaid three heifers, under colour of the ſaid writ againſt him the ſaid Edward Coney, which he is ready to verify, which matter the ſaid John Burgeſs hath not denied, nor to the ſame in any manner hath anſwered, but altogether refuſes to admit that averment, as before prays judgment, and that the ſaid John may be precluded from having reſtitution of the ſaid three heifers, againſt</td></tr></table>

him

him the ſaid Edward, &c. but becauſe the juſtices and the court of the ſaid lord the now king here, are not yet adviſed to give their judgment of and upon the premiſes, day there-upon is given as well to the ſaid J. Burgeſs, as to the ſaid E. Coney, in the ſtate in which now, &c. until the next delivery of the goal of the ſaid lord the king of Newgate, to be held for the county of Middleſex, on Wedneſday, to wit, the 24th day of February now next enſuing, to be held at Juſtice-hall afore-ſaid, before the ſaid juſtices, to hear their judgment of and upon the premiſes aforeſaid, &c. Becauſe that the juſtices and the court here of their judgment of and upon the premiſes afore-ſaid, here thereon not as yet, &c. unto which day and place the court here, by the ſaid juſtices, &c. is adjourned, then to be held before the ſaid juſtices, &c. to give their judgment of and upon the premiſes, &c. And afterwards, to wit, at the delivery of the goal of the ſaid lord the king of Newgate, held by the adjournment aforeſaid, for the county of Middle-ſex, at Juſtice-hall in the Old-baily, in the ſuburbs of the city of London, on the ſaid 24th day of February, in the 9th year of the reign of the ſaid lord the now king, before Edw. Clark, kt. mayor of the city of London, Edward Nevill, kt. one of the juſtices of the ſaid lord the king of the bench, and others their fellows, juſtices of the ſaid lord the king, aſſign-ed to deliver his goal of Newgate of the priſoners being there-in, come as well the ſaid J. Burgeſs, as the ſaid E. Coney, in their proper perſons; but becauſe the juſtices and the court here are not yet adviſed to give their judgment upon the pre-miſes, day thereon is further given, as well to the ſaid J. Burgeſs, as to the ſaid E. Coney, in the ſtate in which now, &c. until the next goal delivery of the ſaid lord the king of New-gate, to be held for the county of Middleſex, on Wedneſday the 24th day of April, now next enſuing, to be held at Juſ-tice-hall aforeſaid, before the ſaid juſtices, to hear their judg-ment of and upon the premiſes; becauſe that the juſtices and the court here, of their judgment of and upon the ſaid premiſes here thereon, not as yet, &c. unto which day and place the court here, by the ſaid juſtices, &c. is adjourned to be held before the ſaid juſtices, &c. to give their judgment of and up-on the premiſes, &c.

*After ſeveral more continuances, this caſe was argued by coun-cil at the old Baily, before Holt, Lrd C. J. of the King's bench, and other judges there; It * was argued for the defendant, that the proſecutor could have no reſtitution after ſale in the market overt, for that thereby the property was altered; and cited ſir William Jones, 148, where the judges obiter agree the law to be ſo, 5 Co. 83, b, and Dalton's juſtice, 410: but the council for the proſecu-tor inſiſted on the expreſs words of the ſtatute 21. H. 8. c. 11; and 2 Inſtitute, 741, and the notes in the margin there; and as to Dalton, it was ſaid, he grounded his opinion on the Year book,*

*P. 320

3 D 2

12:

12 H. 8 10 b. which is before the ſtatute ; and on 3 Coke, 78 by which is nothing to the purpoſe, as to reſtitution on the ſtatute. the Chief juſtice ſaid it had been expreſsly adjudged in the time of Kelynge. Chief juſtice, that ſale in market overt, was no plea to a writ of reſtitution on this ſtatute, but that the proſecutor ſhould be reſtored, notwithſtanding ſuch ſale, and ſo it was adjudged in this caſe, and in five other writs of reſtitution, on five ſeveral other convictions of the ſame perſon. Vide Kelynge's rep. 35, 36, 48.

The King *againſt* Lever.

Michaelmas, the 4th of James the 2d.

One Lever was convicted of Barratry, at Lancaſter, and there fined 600l. & the judgment being removed into the K's. B. by writ of error, it was reverſed, and judgment given that he ſhould be reſtored, ad omnia que, &c. Whereupon this writ iſſued, reciting the judgment and reverſal, and ſuggeſting that the parties to whom it was directed had by colour of the judgment, ſeized goods and chattels of Lever's to the value of 1000l and therefore commands them to reſtore the ſame to him

***P. 321.**

Lancaſter, To wit. } ——THE king, &c. to Gervaiſe Staniford, gent. John Waite, gent. and twelve others, and to every of them greeting. Whereas at the late general quarter ſeſſion of the peace, held for the county Palatine of Lancaſter, on Thurſday, to wit, the nineteenth day of July, in the 29th year of the reign of the lord Charles the 2d, late king of England, before the juſtices of the ſaid lord the late king, aſſigned to preſerve the peace of the ſaid lord the king, in the ſaid county, and alſo to hear and determine divers felonies, treſpaſſes and other miſdeeds in the ſaid county, perpetrated, it was preſented that Robert Lever of Awerington, in the county of Lancaſter, gent. on the tenth day of July, in the twentyninth year of the reign of the lord Charles the ſecond, late king of England, &c. and at divers other days and times, as well before as after at Awerington in the ſaid county, was and as yet is a common barrator, and a daily, and publick diſturber of the peace of the ſaid lord the king, and alſo a common and turbulent challenger, railer and fighter, and a ſower of ſuits, and diſcords among his neighbours, and a common oppreſſor of his neighbours, and that the ſaid Robert Lever, at Awerington aforeſaid, and elſewhere, divers diſputes, controverſies, ſuits, and alſo railings, fights and diſcords among divers liege ſubjects of the ſaid lord the king, then and there, and elſewhere in the ſaid county of Lancaſter, unjuſtly did move, procure and ſtir up to the great oppreſſion of his neighbours, and to the diſturbance of the peace of the ſaid lord the king, and alſo againſt the form of divers ſtatutes, in ſuch caſe made and provided. Which * record and proceſs

there-

thereon, the ſaid lord the late king, for certain cauſes, before Certiorari to the judges of aſſize. William Montague, eſquire, chief baron of the Exchequer of the ſaid lord the late king, at Weſtminſter, chief juſtice to hear and determine all pleas, as well of the crown, as aſſizes of novel diſſeiſin mort d'anceſtor, juris utrum, certificates, attainders and all other pleas whatſoever, to be arrayed or proſecuted within the county Palatine of Lancaſter, to be held at Lancaſter or elſewhere in the ſaid county, and Timothy Littleton, knight, one of the barons of the Exchequer, of the ſaid lord the late king, at Weſtminſter aforeſaid, one other juſtice, to hear and determine all pleas, as well of the crown, as aſſizes of novel diſſeiſin, mort d'anceſtor, juris utrum, certificates, attainders, and all other pleas whatſoever, to be arrayed or proſecuted within the county Palatine of Lancaſter, to be held at Lancaſter aforeſaid, or elſewhere in the ſaid county, cauſed to come at the general ſeſſions of the aſſizes for the county Palatine of Lancaſter aforeſaid, at the city of Lancaſter, in the ſaid county, on Thurſday, to wit, the 6th day of September, in the 29th year of the reign of the ſaid lord the late king, in the form of law to be determined, &c. And whereas afterwards the proceſs was thereupon continued to the next general ſeſſion of the ſaid lord the late king, to hear and determine pleas of the crown in the ſaid county, held for the county aforeſaid, at the city of Lancaſter, in the ſaid county, on Saturday, to wit, the 16th day of March, in the 30th year of the reign of the ſaid lord the late king, before William Wilde, knight and baronet, one of the juſtices of the ſaid late lord the king, aſſigned to hold pleas before the ſaid late king himſelf, chief juſtice to hear and determine all pleas as well of the crown, as aſſizes of novel diſſeiſin, mort d'anceſtor, juris utrum, certificates and attainders, and all other pleas whatſoever, to be arrayed or proſecuted within the ſaid county Palatine of Lancaſter, to be held at Lancaſter aforeſaid, or elſewhere, in the ſaid county, and Vere Beche, eſquire, one of the barons of the Exchequer, of the ſaid lord the king at Weſtminſter, one other juſtice to hear and determine all pleas as well of the crown, as aſſizes of novel diſſeiſin, mort d'anceſtor, juris utrum, certificates, attainders, and all pleas whatſoever, to be arrayed or proſecuted within the county Palatine of Lancaſter, to be held at Lancaſter aforeſaid, or elſewhere in the ſaid county; and at the ſaid general ſeſſion, the ſaid R. Lever, by a jury of the country was tried and convicted of the treſpaſs, contempt and offence aforeſaid, in the indictment aforeſaid ſpecified, to him then charged as above, in the manner and form as by the indictment aforeſaid, above againſt him, then was ſuppoſed; whereupon then and there all and ſingular the premiſes being ſeen, and by the ſaid court then fully underſtood, it was then conſidered by the ſaid court, that the ſaid R. Lever ſhould pay to the ſaid lord the king, for his fine for the treſpaſs, contempt and offence aforeſaid, the ſum of 600*l.* of the lawful money of England, and that the ſaid R. Lever be taken, &c. which record, for certain cauſes we have afterwards cauſed to come before us, by our writ for correcting error in the record and proceſs of the judgment aforeſaid, &c. and whereas afterwards, to wit, in the term of St. Michæl, in the third year of our reign, before us at Weſtminſter, the ſaid R. Lever, perſonally appearing then and there in his proper perſon, did aſſign ſeveral errors in the record and proceſs of the judgment aforeſaid, and thereupon it was in ſuch wiſe proceeded that afterwards, to wit, in the term of St. Michael, in the 4th year of our reign, becauſe that it manifeſtly appeared

P.322. * to the court here that in the record and proceſs of the judgment aforeſaid, there was manifeſt error, and that the record and proceſs of the judgment aforeſaid, were not ſufficient in law any further to charge the ſaid R. Lever, of and upon the premiſes, it was conſidered by our ſaid court, that the judgment aforeſaid, for error in the record and proceſs of the ſaid judgment being found, be reverſed, annulled and held as entirely void, and that he the ſaid R. Lever, be reſtored to all which he hath loſt by occaſion of the ſaid judgment, and that he the ſaid R. Lever be diſcharged of the ſaid judgment, and that he go thereof without day, as fully appears of record in our court before us, and becauſe now on the behalf of the ſaid R. Lever, heavily complaining to us we have underſtood that you Gervaiſe Staniford, John Waite, &c. or ſome of you, or ſome one of you, have taken and ſeized goods and chattels of the ſaid R. Lever, to the value of 1000*l.* of the good and lawful money of England, under colour of the ſaid inſufficient and erroneous judgment given as aforeſaid, to the great damage of the ſaid R. Lever, we willing that juſtice be done to every perſon according to the laws and cuſtoms of this kingdom of England, command you in this behalf as it is juſt that you reſtore, and that each and every of you reſtore the goods and chattels of the ſaid R. Lever, by you or by any of you, or by any one of you, for the occaſion aforeſaid, taken and ſeized, or the true value of the ſame, to the ſaid R. Lever, without delay, and how you ſhall execute this our command, certify to us on the octave of St. Hilary, whereſoever we ſhall be in England, then returning to us this our writ. Witneſs R. Wright, knight, at Weſtminſter, the 16th day of November, in the 4th year of our reign.

Aſtry.

There is a note of this caſe, as to the writ of Error, 2 Lev. 223. But as to this writ of Reſtitution, it was quaſhed by the lord chief juſtice Holt, and the whole court of King's Bench; for that no ſuch
writ

writ lies to ſtrangers to the Record, but that a Scire Facias ſhould iſ-
ſue to make them parties, according to the caſe of Veſe and Harris,
Cro. Car. 328. This caſe of the writ of Reſtitution is reported,
1 Show, 261, 2 Salk. 587.

The King *againſt* Fletcher.

The King, } TO the keepers of our peace, aſſigned to hear
&c. and determine divers felonies, treſpaſſes and
other miſdeeds in our county of Cumberland perpetrated, and
to the ſheriff of the ſaid county, and to every of them, greeting.
Whereas, at the late general ſeſſion of our peace, held at
Cockermouth, on Wedneſday, in the week next after the feaſt
of Eaſter, to wit, on the 8th day of April, in the 22d year of
our reign, before William Briſcoe, J. B. and others, then
keepers of our peace ; and our juſtices aſſigned to hear and determine divers felonies, treſpaſſes and other miſdeeds in the
county aforeſaid perpetrated, it was preſented by the oath of
J. Cockplace, and 14 others, that L. Fletcher* of Deane, in the
county of Cumberland, clk. on the 6th day of Feb. in the 21ſt
year of our reign, with force and arms, and with ſtrong hand
at Ultack in the ſaid county, in and upon the poſſeſſion of
one tenement with the appurtenances, of one Lancelot Woodall, at U. aforeſaid, in the ſaid county did enter and make
an entry, (the ſaid L. W. being poſſeſſed thereof, until the
ſaid L. F. with force and arms, and with ſtrong hand did enter and make an entry) and him, the ſaid L. W. from his poſſeſſion did expel, eject and hold out, and then did hold out,
in contempt of us, and to the great damage of the ſaid L. W.
and againſt our peace, our crown and dignity ; and whereas
afterwards, to wit, at the ſame ſeſſion of our peace, held at
C. in the ſaid county, on the day and year aforeſaid, before
the keepers of our peace, and our juſtices, aſſigned to hear
and determine divers felonies, treſpaſſes and miſdeeds in the
ſaid county perpetrated, came the ſaid L. F. in his proper perſon, and then having heard the indictment aforeſaid, then
ſaid, that he was not guilty thereof, and of this put himſelf
upon the country, and the ſaid L. W. who as well, &c. did
the like, &c. therefore that a jury come thereupon before the
ſaid juſtices, &c. the ſame day was given to the parties aforeſaid there, &c. And whereas, at the general ſeſſion of our
peace, held at C. in the ſaid county, on Wedneſday, in the
week next after the feaſt of St. Thomas the martyr, to wit,
on

P. 323.
An inquiſiti-
on for forcible
entry,
was found at
the ſeſſions
againſt the
defendant
which he
traverſed,
and on the
trial was
found guilty,
and there-
upon the
juſtices
granted a
writ of reſ-
titution to
Woodall, on
whole poſ-
ſeſſion the
force was
committed,
afterwards
the record
was remov-
ed into the
King'sbench
and there-
upon a writ
of error was
brought, and
the judg-
ment was
reverſed,
then this
writ of reſ-
titution iſſu-
ed thence,
directed to
the juſtices
of peace and
ſheriff to
put the de-
fendant
Fletcher, in-
to poſſeſſion.

on the 15th day of July, in the 22d year of our reign, before W. Briſcoe and others, then keepers of our peace, and our juſtices aſſigned to hear and determine divers felonies, treſpaſſes and other miſdeeds, in the ſaid county perpetrated, came the ſaid L. W. who as well, &c. as the ſaid L. F. in his proper perſon, and the jurors by the ſheriff of the ſaid county, for that purpoſe impanelled being called to wit, John Birkett, and 11 others, in like manner came, who being tried and ſworn to ſpeak the truth of and concerning the premiſes, ſaid upon their oath, that the ſaid L. F. was guilty of the treſpaſs, contempt and entry aforeſaid, in the ſaid indictment above ſpecified in the manner and form as above againſt him was ſuppoſed. Therefore it was conſidered by the court there, that the ſaid L. F. ſhould be taken and ſhould ſatisfy us for his fines, by occaſion of the treſpaſs, contempt and entry aforeſaid, which Lancelot then and there preſent in court did pray, that he ſhould be admitted to a fine with the ſaid lord the king, for the occaſion aforeſaid, and thereupon to be put in our mercy, and the fine of the ſaid Lancelot was aſſeſſed by the ſaid juſtices to 12d. to our uſe and behoof; which record we for certain cauſes afterwards, have cauſed to come before us to be determined. And whereas afterwards, to wit, in this ſame term before us at Weſtminſter, the ſaid L. F. perſonally appearing then and there in his proper perſon, produced our certain writ for correcting errors in the record and proceſs of the judgment aforeſaid; and whereas alſo, becauſe that it manifeſtly appeared to the court here, that in the record and proceſs of the judgment aforeſaid, there was manifeſt error; and that the record and proceſs aforeſaid, of the judgment aforeſaid, was not ſufficient in law to charge the ſaid L. F. any further of and upon the premiſes; as the ſaid L. F. upon the allowance of our ſaid writ, for correcting errors in our court before us, in the ſaid term, hath alledged; it was conſidered then and there, by our ſaid court, that the judgment aforeſaid, for the errors by the ſaid L. F. in the record and proceſs of the judgment aforeſaid, aſſigned, and others in the ſaid record and proceſs of the judgment aforeſaid being found

*P. 324. *be reverſed, annulled and held as entirely void; and that he the ſaid L. F. be reſtored to all things which he hath loſt by occaſion of the ſaid judgment, and that he the ſaid L. F. be diſcharged from the ſaid judgment, and that he go thereof without day, as fully appears of record in our court before us. And becauſe now, on the behalf of the ſaid L. F. heavily complaining to us, we have underſtood, that you the ſaid juſtices under colour of the ſaid inſufficient and erroneous judgment given before you, by a certain writ of reſtitution, to you the ſaid ſheriff, or to your officers in this behalf directed, have cauſed the ſaid tenements with the appurtenances to be reſeized, and have put the ſaid L. W. in full poſſeſſion thereof, according to the form and ef-

fect

ſeſt of the writ aforeſaid, to the great damage of the ſaid L. F. and we willing that juſtice be done to every perſon according to the law and cuſtom of this our kingdom of England, command you and each of you, in this behalf as is juſt; that if by virtue of our ſaid writ of reſtitution, to you the ſaid ſheriff, or to your officers in this behalf directed, you have cauſed the ſaid tenements with the appurtenances to be reſeized, and have cauſed the ſaid L. W. to be put in full poſſeſſion thereof, according to the force, form and effect of the ſaid writ, then that you cauſe the tenements aforeſaid, with the appurtenances to be reſeized, and that without delay you cauſe the ſaid L. F. again to be put into his full and peaceable poſſeſſion of the tenements aforeſaid, with the appurtenances, our ſaid writ of reſtitution, ſo by you the ſaid juſtices, to you the ſaid ſheriff or your officers, before thereupon directed, in any wiſe notwithſtanding, and if by colour of our ſaid writ of reſtitution you have not cauſed the tenements aforeſaid, with the appurtenances to be reſeized, nor have cauſed the ſaid L. W. to be put into full poſſeſſion thereof, then altogether that you omit to reſeize the tenements aforeſaid, with the appurtenances, and to put the ſaid L. W. into the full poſſeſſion thereof, and how you ſhall execute this our command, certify to us on the morrow of the Holy Trinity, whereſoever we ſhall then be in England, then returning to us this our writ. Witneſs Francis Bacon, at Weſtminſter, the 25th day of May, in the 23d year of our reign.

The King againſt Jackſon.

The King, &c. } TO the keepers of our peace, and to our juſtices aſſigned to hear and determine divers felonies, treſpaſſes and other miſdeeds in the ſaid county of Cumberland perpetrated, and to the ſheriff of the ſaid county, and to every of them greeting. Whereas at the late general ſeſſions of our peace, held at Cockermouth, in the ſaid county on Wedneſday, in the week next after the feaſt of St. Thomas the martyr, to-wit, on the 15th day of July, in the 23d year of our reign, before William Briſco, John Barwis and others, then keepers of our peace and our juſtices aſſigned

An indictment of forcible entry and forcible detainer was found at the ſeſſions againſt the defendant who thereupon (by proteſtation that to he is not

3 E

to hear and determine divers felonies, treſpaſſes and other miſdeeds in the ſaid county perpetrated, by the oath of William
Brownrigg and 14 others, good and lawful men of the ſaid
county, ſworn and impannelled to enquire for the body of the
ſaid * county, it was preſented that Henry Jackſon, of Ul-
lack, in the pariſh of Deane, in the county of C. yeoman,
on the 28th day of September, in the 21ſt year of our reign,
with force and arms, &c. at U. aforeſaid, in the pariſh of D.
aforeſaid, in the county of C. aforeſaid, in and upon one
Elinor Woodall, in the peace of God and of our peace then
and there being, did make an aſſault and affray, and alſo then
and there with force and arms, and unlawfully into one meſſuage and 40 acres of land, meadow and paſture, with the
appurtenances commonly called the Hill tenement at U. aforeſaid, in the pariſh of D. aforeſaid, in the county of C. aforeſaid, then and there in the quiet and peaceable poſſeſſion of the
ſaid E. W. being, and then being the freehold of the ſaid
E. W. with force and arms, &c. unlawfully and with a ſtrong
hand did enter and make an entry, and her the ſaid E. W.
from her poſſeſſion thereof then and there, at U. aforeſaid,
in the pariſh of D. aforeſaid, in the county of C. aforeſaid,
with force and arms, unlawfully and with ſtrong hand, did
hold out, and as yet doth hold out, to the great damage of
the ſaid E. W. in contempt of us, and of our peace, our
crown and dignity, and alſo againſt the form of the ſtatute
in ſuch caſe, thereupon lately made and provided; and whereas afterwards at the general ſeſſion of our peace of the ſaid
county held at C. in the ſaid county on the Wedneſday in the
week next after the feaſt of St. Michael, to wit, on the 7th
day of October, in the 22d year of our reign aforeſaid, before Thomas Lamplugh, and others, then keepers of our peace
and juſtices aſſigned to preſerve the peace in the ſaid county,
and alſo to hear and determine divers felonies, treſpaſſes,
and other miſdeeds, in the ſaid county perpetrated, came the
ſaid H. J. in his proper perſon, and then and there having
heard the ſaid indictment by proteſtation, then ſaid that he
was not guilty thereof, but ſubmitted himſelf to a fine with
us, and by the favour of the ſaid court, and by the ſaid juſtices the fine of the ſaid H. was aſſeſſed at ſix pence, which
record we for certain cauſes, have cauſed to be ſent before us
to be determined, and we in our court before us on the behalf of the ſaid E. W. heavily complaining to us, have
underſtood that altho ſhe as aforeſaid, is not poſſeſſed of
the ſaid meſſuage and 40 acres of land, meadow and paſture aforeſaid, with the appurtenances, neverthele ſs reſtitution
thereof, as yet remains to be made to the ſaid E. W. ſupplica-

ting

ting us to give her ſuitable remedy in this behalf, and we being willing that the ſtatute aforeſaid, according to the form of
the ſame, be fulfilled in all things, command you and every of
you, that you cauſe the ſaid meſſuage, with 40 acres of land,
meadow and paſture to be re-ſeized, and that you cauſe the ſaid
E.W. to be put into the peaceable and full poſſeſſion of the ſaid
meſſuage and 40 acres of land, meadow and paſture aforeſaid,
according to the form of the ſaid ſtatute, and how you ſhall
execute this our command, certify to us, from the day of St.
Michael, in three weeks, whereſoever we ſhall then be in
England, then returning to us this our writ. Witneſs Francis Bacon, at Weſtminſter, the 5th day of July, in the 23d
year of our reign.

Convictions

* *The* King *against* J. S. *and others.*

Easter, the 35th of Charles 2d. *Roll* 154.

Conviction at the Quarter Sessions, upon oath of two witnesses, for hunting and killing a red deer, in a wood where red deer was usually kept, contra for mam statuti. The subsequent statutes in England ar 3 W & M. c. 10 & the 3 , &c. 3. c. 30.

BE it remembered, that at the general Quarter-sessions of the peace of the lord the king, held at the town of Hertford, in and for the said county, on Monday in the first week next after the Epiphany of our Lord, to wit, on the 8th day of January, in the 34th year, &c. before C. C. kt. &c. and others their fellows, justices of the said lord the now king, assigned to preserve the peace in and for the said county; and also to hear and determine divers felonies, trespasses and other misdeeds in the said county perpetrated, comes one James Lewin, and gives the justices aforesaid here to understand and to be informed, that one J. S. of, &c. ard T. W. of, &c. on the 5th day of January, in the 34th year aforesaid, with force and arms, &c. at H. in the county of H. aforesaid, unlawfully did hunt a certain red-deer, in a certain wood of the most noble John earl of Sarum, commonly called Hoddesdon-woods, in the county of H. aforesaid, where red-deer then were, and before that time usually were kept, without the licence or consent of the said most noble J. earl of S. possessor and proprietor of the said wood, or of any other person specially entrusted with the custody thereof; and the said red-deer then out of the said wood did chase and drive away unto, &c. in the county aforesaid, and the said red-deer at, &c. did kill, against the form of the statute in such case made and provided. And thereupon upon the examination of two credible witnesses, testifying upon their oaths, of and upon the premises, it appears to the justices aforesaid, at the session of the peace aforesaid, held in and for the said county, that the said J. S. and W. T. are guilty and convicted, and that each of them is guilty and convicted of the said premises; and the said justices here declare and adjudge them the said J. S. and T. W. and each of them, to be convicted thereof; therefore it is considered by the justices aforesaid, at the session of the peace aforesaid here, that each of them, the said J. S, and
T. W.

T. W. pay the fum of 20*l*. to wit, one moiety thereof to the
faid earl of Sarum, and the other moiety thereof to the faid
James Lewin, according to the form and effect of the faid flatute.

---

* *The* King *against* White *and others.*   *P. 327.

Michaelmas, 35th Charles 2d.

Essex, } BE it remembered, that on the 11th day of July,   Conviction
to wit, }   in the 35th year, &c. one Laurence Herd, of, &c.   before one
comes in his proper perfon, before John Meade, of, &c. efq;   juftice of
then and as yet one of the juftices of the faid lord the king,   peace, on
affigned to preferve the peace of the faid lord the king in the   the oath of
faid county of Effex, at Chelmsford in the faid county, and   one witnefs,
gives the faid juftice of the peace to underftand, and to be   for hunting
informed, that one Jn. White, of, &c. T. W. of, &c. J. W.   and chafing
of, &c. and H. B. of, &c. on the 12th day of February,   a fallow deer
in the thirtyfifth year aforefaid, in a certain park, then   in a park.
and long before, and as yet, of one Catherine Turner, widow, called Newman-hall-park, in the parifh of Quinden,
in the county of Effex, aforefaid, then, and long before, and
as yet being land in which fallow-deer then were, and long
before, and as yet have been ufually kept, unlawfully did
hunt and chafe the fallow-deer there, without the confent of
the faid Catherine Turner, then proprietor of the faid park,
againft the form of the ftatute in fuch cafe made and provided.
And afterwards, to wit, on the faid 11th day of July, in the
35th year aforefaid, one credible witnefs, to wit, William
Catimer, of, &c. came before the faid J. Meade, then and
there as aforefaid being a juftice of the peace at Chelmsford,
in the faid county of Effex, and before the faid juftice of the
peace, upon his oath upon the Holy Gofpel of God, to him
then and there by the faid juftices of the faid lord the king of
the peace, given and adminifter'd according to the command of
the faid ftatute, did depofe, fwear and fay, that the faid J. W.
T. W. J. W. and H. B. on the faid 12th day of February,
in the 35th year aforefaid, in the faid park and land afore-
                                                            faid,

said, one fallow-deer of the said C. T. in the parish of Quinden aforesaid, unlawfully did hunt and chase, without the consent of the said C. T. then proprietor of the said park, or of any other person, having the custody of fallow deer there, and thereupon the said J. W. T. W. J. W. and H. B. on the said 11th day of July, in the 35th year aforesaid, at Chelmsford aforesaid, before the said justice of the peace, by the oath of one witness aforesaid, according to the form of the said statute thereupon made and provided, are convicted, and each and every of them is convicted; and for the offence aforesaid, each and every of them, to wit, the said J. W. T. W. J. W. and H.B. according to the form of the said statute, severally hath forfeited the sum of twenty pounds, one moiety thereof to the said L. H. the informer as aforesaid in this behalf, and the other moiety thereof to the said C. T. the proprietor as aforesaid, of the said fallow-deer. In witness whereof, I, the said justice, have set my hand hereunto, on the day, year and place first above mentioned.

John Meade.

---

*P. 328.

* The King *against* Dobson.

Hilary, 32d. & 33d. Charles 2d.   *Roll* 81.

Conviction before one justice, for hunting and killing a fallow deer.

Cumberland, To wit. } **B**E it remembered that on the 3d day of September, in the 32d year of the reign of the lord Charles the 2d, late king of England, &c. one Benjamin Granger, of, &c. gent. comes before John Aglionby, esquire, one of the justices of the lord the king, assigned to preserve the peace of the said lord the king, in the said county of Cumberland, at G. in the said county, and gives the said justice of the peace to understand and to be informed, that one James Dobson, late of, &c. J. B. late of, &c. L. M. late of, &c. on the 25th day of August, in the 32d year of the reign of the said lord the now king aforesaid, in a certain park, then of the most noble Hen. duke of Norfolk, called G. park, in the parish of G. aforesaid, then and long before, and as yet being land in which deer then were, and long before usually were kept, unlawfully did hunt, and a certain fallow deer of the said duke, then being in the said park, did kill, take and carry away, without the consent of the said duke,

then

then proprietor of the said park, or of Andrew Huddleston, esquire, then being especially entrusted with the custody of the said park, against the form of the statute in such case made and provided, and afterwards, to wit, on the said 3d day of September, in the 32d year aforesaid, two credible witnesses, to wit, J. H. of, &c. and T. B. of, &c. came before the said justice of the peace, at G. aforesaid, and before the said justice of the peace upon their oath, upon the holy Gospel of God, to them then and there, by the said justice of the peace, according to the command of the said statute given and administered, did depose, swear and say, and each of them then and there did depose, swear and say, upon the said oath, that the said J. D. J. B. and L. M. on the said 25th day of August, in the 32d year aforesaid, in the said park and land, of the said duke of Norfolk, in the parish of G. aforesaid, unlawfully did hunt, and the said deer called a fallow deer, of the said duke, then in the said park or land, did take, kill and carry away, without the consent of the said duke, then proprietor of the said park, or of the said A. H. esquire, then specially entrusted with the custody of the said park and land as aforesaid, and thereupon they the said J. D. J. B. and L. M. on the said 3d day of September, in the 32d year aforesaid, at G. aforesaid, before the said justice of the peace, by the oath of the said two witnesses, according to the form of the said statute, thereupon made and provided, are convicted, and each and every of them is convicted, and for the said offence, each and every of them, the said J. D. J. B. and L. M. according to the form of the statute aforesaid, severally have forfeited the sum of 20l. one moiety thereof to the said B. G. the informer, in this behalf as aforesaid, and the other moiety thereof to the said duke, the proprietor of the said fallow deer as aforesaid, &c.

---

* Stiles *against* Felton *and others.*   *P. 329.

Suffolk, } BE it remembered, that on the 1st day of March,
To wit. } in the 23d year of the reign of the lord Charles the 2d, the now king of England, &c. T. Styles of, &c. at Marlford, in the said county, in his proper person, came before me, S. Allton, esquire, one of the justices of the said lord the king, assigned to preserve the peace in the said county, and then and there gave me to understand, and to be informed of the unlawful hunting of a certain fallow-deer, in the

park

Conviction upon the oaths of several witnesses, for hunting a deer in a park.

park of one Anthony Gaudy, esquire, within the parish, &c. in the county of Suffolk aforesaid, commonly called Grimfted-park, by H. Felton of, &c. baronet, A. Felton of, &c. esquire, J. Golfe, of, &c. labourer, J. Howard, of, &c. W. Numi, of, &c. done and committed without the licence and consent of the said Anthony Gaudy, esq; possessor and proprietor of the said park, or of any other person specially entrusted with the custody thereof, and afterwards to wit, on the said 1st day of March, in the 23d year of the reign of the said lord Charles the 2d the now king of England, &c. aforesaid, at Marlford aforesaid, in the said county of Suffolk, before me the said S. Alston, esquire, being as aforesaid, one of the justices of the said lord the king, assigned to preserve the peace in the said county, and at the prosecution of the said T. Styles, came J. Knight of, &c. T. Fenn of, &c. and J. Sadd, of, &c. being witnesses credible and worthy of credit, in their proper persons, and then and there before me the said justice of the peace, &c. upon the Holy Gospel of God, were sworn, and each and every of them was sworn, and did take his corporal oath by me the said justice of the peace, &c. to them and to each and every of them, administered by the authority of a certain statute, made and provided in the parliament of the said lord the now king, held at Westminster, in the said county of Middlesex, on the 8th day of May, in the 13th year of his reign; and they the said J. K. T. F. and J. F. so as aforesaid, being sworn, then and there upon their oaths did say, depose and swear, and each and every of them then and there before me the said justice of the peace, &c. did say, depose and swear upon his oath aforesaid, that the said H. F. A. F. J. G. J. H. and W. N. after the first day of August, in the 13th year of the reign of the said lord the now king aforesaid, and within six months next before the said information to me, the said justice so as aforesaid given, to wit, upon the 26th day of September, in the 22d year of the reign of the said lord the now king, with force and arms, &c. unlawfully and unjustly, in the park of the said Anthony Gaudy, esquire, called G. park, in the parish of T. St. Martin, in the county of Suffolk aforesaid, without the licence or consent of the said A. G. then being possessor and proprietor of the said park, or of any other person entrusted with the custody of the said park, one fallow deer, being in the said park, did hunt, and each and every of them did hunt, whereby I the said justice, to preserve the peace, &c. do declare and adjudge them the said H. F. A. F. J. G. J. H. and W. N. to be guilty and convicted, and each and every of them to be guilty and convicted of the said unlawful hunting, in the said park, of the

said

said A. G. esquire, without the licence or consent of the said A. G. then and as yet possessor and proprietor of the said park, or of any other person entrusted with the custody of the said park, * against the form and effect of the said statute, and therefore they the said H. F. A. F. J. G. J. H. and W. N. and each and every of them by me the said justice to preserve the peace, &c. by force of the said statute of the said unlawful hunting against the form of the said statute are convicted, and each and every of them separately by himself is convicted. In witness whereof to this present record of the conviction aforesaid, I have set my hand and seal at Marlford aforesaid, the day and year first above written.

*P. 330.

Samuel Alston, (L S).
one of the justices of the lord the king of the said county.

The King against Dennis.

To wit. **H**ERETOFORE to wit, at the general session of the peace held at the castle of Exeter in the said county on the 30th day of the month of September, in the 42d year of the reign of the lady Elizabeth the late queen of England, &c. before W. Courtenay, knight, W. S. knight, J. H. serjeant at law and others, their fellows justices of the said lady the queen, assigned to preserve the peace in the said county, and also to hear and determine divers felonies, trespasses, and other misdeeds in the said county perpetrated, there was exhibited in the open court at same session of the peace by the said J. H. serjeant at law, and under the hand and seal of the said J. the record of the conviction of Thomas Dennis of Y. in the said county, husbandman, for certain trespasses and contempts against the form of the statute, enacted against using a dagg or hand gun, the tenor of which conviction follows, in these words, to wit, "*Devonshire, to wit, on the 29th day of July, in the 42d year of the reign of the lady Elizabeth, by the grace of God, the now queen of England, &c. Thomas Dennis, of Telhampton in the county of Devon, was brought before me John Heale, serjeant at law, one of her majesty's justices of the peace for the said county, by John Welsh, of Y. aforesaid, yeoman, for that he the said T. D. in the full court of the manor of Telhampton, in the parish of Y. aforesaid, holden, sithence her majesty's last general pardon, had secretly about him a pistol (far under*

Conviction
before a jus-
tice of the
peace (on
th defen-
dant's con-
fession) for
carrying a-
bout him a
dagg or hand
gun, against
th statute;
the justice
made a war-
rant and
committed
him to gaol
and returned
the convicti-
on to the
quarter sessi-
ons.

3 F

the

*the length mentioned in the statute, in that behalf made) by some called a dagg or hand gun, to the offence and disturbance of her majesty's subjects then assembled, and upon examination before me being the next justice of the peace, within the said county, and by the confession of the said Dennis, that was found to be true, that he the said T. Dennis had secretly about him, sithence the said pardon, a pistol under the length aforesaid, by some called a dagg or hand gun, contrary to the laws and statutes in that behalf made, wherefore I do by these presents commit the said T. Dennis to the goal of the castle of Exeter, there to remain until the said T. D. hath satisfied or paid the penalty or forfeiture, for the said offence the one moiety to her majesty, the other moiety to the said J. Welsh, and I do hereby will and command the goaler of the said goal, and his lawful deputy in that behalf to take the said T. Dennis into * his custody, and keep him 'til he be deliver'd according to the laws and statutes of this realm. In witness whereof I have hereunto set my hand and seal the day and year first above written."* Whereupon the said T. D. being called appeared at the said session, and by the consideration and by the judgment of the court, was committed for the said trespass and contempt to the said goal of the lady the queen, of the castle of Exeter, there to remain until that he should pay the sum of ten pounds of the lawful money of England, forfeited by the said statute, to the use as well of the said lady the queen, as of the said J. Welsh, of Y. aforesaid, according to the tenor and effect of the said statute. Afterwards to wit, on the 3d day of October, in the 42d year of the reign of the said lady the queen aforesaid, the said T. D. satisfied and paid T. R. knight, then sheriff of the said county, the said sum of ten pounds to the use aforesaid, and thereupon was discharged and delivered out of the said goal, which record the lady the now queen, for certain causes hath caused to come before her to be determined, &c. And now to wit, on the Wednesday, next after fifteen days of Easter, in this same term before the lady the queen at Westminster, comes the said T. D. in his proper person, and having had oyer of the record of the conviction aforesaid, saith that he doth not apprehend, that the said lady the queen, nor the said J. W. who as well, &c. ought to have the said 10l. in the said record specified, or one penny thereof; because he saith, that the said record is not sufficient in law to put the said T. D. to answer to the said record, and that no process against him upon the said record by the law of the land, ought to be made, for this, to wit, because that it doth not appear by the said record, that the said J. Welsh took the said pistol, called a dagg or hand gun, about the said T. D. nor at what day, year, and certain place, the said T. D. had the said pistol about him, as by the law and statute thereupon made and provided, ought to be made. Whereupon for the insufficiency of the said record, he prays judgment, and that

**P. 331.*

Defend nt appeared at the sessions & was committed to the goal, till he paid the fine, afterwards defendant pays the fine to the sheriff & is discharg'd out of custody, the record is afterwards certified to the Queen's Bench, defendant appears there, and demurs to the record.

he

he of the premises, by the court here may be discharged, &c. Whereupon all and singular the premises being seen, and by the court here understood, because that it seems to the court here, that the said record is not sufficient in law, as the said T. D. for his discharge from the premises above, by pleading hath alledged, it is confidered, that the said T. go thereof without day, &c.

Judgment quod eat fine die.

* * *

* The King *against* Roberts.   *P. 332.

Michaelmas, 27th Charles 2d.

County of the city of Canterbury, to wit. } BE it remembered, that on the 24th day of June, in the 27th year of the reign of the lord Charles the 2d, the now king of England, &c. we, Squire Beverton the elder, gent. and T. Fidge, gent. two justices of the said lord the king, assigned to preserve his peace in the said city, and in the county of the said city, and W. Pysing, gent. sheriff of the said city, at the heavy complaint and humble petition of Richard Harding, of the city aforesaid, vintner, in our proper persons repaired to the publick street, called High-street, in the parish of St. Mary, Bredman, and of all Saints, in the ward of Westgate, of the said city, and in the county of the said city, and then and there we found Joseph Roberts, of, &c. gent. W. Porter, of, &c. H. Mason, of, &c. and R. Ellis, of, &c. and other malefactors and disturbers of the peace of the said lord the now king, to the number of 200 persons and more, to us entirely unknown, armed in a warlike manner, to wit, with swords and staves, and with other arms as well offensive as defensive, unlawfully, riotously, and routously assembled and collected, to disturb the peace of the said lord the now king, and to have and bring the said Richard Harding and Elizabeth his wife into difgrace, contempt and public derifion ; and by the procurement of the said J. Roberts, the said W. Porter, then and there did clothe himself in womens apparel, and the said H. Mason and R. Ellis, then and there did clothe themfelves in unusual apparel, and so being apparelled by the procurement and instigation of the said J. Roberts, (who then and there did affociate himself with them) then and there in the said street, with force and arms, hither and thither,

Record of conviction before two justices of the peace & the sheriff of the county upon their view for riding Skymington.

3 F 2   unlawfully

unlawfully, riotously and routously, and with a great clamour did ride. calling and declaring that their riding aforesaid, was riding of Skymington, for the said R. H. and Eliz. his wife, and did strike each other there, and did speak, utter and pronounce then and there openly and publicly, and with a loud voice, obscene and scandalous words, and these unlawful riotous acts they the said, W. P. H. M. and R. E. by the unlawful procurement and instigation of the said J. R. then and there with force and arms, unlawfully did commit and perpetrate, to the abuse and derision of the said R. H. and E. his wife, and in contempt of the said lord the now king, and of his laws, (although they by us S. Beverton and T. Fidge, then being two justices of the said lord the king, assigned to preserve the peace in the said city, and in the county of the said city, were commanded to abstain from the perpetration of such their unlawful and riotous acts) against the form of the statute in such case lately made and provided, and against the peace of the said lord the now king his crown and dignity, &c. and we the said S. B. and T. F. two of the justices of the said lord the king, assigned to preserve the peace in the county of the said city, them the said J. Roberts, W. Porter, H. * Mason and R. Ellis, of the unlawful meeting, assembly and riot aforesaid, by our view and record have convicted, and we, them the said J. Roberts, W. Porter, H. Mason and R. Ellis, and the other persons so unlawfully and riotously assembled, then and there, as much as in us lay, and with the whole power of the constables, and of other persons of the said city, (whom we summoned to our aid,) endeavoured to arrest, and to bring to the next goal of the said lord the king, in the county of the said city, as being convicted by our view and record, of the unlawful assembly and riot aforesaid, there to remain until that they should pay fine to the said lord the king thereupon, but by reason of the number of the persons so unlawfully, riotously and routously assembled, we were not able; but the said J. R. W. P. H. M. and R. E. and the other persons so unlawfully, riotously and routously. assembled, from us with force and arms did escape. In witness whereof, to this our present record we have put our seals, dated at the said city of Canterbury, the day and year aforesaid, &c.

P. 333.

On motion to quash this conviction, the court adjudged the conviction good, and affirmed it, and fined Roberts, the ringleader 40l. and the rest 10l. a piece, it is reported, 3 Keble, 587.

Proceedings

Proceedings upon the Statute of Weſtminſter, 2d chap. 46, againſt perſons for throwing down fences in the night.

The King *and* Street *againſt the Inhabitants of* Hil-vil, *and others.*

Trinity, 30th Charles 2d.

Writ to the ſheriff to diſtrain the adjacent vills.

Recital of a former writ to enquire who were the malefac-tors that proſtrated the hedges, &c.

Dorſet, } THE lord the king hath ſent to the ſheriff of
to wit, } the county aforeſaid, his writ cloſe in theſe words : Charles the Second, &c. To the ſheriff of Dorſet, greeting. Whereas lately by-our writ, iſſuing out of our court of Chancery, we commanded John Every, eſquire, late ſheriff of the county of Dorſet aforeſaid, by the oaths of good and lawful men of the county aforeſaid, by whom the truth of the matter might be the better known, diligently to enquire, what malefactors and diſturbers of our peace, at the pariſh of Hermitage, in the county aforeſaid, with force and arms, the hedges, ditches, gates, rails, and ſtiles of John Street, gent. there lately by him raiſed and erected by night or at ſuch time as they believed their deeds could not be known, had proſtra-ted, and other wrongs to him had done, to the great damage of the ſaid John Street, and againſt our peace, and if the ſaid John Street * ſhould give ſecurity to the ſaid late ſheriff of proſecuting his complaint, then that the ſaid late ſheriff ſhould put by gages and ſafe pledges, all thoſe whom he ſhould find guilty thereof, that they ſhould be before us on the morrow of the Holy Trinity laſt paſt, whereſoever we ſhould then be in England, to anſwer as well to us for the breaking of our peace, as to the ſaid John Street of the treſpaſs aforeſaid ; and the ſaid late ſheriff hath returned to us at that day, a cer-tain inquiſition indented, taken before him at Dorcheſter in the ſame county, on the 9th day of July, in the 29th year of our reign, by virtue of the ſaid writ to him directed, and annexed to the ſaid inquiſition, by which it was found by the oath of twelve jurors, good and lawful men of the ſaid

* P. 334

Recital of the inquiſi-tion, taken by virtue of the recited writ, by the for-mer ſheriff

county

county of Dorſet, that the ſaid J. Street in the ſaid writ named on the firſt day of January, in the 24th year of our reign, and always afterwards until then, was intereſted, and then was intereſted, for the remainder of a certain term of 31 years, then and as yet to come and unexpired, of and in a certain waſte or common, commonly called Hermitage-Common, containing by eſtimation 300 acres or thereabouts, ſituate, lying and being within the pariſh of Hermitage in the county aforeſaid, parcel of the manor of Fotherington in the ſaid county, and alſo parcel of the dutchy of Cornwall; and that he the ſaid John Street, being as aforeſaid intereſted, afterwards, to wit, on the 1ſt day of June in the 25th year of the our reign, at Hermitage aforeſaid, in the county aforeſaid, the ſaid waſte with hedges, ditches, gates, rails, and ſtiles did incloſe, and after the incloſure thereof, certain malefactors and diſturbers of the peace, to the jurors aforeſaid altogether unknown, afterwards, to wit, on the 10th day of June, in the 25th year of our reign, at Hermitage aforeſaid, in the county aforeſaid, by night, or at ſuch time as they believed their deeds could not be known, with force and arms, &c. 12 perches of the ſaid ditches in and about the waſte aforeſaid, lately before by him the ſaid John Street raiſed and erected, had proſtrated; and that certain other malefactors and diſturbers of our peace, to the jurors aforeſaid altogether unknown, afterwards, to wit, in the 26th year of our reign, at the pariſh of Hermitage aforeſaid, in the county aforeſaid, by night, or at ſuch time as they believed their deeds could not be known, with force and arms, &c. 15 other perches of dead hedges, gates and ſtiles, lately before by him the ſaid John Street, in and about the waſte aforeſaid, raiſed and erected, had proſtrated and thrown down; and that afterwards, to wit, in the 27th year of our reign, certain other malefactors and diſturbers of our peace, to the jurors aforeſaid in the like manner unknown, at the pariſh of H. aforeſaid, by night, or at ſuch time as they believed their deeds could not be known, with force and arms, &c. 20 perches of dead hedges and gates, and ſtiles, lately by him the ſaid John Street, in and about the ſaid waſte, in like manner raiſed and erected, had proſtrated and thrown down; and that upon the 20th day of April laſt paſt, certain other malefactors and diſturbers of our peace, to the jurors aforeſaid in like manner unknown, at the pariſh of Hermitage aforeſaid, in the county aforeſaid, by night, or at ſuch time as they believed their deeds could not be known, with force and arms, &c. 10 perches of hedges and ditches, and gates and rails, late before by him the ſaid John Street in and about the ſaid waſte, in like manner raiſed and erected, had proſtrated and cut down; and as by inſpection of the ſaid writ, and of the ſaid inquiſition by the ſaid late ſheriff returned, by virtue

* of the ſaid writ before us, and there of record now remaining

ing, to us manifeſtly appears; we command you that you do not omit by reaſon of any liberty in your bailiwick, but that you diſtrain the vills next adjacent to the ſaid hedges, ditches, gates, rails, and ſtiles ſo proſtrated as aforeſaid; alſo we command you, that by the oath of good and lawful men of your co. by whom the truth of the matter may be the better known, you diligently enquire, what damages the ſaid John Street hath ſuſtained, by occaſion of the proſtration of the ſaid hedges, ditches, gates, rails and ſtiles; and that you reſtore thoſe damages to the ſaid John Street, and how you ſhall have executed this our command certify to us, from the day of Ealter, in fifteen days, whereſoever we ſhall then be in England, under your ſeal, and the ſeals of thoſe by whoſe oath you ſhall take the ſaid inquiſition, then returning to us this our writ. Witneſs, K. Raynsford at Weſtminſter, the 22d day of February, in the 30th year of our reign. At which fifteen days of Eaſter, Robert Pelham, eſquire, ſheriff of the ſaid county, before the lord the king, at Weſtminſter, returns to the lord the king, as follows, to wit; Mainpernors of the inhabitants of Holneſt, Hillvill, Sydling, Hartley, Great Minterne, and Middlemarſh, in the within written county of Dorſet, being the vills next adjacent to the ſaid hedges, ditches, gates, rails and ſtiles, John Doe and Richard Roe, the iſſues of the inhabitants of the vill of Holneſt aforeſaid, 10l. the iſſues of the inhabitants of the vill of Hillvill aforeſaid, 10l. the iſſues of the inhabitants of the vill of Sydling aforeſaid, 10l. the iſſues of the inhabitants of the vill of Hartley aforeſaid, 10l. the iſſues of the inhabitants of the vill of Great Minterne aforeſaid, 10l. the iſſues of the inhabitants of the vill of Middlemarſh aforeſaid, 10l. and further I certify to the lord the king, that, that writ was delivered to me ſo late, that by reaſon of the ſhortneſs of the time, I could not reſtore to the within named John Street, the damages in the inquiſition annexed to this writ; the reſidue of the execution of this writ, appears in the ſaid inquiſition, Robert Pelham, eſquire, ſheriff; Inquiſition indented, taken at Dorcheſter, in the county of Dorſet, on the 13th day of April, in the 30th year of the reign of our lord Charles the 2d, the now king of England, &c. before me Robert Pelham, eſquire, ſheriff of the ſaid county, by virtue of the writ of the lord the king, to this writ annexed, by the oath of John Cardrowe, and 11 others, good and lawful men of the ſaid county, who being ſworn and charged upon the premiſes, in the ſaid writ to this inquiſition annexed, ſay upon their oath, that J. Street, in the ſaid writ, to this inquiſition annexed, mentioned, hath ſuſtained damages by the occaſion of the premiſes in the ſaid writ mentioned, to 360l. In witneſs whereof, as well I the ſaid ſheriff, as the ſaid jurors, to this inquiſition have

ſeverally

feverally put our feals, on the day, year and place aforefaid, Robert Pelham, efquire, fheriff, (L.S.) &c. And now, to wit, on the Friday next after the morrow of the Holy Trinity, in this fame term, before the lord the king, at Weftminfter, come Nathaniel Rawles and Robert Day, two inhabitants of the vill of Holneft aforefaid, in the name of all the inhabitants of the faid vill, C. Whiffen and A. Flambert, two inhabitants of the vill of Hilvill aforefaid, in the name of all the inhabitants of the faid vill, T. Hayne and T. Croade, two inhabitants of the vill of Sydling aforefaid, in the name of all the inhabitants of the faid vill, T. Scutt and W. Fox, two inhabitants of the vill of Hartley aforefaid, in the name of all the inhabitants of the faid vill, * R. Harris and W. Gould, two inhabitants of the vill of Great Minterne aforefaid, in the name of all the inhabitants of the faid vill, and W. Granger and J. Granger, two inhabitants of the vill of Middlemarfh aforefaid, in the name of all the inhabitants of the faid vill, by William Eyre, their attorney, and having had oyer of the faid writ of diftringas and the return thereto made, they the faid N. Rawles and R. Day, two inhabitants of the vill of Holneft aforefaid, in the name of all the inhabitants of the faid vill, and T. Hayne and T. Croade, two inhabitants of the vill of Sydling aforefaid, in the name of all the inhabitants of the faid vill, fay that they do not apprehend that the faid lord the now king, will or ought to impeach or trouble the inhabitants of the vills of Holneft, and Sydling aforefaid, becaufe of the premifes, becaufe they fay that the vills of Hilvill, Hartley, Great Minterne and Middlemarfh, at the time of the proftration of the hedges, ditches, gates, and rails, in the inquifition aforefaid, mentioned, were the only four vills next adjacent to the faid place inclofed by the faid John Street, in the faid inquifition mentioned, and that the faid vills of Holneft and Sydling, at the fame time were and as yet are more remote, from the faid place inclofed than the faid vills of Hilvill, Hartley, Great Minterne, and Middlemarfh, then were or are, and this they are ready to verify, &c. wherefore they pray judgment, &c. And the faid C. Whiffen and A. Flambert, two inhabitants of the vill of Hilvill aforefaid, in the name of all the inhabitants of the faid vill, T. Scutt and W. Fox, two inhabitants of the vill of Hartley aforefaid, in the name of all the inhabitants of the faid vill, T. Harris and W. Gould, two inhabitants of the vill of Great Minterne, in the name of all the inhabitants of the faid vill, and the faid W. Granger and J. Granger, two inhabitants of the vill of Middlemarfh aforefaid, in the name of all the inhabitants of the faid vill, fay that they do not apprehend that the faid lord the

now

Side notes:

Two inhabitants of each vill appear in the name of all the inhabitants of the refpective vills.

* P. 336.

The inhabitants of 2 of the vills plead, that the other 4 vills are the next vills, &c.

The inhabitants of the other 4 vills demur to the diftringas & return.

now king, will or ought any further impeach or trouble, becauſe of the premiſes, the inhabitants of the vills of Hilvill, Hartley, great Minterne and Middlemarſh, becauſe they ſay that the writ of diſtringas aforeſaid, and the return thereto made are not ſufficient in law, to which they have no neceſſity, neither are they bound by the law of the land, in any manner to anſwer, and this they are ready to verify, wherefore for the inſufficiency of the ſaid writ of diſtringas, and the return thereto made they pray judgment, and that they by the court here may be diſmiſſed, &c. and for cauſes of their demurrer in law, they the ſaid C. Whiffen and A. Flambert, in their own names and in the names of all the inhabitants of the vill of Hilvill aforeſaid, T. Scutt and W. Fox, in their own names and in the names of all the inhabitants of the vill of Hartley aforeſaid, R. Harris and W. Gould, in their own names and in the names of all the inhabitants of the vill of great Minterne aforeſaid, and W. Granger and J. Granger, in their own names and in the names of all the inhabitants of the vill of Middlemarſh aforeſaid, ſhew theſe cauſes following to wit, for this becauſe that it doth not appear by the inquiſition in the ſaid writ mentioned, that the ſaid place mentioned in the ſaid inquiſition to have been incloſed by the ſaid John Street, was a place in which a the time of ſuch incloſure, any perſon had a right of commonage; nor that he the ſaid J. Street, at the time of the ſaid incloſure or at any time afterwards, was lord of any manor of * which the place ſo incloſed was parcel; nor that he the ſaid John Street, at the time of the incloſure thereof, or ever afterwards had any right of incloſing the place ſo by him incloſed; and for this, becauſe that it appears by the ſaid inquiſition that the ſaid John Street, incloſed the whole place in the ſaid inquiſition mentioned, and it doth not appear by the ſaid inquiſition, that he hath left as much paſture for thoſe who have right of commonage there as is ſufficient for their tenements, with free ingreſs and egreſs as by the form of the ſtatute upon which the ſaid writ is grounded, ought to be made; and finally, becauſe that it doth not appear by the ſaid inquiſition but that the ſaid John Street, hath determined his eſtate of and in the ſaid place ſo incloſed, before the iſſuing of this writ And Samuel Aſtry, eſquire, coroner, and attorney of the lord the king, in the court of the ſaid lord the king, before the king himſelf, who for the ſaid lord the king, in his behalf proſecutes, and the ſaid John Street for himſelf, having heard as well the plea by the ſaid N. Rawls, and R. Day, in the name of all the inhabitants of the vill of Holneſt aforeſaid, and by the ſaid T. Hayne and T. Croade, in the name of all the inhabitants of the vill of Sydling aforeſaid,

3 G

Side notes:

Special cauſes of demurrer.

1ſt cauſe.

2d cauſe.

*P. 337.

3d cauſe.

4th cauſe.

5th cauſe.

6th cauſe.

The king's coroner and attorney and the plaintiff reply as to the plea of the two vills, that all the 6 vills were the next vills, and traverſe that the *other four vills are the only next vills.* in the manner and form aforeſaid, above pleaded, as the ſaid plea by the ſaid C. Whiffen and A. Flambert, in the name of all the inhabitants of the vill of Hilvill, and by the ſaid T. Scutt and W. Fox, in the name of all the inhabitants of the vill of Hartley aforeſaid, and by the ſaid R. Harris and W. Gould, in the name of all the inhabitants of great Minterne aforeſaid, and by the ſaid W. Granger and J. Granger, in the name of all the inhabitants of the vill of Middlemarſh aforeſaid, in the manner and form aforeſaid, above pleaded, ſay that the ſaid lord the now king, and the ſaid John Street, by any thing by the ſaid N. R. R. D. T. H. and T. C. above by pleading alledged, ought not to be precluded from the ſaid writ of diſtringas, and the return made thereto againſt the inhabitants of the vills of Holneſt and Sydling aforeſaid, becauſe they ſay that as well the ſaid vills of Holneſt and Sydling aforeſaid, as the ſaid vills of Hilvill, Hartley, great Minterne and Middlemarſh, at the time of the proſtration of the hedges, ditches, gates, rails, and ſtiles, in the inquiſition mentioned, are the vills, next to ſaid place ſo incloſed, without this, that the ſaid vills called Hilvill, Hartley, great Minterne and Middlemarſh, at the time of the proſtration of the hedges, ditches, gates, rails and ſtiles, in the inquiſition mentioned, are the only next vills, next adjacent to ſaid place ſo incloſed as the ſaid N.R.R.D.T. H. and T. C. above by pleading, have alledged, and this they are ready to verify as the court, &c. whereupon they pray judgment and that the inhabitants of the vills of Holneſt

And join in demurrer with the other 4 vills. and Sydling aforeſaid, may be convicted of the premiſes by the court here. And they further ſay that the ſaid writ of diſtringas, and the return thereto made, are good and ſufficient in law, to which the inhabitants of the vills of Hilvill, Hartley, great Minterne, and Middlemarſh aforeſaid, have neceſſity and by the law of the land are bound to anſwer, wherefore becauſe that the ſaid inhabitants of the ſaid vills of Hilvill, Hartley, great Minterne, and Middlemarſh aforeſaid, have not anſwer'd to the ſaid writ of diſtringas and to the return thereto made nor them in any manner have denied they pray judgment and that the inhabitants of the vills of Hilvill, Hartley, great Minterne and Middlemarſh aforeſaid, of the premiſſes by the court here may be convicted, &c. &c.

***P. 338.** — The King *againſt* the Inhabitants of Hannam.

Hilary, the 33d and 34th Charles 2d.

Writ to the ſheriff to enquire of *Charles the 2d, &c.* } TO the ſheriff of Glouceſter, greeting. We command you by the oath of good and lawful

ful men of your county, by whom the truth of the matter the breakets of the hed-ges, &c. may be the better known, diligently to enquire what male-factors and disturbers of your peace at West-hannam, within the parish of Bitton, in our county, with force and arms, the hedges, ditches, walls, gates, rails and stiles of Francis Creswick, esquire, there lately by him raised and erected, by night or at such time as they believed that their deeds could not be known, did prostrate and fill up, and other wrongs to him did, to the great damage of the said Francis, and against our peace, and if the said Francis shall give you security for prosecuting his complaint, then put by gages and sate pledges, all those whom you shall find guilty thereof, that they be before us on the morrow of the purification of the blessed Virgin Mary, wheresoever we shall then be in England, to answer as well to us of the breach of our peace, as to the said Francis of the said trespass, and have there the names of those by whose oath you shall make that inquisition, and this writ. Witness our self at Westminster, the 16th day of December, in the 33d year of our reign.

Adderley.

The execution of this writ appears in a certain inquisition to this writ annexed, W. W. esquire, sheriff.

Gloucester, } **INQUISITION** indented taken at Tetbury, Inquisition finds the hedges broke.
To wit, } in the said county, on the 2d day of February in the 34th year of the reign of our lord Charles the 2d, the now king of England, &c. before me W. Wall, esquire she-riff of the said county, by virtue of the writ of the lord the king to me directed, and to this inquisition annexed by the oath of C. H. &c. good and lawful men of my bailiwick who say upon their oath that certain malefactors and distur-bers of the peace of the said lord the king, on the first day of February, in the 32d year of the reign of the said lord the now king, and at divers other days and times, between the said 1st day of February, and the 21st day of December, in the 33d year of the reign of the said lord the now king, at West-hannam in the said county, with force and arms, &c. with a multitude of persons unknown, sixty perches of rails 30 perches of wall, three hundred and eighty feet of ditch and fence, ten gates and three stiles of the said Francis Creswick, in the said writ named at West-hannam aforesaid, lately raised and erected in the nights of the said days, did prostrate and also 15 trees of the said Francis did cut down, to the great damage of the said Francis Creswick, but who so prostrated the hedges, ditches, fences, gates and stiles, or any part of them the said jurors aforesaid, are entirely ignorant, and in P. 558. like manner say upon their oath that the malefactors afore-

3 G 2
said.

ſaid, who committed the miſdeeds aforeſaid, ſo as aforeſaid, came with ſuch power and multitude of perſons, and committed the ſaid miſdeeds in the night time, ſo that no perſon dare approach nigh to them, to diſcover them. In witneſs whereof, to this inquiſition as well I the ſaid ſheriff, as the ſaid jurors, have put our ſeveral ſeals, the day and year aforeſaid, W. Wall, eſquire, ſheriff, (L.S.) &c. Charles the 2d, &c. To the ſheriff of Gloucelter, greeting. Whereas lately by our writ, we commanded you by the oath of good and lawful men of your county, by whom the truth of the matter might be the better known, diligently to enquire what malefactors and diſturbers of our peace at Weſt-hannam, within the pariſh of Bitton in your county, with force and arms, the hedges, ditches, walls, gates, rails and ſtiles of Francis Creſwick, eſq; there lately by him raiſed and erected by night, or at ſuch time as they believed that their deeds could not be known, had proſtrated and filled up and other wrongs to him had done, to the great damage of the ſaid Francis, and againſt our peace ; and if the ſaid Francis ſhould give you ſecurity to proſecute his complaint, then that you ſhould put by gages and ſafe pledges, all thoſe whom you ſhould find guilty thereof, that they ſhould be before us on the morrow of the purification of the bleſſed Virgin Mary laſt paſt, whereſoever we ſhould then be in England, to anſwer as well to us of the breach of the peace, as the ſaid Francis of the treſpaſs aforeſaid, and you at that day returned to us, that by a certain inquiſition indented, taken at Tetbury, in your county, on the 2d day of February, in the 34th year of our reign, before you, by virtue of the ſaid writ, it is found by the oath of twelve jurors, good and lawful men of your ſaid county, that certain malefactors and diſturbers of our peace, on the 1ſt day of February, in the 32d year of our reign, and at divers other days and times, between the ſaid 1ſt day of February and the 21ſt day of December, in the 33d year of our reign, at Weſt-hannam, in the ſaid county, with force and arms, &c. with a multitude of perſons unknown, 60 perches of rails, 30 perches of walls, 380 feet of ditch and fence, 10 gates and 3 ſtiles, of the ſaid Francis Creſwick, at Weſt-hannam aforeſaid, lately raiſed and erected, in the nights of the ſaid days had proſtrated, and alſo 15 trees of the ſaid Francis, had cut down, to the great damage of the ſaid Francis Creſwick, but thoſe who had ſo proſtrated the ſaid hedges, ditches, fences, gates and ſtiles, the ſaid jurors were entirely ignorant, and in like manner they ſaid upon their oath, that the malefactors aforeſaid, who had ſo committed the miſdeeds aforeſaid, ſo as aforeſaid, had came with ſuch power and multitude of perſons, and had committed the ſaid miſdeeds in the night time, ſo that no perſon

dare

Writ to diſtrai the next vills & to enquire what damage the plaintiff hath ſuſtained.

dare to approach nigh to them, to difcover them, as by infpection of the writ aforefaid, and of the inquifition aforefaid, by you, by virtue of the writ aforefaid, returned before us, and there now remaining of record, manifeftly appears to us; we command you, that you do not omit, by
reafon of any liberty in your bailiwick, but that you diftrain
the vills next adjacent to the faid hedges, ditches, walls,
fences, gates and ftiles, to raife the faid hedges, ditches,
walls, fences, gates and ftiles, at their own proper coft, alfo
we * command you, by the oath of good and lawful men of `*P. 340.`
your county, by whom the truth of the matter may be the
better known, to enquire diligently, what damages the faid
Francis Crefwick hath fuftained, by occafion of the faid
proftration, of the faid 60 perches of rails, 30 perches of
wall, 380 feet of ditch and fence, 10 gates, 3 ftiles and 15
trees, and that you reftore thofe damages to the faid Francis,
and how you fhall have executed this our command certify
to us, from the day of Eafter in 15 days, wherefoever we
fhall then be in England, under your feal and the feals of
thofe by whofe oath you fhall take the faid inquifition, then
returning to us this our writ. Witnefs F. Pemberton, kt.
at Weftminfter, the 13th day of February, in the 34th year
of our reign.

Aftry.

Pledges to profecute John Doe and Richard Roe, the if- Return of
the writ.
fues of the lands of the inhabitants of Bitton, Hannam and
Odland, the vills next to the within written hedges, 40s. Iffues re-
turned upon
the next
vills.
feverally; the refidue of the execution of this writ appears
in a certain inquifition to this writ annexed.

W. W. efquire, fheriff.

Gloucefter,   A N inquifition indented, taken at the caftle Inquifition.
to wit.   of Gloucefter, in the county of Gloucefter,
on the 27th day of April, in the 34th year of the reign of
our lord Charles the 2d, the now king of England, &c. before me W. W. efquire, fheriff of the faid county, by virtue
of the writ of the lord the king, to me directed, and to
this inquifition annexed, by the oath of H. L. &c. good
and lawful men of the faid county, who fay upon their
oath aforefaid, that the faid F. C. efquire, in the faid writ
named, hath fuftained damages by occafion of the proftration of 60 perches of rails, 30 perches of wall, 380 feet of
ditch and fence, 10 gates, 3 ftiles and 25 trees in the faid writ
mentioned, to the value of 36l. 13s. in teftimony whereof as Damages
found 36'
13s.
well I the faid fheriff as the faid jurors have fet our feals to
this inquifition the day and year aforefaid.

And now to wit, on the Tuefday next after fifteen days of Plea to the
diftringas by
three inha-
the Holy Trinity, in this fame term before the lord the king
at Weftminfter come J. Liddiard, John Harding and William

Fox,

Fox, men, inhabitants in the vills of Bitton, Hannam and Od-lands by Robert Seyliard their attorney, and having heard the ſeveral writs and inquiſitions aforeſaid, ſay that they by reaſon of the writs and inquiſitions aforeſaid, by the ſaid lord the king ought not to be diſquieted or troubled, becauſe they ſay, that the place in which the proſtration and cutting down in the firſt inquiſition mentioned, are ſuppoſed to be done at the ſaid times, in which the ſaid proſtration and cutting down were committed, did contain, and as yet doth contain 100 acres of paſture, in Weſt-hannam aforeſaid, called or known by the name of Hannam's heath, otherwiſe Hannam's common, and that before the times, and alſo at the times of the proſtration and cutting down aforeſaid, the ſaid J. Lid-diard, J. Harding and W. Fox, and divers other perſons were tenants of one John Newton, baronet, and of divers tenements, parcel of his manors of Bitton, Hannam and

Odlands, in the county of Glouceſter, * which John New-ton, then was and yet is ſeized of, and in the ſaid manors in his demeſne as of fee, and that the ſaid John Newton, and all thoſe whoſe eſtate he then had, and now has, of and in the manors aforeſaid, before the ſaid times in which, &c. and at the ſaid times in which, &c. hath and have had, and alſo hath and have been accuſtomed to have, from the time whereof the memory of man is not to the contrary, for themſelves, and for their tenants, of the ſeveral tenements, parcel of their manors aforeſaid, common of paſture for all their commonable cattle, and for all the commonable cattle of

their tenants, levant and couchant upon the ſaid manors, and the ſeveral tenements, parcel of the ſaid manors, of and in the ſaid place in which, &c. called Hannam's heath, or Hannam's common, at all times of the year as appendant and appurtenant to the manors aforeſaid; and the ſaid in-habitants further ſay, that afterwards and before the time of the proſtration and cutting down aforeſaid, to wit, on the 1ſt day of November, in the 31ſt year of the reign of the lord Charles the 2d, the now king, &c. the ſaid F. C. in the ſaid writs named, did incloſe a great part of the place in which, &c. with the hedges, ditches, fences, rails, walls, ſtiles and gates, in the ſaid inquiſition mentioned, whereby

the ſaid J. Lyddiard, J. Harding and W. Fox, and the other tenants of the ſaid John Newton, of his manors aforeſaid, from having their common aforeſaid, within the ſaid place in which, &c. ſo incloſed were excluded, whereupon the
said

There ſeems to be an inaccuracy in theſe pleadings, as here the defendants plead for themſelves, and afterwards demur in behalf of the inhabitants of the vills, and if it be ſaid that the pleadings ſhould be ſo tranſlated as to make the inhabitants of the vills partys to this plea, then they ſhould have demurred jointly with the defendants, and the defendants ſhould not have de-murred for them. beſides it is apprehended that the original text would not warrant ſuch tranſlation.

faid John, John and William, afterwards to wit, on the said day and year laft mentioned, at Wefthannam aforefaid, gave notice to the faid Francis, that he fhould open the faid inclofure, and that if he would not do it, that they would open the faid inclofure, to have their faid common there, and becaufe the faid Francis, after fuch notice did not open the faid inclofure, they the faid John, John and William, and divers men, labourers, at their command and at the command of the faid John Newton, to the number only of eight perfons, afterwards, to wit, on the ift day of February, in the 32d year of the reign of our lord Charles the 2d, &c. and at the faid other days and times in the faid inquifition mentioned, peaceably, openly and publickly and in the day time and before the fetting of the fun of the faid days, one perch of rails, fix feet of ditch and fence, two gates and one ftile of the faid inclofure at Weft-hannam aforefaid, in the faid place, in which aforefaid, fo as aforefaid, raifed and erected, did proftrate, and two trees did cut down, which was neceffary for them to cut down and proftrate, to open their way to have their faid common there, as it was lawful for them to do, without this that any malefactors at any of the times in the faid inquifitions mentioned, fixty perches of rails, thirty perches of wall, three hundred and 80 feet of ditch and fence, ten gates and three ftiles of him the faid Francis Crefwick, at Wefthannam aforefaid, lately raifed in the nights of the faid days in the faid inquifition mentioned, or at any time in which they believed their deeds could not be known did proftrate, and alfo fifteen trees of the faid Francis Crefwick, then did cut down in the manner and form as in the faid firft inquifition aforefaid, is contained, and this the faid inhabitants are ready to verify, &c. wherefore they pray judgment if the faid lord the king will any further trouble the faid inhabitants thereon, and that they from any further profecution upon * the faid writs and the faid inquifitions thereon by the court of the faid lord the king, here may be difmiffed, &c.   *W. Pawlett.*

And the faid Francis Crefwick, who as well for the lord the king as for himfelf, in this behalf profecutes, faith, that the faid men, inhabitants in the vills of Bitton, Hannam and Odlands, by any thing by them above by pleading alledged ought not to be difcharged from raifing the hedges, ditches, fences, walls, gates, or ftiles aforefaid, fo as aforefaid proftrated, at their own proper cofts, or from yielding and paying to the faid Francis Crefwick his damages, by occafion of the proftration of the rails, walls, ditches, fences, gates, and ftiles aforefaid, and of the cutting down of the faid trees, by the faid inquifition found, or to anfwer to the faid lord the king, for the breach of the peace of the faid lord the king, becaufe protefting that the faid plea of the faid inhabitants

of

time threw
them down.

and traverfe
their doing
it in the
night.

*P. 342.

Plaintiff re-
plies that
the place
where, &c.
is his free-
hold, and
traverfes the
right of
common.

of the vills of Bitton, Hannam, and Odlands, and the matter in the ſame contained, are not ſufficient in law to diſcharge or acquit them, from raiſing the hedges, ditches, fences, walls, gates, and ſtiles aforeſaid, or from yielding or paying to the ſaid Francis his damages aforeſaid, or from anſwering to the ſaid lord the king of and upon the premiſes, for plea ſaith, that the ſaid place called Hannam-Heath, otherwiſe Hannam's-common is, and at the ſaid time in which the ſaid treſpaſs is ſuppoſed to be done, was within the pariſh of Bitton aforeſaid, in the ſaid county, and the ſeveral ſoil and freehold of him the ſaid Francis Creſwick, eſq; without this, that the ſaid J. Newton, and all thoſe whoſe eſtate at the ſaid times in which, &c. he had and now has, of and in the ſaid manors with their appurtenances, from the time whereof the memory of man is not to the contrary, have had and have been accuſtomed to have, for themſelves, and their tenants of the ſeveral tenements, parcel of the ſaid manors, common of paſture, for all their commonable cattle, and the commonable cattle of their tenants, levant and couchant, upon the ſaid manors, and the ſeveral tenements, parcel of the ſaid manors of and in the ſaid place in which, &c. at all times of the year, as appendant and appurtenant to the ſaid manors, and this he is ready to verify, wherefore he prays judgment, and that the ſaid men, inhabitants in the ſaid vills of Bitton, Hannam, and Odlands, may not be diſcharged from raiſing, paying and anſwering in the form aforeſaid.

Jchh Powell.

Demurrer.

And the ſaid J. Liddiard, J. Harding, and W. Fox, for and on behalf of the ſaid inhabitants ſay, that they by any thing, by the ſaid lord the king above, by replying alledged, ought not to be compelled to raiſe and erect the hedges, ditches, fences, walls, gates, and ſtiles aforeſaid; or to pay to the ſaid Francis Creſwick any damages, coſts and charges, for the occaſion aforeſaid, * becauſe they ſay that the replication aforeſaid, in the form aforeſaid, above pleaded, and the matter in the ſame contained, are not ſufficient in law, to compel them to anſwer to the ſaid lord the king thereupon, to which replication in the manner and form aforeſaid pleaded, they the ſaid John, Jn. and Wm. have no neceſſity, neither are they bound by the law of the land in any manner to anſwer, and this they are ready to verify; wherefore for want of a ſufficient replication in this behalf, they the ſaid John, John and William pray judgment of the inquiſition aforeſaid, and that they and the ſaid inhabitants may go thereof quit; and for cauſe of their demurrer in law, they ſhew the following cauſe, to wit, that the ſaid lord the king hath not joined iſſue upon the traverſe tendered, but has tendered another iſſue, which is immaterial, in reſpect to the writ and inquiſition aforeſaid;

P. 343.

Cauſes of demurrer.

becauſe

becaufe if the faid proftrations were not done in the night, or at fome time fo fecretly, that the actors of the deed believed that their deeds could not be known, fuch trefpaffers are punifhable by indictment, or action of trefpafs at the common law, but neither they nor the neighbouring vills in that cafe are punifhable, by fuch writs and inquifitions in the country by the ftatute, upon which the faid writs are grounded. And if the faid proftrations were committed by night, or in the day time fecretly, by thofe who had the right of proftration, it is probable that they would be punifhable by the faid ftatute. *W. Bowen.*

And the faid Francis Crefwick, who as well, &c. becaufe he above by replying hath alledged fufficient matter in the law to compel the faid men inhabitants in the vills aforefaid, of Bitton, Hannam and Odlands, to raife at their own proper coft the hedges, ditches, fences, walls, gates and ftiles aforefaid fo as aforefaid, proftrated, and to yield and pay to the faid F. Crefwick, his damages by occafion of the proftration of the rails, walls, ditches, fences, gates and ftiles aforefaid, and of the cutting down of the trees aforefaid, by the inquifition aforefaid found, and to anfwer to the faid lord the king, of and for the breach of the peace of the faid lord the king, which he is ready to verify, which matter the faid men inhabitants in the faid vills of Bitton, Hannam and Odlands have not denied, nor to the fame in any manner have anfwered, but altogether refufe to admit the faid averment as before prays judgment, and that the faid men inhabitants in the faid vills of Bitton, Hannam and Odlands, may be charged to raife, pay and anfwer in the form aforefaid, &c. &c.

Joinder in demurrer.

---

* The King and lord Matravers, and others *P. 344.

againft the Inhabitants of Darking.

Surrey, } THE lord the king, hath fent to the fheriff of
To wit. } the county aforefaid, his writ clofe in thefe
words to wit, Charles by the grace of God, &c. to the therif
of Surrey greeting. Whereas lately by our writ iffuing out
of our court of Chancery, we commanded you by the oath of
good and lawful men of your county, by whom the truth of

Writ to the fheriff to diftrain the adjacent vills.

the

Recital of the writ of enquiry.

the matter might be the better known, diligently to enquire what malefactors and diſturbers of our peace, at Darking in your court with force and arms, the hedges and ditches of Henry lord Matravers and Ambroſe Brown, baronet, there by them lately raiſed, in the night or at ſuch time as they believed their deeds could not be known, had proſtrated, and other wrongs to them had done to the great damage of the ſaid Henry and Ambroſe, and againſt the peace, and if the ſaid Henry and Ambroſe ſhould give you ſecurity to proſecute their complaint then that you ſhould put by gages and ſafe pledges all thoſe whom you ſhould find guilty thereof, that they ſhould be before us on the octave of St. Michael laſt paſt, whereſoever we ſhould then be in England, as well to anſwer to us of the breach of our peace, as to the ſaid Henry and Ambroſe, of the treſpaſs aforeſaid, and you at that day returned to us, that

Recital of the inquſition.

by a certain inquiſition indented, taken before you by virtue of the ſaid writ at Darking in the county aforeſaid, on Wedneſday, the 21ſt day of Auguſt, in the 15th year of our reign, it is found by the oath of twelve jurors good and lawful men of your county, that certain malefactors and diſturbers of our peace, on the 27th day of May, in the 15th year of our reign aforeſaid, at D. aforeſaid, in the ſaid county, with force and arms, 260 perches of hedges, and 260 perches of ditches of the ſaid H. lord Matravers, and of Ambroſe B. baronet, then lately before that time by them raiſed in the night or at ſuch time as they believed that their deeds could not be known, had proſtrated againſt our peace, but who had proſtrated the hedges and ditches aforeſaid, the ſaid jurors were entirely ignorant, as by inſpection of the writ aforeſaid, and inquiſition aforeſaid, by you, by virtue of the writ aforeſaid, returned before us and there now remaining of record manifeſtly appears to us, we command you that you do not omit

Command of this writ.

by reaſon of any liberty with your bailiwick, but that you diſtrain the vills next adjacent to the hedges and ditches aforeſaid, at their own proper coſts to raiſe the hedges and ditches, aforeſaid proſtrated, we alſo command you that by the oath of good and lawful men, in your county, by whom the truth of the matter may be the better known, diligently to enquire what damages the ſaid H. lord M and A. B. baronet, have ſuſtained by occaſion of the proſtration aforeſaid, of the ſaid 260 perches of hedges, and of the ſaid 260 perches of ditches and that you reſtore thoſe damages to the ſaid H. lord M. and A. B baronet, and how you ſhall have executed this our command, certify to us on the octave of St. Hilary, whereſoever we ſhall then be in England, under your ſeal and the ſeals of thoſe by whoſe oath you ſhall take the inquiſition aforeſaid, then returning to us this our writ. Witneſs J. Brampſton

ton at Weftminfter, the 25th day of October, in the 15th year of our reign.

* Mainpernors of the feveral inhabitants of Darking and Capell, being the vills next adjacent to the within written, hedges and ditches, John Roe and Richard Roe, iffues of the inhabitants of Darking, 6l. 13s. 4d. iffues of the inhabitants of Capell, 6l. 6s. 8d. and further, I certify to the within written lord the king, that that writ was delivered to me fo late that becaufe of the fhortnefs of the time I cannot reftore the damages, in the inquifition, to this writ annexed mentioned, to the within named H. lord M. and A. B. baronet. The refidue of the execution of this writ appears in the inquifition aforefaid, John Grefham, knight, fheriff, that writ as above indorfed was delivered to me by indenture, between me and the faid late fheriff on his departure from his office, John Howland, efquire, fheriff. Surrey to wit, inquifition indented, taken at Southwark, in the faid county, on the 25th day of November, in the 15th year of the reign of our lord Charles, now king of England, &c. before me John Grefham, knight, fheriff of the faid county, by virtue of the writ of the lord the king, to me directed and to this inquifition annexed it is found by the oath of J. L. T. G, &c. good and lawful men of the faid county, who fay upon their oath that H. lord M. and A. B. baronet, in the writ to this inquifition annexed named, have fuftained damage by the occafion in the faid writ fpecified to 26l. 6s. 8d. in witnefs whereof as well, I the faid fheriff as the jurors aforefaid, have feverally put our feals to this inquifition, on the day and year aforefaid ; John Grefham, knight, fheriff. Afterwards to wit, on the Wednefday next after 15 days of Eafter, in this fame term before the lord the king, at Weftminfter, the fheriff was commanded as often times, &c. that he do not omit, &c. but that he diftrain the feveral inhabitants of D. and C. aforefaid, being the vills next adjacent to the hedges and ditches aforefaid, to raife at their own proper coft, the faid hedges and ditches, proftrated, alfo the fheriff was commanded that he do not omit, &c, but that of the goods and chattels of the feveral inhabitants of D. and C. he caufe to be made the faid 26l. 6s. 8d. in the faid inquifition fpecified, and that he have that money before the lord the king, on the morrow of the Holy Trinity, wherefoever, &c. to reftore it to the faid H. lord M. and A. B. baronet. At which morrow of the Holy Trinity, before the lord the king, at Weftminfter, John Howland, efquire, fheriff hath returned, mainpernors of the feveral inhabitants of D. and C. aforefaid, John Doe and Richard Roe, the iffues of the faid inhabitants of Darking, 10l. the iffues of the faid inhabitants of C. 5l. and alfo that he hath taken into his hands

3 H 2

Marginal notes:

* P. 345.

Iffues returned upon 2 vills.

Tarde.

Pluries diftringas againft the vills and a fcire facias, as to the damages.

More iffues returned on the vills.

hands goods and chattels of the inhabitants of D. and C. to the value of 26l. 6s. 8d. which goods and chattels remain in his hands unsold for the want of buyers, so that he could not have the said 26l. 6s. 8d. before the said lord the king, on the day aforesaid, to restore to the said H. lord M. and A. B. baronet, as to him above was commanded. And on the said morrow of the Holy Trinity, before the lord the king at Westminster, come as well John Keeling, esquire, who prosecutes, &c. as Jasper Goodwin and H. S. two inhabitants and freeholders of the manor of D. aforesaid, in the name of all and singular the inhabitants and freeholders of the said manor, and the said Jasper Goodwin and William Arnold, two inhabitants and customary tenants by copy of court roll of the said manor, in the name of all and singular the customary tenants of the said manor by John Redwood their attorney, and having having had oyer of the inquisition * and the several writs of distringas aforesaid, say that they do not apprehend that the said lord the now king will or ought any further impeach or trouble the inhabitants, and freeholders and customary tenants or any of them for occasion of the premises, because they say that long before the time of the taking of the inquisition aforesaid, to wit, on the 27th day of May, in the 15th year of the reign of the said lord the now king, H. lord M. and A. B. baronet, were seized of the manner of Darking with the appurtenances, in the county of Surrey aforesaid, whereof a certain waste or common called Homewood-common lately containing 1000 acres of pasture with the appurtenances in D. aforesaid, is, and at the said time of the taking of the said inquisition, and also from the time whereof the memory of man is not to the contrary, was and as yet is parcel, in their demesne as of fee, and that within the said manor aforesaid, there then and as yet are as well forty freeholders who then were and as yet, are seized to them and to their heirs in their demesne as of fee, of divers messuages and freeholds with the appurtenances within the manor, and held of the said manor aforesaid, as sixty customary tenants who then were and as yet are seized to them and to their heirs by copy of the rolls of the court of the manor aforesaid, at the will of the lord or lords of the manor aforesaid, according to the custom of the manor aforesaid, of divers customary, messuages and tenements with the appurtenances within the said manor, and held of the said manor, and parcel of the said manor, and that all and singular the men, tenants of the messuages and freeholds aforesaid, with the appurtenances for the time being, and all those whose estates, the said freeholders now have, and also at the said time in which, &c. had in the said freeholds, messuages, and tenements with the appurtenances

purtenances from the time whereof, the memory of man is not to the contrary have had and have been accuſtomed to have common of paſture in the ſaid waſte or common for all their commonable cattle (ſheep only excepted) upon their freeholds aforeſaid, reſpectively levant and couchant every year and at all times of the year, as to their freeholds aforeſaid, with the appurtenances, appurtenant, and that within the manor aforeſaid, there is, had, and alſo from the time whereof the memory of man is not to the contrary, was had, and there was, and is a certain cuſtom, to wit, that all and ſingular the men, cuſtomary tenants of the cuſtomary tenements aforeſaid, with the appurtenances for the time being have had and have been accuſtomed to have common of paſture in the ſaid waſte or common for all their commonable cattle (ſheep only excepted) upon the ·cuſtomary tenements aforeſaid, reſpectively levant and couchant every year and at all times of the year, as appurtenant to their cuſtomary tenements aforeſaid ; and becauſe the ſaid H. lord M. and A. B. baronet, before the ſaid time of the taking of the inquiſition aforeſaid, to wit, on the ſaid 27th day of May, in the 15th year aforeſaid, 200 acres, parcel of the ſaid one thouſand acres of paſture in Darking aforeſaid, had incloſed with hedges and ditches, not leaving ſufficient common of paſture for the tenants and inhabitants aforeſaid, to their freeholds and cuſtomary tenements aforeſaid, reſpectively appurtenant they the ſaid Jaſper and Henry, then being freeholders of the manor aforeſaid, to them and to their heirs of and in eight free meſſuages or freeholds and 300 acres of land and paſture, with the appurtenances lying within the manor aforeſaid, and the ſaid Jaſper and William, then being cuſtomary tenants to them and their heirs by * copy of the rolls of the court of the manor aforeſaid, at the will of the lord or lords of the manor aforeſaid, according to the cuſtom of the ſaid manor of and in five cuſtomary meſſuages, and 130 acres of cuſtomary land with the appurtenances within the manor, and held of the manor aforeſaid, and parcel of the ſaid manor; in their own proper right, and in the name of all and ſingular the freehold and cuſtomary tenants, aforeſaid, as well for the maintenance of their right and title to the ſaid common of paſture in the ſaid 200 acres of paſture ſo as aforeſaid incloſed, as for the free uſe and enjoyment of the ſaid common to be had and perceived by them reſpectively with their cattle aforeſaid, upon their freehold tenements and cuſtomary tenements aforeſaid, reſpectively levant and couchant, on the ſaid 27th day of May, in the 15th year aforeſaid, in the inquiſition aforeſaid, ſpecified, at Darking aforeſaid, in the county of Surrey aforeſaid, 260 perches of hedges, and 260 perches of ditches, by the ſaid H. lord M. and A. B. there then erected, and conſtructed and incloſing the ſaid 200 acres of paſture in the form aforeſaid,

That the plaintiffs incloſed part of the waſte and did not leave ſufficient common, wherefore the defendants juſtify the proſtration.

*P. 347.

aforesaid, did prostrate as it was lawful for them to do, and this they are ready to verify as the court, &c. wherefore they pray judgment, and that they of the issues in the premises by the court here may be dismissed, &c. &c.

Imparlance to reply. And the said John Keeling, who prosecutes, &c. having heard the plea aforesaid, for the said lord the king, prays day to imparl thereto, unto the octave of St. Michael, and it is granted to him, before the said lord the king, wheresoever, &c. the same day is given as well to the said John Keeling, who prosecutes, &c. as to the said Jasper Goodwin and Henry Stone, in the name of all and singular the inhabitants and freeholders of the manor aforesaid, and to the said Jasper Goodwin and William Arnold, in the name of all and singular the customary tenants of the manor aforesaid; at which octave of St. Michael, before the lord the king, at Westminster, come as well the said John Keeling, who prosecutes, as the said Jasper Goodwin and Henry Stone, in the name of all and singular the freeholders of the manor aforesaid, and the said Jasper Goodwin and William Arnold, in the name of all and singular the customary tenants of the manor aforesaid, by their attorney aforesaid, and the said John Keeling, who prosecutes, &c. having heard the said plea, by the said Jasper Goodwin and Henry Stone, in the name of all and singular the inhabitants and freeholders of the manor of Darking aforesaid, and by the said Jasper Goodwin and William Arnold, in the name of all and singular the customary tenants of the manor aforesaid, above in the form aforesaid pleaded, saith, that the *Demurrer to the plea.* said lord the now king, by any thing, by them the said Jasper Goodwin and Henry Stone, and William Arnold above pleaded, ought not to be precluded from having the writ of Venditioni exponas, to the sheriff of the county of Surrey directed, to sell the goods and chattels remaining in his hands unsold, for want of buyers, and from having the writ of distringas, to distrain the several inhabitants of Darking and Capell aforesaid, to raise at their own proper cost, the hedges and ditches aforesaid, because he saith, that the plea aforesaid, by them above in the form aforesaid pleaded, and the matter in the same contained, are not sufficient in law, to which he hath no necessity, neither is he bound by the law of the land, in any manner to answer, wherefore for want of a sufficient plea in this behalf, he prays judgment, and that the writ of Venditioni exponas may be made, directed to the sheriff of Surrey aforesaid, to sell the goods and chattels aforesaid, remaining in the hands of the sheriff aforesaid, unsold, for want of buyers, and that the writ of distringas may be made, to distrain the several inhabitants of Darking and Capell aforesaid, to raise at their own proper cost, the *P. 348.* hedges and * ditches aforesaid. And the said Jasper Goodwin

of

and Henry Stone, in the name of all and ſingular the inha- *Joinder in*
bitants and freeholders of the manor of D. aforeſaid. And *demurrer.*
the ſaid Jaſper Goodwin and William Arnold, in the name
of all and ſingular the cuſtomary tenants of the manor aforeſaid, ſay, that the plea aforeſaid, by them in the form aforeſaid above pleaded, and the matter in the ſame contained,
are good and ſufficient in law, to preclude the ſaid lord the
king from the writ of Venditioni exponas, directed to the
ſheriff of Surrey, to ſell the goods and chattels aforeſaid,
remaining in his hands unſold, for want of buyers, and
from the writ of diſtringas, to diſtrain the ſeveral inhabitants
of Darking and Capell aforeſaid, to raiſe at their own proper coſt, the hedges and ditches aforeſaid, wherefore, becauſe that the ſaid attorney of the ſaid lord the king hath
not anſwered to the ſaid plea, nor it in any manner hath denied, but altogether refuſes to admit the ſaid averment, they
pray judgment, and that the ſaid inhabitants of Darking and
Capell may be diſmiſſed by the court here, &c. and becauſe
the court of the lord the king here, is not yet adviſed to
give their judgment of and upon the premiſes, day is given
thereupon, as well to the ſaid John Keeling, who proſe- *Curia non-*
cutes, &c. as to the ſaid Jaſper Goodwin and Henry Stone, *dum adviſ-*
in the name of all and ſingular the freeholders of the manor *tum.*
aforeſaid, and to the ſaid Jaſper Goodwin and William
Arnold, in the name of all and ſingular the cuſtomary tenants of the manor aforeſaid, unto the octave of St. Hilary,
before the lord the king, whereſoever, &c. to hear their
judgment thereupon, becauſe that the court here, not as
yet, &c. &c.

The King *againſt the* Inhabitants *of* Eaſt Grinſtead.

Charles the 2d, TO the ſheriff of Suſſex, greeting. Where- *Diſtringas*
&c. as lately by our writ iſſuing out of our *againſt the*
court of Chancery, we commanded the late ſheriff of your *adjacent vills*
county, by the oath of good and lawful men of your county, *to repair the*
fences.
by whom the truth of the matter might be the better known,
diligently to enquire what malefactors and diſturbers of our *Recital of*
peace, at the foreſt or chaſe of Aſhdown, otherwiſe Lancaſ- *the writ of*
ter great park, in your county, the hedges and ditches of *enquiry.*
Edward

Edward Andrews, efquire, there lately by him raifed, in the night, or at fuch time as they believed their deeds could not be known, had proftrated and other wrongs to the faid Edward Andrews had done, to the great damage of the faid Edward, and againft our peace, and that he fhould put, by gages and fafe pledges, all thofe whom he fhould find guilty thereof, that they fhould be before us on a certain day now paft, wherefoever we fhould then be, in England, to anfwer as well to us, of the breach of our peace, as to the faid Edward Andrews, of the trefpafs aforefaid; and our faid late fheriff of our county of Suffex, to wit, William Spence, efquire, at that day returned to us, that by a certain inquifition, taken before him, by virtue of the faid writ, at Lewes, in the county of Suffex aforefaid, on the 27th day of March, in the 17th year of our reign, by the oath of twelve jurors, good and lawful men of the faid county, it is found that certain malefactors and difturbers of our peace, on the 1ft day of March, in the 16th year of our reign, and at divers other days and times, as well before as after, before the iffuing of the faid writ, at the foreft or chafe of Afhdown, otherwife Lancafter great park, in your county, with force and arms, 1690 perches of hedges and ditches, by the faid Edward Andrews, there late before that time by him raifed, in the night, or at fuch time that they believed their deeds could not be * known, had proftrated againft our peace, but who had proftrated the hedges and ditches aforefaid, the faid jurors were entirely ignorant of, as by infpection of the faid writ and of the faid inquifition by the faid fheriff taken, by virtue of the faid writ, and returned before us, and there now remaining of record manifeftly appears; and whereas alfo thereupon, by our writ iffuing out of our court before us, we commanded the late fheriff of your county, that he fhould not omit, by reafon of any liberty within his bailiwick, but that he fhould diftrain the vills next adjacent to the faid hedges and ditches, to raife the hedges and ditches aforefaid, at their own proper coft, and whereas thereupon, by our faid writ, we command the late fheriff, by the oath of good and lawful men of your county, by whom the truth of the matter might be the better known, diligently to enquire what damages the faid Edward Andrews had fuftained, by occafion of the proftration of the faid 1690 perches of hedges and ditches, and that he fhould reftore thofe damages to the faid E. A. and that he fhould certify to us, how he fhould have executed our faid command, at a certain day now paft, wherefoever we fhould then be, in England, under his feal and the feals of thofe by whofe oath he fhould take the faid inquifition, then returning to us the faid writ; and the faid late fheriff

P. 349.

Recital of the inquifition thereon

Recital of a former diftringas and writ of enquiry of damages.

at

of our county of Suffex, to wit, Walter Devell, efquire, at that day returned to us, that the inhabitants of Eaftgrinftead, Hartfield, Buxfield, Marisfield, Fletching, Horfted Haynes and Wefthoadly, are the vills next adjacent to the faid hedges and ditches, and that by a certain inquifition taken before him, by virtue of the faid writ laft mentioned at Horfham in the faid county, on the 8th day of April, in the 22d year of our reign, by the oath of twelve jurors good and lawful men of the county aforefaid, it is found that the faid E. A. hath fuftained damages by occafion of the premifes to 1600*l.* And whereas alfo on the Friday, next after the morrow of the Holy Trinity, before us at Weftminfter, came G B. and E. W. two inhabitants of Eaftgrinfted aforefaid, R. F. and T. K. two inhabitants of the vill of Hartfield aforefaid, J. A and W. C. two inhabitants of the vill of Buxfield aforefaid, J. K. and W. P. two inhabitants of the vill of Marisfield aforefaid, J. S. and W. J. two inhabitants of the vill of Fletching aforefaid, W. J. and W. S. two inhabitants of the vill of Horfted Haynes aforefaid, and J. R. and T. C. two inhabitants of the vill of Weft hoadly, in the name of all the inhabitants of all the faid feveral vills by John Godden their attorney, and having had oyer of the writs and inquifitions aforefaid, faid that the faid E. A. did not fuftain damages by occafion of the proftration of the hedges and ditches aforefaid, to 1600*l.* or to one penny thereof, as by the faid inquifition is above found, and of this they did put themfelves upon the country. And Thomas Fanfhaw, knight, our coroner and attorney, in our court before us, who for us in that behalf profecuted, and the faid E. Andrews, for himfelf did the like, &c. which iffue fo as aforefaid joined, afterwards, to wit, on the Thurfday next after the * morrow of St. Martin, laft paft, in our court, before us, by a jury of the country, was tried, and by the faid jury it was found, that the faid E. A. fuftained damages by occafion of the premifes, to 100l. as by the record in our court before us, remaining fully appears, and now on behalf of the faid E. Andrews, it is fhown to us, that the hedges and ditches proftrated as aforefaid, are not as yet raifed, therefore we command you, that you do not omit by reafon of any liberty within your bailiwick, but that you diftrain the inhabitants of the feveral vills of Eaft-grinftead, Hartfield, Buxfield, Marisfield, Fletching, Horfted Haynes and Weft-hoadly, being the vills next adjacent to the faid hedges and ditches, by all their lands and chattels in your bailiwick, fo that neither they nor any one for them, do intermeddle therewith, until that you have other command from us thereupon, and that you anfwer to us for the iffues of the fame, fo that they well and fufficiently raife at their own proper coft, the hedges

3 I   and

1600*l.* damages found

Recital that 2 inhabitants of each vill in the name of all the inhabitants appear and traverfe the damages found in th inquifition.

The cafe of the king againft the vills of Upwood, &c.
1 Sid. 212.
mentioned 1ft Lutw che,
156 feems to warrant this plea.

*P. 350.
Trial at bar.

Verdict for 100l damages.

Command of this writ

and ditches proſtrated as aforeſaid. if before that time they have not been be raiſed by them, and how you ſhall have executed this our command certify to us, from the day of Eaſter in one month, whereſoever we ſhall then be, in England, then returning to us this our writ. Witneſs, T. Twyſden, at Weſtminſter, the 10th day of May, in the 23d year of our reign.

By the court

Fanſhawe.

This caſe is reported, 2d Keble, 663 683. 723.

End of Part the Firſt.

I N D E X

TO

PART the FIRST,

FROM PAGE 1 TO PAGE 350 INCLUSIVE.

ABATEMENT.

ACCESSARY.

ADULTERY. Vide MISDEMEANOR.

APPEAL.

ARTIST.

Seducing artists. Vide MISDEMEANOR.

ASSAULT

INDEX.

ASSAULT. Vide MISDEMEANOR.

BANKRUPT. Vide MISDEMEANOR.

BARRATRY. Vide MISDEMEANOR.

BLASPHEMY. Vide MISDEMEANOR.

BUGGERY.

CAPTION.

CATTLE.

CERTIORARI.

CHALLENGE to FIGHT. Vide LIBEL.

CHEATS

I N D E X.

CHEATS. Vide MISDEMEANOR.

COINING.

CONSPIRACY.

CONSTABLE. Vide MISDEMEANOR.

CONTI-

D I S C O N T I N U A N C E.

D I S T R I N G A S.

E M B R A C E R Y.—Vide Perjury,

E R R O R.

Writ

An

GAMING. Vide MISDEMEANOR.

HEIRESS.

HIGH STEWARD.

INFORMATION. Vide ASSAULT, CHEATS, ESCAPE, FORGERY, LIBEL, MAINTENANCE, MISDEMEANOR, NUISANCE, PERJURY, RIOT, SCANDALOUS WORDS, SEDITION.

INQUISITION. Vide FENCES and MISDEMEANOR.

ISSUE.   194

JUDGMENT.

JURISDICTION.

INDEX.

I N D E X.

 Information

MONOPOLY.

MUR-

M U R D E R.

N O L L E P R O S E Q U I.   318

N O N M I S I T B R E V E.   184

N O N T E N U R E

N U I S A N C E.

O Y E R and T E R M I N E R

O U T L A W R Y.

P A R D O N

PERJURY.

INDEX.

PERJURY.

For

PHYSICIAN.

PLEA.

Son

POLICIES OF ASSURANCE.

Vide MISDEMEANOR.

POSTEA.

PROCLAMATION.

PROTESTATION.

REJOINDER.

REPLICATION.

To a plea to an indictment for murder that defendant's petition

R E S P O N D E A S. Ouster.

R E S T I T U T I O N.

R I O T.

R O B B E R Y.

I N D E X.

INDEX.

WOMEN.

Vide Heiress—Misdemeanor.

WORDS.

Vide Scandalous Words and Sedition.